D0131116

RIVALS OF SHERLOCK HOLMES

RIVALS OF SHERLOCK HOLMES

Forty Stories of Crime and Detection from Original Illustrated Magazines
by

GRANT ALLEN ROBERT BARR

ARNOLD BENNETT RICHARD HARDING DAVIS

ARTHUR CONAN DOYLE L.T. MEADE & ROBERT EUSTACE

L.T. MEADE & CLIFFORD HALIFAX, M.D. ARTHUR MORRISON

NEWTON MacTAVISH BARONESS E. ORCZY C.L. PIRKIS

CLARENCE ROOK H.G. WELLS

FRED M. WHITE

Selected and introduced by ALAN K. RUSSELL

CASTLE BOOKS

ISBN 0-89009-207-9 September—1978

Manufactured in the United States of America

CONTENTS

A GOLDEN ERA
OF
CRIME AND DETECTION

YOU ARE INVITED to enter the world of gas-lit London, with spies and anarchists, visiting American heiresses, con-men, murderers, tricksters, jewel thieves—and private detectives. While the streets resound to the clatter of horses' hooves, and the breath of a running man hangs in the cold night air, who knows what menace may lurk in the silent shadows of midnight alleys? In a world of contrasts—a world drawn in black and white—the trail of a criminal may lead from luxury in Mayfair to squalor in London's foggy dockland or to the playgrounds of Europe. Whichever it may be, we know that Good will always triumph in the end.

Rivals of Sherlock Holmes presents forty rare stories by authors who competed with Arthur Conan Doyle in entertaining the public. In the thrilling tales in this book you will find:

—Miss Loveday Brooke, who has (the chief of the detective agency declaims) "the faculty—so rare among women—of carrying out orders to the very letter . . ."
—Martin Hewitt, Investigator.
—Dr. Halifax, who recounts adventures of crime in which the medical evidence solves the case.
—Rare stories of detection by Arthur Conan Doyle.
—The thin and bony old man with large spectacles, who sits in the corner of a tea shop and solves mysteries.
—Madame Sara, the most wicked woman in the world.
—The adventures of an American millionaire in Europe.
—A lady detective from New York making an arrest in London.

Creative talent, which today is spread over a wide variety of media—radio, television, cinema—was only seven decades ago virtually monopolized by popular monthly magazines. Each issue was as keenly read and talked about as a new television series is today. Each month for many years, famous and popular magazines were published, including *The Strand Magazine*, *The Windsor Magazine* ("An illustrated Monthly for Men and Women"), *Pearson's Magazine*, *The Royal*

Magazine, *Cassell's Magazine*, *The Ludgate Monthly*, *The Harmsworth Magazine*, *The Idler*, and many more. It is from these popular magazines, with stories by some of the most creative talent of the day, that we present for you—complete and exactly as they originally appeared—forty exciting stories.

Reading *Rivals of Sherlock Holmes*, you are as close to the creation of a whole genre of fiction as if you had gone back in time and were reading the magazines afresh from the newsstands.

One last note: Most of the stories in this volume were originally published while Sherlock Holmes was "dead". In 1893 he fell over the Reichenback Falls in a fight with the evil Dr. Moriarty, and it was not until 1901 that *The Strand* started to serialize *The Hound of the Baskervilles.* A companion volume to *Rivals of Sherlock Holmes* presents *The Complete Original Illustrated Sherlock Holmes* as the original stories appeared in *The Strand*, illustrated by Sidney Paget.

But enough of background; now to the stories.

ALAN K. RUSSELL

THE AUTHORS AND SOME BIBLIOGRAPHICAL NOTES

TO TRACK DOWN background about authors or to provide bibliographical details (without which no collection of short stories should ever be permitted to be published), one needs to be something of a detective oneself.

There is no ready source of biographical information about the authors: many had long careers and their background is known, but others wrote for only a short time and are not easy to trace. Bibliographical information is easier to find, and some fine reference works have been published. Here are some brief notes about the authors whose work is presented in *Rivals of Sherlock Holmes*, plus details of the magazines from which their stories have been reproduced.

Grant Allen (Charles Grant Blairfindie Allen) was born in Canada in 1848 and died in 1899. He wrote on a variety of subjects and was a Professor of Mental and Moral Philosophy at one time in his career, but is best remembered for his detective fiction. His book *Hilda Wade* is cited by many as being a noteworthy volume of detective stories, but is weak stuff. In the present volume, we present two of the enjoyable episodes from *An African Millionaire* (*Strand*, June and July 1896), and *The Great Ruby Robbery* (*Strand*, September 1892). The stories of *An African Millionaire* were published in volume form in 1897 and the book is included in *Queen's Quorum* (1951 and 1969), a descriptive listing of the 125 most important detective-crime short story books chosen by Ellery Queen. Queen comments: "The 'illustrious' Colonel Clay has been shamefully neglected . . . The Adam of yeggmen . . . [is entitled] to top honors as the first great short story thief on the criminaliteracy scene."

The Experiences of Loveday Brooke, Lady Detective are from *The Ludgate Monthly*, issues of February and March 1893, and were published in volume form in 1894. Mrs. Catherine Louisa Pirkis wrote no further stories about her prim, Quaker-like lady detective. She published 14 novels between 1877 and 1894, and died in 1910. Queen mentions *The Experiences of Loveday Brooke, Lady Detective*, but it is not one of his chosen titles.

You have in this book six stories by the prolific Mrs. Meade (1854-1914), three written with each of her two medical collaborators. Her *Stories from the Diary of a Doctor*, written with "Dr. Clifford Halifax" and one of Queen's selected books, are reproduced from *The Strand Magazine* issues of March, April, and June 1894. The book was published in Britain in 1894 and in the United States the following year. A second volume of stories was published a year later. The melodramatic and memorable *Sorceress of the Strand* was first published in *The Strand Magazine*, the three episodes here in the issues of October, November, and December 1902. (Ellery Queen says that Madame Sara "made rogues like Colonel Clay and Raffles look like sissies".) "The Strand" of both series is the half-mile street in central London that runs between Trafalgar Square and Fleet Street. Upon it stands the Savoy Hotel, but a few yards from the River Thames; and off the Strand runs Norfolk Street, at the corner of which was the ABC tea shop in which the old man in the corner sat and solved his cases. It is as busy and thronged today as it was when these stories and the magazine were originally published.

"Clifford Halifax" was a pseudonym, but the medical qualification was not an invention, for the real person was Dr. Edgar Beaumont (1860-1921). "Robert Eustace" was also a pseudonym—this time for a person whom it has been difficult to track down, but is now believed to have been a Dr. Eustace Robert Barton. Mrs. Meade (Mrs. Alfred Toulmin-Smith) also wrote some 250 stories for children and teenage girls, such as *Girls of Merton College* and *Sweet Girl Graduate*.

Close to the Strand, near Charing Cross station, lay the offices of Arthur Morrison's hero, Martin Hewitt. Although Morrison (1863-1945) wrote quite a number of stories about Hewitt, his first were the best, and we present four complete stories from the April, May, June, and August 1894 issues of *The Strand Magazine*, illustrated by Sidney Paget (who, of course, also illustrated the stories of Sherlock Holmes). The book *Martin Hewitt, Investigator* (London and New York, 1894) is cited as one of *Queen's Quorum*, in which Queen says: "Of Doyle's contemporary imitators, the most durable (indeed, the only important one to survive over the ages) is the private investigator, a man of awe-inspiring technical and statistical knowledge, in *Martin Hewitt, Investigator*." Read these four stories, and this whole book through, and see if you agree with this judgment.

Arthur Conan Doyle (1859-1930) was, of course, the creator of the immortal Sherlock Holmes. But, apart from the short stories and novels about the great detective of Baker Street, Doyle wrote a series of crime and horror stories without his celebrated hero, entitled *Round The Fire Stories*. Four are presented in this volume and, as Barzun and Taylor say in their fine *Catalogue of Crime* (1971), they are "worth reading even around a radiator". We reproduce the stories from the July, August, and October 1898 and February 1899 issues of *The Strand Magazine*. They were published in a volume of the same title with additional stories in 1908. In two of the stories, *The Man with the Watches* and *The Lost Special*, Sherlock Holmes is, according to Vincent Starrett, "obliquely referred to—offstage—but not by name". Doyle also retold some dramatic true stories of crime for readers of *The Strand*.

Clarence Rook's story about Miss Van Snoop is from *The Harmsworth Magazine*, September 1898. Eric Quayle, in *The Collector's Book of Detective Fiction* (1972), says that "this was probably Miss Van Snoop's one and only case, for I have not been able to track the lady detective's next appearance".

Newton MacTavish's *An Unposted Letter* is from *Pearson's Magazine*, September 1901.

We include in *Rivals of Sherlock Holmes* one of Fred M. White's few stories of crime detection, *The Black Narcissus*, which is from *The Windsor Magazine*, December 1901. White wrote some fine science fiction, which has but rarely been reprinted—a deficiency that should be repaired.

Baroness Emmuska Orczy (Mrs. Montagu Barstow) created in *The Old Man in the Corner* "one of the truly conspicuous contributions to detective literature", according to Ellery Queen. Of Hungarian extraction, Baroness Orczy was born in Tarna-Örs in 1865, and claimed to be able to trace her descent back to the ninth century. She came to England at the age of 14. Her first literary work was detective fiction, and she went on to create the famous Scarlet Pimpernel, the idea of which came to her one day while she was sitting, fog-bound, in a London horse omnibus. The seven stories in this volume form a complete sequence of *Mysteries of Great Cities*, first published in *The Royal Magazine* from April to October 1902. The two books of *The Old Man in the Corner* and *The Case of Miss Elliott* present an odd little mystery in themselves: the first book in the sequence was not published until 1909, but the second appeared in 1905.

Barzun and Taylor's *Catalogue of Crime* applauds *In The Fog* by Richard Harding Davis as a "classic novella . . . [which] deserves a place of honor in any collection". Ellery Queen, in selecting *In The Fog* as one of his *Quorum*, says it is "a memorable book containing three connected tales and representing a perfect blend of Anglo-American storytelling". We reproduce all three, the complete work, from *The Windsor Magazine*, March to May issues, 1902. They appeared in Great Britain a year after the unillustrated first edition of the book was published in America by H.R. Russell.

Robert Barr (1850-1912) was a journalist who worked in both the United States and Great Britain, and collaborated with Jerome K. Jerome and Stephen Crane. *The Mystery of the Five Hundred Diamonds* is from the November 1904 issue of *The Windsor Magazine*. Barr is best remembered for his book, *The Triumphs of Eugene Valmont* (London and New York, 1906).

We present the complete book *The Loot of Cities*, the entertaining contribution Arnold Bennett (1867-1931) made to crime literature in the style of the Raffles books. Bennett wrote many other (and famous) books, including *The Old Wives' Tale*, *Clayhanger*, and *Hilda Lessways*, but *The Loot of Cities*, which he wrote while he was living in France, is, as Ellery Queen says in selecting the book for his *Quorum*, "a book of unusual interest, both as an example of Arnold Bennett's early work and as an example of dilettante detectivism". The six stories are reproduced from *The Windsor Magazine*, June to November 1905. They were published in volume form in 1905.

H.G. Wells' *The Hammerpond Mystery* is, say Barzun and Taylor, "a story of criminal activity with strongly social and moral implications. This tale also appears to be an attempt to bring back naturalistic detail into descriptions of felony, after the gallant nonsense of Raffles and his peers". It is reproduced from *Pearson's Magazine*, January to June 1905. H.G. Wells (1866-1946) is today best remembered for his innovative and imaginative science fiction, although he was a prolific writer and concentrated much of his efforts on work to promote peace and international understanding.

Four of the forty stories in this volume also appear amongst the three volumes of thirteen stories edited by Hugh Greene (brother of Grahame Greene), who has done much to re-introduce early detective stories to modern readers. These are coincidentally entitled *The Rivals of Sherlock Holmes* (1970), *More Rivals of Sherlock Holmes* (1971), and *The Crooked Counties* (1973). There has been a British television series based on his selection. His three books each have an urbane and knowledgeable introduction.

ALAN K. RUSSELL

I

The Great Ruby Robbery

GRANT ALLEN

The Great Ruby Robbery: a Detective Story.

BY GRANT ALLEN.

I.

ERSIS REMANET was an American heiress. As she justly remarked, this was a commonplace profession for a young woman nowadays; for almost everybody of late years has been an American and an heiress. A poor Californian, indeed, would be a charming novelty in London society. But London society, so far, has had to go without one.

Persis Remanet was on her way back from the Wilcoxes' ball. She was stopping, of course, with Sir Everard and Lady Maclure at their house at Hampstead. I say "of course" advisedly; because if you or I go to see New York, we have to put up at our own expense (five dollars a day, without wine or extras) at the Windsor or the Fifth Avenue; but when the pretty American comes to London (and every American girl is *ex officio* pretty, in Europe at least; I suppose they keep their ugly ones at home for domestic consumption) she is invariably the guest either of a dowager duchess or of a Royal Academician, like Sir Everard, of the first distinction. Yankees visit Europe, in fact, to see, among other things, our art and our old nobility; and by dint of native persistence they get into places that you and I could never succeed in penetrating, unless we devoted all the energies of a long and blameless life to securing an invitation.

Persis hadn't been to the Wilcoxes with Lady Maclure, however. The Maclures were too really great to know such people as the Wilcoxes, who were something tremendous in the City, but didn't buy pictures; and Academicians, you know, don't care to cultivate City people—unless they're customers. ("Patrons," the Academicians more usually call them; but I prefer the simple business word myself, as being a deal less patronizing.) So Persis had accepted an invitation from Mrs. Duncan Harrison, the wife of the well-known member for the Hackness Division of Elmetshire, to take a seat in her carriage to and from the Wilcoxes. Mrs. Harrison knew the habits and manners of American heiresses too well to offer to chaperon Persis; and indeed, Persis, as a free-born American citizen, was quite as well able to take care of herself, the wide world over, as any three ordinary married Englishwomen.

Now, Mrs. Harrison had a brother, an Irish baronet, Sir Justin O'Byrne, late of the Eighth Hussars, who had been with them to the Wilcoxes, and who accompanied them home to Hampstead on the back seat of the carriage. Sir Justin was one of those charming, ineffective, elusive Irishmen whom everybody likes and everybody disapproves of. He had been everywhere, and done everything—except to earn an honest livelihood. The total absence of rents during the sixties and seventies had never prevented his father, old Sir Terence O'Byrne, who sat so long for Connemara in the unreformed Parliament, from sending his son Justin in state to Eton, and afterwards to a fashionable college at Oxford. "He gave me the education of a gentleman," Sir Justin was wont regretfully to observe; "but he omitted to give me also the income to keep it up with."

Nevertheless, society felt O'Byrne was the sort of man who must be kept afloat somehow; and it kept him afloat accordingly in those mysterious ways that only society understands, and that you and I, who are not society, could never get to the bottom of if we tried for a century. Sir Justin himself had essayed Parliament, too, where he sat for a while behind the great Parnell without for a moment forfeiting society's regard even in those earlier days when it was held as a prime article of faith by the world that no gentleman could possibly call himself a Home-Ruler. 'Twas only one of O'Byrne's wild Irish tricks, society said, complacently, with that singular indulgence it always extends to its special favourites, and which is, in fact, the correlative of that unsparing cruelty it shows in turn to those who happen to offend against its unwritten precepts. If Sir Justin had blown up a Czar or two in a fit of political exuberance, society would only have regarded the escapade as "one of O'Byrne's eccentricities." He had also held a commission for a while in a cavalry regiment, which he left, it was understood, owing to a difference of opinion about a lady with the colonel; and he was now a gentleman-at-large on London society, supposed by those who know more about everyone than one knows about oneself, to be on the look-out for a nice girl with a little money.

"SIR JUSTIN HAD PAID PERSIS A GREAT DEAL OF ATTENTION."

Sir Justin had paid Persis a great deal of attention that particular evening; in point of fact, he had paid her a great deal of attention from the very first, whenever he met her; and on the way home from the dance he had kept his eyes fixed on Persis's face to an extent that was almost embarrassing. The pretty Californian leaned back in her place in the carriage and surveyed him languidly. She was looking her level best that night, in her pale pink dress, with the famous Remanet rubies in a cascade of red light setting off that snowy neck of hers. 'Twas a neck for a painter. Sir Justin let his eyes fall regretfully more than once on the glittering rubies. He liked and admired Persis, oh! quite immensely. Your society man who has been through seven or eight London seasons could hardly be expected to go quite so far as falling in love with any woman; his habit is rather to look about him critically among all the nice girls trotted out by their mammas for his lordly inspection, and to reflect with a faint smile that this, that, or the other one might perhaps really suit him—if it were not for—and there comes in the inevitable *But* of all human commendation. Still, Sir Justin admitted with a sigh to himself that he liked Persis ever so much; she was so fresh and original! and she talked so cleverly! As for Persis, she would have given her eyes (like every other American girl) to be made "my lady"; and she had seen no man yet, with that auxiliary title in his gift, whom she liked half so well as this delightful wild Irishman.

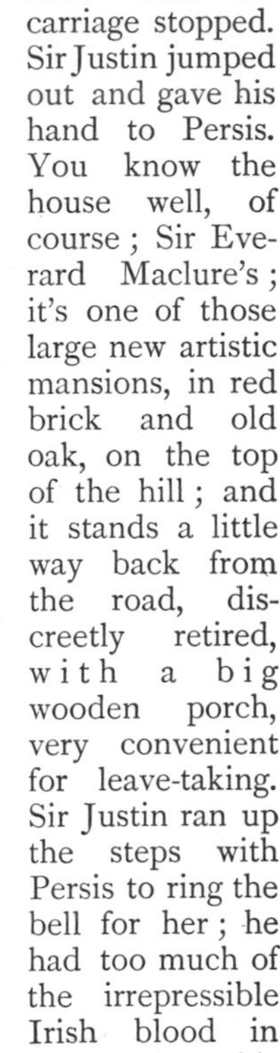

At the Maclures' door the carriage stopped. Sir Justin jumped out and gave his hand to Persis. You know the house well, of course; Sir Everard Maclure's; it's one of those large new artistic mansions, in red brick and old oak, on the top of the hill; and it stands a little way back from the road, discreetly retired, with a big wooden porch, very convenient for leave-taking. Sir Justin ran up the steps with Persis to ring the bell for her; he had too much of the irrepressible Irish blood in his veins to leave that pleasant task to his sister's footman. But he didn't ring it at once; at the risk of keeping Mrs. Harrison waiting outside for nothing, he stopped and talked a minute or so with the pretty American. "You looked charming to-night, Miss Remanet," he said, as she threw back her light opera wrap for a moment in the porch and displayed a single flash of that snowy neck with the famous rubies; "those stones become you so."

Persis looked at him and smiled. "You think so?" she said, a little tremulous, for even your American heiress, after all, is a woman. "Well, I'm glad you do. But it's good-bye to-night, Sir Justin, for I go next week to Paris."

Even in the gloom of the porch, just lighted by an artistic red and blue lantern in wrought iron, she could see a shade of disappointment pass quickly over his handsome face as he answered, with a little gulp, "No! you don't mean that? Oh, Miss Remanet, I'm so sorry!" Then he paused and drew back: "And yet . . . . after all," he continued, "perhaps——," and there he checked himself.

Persis looked up at him hastily. "Yet, after all, what?" she asked, with evident interest.

The young man drew an almost inaudible sigh. "Yet, after all—nothing," he answered, evasively.

"That might do for an Englishwoman," Persis put in, with American frankness, "but it won't do for me. You must tell me what you mean by it." For she reflected sagely that the happiness of two lives might depend upon those two minutes; and how foolish to throw away the chance of a man you really like (with a my-ladyship to boot), all for the sake of a pure convention!

Sir Justin leaned against the woodwork of that retiring porch. She was a beautiful girl. He had hot Irish blood. . . . Well, yes; just for once—he would say the plain truth to her.

"Miss Remanet," he began, leaning forward, and bringing his face close to hers, "Miss Remanet—Persis—shall I tell you the reason why? Because I like you so much. I almost think I love you!"

Persis felt the blood quiver in her tingling cheeks. How handsome he was—and a baronet!

"And yet you're not altogether sorry," she said, reproachfully, "that I'm going to Paris!"

"SIR JUSTIN HESITATED A SECOND."

"No, not altogether sorry," he answered, sticking to it; "and I'll tell you why, too, Miss Remanet. I like you very much, and I think you like me. For a week or two, I've been saying to myself, 'I really believe I *must* ask her to marry me.' The temptation's been so strong I could hardly resist it."

"And why do you want to resist it?" Persis asked, all tremulous.

Sir Justin hesitated a second; then with a perfectly natural and instinctive movement (though only a gentleman would have ventured to make it) he lifted his hand and just touched with the tips of his fingers the ruby pendants on her necklet. "*This* is why," he answered simply, and with manly frankness. "Persis, you're so rich! I never dare ask you."

"Perhaps you don't know what my answer would be," Persis murmured very low, just to preserve her own dignity.

"Oh, yes; I think I do," the young man replied, gazing deeply into her dark eyes. "It isn't that; if it were only that, I wouldn't so much mind it. But I think you'd take me." There was moisture in her eye. He went on more boldly: "I know you'd take me, Persis, and that's why I don't ask you. You're a great deal too rich, and *these* make it impossible."

"Sir Justin," Persis answered, removing his hand gently, but with the moisture growing thicker, for she really liked him, "it's most unkind of you to say so; either you oughtn't to have told me at all, or else—if you did——" She stopped short. Womanly shame overcame her.

The man leaned forward and spoke earnestly. "Oh, don't say that!" he cried, from his heart. "I couldn't bear to offend you. But I couldn't bear, either, to let you go away—well—without having ever told you. In that case you might have thought I didn't care at all for you, and was only flirting with you. But, Persis, I've cared a great deal for you—a great, great deal—and had hard work many times to prevent myself from asking you. And I'll tell you the plain reason why I haven't asked you. I'm a man about town, not much good, I'm afraid, for anybody or anything; and everybody says I'm on the look-out for an heiress—which happens not to be true; and if I married you, everybody'd say, 'Ah, there! I told you so!' Now, I wouldn't mind that for myself; I'm a man, and I could snap my fingers at them; but I'd mind it for *you*, Persis, for I'm enough in love with you to be very, very jealous, indeed, for your honour. I couldn't bear to think people should say, 'There's that pretty American girl, Persis Remanet that was, you know; she's thrown herself away upon that good-for-nothing Irishman, Justin O'Byrne, a regular fortune-hunter, who's married her for her money.' So for your sake, Persis, I'd rather not ask you; I'd rather leave you for some better man to marry."

"But *I* wouldn't," Persis cried aloud. "Oh, Sir Justin, you must believe me. You must remember——"

At that precise point, Mrs. Harrison put her head out of the carriage window and called out rather loudly:—

"Why, Justin, what's keeping you? The horses'll catch their deaths of cold; and they were clipped this morning. Come back at once, my dear boy. Besides, you know, *les convenances!*"

"All right, Nora," her brother answered; "I won't be a minute. We can't get them to answer this precious bell. I believe it don't ring! But I'll try again, anyhow." And half forgetting that his own words weren't strictly true, for he hadn't yet tried, he pressed the knob with a vengeance.

"Is that your room with the light burning, Miss Remanet?" he went on, in a fairly loud official voice, as the servant came to answer. "The one with the balcony, I mean? Quite Venetian, isn't it? Reminds one of Romeo and Juliet. But most convenient for a burglary, too! Such nice low rails! Mind you take good care of the Remanet rubies!"

"I don't want to take care of them," Persis answered, wiping her dim eyes hastily with her lace pocket-handkerchief, "if they make you feel as you say, Sir Justin. I don't mind if they go. Let the burglar take them!"

And even as she spoke, the Maclure footman, immutable, sphinx-like, opened the door for her.

II.

Persis sat long in her own room that night before she began undressing. Her head was full of Sir Justin and these mysterious hints of his. At last, however, she took her rubies off, and her pretty silk bodice. "I don't care for them at all," she thought, with a gulp, "if they keep from me the love of the man I'd like to marry."

It was late before she fell asleep; and when she did, her rest was troubled. She dreamt a great deal; in her dreams, Sir Justin, and dance music, and the rubies, and burglars were incongruously mingled. To make up for it, she slept late next morning; and Lady Maclure let her sleep on, thinking she was probably wearied out with much dancing the previous evening—as though any amount of excitement could ever weary a pretty American! About ten o'clock she woke with a start. A vague feeling oppressed her that somebody had come in during the night and stolen her rubies. She rose hastily and went to her dressing-table to look for them. The case was there all right; she opened it and looked at it. Oh, prophetic soul! the rubies were gone, and the box was empty!

Now, Persis had honestly said the night before the burglar might take her rubies if he chose, and she wouldn't mind the loss of them. But that was last night, and the rubies hadn't then as yet been taken. This morning, somehow, things seemed quite different. It would be rough on us all (especially on politicians) if we must always be bound by what we said yesterday. Persis was an American, and no American is insensible to the charms of precious stones; 'tis a savage taste which the European immigrants seem to have inherited obliquely from their Red Indian predecessors. She rushed over to the bell and rang it with feminine violence. Lady Maclure's maid answered the summons, as usual. She was a clever, demure-looking girl, this maid of Lady Maclure's; and when Persis cried to her wildly, "Send for the police at once, and tell Sir Everard my jewels are stolen!" she answered "Yes, miss," with such sober acquiescence that Persis, who was American, and therefore a bundle of nerves, turned round and stared at her as an incomprehensible mystery. No Mahatma could have been more unmoved. She seemed quite to expect those rubies would be stolen, and to take no more notice of the incident than if Persis had told her she wanted hot water.

Lady Maclure, indeed, greatly prided herself on this cultivated imperturbability of Bertha's; she regarded it as the fine flower of English domestic service. But Persis was American, and saw things otherwise; to her, the calm repose with which Bertha answered, "Yes, miss; certainly, miss; I'll go and tell Sir Everard," seemed nothing short of exasperating.

Bertha went off with the news, closing the door quite softly; and a few minutes later Lady Maclure herself appeared in the Californian's room, to console her visitor under this severe domestic affliction. She found Persis sitting up in bed, in her pretty French dressing jacket (pale blue with *revers* of fawn colour), reading a book of verses. "Why, my dear!" Lady Maclure exclaimed, "then you've found them again, I suppose? Bertha told us you'd lost your lovely rubies!"

"So I have, dear Lady Maclure," Persis answered, wiping her eyes; "they're gone. They've been stolen. I forgot to lock my door when I came home last night, and the window was open; somebody must have come in, this way or that, and taken them. But whenever I'm in trouble, I try a dose of Browning. He's splendid for the nerves. He's so consoling, you know; he brings one to anchor."

"LADY MACLURE WAS STARTLED.

She breakfasted in bed; she wouldn't leave the room, she declared, till the police arrived. After breakfast she rose and put on her dainty Parisian morning wrap—Americans have always such pretty bedroom things for these informal receptions—and sat up in state to await the police officer. Sir Everard himself, much disturbed that such a mishap should have happened in his house, went round in person to fetch the official. While he was gone, Lady Maclure made a thorough search of the room, but couldn't find a trace of the missing rubies.

"Are you sure you put them in the case, dear?" she asked, for the honour of the household.

And Persis answered: "Quite confident, Lady Maclure; I always put them there the moment I take them off; and when I came to look for them this morning, the case was empty."

"They were *very* valuable, I believe?" Lady Maclure said, inquiringly.

"Six thousand pounds was the figure in your money, I guess," Persis answered, ruefully. "I don't know if you call that a lot of money in England, but we do in America."

There was a moment's pause, and then Persis spoke again:—

"Lady Maclure," she said, abruptly, "do you consider that maid of yours a Christian woman?"

Lady Maclure was startled. That was hardly the light in which she was accustomed to regard the lower classes.

"Well, I don't know about that," she said, slowly; "that's a great deal, you know, dear, to assert about *anybody*, especially one's maid. But I should think she was honest, quite decidedly honest."

"Well, that's the same thing, about, isn't it?" Persis answered, much relieved. "I'm glad you think that's so; for I was almost half afraid of her. She's too quiet for my taste, somehow; so silent, you know, and inscrutable."

"Oh, my dear," her hostess cried, "don't blame her for silence; that's just what I like about her. It's exactly what I chose her for. Such a nice, noiseless girl; moves about the room like a cat on tiptoe; knows her proper place, and never dreams of speaking unless she's spoken to."

"Well, you may like them that way in Europe," Persis responded, frankly; "but in America, we prefer them a little bit human."

Twenty minutes later the police officer arrived. He wasn't in uniform. The inspector, feeling at once the gravity of the case, and recognising that this was a Big Thing, in which there was glory to be won, and perhaps promotion, sent a detective at once, and advised that if possible nothing should be said to the household on the subject for the present, till the detective had taken a good look round the premises. That was useless, Sir Everard feared, for the lady's-maid knew; and the lady's-maid would be sure to go down, all agog with the news, to the servants' hall immediately. However, they might try; no harm in trying; and the sooner the detective got round to the house, of course, the better.

The detective accompanied him back—a keen-faced, close-shaven, irreproachable-looking man, like a vulgarized copy of Mr. John Morley. He was curt and business-like. His first question was, "Have the servants been told of this?"

Lady Maclure looked inquiringly across at Bertha. She herself had been sitting all the time with the bereaved Persis, to console her (with Browning) under this heavy affliction.

"No, my lady," Bertha answered, ever calm (invaluable servant, Bertha!), "I didn't mention it to anybody downstairs on purpose, thinking perhaps it might be decided to search the servants' boxes."

The detective pricked up his ears. He was engaged already in glancing casually round the room. He moved about it now, like a conjurer, with quiet steps and slow. "He doesn't get on one's nerves," Persis remarked, approvingly, in an undertone to her friend; then she added, aloud: "What's your name, please, Mr. Officer?"

The detective was lifting a lace handkerchief on the dressing-table at the side. He turned round softly. "Gregory, madam," he answered, hardly glancing at the girl, and going on with his occupation.

"The same as the powders!" Persis interposed, with a shudder. "I used to take them when I was a child. I never could bear them."

"We're useful, as remedies," the detective replied, with a quiet smile; "but nobody likes us." And he relapsed contentedly into his work once more, searching round the apartment.

"The first thing we have to do," he said, with a calm air of superiority, standing now by the window, with one hand in his pocket, "is to satisfy ourselves whether or not there has really, at all, been a robbery. We must look through the room well, and see you haven't left the rubies lying about loose somewhere. Such things often happen. We're constantly called in to investigate a case, when it's only a matter of a lady's carelessness."

At that Persis flared up. A daughter of the great republic isn't accustomed to be doubted like a mere European woman. "I'm quite sure I took them off," she said, "and put them back in the jewel case. Of that I'm just confident. There isn't a doubt possible."

Mr. Gregory redoubled his search in all likely and unlikely places. "I should say that settles the matter," he answered, blandly. "Our experience is that whenever a lady's perfectly certain, beyond the possibility of doubt, she put a thing away safely, it's absolutely sure to turn up where she says she didn't put it."

Persis answered him never a word. Her manners had not that repose that stamps the caste of Vere de Vere; so, to prevent an outbreak, she took refuge in Browning.

Mr. Gregory, nothing abashed, searched the room thoroughly, up and down, without the faintest regard to Persis's feelings; he was a detective, he said, and his business was first of all to unmask crime, irrespective of circumstances. Lady Maclure stood by, meanwhile, with the imperturbable Bertha. Mr. Gregory investigated every hole and cranny, like a man who wishes to let the world see for itself he performs a disagreeable duty with unflinching thoroughness. When he had finished, he turned to Lady Maclure. "And now, if you please," he said, blandly, "we'll proceed to investigate the servants' boxes."

Lady Maclure looked at her maid. "Bertha," she said, "go downstairs, and see that none of the other servants come up, meanwhile, to their bedrooms." Lady Maclure was not quite to the manner born, and had never acquired the hateful aristocratic habit of calling women servants by their surnames only.

But the detective interposed. "No, no," he said, sharply. "This young woman had better stop here with Miss Remanet—strictly under her eye—till I've searched the boxes. For if I find nothing there, it may perhaps be my disagreeable duty, by-and-by, to call in a female detective to search her."

It was Lady Maclure's turn to flare up now. "Why, this is my own maid," she said, in a chilly tone, "and I've every confidence in her."

"Very sorry for that, my lady," Mr. Gregory responded, in a most official voice; "but our experience teaches us that if there's a person in the case whom nobody ever

"THE DETECTIVE WAS LIFTING A LACE HANDKERCHIEF.

indifference. "You can search me if you like—when you've got a warrant for it."

The detective looked up sharply; so also did Persis. This ready acquaintance with the liberty of the subject in criminal cases impressed her unfavourably. "Ah! we'll see about that," Mr. Gregory answered, with a cool smile. "Meanwhile, Lady Maclure, I'll have a look at the boxes."

III.

THE search (strictly illegal) brought out nothing. Mr. Gregory returned to Persis's bedroom, disconsolate. "You can leave the room," he said to Bertha; and Bertha glided out. "I've set another man outside to keep a constant eye on her," he added in explanation.

By this time Persis had almost made her mind up as to who was the culprit; but she said nothing overt, for Lady Maclure's sake, to the detective. As for that immovable official, he began asking questions—some of them, Persis thought, almost bordering on the personal. Where had she been last night? Was she sure she had really worn the rubies? How did she come home? Was she certain she took them off? Did the maid help her undress? Who came back with her in the carriage?

To all these questions, rapidly fired off with cross-examining acuteness, Persis answered in the direct American fashion. She was sure she had the rubies on when she came home to Hampstead, because Sir Justin O'Byrne, who came back with her in his sister's carriage, had noticed them the last thing, and had told her to take care of them.

At mention of that name the detective smiled meaningly. (A meaning smile is stock-in-trade to a detective.) "Oh, Sir Justin O'Byrne!" he repeated, with quiet self-constraint. "*He* came back with you in the carriage, then? And did he sit the same side with you?"

Lady Maclure grew indignant (that was Mr. Gregory's cue). "Really, sir," she said, angrily, "if you're going to suspect gentlemen in Sir Justin's position, we shall none of us be safe from you."

"The law," Mr. Gregory replied, with an

dreams of suspecting, that person's the one who has committed the robbery."

"Why, you'll be suspecting myself next!" Lady Maclure cried, with some disgust.

"Your ladyship's just the last person in the world I should think of suspecting," the detective answered, with a deferential bow—which, after his previous speech, was to say the least of it equivocal.

Persis began to get annoyed. She didn't half like the look of that girl Bertha, herself; but still, she was there as Lady Maclure's guest, and she couldn't expose her hostess to discomfort on her account.

"The girl shall *not* be searched," she put in, growing hot. "I don't care a cent whether I lose the wretched stones or not. Compared to human dignity, what are they worth? Not five minutes' consideration."

"They're worth just seven years," Mr. Gregory answered, with professional definiteness. "And as to searching, why, that's out of your hands now. This is a criminal case. I'm here to discharge a public duty."

"I don't in the least mind being searched," Bertha put in obligingly, with an air of air of profound deference, "is no respecter of persons."

"But it ought to be of characters," Lady Maclure cried, warmly. "What's the good of having a blameless character, I should like to know, if—if——"

"If it doesn't allow you to commit a robbery with impunity?" the detective interposed, finishing her sentence his own way. "Well, well, that's true. That's per-fectly true—but Sir Justin's character, you see, can hardly be called blameless."

"He's a gentleman," Persis cried, with flashing eyes, turning round upon the officer; "and he's quite incapable of such a mean and despicable crime as you dare to suspect him of."

"Oh, I see," the officer answered, like one to whom a welcome ray of light breaks suddenly through a great darkness. "Sir Justin's a friend of yours! Did he come into the porch with you?"

"He did," Persis answered, flushing crimson; "and if you have the insolence to bring a charge against him——"

"Calm yourself, madam," the detective replied, coolly. "I do nothing of the sort—at this stage of the proceedings. It's possible there may have been no robbery in the case at all. We must keep our minds open for the present to every possible alternative. It's—it's a delicate matter to hint at; but before we go any further—do you think, perhaps, Sir Justin may have carried the rubies away by mistake, entangled in his clothes?—say, for example, his coat-sleeve?"

It was a loophole of escape; but Persis didn't jump at it.

"He had never the opportunity," she answered, with a flash. "And I know quite well they were there on my neck when he left me, for the last thing he said to me was, looking up at this very window: 'That balcony's awfully convenient for a burglary. Mind you take good care of the Remanet rubies.' And I remembered what he'd said when I took them off last night; and that's what makes me so sure I really had them."

"*And* you slept with the window open!" the detective went on, still smiling to himself. "Well, here we have all the materials, to be sure, for a first-class mystery!"

IV.

For some days more, nothing further turned up of importance about the Great Ruby Robbery. It got into the papers, of course, as everything does nowadays, and all London was talking of it. Persis found herself quite famous as the American lady who had lost her jewels. People pointed her out in the park; people stared at her hard through their opera-glasses at the theatre. Indeed, the possession of the celebrated Remanet rubies had never made her half so conspicuous in the world as the loss of them made her. It was almost worth while losing them, Persis thought, to be so much made of as she was in society in consequence. All the world knows a young lady must be somebody when she can offer a reward of five hundred pounds for the recovery of gewgaws valued at six thousand.

Sir Justin met her in the Row one day. "Then you don't go to Paris for awhile yet—until you get them back?" he inquired very low.

And Persis answered, blushing, "No, Sir Justin; not yet; and—I'm almost glad of it."

"No, you don't mean that!" the young man cried, with perfect boyish ardour. "Well, I confess, Miss Remanet, the first thing I thought myself when I read it in *The Times* was just the very same: 'Then, after all, she won't go yet to Paris!'"

Persis looked up at him from her pony with American frankness. "And I," she, said, quivering, "I found anchor in Browning. For what do you think I read?

'And learn to rate a true man's heart
Far above rubies.'

The book opened at the very place; and *there* I found anchor!"

But when Sir Justin went round to his rooms that same evening his servant said to him, "A gentleman was inquiring for you here this afternoon, sir. A close-shaven gentleman. Not very prepossessin'. And it seemed to me somehow, sir, as if he was trying to pump me."

Sir Justin's face was grave. He went to his bedroom at once. He knew what that man wanted; and he turned straight to his wardrobe, looking hard at the dress coat he had worn on the eventful evening. Things may cling to a sleeve, don't you know—or be entangled in a cuff—or get casually into a pocket! Or someone may put them there.

V.

For the next ten days or so Mr. Gregory was busy, constantly busy. Without doubt, he was the most active and energetic of detectives. He carried out so fully his own official principle of suspecting everybody, from China to Peru, that at last poor Persis got fairly mazed with his web of possibilities. Nobody was safe from his cultivated and highly-trained suspicion—not Sir Everard in his studio, nor

"SIR JUSTIN MET HER IN THE ROW."

course, the laziest of her kind; for she had taken an unaccountable dislike, somehow, to that quiet girl Bertha. On this particular morning, however, when Persis looked out, she saw Bertha engaged in close, and apparently very intimate, conversation with the Hampstead postman. This sight disturbed the unstable equilibrium of her equanimity not a little. Why should Bertha go to the door to the postman at all? Surely it was no part of the duty of Lady Maclure's maid to take in the letters! And why should she want to go prying into the question of who wrote to Miss Remanet? For Persis, intensely conscious herself that a note from Sir Justin

Lady Maclure in her boudoir, nor the butler in his pantry, nor Sir Justin O'Byrne in his rooms in St. James's. Mr. Gregory kept an open mind against everybody and everything. He even doubted the parrot, and had views as to the intervention of rats and terriers. Persis got rather tired at last of his perverse ingenuity; especially as she had a very shrewd idea herself who had stolen the rubies. When he suggested various doubts, however, which seemed remotely to implicate Sir Justin's honesty, the sensitive American girl "felt it go on her nerves," and refused to listen to him, though Mr. Gregory never ceased to enforce upon her, by precept and example, his own pet doctrine that the last person on earth one would be likely to suspect is always the one who turns out to have done it.

A morning or two later, Persis looked out of her window as she was dressing her hair. She dressed it herself now, though she was an American heiress, and, therefore, of

lay on top of the postman's bundle—she recognised it at once, even at that distance below, by the peculiar shape of the broad rough envelope—jumped to the natural feminine conclusion that Bertha must needs be influenced by some abstruse motive of which she herself, Persis, was, to say the very least, a component element. 'Tis a human fallacy. We're all of us prone to see everything from a personal standpoint; indeed, the one quality which makes a man or woman into a possible novelist, good, bad, or indifferent, is just that special power of throwing himself or herself into a great many people's personalities alternately. And this is a power possessed on an average by not one in a thousand men or not one in ten thousand women.

Persis rang the bell violently. Bertha came up, all smiles: "Did you want anything, miss?" Persis could have choked her. "Yes," she answered, plainly, taking the bull by the horns; "I want to know what you were doing down there, prying into other people's letters with the postman?"

Bertha looked up at her, ever bland; she answered at once, without a second's hesitation: "The postman's my young man, miss; and we hope before very long now to get married."

"Odious thing!" Persis thought. "A glib lie always ready on the tip of her tongue for every emergency."

But Bertha's full heart was beating violently. Beating with love and hope and deferred anxiety.

A little later in the day Persis mentioned the incident casually to Lady Maclure—mainly in order to satisfy herself that the girl had been lying. Lady Maclure, however, gave a qualified assent:—

"I *believe* she's engaged to the postman," she said. "I *think* I've heard so; though I make it a rule, you see, my dear, to know as little as I can of these people's love affairs. They're so very uninteresting. But Bertha certainly told me she wouldn't leave me to get married for an indefinite period. That was only ten days ago. She said her young man wasn't just yet in a position to make a home for her."

"Perhaps," Persis suggested, grimly, "something has occurred meanwhile to better her position. Such strange things crop up. She may have come into a fortune!"

"Perhaps so," Lady Maclure replied, languidly. The subject bored her. "Though, if so, it must really have been very sudden; for I think it was the morning before you lost your jewels she told me so."

Persis thought that odd, but she made no comment.

Before dinner that evening she burst suddenly into Lady Maclure's room for a minute. Bertha was dressing her lady's hair. Friends were coming to dine—among them Sir Justin. "How do these pearls go with my complexion, Lady Maclure?" Persis asked rather anxiously; for she specially wished to look her best that evening, for one of the party.

"Oh, charming!" her hostess answered, with her society smile. "Never saw anything suit you better, Persis."

"Except my poor rubies!" Persis cried rather ruefully, for coloured gewgaws are dear to the savage and the woman. "I wish I could get them back! I wonder that man Gregory hasn't succeeded in finding them."

"Oh! my dear," Lady Maclure drawled out, "you may be sure by this time they're safe at Amsterdam. That's the only place in Europe now to look for them."

"Why to Amsterdam, my lady?" Bertha interposed suddenly, with a quick side-glance at Persis.

Lady Maclure threw her head back in surprise at so unwonted an intrusion. "What do you want to know that for, child?" she asked, somewhat curtly. "Why, to be cut, of course. All the diamond-cutters in the world are concentrated in Amsterdam; and the first thing a thief does when he steals big jewels is to send them across, and have them cut in new shapes so that they can't be identified."

"I shouldn't have thought," Bertha put in, calmly, "they'd have known who to send them to."

Lady Maclure turned to her sharply. "Why, these things," she said, with a calm air of knowledge, "are always done by experienced thieves, who know the ropes well, and are in league with receivers the whole world over. But Gregory has his eye on Amsterdam, I'm sure, and we'll soon hear something."

"Yes, my lady," Bertha answered, in her acquiescent tone, and relapsed into silence.

VI.

Four days later, about nine at night, that hard-worked man, the posty on the beat, stood loitering outside Sir Everard Maclure's house, openly defying the rules of the department, in close conference with Bertha.

"Well, any news?" Bertha asked, trembling over with excitement, for she was a very different person outside with her lover from the demure and imperturbable model maid who waited on my lady.

"Why, yes," the posty answered, with a low laugh of triumph. "A letter from Amsterdam! And I think we've fixed it!"

Bertha almost flung herself upon him. "Oh, Harry!" she cried, all eagerness, "this is too good to be true! Then in just one other month we can really get married!"

There was a minute's pause, inarticulately filled up by sounds unrepresentable through the art of the type-founder. Then Harry spoke again. "It's an awful lot of money!" he said, musing. "A regular fortune! And what's more, Bertha, if it hadn't been for your cleverness we never should have got it!"

Bertha pressed his hand affectionately. Even ladies'-maids are human.

"Well, if I hadn't been so much in love with you," she answered, frankly, "I don't think I could ever have had the wit to manage it. But, oh! Harry, love makes one do or try anything!"

If Persis had heard those singular words, she would have felt no doubt was any longer possible.

VII.

NEXT morning, at ten o'clock, a policeman came round, post haste, to Sir Everard's. He asked to see Miss Remanet. When Persis came down, in her morning wrap, he had but a brief message from head quarters to give her: "Your jewels are found, Miss. Will you step round and identify them?"

Persis drove back with him, all trembling. Lady Maclure accompanied her. At the police-station they left their cab, and entered the ante-room.

A little group had assembled there. The first person Persis distinctly made out in it was Sir Justin. A great terror seized her. Gregory had so poisoned her mind by this time with suspicion of everybody and everything she came across, that she was afraid of her own shadow. But next moment she saw clearly he wasn't there as prisoner, or even as witness; merely as spectator. She acknowledged him with a hasty bow, and cast her eye round again. The next person she definitely distinguished was Bertha, as calm and cool as ever, but in the very centre of the group, occupying as it were the place of honour which naturally belongs to the prisoner on all similar occasions. Persis was not surprised at that; she had known it all along; she glanced meaningly at Gregory, who stood a little behind, looking by no means triumphant. Persis found his dejection odd; but he was a proud detective, and perhaps someone else had effected the capture!

"These are your jewels, I believe," the inspector said, holding them up; and Persis admitted it.

"This is a painful case," the inspector went on. "A very painful case. We grieve to have discovered such a clue against one of our own men; but as he owns to it himself, and intends to throw himself on the mercy of the Court, it's no use talking about it. He won't attempt to defend it; indeed, with such evidence, I think he's doing what's best and wisest."

"LOVE MAKES ONE DO OR TRY ANYTHING."

Persis stood there, all dazed. "I—I don't understand," she cried, with a swimming brain. "Who on earth are you talking about?"

The inspector pointed mutely with one hand at Gregory; and then for the first time Persis saw he was guarded. She clapped her hand to her head. In a moment it all broke in upon her. When she had called in the police, the rubies had never been stolen at all. It was Gregory who stole them!

She understood it now, at once. The real facts came back to her. She had taken her necklet off at night, laid it carelessly down on the dressing-table (too full of Sir Justin), covered it accidentally with her lace pocket-handkerchief, and straightway forgotten all about it. Next day she missed it, and jumped at conclusions. When Gregory came, he spied the rubies askance under the corner of the handkerchief—of course, being a woman, she had naturally looked everywhere except in the place where she laid them—and knowing it was a safe case he had quietly pocketed them before her very eyes, all unsuspected. He felt sure nobody could accuse him of a robbery which was committed before he came, and which he had himself been called in to investigate.

"The worst of it is," the inspector went on, "he had woven a very ingenious case against Sir Justin O'Byrne, whom we were on the very point of arresting to-day, if this young woman hadn't come in at the eleventh hour, in the very nick of time, and earned the reward by giving us the clue that led to the discovery and recovery of the jewels. They were brought over this morning by an Amsterdam detective."

"THESE ARE YOUR JEWELS, I BELIEVE."

Persis looked hard at Bertha. Bertha answered her look. "My young man was the postman, miss," she explained, quite simply; "and after what my lady said, I put him up to watch Mr. Gregory's delivery for a letter from Amsterdam. I'd suspected him from the very first; and when the letter came, we had him arrested at once, and found out from it who were the people at Amsterdam who had the rubies."

Persis gasped with astonishment. Her brain was reeling. But Gregory in the background put in one last word :—

"Well, I was right, after all," he said, with professional pride. "I told you the very last person you'd dream of suspecting was sure to be the one that actually did it."

Lady O'Byrne's rubies were very much admired at Monte Carlo last season. Mr. Gregory has found permanent employment for the next seven years at Her Majesty's quarries on the Isle of Portland. Bertha and her postman have retired to Canada with five hundred pounds to buy a farm. And everybody says Sir Justin O'Byrne has beaten the record, after all, even for Irish baronets, by making a marriage at once of money and affection.

II

The Experiences of Loveday Brooke, Lady Detective

C.L. PIRKIS

The Experiences of Loveday Brooke, Lady Detective.

By C. L. PIRKIS

THE BLACK BAG LEFT ON A DOOR-STEP.

"IT'S a big thing," said Loveday Brooke, addressing Ebenezer Dyer, chief of the well-known detective agency in Lynch Court, Fleet Street; "Lady Cathrow has lost £30,000 worth of jewellery, if the newspaper accounts are to be trusted."

"They are fairly accurate this time. The robbery differs in few respects from the usual run of country-house robberies. The time chosen, of course, was the dinner-hour, when the family and guests were at table and the servants not on duty were amusing themselves in their own quarters. The fact of its being Christmas Eve would also of necessity add to the business and consequent distraction of the household. The entry to the house, however, in this case was not effected in the usual manner by a ladder to the dressing-room window, but through the window of a room on the ground floor—a small room with one window and two doors, one of which opens into the hall, and the other into a passage that leads by the back stairs to the bedroom floor. It is used, I believe, as a sort of hat and coat room by the gentlemen of the house."

"It was, I suppose, the weak point of the house?"

"Quite so. A very weak point indeed. Craigen Court, the residence of Sir George and Lady Cathrow, is an oddly-built old place, jutting out in all directions, and as this window looked out upon a blank wall, it was filled in with stained glass, kept fastened by a strong brass catch, and never opened, day or night, ventilation being obtained by means of a glass ventilator fitted in the upper panes. It seems absurd to think that this window, being only about four feet from the ground, should have had neither iron bars nor shutters added to it; such, however, was the case. On the night of the robbery, someone within the house must have deliberately, and of intention, unfastened its only protection, the brass catch, and thus given the thieves easy entrance to the house."

"Your suspicions, I suppose, centre upon the servants?"

"Undoubtedly; and it is in the servants' hall that your services will be required. The thieves, whoever they were, were perfectly cognizant of the ways of the house. Lady Cathrow's jewellery was kept in a safe in her dressing-room, and as the dressing-room was over the dining-room, Sir George was in the habit of saying that it was the 'safest' room in the house. (Note the pun, please, Sir George is rather proud of it.) By his orders the window of the dining-room immediately under the dressing-room window was always left unshuttered and without blind during dinner, and as a full stream of light thus fell through it on to the outside terrace, it would have been impossible

WINDOW ON THE GROUND FLOOR.

for anyone to have placed a ladder there unseen."

"I see from the newspapers that it was Sir George's invariable custom to fill his house and give a large dinner on Christmas Eve."

"Yes. Sir George and Lady Cathrow are elderly people, with no family and few relatives, and have consequently a large amount of time to spend on their friends."

"I suppose the key of the safe was frequently left in the possession of Lady Cathrow's maid?"

A HABIT OF DROPPING HER EYELIDS.

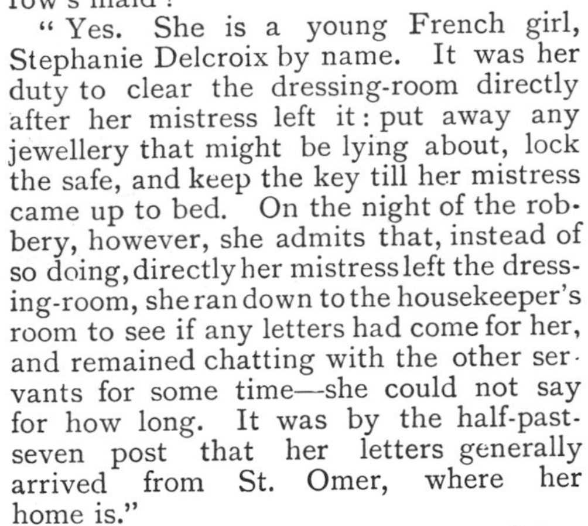

"Yes. She is a young French girl, Stephanie Delcroix by name. It was her duty to clear the dressing-room directly after her mistress left it: put away any jewellery that might be lying about, lock the safe, and keep the key till her mistress came up to bed. On the night of the robbery, however, she admits that, instead of so doing, directly her mistress left the dressing-room, she ran down to the housekeeper's room to see if any letters had come for her, and remained chatting with the other servants for some time—she could not say for how long. It was by the half-past-seven post that her letters generally arrived from St. Omer, where her home is."

"Oh, then, she was in the habit of thus running down to enquire for her letters, no doubt, and the thieves, who appear to be so thoroughly cognizant of the house, would know this also."

"Perhaps; though at the present moment I must say things look very black against the girl. Her manner, too, when questioned, is not calculated to remove suspicion. She goes from one fit of hysterics into another; contradicts herself nearly every time she opens her mouth, then lays it to the charge of her ignorance of our language; breaks into voluble French; becomes theatrical in action, and then goes off into hysterics once more."

"All that is quite Français, you know," said Loveday. "Do the authorities at Scotland Yard lay much stress on the safe being left unlocked that night?"

"They do, and they are instituting a keen enquiry as to the possible lovers the girl may have. For this purpose they have sent Bates down to stay in the village and collect all the information he can outside the house. But they want someone within the walls to hob-nob with the maids generally, and to find out if she has taken any of them into her confidence respecting her lovers. So they sent to me to know if I would send down for this purpose one of the shrewdest and most clear-headed of my female detectives. I, in my turn, Miss Brooke, have sent for you—you may take it as a compliment if you like. So please now get out your note-book, and I'll give you sailing orders."

Loveday Brooke, at this period of her career, was a little over thirty years of age, and could be best described in a series of negations.

She was not tall, she was not short; she was not dark, she was not fair; she was neither handsome nor ugly. Her features were altogether nondescript; her one noticeable trait was a habit she had, when absorbed in thought, of dropping her eyelids over her eyes till only a line of eyeball showed, and she appeared to be looking out at the world through a slit, instead of through a window.

Her dress was invariably black, and was almost Quaker-like in its neat primness.

Some five or six years previously, by a jerk of Fortune's wheel, Loveday had been thrown upon the world penniless and all but friendless. Marketable accomplishments she had found she had none, so she had forthwith defied convention, and had chosen for herself a career that had cut her off sharply from her former associates and her position in society. For five or six years she drudged away patiently in the lower walks of her profession; then chance, or, to speak more precisely, an intricate criminal case, threw her in the way of the experienced head of the flourishing detective agency in Lynch Court. He quickly enough found out the stuff she was made of, and threw her in the way of better-class work—work, indeed, that brought increase of pay and of reputation alike to him and to Loveday.

Ebenezer Dyer was not, as a rule, given to enthusiasm; but he would at times wax eloquent over Miss Brooke's qualifications for the profession she had chosen.

"Too much of a lady, do you say?" he would say to anyone who chanced to call in question those qualifications. "I don't care twopence-halfpenny whether she is or is not a lady. I only know she is the most sensible and practical woman I ever met. In the first place, she has the faculty—so rare among women—of carrying out orders to the very letter; in the second place, she has a clear, shrewd brain, unhampered by any hard-and-fast theories; thirdly, and most important item of all, she has so much common sense that it amounts to genius—positively to genius, sir."

"HAVE YOU SEEN THIS?"

But although Loveday and her chief as a rule, worked together upon an easy and friendly footing, there were occasions on which they were wont, so to speak, to snarl at each other.

Such an occasion was at hand now.

Loveday showed no disposition to take out her note-book and receive her "sailing orders."

"I want to know," she said, "if what I saw in one newspaper is true—that one of the thieves before leaving, took the trouble to close the safe-door, and to write across it in chalk: 'To be let, unfurnished'?"

"Perfectly true; but I do not see that stress need be laid on the fact. The scoundrels often do that sort of thing out of insolence or bravado. In that robbery at Reigate, the other day, they went to a lady's Davenport, took a sheet of her note-paper, and wrote their thanks on it for her kindness in not having had the lock of her safe repaired. Now, if you will get out your note-book ——"

"Don't be in such a hurry," said Loveday calmly; "I want to know if you have seen this?" She leaned across the writing-table at which they sat, one either side, and handed to him a newspaper cutting which she took from her letter-case.

Mr. Dyer was a tall, powerfully-built man with a large head, benevolent bald forehead and a genial smile. That smile, however, often proved a trap to the unwary, for he owned a temper so irritable that a child with a chance word might ruffle it.

The genial smile vanished as he took the newspaper cutting from Loveday's hand.

"I would have you to remember, Miss Brooke," he said severely, "that although I am in the habit of using despatch in my business, I am never known to be in a hurry; hurry in affairs I take to be the especial mark of the slovenly and unpunctual."

Then, as if still further to give contradiction to her words, he very deliberately unfolded her slip of newspaper and slowly, accentuating each word and syllable, read as follows:—

"Singular Discovery.

"A black leather bag, or portmanteau, was found early yesterday morning by one of Smith's newspaper boys on the doorstep of a house in the road running between Easterbrook and Wreford, and inhabited by an elderly spinster lady. The contents of the bag include a clerical collar and necktie, a Church Service, a book of sermons, a copy of the works of Virgil, a *facsimile* of Magna Charta, with translations, a pair of black kid gloves, a brush and comb, some newspapers, and several small articles suggesting clerical ownership. On the top of the bag the following extraordinary letter, written in pencil on a long slip of paper, was found:

'The fatal day has arrived. I can exist no longer. I go hence and shall be no more seen. But I would have Coroner and Jury know that I am a sane man, and a verdict of temporary insanity in my case would be an error most gross after this intimation. I care not if it is *felo de se*, as I shall have passed all suffering. Search diligently for my poor lifeless body in the immediate neighbourhood—on the cold heath, the rail, or the river by yonder bridge—a few moments will decide how I shall depart. If I had walked aright I might have been a power in the Church of which I am now an unworthy member and priest; but the damnable sin of gambling got hold on me, and betting has been my ruin, as it has been the ruin of thousands who have preceded me. Young man, shun the bookmaker and the race-course as you would shun the devil and hell. Farewell, chums of Magdalen. Farewell, and take warning. Though I can claim relationship with a Duke, a Marquess, and a Bishop, and though I am the son of a noble woman, yet am I a tramp and an outcast, verily and indeed. Sweet death, I greet thee. I dare not sign my name. To one and all, farewell. O, my poor Marchioness mother, a dying kiss to thee. R.I.P.'

"The police and some of the railway officials have made a 'diligent search' in the neighbourhood of the railway station, but no 'poor lifeless body' has been found. The police authorities are inclined to the belief that the letter is a hoax, though they are still investigating the matter."

In the same deliberate fashion as he had opened and read the cutting, Mr. Dyer folded and returned it to Loveday.

"May I ask," he said sarcastically, "what you see in that silly hoax to waste your and my valuable time over?"

"I wanted to know," said Loveday, in the same level tones as before, "if you saw anything in it that might in some way connect this discovery with the robbery at Craigen Court?"

Mr. Dyer stared at her in utter, blank astonishment.

"When I was a boy," he said sarcastically as before, "I used to play at a game called 'what is my thought like?' Someone would think of something absurd—say the top of the monument—and someone else would hazard a guess that his thought might be — say the toe of his left boot, and that unfortunate individual would have to show the connection between the toe of his left boot and the top of the monument. Miss Brooke, I have no wish to repeat the silly game this evening for your benefit and mine."

"Oh, very well," said Loveday, calmly; "I fancied you might like to talk it over, that was all. Give me my 'sailing orders,' as you call them, and I'll endeavour to concentrate my attention on the little French maid and her various lovers."

Mr. Dyer grew amiable again.

"That's the point on which I wish you to fix your thoughts," he said; "you had better start for Craigen Court by the first train to-morrow—it's about sixty miles down the Great Eastern line. Huxwell is the station you must land at. There one of the grooms from the Court will meet you, and drive you to the house. I have arranged with the housekeeper there—Mrs. Williams, a very worthy and discreet person—that you shall pass in the house for a niece of hers, on a visit to recruit, after severe study in order to pass board-school teachers' exams. Naturally you have injured your eyes as well as your health with overwork; and so you can wear your blue spectacles. Your name, by the way, will be Jane Smith—better write it down. All your work will lie among the servants of the establishment, and there will be no necessity for you to see either Sir George or Lady Cathrow—in fact, neither of them have been apprised of your intended visit—the fewer we take into our confidence the better. I've no doubt, however, that Bates will hear from Scotland Yard that you are in the house, and will make a point of seeing you."

"Has Bates unearthed anything of importance?"

"Not as yet. He has discovered one of the girl's lovers, a young farmer of the name of Holt; but as he seems to be an honest, respectable young fellow, and entirely above suspicion, the discovery does not count for much."

"I think there's nothing else to ask," said Loveday, rising to take her departure. "Of course, I'll telegraph, should need arise, in our usual cipher."

The first train that left Bishopsgate for Huxwell on the following morning included, among its passengers, Loveday Brooke, dressed in the neat black supposed to be appropriate to servants of the upper class. The only literature with which she had provided herself in order to beguile the tedium of her journey was a small volume bound in paper boards, and entitled, "The Reciter's Treasury." It was published at the low price of one shilling, and seemed specially designed to meet the requirements of third-rate amateur reciters at penny readings.

Miss Brooke appeared to be all-absorbed in the contents of this book during the first half of her journey. During the second, she lay back in the carriage with closed eyes, and motionless as if asleep or lost in deep thought.

The stopping of the train at Huxwell aroused her, and set her collecting together her wraps.

It was easy to single out the trim groom from Craigen Court from among the country loafers on the platform. Someone else beside the trim groom at the same moment caught her eye—Bates, from Scotland Yard, got up in the style of a commercial traveller, and carrying the orthodox "commercial bag" in his hand. He was a small, wiry man, with red hair and whiskers, and an eager, hungry expression of countenance.

"I am half-frozen with cold," said Loveday, addressing Sir George's groom; "if you'll kindly take charge of my portmanteau, I'd prefer walking to driving to the Court."

The man gave her a few directions as to the road she was to follow, and then drove off with her box, leaving her free to indulge Mr. Bates's evident wish for a walk and confidential talk along the country road.

RECITING THE "NOBLE CONVICT."

Bates seemed to be in a happy frame of mind that morning.

"Quite a simple affair, this, Miss Brooke," he said; "a walk over the course, I take it, with you working inside the castle walls and I unearthing without. No complications as yet have arisen, and if that girl does not find herself in jail before another week is over her head, my name is not Jeremiah Bates."

"You mean the French maid?"

"Why, yes, of course. I take it there's little doubt but what she performed the double duty of unlocking the safe and the window too. You see I look at it this way, Miss Brooke: all girls have lovers, I say to myself, but a pretty girl like that French maid, is bound to have double the number of lovers than the plain ones. Now, of course, the greater the number of lovers, the greater the chance there is of a criminal being found among them. That's plain as a pikestaff, isn't it?"

"Just as plain."

Bates felt encouraged to proceed.

"Well, then, arguing on the same lines, I say to myself, this girl is only a pretty, silly thing, not an accomplished criminal, or she wouldn't have admitted leaving open the safe door; give her rope enough and she'll hang herself. In a day or two, if we let her alone, she'll be bolting off to join the fellow whose nest she has helped to feather, and we shall catch the pair of them 'twixt here and Dover Straits, and also possibly get a clue that will bring us on the traces of their accomplices. Eh, Miss Brooke, that'll be a thing worth doing?"

"Undoubtedly. Who is this coming along in this buggy at such a good pace?"

The question was added as the sound of wheels behind them made her look round.

Bates turned also. "Oh, this is young Holt; his father farms land about a couple of miles from here. He is one of Stephanie's lovers, and I should imagine about the best of the lot. But he does not appear to be first favourite; from what I hear someone else must have made the running on the sly. Ever since the robbery I'm told the young woman has given him the cold shoulder."

As the young man came nearer in his buggy he slackened pace, and Loveday could not but admire his frank, honest expression of countenance.

"Room for one—can I give you a lift?" he said, as he came alongside of them.

And to the ineffable disgust of Bates, who had counted upon at least an hour's confidential talk with her, Miss Brooke accepted the young farmer's offer, and mounted beside him in his buggy.

As they went swiftly along the country road, Loveday explained to the young man that her destination was Craigen Court, and that as she was a stranger to the place, she must trust to him to put her down at the nearest point to it that he would pass.

At the mention of Craigen Court his face clouded.

"They're in trouble there, and their trouble has brought trouble on others," he said a little bitterly.

"I know," said Loveday sympathetically; "it is often so. In such circumstances as these suspicion frequently fastens on an entirely innocent person."

"That's it! that's it!" he cried excitedly; "if you go into that house you'll hear all sorts of wicked things said of her, and see everything setting in dead against her. But she's innocent. I swear to you she is as innocent as you or I are."

His voice rang out above the clatter of his horse's hoofs. He seemed to forget that he had mentioned no name, and that Loveday, as a stranger, might be at a loss to know to whom he referred.

"Who is guilty Heaven only knows," he went on after a moment's pause; "it isn't for me to give an ill name to anyone in that house; but I only say she is innocent, and that I'll stake my life on."

"She is a lucky girl to have found one to believe in her, and trust her as you do," said Loveday, even more sympathetically than before.

"Is she? I wish she'd take advantage of her luck, then," he answered bitterly. "Most girls in her position would be glad to have a man to stand by them through thick and thin. But not she! Ever since the night of that accursed robbery she has refused to see me—won't answer my letters—won't even send me a message. And, great Heavens! I'd marry her to-morrow, if I had the chance, and dare the world to say a word against her."

He whipped up his pony. The hedges seemed to fly on either side of them, and before Loveday realised that half her drive was over, he had drawn rein, and was helping her to alight at the servants' entrance to Craigen Court.

"You'll tell her what I've said to you, if you get the opportunity, and beg her to see me, if only for five minutes?" he petitioned before he re-mounted his buggy. And Loveday, as she thanked the young man for his kind attention, promised to make an opportunity to give his message to the girl.

Mrs. Williams, the housekeeper, welcomed Loveday in the servants' hall, and then took her to her own room to pull off her wraps. Mrs. Williams was the widow of a London tradesman, and a little beyond the average housekeeper in speech and manner.

She was a genial, pleasant woman, and readily entered into conversation with Loveday. Tea was brought in, and each seemed to feel at home with the other. Loveday in the course of this easy, pleasant talk, elicited from her the whole history of the events of the day of the robbery, the number and names of the guests who sat down to dinner that night, together with some other apparently trivial details.

The housekeeper made no attempt to disguise the painful position in which she and every one of the servants of the house felt themselves to be at the present moment.

"We are none of us at our ease with each other now," she said, as she poured out hot tea for Loveday, and piled up a blazing fire. "Everyone fancies that everyone else is suspecting him or her, and trying to rake up past words or deeds to bring in as evidence. The whole house seems under a cloud. And at this time of year, too; just when everything as a rule is at its merriest!" and here she gave a doleful glance to the big bunch of holly and mistletoe hanging from the ceiling.

"I suppose you are generally very merry downstairs at Christmas time?" said Loveday. "Servants' balls, theatricals, and all that sort of thing?"

"I should think we were! When I think of this time last year and the fun we all had, I can scarcely believe it is the same house. Our ball always follows my lady's ball, and we have permission to ask our friends to it, and we keep it up as late as ever we please. We begin our evening with a concert and recitations in character, then we have a supper and then we dance right on till morning; but this year!"—she broke off, giving a long, melancholy shake of her head that spoke volumes.

"I suppose," said Loveday, "some of your friends are very clever as musicians or reciters?"

"Very clever indeed. Sir George and my lady are always present during the early part of the evening, and I should like you to have seen Sir George last year laughing fit to kill himself at Harry Emmett dressed in prison dress with a bit of oakum in his hand, reciting the "Noble Convict!" Sir George said if the young man had gone on the stage, he would have been bound to make his fortune."

"Half a cup, please," said Loveday, presenting her cup. "Who was this Harry Emmett then—a sweetheart of one of the maids?"

"Oh, he would flirt with them all, but he was sweetheart to none. He was footman to Colonel James, who is a great friend of Sir George's, and Harry was constantly backwards and forwards bringing messages from his master. His father, I think, drove a cab in London, and Harry for a time did so also; then he took it into his head to be a gentleman's servant, and great satisfaction he gave as such. He was always such a bright, handsome young fellow and so full of fun, that everyone liked him. But I shall tire you with all this; and you, of course, want to talk about something so different;" and the housekeeper sighed again, as the thought of the dreadful robbery entered her brain once more.

"TO BE LET, UNFURNISHED."

"Not at all. I am greatly interested in you and your festivities. Is Emmett still in the neighbourhood? I should amazingly like to hear him recite myself."

"I'm sorry to say he left Colonel James about six months ago. We all missed him very much at first. He was a good, kind-hearted young man, and I remember he told me he was going away to look after his dear old grandmother, who had a sweet-stuff shop somewhere or other, but where I can't remember."

Loveday was leaning back in her chair now, with eyelids drooped so low that she literally looked out through "slits" instead of eyes.

Suddenly and abruptly she changed the conversation.

"When will it be convenient for me to see Lady Cathrow's dressing-room?" she asked.

The housekeeper looked at her watch. "Now, at once," she answered; "it's a quarter to five now and my lady sometimes goes up to her room to rest for half an hour before she dresses for dinner."

"Is Stephanie still in attendance on Lady Cathrow?" Miss Brooke asked as she followed the housekeeper up the back stairs to the bedroom floor.

"Yes. Sir George and my lady have been goodness itself to us through this trying time, and they say we are all innocent till we are proved guilty, and will have it that none of our duties are to be in any way altered."

"Stephanie is scarcely fit to perform hers, I should imagine?"

"Scarcely. She was in hysterics nearly from morning till night for the first two or three days after the detectives came down, but now she has grown sullen, eats nothing and never speaks a word to any of us except when she is obliged. This is my lady's dressing-room, walk in please."

Loveday entered a large, luxuriously furnished room, and naturally made her way straight to the chief point of attraction in it—the iron safe fitted into the wall that separated the dressing-room from the bedroom.

It was a safe of the ordinary description, fitted with a strong iron door and Chubb lock. And across this door was written with chalk in characters that seemed defiant in their size and boldness, the words: "To be let, unfurnished."

Loveday spent about five minutes in front of this safe, all her attention concentrated upon the big, bold writing.

She took from her pocket-book a narrow strip of tracing-paper and compared the writing on it, letter by letter, with that on the safe door. This done she turned to Mrs. Williams and professed herself ready to follow her to the room below.

Mrs. Williams looked surprised. Her opinion of Miss Brooke's professional capabilities suffered considerable diminution.

"The gentlemen detectives," she said, "spent over an hour in this room; they paced the floor, they measured the candles, they ——"

"Mrs. Williams," interrupted Loveday, "I am quite ready to look at the room below." Her manner had changed from gossiping friendliness to that of the business woman hard at work at her profession.

Without another word, Mrs. Williams led the way to the little room which had proved itself to be the "weak point" of the house.

They entered it by the door which opened into a passage leading to the back-stairs of the house. Loveday found the room exactly what it had been described to her by Mr. Dyer. It needed no second glance at the window to see the ease with which anyone could open it from the outside, and swing themselves into the room, when once the brass catch had been unfastened.

Loveday wasted no time here. In fact, much to Mrs. Williams's surprise and disappointment, she merely walked across the room, in at one door and out at the opposite one, which opened into the large inner hall of the house.

Here, however, she paused to ask a question:

"Is that chair always placed exactly in that position?" she said, pointing to an oak chair that stood immediately outside the room they had just quitted.

The housekeeper answered in the affirmative. It was a warm corner. "My lady" was particular that everyone who came to the house on messages should have a comfortable place to wait in.

"I shall be glad if you will show me to my room now," said Loveday, a little abruptly; "and will you kindly send up to me a county trade directory, if, that is, you have such a thing in the house?"

Mrs. Williams, with an air of offended dignity, led the way to the bedroom quarters once more. The worthy housekeeper felt as if her own dignity had, in some sort, been injured by the want of interest Miss Brooke had evinced in the rooms which, at the present moment, she considered the "show" rooms of the house.

"Shall I send someone to help you unpack?" she asked, a little stiffly, at the door of Loveday's room.

"No, thank you; there will not be much unpacking to do. I must leave here by the first up-train to-morrow morning."

"To-morrow morning! Why, I have told everyone you will be here at least a fortnight!"

"Ah, then you must explain that I have been suddenly summoned home by telegram. I'm sure I can trust you to make excuses for me. Do not, however, make them before supper-time. I shall like to sit down to that meal with you. I suppose I shall see Stephanie then?"

The housekeeper answered in the affirmative, and went her way, wondering over the strange manners of the lady whom, at first, she had been disposed to consider "such a nice, pleasant, conversable person!"

At supper-time, however, when the upper-servants assembled at what was, to them, the pleasantest meal of the day, a great surprise was to greet them.

Stephanie did not take her usual place at table, and a fellow-servant, sent to her room to summon her, returned, saying that the room was empty, and Stephanie was nowhere to be found.

Loveday and Mrs. Williams together went to the girl's bed-room. It bore its usual appearance: no packing had been done in it, and, beyond her hat and jacket, the girl appeared to have taken nothing away with her.

On enquiry, it transpired that Stephanie had, as usual, assisted Lady Cathrow to dress for dinner; but after that not a soul in the house appeared to have seen her.

Mrs. Williams thought the matter of sufficient importance to be at once reported to her master and mistress; and Sir George, in his turn, promptly despatched a messenger to Mr. Bates, at the "King's Head," to summon him to an immediate consultation.

Loveday despatched a messenger in another direction—to young Mr. Holt, at his farm, giving him particulars of the girl's disappearance.

Mr. Bates had a brief interview with Sir George in his study, from which he emerged radiant. He made a point of seeing Loveday before he left the Court, sending a special request to her that she would speak to him for a minute in the outside drive.

Loveday put her hat on, and went out to him. She found him almost dancing for glee.

"Told you so! told you so! Now, didn't I, Miss Brooke?" he exclaimed. "We'll come upon her traces before morning, never fear. I'm quite prepared. I knew what was in her mind all along. I said to myself, when that girl bolts it will be after she has dressed my lady for dinner—when she has two good clear hours all to herself, and her absence from the house won't be noticed, and when, without much difficulty, she can catch a train leaving Huxwell for Wreford. Well, she'll get to Wreford safe enough; but from Wreford she'll be followed every step of the way she goes. Only yesterday I set a man on there—a keen fellow at this sort of thing—and gave him full directions; and he'll hunt her down to her hole properly. Taken nothing with her, do you say? What does that matter? She thinks she'll find all she wants where she's going—'the feathered nest' I spoke to you about this morning. Ha! ha! Well, instead of stepping into it, as she fancies she will, she'll walk straight into a detective's arms, and land her pal there into the bargain. There'll be two of them netted before another forty-eight hours are over our heads, or my name's not Jeremiah Bates."

AN OLD GENTLEMAN WRITING.

"What are you going to do now?" asked Loveday, as the man finished his long speech.

"Now! I'm back to the "King's Head" to wait for a telegram from my colleague at Wreford. Once he's got her in front of him he'll give me instructions at what point to meet him. You see, Huxwell being such an out-of-the-way place, and only one train leaving between 7.30 and 10.15, makes us really positive that Wreford must be the girl's destination and relieves my mind from all anxiety on the matter."

"Does it?" answered Loveday gravely. "I can see another possible destination for the girl—the stream that runs through the wood we drove past this morning. Good night, Mr. Bates, it's cold out here. Of course so soon as you have any news you'll send it up to Sir George."

The household sat up late that night, but no news was received of Stephanie from any quarter. Mr. Bates had impressed upon Sir George the ill-advisability of setting up a hue and cry after the girl that might possibly reach her ears and scare her from joining the person whom he was pleased to designate as her "pal."

"We want to follow her silently, Sir George, silently as, the shadow follows the man," he had said grandiloquently, "and then we shall come upon the two, and I trust upon their booty also." Sir George in his turn had impressed Mr. Bates's wishes upon his household, and if it had not been for Loveday's message, despatched early in the evening to young Holt, not a soul outside the house would have known of Stephanie's disappearance.

Loveday was stirring early the next morning, and the eight o'clock train for Wreford numbered her among its passengers. Before starting, she despatched a telegram to her chief in Lynch Court. It read rather oddly, as follows:—

"Cracker fired. Am just starting for Wreford. Will wire to you from there. L.B."

Oddly though it might read, Mr. Dyer did not need to refer to his cipher book to interpret it. "Cracker fired" was the easily remembered equivalent for "clue found" in the detective phraseology of the office.

"Well, she has been quick enough about it this time!" he soliloquised as he speculated in his own mind over what the purport of the next telegram might be.

Half an hour later there came to him a constable from Scotland Yard to tell him of Stephanie's disappearance and the conjectures that were rife on the matter, and he then, not unnaturally, read Loveday's telegram by the light of this information, and concluded that the clue in her hands related to the discovery of Stephanie's whereabouts as well as to that of her guilt.

A telegram received a little later on, however, was to turn this theory upside down. It was, like the former one, worded in the enigmatic language current in the Lynch Court establishment, but as it was a lengthier and more intricate message, it sent Mr. Dyer at once to his cipher book.

"Wonderful! She has cut them all out this time!" was Mr. Dyer's exclamation as he read and interpreted the final word.

In another ten minutes he had given over his office to the charge of his head clerk for the day, and was rattling along the streets in a hansom in the direction of Bishopsgate Station.

There he was lucky enough to catch a train just starting for Wreford.

"The event of the day," he muttered, as he settled himself comfortably in a corner seat, "will be the return journey when she tells me, bit by bit, how she has worked it all out."

It was not until close upon three o'clock in the afternoon that he arrived at the old-fashioned market town of Wreford. It chanced to be cattle-market day, and the station was crowded with drovers and farmers. Outside the station Loveday was waiting for him, as she had told him in her telegram that she would, in a four-wheeler.

"It's all right," she said to him as he got in; "he can't get away, even if he had an idea that we were after him. Two of the local police are waiting outside the house door with a warrant for his arrest, signed by a magistrate. I did not, however, see why the Lynch Court office should not have the credit of the thing, and so telegraphed to you to conduct the arrest."

They drove through the High Street to the outskirts of the town, where the shops became intermixed with private houses let out in offices. The cab pulled up outside one of these, and two policemen in plain clothes came forward, and touched their hats to Mr. Dyer.

"He's in there now, sir, doing his office work," said one of the men pointing to a door, just within the entrance, on which was painted in black letters, "The United Kingdom Cab-drivers' Beneficent Association." "I hear, however, that this is the last time he will be found there, as a week ago he gave notice to leave."

As the man finished speaking, a man, evidently of the cab-driving fraternity, came up the steps. He stared curiously at the little group just within the entrance, and then chinking his money in his hand, passed on to the office as if to pay his subscription.

"Will you be good enough to tell Mr. Emmett in there," said Mr. Dyer, addressing the man, "that a gentleman outside wishes to speak with him."

The man nodded and passed into the office. As the door opened, it disclosed to view an old gentleman seated at a desk apparently writing receipts for money. A little in his rear at his right hand, sat a young and decidedly good-looking man, at a table on which were placed various little piles of silver and pence. The get-up of this young man was gentleman-like, and his manner was affable and pleasant as he responded, with a nod and a smile, to the cab-driver's message.

"I sha'n't be a minute," he said to his colleague at the other desk, as he rose and crossed the room towards the door.

But once outside that door it was closed firmly behind him, and he found himself in the centre of three stalwart individuals, one of whom informed him that he held in his hand a warrant for the arrest of Harry Emmett on the charge of complicity in the Craigen Court robbery, and that he had "better come along quietly, for resistance would be useless."

Emmett seemed convinced of the latter fact. He grew deadly white for a moment, then recovered himself.

"Will someone have the kindness to fetch my hat and coat," he said in a lofty manner. "I don't see why I should be made to catch my death of cold because some other people have seen fit to make asses of themselves."

HE GREW DEADLY WHITE.

His hat and coat were fetched, and he was handed into the cab between the two officials.

"Let me give you a word of warning, young man," said Mr. Dyer, closing the cab door and looking in for a moment through the window at Emmett. "I don't suppose it's a punishable offence to leave a black bag on an old maid's doorstep, but let me tell you, if it had not been for that black bag you might have got clean off with your spoil."

Emmett, the irrepressible, had his answer ready. He lifted his hat ironically to Mr. Dyer; "You might have put it more neatly, guv'nor," he said; "if I had been in your place I would have said: 'Young man, you are being justly punished for your misdeeds; you have been taking off your fellow-creatures all your life long, and now they are taking off you.' "

Mr. Dyer's duty that day did not end with the depositing of Harry Emmett in the local jail. The search through Emmett's lodgings and effects had to be made, and at this he was naturally present. About a third of the lost jewellery was found there, and from this it was consequently concluded that his accomplices in the crime had considered that he had borne a third of the risk and of the danger of it.

Letters and various memoranda discovered in the rooms, eventually led to the detection of those accomplices, and although Lady Cathrow was doomed to lose the greater part of her valuable property, she had ultimately the satisfaction of knowing that each one of the thieves received a sentence proportionate to his crime.

It was not until close upon midnight that Mr. Dyer found himself seated in the train, facing Miss Brooke, and had leisure to ask for the links in the chain of reasoning that had led her in so remarkable a manner to connect the finding of a black bag, with insignificant contents, with an extensive robbery of valuable jewellery.

Loveday explained the whole thing, easily, naturally, step by step in her usual methodical manner.

"I read," she said, "as I dare say a great many other people did, the account of the two things in the same newspaper, on the same day, and I detected, as I dare say a great many other people did not, a sense of fun in the principal actor in each incident. I notice while all people are agreed as to the variety of motives that instigate crime, very few allow sufficient margin for variety of character in the criminal. We are apt to imagine that he stalks about the world with a bundle of deadly motives under his arm, and cannot picture him at his work with a twinkle in his eye and a keen sense of fun, such as honest folk have sometimes when at work at their calling."

Here Mr. Dyer gave a little grunt; it might have been either of assent or dissent.

Loveday went on:

"Of course, the ludicrousness of the

diction of the letter found in the bag would be apparent to the most casual reader; to me the high falutin sentences sounded in addition strangely familiar; I had heard or read them somewhere I felt sure, although where I could not at first remember. They rang in my ears, and it was not altogether out of idle curiosity that I went to Scotland Yard to see the bag and its contents, and to copy, with a slip of tracing paper, a line or two of the letter. When I found that the handwriting of this letter was not identical with that of the translations found in the bag, I was confirmed in my impression that the owner of the bag was not the writer of the letter; that possibly the bag and its contents had been appropriated from some railway station for some distinct purpose; and, that purpose accomplished, the appropriator no longer wished to be burthened with it, and disposed of it in the readiest fashion that suggested itself. The letter, it seemed to me, had been begun with the intention of throwing the police off the scent, but the irrepressible spirit of fun that had induced the writer to deposit his clerical adjuncts upon an old maid's doorstep had proved too strong for him here, and had carried him away, and the letter that was intended to be pathetic ended in being comic."

"Very ingenious, so far," murmured Mr. Dyer: "I've no doubt when the contents of the bag are widely made known through advertisements a claimant will come forward, and your theory be found correct."

"When I returned from Scotland Yard," Loveday continued, "I found your note, asking me to go round and see you respecting the big jewel robbery. Before I did so I thought it best to read once more the newspaper account of the case, so that I might be well up in its details. When I came to the words that the thief had written across the door of the safe, 'To be Let, Unfurnished,' they at once connected themselves in my mind with the 'dying kiss to my Marchioness Mother,' and the solemn warning against the race-course and the book-maker, of the black-bag letter-writer. Then, all in a flash, the whole thing became clear to me. Some two or three years back my professional duties necessitated my frequent attendance at certain low-class penny-readings, given in the South London slums. At these penny-readings young

A YOUNG CLERGYMAN PRESENTED HIMSELF.

shop-assistants, and others of their class, glad of an opportunity for exhibiting their accomplishments, declaim with great vigour; and, as a rule, select pieces which their very mixed audience might be supposed to appreciate. During my attendance at these meetings, it seemed to me that one book of selected readings was a great favourite among the reciters, and I took the trouble to buy it. Here it is."

Here Loveday took from her cloak-pocket "The Reciter's Treasury," and handed it to her companion.

"Now," she said, "if you will run your eye down the index column you will find the titles of those pieces to which I wish to draw your attention. The first is 'The Suicide's Farewell;' the second, 'The Noble Convict;' the third, 'To be Let, Unfurnished.'"

"By, Jove! so it is!" ejaculated Mr. Dyer.

"In the first of these pieces, 'The Suicide's Farewell,' occur the expressions with which the black-bag letter begins—'The fatal day has arrived,' etc., the warnings against gambling, and the allusions to the 'poor lifeless body.' In the second, 'The Noble Convict,' occur the allusions to the aristocratic relations and the dying kiss to the marchioness mother. The third piece, 'To be Let, Unfurnished,' is a foolish little poem enough, although I dare say it has often raised a laugh in a not too-discriminating audience.

It tells how a bachelor, calling at a house to enquire after rooms to be let unfurnished, falls in love with the daughter of the house, and offers her his heart, which, he says, is to be let unfurnished. She declines his offer, and retorts that she thinks his head must be to let unfurnished, too. With these three pieces before me, it was not difficult to see a thread of connection between the writer of the black-bag letter and the thief who wrote across the empty safe at Craigen Court. Following this thread, I unearthed the story of Harry Emmett—footman, reciter, general lover and scamp. Subsequently I compared the writing on my tracing-paper with that on the safe-door, and, allowing for the difference between a bit of chalk and a steel nib, came to the conclusion that there could be but little doubt but what both were written by the same hand. Before that, however, I had obtained another, and what I consider the most important, link in my chain of evidence — how Emmett brought his clerical dress into use."

"Ah, how did you find out that now?" asked Mr. Dyer, leaning forward with his elbows on his knees.

"In the course of conversation with Mrs. Williams, whom I found to be a most communicative person, I elicited the names of the guests who had sat down to dinner on Christmas Eve. They were all people of undoubted respectability in the neighbourhood. Just before dinner was announced, she said, a young clergyman had presented himself at the front door, asking to speak with the Rector of the parish. The Rector, it seems, always dines at Craigen Court on Christmas Eve. The young clergyman's story was that he had been told by a certain clergyman, whose name he mentioned, that a curate was wanted in the parish, and he had travelled down from London to offer his services. He had been, he said, to the Rectory and had been told by the servants where the Rector was dining, and fearing to lose his chance of the curacy, had followed him to the Court. Now the Rector had been wanting a curate and had filled the vacancy only the previous week; he was a little inclined to be irate at this interruption to the evening's festivities, and told the young man that he didn't want a curate. When, however, he saw how disappointed the poor young fellow looked—I believe he shed a tear or two—

LOVEDAY EXPLAINED THE WHOLE THING.

his heart softened; he told him to sit down and rest in the hall before he attempted the walk back to the station, and said he would ask Sir George to send him out a glass of wine. The young man sat down in a chair immediately outside the room by which the thieves entered. Now I need not tell you who that young man was, nor suggest to your mind, I am sure, the idea that while the servant went to fetch him his wine, or, indeed, so soon as he saw the coast clear, he slipped into that little room and pulled back the catch of the window that admitted his confederates, who, no doubt, at that very moment were in hiding in the grounds. The housekeeper did not know whether this meek young curate had a black bag with him. Personally I have no doubt of the fact, nor that it contained the cap, cuffs, collar, and outer garments of Harry Emmett, which were most likely re-donned before he returned to his lodgings at Wreford, where I should say he repacked the bag with its clerical contents, and wrote his serio-comic letter. This bag, I suppose, he must have deposited in the very early morning, before anyone was stirring, on the door-step of the house in the Easterbrook Road."

Mr. Dyer drew a long breath. In his heart was unmitigated admiration for his colleague's skill, which seemed to him to fall little short of inspiration. By-and-by, no doubt, he would sing her praises to the first person who came along with a hearty good will; he had not, however, the slightest intention of so singing them in her own ears—excessive praise was apt to have a bad effect on the rising practitioner.

So he contented himself with saying :

"Yes, very satisfactory. Now tell me how you hunted the fellow down to his diggings ? "

"Oh, that was mere A B C work," answered Loveday. "Mrs. Williams told me he had left his place at Colonel James's about six months previously, and had told her he was going to look after his dear old grandmother, who kept a sweet-stuff-shop ; but where she could not remember. Having heard that Emmett's father was a cabdriver, my thoughts at once flew to the cabman's vernacular—you know something of it, no doubt—in which their provident association is designated by the phrase, 'the dear old grandmother,' and the office where they make and receive their payments is styled 'the sweet stuff-shop.'"

"Ha, ha, ha ! And good Mrs. Williams took it all literally, no doubt ? "

"She did ; and thought what a dear, kind-hearted fellow the young man was. Naturally I supposed there would be a branch of the association in the nearest market town, and a local trades' directory confirmed my supposition that there was one at Wreford. Bearing in mind where the black bag was found, it was not difficult to believe that young Emmett, possibly through his father's influence and his own prepossessing manners and appearance, had attained to some position of trust in the Wreford branch. I must confess I scarcely expected to find him as I did, on reaching the place, installed as receiver of the weekly moneys. Of course, I immediately put myself in communication with the police there, and the rest I think you know."

Mr. Dyer's enthusiasm refused to be longer restrained.

"It's capital, from first to last," he cried; "you've surpassed yourself this time ! "

"The only thing that saddens me," said Loveday, "is the thought of the possible fate of that poor little Stephanie."

Loveday's anxieties on Stephanie's behalf were, however, to be put to flight before another twenty-four hours had passed. The first post on the following morning brought a letter from Mrs. Williams telling how the girl had been found before the night was over, half dead with cold and fright, on the verge of the stream running through Craigen Wood—"found too"—wrote the housekeeper, "by the very person who ought to have found her, young Holt, who was, and is so desperately in love with her. Thank goodness! at the last moment her courage failed her, and instead of throwing herself into the stream, she sank down, half-fainting, beside it. Holt took her straight home to his mother, and there, at the farm, she is now, being taken care of and petted generally by everyone."

FOUND ON THE VERGE OF THE STREAM.

The Experiences of Loveday Brooke, Lady Detective.

By C. L. PIRKIS

THE MURDER AT TROYTE'S HILL.

"GRIFFITHS, of the Newcastle Constabulary, has the case in hand," said Mr. Dyer; "those Newcastle men are keen-witted, shrewd fellows, and very jealous of outside interference. They only sent to me under protest, as it were, because they wanted your sharp wits at work inside the house."

"I suppose throughout I am to work with Griffiths, not with you?" said Miss Brooke.

"Yes; when I have given you in outline the facts of the case, I simply have nothing more to do with it, and you must depend on Griffiths for any assistance of any sort that you may require."

Here, with a swing, Mr. Dyer opened his big ledger and turned rapidly over its leaves till he came to the heading "Troyte's Hill" and the date "September 6th."

"I'm all attention," said Loveday, leaning back in her chair in the attitude of a listener.

"The murdered man," resumed Mr. Dyer, "is a certain Alexander Henderson—usually known as old Sandy—lodge-keeper to Mr. Craven, of Troyte's Hill, Cumberland. The lodge consists merely of two rooms on the ground floor, a bed-room and a sitting-room; these Sandy occupied alone, having neither kith nor kin of any degree. On the morning of September 6th, some children going up to the house with milk from the farm, noticed that Sandy's bed-room window stood wide open. Curiosity prompted them to peep in; and then, to their horror, they saw old Sandy, in his night-shirt, lying dead on the floor, as if he had fallen backwards from the window. They raised an alarm; and on examination, it was found that death had ensued from a heavy blow on the temple, given either by a strong fist or some blunt instrument. The room, on being entered, presented a curious appearance. It was as if a herd of monkeys had been turned into it and allowed to work their impish will. Not an article of furniture remained in its place: the bed-clothes had been rolled into a bundle and stuffed into the chimney; the bedstead—a small iron one—lay on its side; the one chair in the room stood on the top of the table; fender and fire-irons lay across the washstand, whose basin was to be found in a farther corner, holding bolster and pillow. The clock stood on its head in the middle of the mantelpiece; and the small vases and ornaments, which flanked it on either side, were walking, as it were, in a straight line towards the door. The old man's clothes had been rolled into a ball and thrown on the top of a high cupboard in which he kept his savings and whatever valuables he had. This cupboard, however, had not been meddled with, and its contents remained intact, so it was evident that robbery was not the motive for the crime. At the inquest, subsequently held, a verdict of 'wilful murder' against some person or persons unknown was returned. The local police are diligently investigating the affair, but, as yet, no arrests have been made. The opinion that at present prevails in the neighbourhood is that the crime has been perpetrated by some lunatic, escaped or otherwise, and enquiries are being made at the local asylums as to missing or lately released inmates. Griffiths, however, tells me that his suspicions set in another direction."

"Did anything of importance transpire at the inquest?"

"Nothing specially important. Mr. Craven broke down in giving his evidence when he alluded to the confidential relations that had always subsisted between Sandy and himself, and spoke of the last time that he had seen him alive. The evidence of the butler, and one or two of the female servants, seems clear enough, and they let fall something of a hint that Sandy was not altogether a favourite among them, on account of the overbearing manner in which he used his influence with his master. Young Mr. Craven, a youth of about nineteen, home from Oxford for the long vacation, was not present at the inquest; a doctor's certificate was put in stating that he was suffering from typhoid fever, and could not leave his bed without risk to his life. Now this young man is a thoroughly bad sort, and as much a gentleman-blackleg as it is possible for such a young fellow to be. It seems to Griffiths that there is something suspicious about this illness of his. He came back from Oxford on the verge of delirium tremens, pulled round from that, and then suddenly, on the day after the murder, Mrs. Craven rings the bell, announces that he has developed typhoid fever and orders a doctor to be sent for."

"What sort of man is Mr. Craven senior?"

"He seems to be a quiet old fellow, a scholar and learned philologist. Neither his neighbours nor his family see much of him; he almost lives in his study, writing a treatise, in seven or eight volumes, on comparative philology. He is not a rich man. Troyte's Hill, though it carries position in the county, is not a paying property, and Mr. Craven is unable to keep it up properly. I am told he has had to cut down expenses in all directions in order to send his son to college, and his daughter from first to last, has been entirely educated by her mother. Mr. Craven was originally intended for the church, but for some reason or other, when his college career came to an end, he did not present himself for ordination—went out to Natal instead, where he obtained some civil appointment and where he remained for about fifteen years. Henderson was his servant during the latter portion of his Oxford career, and must have been greatly respected by him, for although the remuneration derived from his appointment at Natal was small, he paid Sandy a regular yearly allowance out of it. When, about ten years ago, he succeeded to Troyte's Hill, on the death of his elder brother, and returned home with his family, Sandy was immediately installed as lodge-keeper, and at so high a rate of pay that the butler's wages were cut down to meet it."

"Ah, that wouldn't improve the butler's feelings towards him," ejaculated Loveday.

Mr. Dyer went on: "But, in spite of his high wages, he doesn't appear to have troubled much about his duties as lodge-keeper, for they were performed, as a rule, by the gardener's boy, while he took his meals and passed his time at the house, and, speaking generally, put his finger into every pie. You know the old adage respecting the servant of twenty-one years' standing: 'Seven years my servant, seven years my equal, seven years my master.' Well, it appears to have held good in the case of Mr. Craven and Sandy. The old gentleman, absorbed in his philological studies, evidently let the reins slip through his fingers, and Sandy seems to have taken easy possession of them. The servants frequently had to go to him for orders, and he carried things, as a rule, with a high hand."

"Did Mrs. Craven never have a word to say on the matter?"

"I've not heard much about her. She seems to be a quiet sort of person. She is a Scotch missionary's daughter; perhaps she spends her time working for the Cape mission and that sort of thing."

"And young

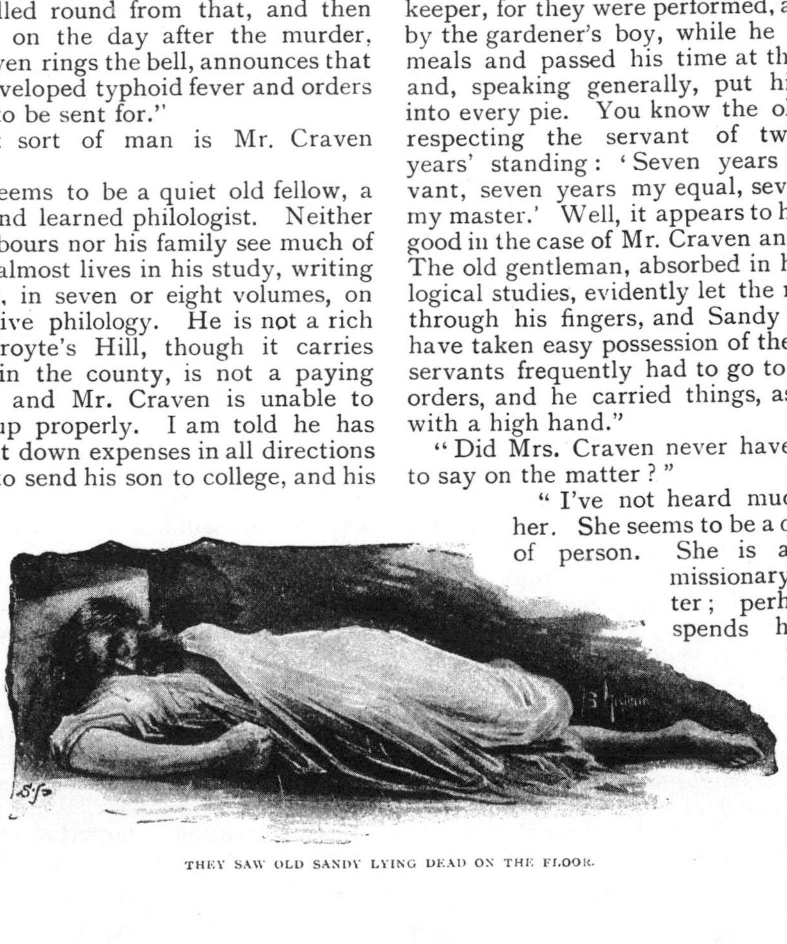

THEY SAW OLD SANDY LYING DEAD ON THE FLOOR.

Mr. Craven: did he knock under to Sandy's rule?"

"Ah, now you're hitting the bull's eye and we come to Griffiths' theory. The young man and Sandy appear to have been at loggerheads ever since the Cravens took possession of Troyte's Hill. As a schoolboy Master Harry defied Sandy and threatened him with his hunting-crop; and subsequently, as a young man, has used strenuous endeavours to put the old servant in his place. On the day before the murder, Griffiths says, there was a terrible scene between the two, in which the young gentleman, in the presence of several witnesses, made use of strong language and threatened the old man's life. Now, Miss Brooke, I have told you all the circumstances of the case so far as I know them. For fuller particulars I must refer you to Griffiths. He, no doubt, will meet you at Grenfell—the nearest station to Troyte's Hill, and tell you in what capacity he has procured for you an entrance into the house. By-the-way, he has wired to me this morning that he hopes you will be able to save the Scotch express to-night."

Loveday expressed her readiness to comply with Mr. Griffiths' wishes.

"I shall be glad," said Mr. Dyer, as he shook hands with her at the office door, "to see you immediately on your return—that, however, I suppose, will not be yet awhile. This promises, I fancy, to be a longish affair?" This was said interrogatively.

"I haven't the least idea on the matter," answered Loveday. "I start on my work without theory of any sort—in fact, I may say, with my mind a perfect blank."

And anyone who had caught a glimpse of her blank, expressionless features, as she said this, would have taken her at her word.

Grenfell, the nearest post-town to Troyte's Hill is a fairly busy, populous little town—looking south towards the black country, and northwards to low, barren hills. Pre-eminent among these stands Troyte's Hill, famed in the old days as a border keep, and possibly at a still earlier date as a Druid stronghold.

At a small inn at Grenfell, dignified by the title of "The Station Hotel," Mr. Griffiths, of the Newcastle constabulary, met Loveday and still further initiated her into the mysteries of the Troyte's Hill murder.

"A little of the first excitement has subsided," he said, after preliminary greetings had been exchanged; "but still the wildest rumours are flying about and repeated as solemnly as if they were Gospel truths. My chief here and my colleagues generally adhere to their first conviction, that the criminal is some suddenly crazed tramp or else an escaped lunatic, and they are confident that sooner or later we shall come upon his traces. Their theory is that Sandy, hearing some strange noise at the Park Gates, put his head out of the window to ascertain the cause and immediately had his death blow dealt him; then they suppose that the lunatic scrambled into the room through the window and exhausted his frenzy by turning things generally upside down. They refuse altogether to share my suspicions respecting young Mr. Craven."

Mr. Griffiths was a tall, thin-featured man, with iron-grey hair, cut so close to his head that it refused to do anything but stand on end This gave a somewhat comic expression to the upper portion of his face and clashed oddly with the melancholy look that his mouth habitually wore.

"I have made all smooth for you at Troyte's Hill," he presently went on. "Mr. Craven is not wealthy enough to allow himself the luxury of a family lawyer, so he occasionally employs the services of Messrs. Wells and Sugden, lawyers in this place, and who, as it happens, have, off and on, done a good deal of business for me. It was through them I heard that Mr. Craven was anxious to secure the assistance of an amanuensis. I immediately offered your services, stating that you were a friend of mine, a lady of impoverished means, who would gladly undertake the duties for the munificent sum of a guinea a month, with board and lodging. The old gentleman at once jumped at the offer, and is anxious for you to be at Troyte's Hill at once.

Loveday expressed her satisfaction with the programme that Mr. Griffiths had sketched for her, then she had a few questions to ask.

"Tell me," she said, "what led you, in the first instance, to suspect young Mr. Craven of the crime?"

"The footing on which he and Sandy stood towards each other, and the terrible scene that occurred between them only the day before the murder," answered Griffiths, promptly. "Nothing of this, however, was elicited at the inquest, where a very fair face was put on Sandy's relations with the whole of the Craven family. I have subsequently unearthed a good deal respecting the private life of Mr. Harry Craven, and, among other things, I have found out that on the night of the murder he left the house shortly after ten o'clock, and no one, so far as I have been able to ascertain, knows at what hour he returned. Now I must draw your attention, Miss Brooke, to the fact that at the inquest the medical evidence went to prove that the murder had been committed between ten and eleven at night."

PRETTY MISS CRAVEN

"Do you surmise, then, that the murder was a planned thing on the part of this young man?"

"I do. I believe that he wandered about the grounds until Sandy shut himself in for the night, then aroused him by some outside noise, and, when the old man looked out to ascertain the cause, dealt him a blow with a bludgeon or loaded stick, that caused his death."

"A cold-blooded crime that, for a boy of nineteen?"

"Yes. He's a good-looking, gentlemanly youngster, too, with manners as mild as milk, but from all accounts is as full of wickedness as an egg is full of meat. Now, to come to another point—if, in connection with these ugly facts, you take into consideration the suddenness of his illness, I think you'll admit that it bears a suspicious appearance and might reasonably give rise to the surmise that it was a plant on his part, in order to get out of the inquest."

"Who is the doctor attending him?"

"A man called Waters; not much of a practitioner, from all accounts, and no doubt he feels himself highly honoured in being summoned to Troyte's Hill. The Cravens, it seems, have no family doctor. Mrs. Craven, with her missionary experience, is half a doctor herself, and never calls in one except in a serious emergency."

"The certificate was in order, I suppose?"

"Undoubtedly. And, as if to give colour to the gravity of the case, Mrs. Craven sent a message down to the servants, that if any of them were afraid of the infection they could at once go to their homes. Several of the maids, I believe, took advantage of her permission, and packed their boxes. Miss Craven, who is a delicate girl, was sent away with her maid to stay with friends at Newcastle, and Mrs. Craven isolated herself with her patient in one of the disused wings of the house."

"Has anyone ascertained whether Miss Craven arrived at her destination at Newcastle?"

Griffiths drew his brows together in thought.

"I did not see any necessity for such a thing," he answered. "I don't quite follow you. What do you mean to imply?"

"Oh, nothing. I don't suppose it matters much: it might have been interesting as a side-issue." She broke off for a moment, then added:

"Now tell me a little about the butler, the man whose wages were cut down to increase Sandy's pay."

"Old John Hales? He's a thoroughly worthy, respectable man; he was butler for five or six years to Mr. Craven's brother, when he was master of Troyte's Hill, and then took duty under this Mr. Craven. There's no ground for suspicion in that quarter. Hales's exclamation when he heard of the murder is quite enough to stamp him as an innocent man: 'Serve the old idiot right,' he cried: 'I couldn't pump up a tear for him if I tried for a month of Sundays!' Now I take it, Miss Brooke, a guilty man wouldn't dare make such a speech as that!"

THE BUTLER.

"You think not?"

Griffiths stared at her. "I'm a little disappointed in her," he thought. "I'm afraid her powers have been slightly exaggerated if she can't see such a straightforward thing as that."

Aloud he said, a little sharply, "Well, I don't stand alone in my thinking. No one yet has breathed a word against Hales, and if they did I've no doubt he could prove an *alibi* without any trouble, for he lives in the house, and everyone has a good word for him."

"I suppose Sandy's lodge has been put into order by this time?"

"Yes; after the inquest, and when all possible evidence had been taken, everything was put straight."

"At the inquest it was stated that no marks of footsteps could be traced in any direction?"

"The long drought we've had would render such a thing impossible, let alone the fact that Sandy's lodge stands right on the gravelled drive, without flower-beds or grass borders of any sort around it. But look here, Miss Brooke, don't you be wasting your time over the lodge and its surroundings. Every iota of fact on that matter has been gone through over and over again by me and my chief. What we want you to do is to go straight into the house and concentrate attention on Master Harry's sick-room, and find out what's going on there. What he did outside the house on the night of the 6th, I've no doubt I shall be able to find out for myself. Now, Miss Brooke, you've asked me no end of questions, to which I have replied as fully as it was in my power to do; will you be good enough to answer one question that I wish to put, as straightforwardly as I have answered yours? You have had fullest particulars given you of the condition of Sandy's room when the police entered it on the morning after the murder. No doubt, at the present moment, you can see it all in your mind's eye—the bedstead on its side, the clock on its head, the bedclothes half-way up the chimney, the little vases and ornaments walking in a straight line towards the door?"

Loveday bowed her head.

"Very well. Now will you be good enough to tell me what this scene of confusion recalls to your mind before anything else?"

"The room of an unpopular Oxford freshman after a raid upon it by undergrads.," answered Loveday promptly.

Mr. Griffiths rubbed his hands.

"Quite so!" he ejaculated. "I see, after all, we are one at heart in this matter, in spite of a little surface disagreement of ideas. Depend upon it, by-and-bye, like the engineers tunnelling from different quarters under the Alps, we shall meet at the same point and shake hands. By-the-way, I have arranged for daily communication between us through the postboy who takes the letters to Troyte's Hill. He is trustworthy, and any letter you give him for me will find its way into my hands within the hour."

It was about three o'clock in the afternoon when Loveday drove in through the park gates of Troyte's Hill, past the lodge where old Sandy had met with his death. It was a pretty little cottage, covered with Virginia creeper and wild honeysuckle, and showing no outward sign of the tragedy that had been enacted within.

The park and pleasure-grounds of Troyte's Hill were extensive, and the house itself was a somewhat imposing red brick structure, built, possibly, at the time when Dutch William's taste had grown popular in the country. Its frontage presented a somewhat forlorn appearance, its centre windows—a square of eight—alone seeming to show signs of occupation. With the exception of two windows at the extreme end of the bedroom floor of the north wing, where, possibly, the invalid and his mother were located, and two windows at the extreme end of the ground floor of the south wing, which Loveday ascertained subsequently were those of Mr. Craven's study, not a single window in either wing owned blind or curtain. The wings were extensive, and it was easy to understand that at the extreme end of the one the fever patient would be isolated from the rest of the household, and that at the extreme end of the other Mr. Craven could secure the quiet and freedom from interruption which, no doubt, were essential to the due prosecution of his philological studies.

Alike on the house and ill-kept grounds were present the stamp of the smallness of the income of the master and owner of the place. The terrace, which ran the length of the house in front, and on to which every window on the ground floor opened, was miserably out of repair: not a lintel or door-post, window-ledge or balcony but what seemed to cry aloud for the touch of the painter. "Pity me! I have seen better days," Loveday could fancy written as a legend across the red-brick porch that gave entrance to the old house.

The butler, John Hales, admitted Loveday, shouldered her portmanteau and told her he would show her to her room. He was a tall, powerfully-built man, with a ruddy face and dogged expression of countenance. It was easy to understand that, off and on, there must have been many a sharp encounter between him and old Sandy. He treated Loveday in an easy, familiar fashion, evidently considering that an amanuensis took much the same rank as a nursery governess—that is to say, a little below a lady's maid and a little above a housemaid.

"We're short of hands, just now," he said, in broad Cumberland dialect, as he led the way up the wide staircase. "Some of the lasses downstairs took fright at the fever and went home. Cook and I are single-handed, for Moggie, the only maid left, has been told off to wait on Madam and Master Harry. I hope you're not afeared of fever?"

Loveday explained that she was not, and asked if the room at the extreme end of the north wing was the one assigned to "Madam and Master Harry."

"Yes," said the man; "it's convenient for sick nursing; there's a flight of stairs runs straight down from it to the kitchen quarters. We put all Madam wants at the foot of those stairs and Moggie comes down and fetches it. Moggie herself never enters the sick-room. I take it you'll not be seeing Madam for many a day, yet awhile."

"When shall I see Mr. Craven? At dinner to-night?"

"That's what naebody could say," answered Hales. "He may not come out of his study till past midnight; sometimes he sits there till two or three in the morning. Shouldn't advise you to wait till he wants his dinner—better have a cup of tea and a chop sent up to you. Madam never waits for him at any meal."

As he finished speaking he deposited the portmanteau outside one of the many doors opening into the gallery.

"This is Miss Craven's room," he went on; "cook and me thought you'd better have it, as it would want less getting ready than the other rooms, and work is work when there are so few hands to do it. Oh, my stars! I do declare there is cook putting it straight for you now."

The last sentence was added as the opened door laid bare to view, the cook, with a duster in her hand, polishing a mirror; the bed had been made, it is true, but otherwise the room must have been much as Miss Craven left it, after a hurried packing up.

To the surprise of the two servants Loveday took the matter very lightly.

"I have a special talent for arranging rooms and would prefer getting this one straight for myself," she said. "Now, if you will go and get ready that chop and cup of tea we were talking about just now, I shall think it much kinder than if you stayed here doing what I can so easily do for myself."

IN SILENCE AND SOLITUDE SHE PARTOOK OF THE SIMPLE REPAST.

When, however, the cook and butler had departed in company, Loveday showed no disposition to exercise the "special talent" of which she had boasted.

She first carefully turned the key in the lock and then proceeded to make a thorough and minute investigation of every corner of the room. Not an article of furniture, not an ornament or toilet accessory, but what was lifted from its place and carefully scrutinised. Even the ashes in the grate, the debris of the last fire made there, were raked over and well looked through.

This careful investigation of Miss Craven's late surroundings occupied in all about three quarters of an hour, and Loveday, with her hat in her hand, descended the stairs to see Hales crossing the hall to the dining-room with the promised cup of tea and chop.

In silence and solitude she partook of the simple repast in a dining-hall that could with ease have banqueted a hundred and fifty guests.

"Now for the grounds before it gets dark," she said to herself, as she noted that already the outside shadows were beginning to slant.

The dining-hall was at the back of the house; and here, as in the front, the windows, reaching to the ground, presented easy means of egress. The flower-garden was on this side of the house and sloped downhill to a pretty stretch of well-wooded country.

Loveday did not linger here even to admire, but passed at once round the south corner of the house to the windows which she had ascertained, by a careless question to the butler, were those of Mr. Craven's study.

Very cautiously she drew near them, for the blinds were up, the curtains drawn back. A side glance, however, relieved her apprehensions, for it showed her the occupant of the room, seated in an easy-chair, with his back to the windows. From the length of his outstretched limbs he was evidently a tall man. His hair was silvery and curly, the lower part of his face was hidden from her view by the chair, but she could see one hand was pressed tightly across his eyes and brows. The whole attitude was that of a man absorbed in deep thought. The room was comfortably furnished, but presented an appearance of disorder from the books and manuscripts scattered in all directions. A whole pile of torn fragments of foolscap sheets, overflowing from a waste-paper basket beside the writing-table, seemed to proclaim the fact that the scholar had of late grown weary of, or else

SEATED IN AN EASY-CHAIR WITH HIS BACK TO THE WINDOW.

dissatisfied with his work, and had condemned it freely.

Although Loveday stood looking in at this window for over five minutes, not the faintest sign of life did that tall, reclining figure give, and it would have been as easy to believe him locked in sleep as in thought.

From here she turned her steps in the direction of Sandy's lodge. As Griffiths had said, it was gravelled up to its doorstep. The blinds were closely drawn, and it presented the ordinary appearance of a disused cottage.

A narrow path beneath over-arching boughs of cherry-laurel and arbutus, immediately facing the lodge, caught her eye, and down this she at once turned her footsteps.

This path led, with many a wind and turn, through a belt of shrubbery that skirted the frontage of Mr. Craven's grounds, and eventually, after much zigzagging, ended in close proximity to the stables. As Loveday entered it, she seemed literally to leave daylight behind her.

"I feel as if I were following the course of a circuitous mind," she said to herself as the shadows closed around her. "I could not fancy Sir Isaac Newton or Bacon planning or delighting in such a windabout-alley as this!"

The path showed greyly in front of her out of the dimness. On and on she followed it; here and there the roots of the old laurels, struggling out of the ground, threatened to trip her up. Her eyes, however, had now grown accustomed to the half-gloom, and not a detail of her surroundings escaped her as she went along.

A bird flew from out the thicket on her right hand with a startled cry. A dainty little frog leaped out of her way into the shrivelled leaves lying below the laurels. Following the movements of this frog, her eye was caught by something black and solid among those leaves. What was it? A bundle—a shiny black coat? Loveday knelt down, and using her hands to assist her eyes, found that they came into contact with the dead, stiffened body of a beautiful black retriever. She parted, as well as she was able, the lower boughs of the evergreens, and minutely examined the poor animal. Its eyes were still open, though glazed and bleared, and its death had, undoubtedly, been caused by the blow of some blunt, heavy instrument, for on one side its skull was almost battered in.

"Exactly the death that was dealt to Sandy," she thought, as she groped hither and thither beneath the trees in hopes of lighting upon the weapon of destruction.

She searched until increasing darkness warned her that search was useless. Then, still following the zig-zagging path, she made her way out by the stables and thence back to the house.

She went to bed that night without having spoken to a soul beyond the cook and butler. The next morning, however, Mr. Craven introduced himself to her across the breakfast-table. He was a man of really handsome personal appearance, with a fine carriage of the head and shoulders, and eyes that had a forlorn, appealing look in them. He entered the room with an air of great energy, apologized to Loveday for the absence of his wife, and for his own remissness in not being in the way to receive her on the previous day. Then he bade her make herself at home at the breakfast-table, and expressed his delight in having found a coadjutor in his work.

"I hope you understand what a great—a stupendous work it is?" he added, as he sank into a chair. "It is a work that will leave its impress upon thought in all the ages to come. Only a man who has studied comparative philology as I have for the past thirty years, could gauge the magnitude of the task I have set myself."

With the last remark, his energy seemed spent, and he sank back in his chair, covering his eyes with his hand in precisely the same attitude as that in which Loveday had seen him over-night, and utterly oblivious of the fact that breakfast was before him and a stranger-guest seated at table. The butler entered with another dish. "Better go on with your breakfast," he whispered to Loveday, "he may sit like that for another hour."

He placed his dish in front of his master.

"Captain hasn't come back yet, sir," he said, making an effort to arouse him from his reverie.

"Eh, what?" said Mr. Craven, for a moment lifting his hand from his eyes.

"Captain, sir—the black retriever," repeated the man.

The pathetic look in Mr. Craven's eyes deepened.

"Ah, poor Captain!" he murmured; "the best dog I ever had."

Then he again sank back in his chair, putting his hand to his forehead.

The butler made one more effort to arouse him.

"Madam sent you down a newspaper, sir, that she thought you would like to see," he shouted almost into his master's ear, and at the same time laid the morning's paper on the table beside his plate.

"Confound you! leave it there," said Mr. Craven irritably. "Fools! dolts that you all are! With your trivialities and interruptions you are sending me out of the world with my work undone!"

And again he sank back in his chair, closed his eyes and became lost to his surroundings.

Loveday went on with her breakfast.

HE LAID THE MORNING'S PAPER BESIDE HIS PLATE.

She changed her place at table to one on Mr. Craven's right hand, so that the newspaper sent down for his perusal lay between his plate and hers. It was folded into an oblong shape, as if it were wished to direct attention to a certain portion of a certain column.

A clock in a corner of the room struck the hour with a loud, resonant stroke. Mr. Craven gave a start and rubbed his eyes.

"Eh, what's this?" he said. "What meal are we at?" He looked around with a bewildered air. "Eh!—who are you?" he went on, staring hard at Loveday. "What are you doing here? Where's Nina?—Where's Harry?"

Loveday began to explain, and gradually recollection seemed to come back to him.

"Ah, yes, yes," he said. "I remember; you've come to assist me with my great work. You promised, you know, to help me out of the hole I've got into. Very enthusiastic, I remember they said you were, on certain abstruse points in comparative philology. Now, Miss—Miss—I've forgotten your name—tell me a little of what you know about the elemental sounds of speech that are common to all languages. Now, to how many would you reduce those elemental sounds—to six, eight, nine? No, we won't discuss the matter here, the cups and saucers distract me. Come into my den at the other end of the house; we'll have perfect quiet there."

And utterly ignoring the fact that he had not as yet broken his fast, he rose from the table, seized Loveday by the wrist, and led her out of the room and down the long corridor that led through the south wing to his study.

But seated in that study his energy once more speedily exhausted itself.

He placed Loveday in a comfortable chair at his writing-table, consulted her taste as to pens, and spread a sheet of foolscap before her. Then he settled himself in his easy-chair, with his back to the light, as if he were about to dictate folios to her.

In a loud, distinct voice he repeated the title of his learned work, then its subdivision, then the number and heading of the chapter that was at present engaging his attention. Then he put his hand to his head. "It's the elemental sounds that are my stumbling-block," he said. "Now, how on earth is it possible to get a notion of a sound of agony that is not in part a sound of terror? or a sound of surprise that is not in part a sound of either joy or sorrow?"

With this his energies were spent, and although Loveday remained seated in that study from early morning till daylight began to fade, she had not ten sentences to show for her day's work as amanuensis.

Loveday in all spent only two clear days at Troyte's Hill.

On the evening of the first of those days Detective Griffiths received, through the trustworthy post-boy, the following brief note from her:

"I have found out that Hales owed Sandy close upon a hundred pounds, which he had borrowed at various times. I don't know whether you will think this fact of any importance.—L. B."

Mr. Griffiths repeated the last sentence blankly. "If Harry Craven were put upon his defence, his counsel, I take it, would consider the fact of first importance," he muttered. And for the remainder of that day Mr. Griffiths went about his work in a perturbed state of mind, doubtful whether to hold or to let go his theory concerning Harry Craven's guilt.

The next morning there came another brief note from Loveday which ran thus:

"As a matter of collateral interest, find out if a person, calling himself Harold Cousins, sailed two days ago from London Docks for Natal in the *Bonnie Dundee?*"

To this missive Loveday received, in reply, the following somewhat lengthy despatch:

"I do not quite see the drift of your last note, but have wired to our agents in London to carry out its suggestion. On my part, I have important news to communicate. I have found out what Harry Craven's business out of doors was on the night of the murder, and at my instance a warrant has been issued for his arrest. This warrant it will be my duty to serve on him in the course of to-day. Things are beginning to look very black against him, and I am convinced his illness is all a sham. I have seen Waters, the man who is supposed to be attending him, and have driven him into a corner and made him admit that he has only seen young Craven once—on the first day of his illness—and that he gave his certificate entirely on the strength of what Mrs. Craven told him of her son's condition. On the occasion of this, his first and only visit, the lady, it seems, also told him that it would not be necessary for him to continue his attendance, as she quite felt herself competent to treat the case, having had so much experience in fever cases among the blacks at Natal.

"As I left Waters's house, after eliciting this important information, I was accosted by a man who keeps a low-class inn in the place, McQueen by name. He said that he wished to speak to me on a matter of importance. To make a long story short, this McQueen stated that on the night of the sixth, shortly after eleven o'clock, Harry Craven came to his house, bringing with him a valuable piece of plate—a handsome epergne—and requested him to lend him a hundred pounds on it, as he hadn't a penny in his pocket. McQueen complied with his request to the extent of ten sovereigns, and now, in a fit of nervous terror, comes to me to confess himself a receiver of stolen goods and play the honest man! He says he noticed that the young gentleman was very much agitated as he made the request, and he also begged him to mention his visit to no one. Now, I am curious to learn how Master Harry will get over the fact that he passed the lodge at the hour at which the murder was most probably committed; or how he will get out of the dilemma of having repassed the lodge on his way back to the house, and not noticed the wide-open window with the full moon shining down on it?

"Another word! Keep out of the way when I arrive at the house, somewhere between two and three in the afternoon, to serve the warrant. I do not wish your professional capacity to get wind, for you will most likely yet be of some use to us in the house.

"S. G."

Loveday read this note, seated at Mr. Craven's writing-table, with the old gentleman himself reclining motionless beside her in his easy-chair. A little smile played about the corners of her mouth as she read over again the words—"for you will most likely yet be of some use to us in the house."

Loveday's second day in Mr. Craven's study promised to be as unfruitful as the first. For fully an hour after she had received Griffiths' note, she sat at the writing-table with her pen in her hand, ready to transcribe Mr. Craven's inspirations. Beyond, however, the phrase, muttered with closed eyes—"It's all here, in my brain, but I can't put it into words"—not a half-syllable escaped his lips.

At the end of that hour the sound of footsteps on the outside gravel made her turn her head towards the window. It was Griffiths approaching with two constables. She heard the hall door opened to admit them, but, beyond that, not a sound reached her ear, and she realised how fully she was cut off from communication with the rest of the household at the farther end of this unoccupied wing.

Mr. Craven, still reclining in his semi-trance, evidently had not the faintest suspicion that so important an event as the arrest of his only son on a charge of murder was about to be enacted in the house.

Meantime, Griffiths and his constables had mounted the stairs leading to the north wing, and were being guided through the corridors to the sick-room by the flying figure of Moggie, the maid.

"Hoot, mistress!" cried the girl, "here are three men coming up the stairs—policemen, every one of them—will ye come and ask them what they be wanting?"

Outside the door of the sick-room stood Mrs. Craven—a tall, sharp-featured woman with sandy hair going rapidly grey.

"What is the meaning of this? What is your business here?" she said haughtily, addressing Griffiths, who headed the party.

Griffiths respectfully explained what his business was, and requested her to stand on one side that he might enter her son's room.

"This is my daughter's room; satisfy yourself of the fact," said the lady, throwing back the door as she spoke.

And Griffiths and his confrères entered, to find pretty Miss Craven, looking very white and scared, seated beside a fire in a long flowing robe de chambre.

Griffiths departed in haste and confusion, without the chance of a professional talk with Loveday. That afternoon saw him telegraphing wildly in all directions, and despatching messengers in all quarters. Finally he spent over an hour drawing up an elaborate report to his chief at Newcastle, assuring him of the identity of one, Harold Cousins, who had sailed in the *Bonnie Dundee* for Natal, with Harry Craven, of Troyte's Hill, and advising that the police authorities in that far-away district should be immediately communicated with.

The ink had not dried on the pen with which this report was written before a note, in Loveday's writing, was put into his hand.

Loveday evidently had had some difficulty in finding a messenger for this note, for it was brought by a gardener's boy, who informed Griffiths that the lady had said he would receive a gold sovereign if he delivered the letter all right.

Griffiths paid the boy and dismissed him, and then proceeded to read Loveday's communication.

It was written hurriedly in pencil, and ran as follows:

"Things are getting critical here. Directly you receive this, come up to the house with two of your men, and post yourselves anywhere in the grounds where you can see and not be seen. There will be no difficulty in this, for it will be dark by the time you are able to get there. I am not sure whether I shall want your aid to-night, but you had better keep in the grounds until morning, in case of need; and above all, never once lose sight of the study windows." (This was underscored.) "If I put a lamp with a green shade in one of those windows, do not lose a moment in entering by that window, which I will contrive to keep unlocked."

Detective Griffiths rubbed his forehead—rubbed his eyes, as he finished reading this.

"Well, I daresay it's all right," he said, "but I'm bothered, that's all, and for the life of me I can't see one step of the way she is going."

He looked at his watch; the hands pointed to a quarter past six. The short September day was drawing rapidly to a close. A good five miles lay between him and Troyte's Hill—there was evidently not a moment to lose.

At the very moment that Griffiths, with his two constables, were once more starting along the Grenfell High Road behind the best horse they could procure, Mr. Craven was rousing himself from his long slumber, and beginning to look around him. That slumber, however, though long, had not been a peaceful one, and it was sundry of the old gentleman's muttered exclamations, as he had started uneasily in his sleep, that had caused Loveday to pen, and then to creep out of the room to despatch, her hurried note.

MISS CRAVEN LOOKING VERY WHITE AND SCARED.

What effect the occurrence of the morning had had upon the household generally, Loveday, in her isolated corner of the house, had no means of ascertaining. She only noted that when Hales brought in her tea, as he did precisely at five o'clock, he wore a particularly ill-tempered expression of countenance, and she heard him mutter, as he set down the tea-tray with a clatter, something about being a respectable man, and not used to such "goings on."

It was not until nearly an hour and a half after this that Mr. Craven had awakened with a sudden start, and, looking wildly around him, had questioned Loveday who had entered the room.

Loveday explained that the butler had brought in lunch at one, and tea at five, but that since then no one had come in.

"Now that's false," said Mr. Craven, in a sharp, unnatural sort of voice; "I saw him sneaking round the room, the whining, canting hypocrite, and you must have seen him, too! Didn't you hear him say, in his squeaky old voice: 'Master, I knows your secret——' He broke off abruptly, looking wildly round. "Eh, what's this?" he cried. "No, no, I'm all wrong—Sandy is dead and buried—they held an inquest on him, and we all praised him up as if he were a saint."

"He must have been a bad man, that old Sandy," said Loveday sympathetically.

"You're right! you're right!" cried Mr. Craven, springing up excitedly from his chair and seizing her by the hand. "If ever a man deserved his death, he did. For thirty years he held that rod over my head, and then—ah where was I?"

He put his hand to his head and again sank, as if exhausted, into his chair.

"I suppose it was some early indiscretion of yours at college that he knew of?" said Loveday, eager to get at as much of the truth as possible while the mood for confidence held sway in the feeble brain.

"That was it! I was fool enough to marry a disreputable girl—a barmaid in the town—and Sandy was present at the wedding, and then——" Here his eyes closed again and his mutterings became incoherent.

For ten minutes he lay back in his chair, muttering thus; "A yelp—a groan," were the only words Loveday could distinguish among those mutterings, then, suddenly, slowly and distinctly, he said, as if answering some plainly-put question: "A good blow with the hammer and the thing was done."

GRIFFITHS LOOKED AT HIS WATCH.

"I should like amazingly to see that hammer," said Loveday; "do you keep it anywhere at hand?"

His eyes opened with a wild, cunning look in them.

"Who's talking about a hammer? I did not say I had one. If anyone says I did it with a hammer, they're telling a lie."

"Oh, you've spoken to me about the hammer two or three times," said Loveday calmly; "the one that killed your dog, Captain, and I should like to see it, that's all."

The look of cunning died out of the old man's eye—"Ah, poor Captain! splendid dog that! Well, now, where were we? Where did we leave off? Ah, I remember, it was the elemental sounds of speech that bothered me so that night. Were you here then? Ah, no! I remember. I had been trying all day to assimilate a dog's yelp of pain to a human groan, and I couldn't do it. The idea haunted me—followed me about wherever I went. If they were both elemental sounds, they must have something in common, but the link between them I could not find; then it occurred to me, would a well-bred, well-trained dog like my Captain in the stables, there, at the moment of death give an unmitigated currish yelp; would there not be something of a human note in his death-cry? The thing was worth putting to the test. If I could hand down in my treatise a fragment of fact on the matter, it would be worth a dozen dogs' lives. So I went out into the moonlight—ah, but you know all about it—now, don't you?"

"Yes. Poor Captain! did he yelp or groan?"

"Why, he gave one loud, long, hideous yelp, just as if he had been a common cur. I might just as well have let him alone; it only set that other brute opening his window and spying out on me, and saying in his cracked old voice: 'Master, what are you doing out here at this time of night?'

Again he sank back in his chair, muttering incoherently with half-closed eyes.

Loveday let him alone for a minute or so; then she had another question to ask.

"And that other brute—did he yelp or groan when you dealt him his blow?"

"What, old Sandy—the brute? he fell back—Ah, I remember, you said you would like to see the hammer that stopped his babbling old tongue—now, didn't you?"

He rose a little unsteadily from his chair, and seemed to drag his long limbs with an effort across the room to a cabinet at the farther end. Opening a drawer in this cabinet, he produced, from amidst some specimens of strata and fossils, a large-sized geological hammer.

He brandished it for a moment over his head, then paused with his finger on his lip.

"Hush!" he said, "we shall have the fools creeping in to peep at us if we don't take care." And to Loveday's horror he suddenly made for the door, turned the key in the lock, withdrew it and put it into his pocket.

She looked at the clock; the hands pointed to half-past seven. Had Griffiths received her note at the proper time, and were the men now in the grounds? She could only pray that they were.

"The light is too strong for my eyes," she said, and rising from her chair, she lifted the green-shaded lamp and placed it on a table that stood at the window.

"No, no, that won't do," said Mr. Craven; "that would show everyone outside what we're doing in here." He crossed to the window as he spoke and removed the lamp thence to the mantelpiece.

Loveday could only hope that in the few seconds it had remained in the window it had caught the eye of the outside watchers.

The old man beckoned to Loveday to come near and examine his deadly weapon. "Give it a good swing round," he said, suiting the action to the word, "and down it comes with a splendid crash." He brought the hammer round within an inch of Loveday's forehead.

She started back.

"Ha, ha," he laughed harshly and unnaturally, with the light of madness dancing in his eyes now; "did I frighten you? I wonder what sort of sound you would make if I were to give you a little tap just there." Here he lightly touched her forehead with the hammer. "Elemental, of course, it would be, and —— "

Loveday steadied her nerves with difficulty. Locked in with this lunatic, her only chance lay in gaining time for the detectives to reach the house and enter through the window.

"Wait a minute," she said, striving to divert his attention; "you have not yet told me what sort of an elemental sound old Sandy made when he fell. If you'll give me pen and ink, I'll write down a full account of it all, and you can incorporate it afterwards in your treatise."

For a moment a look of real pleasure flitted across the old man's face, then it faded. "The brute fell back dead without a sound," he answered; "it was all for nothing, that night's work; yet not altogether for nothing. No, I don't mind owning I would do it all over again to get the wild thrill of joy at my heart that I had when I looked down into that old man's dead face and felt myself free at last! Free at last!" his voice rang out

WITH HIS LIPS CLOSE TO LOVEDAY'S EAR.

excitedly — once more he brought his hammer round with an ugly swing.

"For a moment I was a young man again; I leaped into his room—the moon was shining full in through the window—I thought of my old college days, and the fun we used to have at Pembroke—topsy turvey I turned everything—— " He broke off abruptly, and drew a step nearer to Loveday. "The pity of it all was," he said, suddenly dropping from his high, excited tone to a low, pathetic one, "that he fell without a sound of any sort." Here he drew another step nearer. "I wonder —" he said, then broke off again, and came close to Loveday's side. "It has only this moment occurred to me," he said, now with his lips close to Loveday's ear, "that a woman, in her death agony, would be much more likely to give utterance to an elemental sound than a man."

He raised his hammer, and Loveday fled to the window, and was lifted from the outside by three pairs of strong arms.

"I thought I was conducting my very last case—I never had such a narrow escape before!" said Loveday, as she stood talking with Mr. Griffiths on the Grenfell platform, awaiting the train to carry her back to London. "It seems strange that no one before suspected the old gentleman's sanity—I suppose, however, people were so used to his eccentricities that they did not notice how they had deepened into positive lunacy. His cunning evidently stood him in good stead at the inquest."

"It is possible," said Griffiths thoughtfully, "that he did not absolutely cross the very slender line that divides eccentricity from madness until after the murder. The excitement consequent upon the discovery of the crime may just have pushed him over the border. Now, Miss Brooke, we have exactly ten minutes before your train comes in. I should feel greatly obliged to you if you would explain one or two things that have a professional interest for me."

"With pleasure," said Loveday. "Put your questions in categorical order and I will answer them."

"Well, then, in the first place, what suggested to your mind the old man's guilt?"

"The relations that subsisted between him and Sandy seemed to me to savour too much of fear on the one side and

WANTED A HUNDRED POUNDS.

power on the other. Also the income paid to Sandy during Mr. Craven's absence in Natal bore, to my mind, an unpleasant resemblance to hush-money."

"Poor wretched being! And I hear that, after all, the woman he married in his wild young days died soon afterwards of drink. I have no doubt, however, that Sandy sedulously kept up the fiction of her existence, even after his master's second marriage. Now for another question: how was it you knew that Miss Craven had taken her brother's place in the sick-room?"

"On the evening of my arrival I discovered a rather long lock of fair hair in the unswept fireplace of my room, which, as it happened, was usually occupied by Miss Craven. It at once occurred to me that the young lady had been cutting off her hair and that there must be some powerful motive to induce such a sacrifice. The suspicious circumstances attending her brother's illness soon supplied me with such a motive."

"Ah! that typhoid fever business was very cleverly done. Not a servant in the house, I verily believe, but who thought Master Harry was upstairs, ill in bed, and Miss Craven away at her friends' in Newcastle. The young fellow must have got a clear start off within an hour of the murder. His sister, sent away the next day to Newcastle, dismissed her maid there, I hear, on the plea of no accommodation at her friends' house—sent the girl to her own home for a holiday and herself returned to Troyte's Hill in the middle of the night, having walked the five miles from Grenfell. No doubt her mother admitted her through one of those easily-opened front windows, cut her hair and put her to bed to personate her brother without delay. With Miss Craven's strong likeness to Master Harry, and in a darkened room, it is easy to understand that the eyes of a doctor, personally unacquainted with the family, might easily be deceived. Now, Miss Brooke, you must admit that with all this elaborate chicanery and double dealing going on, it was only natural that my suspicions should set in strongly in that quarter."

"I read it all in another light, you see," said Loveday. "It seemed to me that the mother, knowing her son's evil proclivities, believed in his guilt, in spite, possibly, of his assertions of innocence. The son, most likely, on his way back to the house after pledging the family plate, had met old Mr. Craven with the hammer in his hand. Seeing, no doubt, how impossible it would be for him to clear himself without incriminating his father, he preferred flight to Natal to giving evidence at the inquest."

"Now about his alias?" said Mr. Griffiths briskly, for the train was at that moment steaming into the station. "How did you know that Harold Cousins was identical with Harry Craven, and had sailed in the *Bonnie Dundee?*"

"Oh, that was easy enough," said Loveday, as she stepped into the train; "a newspaper sent down to Mr. Craven by his wife, was folded so as to direct his attention to the shipping list. In it I saw that the *Bonnie Dundee* had sailed two days previously for Natal. Now it was only natural to connect Natal with Mrs. Craven, who had passed the greater part of her life there; and it was easy to understand her wish to get her scapegrace son among her early friends. The alias under which he sailed came readily enough to light. I found it scribbled all over one of Mr. Craven's writing pads in his study; evidently it had been drummed into his ears by his wife as his son's alias, and the old gentleman had taken this method of fixing it in his memory. We'll hope that the young fellow, under his new name, will make a new reputation for himself—at any rate, he'll have a better chance of doing so with the ocean between him and his evil companions. Now it's good-bye, I think."

"No," said Mr. Griffiths; "it's au revoir, for you'll have to come back again for the assizes, and give the evidence that will shut old Mr. Craven in an asylum for the rest of his life."

III

Stories from the Diary of a Doctor

L.T. MEADE & CLIFFORD HALIFAX, M.D.

Stories from the Diary of a Doctor.

BY L.T. MEADE AND CLIFFORD HALIFAX, M.D.

AN OAK COFFIN.

N a certain cold morning in early spring, I was visited by two ladies, mother and daughter. The mother was dressed as a widow. She was a tall, striking-looking woman, with full, wide-open dark eyes, and a mass of rich hair turned back from a white and noble brow. Her lips were firm, her features well formed. She seemed to have plenty of character, but the deep lines of sadness under her eyes and round her lips were very remarkable. The daughter was a girl of fourteen, slim to weediness. Her eyes were dark, like her mother's, and she had an abundance of tawny brown and very handsome hair. It hung down her back below her waist, and floated over her shoulders. She was dressed, like her mother, in heavy mourning, and round her young mouth and dark, deep eyes there lingered the same inexpressible sadness.

I motioned my visitors to chairs, and waited as usual to learn the reason of their favouring me with a call.

"My name is Heathcote," said the elder lady. "I have lately lost my husband. I have come to you on account of my daughter—she is not well."

I glanced again more attentively at the young girl. I saw that she looked overstrained and nervous. Her restlessness, too, was so apparent that she could scarcely sit still, and catching up a paper-knife which stood on the table near, she began twirling it rapidly between her finger and thumb.

"It does me good to fidget with something," she said, glancing apologetically at her mother.

"What are your daughter's symptoms?" I asked.

Mrs. Heathcote began to describe them in the vague way which characterizes a certain class of patient. I gathered at last from her words that Gabrielle would not eat—she slept badly—she was weak and depressed—she took no interest in anything.

"How old is Miss Gabrielle?" I asked.

"She will be fifteen her next birthday," replied her mother.

All the while Mrs. Heathcote was speaking, the young daughter kept her eyes fixed on the carpet—she still twirled the paper-knife, and once or twice she yawned profoundly.

I asked her to prepare for the usual medical examination. She complied without any alacrity, and with a look on her face which said plainly, "Young as I am, I know how useless all this fuss is—I only submit because I must."

I felt her pulse and sounded her heart and lungs. The action of the heart was a little weak, but the lungs were perfectly healthy. In short, beyond a general physical and mental debility, I could find nothing whatever the matter with the girl.

After a time, I rang the bell to desire my servant to take Miss Heathcote into another room, in order that I might speak to her mother alone.

The young lady went away very unwillingly. The sceptical expression on her face was more apparent than ever.

"You will be sure to tell me the exact truth?" said Mrs. Heathcote, as soon as we were alone.

"I have very little to tell," I replied. "I have examined your daughter carefully. She is suffering from no disease to which a name can be attached. She is below par, certainly; there is weakness and general depression, but a tonic ought to set all these matters right."

"I have tried tonics without avail," said Mrs. Heathcote.

"Has not your family physician seen Miss Heathcote?"

"Not lately." The widow's manner became decidedly hesitating. "The fact is, we have not consulted him since—since Mr. Heathcote's death," she said.

"When did that take place?"

"Six months ago."

Here she spoke with infinite sadness, and her face, already very pale, turned perceptibly paler.

"Is there nothing you can tell me to give me a clue to your daughter's condition? Is there anything, for instance, preying on her mind?"

"Nothing whatever."

"The expression of her face is very sad for so young a girl."

"I FELT HER PULSE."

"I have felt my sorrow acutely," she replied.

I made a few more general remarks, wrote a prescription for the daughter, and bade Mrs. Heathcote good-bye. About the same hour on the following morning I was astonished when my servant brought me a card on which was scribbled in pencil the name *Gabrielle Heathcote*, and underneath, in the same upright, but unformed hand, the words, "I want to see you most urgently."

A few moments later, Miss Gabrielle was standing in my consulting-room. Her appearance was much the same as yesterday, except that now her face was eager, watchful, and all awake.

"How do you do?" she said, holding out her hand, and blushing. "I have ventured to come alone, and I haven't brought a fee. Does that matter?"

"Not in the least," I replied. "Pray sit down and tell me what you want."

"I would rather stand," she answered; "I feel too restless and excited to sit still. I stole away from home without letting mother know. I liked your look yesterday and determined to see you again. Now, may I confide in you?"

"You certainly may," I replied.

My interest in this queer child was a good deal aroused. I felt certain that I was right in my conjectures of yesterday, and that this young creature was really burdened with some secret which was gravely undermining her health.

"I am willing to listen to you," I continued. "You must be brief, of course, for I am a very busy man, but anything you can say which will throw light on your own condition, and so help me to cure you, will, of course, be welcome."

"You think me very nervous?" said Miss Gabrielle.

"Your nerves are out of order," I replied.

"You must remember," said Mrs. Heathcote, "that she has lately lost her father."

"Even so," I replied; "that would scarcely account for her nervous condition. A healthy-minded child will not be overcome with grief to the serious detriment of health after an interval of six months. At least," I added, "that is my experience in ordinary cases."

"I am grieved to hear it," said Mrs. Heathcote.

She looked very much troubled. Her agitation was apparent in her trembling hands and quivering lips.

"Your daughter is in a nervous condition," I said, rising. "She has no disease at present, but a little extra strain might develop real disease, or might affect her nerves, already overstrung, to a dangerous degree. I should recommend complete change of air and scene immediately."

Mrs. Heathcote sighed heavily.

"You don't look very well yourself," I said, giving her a keen glance.

She flushed crimson.

"You know that I don't sleep at night?"

"Yes."

Miss Gabrielle looked towards the door.

"Is it shut?" she asked, excitedly

"Of course it is."

She came close to me, her voice dropped to a hoarse whisper, her face turned not only white but grey.

"I can stand it no longer," she said. "I'll tell you the truth. You wouldn't sleep either if you were me. *My father isn't dead!*"

"Nonsense," I replied. "You must control such imaginings, Miss Gabrielle, or you will really get into a very unhealthy condition of mind."

"That's what mother says when I speak to her," replied the child. "But I tell you, this thing is true. My father is not dead. I know it."

"How can you possibly know it?" I asked.

"I have seen him—there!"

"You have seen your father!—but he died six months ago?"

"Yes. He died—and was buried, and I went to his funeral. But all the same he is not dead now."

"My dear young lady," I said, in as soothing a tone as I could assume, "you are the victim of what is called a hallucination. You have felt your father's death very acutely."

"I have. I loved him beyond words. He was so kind, so affectionate, so good to me. It almost broke my heart when he died. I thought I could never be happy again. Mother was as wretched as myself. There weren't two more miserable people in the wide world. It seemed impossible to either of us to smile or be cheerful again. I began to sleep badly, for I cried so much, and my eyes ached, and I did not care for lessons any more."

"All these feelings will pass," I replied; "they are natural, but time will abate their violence."

"You think so?" said the girl, with a strange smile. "Now let me go on with my story: It was at Christmas time I first saw my father. We live in an old house at Brixton. It has a walled-in garden. I was standing by my window about midnight. I had been in bed for an hour or more, but I could not sleep. The house was perfectly quiet. I got out of bed and went to the window and drew up the blind. I stood by the window and looked out into the garden, which was covered with snow. There, standing under the window, with his arms folded, was father. He stood perfectly still, and turned his head slowly, first in the direction of my room and then in that of mother's. He stood there for quite five minutes, and then walked across the grass into the shelter of the shrubbery. I put a cloak on and rushed downstairs. I unbolted the front door and went into the garden. I shouted my father's name and ran into the shrubbery to look for him, but he wasn't there, and I—I think I fainted. When I came to myself I was in bed and mother was bending over me. Her face was all blistered as if she had been crying terribly. I told her that I had just seen father, and she said it was a dream."

"So it was," I replied.

Miss Gabrielle's dark brows were knit in some pain.

"I did not think you would take that commonplace view," she responded.

"I am sorry I have offended you," I answered. "Girls like you do have bad dreams when they are in trouble, and those dreams are often so vivid, that they mistake them for realities."

"Very well, then, I have had more of those vivid dreams. I have seen my father again. The last time I saw him he was in the house. It was about a month ago. As usual, I could not sleep, and I went downstairs quite late to get the second volume of a novel which interested me. There was father walking across the passage. His back was to me. He opened the study door and went in. He shut it behind him. I rushed to it in order to open it and follow him. It was locked, and though I screamed through the key-hole, no one replied to me. Mother found me kneeling by the study door and shouting through the key-hole to father. She was up and dressed, which seemed strange at so late an hour. She took me upstairs and put me to bed, and pretended to be angry with me, but when I told her that I had seen father she burst into the most awful bitter tears and said:—

"'Oh, Gabrielle, he is dead—dead—quite dead!'

"'Then he comes here from the dead,' I said. 'No, he is not dead. I have just seen him.'

"'My poor child,' said mother, 'I must take you to a good doctor without delay. You must not get this thing on your brain.'

"'Very well,' I replied; 'I am quite willing to see Dr. Mackenzie.'"

I interrupted the narrative to inquire who Dr. Mackenzie was.

"I SCREAMED THROUGH THE KEY-HOLE."

"He is our family physician," replied the young lady. "He has attended us for years."

"And what did your mother say when you proposed to see him?"

"She shivered violently, and said: 'No, I won't have him in the house.' After a time she decided to bring me to you."

"And have you had that hallucination again?" I inquired.

"It was not a hallucination," she answered, pouting her lips.

"I will humour you," I answered. "Have you seen your father again?"

"No, and I am not likely to."

"Why do you think that?"

"I cannot quite tell you—I think mother is in it. Mother is very unhappy about something, and she looks at me at times as if she were afraid of me." Here Miss Heathcote rose. "You said I was not to stay long," she remarked. "Now I have told you everything. You see that it is absolutely impossible for ordinary medicines to cure me, any more than ordinary medicines can cure mother of her awful dreams."

"I did not know that your mother dreamt badly," I said.

"She does—but she doesn't wish it spoken of. She dreams so badly, she cries out so terribly in her sleep, that she has moved from her old bedroom next to mine, to one in a distant wing of the house. Poor mother, I am sorry for her, but I am glad at least that I have had courage to tell you what I have seen. You will make it your business to find out the truth now, won't you?"

"What do you mean?" I asked.

"Why, of course, my father is alive," she retorted. "You have got to prove that he is, and to give him back to me again. I leave the matter in your hands. I know you are wise and very clever. Good-bye, good-bye!"

The queer girl left me, tears rolling down her cheeks. I was obliged to attend to other patients, but it was impossible for me to get Miss Heathcote's story out of my head. There was no doubt whatever that she was telling me what she firmly believed to be the truth. She had either seen her father once more in the flesh, or she was the victim of a very strong hallucination. In all probability the latter supposition was the correct one. A man could not die and have a funeral and yet still be alive: but, then, on the other hand, when Mrs. Heathcote brought Gabrielle to see me yesterday, why had she not mentioned this central and principal feature of her malady? Mrs. Heathcote had said nothing whatever with regard to Gabrielle's delusions. Then why was the mother so nervous? Why did she say nothing about her own bad dreams, dreams so disturbing, that she was obliged to change her bedroom in order that her daughter should not hear her scream?

"I leave the matter in your hands!" Miss Heathcote had said. Poor child, she had done so with a vengeance. I could not get the story out of my thoughts, and so uncomfortable did the whole thing make me that I determined to pay Dr. Mackenzie a visit.

Mackenzie was a physician in very large

practice at Brixton. His name was already familiar to me—on one or two occasions I had met him in consultation. I looked up his address in the Medical Directory, and that very evening took a hansom to his house. He happened to be at home. I sent in my card and was admitted at once.

Mackenzie received me in his consulting-room, and I was not long in explaining the motive of my visit. After a few preliminary remarks, I said that I would be glad if he would favour me with full particulars with regard to Heathcote's death.

"I can easily do so," said Mackenzie. "The case was a perfectly straightforward one—my patient was consumptive, had been so for years, and died at last of hemoptysis."

"What aged man was he?" I asked.

"Not old—a little past forty—a tall, slight, good-looking man, with a somewhat emaciated face. In short, his was an ordinary case of consumption."

I told Mackenzie all about the visit which I had received from Mrs. Heathcote, and gave him a faithful version of the strange story which Miss Gabrielle Heathcote had told me that day.

"Miss Gabrielle is an excitable girl," replied the doctor. "I have had a good deal to do with her for many years, and always thought her nerves highly strung. She is evidently the victim of a delusion, caused by the effect of grief on a somewhat delicate organism. She probably inherits her father's disease. Mrs. Heathcote should take her from home immediately."

"Mrs. Heathcote looks as if she needed change almost as badly as her daughter," I answered; "but now you will forgive me if I ask you a few more questions. Will you oblige me by describing Heathcote's death as faithfully as you can?"

"I WAS PAYING THE CABMAN HIS FARE."

"Certainly," replied the physician.

He sank down into a chair at the opposite side of the hearth as he spoke.

"The death, when it came," he continued, "was, I must confess, unexpected. I had sounded Heathcote's lungs about three months previous to the time of his death seizure. Phthisis was present, but not to an advanced degree. I recommended his wintering abroad. He was a solicitor by profession, and had a good practice. I remember his asking me, with a comical rise of his brows, how he was to carry on his profession so many miles from Chancery Lane. But to come to his death. It took place six months ago, in the beginning of September. It had been a hot season, and I had just returned from my holiday. My portmanteau and Gladstone bag had been placed in the hall, and I was paying the cabman his fare, when a servant from the Heathcotes arrived, and begged of me to go immediately to her master, who was, she said, dying.

"I hurried off to the house without a moment's delay. It is a stone's throw from here. In fact, you can see the walls of the garden from the windows of this room in the daytime. I reached the house. Gabrielle was standing in the hall. I am an old friend of hers. Her face was quite white and had a stunned expression. When she saw me she rushed to me, clasped one of my hands in both of hers, and burst into tears.

"'Go and save him!' she gasped, her voice choking with sobs, which were almost hysterical.

"A lady who happened to be staying in the house came and drew the girl away into one of the sitting-rooms, and I went upstairs. I found Heathcote in his own room. He was lying on the bed—he was a ghastly sight. His face wore the sick hue of death itself; the sheet, his hair, and even his face were all covered with blood. His wife was standing over him, wiping away the blood, which oozed from his lips. I saw, of course, immediately what was the matter. Hemoptysis had set in, and I felt that his hours were numbered.

"'He has broken a blood vessel,' exclaimed Mrs. Heathcote. 'He was standing here, preparing to go down to dinner, when he coughed violently—the blood began to pour from his mouth; I got him on the bed and sent for you. The hemorrhage seems to be a little less violent now.'

"I examined my patient carefully, feeling his pulse, which was very weak and low; I cautioned him not to speak a single word, and asked Mrs. Heathcote to send for some ice immediately. She did so. I packed him in ice and gave him a dose of ergotine. He seemed easier, and I left him, promising to return again in an hour or two. Miss Gabrielle met me in the hall as I went out.

"'Is he any better? Is there any hope at all?' she asked, as I left the house.

"'Your father is easier now,' I replied; 'the hemorrhage has been arrested. I am coming back soon. You must be a good girl and try to comfort your mother in every way in your power.'

"'Then there is no hope?' she answered, looking me full in the face.

"I could not truthfully say that there was. I knew poor Heathcote's days were numbered, although I scarcely thought the end would come so quickly."

"What do you mean?" I inquired.

"Why this," he replied. "Less than an hour after I got home, I received a brief note from Mrs. Heathcote. In it she stated that fresh and very violent hemorrhage had set in almost immediately after I left, and that her husband was dead."

"And——" I continued.

"Well, that is the story. Poor Heathcote had died of hemoptysis."

"Did you see the body after death?" I inquired, after a pause.

"No—it was absolutely unnecessary—the cause of death was so evident. I attended the funeral, though. Heathcote was buried at Kensal Green."

I made no comment for a moment or two.

"I am sorry you did not see the body after death," I said, after a pause.

My remark seemed to irritate Mackenzie. He looked at me with raised brows.

"Would you have thought it necessary to do so?" he asked. "A man known to be consumptive dies of violent hemorrhage of the lungs. The family are in great trouble—there is much besides to think of. Would you under the circumstances have considered it necessary to refuse to give a certificate without seeing the body?"

I thought for a moment.

"I make a rule of always seeing the body," I replied; "but, of course, you were justified, as the law stands. Well, then, there is no doubt Heathcote is really dead?"

"Really dead?" retorted Mackenzie. "Don't you understand that he has been in his grave for six months?—That I practically saw him die?—That I attended his funeral? By what possible chance can the man be alive?"

"None," I replied. "He is dead, of course. I am sorry for the poor girl. She ought to leave home immediately."

"Girls of her age often have delusions," said Mackenzie. "I doubt not this will pass in time. I am surprised, however, that the Heathcotes allowed the thing to go on so long. I remember now that I have never been near the house since the funeral. I cannot understand their not calling me in."

"That fact puzzles me also," I said. "They came to me, a total stranger, instead of consulting their family physician, and Mrs. Heathcote carefully concealed the most important part of her daughter's malady. It is strange altogether; and, although I can give no explanation whatever, I am convinced there is one if we could only get at it. One more question before I go, Mackenzie. You spoke of Heathcote as a solicitor: has he left his family well off?"

"They are not rich," replied Mackenzie; "but as far as I can tell, they don't seem to want for money. I believe their house, Ivy Hall is its name, belongs to them. They live there very quietly, with a couple of maidservants. I should say they belonged to the well-to-do middle classes."

"Then money troubles cannot explain the mystery?" I replied.

"Believe me, there is no mystery," answered Mackenzie, in an annoyed voice.

I held out my hand to wish him good-bye, when a loud peal at the front door startled us both. If ever there was frantic haste in anything, there was in that ringing peal.

"Someone wants you in a hurry," I said to the doctor.

He was about to reply, when the door of the consulting-room was flung wide open, and Gabrielle Heathcote rushed into the room.

"Mother is very ill," she exclaimed. "I think she is out of her mind. Come to her at once."

"GABRIELLE HEATHCOTE RUSHED INTO THE ROOM."

She took Mackenzie's hand in hers

"There isn't a minute to lose," she said, "she may kill herself. She came to me with a carving-knife in her hand; I rushed away at once for you. The two servants are with her now, and they are doing all they can; but, oh! pray, do be quick."

At this moment Gabrielle's eyes rested on me. A look of relief and almost ecstasy passed over her poor, thin little face.

"You are here!" she exclaimed. "You will come, too? Oh, how glad I am."

"If Dr. Mackenzie will permit me," I replied, "I shall be only too pleased to accompany him."

"By all means come, you may be of the greatest use," he answered.

We started at once. As soon as we left the house Gabrielle rushed from us.

"I am going to have the front door open for you both when you arrive," she exclaimed. She disappeared as if on the wings of the wind.

"That is a good girl," I said, turning to the other doctor.

"She has always been deeply attached to both her parents," he answered.

We did not either of us say another word until we got to Ivy Hall. It was a rambling old house, with numerous low rooms and a big entrance-hall. I could fancy that in the summer it was cheerful enough, with its large, walled-in garden. The night was a dark one, but there would be a moon presently.

Gabrielle was waiting in the hall to receive us.

"I will take you to the door of mother's room," she exclaimed.

Her words came out tremblingly, her face was like death. She was shaking all over. She ran up the stairs before us, and then down a long passage which led to a room a little apart from the rest of the house.

"I told you mother wished to sleep in a room as far away from me as possible," she said, flashing a glance into my face as she spoke.

I nodded in reply. We opened the door and went in. The sight which met our eyes was one with which most medical men are familiar.

The patient was lying on the bed in a state of violent delirium. Two maid-servants were bending over her, and evidently much exciting her feelings in their efforts to hold her down. I spoke at once with authority.

"You can leave the room now," I said—"only remain within call in case you are wanted."

They obeyed instantly, looking at me with surprised glances, and at Mackenzie with manifest relief.

I shut the door after them and approached the bed. One glance showed that Mrs.

Heathcote was not mad in the ordinary sense, but that she was suffering at the moment from acute delirium. I put my hand on her forehead: it burned with fever. Her pulse was rapid and uneven. Mackenzie took her temperature, which was very nearly a hundred and four degrees. While we were examining her she remained quiet, but presently, as we stood together and watched her, she began to rave again.

"What is it, Gabrielle? No, no, he is quite dead, child. I tell you I saw the men screw his coffin down. He's dead—quite dead. Oh, God! oh, God! yes, dead, dead!"

She sat up in bed and stared straight before her.

"You mustn't come here so often," she said, looking past us into the centre of the room, and addressing someone whom she seemed to see with distinctness, "I tell you it isn't safe. Gabrielle suspects. Don't come so often — I'll manage some other way. Trust me. Do trust me. You know I won't let you starve. Oh, go away, go away."

She flung herself back on the bed and pressed her hands frantically to her burning eyes.

"Your father has been dead six months now, Gabrielle," she said, presently, in a changed voice.

"No one was ever more dead. I tell you I saw him die; he was buried, and you went to his funeral." Here again her voice altered. She sat upright and motioned with her hand. "Will you bring the coffin in here, please, into this room? Yes; it seems a nice coffin — well finished. The coffin is made of oak. That is right. Oak lasts. I can't bear coffins that crumble away very quickly. This is a good one— you have taken pains with it—I am pleased. Lay him in gently. He is not very heavy, is he? You see how worn he is. Consumption! — yes, consumption. He had been a long time dying, but at the end it was sudden. Hemorrhage of the lungs. We did it to save Gabrielle, and to keep away—what, what, *what* did we want to keep away?—Oh, yes, dishonour! The—the——" Here she burst into a loud laugh.

"You don't suppose, you undertaker's men, that I'm going to tell you what we did it for? Dr. Mackenzie was there—he saw him just at the end. Now you have placed him nicely in his coffin, and you can go. Thank you, you can go now. I don't want you to see his face. A dead face is too sacred. You must not look on it. He is peaceful, only pale, very pale. All dead people look pale. Is he as pale as most dead people? Oh, I forgot—you can't see him. And as cold? Oh, yes, I think so, quite. You want to screw the coffin down, of course, of course— I was forgetting. Now, be quick about it. Why, do you know, I was very nearly having him buried with the coffin open! Screw away now, screw away. Ah, how that noise grates on my nerves. I shall go mad if you are not quick. Do be quick—be *quick*, and leave me alone with my dead. Oh, God, with my dead, my dead!"

The wretched woman's voice sank to a

"HAVE MERCY UPON ME AND UPON MY DEAD."

hoarse whisper. She struggled on to her knees, and folding her hands, began to pray.

"God in Heaven have mercy upon me and upon my dead," she moaned. "Now, now, now! where's the screwdriver? Oh, *heavens*, it's lost, it's lost! We are undone! My God, what is the matter with me? My brain reels. Oh, my God, my God!"

She moaned fearfully. We laid her back on the bed. Her mutterings became more rapid and indistinct. Presently she slept.

"She must not be left in this condition," said Mackenzie to me. "It would be very bad for Gabrielle to be with her mother now. And those young servants are not to be trusted. I will go and send in a nurse as soon as possible. Can you do me the inestimable favour of remaining here until a nurse arrives?"

"I was going to propose that I should, in any case, spend the night here," I replied.

"That is more than good of you," said the doctor.

"Not at all," I answered; "the case interests me extremely."

A moment or two later Mackenzie left the house. During his absence Mrs. Heathcote slept, and I sat and watched her. The fever raged very high—she muttered constantly in her terrible dreams, but said nothing coherent. I felt very anxious about her. She had evidently been subjected to a most frightful strain, and now all her nature was giving way. I dared not think what her words implied. My mission was at present to do what I could for her relief.

The nurse arrived about midnight. She was a sensible, middle-aged woman, very strong too, and evidently accustomed to fever patients. I gave her some directions, desired her to ring a certain bell if she required my assistance, and left the room. As I went slowly downstairs I noticed the moon had risen. The house was perfectly still—the sick woman's moans could not be heard beyond the distant wing of the house where she slept. As I went downstairs I remembered Gabrielle's story about the moonlit garden and her father's figure standing there. I felt a momentary curiosity to see what the garden was like, and, moving aside a blind, which concealed one of the lobby windows, looked out. I gave one hurried glance and started back. Was I, too, the victim of illusion? Standing in the garden was the tall figure of a man with folded arms. He was looking away from me, but the light fell on his face: it was cadaverous and ghastly white; his hat was off; he moved into a deep shadow. It was all done in an instant—he came and went like a flash.

I pursued my way softly downstairs. This man's appearance seemed exactly to coincide with Mackenzie's description of Heathcote; but was it possible, in any of the wonderful possibilities of this earth, that a man could rise from his coffin and walk the earth again?

Gabrielle was waiting for me in the cheerful drawing-room. A bright fire burned in the grate, there were candles on brackets, and one or two shaded lamps placed on small tables. On one table, a little larger than the rest, a white cloth was spread. It also contained a tray with glasses, some claret and sherry in decanters, and a plate of sandwiches.

"You must be tired," said Gabrielle. "Please have a glass of wine, and please eat something. I know those sandwiches are good—I made them myself."

She pressed me to eat and drink. In truth, I needed refreshment. The scene in the sick room had told even on my iron nerves, and the sight from the lobby window had almost taken my breath away.

Gabrielle attended on me as if she were my daughter. I was touched by her solicitude, and by the really noble way in which she tried to put self out of sight. At last she said, in a voice which shook with emotion:—

"I know, Dr. Halifax, that you think badly of mother."

"Your mother is very ill indeed," I answered.

"It is good of you to come and help her. You are a great doctor, are you not?"

I smiled at the child's question.

"I want you to tell me something about the beginning of your mother's illness," I said, after a pause. "When I saw her two days ago, she scarcely considered herself ill at all—in fact, you were supposed to be the patient."

Gabrielle dropped into the nearest chair.

"There is a mystery somewhere," she said, "but I cannot make it out. When I came back, after seeing you to-day, mother seemed very restless and troubled. I thought she would have questioned me about being so long away, and ask me at least what I had done with myself. Instead of that, she asked me to tread softly. She said she had such an intolerable headache that she could not endure the least sound. I saw she had been out, for she had her walking boots on, and they were covered with mud. I tried to coax her to eat something, but she would not, and as I saw she really wished to be alone, I left her.

"At tea-time, our parlour-maid, Peters, told me that mother had gone to bed and had given directions that she was on no account to be disturbed. I had tea alone, and then came in here and made the place as bright and comfortable as I could. Once or twice before, since my father's death, mother has suffered from acute headaches, and has gone to bed; but when they got better, she has dressed and come downstairs again. I thought she might like to do so to-night, and that she would be pleased to see a bright room and everything cheerful about her.

"I got a story-book and tried to read, but my thoughts were with mother, and I felt dreadfully puzzled and anxious. The time seemed very long too, and I heartily wished that the night were over. I went upstairs about eight o'clock, and listened outside mother's door. She was moaning and talking to herself. It seemed to me that she was saying dreadful things. I quite shuddered as I listened. I knocked at the door, but there was no answer. Then I turned the handle and tried to enter, but the door was locked. I went downstairs again, and Peters came to ask me if I would like supper. She was still in the room, and I had not made up my mind whether I could eat anything or not, when I heard her give a short scream, and turning round, I saw mother standing in the room in her nightdress. She had the carving-knife in her hand.

"'Gabrielle,' she said, in a quiet voice, but with an awful look in her eyes, 'I want you to tell me the truth. Is there any blood on my hands?'

"'No, no, mother,' I answered.

"She gave a deep sigh, and looked at them as if she were Lady Macbeth.

"'Gabrielle,' she said again, 'I can't live any longer without your father. I have made this knife sharp, and it won't take long.'

"Then she turned and left the room. Peters ran for cook, and they went upstairs after her, and I rushed for Dr. Mackenzie."

"It was a fearful ordeal for you," I said, "and you behaved very bravely; but you must not think too much about your mother's condition, nor about any words which she happened to say. She is highly feverish at present, and is not accountable for her actions. Sit down now, please, and take a glass of wine yourself."

"No, thank you—I never take wine."

"I'm glad to hear you say so, for in that case a glass of this good claret will do wonders for you. Here, I'm going to pour one out—now drink it off at once."

She obeyed me with a patient sort of smile. She was very pale, but the wine brought some colour into her cheeks.

"I am interested in your story," I said, after a pause. "Particularly in what you told me about your poor father. He must have been an interesting man, for you to treasure his memory so deeply. Do you mind describing him to me?"

She flushed up when I spoke. I saw that tears were very near her eyes, and she bit her lips to keep back emotion.

"My father was like no one else," she said. "It is impossible for me to make a picture of him for one who has not seen him."

"But you can at least tell me if he were tall or short, dark or fair, old or young?"

"No, I can't," she said, after another pause. "He was just father. When you love your father, he has a kind of eternal youth to you, and you don't discriminate his features. If you are his only child,

"IS THERE ANY BLOOD ON MY HANDS?"

his is just the one face in all the world to you. I find it impossible to describe the face, although it fills my mind's eye, waking and sleeping. But, stay, I have a picture of him. I don't show it to many, but you shall see it."

She rushed out of the room, returning in a moment with a morocco case. She opened it, and brought over a candle at the same time so that the light should fall on the picture within. It represented a tall, slight man, with deep-set eyes and a very thin face. The eyes were somewhat piercing in their glance; the lips were closely set and firm; the chin was cleft. The face showed determination. I gave it a quick glance, and, closing the case, returned it to Gabrielle.

The face was the face of the man I had seen in the garden.

My patient passed a dreadful night. She was no better the next morning. Her temperature was rather higher, her pulse quicker, her respiration more hurried. Her ravings had now become almost incoherent. Mackenzie and I had an anxious consultation over her. When he left the house I accompanied him.

"I am going to make a strange request of you," I said. "I wish for your assistance, and am sure you will not refuse to give it to me. In short, I want to take immediate steps to have Heathcote's coffin opened."

I am quite sure Mackenzie thought that I was mad. He looked at me, opened his lips as if to speak, but then waited to hear my next words.

"I want to have Heathcote's body exhumed," I said. "If you will listen to me, I will tell you why."

I then gave him a graphic account of the man I had seen in the garden.

"There is foul play somewhere," I said, in conclusion. "I have been dragged into this thing almost against my will, and now I am determined to see it through."

Mackenzie flung up his hands.

"I don't pretend to doubt your wisdom," he said; "but to ask me gravely to assist you to exhume the body of a man who died of consumption six months ago, is enough to take my breath away. What reason can you possibly give to the authorities for such an action?"

"That I have strong grounds for believing that the death never took place at all," I replied. "Now, will you co-operate with me in this matter, or not?"

"Oh, of course, I'll co-operate with you," he answered. "But I don't pretend to say that I like the business."

We walked together to his house, talking over the necessary steps which must be taken to get an order for exhumation. Mackenzie promised to telegraph to me as soon as ever this was obtained, and I was obliged to hurry off to attend to my own duties. As I was stepping into my hansom I turned to ask the doctor one more question.

"Have you any reason to suppose that Heathcote was heavily insured?" I asked.

"No; I don't know anything about it," he answered.

"You are quite sure there were no money troubles anywhere?"

"I do not know of any; but that fact amounts to nothing, for I was not really intimate with the family, and, as I said yesterday evening, never entered the house until last night from the day of the funeral. I have never *heard* of money troubles; but, of course, they might have existed."

"As soon as ever I hear from you, I will make an arrangement to meet you at Kensal Green," I replied, and then I jumped into the hansom and drove away.

In the course of the day I got a telegram acquainting me with Mrs. Heathcote's condition. It still remained absolutely unchanged, and there was, in Mackenzie's opinion, no necessity for me to pay her another visit. Early the next morning, the required order came from the coroner. Mackenzie wired to apprise me of the fact, and I telegraphed back, making an appointment to meet him at Kensal Green on the following morning.

I shall not soon forget that day. It was one of those blustering and intensely cold days which come oftener in March than any other time of the year. The cemetery looked as dismal as such a place would on the occasion. The few wreaths of flowers which were scattered here and there on newly-made graves were sodden and deprived of all their frail beauty. The wind blew in great gusts, which were about every ten minutes accompanied by showers of sleet. There was a hollow moaning noise distinctly audible in the intervals of the storm.

I found, on my arrival, that Mackenzie was there before me. He was accompanied by one of the coroner's men and a police-constable. Two men who worked in the cemetery also came forward to assist. No one expressed the least surprise at our strange errand. Around Mackenzie's lips, alone, I read an expression of disapproval.

Kensal Green is one of the oldest cemeteries which surround our vast Metropolis, and the Heathcotes' burying-place was quite in the oldest portion of this God's acre. It was one of the hideous, ancient, rapidly-going-out-of-date vaults. A huge brick erection was placed over it, at one side of which was the door of entrance.

The earth was removed, the door of the vault opened, and some of the men went down the steps, one of them holding a torch, in order to identify the coffin. In a couple of minutes' time it was borne into the light of day. When I saw it I remembered poor Mrs. Heathcote's wild ravings.

"A good, strong oak coffin, which wears well," she had exclaimed.

Mackenzie and I, accompanied by the police-constable and the coroner's man, followed the bearers of the coffin to the mortuary.

As we were going there, I turned to ask Mackenzie how his patient was.

He shook his head as he answered me.

"I fear the worst," he replied. "Mrs. Heathcote is very ill indeed. The fever rages high and is like a consuming fire. Her temperature was a hundred and five this morning."

"I should recommend packing her in sheets wrung out of cold water," I answered. "Poor woman!—how do you account for this sudden illness, Mackenzie?"

He shrugged his shoulders.

"Shock of some sort," he answered. Then he continued: "If she really knew of this day's work, it would kill her off pretty quickly. Poor soul," he added, "I hope it may never reach her ears."

We had now reached the mortuary. The men who had borne the coffin on their shoulders lowered it on to a pair of trestles. They then took turn-screws out of their pockets, and in a business-like and callous manner unscrewed the lid. After doing this they left the mortuary, closing the door behind them.

The moment we found ourselves alone, I said a word to the police-constable, and then going quickly up to the coffin, lifted the lid. Under ordinary circumstances, such a proceeding would be followed by appalling results, which need not here be described. Mackenzie, whose face was very white, stood near me. I looked at him for a moment, and then flung aside the pall which was meant to conceal the face of the dead.

The dead truly! Here was death, which had never, in any sense, known life like ours. Mackenzie uttered a loud exclamation. The constable and the coroner's man came close. I lifted a bag of flour out of the coffin!

There were many similar bags there. It had been closely packed, and evidently with a view to counterfeit the exact weight of the dead man.

Poor Mackenzie was absolutely speechless. The coroner's man began to take copious notes; the police-constable gravely did the same.

Mackenzie at last found his tongue.

"I never felt more stunned in my life," he said. "In very truth, I all but saw the man die. Where is he? In the name of Heaven, what has become of him? This is the most monstrous thing I have ever heard of in the whole course of my life, and—and I attended the funeral of those *bags of flour!* No wonder that woman never cared to see me inside the house again. But what puzzles me," he continued, "is the motive—what *can* the motive be?"

"Perhaps one of the insurance companies can tell us that," said the police-officer. "It is my duty to report this thing, sir," he con-

"THEY UNSCREWED THE LID."

tinued, turning to me. "I have not the least doubt that the Crown will prosecute."

"I cannot at all prevent your taking what steps you think proper," I replied, "only pray understand that the poor lady who is the principal perpetrator in this fraud lies at the present moment at death's door."

"We must get the man himself," murmured the police-officer. "If he is alive we shall soon find him."

Half an hour later, Mackenzie and I had left the dismal cemetery.

I had to hurry back to Harley Street to attend to some important duties, but I arranged to meet Mackenzie that evening at the Heathcotes' house. I need not say that my thoughts were much occupied with Mrs. Heathcote and her miserable story. What a life that wretched Heathcote must have led during the last six months. No wonder he looked cadaverous as the moonlight fell over his gaunt figure. No ghost truly was he, but a man of like flesh and blood to ourselves—a man who was supposed to be buried in Kensal Green, but who yet walked the earth.

It was about eight o'clock when I reached the Heathcotes' house. Mackenzie had already arrived—he came into the hall to meet me.

"Where is Miss Gabrielle?" I asked at once.

"Poor child," he replied; "I have begged of her to stay in her room. She knows nothing of what took place this morning, but is in a terrible state of grief about her mother. That unfortunate woman's hours are numbered. She is sinking fast. Will you come to her at once, Halifax—she has asked for you several times."

Accompanied by Mackenzie, I mounted the stairs and entered the sick room. One glance at the patient's face showed me all too plainly that I was in the chamber of death. Mrs. Heathcote lay perfectly motionless. Her bright hair, still the hair of quite a young woman, was flung back over the pillow. Her pale face was wet with perspiration. Her eyes, solemn, dark, and awful in expression, turned and fixed themselves on me as I approached the bedside. Something like the ghost of a smile quivered round her lips. She made an effort to stretch out a shadowy hand to grasp mine.

"Don't stir," I said to her. "Perhaps you want to say something? I will stoop down to listen to you. I have very good hearing, so you can speak as low as you please."

She smiled again with a sort of pleasure at my understanding her.

"I have something to confess," she said, in a hollow whisper. "Send the nurse and—and Dr. Mackenzie out of the room."

I was obliged to explain the dying woman's wishes to my brother physician. He called to the nurse to follow him, and they immediately left the room.

As soon as they had done so, I bent my head and took one of Mrs. Heathcote's hands in mine.

"Now," I said, "take comfort—God can forgive sin. You have sinned?"

"Oh, yes, yes; but how can you possibly know?"

"Never mind. I am a good judge of character. If telling me will relieve your conscience, speak."

"My husband is alive," she murmured.

"Yes," I said, "I guessed as much."

"He had insured his life," she continued, "for—for about fifteen thousand pounds. The money was wanted to—to save us from dishonour. We managed to counterfeit—death."

She stopped, as if unable to proceed any further. "A week ago," she continued, "I—I saw the man who is supposed to be dead. He is really dying now. The strain of knowing that I could do nothing for him—nothing to comfort his last moments—was too horrible. I felt that I could not live without him. On the day of my illness I took—poison, a preparation of Indian hemp. I meant to kill myself. I did not know that my object would be effected in so terrible a manner."

Here she looked towards the door. A great change came over her face. Her eyes shone with sudden brightness. A look of awful joy filled them. She made a frantic effort to raise herself in bed.

I followed the direction of her eyes, and then, indeed, a startled exclamation passed my lips.

Gabrielle, with her cheeks crimson, her lips tremulous, her hair tossed wildly about her head and shoulders, was advancing into the room, leading a cadaverous, ghastly-looking man by the hand. In other words, Heathcote himself in the flesh had come into his wife's dying chamber.

"Oh, Horace!" she exclaimed; "Horace—to die in your arms—to know that you will soon join me. This is too much bliss—this is too great joy!"

The man knelt by her, put his dying arms round her, and she laid her head on his worn breast.

"We will leave them together," I said to Gabrielle.

"LEADING A CADAVEROUS, GHASTLY-LOOKING MAN BY THE HAND."

I took the poor little girl's hand and led her from the room.

She was in a frantic state of excitement.

"I said he was not dead," she repeated—"I always said it. I was sitting by my window a few minutes ago, and I saw him in the garden. This time I was determined that he should not escape me. I rushed downstairs. He knew nothing until he saw me at his side. I caught his hand in mine. It was hot and thin. It was like a skeleton's hand—only it burned with living fire. 'Mother is dying—come to her at once,' I said to him, and then I brought him into the house."

"You did well—you acted very bravely," I replied to her.

I took her away to a distant part of the house.

An hour later, Mrs. Heathcote died. I was not with her when she breathed her last. My one object now was to do what I could for poor little Gabrielle. In consequence, therefore, I made arrangements to have an interview with Heathcote. It was no longer possible for the wretched man to remain in hiding. His own hours were plainly numbered, and it was more than evident that he had only anticipated his real death by some months.

I saw him the next day, and he told me in a few brief words the story of his supposed death and burial.

"I am being severely punished now," he said, "for the one great sin of my life. I am a solicitor by profession, and when a young man was tempted to appropriate some trust funds—hoping, like many another has done before me, to replace the money before the loss was discovered. I married, and had a happy home. My wife and I were devotedly attached to each other. I was not strong, and more than one physician told me that I was threatened with a serious pulmonary affection. About eight months ago, the blow which I never looked for fell. I need not enter into particulars. Suffice it to say that I was expected to deliver over twelve thousand pounds, the amount of certain trusts committed to me, to their rightful owners within three months' time. If I failed to realize this money, imprisonment, dishonour, ruin, would be mine. My wife and child would also be reduced to beggary. I had effected an insurance on my life for fifteen thousand pounds. If this sum could be realized, it would cover the deficit in the trust, and also leave a small overplus for the use of my wife and daughter. I knew that my days were practically numbered, and it did not strike me as a particularly heinous crime to forestall my death by a few months. I talked the matter over with my wife, and at last got her to consent to help me. We managed everything cleverly, and not a soul suspected the fraud which was practised on the world. Our old servants, who had lived with us for years, were sent away on a holiday. We had no servant in the house except a charwoman, who came in for a certain number of hours daily."

"You managed your supposed dying condition with great skill," I answered. "That hemorrhage, the ghastly expression of your face, were sufficiently real to deceive even a keen and clever man like Mackenzie."

Heathcote smiled grimly.

"After all," he said, "the fraud was simple enough. I took an emetic, which I knew would produce the cadaverous hue of approaching death, and the supposed hemorrhage was managed with some bullock's blood. I got it from a distant butcher, telling him that I wanted it to mix with meal to feed my dogs with."

"And how did you deceive the undertaker's men?" I asked.

"My wife insisted on keeping my face covered, and I managed to simulate rigidity. As to the necessary coldness, I was cold enough lying with only a sheet over me. After I was placed in the coffin my wife would not allow anyone to enter the room but herself: she brought me food, of course. We bored holes, too, in the coffin lid. Still, I shall never forget the awful five minutes during which I was screwed down.

"It was all managed with great expedition. As soon as ever the undertaker's men could be got out of the way, my wife unscrewed the coffin and released me. We then filled it with bags of flour, which we had already secured and hidden for the purpose. My supposed funeral took place with due honours. I left the house that night, intending to ship to America. Had I done this, the appalling consequences which have now ended in the death of my wife might never have taken place, but, at the eleventh hour, my courage failed me. I could do much to shield my wife and child, but I could not endure the thought of never seeing them again. Contrary to all my wife's entreaties, I insisted on coming into the garden, for the selfish pleasure of catching even a glimpse of Gabrielle's little figure, as she moved about her bedroom. She saw me once, but I escaped through the shrubbery and by a door which we kept on purpose unlocked, before she reached me. I thought I would never again transgress, but once more the temptation assailed me, and I was not proof against it. My health failed rapidly. I was really dying, and on the morning when my wife's illness began, had suffered from a genuine and very sharp attack of hemorrhage. She found me in the wretched lodging where I was hiding in a state of complete misery, and almost destitution. Something in my appearance seemed suddenly to make her lose all self-control.

"'Horace,' she exclaimed, 'I cannot stand this. When you die, I will die. We will carry our shame and our sorrow and our unhappy love into the grave, where no man can follow us. When you die, I will die. Oh, to see you like this drives me mad!'

"She left me. She told me when I saw her during those last few moments yesterday, that she had hastened her end by a powerful dose of Indian hemp. That is the story. I know that I have laid myself open to criminal prosecution of the gravest character, but I do not think I shall live to go through it."

"WHEN YOU DIE, I WILL DIE."

Heathcote was right. He passed away that evening quite quietly in his sleep.

Poor little Gabrielle! I saw her once since her parents' death, but it is now a couple of years since I have heard anything about her. Will she ever get over the severe shock to which she was subjected? What does the future hold in store for her? I cannot answer these questions. Time alone can do that.

Stories from the Diary of a Doctor.

BY L. T. MEADE AND CLIFFORD HALIFAX, M.D.

WITHOUT WITNESSES.

IN the October of 1890 I went to pay a short visit to my friends, the Brabazons, of Penporran, in Cornwall. I could only spare a week out of town, and looked forward to my visit with the pleasure which a busy man must feel when he can relax his labours for a short time.

Brabazon was an old college friend, and on the first evening of my stay we had many memories to revive and many friends to talk over. We sat until the small hours in his smoking-room, and it was early morning before we retired to bed. Just as I was leaving the room, he said to me :—

"WE HAD MANY MEMORIES TO REVIVE."

"By the way, you will find some disturbing elements at work here. I know you are fond of attributing everything to some psychological cause. I wonder what you will say to the love affairs of Randall, Carleton, and Miss Farnham."

I naturally asked what my host meant.

"Randall and Carleton are both desperately in love with the same girl," he replied. "Did you not notice the state of affairs this evening at dinner?"

"I naturally noticed Miss Farnham," I answered at once. "It would be difficult not to be attracted by so striking a personality."

"Barbara Farnham is, without exception, the most dangerous girl of my acquaintance," replied Brabazon, with a slight laugh. "Before her advent on the scene, Randall and Carleton were the best possible friends. Now they are at daggers drawn."

"I confess I did not particularly observe them," I answered.

"Oh, they are just ordinary good young fellows," replied Brabazon. "I am sorry for Carleton, of course, for I don't think he has the ghost of a chance with Miss Farnham. He is not particularly good looking, and he has the misfortune to be poor. Randall is a handsome lad, and has considerable expectations. His father is Lord Hartmore—but the fact is, I don't think the girl means to marry either of them—she is simply playing one against the other for her own ends. She is a handsome witch, and a dangerous one. She plays as carelessly with edged tools—as carelessly and unconcernedly as a baby would with its rattle."

I said nothing further. Brabazon conducted me to my room, and wished me good-night. I sat down by the fire, and thought in an idle manner over the events of the evening. There was a large house party at Penporran. Shooting was going on vigorously, and cub-hunting had begun. Some of the guests were acquaintances of mine. In short, I looked forward to a pleasant week in this genial house. As I laid my head on my pillow I thought again, but without any specially keen interest, of Brabazon's story about the disturbing elements which were now agitating the air of this otherwise peaceful mansion.

Two young men were in love with the same girl. Surely the situation was a very ordinary one. Such a complication happened daily.

I wondered why Brabazon should have troubled himself to mention such an ordinary event, but as I was dropping off to sleep, I saw rising up before me, in my mind's eye, the proud, beautiful face of Barbara Farnham, and a kind of intuition told me that these commonplace incidents might assume the form of tragedy in her cruel and careless hands.

I dreamt of Miss Farnham that night, and came down to breakfast the next morning with my curiosity considerably aroused about her.

She was in the room when I entered, and was idly helping herself to a cup of coffee, which she carried to a distant window where a small table was also laid for breakfast. She sat down, and, sipping it leisurely, looked around her with a careless glance. Her eyes fell on me—she smiled and motioned to me to approach.

"Pray bring your breakfast to this table," she said, in a light tone. "I was immensely interested in you when I heard you were coming. I adore doctors, particularly if they are clever. Are you going to ride this morning?"

I answered in the affirmative, and asked her if she was fond of horses.

"Fond?" she replied, a flash of added warmth lighting up her peculiar red-brown eyes. "I am going to whisper a secret to you—I never could compare horses and human beings. I consider the horse the infinitely nobler creature of the two."

I laughed, and we entered into an animated conversation.

While we were talking, Carleton came into the room. He was a squarely built young man, with deeply set dark eyes, and a determined chin and mouth. His figure was slightly above the middle height; he was extremely spare, but had good shoulders and was well set up. As soon as ever he appeared in sight, Miss Farnham, by an almost imperceptible movement, slightly turned her back to him and her talk with me became even more animated and full of wit than before. Her gay, light laugh must have reached Carleton, who came straight across the room to her side.

"You are in your favourite seat," he said.

"Yes," she replied, "and Dr. Halifax is having breakfast with me."

Then she turned to continue her conversation with me, while Carleton stood perfectly erect and silent by her side.

"Why don't you eat something?" she said to him, presently.

"There is time enough," he answered.

Finding he would not go away she tried to draw him into conversation, but he was evidently not in the humour to make himself agreeable. His answers were confined to monosyllables, and to some of Miss Farnham's remarks he did not reply at all.

I confess that I began to think him an unmitigated bore.

A change was, however, quickly to take place in the situation—Randall, the other lover, appeared on the scene, and his coming acted like a flash of sunshine. He was a gay, handsome, debonair-looking young fellow. He had good teeth, good eyes, a genial smile, a hearty manner. His voice was musical, and he knew well how to use it. He nodded carelessly to one or two acquaintances when he entered the room, and then came straight to Miss Farnham's table.

She shook hands with him, and he nodded a cheerful good morning to Carleton and me.

"That is right," he said, smiling brightly at the handsome girl; "you promised to reserve a seat for me at this table, and I see you have kept your word. Have you done breakfast, Carleton?"

"I had something an hour ago," replied Carleton.

Randall went to a sideboard to help himself to a generous portion of a dish which was being kept hot with a spirit lamp. On his return our conversation became gayer and more lively than ever.

I must confess that I saw nothing to object to in Miss Farnham's manners. I could not imagine why Brabazon spoke of her as a dangerous witch. She tried to be polite to both men—or rather, she was polite without effort, but there was not a trace of the flippant in her manner or bearing. Her beauty was undoubtedly of a remarkable order. Her eyes were her most striking characteristic. There was a great deal of red in their brown, which was further accentuated by the red-brown of her long eyelashes. The eyes were capable of every shade of expression, and could be at times as eloquent and as full of meaning as those of that bewitching creature, the collie. Her eyebrows were dark and delicately pencilled. Her hair was tawny in shade — she had quantities of it, and she wore it picturesquely round her stately, statuesque head. In some lights that brilliantly coloured hair looked as if a sunbeam had been imprisoned in it. Her complexion was of a warm, creamy whiteness. Her figure was slight and graceful. But for her eyes she might have been simply remarked as a handsome girl; but those eyes made her beautiful, and lifted her completely out of the commonplace.

We had nearly finished breakfast, when I was startled by seeing Randall suddenly press his hand to his eyes, and turn so white that I thought he was going to lose consciousness. He recovered himself almost immediately, however, and so completely, that no one else remarked the circumstance. Miss Farnham rose from the breakfast-table.

"I am going to ride with you, Dr. Halifax," she said, nodding brightly to me. "I shall come downstairs in my habit in half an hour."

She was crossing the room to speak to some of the other guests when Carleton came up to her.

"I want to say something to you," he said—"can we go to some room where we shall be quite undisturbed?"

His words were distinctly audible, not only to me, but to several other people in the room.

Randall in particular heard them, and I could see that he was waiting anxiously for the reply.

"I want to ride this morning—I have no time for private confidences," replied Miss Farnham, in a distinctly vexed tone.

"I won't keep you long," replied Carleton—"what I have to say is of great importance, at least to me."

"I will give you ten minutes after lunch; will that suffice?"

"Five minutes now will do better. I am very much in earnest when I make this request."

"Very well," said Miss Farnham, in a light tone; "importunate people generally have their way. Come into the conservatory—there is a rose there on which I have set my heart; it is too high for me to reach."

She left the room as she spoke, and Carleton quickly followed her. As they disappeared, I noticed more than one guest looking significantly after them. Carleton's pluck was distinctly approved of—I could see that by the expression on some of the ladies' faces—and one, as she passed close to Randall's side, was heard to murmur, audibly:—

"Faint heart never won fair lady."

Randall came up to me and asked me to join him in a smoke on the balcony. As we walked up and down, he talked cheerfully, and, whatever anxiety he may inwardly have felt, was careful not to betray a trace of it.

In less than half an hour Miss Farnham joined us. She was in a dark brown riding-habit, which toned perfectly with her rich and peculiar colouring. Her spirits were gay, not to say wild, and the warm, creamy whiteness of her face seemed to glow now as if with hidden fire.

"Are you not ready for your ride?" she said, looking at me with a certain reproach. "The horses will be round in less than ten minutes. It is a splendid morning for a gallop. You are coming, too?" she added, turning suddenly to Randall.

"I only waited for you to invite me," he said. "Of course I shall come, with pleasure. But I thought," he added, in a low tone, coming close to her side as he spoke, "that you arranged to ride with Ronald Carleton this morning?"

"That is off," she replied, in a light tone. "Mr. Carleton has, I believe, another engagement."

The balcony on which we were walking led round to one of the entrances to the house; at this moment a groom was seen leading a smart mare up to the door, and at the same instant Carleton ran down the steps, and sprang lightly into the saddle.

"Where are you off to?" exclaimed Randall, bending out of the balcony to speak to him. "Miss Farnham, Dr. Halifax, and I are all going out immediately. Won't you join us?"

"Not this morning, I think," said Carleton, constraint in his tone. He gathered up the reins, and the mare began to prance about.

"You are holding her too much on the curb," exclaimed Randall.

"Thanks, I think I know what I'm about," replied Carleton, with evident temper. "Quiet, you brute, quiet," he continued, vainly endeavouring to restrain the movements of the impatient animal.

"I tell you, that mare won't stand the curb," shouted Randall. "Give her her head, and she'll do anything you ask her. I know, for I've often ridden her."

"When I require a riding lesson from you, I'll inform you of the fact," answered Carleton, in a sulky voice, which was rendered almost ridiculous by the frantic movements of the mare, now thoroughly upset.

Miss Farnham, who had been standing in the background, came up at this juncture, and took her place conspicuously by Randall's side.

"Mr. Randall is right and you are wrong," she exclaimed. "It is absolutely cruel to ride that mare on the curb."

Carleton looked up with a scowl, which anything but improved him. He would not even glance at Miss Farnham, but his eyes

"CARLETON LOOKED UP WITH A SCOWL."

flashed an angry fire at his more fortunate rival.

"Of course, Randall is right," he exclaimed. "All the odds are in his favour."

"Nonsense," retorted Randall, with heat.

"Come, come, gentlemen, pray don't quarrel on this lovely morning," said Miss Farnham. "Mr. Carleton, I wish you a pleasant ride."

She left the balcony as she spoke, and Randall and I immediately followed her example.

We had a splendid ride over an extensive moorland country, and returned to lunch in excellent spirits and in high good humour with each other. Carleton had not yet come back, but his absence did not seem to depress anyone, certainly not Miss Farnham, whose bright eyes and gay, animated manner made her the life of the party. Randall was radiant in the sunshine of her presence. She was confidential and almost affectionate in her manner to him; and he undoubtedly looked, and was, at his best.

I could not help cordially liking him and thinking that the pair were well matched. Notwithstanding Brabazon's words of the night before, I had no doubt that Miss Farnham was sincerely attached to Randall, and would tell him so presently.

I spent the greater part of the afternoon alone with my host, and did not see the rest of the guests until we met at dinner. Carleton had then returned. He sat between a red-haired girl and a very fat old lady, and looked as *distrait* and bored as man well could. Randall, on the other hand, was in his best form. His clothes sat well on him. He was, undoubtedly, a handsome, striking-looking man.

I cannot describe Miss Farnham's dress. It was ethereal in texture and suited her well. She was not seated in the neighbourhood of either Randall or Carleton, but once or twice I noticed that her eyes wandered down to their part of the table. For some reason, she was not in such high spirits as she had been in the early part of the day. My neighbour, a quiet, middle-aged spinster, began suddenly to talk to me about her.

"I see you are interested in Barbara Farnham," she began. "I am not the least surprised—you but follow the example of all the other men who know her."

"Miss Farnham is a very beautiful girl," I replied.

Miss Derrick gave a short sigh.

"Yes," she replied, "Barbara has a beautiful face. She is a fine creature too, although of course terribly spoilt."

"Have you known her long?" I asked.

"Yes; since she was a child. Of course you must notice, Dr. Halifax, the state of matters. Barbara's conduct is more or less the talk of the whole house. I presume from his manner that poor Mr. Carleton's chances of success are quite over, and for my part I am sorry. He is not rich, but he is a good fellow—he is devotedly attached to Barbara, and his abilities are quite above the average. Yes, I am sorry for Mr. Carleton. Barbara might have done worse than return his affection."

I did not feel inclined to pursue the subject any further with this somewhat garrulous lady. After a pause, I remarked:—

"Miss Farnham looks tired, and does not seem in her usual spirits."

Miss Derrick shrugged her thin shoulders.

"What else can you expect?" she

answered. "Barbara is a creature of moods. She was quite *exaltée* all the morning; now she will be correspondingly dull, until a fresh wave of excitement raises her spirits."

At this moment the signal for the ladies to withdraw was given. After their departure, Carleton and Randall found themselves sitting close together. I noticed that neither man spoke to the other, and also observed that after a time Carleton deliberately changed his seat for one at a distant part of the table.

"CARLETON DELIBERATELY CHANGED HIS SEAT."

We did not sit long over wine, and when we came into the drawing-room a lady was playing some classical music with precision and sufficient brilliancy to attract several musical men to the vicinity of the piano. Her place was quickly taken by the droll man of the party, who entertained the company with comic songs. The evening dragged on in the usual manner. For some unaccountable reason no one seemed quite in good spirits. As for me, I found myself constantly looking in the direction of the door. I heartily wished that either Carleton or Randall would come in—I acknowledged to myself that the presence of one at least of these gentlemen in the room would give me relief.

An hour and more passed away, however, and neither of them appeared. I glanced towards Miss Farnham. She was standing near the piano, idly playing with a large feather fan. I thought I read both solicitude and expectation in her eyes.

The funny man was trolling out a sea-song to which a lively chorus was attached. Brabazon came up and touched my arm.

"When that is over," he said, in a low voice, "I will ask Barbara Farnham to sing."

"Can she sing?" I asked.

"Can she!" he reiterated. "Yes, she sings," he replied, emphatically. "Wait—you will hear her in a moment. Her voice is the most absolutely sympathetic I have ever listened to."

Soon afterwards Miss Farnham went to the piano. She played her own accompaniment. One grand sweep her hands seemed to take of the instrument, as if they meant to embrace it, and then a voice, high, full, sweet, magnificent in its volume of melody, rose on the air and seemed to fill the room.

Brabazon was right. Barbara Farnham could sing. As the words fell from her lips, there was no other sound in the listening room.

I jotted those words down afterwards from memory—they seemed to me to be a fit prelude to the scene which was immediately to follow:—

Thou hast filled me a golden cup
  With a drink divine that glows,
With the bloom that is flowing up
  From the heart of the folded rose.
The grapes in their amber glow,
  And the strength of the blood-red wine,
All mingle and change and flow
  In this golden cup of thine
With the scent of the curling wine,
  With the balm of the rose's breath—
For the voice of love is thine,
  And thine is the Song of Death!

The voice of the singer sank low as she approached the end of her song. The final words were in a minor key. I looked full at Miss Farnham, and her dark eyes met mine. They were full of apprehension. A kind of premonition of coming sorrow might well have filled her breast from the look in their depths.

There was a noise and sense of confusion in the outer drawing-room. People stood back to make way for someone, and hurrying steps came quickly towards the piano.

Miss Farnham sprang to her feet, the last notes of the song arrested on her lips.

Carleton, an overcoat covering his evening dress, his hair dishevelled, his eyes wild, had come hastily to her side.

"You will think that I have killed him, Barbara; but, before God, it is not true!" he said in a hoarse whisper—then he grasped my arm.

"Come, I want you," he said, and he dragged me, as if he were a young fury, out of the room.

"What, in the name of Heaven, is the matter?" I asked of him when we found ourselves in the hall.

"Randall has fallen over the cliff down by Porran's field," he gasped. "I have found the—the body. Oh! no, no, what am I saying? Not the body yet—not a body when I left it—it breathed—it just breathed when I left. I tried to drag it up here, but it was too heavy. Come at once, for the love of Heaven."

Other people had followed us out of the drawing-room. I encountered a glance of fire from Miss Farnham's dark eyes—her face was like death itself. Brabazon, in a tone full of authority, as befitted the host, began to speak.

"Come!" he said. "Accident or no, there is not a moment to be lost in trying to help the poor fellow. You will lead us to the spot at once, Carleton. Come, Halifax; what a blessing that you happen to be on the spot!"

"Get some brandy and something which we can improvise into a litter or shutter," I exclaimed. "I am going to my room to fetch my surgical case."

I ran upstairs. A moment or two later we were on our way to the scene of the accident. Every man of the party accompanied us, and several of the ladies. The foremost of the group was Miss Farnham herself. She had hastily flung a shawl over her head, and the train of her rich dinner dress was slung across her arm. She looked at Carleton, and with a peremptory gesture seemed to invite him to come to her side. He did so, and they rushed on—too quickly for many of the rest of the party to keep up with them.

It was a bright, moonlight night, and we had scarcely any need of the lantern which Brabazon was thoughtful enough to bring with him. We had to go some distance to reach the spot where poor Randall was lying, but by-and-by we found him stretched partly on his back, partly rolled over on his left side, on a little strip of sand which gleamed cold in the moonlight.

"Yes, it was here I left him," exclaimed Carleton. He fell on his knees as he spoke and looked intently into the poor lad's face.

"Thank God!" he exclaimed, looking up at me, "he can't be dead. I dragged him as far as this, and then left him lying on his back. See, he has moved—he is partly on his side now!"

I motioned to Carleton to make way for me to approach. I felt for the pulse in the limp and powerless wrist. I laid my hand on the heart—then I gently raised the head, and felt along the region of the skull.

"You will give him a little brandy," exclaimed Brabazon; "here is the flask."

Miss Farnham took it out of Brabazon's

"I FELT FOR THE PULSE IN THE LIMP AND POWERLESS WRIST."

hands, unscrewed it, and began to pour some into the cup. As she did so, she knelt also on the sand. I looked at her and felt that she would probably need the stimulant which could avail nothing now to the dead.

"It is all over," I said; "he is dead, poor fellow!"

As I spoke, I stretched out my hand and took the brandy flask from Miss Farnham. She looked wildly round, glanced at Carleton, gave a piercing cry, and fell forward over Randall's body. She had completely lost consciousness. I laid her flat on the sand, and, applying some restoratives, she quickly came to her senses.

The body of the dead man was lifted up and laid on some boards which we had brought with us, and we returned slowly to the house. Brabazon gave his arm to Miss Farnham, who truly needed it, for she staggered as she walked. I looked round for Carleton. There was a wild expression in his eyes, which made me anxious about him. I saw, too, that he wished to linger behind the others.

"Come," I said, going up to him, "this has given you a terrible shock; why, you are just as much overcome as Miss Farnham."

I dragged his hand through my arm, and we followed in the rear of the sad procession. All the way up to the house he did not speak, nor did I trouble him with questions. I saw that his misery had made him dumb for the time being—in short, he was in a stunned condition. I dreaded, however, the return tide of strong emotion which must inevitably follow this apparent calm. I guessed that Carleton was a man of strong sensibilities. I could read character well—most men in my profession have much practice in this art. The human eye tells a doctor a good deal. The lips may falter out certain utterances, which the eyes will belie. I read truth and sincerity in the honest eyes of this young man. He was intensely reserved—he was jealous to a morbid degree—he in all probability possessed anything but a good temper; nevertheless, his eyes were honest, and I felt certain that he had nothing whatever to do with poor Randall's death. Nevertheless, I knew well that appearances were strongly against him.

When we got to the house I turned to him and said, abruptly:—

"I should like to see you in Brabazon's smoking-room in about half an hour."

He raised sullen eyes to my face.

"Come," I said, laying my hand on his shoulder, "I tell you at once I do not believe that you killed that poor fellow, but we must talk the matter over. I am anxious to be your friend. It is absolutely necessary that you should confide in someone. I am as unbiased in my views of the whole situation as man can be. Come and talk to me in half an hour in the smoking-room."

He did not say a word, but I knew by the way in which he suddenly grasped my hand that he would come.

The dead man was carried into the library, where he was laid reverently on a table. Brabazon then had a consultation with me as to the best means of breaking the news to Lord and Lady Hartmore. Poor Randall was their only son; it was a terrible business altogether, and Brabazon was naturally greatly distressed.

I asked after Miss Farnham. He told me that she had gone straight to her room. His tone was scarcely sympathetic, and I looked at him in wonder.

"I have no patience with her," he exclaimed. "She has behaved very badly—this awful thing would not have occurred but for her. She has driven poor Carleton——"

I put up my hand to arrest the words.

"Hush!" I exclaimed. "You surely don't——?"

He laughed aloud in his agitation.

"I surely do," he began. "There, Halifax, we won't give the thing a name to-night. Of course, there must be a coroner's inquest."

"Yes," I replied.

"It is a terrible thing altogether," continued Brabazon; "and to think of its happening here. And to Randall, of all people—a man with his expectations. Well, it is a lesson which Miss Farnham may well lay to heart."

We were standing together in the library—the hour was now nearly midnight. The body of the dead man lay on the centre table covered with a white sheet. There came a knock at the door, and to my dismay and astonishment I saw Carleton enter the room.

"I heard voices, and guessed you would be here," he exclaimed. "I have recovered my nerves to a certain extent, and wish to tell you, sir," looking at his host, "and you also, Dr. Halifax, exactly what has occurred."

"Come into the smoking-room," said Brabazon, not unkindly.

"No," answered the poor lad. "If you will allow me, I will tell my story here. There is not much to tell, but what there is had best be told in the presence of——" his lip trembled—he could not get further words out. He sank suddenly into a chair, and covered his white face with his shaking hands. "We must humour him," I said, turning and speaking in a whisper to Brabazon—"and before God," I continued, impulsively,

"HE COVERED HIS WHITE FACE WITH HIS SHAKING HANDS."

"I believe he is as innocent as I am."

I drew forward a chair for myself as I spoke, but Brabazon stood by the hearth.

Carleton began to speak almost directly—his emotion was quickly mastered.

"I have loved Barbara Farnham for two years. At intervals she has given me great encouragement, and I had fair hopes of winning her until she met Randall in this house a fortnight ago. This morning I felt desperate, and resolved to put my fortunes to the test. I asked her to give me an interview after breakfast, as you doubtless noticed." He paused, and looked at me—I nodded my head, and he continued: "We went into the conservatory, and I—I spoke to her. I told her the naked truth, perhaps a little too bluntly. I asked her if she really meant to—no, I must not say what I did ask her. It is unfair—unfair to her. From her manner and her words I plainly gathered that she preferred Randall to me, and that I had no chance whatever of winning her. Perhaps I lost my temper—anyhow, it was unmanly of me to say what I did. I accused her of valuing Randall's position. I told her plainly that if Randall and I could change places, I should be the favoured one. We had a disagreement; our interview was full of pain, at least to me. When I left Miss Farnham the Evil One seemed to enter into me, and I hated Randall as I never knew before that I could hate anyone. I would not ride with the others, but went away by myself, and the whole day has been a long agony to me.

"My hatred to Randall grew worse and worse, until its vehemence half frightened me. We used to be good friends, too. After dinner I felt that I could not bear a couple of conventional hours in the drawing-room, and went out to nurse my misery in the open air. I had no idea that Randall was also out. I went along by the shore, but mounted to the higher cliffs on my way back. I intended to leave Penporran early to-morrow, and felt impatient for the hour when I could get away from the loathsome sight of my successful rival.

"As I was walking along by the edge of the cliffs, and had just entered Porran's field, I felt my heart jump into my mouth, for Randall was coming to meet me. He was about a hundred yards away when I first saw him. He is a taller man than I, and he seemed to stand out sharply between me and the sky. I knew by his attitude that he was smoking a cigar. I stood still for a moment. I did not want to pass him. My heart was full of torment, and I hated to meet him out there, with not a soul to stand between us. You know that part of the cliff, Mr. Brabazon? Randall had just come to that portion of it which is railed in to keep the cattle from tumbling over. I don't know what possessed him to take the outside path, which is very narrow and slippery. He did so, however; and now, for the first time, he must have noticed me. I was within fifty yards of him, coming also along the edge of the cliff. He stood stock still, as if something or somebody had shot him. I thought he was about to shout to me, but instead of doing so, he threw up one hand and clutched his brow. The next instant he began to sway from side to side, and before I could approach him, he had fallen over the cliff, sheer down that awful height!

"My absolute surprise stunned me for a moment—then I ran up to the spot where he had fallen, and throwing myself on my face and hands, looked over the cliff, in the hopes that he might have clung on to something. The moon was bright, but I could not see him. Looking down from that height made me dizzy, and I saw there was nothing for it but to retrace my steps as fast as possible to the shore. I ran quickly, and was breathless when I got up to him. He was lying on his back, with his arms stretched out—some blood was oozing from his mouth. I wiped it away and called to him, and putting my arms under his head, tried to lift him. He moaned and moved faintly. I felt his limbs—they seemed all right. I had a wild hope that he was only stunned, and tried to drag him along the shore. He was too heavy for me, however, and I feared that I was only injuring him in my attempt to get him back to the house. I laid him as easily as I could on a piece of sand above high-water mark, and then ran back to Penporran. It was on my way back that the awful idea first occurred to me that Barbara would think I had killed him. I seemed to see all the circumstances of his terrible death with preternatural clearness, and I felt sure that the gravest suspicion would attach to me. I have come to this room now to tell you both, before Heaven, and in the presence of the dead man, the solemn truth. Of course, I cannot compel you to believe me."

Carleton stood up as he uttered these last words. His attitude was very manly, and the look on his face was at once straightforward and quiet. I liked him better than I thought I ever could have liked him. I felt deep sympathy for him, and looked at Brabazon, expecting him to share my sentiments. To my surprise, however, I saw by the expression round his lips that he was not favourably impressed by Carleton, and that his feelings towards him were the reverse of sympathetic.

Carleton looked full at him, expecting him to speak. When he did not, the poor fellow repeated his last remark, a faint quaver perceptible in his voice:—

"Of course, I cannot compel you to believe me."

"Thank you for coming to see us," said Brabazon then; "you have been the first to give name to a suspicion which will, doubtless, be harboured by more than one person who has known all the circumstances of this unhappy case. I sincerely pity you, Carleton, but I prefer to keep my judgment in abeyance for the time being. Halifax will tell you that a coroner's inquest will be necessary. At the inquest the whole matter will be gone carefully into. You may be certain that all possible justice will be done you."

"Justice!" exclaimed Carleton, a faint smile playing for an instant round his lips. "Justice, when there were no witnesses! Oh, that the dead could speak!" He turned abruptly and prepared to leave the room.

Brabazon called after him.

"You must give me your word of honour that you will not attempt to leave Penporran before the inquest."

"You may rest assured on that point," said Carleton.

He left the room. The restraint he was putting upon himself gave a dignity to his whole bearing which impressed me much.

"I fully believe in that poor fellow's innocence," I said, as soon as the door had closed behind him. Brabazon gave me a keen glance.

"You are a good judge of character," he said, after a pause; "still, I prefer to keep my judgment in abeyance."

Shortly afterwards he bade me good-night, and I retired to my own room. I closed the door and stood by the hearth, where the ashes of the fire, which had been lit some hours previous and had long ago burnt itself out, were to be seen.

I felt too restless to go to bed, and wished the morning would come. I was standing so, thinking over all the circumstances which had turned our gay party into one of mourning, when I heard a footfall outside my door. I thought it might possibly be Carleton, and going across the room, I opened the door and went out into the corridor. To my astonishment, Miss Farnham, still wearing her gay evening dress, stood before me.

"I was thinking of knocking at your door," she said, "but had scarcely courage to do so. I want to speak to you."

"I will see you in the morning," I said.

"It is morning already," she replied. "This is no time for conventionality, Dr. Halifax; I wish to speak to you now. You cannot sleep, and no more can I. Please follow me to Mrs. Brabazon's sitting-room, where a fire and a lamp are still burning."

She led the way, and I obeyed her without a word.

"Now tell me the truth," she said, the moment we found ourselves in the room. "Will Mr. Carleton be accused of having murdered poor Arthur Randall?"

"PLEASE FOLLOW ME."

"You believe all this?" she said, with intense eagerness, when I had done speaking.

"Yes."

"How do you account for Mr. Randall's death?"

I could not help sighing deeply.

"You allude now to the difficulty of the position," I said. "At the present moment I cannot account for Randall's death. A man in perfect health is not often attacked with such violent vertigo as to cause him to lose the power of keeping himself upright." Then I paused—I was thinking deeply. "Undoubtedly there have been such cases," I said, "but they are rare."

I remembered, as I spoke, Randall's change of colour and the sudden pressure of his hand to his head that morning at breakfast.

"You have seen a good deal of the poor fellow," I said. "Did he ever at any time complain of peculiar symptoms to you? Did you ever notice anything about him which would lead you not to suppose him in perfect health?"

"Never," she said at once, emphatically. "He always seemed to me to be the perfect embodiment of the rudest health and strength."

"The death is very mysterious," I said; "and while I personally believe poor Carleton's story, I fear matters will go hard with him."

I was about to leave the room, as I did not imagine Miss Farnham could have anything further to say to me, when she exclaimed, impulsively, her eyes filled with the most terrible anguish, her face turning white as death: "If, indeed, this thing is true, and if Ronald Carleton has to suffer in consequence of Mr. Randall's death, I shall put an end to my own life."

"Nonsense!" I said, sharply. "You must not speak in that wild way. You know you don't mean a word that you say."

"You mistake me," she replied. "I exaggerate nothing. I state a simple fact when I tell you that if Ronald Carleton suffers for this, my remorse will be greater than I can bear. I have behaved badly to him."

"Yes, God knows you have!" I interrupted. I felt angry with her, and did not want to spare her at that moment. "You have

"There is no doubt that grave suspicion will attach to him," I answered, without hesitation.

"But you think him innocent?" she queried.

"I think him innocent. As innocent as you or I."

"Oh, don't speak of me," she said, sinking suddenly on the sofa. "Pray don't mention my innocence. But for me this tragedy would never have happened."

I looked long at her before I replied.

"In one sense you may be right," I answered; "it is quite possible that but for you Carleton would not have witnessed Randall's death. Still, you must not be unfair to yourself—you are not accountable for the sudden brain seizure which must have caused Randall to reel and fall over the cliff."

"What do you mean?" she demanded.

"Carleton has just described the accident to Brabazon and me," I answered. "He saw Randall sway and fall over the cliff. I believe his story, although I fear few people will agree with me."

"I don't know the story," she said, faintly. "Pray tell it to me."

I did so in a few words.

behaved badly to as honest and true-hearted a man as ever breathed. When will beautiful women like you learn that men's hearts are not mere balls to be kicked here and there?"

"Oh, yes, you are right to abuse me," she said. "Go on, go on. I am so unhappy that nothing you can say will add to my pain. My cup of misery is full. I have ruined the man I love."

"The man you love?" I queried, looking at her in astonishment. "Nay, you must not be too hard on yourself. You surely are not accountable for Randall's tragic end. If Carleton's story is true, he died from sudden vertigo. You were kind to him while he lived — you have nothing to reproach yourself with on that score."

"Yes, I have," she answered, with sudden passion. "I deceived him. I made him think that I loved him; in reality, he was nothing to me. It is Ronald Carleton whom I love."

"Then, in the name of the Evil One——" I began.

"Yes, you may well quote the Evil One," she retorted. "I think he has been about the house all day. I think he entered into me this morning when poor Ronald spoke to me. The Evil One held me back then from telling him what I really thought. I gave him to understand that I—I hated him, and all the time I loved him—I loved him then—I love him now—I shall love him for ever! The dead man is nothing to me: less than nothing!"

She began to walk up and down the room; fever spots burnt on her cheeks; her eyes looked wild; she clenched her right hand.

"What can I do for you?" I asked, after a pause. "You have been good enough to confide in me: you must have done so for a reason."

She stopped her restless walk and came close to me.

"I have heard of you before, Dr. Halifax," she said. "This is not the first time you have been asked to help people in trouble. I want you to help me—will you help me?"

"With all my power, if I can."

"You can. Find out what killed Mr. Randall. Save Ronald Carleton."

"I wish I could," I said, reflectively.

"Oh, it won't be difficult," she replied.

I looked at her in surprise.

"What can you mean?" I asked.

To my amazement, she flung herself on her knees at my feet.

"You can invent something," she said, clasping my hand and pressing it frantically

"SHE FLUNG HERSELF ON HER KNEES AT MY FEET."

between both her own. "Oh, it would not be a crime—and it would save a life—two lives. Say you saw symptoms of apoplexy. Say—oh, you will know what to say—and you are a great doctor, and you will be believed."

"Get up," I said, sternly; "I will forgive your wild words, for circumstances have excited you so much that you do not quite know what you are saying. Believe me that nothing would give me more sincere satisfaction than to be able to discover the real cause of poor Randall's death. But you mistake your man utterly when you make the suggestion you do. Now I must leave you. It is almost morning, and I have promised to meet Brabazon downstairs at an early hour."

I went back to my own room, where I sat in anxious thought until the time which Brabazon had appointed for us to meet arrived. I then went down to the smoking-room, where I found him.

He looked harassed and ill—no wonder. The subject we had met to discuss was how best the news of their only son's death was to be broken to Lord and Lady Hartmore. The Hartmores' place was situated about a hundred miles away. Brabazon said that there was nothing whatever for it but to telegraph the unhappy circumstance to them.

"And I fear doing so very much," he added, "for Hartmore is not strong: he has a rather dangerous heart affection."

"Don't telegraph," I said, impulsively; "I will go and see them."

"You!" exclaimed Brabazon. "That would be an immense relief. You will know how to break the news in the least startling way. I should recommend you to see Lady Hartmore if possible first—she is a strong-minded woman, and has a fine character. But, at best, the shock will be terrible—it is good of you, Halifax, to undertake so fearful a mission."

"Not at all," I replied. "Will you come with me?"

"I fear I cannot. My wife is very much shaken, and I ought not to leave her with a house full of people."

"I suppose most of your guests will leave to-day?"

"Probably; still, for the time being, they are here. Then there is the inquest, which will most likely take place to-day."

"I was going to propose," I said, "that a post-mortem examination should precede the inquest."

Brabazon raised his brows—he looked annoyed.

"Is that necessary?" he asked—"a post-mortem examination will only add needlessly to the sufferings of the unfortunate parents. In this case, surely, the cause of death is clearly defined—fracture of the skull?"

"The cause of death *is* clearly defined," I answered, "but not the cause of the sudden vertigo."

"The sudden vertigo, according to Carleton's account," corrected Brabazon. He did not say anything further for a moment—nor did I. After a pause, he continued: "As you are good enough to say you will go to Tregunnel, I will ask you to take poor Randall's last letter with you. I went into his room yesterday evening, and found one directed to his mother on the writing-table. She will prize it, of course. Now I had better look up your train."

He did so, and half an hour afterwards I was driving as fast as a pair of horses could take me to the nearest railway station. I caught an early train to Tregunnel, and arrived there between nine and ten that morning. A cab conveyed me to the castle, which stood on a little eminence above the sleepy-looking town.

My errand was, in truth, a gloomy one. During the journey I had made up my mind for every reason to see Lady Hartmore first. When the servant opened the door, I asked for her, and giving the man my card, told him that I wished to see his mistress alone on a matter of urgent importance. I was shown into a morning-room, and in a very short time Lady Hartmore came in. She was a tall, fine-looking woman, with a likeness to her dead son about her kindly, well-opened eyes and pleasant mouth.

My name and the message I had sent to her by the servant naturally startled her. She gave me a keen glance when she entered the room, which I returned with interest. I saw at once that her heart was strong enough, her nature brave enough, to stand the full weight of the terrible calamity without breaking down.

"I have come to see you on a most painful matter," I began at once. "I am just now visiting the Brabazons at Penporran."

"Then it is something about my son," she exclaimed, instantly. Her face grew very pale; she pressed her hand to her left side, and looked hurriedly towards the door.

"Lord Hartmore may come in, if you are not quick," she said. "He was in the breakfast-room when the servant brought me your card and message. Please tell what you have got to say at once—I can bear a shock, but he cannot."

Poor wife! poor mother! Her eyes looked at me with dumb entreaty, while her lips uttered the words of courage.

"Women like you, Lady Hartmore," I could not help uttering, impulsively, "are always brave. It is my terrible mission to inflict a great blow upon you—your son has met with an accident."

"Is he dead?" she asked. She came close to me as she spoke, her voice had sunk to a hoarse whisper.

"He is dead," I replied, instantly; "sit down."

I motioned her to a chair—she obeyed me.

"Lock the door," she said; "Lord Hartmore must not—must not know of this—quite yet."

I did what she asked me, and then went and stood with my back to her in one of the windows.

As I did so I felt in my pocket for the letter which Brabazon was to have given me. It was not there. I then remembered that in the excitement of my getting off in time to catch the train we must both have forgotten it.

"'IS HE DEAD?' SHE ASKED."

After a time Lady Hartmore's voice, sounding hollow and low, reached my ears.

"Tell me the particulars," she said.

I did so. I sat down near her and told them as briefly as possible. She listened attentively. When I had finished she said, in a puzzled tone:—

"I cannot account for the sudden giddiness. Arthur always had excellent health." Then she looked me full in the face. "Do you believe the story, Dr. Halifax?"

I thought for a moment, then I said, emphatically:—

"Yes, I believe it."

She did not speak at all for the best part of a moment. Then she gave a heavy sigh.

"After all," she said, "the thing that affects us is the death. He is dead. The inevitable has overtaken him. It scarcely matters how it happened—at least not now—not to me."

"Pardon me," I interrupted, "it matters a great deal how it happened. The cause of your son's death will be a question of anxious investigation—of the gravest and most searching inquiries. I fully believe the story which Carleton told us last night, but there are others who will—who must—suspect him of foul play. Is it possible, Lady Hartmore—is it in any way within the province of woman, so completely to forget herself in this moment of terrible anguish, as to live for another? You can do nothing now for the dead, but you can do much, very much, for the living."

"You mean for my husband?" she inquired.

"Not alone for your husband—not even principally for him. You can do much for the man who will be accused of the crime of having murdered your son. I can only repeat my firm conviction of his innocence, but the grounds for my belief, at present, go for nothing; circumstances prove a grave case against him. Your son, to all appearance, was much attached to the girl whom Carleton loved and loves. Yesterday morning Carleton received what he considered a final rejection from Miss Farnham. She spent the day with your son; she gave him every encouragement. Carleton was morose, gloomy, jealous. His jealousy and gloom were noticed by every member of our party. Carleton and your son both absented themselves from the drawing-room after dinner. It was during that time that the accident, which deprived your son of his life, took place. There will, of course, be a coroner's inquest. At the inquest the circumstances which I have just alluded to will come out, and there is no question but that Carleton will be arrested on suspicion and sent to trial—unless, indeed, you will help me."

"How can I help you?" she asked. "What am I to do? You ask me to share your belief, which seems to me to be based on nothing. Suppose I cannot share it?"

I was silent for a moment.

"I will tell you what I want you to do," I said then. "I want you to join me in insisting on having a post-mortem examination."

She gave me a glance of horror.

"Why?" she asked. "Why must the sleep of the dead be disturbed?"

Before I could answer her, Lord Hartmore's voice was heard at the door.

She was a brave woman, but at the sound of her husband's voice her courage for a moment deserted her.

"How—how can I break it to him?" she gasped. "Oh, please, don't leave me."

"No," I said, "I will stay with you.'

I unlocked the door myself, and a white-headed, feeble-looking man came querulously into the room.

His wife rose to meet him. She put her arms round him and some way, somehow, conveyed the terrible tidings to his mind. I need scarcely linger over the hour that followed. At the end of that time I was accompanying the Hartmores back to Penporran. During the journey my companions were almost completely silent. Lady Hartmore kept her veil down, and, I felt sure, wished to avoid speaking to me. The old lord was completely prostrated with grief. Not by word or hint had either parent given me the slightest clue by which I could insist on a post-mortem examination. Their son had evidently enjoyed perfect health during his brief life. I saw that circumstances were very black against Carleton.

It was evening when we reached Penporran. Lord and Lady Hartmore went at once to a private suite of rooms which had been got ready for their reception. As soon as I could I sought an interview with Brabazon.

"Most of our visitors have left us," he said. "But Miss Farnham and, of course, Carleton, remain. The inquest is to take place in the library at an early hour to-morrow."

I was silent for a moment, then I said, abruptly:—

"Even at the risk of annoying you, Brabazon, I must repeat my strong desire that a post-mortem should precede the coroner's inquest."

"Have you spoken to the Hartmores on the subject?" inquired Brabazon.

I told him that I had mentioned my wish to Lady Hartmore.

"And what did she say?" he asked.

"She shrank from the idea with horror," I was obliged to confess.

"You can scarcely blame her," said Brabazon. "Why should the poor fellow's body be unnecessarily disturbed? The fact is, I have the greatest faith in your judgment, Halifax, but I think in the present instance you carry your sympathy for Ronald Carleton too far. The cause of death in the case of poor Randall was so absolutely apparent, that I do not think you will get the coroner to consent to a post-mortem."

"There is one thing that occurred to me," I said: "if Randall met his death by violence, there would be some traces of a struggle at the spot where he fell over. Randall would not tamely submit to murder—he was a big man and muscular. Has the path along the cliff been carefully searched?"

"Yes," replied Brabazon, "and there is no trace anywhere of a struggle. A little blood has been discovered on a sharp point of rock just where Carleton described the fall to have taken place. The marks of a heavy body being dragged along the sands above high-water mark have also been seen. All these evidences are, of course, I am bound to say, quite consistent with Carleton's story. The blood on the rock indicates also the exact spot of the accident."

"That was where the vault of the skull was broken," I said. "By the way, you forgot to give me poor Randall's letter to his mother. Doubtless Lady Hartmore would like to have it without a moment's delay."

Brabazon started, and put his hand in his pocket.

"I put the letter here," he said, "intending to give it to you as you were starting; of course, I forgot it. Here it is: no, though, there is nothing in my pocket. Surely I can't have dropped it anywhere. I know I put it here this morning. I rushed up to the poor fellow's room to fetch it just when the brougham was coming round."

"You did not give it to me," I said; "that letter ought to be found: it may be of the utmost importance. Was that the coat you wore this morning?"

"Yes, I have not been out of it all day; you don't know what a rush and confusion the whole place has been in."

"You will look for the letter, won't you, Brabazon? I cannot quite tell you why, but it will give me a sense of relief to know that it has been found before the inquest takes place to-morrow morning."

Soon afterwards we parted. I went into one of the morning-rooms, where I found Mrs. Brabazon. I made inquiries with regard to Carleton and Miss Farnham.

"I have not seen either of them," replied my hostess. "I believe Mr. Carleton has spent the day in his room, and a servant told me that Barbara Farnham was not well. I hear she has not risen at all to-day."

"Poor girl!" I ejaculated.

Mrs. Brabazon looked at me with languid interest—she was a very lethargic person.

"Yes," she ejaculated, after a pause—"this tragedy will be a sad blow to Barbara. She is as ambitious as she is handsome. She would have made a regal-looking Lady Hartmore."

I said nothing further—I could not betray the poor girl's secret, nor let Mrs. Brabazon know what a small place high position and greatness occupied just now in Miss Farnham's thoughts.

Just before the inquest the next morning, I asked Brabazon if the missing letter had been found.

"No," he said—"I cannot tell you how vexed I am about it. Every conceivable hole and corner both in the house and out has been searched, but no trace of the letter has been discovered. What I fear is that when I was down on the shore yesterday making investigations, it may have dropped out of my pocket and been washed away with the incoming tide. I cannot think of any other cause for its absolute disappearance. I beg of you, Halifax, not to say anything to Lady Hartmore about it for the present."

"Of course not," I answered, in some surprise at the request.

I then ran upstairs. I must, of course, be present at the inquest, but I had still a moment at my disposal. I went boldly to Miss Farnham's door and knocked. After a very brief pause she opened it herself and stood before me. She was fully dressed. Her face was of a dead white—all the beautiful warmth of colour had fled.

"I am told I must be present at the inquest," she said. "Is it time for me to go downstairs? Have you come to fetch me?" She shuddered visibly as she spoke.

"I have come to ask you to help me," I said, eagerly. "I will manage to account for your absence in the library. Put on your hat; I want you to go out at once."

"What do you mean?" she asked, in astonishment.

"I will tell you," I said. "On the day of his death Randall wrote a letter to his mother. That letter has been lost. Brabazon had it in his pocket and has dropped it—no one knows where. There is no saying, Miss Farnham, what important evidence that letter may contain. I am sure it is not in the house. Brabazon believes that he dropped it when exploring the coast yesterday. Will you go at once and look for it? The moment you discover it, bring it to the library. Now, be as quick as ever you can."

"Yes," she replied, the soul in her eyes leaping up with a sudden renewed joy. She turned, pinned a hat on her head, wrapped a shawl round her, and ran downstairs. Her woman's wit grasped the whole situation at a glance. I went to the library, feeling assured that if poor Randall's letter were still in existence, Miss Farnham would find it.

There were present at the inquest Lady Hartmore, Brabazon and his wife, Carleton, and two gentlemen who had not yet left the house. Also, of course, the coroner and the jury. The moment I entered the room I glanced at the coroner; I had not seen him before. He was a little old gentleman, with a somewhat irascible expression of face, and a testy manner. I looked from him to poor Carleton, whom I had not seen since the time when he told his story in this room. The body of the dead man had been placed in a shell, and still occupied the central table of the library. Lady Hartmore sat near it. A sheet covered the face of the dead. Once I saw her raise her hand and touch the sheet reverently. She had the attitude of one who was protecting the body from intended violence. Her position and the look on her face reminded me of Rispah.

I looked again from her to Carleton. It was necessary for me to glance at the poor fellow, and to notice the despair on his face, to enable me to go up to the coroner, and urge upon him the necessity of a post-mortem preceding the inquest. He did not take my suggestion kindly.

"The cause of death is abundantly evident," he said, with irritation. "I cannot counsel a post-mortem examination."

"And I will not hear of it," said Lady Hartmore, looking at me with eyes full of reproach.

"Pray say nothing more about it," exclaimed Carleton.

I bowed, and sat down.

The inquest was conducted with extreme care, but soon Miss Farnham's presence was found necessary, and her absence commented upon. I saw Carleton start when her name was mentioned, and a look of extreme distress filled his eyes.

"I will go and find her," said Mrs. Brabazon, leaving the room.

She returned in a moment to say that Miss Farnham was not in her room, and that no one seemed to know anything about her.

"I have sent several servants into the grounds to look for her," she said.

As Miss Farnham was an important witness, having spent almost the entire day previous to his death with poor Randall, proceedings were delayed during her absence.

The case, however, seemed as black as could be against Carleton, and I had not the least doubt that the coroner would order a warrant to be issued for his arrest on suspicion.

My one last hope now hung on Miss Farnham's being able to find the missing letter, and then on the letter containing evidence which would give a medical cause for poor Randall's extraordinary death.

I seldom found myself in a more torturing position than during the time of this inquest. Relief, however, was at hand. I heard the sound of light and quickly moving feet in the hall. The door of the library was opened, not softly and with reverent hush, but with the eager, impetuous movement of someone in hot haste. Miss Farnham came into the room with a wild colour in her cheeks and a wild, bright light in her eyes. Her skirts were draggled and wet, her hair was loosened and fell over her shoulders—she had cast away both hat and shawl.

"There," she said, going straight up to Lady Hartmore; "there's your letter—the last letter your son ever wrote to you. It was lost, or supposed to be lost, but I found it. I walked along the cliff, close to the edge—very close. There is a part where the cliff is undermined. I lay on my face and hands and looked over. I saw, far below me, a tiny ledge of rock: there was a bush growing there, and, sticking in the bush, something white—it might be a useless rag or a piece of torn paper, or it might be a letter of importance. The tide was coming in fast; still, I thought that I had time. I put wings to my feet and rushed down a narrow path which led to the beach below. The tide had already come up and was wetting the base of the rock above which the bush which contained the white paper stood.

"I waded through the water and climbed the cliff and got the paper. I scrambled down again. When I came back the water was up to my knees. I crossed it safely, and mounted to the higher cliff again. Then, for the first time, I examined my prize. Yes, it was a letter—it was open. I don't know what had become of its covering. I sat on the grass and I read it—yes, I read every word. Here it is now, and you can read it. Read it aloud, please, for it is important — it explains—it saves! Ronald, it saves you!" Here the excited girl paused in her eager narrative, and turned her full gaze upon Carleton, who was bending forward to listen to her. "It saves you," she repeated; "it exonerates you completely!"

"I CLIMBED THE CLIFF AND GOT THE PAPER.

The commotion and interest which Miss Farnham's words and manner excited can be better felt than described. Lady Hartmore stood up and confronted the breathless girl. She held out her hand and clutched the letter, which was torn and dirty from its long exposure to wind and weather. She held it close and looked at it. It was in the beloved writing of the dead. The dead man was her only son—the letter was addressed to her, his mother. It contained a last message from the brain now silent—from the heart now still.

Tears filled her eyes.

"I must read this letter in private," she faltered. "This last letter of my boy's is too sacred for anyone but his mother to hear—I must read it alone."

"No," interrupted Miss Farnham, "it contains important information. I will call upon the coroner to insist on its being read aloud. I risked my life to get it. Another life hangs upon the information it contains. Dr. Halifax, you are a medical man—will you insist on this letter being read aloud?"

I went up to Lady Hartmore and said something to her in a low voice. She listened attentively—she considered my words. After a pause she put the letter into my hands.

"If it must be, it must," she said. "This is the last drop in the bitterness of my cup."

She sat down, and flinging out her two arms, stretched them over the body of the dead man. Once more her attitude and manner reminded me of Rispah.

Miss Farnham stood close to Lady Hartmore. She forgot her dishevelled hair, her disordered appearance. All her soul filled the eyes which she raised expectantly to my face.

I glanced hurriedly through the letter—then I spoke.

"There is a good deal in this sheet of paper which is strictly private," I said, "and need not be read for the benefit of the coroner and the jury; but there are some sentences referring to the state of Mr. Randall's health which are, as Miss Farnham remarked, of the utmost importance. I will now proceed to read that portion of the letter."

I did so in a loud, clear voice.

These were poor Randall's words:—

"As far as I can tell, I am in perfect health, but for the last week or so, I have been suffering at intervals from a strange form of giddiness. I feel as though I were made to turn round and round, or against my will impelled to go forwards, or backwards, or to one side. Sometimes the giddiness takes another form—I fancy that objects are revolving round *me*. I am perfectly conscious all the time, but the giddiness is generally accompanied by a distinct sensation of nausea. Very often the act of closing my eyes removes the vertigo completely for the time being. When the attack goes off I feel perfectly well, only I fancy I am suffering from continued deafness in my right ear. I don't know why I am impelled to tell you this—it is not worth making a fuss over. If I were to consult a medical man, he would probably set it down to a form of indigestion. I had a slight attack this morning at breakfast. If it continues or gets worse, I will take the opportunity of consulting a London doctor who happens to be in the house."

I did not read any more, but folding up the letter returned it to Lady Hartmore. Both Carleton and Miss Farnham had approached each other in their excitement.

I looked beyond them to the coroner.

"I am sure," I said, "that I now express Lady Hartmore's sentiments as well as my own, when I demand that this inquest be adjourned until a post-mortem examination has been made on the body of the dead man. The symptoms which he describes in the letter which I have just read aloud distinctly point to a disease of the inner ear, well known to the medical faculty, although not of common occurrence. I will ask the coroner to take immediate steps to get the services of two independent doctors to conduct the post-mortem, at which I should wish to be present."

My words were followed by a slight pause—the coroner then agreed to my wishes, and the inquest was adjourned.

The post-mortem took place on the afternoon of that same day, and the results amply accounted for the strange symptoms which poor Randall had so faithfully described in his last letter to his mother. On the right side of that portion of the base of the skull which contains the delicate organs of hearing, we found a small, bony excrescence growing down into the labyrinth or inner ear. This, though small, was undoubtedly the cause of the terrible attacks of vertigo which the poor fellow complained of, and in one of which he met with his tragic death.

The coroner's inquest was resumed on the following day, and, of course, Carleton was abundantly exonerated.

It was two years afterwards, however, before I accidentally saw in the *Times* the announcement of his marriage with Miss Farnham.

Stories from the Diary of a Doctor.

BY L. T. MEADE AND CLIFFORD HALIFAX, M.D.

THE PONSONBY DIAMONDS.

FEW cases in their day interested me more than that of Beryl Temple, and this, not so much from the medical point of view as from the character of this strong-minded and brave girl.

It was on the occasion of her mother's death that I first became acquainted with Beryl. She suffered keenly at the time, but her courage and presence of mind and fine self-suppression aroused my interest, and when, a month afterwards, she came to me and told me in the simple manner which always characterized her that she was not only friendless but without means of support, I eagerly asked in what way I could help her.

She replied with a blush, and something like tears in her eyes.

"Of all things in the world," she said, "I should like best to be trained as a hospital nurse—do you think I am suited to the profession?"

"Admirably," I replied. "You have nerve and self-control; you have also good health and, although I am sure that you have plenty of heart, you would never be mawkishly sentimental."

"Oh, no," she answered; "I am glad you approve."

"I cordially approve," I replied. "In many cases the profession of nursing is best undertaken by women who are not too highly cultivated, and whose position is below that of the supposed lady—but you, Miss Temple, will make an admirable nurse. Your peculiar characteristics fit you for this calling."

I saw by the expression on her face that my words pleased her. I helped her to take the necessary steps to become a probationer at one of the large hospitals. She entered on her profession with enthusiasm—her time of training passed without hitch, and in due course I placed her on my own special staff of nurses.

I had been by no means mistaken in Miss Temple's qualifications — her nerve was wonderful, her tact perfect. Although slight and rather delicate looking, she had a great reserve of strength, and I never knew her to break down or fail in any way, even when the case she had to attend to was involved in serious difficulties.

For nervous cases in especial, I found Miss Temple invaluable, and it so happened that she was the first person I applied to in the case of a very peculiar patient, Lady Violet Dalrymple.

I was sent for to the country to see Lady Violet in the autumn of the year 1889.

I remember the night when the telegram came to me from her mother, the Countess of Erstfield. Lady Violet was the only child—a girl of seventeen. Lady Erstfield had

"I CORDIALLY APPROVE."

once brought her to see me in town. I then considered her an overgrown, somewhat nervous girl, had ordered change, a quiet life, plenty of fresh air, plenty of nourishment, plenty of congenial occupation, and had felt assured that if these remedies were systematically followed out, the young girl would quickly recover from the nervous derangements which were just then interfering with her health and happiness.

By the tenor of Lady Erstfield's telegram, however, I feared that this was not the case.

"I am very anxious about Violet. Come without delay," she wired.

I replied by telegram that I would arrive at Beeches by a late train that evening. I did so. Lady Erstfield was up. I had a long interview with her, and got all possible information with regard to my patient's state of health. I did not see Lady Violet herself, however, until the following morning.

At an early hour that day, I was taken into the pretty boudoir, where I found my patient lying on a sofa. It was a room furnished with all that taste, money, and love could suggest. Books, flowers, pictures, birds in cages, all that was gay and bright, surrounded the lovely girl who lay pale and languid on a sofa drawn close to the open window. This window commanded a perfect view of river, wood, and meadow, with a distant peep of low-lying hills against the horizon. To my eyes, accustomed to London bustle and noise, this view alone was restful and delightful.

Drawing a chair forward, I sat down by my patient and entered into a common-place talk with her. I had purposely asked Lady Erstfield to leave us, for I knew by experience that in nervous cases the patient was far more inclined to be confidential and to reply truthfully to questions when alone with the physician.

Having carefully examined Lady Violet, and made certain that she was suffering from no organic disease, it only remained for me to conclude that she was a victim to one of those many ill-defined and misunderstood nervous disorders, which, by their variety and complexity, present the greatest difficulty in medical practice.

The treatment I saw at once must be moral, not medical.

"I don't find much the matter with you," I said, cheerfully; "your disease is more fancy than reality—instead of lying here, you ought to be having a gallop across those moors yonder."

Lady Violet gazed at me with a look of surprise and even faint displeasure in her large brown eyes.

"I love riding," she said, in a gentle voice, "but it is long since I have had the pleasure of a canter over the moors or anywhere else."

"You should not give up riding," I said; "it is a most healthful exercise and a splendid tonic for the nerves."

"I don't think you can realize how very weak I am," she answered, something like tears dimming her eyes. "Did not mother explain to you the strange symptoms from which I suffer?"

"The symptoms of which you complain are clearly due to an over-wrought imagina-

"DRAWING A CHAIR FORWARD, I SAT DOWN BY MY PATIENT."

tion," I replied. "You must try to curb it by every means in your power. I assure you I am only telling you the true state of the case when I say that there is nothing serious the matter with you."

She sighed and looked away from me.

I took her slim hand in mine and felt her pulse. It was weak, fluttering, and uneven. I bent forward and looked into her eyes—the pupils were slightly dilated. Still I held firmly to my opinion that nervous derangement, that most convenient phrase, was at the bottom of all that was wrong.

"Now," I said, rising as I spoke, "I will prescribe a drive for you this afternoon, and in a day or two, I have no doubt, you will be strong enough to get on horseback again. Take no medicines; eat plenty, and amuse yourself in every way in your power."

Soon afterwards I left the room, and saw Lady Erstfield alone.

"Your daughter is an instance of that all too common condition which we call neurasthenia," I said. "Although, unlike the name, the disease is not a coinage of the nineteenth century, still it has greatly increased of late, and claims for its victims those who have fallen out of the ranks of the marching army of women, in the advancing education and culture of their sex."

"I don't understand your placing Violet in that position," said Lady Erstfield, with reddening cheeks.

"My dear madam," I replied, "your daughter is the undoubted victim of over-culture and little to do. Were she a farmer's daughter, or were she obliged in any other way to work for her living, she would be quite well. The treatment which I prescribe is simply this—healthy occupation of every muscle and every faculty. Do all in your power to turn her thoughts outwards, and to arouse an active interest in her mind for something or someone. I assure you that although I am not anxious about her present state, yet cases like hers, if allowed to drift, frequently end in impairment of intellect in some degree, either small or great."

Lady Erstfield looked intensely unhappy. "Violet is our only child," she said; "her father and I are wrapped up in her. Although you seem to apprehend no danger to her life——"

"There is none," I interrupted.

"Yet you allude to other troubles which fill me with terror. There is nothing Lord Erstfield and I would not do for our child. Will you kindly tell me how we are to provide her with the interests and occupations which are to restore her mind to a healthy condition?"

I thought for a moment.

"Lady Violet is very weak just now," I said, "her whole constitution has been so enfeebled with imaginary fears and nervous disorders that a little good nursing would not come amiss for her. I propose, therefore, to send a nurse to look after your daughter."

Lady Erstfield uttered an exclamation of dismay.

"A hospital nurse!" she exclaimed; "the mere word will terrify Violet into hysterics."

"Nothing of the kind," I answered. "The nurse I propose to send here is not an ordinary one. She is a lady—well born and well educated. She is extremely clever, and is remarkable both for her tact and gentleness. She thoroughly understands her duties—in this case they will consist mainly in amusing Lady Violet in the most strengthening and invigorating manner. Her name is Temple. I will ask you to call her Miss Temple, and never to speak of her or to her as nurse. She will soon win her own way with your daughter, and I shall be greatly surprised if she does not become more or less indispensable to her. She is just as healthy-minded, as bright, as strong as Lady Violet is the reverse."

After a little more conversation with Lady Erstfield, it was arranged that Miss Temple was to be telegraphed for at once.

I wrote her a long letter, giving her full directions with regard to the patient. This letter I left with Lady Erstfield, and asked her to deliver it to Miss Temple as soon as ever she arrived. I then went to bid Lady Violet good-bye.

She looked even more wan and exhausted than when I had seen her in the morning. I thought it well to let her know about Miss Temple's arrival.

"She is a thoroughly nice girl," I said. "She will nurse you when you want to be nursed, and amuse you when you wish to be amused, and let you alone when you want quiet, and you will find her so fresh and bright and entertaining that you will soon, I am persuaded, be unable to do without her. Good-bye, now—I hope you will soon be much better, both for your mother's sake and your own."

Lady Violet raised her brows.

"Is mother unhappy about me?" she asked.

"She loves you," I replied, steadily, "and is getting quite worn out with anxiety about you. I wish her mind to be relieved as soon as possible, and I think it is your duty to do what you can towards this end."

"What can you mean?" asked Lady Violet.

"In your mother's presence," I answered, "you ought to endeavour as much as possible to overcome the melancholy which has taken such possession of you. Seem to be gay, even when you don't feel it. Try to appear well, even when you don't think you are. When you are alone with Miss Temple, you can do, of course, exactly as you please. But when with your father and mother, you ought to make a strenuous effort to overcome the morbid feelings, which are due entirely to the nervous weakness from which you are suffering."

Lady Violet looked at me intently.

"I love my father and mother," she exclaimed. "I would not willingly hurt the feelings of either. But, oh! how little you know what I suffer when you speak of my suppressing my trouble and terrible depression. Am I not always—always suppressing my fears? Oh, how hateful life is to me — how distasteful, how hollow. I should like to die beyond anything, and yet I am such a coward that the near approach of death would terrify me. Why was I born to be so miserable?"

"You were born to be happy," I answered, "or, at least, to be useful and contented. Your fear of death is perfectly natural, and I hope it will be many a long day before you are called upon to resign so precious a possession as life. Remember, you have only one life—use it well—you will have to account for it some day; and now, good-bye."

I returned to London, and in about a week's time I received a letter from Miss Temple. It satisfied me thoroughly. Lady Violet was better. She went out for a little daily. She read to herself, and allowed Miss Temple to read to her. She was interested in a fancy fair which was to be held in the neighbourhood, and was helping Miss Temple to work for it. The nurse had also discovered that her patient had a love, almost a passion, for music. Miss Temple was an accomplished pianist before she took up her present profession, and she and Lady Violet spent a considerable portion of each day over the piano.

In short, Miss Temple was doing all that I expected her to do for the young girl whose life was so valuable. Lady Violet was undoubtedly already acquiring that outward view which means health both of mind and body.

Miss Temple's first letter was followed in the course of time by another, which was even more hopeful than the first. Lady Violet was devotedly attached to her, and could scarcely bear her out of her presence. The girls rode together, walked together,

"THE GIRLS RODE TOGETHER."

sketched and played together. The colour of health was coming back to Lady Violet's pale cheeks; she would soon, in Miss Temple's opinion, be restored to perfect health.

Lady Erstfield also wrote to me about this time, and spoke in rapture of the companion whom I had secured for her daughter.

"I cannot tell you what Beryl Temple is to us," she said; "we owe Violet's recovery to her wonderful tact, her sympathy, her genius. She is like no girl I ever met before—she fascinates and subjugates us all—we do not want ever to part with her—as to Violet, it would almost kill her, I think, were Beryl Temple now to leave us."

About a month after receiving these two letters I was astonished and much pleased to see an announcement in the *Morning Post* to the effect that a matrimonial alliance was arranged between Lady Violet Dalrymple, only daughter of the Earl and Countess of Erstfield, and Captain Geoffrey Ponsonby, of the Coldstream Guards, and that the marriage was likely to take place in December.

On reading this short paragraph I turned to my case-book, and under Lady Violet's name made the following note:—

"*A case of neurasthenia, in which environment with moral treatment caused recovery.*"

I then dismissed the subject from my mind, with the final reflection that I should not have much more to do with Lady Violet.

The following circumstances quickly proved my mistake.

On the evening of that same day I had a letter from Miss Temple, confirming the news of the approaching marriage; telling me that it had been contemplated for some time by the parents of the young people, but that a formal engagement had been deferred owing to the state of Lady Violet's health. Captain Ponsonby had arrived at Beeches about a fortnight ago, had proposed for Lady Violet, who had accepted him not without a certain unwillingness, and the marriage was arranged to take place immediately after Christmas.

"Lady Violet is not as well as I could wish," continued Miss Temple, towards the close of her letter. "At first she refused absolutely to engage herself to Captain Ponsonby, but yielded to the entreaties of both her parents, who are most desirous for the match. She is once more languid, and inclined to be uninterested in her surroundings. I am not satisfied about her state, and deeply regret Captain Ponsonby's arrival—she was really in radiant health when he came to the house a fortnight ago. Lord and Lady Erstfield quite fail to observe their daughter's state of depression—they are both in the highest spirits, and active preparations for the wedding are going forward."

This letter caused me uneasiness—it was followed almost immediately by a second.

"Dear Dr. Halifax," wrote Miss Temple, "I am in great, in dreadful, trouble—not alone about Lady Violet, whose condition alarms me much, but on my own account. In short, I am bewildered by the fearful calamity which has suddenly overtaken me. I have not a soul to confide in, and greatly long to see you. I know I must not expect you to come here, and yet it is impossible for me, under existing circumstances, to ask for a day off duty. God help me; I am the most unhappy girl in the world!

"Yours sincerely,

"Beryl Temple."

I received this letter by the last post one night. It caused me some wakeful hours, for I was greatly puzzled how to act. By the morning I resolved to write a line to Lady Erstfield, telling her that I had heard from Miss Temple of Lady Violet's altered condition, and offering to come to see her. That letter was not destined to be written, however. As I was sitting at breakfast a telegram was put into my hand. It was from Lord Erstfield, requesting me to go to Beeches immediately.

I started off by an early train and arrived at my destination about noon. I was shown at once into a reception-room, where Lady Erstfield awaited me.

"It is good of you to respond so quickly to our telegram," she said. "We are in terrible trouble here. Violet is in the strangest condition. She is very feverish: her strength seems completely gone. She lies hour after hour moaning to herself, and takes little notice of anyone."

"How long has this state of things gone on?" I asked.

"The complete breakdown only took place yesterday, but Miss Temple assures me that Violet has been failing for some time. Her father and I noticed on one or two occasions that she seemed pale and languid, but as there was a good deal to excite her, we put her fatigue down to that source. Under your judicious treatment and the admirable care Miss Temple gave her, we considered her perfectly recovered, and it did not enter into our minds that a recurrence of the old attack was possible."

"When you speak of Lady Violet having much to excite her, you doubtless allude to her engagement?" I said. "I saw it officially announced in the *Morning Post.* I judged from it that she had quite recovered."

Lady Erstfield coloured.

"We thought so," she said; "her father and I both thought so. We were much pleased at the contemplated marriage, and we imagined that our child was happy, too. Captain Ponsonby is all that anyone can desire."

"And you have reason not to be satisfied now?" I asked.

"The fact is this," said Lady Erstfield, shortly: "Violet is unhappy—she does not wish the engagement to go on. She told Miss Temple so this morning. I have seen my dear child on the subject an hour ago—we cannot account for her caprice in this matter."

"I will see Lady Violet now, if you will permit me," I said. "The engagement is, doubtless, the cause of this strange break-down. Will you take me to her room?"

Lady Erstfield led the way without a word.

I found my patient even worse than her mother had given me to understand. In addition to much nervous trouble, she had unquestionably taken a chill of some sort, and symptoms of pneumonia were manifesting themselves. When I bent over her, I noticed the deep flush on her cheeks, her eyes were closed—her breathing was short and hurried. Miss Temple was standing by the bedside—she gave me an earnest glance, her face was as pale as Lady Violet's was flushed. I noticed that Lady Erstfield avoided speaking to the nurse, who, on her part, moved slightly away as she approached. The despair, however, which must have filled the poor mother's heart as she watched her suffering child might in itself account for her manner. I was very anxious to see the nurse alone, and asked Lady Erstfield if I could do so.

"Certainly," she answered; "I will watch here until Miss Temple is able to resume her duties."

"I will not be long away," answered Beryl. She took me at once into Lady Violet's pretty little boudoir and shut the door.

"I must be very quick," she said, "my place is with Violet. You think her very ill?"

"I do," I answered. "Her life is in danger. She is threatened with pneumonia. If the symptoms grow worse, she will not have strength to bear up under the attack."

"Oh, then, I must not think of myself—even now I manage to soothe her as no one else can. Let me go back!"

"Sit down," I answered; "you will not be fit long to nurse anyone unless you look after yourself. What is the matter with you? You are greatly changed!"

"Did I not tell you in my letter that I am in great trouble?"

Miss Temple's words were interrupted by a knock at the door of the boudoir.

She said "Come in," and a manservant entered. He approached Lady Violet's little writing-table, disturbed a book or two, and finally retreated with an "A B C" in his hand, apologizing as he did so.

"Do you know who that man is?" asked Miss Temple.

"One of the servants," I replied; "never

"HE APPROACHED LADY VIOLET'S WRITING-DESK AND DISTURBED A BOOK OR TWO.

mind him—tell me your trouble as quickly as possible."

"He is connected with it, unfortunately. He is not one of the usual servants of the house, although he wears the livery. That man is a detective from Scotland Yard, and he came into the room just now to watch me. He, or his fellow detective, for there are two here, watch me wherever I go. On one excuse or another, they enter each room where I am found."

"What do you mean?" I asked.

"I will tell you in as few words as possible—can you wonder that I am changed?"

"I am lost in conjecture as to what you can possibly mean," I answered, looking at her anxiously.

In truth I had cause for my anxiety.

Her fine face looked absolutely aged and worn. Her eyes were almost too large—their expression was strained—they had heavy black lines under them. Her mouth showed extreme dejection. When I remembered the blooming, healthy girl who had gone to Beeches two months ago, I was appalled by the change.

"Speak," I said; "I am deeply interested. You know that I will do everything in my power to help you."

"This is my story," she said: "Lady Violet got quite well—I was much attached to her, we were very happy—it seemed like the old life back again, when my mother was alive and I had a luxurious home. Lord and Lady Erstfield treated me more like a daughter than a nurse; Lady Violet was my dear sister. Then Captain Ponsonby came. He proposed, and was accepted. Immediately after the engagement Lady Violet drooped; she no longer gave me her confidence; she lost her appetite; she became constrained and silent. Once or twice I caught her crying—she turned away when I tried to question her. Lord and Lady Erstfield noticed no change, and Captain Ponsonby came and went as an honoured guest. No one seemed to notice the efforts Lady Violet made to seem at home in his society.

"One morning about ten days ago Lady Erstfield, accompanied by Captain Ponsonby, came into this room, where I was reading aloud to my dear little patient. I could not imagine why they did not observe her pale cheeks and her languor. I saw, however, at a glance that Lady Erstfield was in a high state of excitement and delight. She held a jewel-case in her hand. She opened it and, bending down, showed its glittering contents to her daughter. I was startled at the effect on Lady Violet. She clapped her hands in ecstasy and sat upright on the sofa. Her eyes had grown suddenly bright, and her cheeks rosy.

"'How I adore diamonds,' she said, 'and what beauties these are: oh, you lovely creatures! But, mother, why do you show them to me?'

"'They are my present to you, Violet,' said Captain Ponsonby. 'Those diamonds are heirlooms in the family, and are of great value. They will be yours when we are married.'

"'Come and look at them, Beryl," exclaimed Lady Violet. 'Are they not splendid?' As she spoke she lifted a diamond necklace of extraordinary brilliancy and quaint device out of the case. I knelt down by her and examined the gems with delight almost equal to her own. I have always had a great love for jewels, and for diamonds in particular, and these were quite the most magnificent I had ever seen. The necklace was accompanied by a tiara and earrings, and the gems were worth, Lady Erstfield said, from fifteen to twenty thousand pounds.

"We spent some time examining and criticising them. Violet sent for a looking-glass from one of the bedrooms in order to see the effect of the jewels round her throat. She insisted on my trying them on as well as herself. Lady Violet is fair, but, as you know, I am very dark. I could not help seeing for myself that the jewels suited me. Lady Violet uttered an exclamation when she saw them on me. 'You look beautiful, Beryl,' she said.

"I laughed, and was about to answer her, when I met Captain Ponsonby's eyes. There was something in his expression which I did not quite like. I unfastened the necklace quickly and laid it back in its velvet bed.

"'Thank you for letting me try it on,' I said. 'I feel as if for one brief moment I had imprisoned the rainbow.'

"I don't know why I said those words. They did me no good afterwards, but I was excited at the time. The magnificent diamonds had really cast a spell over me. Lady Erstfield suggested that Violet should go out for her usual ride.

"'No, mother; I am too tired,' she replied. 'I will drive instead, and Beryl shall come with me.'

"'Run and get ready, then,' said Lady Erstfield to me.

"I was leaving the room when she suddenly called me back.

"'My dear,' she said, giving me the case

"YOU LOOK BEAUTIFUL, BERYL!"

which held the diamonds as she spoke, 'will you have the goodness to take these to my room, and lock them up in my jewel safe? Here is the key. You must turn the lock twice, and when the revolving shutter moves back, use this smaller key to unlock the inner compartment. Put the case in there, and bring me back the keys when you have changed your dress.'

"I promised to obey, and ran off with a light heart.

"The safe where Lady Erstfield kept her jewels was built into the wall, and was of a very ingenious device. Following her directions implicitly, I opened it, placed the case within, and locked the safe carefully again. I then went and changed my dress and returned the keys to Lady Erstfield. Captain Ponsonby, Lady Violet, and I had a pleasant drive, and nothing more was said about the diamonds—I really think we all forgot them.

"The next morning Lady Violet came down to breakfast, looking so ghastly pale and so depressed, that even her mother uttered an exclamation of surprise when she saw her.

"'My darling, you look positively ill,' she said, going up and kissing her.

"Lady Violet gave her a startled and queer look. She made some remark in a very low voice, and with a pettish movement. She then crossed the room to my side, and Lady Erstfield did not question her any further.

"Just as we were leaving the breakfast-table, Captain Ponsonby announced his intention of running up to town for the day, and suddenly suggested that he should take the diamonds with him in order to give the jeweller plenty of time to re-set them in the most thorough manner.

"'That is a good thought, Geoffrey,' said Lady Erstfield. Then she turned to me.

"'You know where the jewels are, Beryl,' she said—'here are my keys—run, dear, and fetch them. I don't allow even my own maid to know the secret of my jewel safe,' she continued, looking at Captain Ponsonby as she spoke.

"I ran away, reached Lady Erstfield's room, unlocked the safe, and put in my hand to take out the case. It had vanished. I searched for it at first without any uneasiness, then in bewilderment, then in a sort of frantic terror. There was the empty spot on the floor of the safe where I had placed the case—there were the other cases of jewels pushed aside in some little confusion, but the Ponsonby diamonds had absolutely vanished.

"The full horror of the situation had not yet burst upon me—I had not yet even begun to *think* that anyone would suspect me, but, nevertheless, I felt sick with a sort of nameless terror.

"I locked the safe and returned to the breakfast-room.

"Lord Erstfield was standing by the hearth, talking to Captain Ponsonby—Lady Erstfield was reading the *Times*, and Violet was kneeling on the floor playing with her favourite pug. Their peaceful faces added to my misery. I know I must have looked wild and frightened—I know when I spoke that my voice must have shaken.

"'The diamonds are gone,' I said; 'they are not in the safe.'

"It was just as if I had flung a bomb into the midst of the cheerful party. Lord Erstfield drew himself up with a dazed expression. Captain Ponsonby turned white, and Lady Erstfield, with a sharp cry, rushed from the room, snatching the keys from my hand as she did so.

"'There is no use in Lady Erstfield examining the safe,' I said, 'the diamonds are certainly not there—I have searched all the shelves. The spot where I placed them yesterday is empty; the case has vanished.'

"'I don't believe it,' said Violet. 'The diamonds must be there. You must be mistaken, Beryl.'

"I made no reply, but when the others left the room I followed.

"We all now went up in a body to Lady Erstfield's room, and the safe was carefully examined by Lord Erstfield and Captain Ponsonby. The case containing the diamonds was indeed missing, but not another jewel, not even the smallest ring had been touched. There was no mark of the safe having been tampered with in any way, and as it was made on a perfectly unique pattern, and there was not supposed to be a key in the world to fit it, except the special ones made for it, the whole affair seemed buried in hopeless mystery. No one accused me in any way, and it never occurred to me, as I stood in that room, to accuse myself. We discussed the matter in all its bearings. We stood round the open safe and talked until we were tired. I described the exact position in which I had placed the case. Lady Erstfield was certain that from the moment I returned her the keys they had not been out of her possession until she had again placed them in my hands that morning.

"Finally we left the room in a state of hopeless bewilderment. Violet and I went away by ourselves, and, sitting down together, discussed the strange mystery from every point of view. The loss of the jewels had much excited her. She had regained her colour and her manner was quite animated.

"'I thought, at least, I should have the diamonds,' she said, with a queer sort of desolate echo in her voice, 'and I love diamonds: they seem to comfort me in the strangest way. I feel akin to them. When they sparkle and leap and glitter, they appear to me to be alive; they tell me secrets of the strange things they have witnessed in the course of their long existence. Think, if the Ponsonby diamonds could speak, what stories they could tell of the queer, queer things they have seen and heard; eh, Beryl?'

"I tried to turn the conversation—Lady Violet was always worse after indulging in wild talk of this sort.

"'We have now to consider how to get the Ponsonby diamonds back,' I said. 'Who can have stolen them?'

"We talked the matter threadbare, arriving, of course, at no conclusion.

"At lunch we were surprised to find that Captain Ponsonby had not gone to London. When the servants withdrew, we were told that the affair of the diamonds had been put not only into the hands of the local police, but that the authorities in Scotland Yard had been communicated with, and that in all probability a couple of detectives would be sent to Beeches that night.

"'We have decided,' said Lord Erstfield, 'not to say anything of our loss to the servants. The person who stole those diamonds is quite clever enough to hide them if the least alarm is raised. Our best chance of recovering the treasure is through detectives, who will come here, of course, in plain clothes. We are expecting several fresh guests to-morrow, and in consequence the servants have heard that two new men-servants from London are coming here to help them. We have communicated this fact to Scotland Yard, and the men will be provided with the house livery.'

"After making this statement, which he did very briefly, Lord Erstfield left the room.

"The early part of the afternoon passed listlessly. Lady Violet was once more pale, deadly tired, and too languid to care to do anything. I persuaded her to lie down, and offered to read her to sleep.

"'No,' she answered; 'I don't want anyone to read to me. I will shut my eyes and think of the diamonds. Go and take a walk, Beryl; you look pale and tired yourself.'

"I saw she did not want me, and, putting on my hat, I went out for a stroll. I had gone a little way from the house when I heard footsteps behind me. I turned and saw, to my surprise, that Captain Ponsonby was following me.

"'I noticed that you had gone out,' he said, 'and took the liberty of coming after you.' He grew red as he spoke. 'I want to say something to you,' he said; 'something of importance. Can we go somewhere where we can be alone?'

"I told him that I was going to walk through the shrubbery, and that he might, if he pleased, accompany me there; 'but,' I added, 'I shall not be out long, for I am anxious about Lady Violet and want to return to her.'

"We entered the shrubbery as I spoke. He did not speak at all for a moment; then he said, with a sort of abruptness which surprised me:—

"'I will not keep you long. I am glad of this opportunity.' Here he paused, and, turning, looked me full in the face.

"'If you will give me back the diamonds,' he said, 'I will faithfully promise to arrange matters so that not a breath of suspicion shall rest upon you.'

"I felt as if I were shot. His words took me so completely by surprise that I could not find either breath or speech for a moment.

"'Do you really think,' I said then, in a choking voice—'is it possible that you think, really, that I —I have stolen the diamonds?'

"I suppose my agitation confirmed his suspicions.

"He looked at me with a queer sort of pity.

"'I could see yesterday how struck you were with their beauty,' he said. 'Do you remember what you said about imprisoning the rainbow? The opportunity to take the diamonds was put into your hands. You could not resist the sudden temptation, but I am sure you are sorry now, and would return them if it were possible. I believe I can manage this for you, if you will confide in me.'

"I turned quickly; my face was hot; my heart was beating so fast I thought it would burst.

"'Come with me at once to Lady Erstfield,' I said: 'say those words again in her presence. She shall search all my possessions. Come, don't delay a moment.'

"'You must be mad,' he said. 'For Heaven's sake don't inculpate yourself in that manner. As far as I am aware, I am the only person who, at present, suspects you. It has never, I know, even entered into Violet's head that you could have had anything to do with the robbery, and Lord and Lady Erstfield, I am sure, think you as innocent as themselves—they are the most loyal people in the world—they believe, and rightly, that they owe Violet's life to you. I don't think they could harbour an

"I FELT AS IF I WERE SHOT!"

unkind thought of you. Lord Erstfield and I have talked over the loss for a couple of hours this morning, and your name has not once been mentioned in connection with it—I alone——'

"'You alone,' I interrupted, 'entertain this horrible doubt against a defenceless girl?'

"'I am very sorry,' he replied, in a steady voice, 'but it is not even a doubt.' Here he looked full at me. 'In my mind it takes the form of a certainty. It is absolutely impossible that anyone else could have taken the diamonds. They are gone—you were last seen with them—you put them into the safe. You returned the keys to Lady Erstfield, who did not let them out of her possession until she gave them to you again this morning. You must see for yourself what the logical conclusion is—you are the culprit.'

"'No one else has come to that logical conclusion,' I answered.

"'I am a man of the world,' he replied.

"I stood perfectly still for a moment. His cool assurance seemed to deprive me almost of the power of thought. I turned to walk towards the house, but he barred my path.

"'What can I do to induce you to be guided by my common-sense?' he said. 'I can understand the sudden temptation—if you return the jewels to me, not a shadow of suspicion shall ever rest upon you from any other quarter.'

"'I think,' I said, in a trembling voice, 'that the only thing for me to do will be to adhere to my first resolution, to see Lady Erstfield in your presence—to ask you to accuse me of the theft before her—to insist upon having all my possessions searched, and then to leave Beeches immediately.'

"'You won't screen yourself by any such plan,' said Captain Ponsonby—'nay, your wish to leave Beeches will seem to all interested as a certain proof of your guilt. I wish I could get you to understand that I do not feel unkindly to you—that I am sincerely anxious to be your friend in this matter. I *know you to be guilty*. If you protested from now until Doomsday, the firm conviction in my mind would still be unshaken. May I state the case very briefly to you? Will you try and listen as if I were telling you about some other girl? You took the diamonds in a moment of acute temptation. You are, I presume, a penniless girl. You admired the gems, not only for themselves but also for the effect they produced when they shone like so many suns round your warm, white throat. The price of these jewels was named in your presence. If you could sell them, you would be rich—if you could keep them and wear them, you would be beautiful enough to turn any man's head. Yes, I understand—I pity, and I am most anxious to screen you. No one else suspects you at present at Beeches, but that state of things will not continue there much longer. As soon as the detectives from London arrive, their suspicions will naturally be fastened on you. Your youth and apparent innocence will in no way deceive them. They will whisper doubts into the minds of Lord and Lady Erstfield, and into the mind also of Lady Violet. The Ponsonby diamonds are of immense historical importance—they have been mixed up with the fortunes of the family for a couple of centuries, and it is absolutely impossible that a girl like you can hide them successfully. Go where you will, you will never be able to sell that necklace and pendant. Each diamond has a story, and can be traced by experts into whatever hands it falls. You can never sell the necklace, nor would you ever dare to wear it, except in the privacy of your own room. I beg of you, therefore, to let me have it back, and I solemnly swear that the secret shall never pass my lips.'

"I listened to Captain Ponsonby's speech with great attention. The buzzing in my ears and the great tumult round my heart had now to a considerable extent subsided. I was able to bring my common-sense to bear upon the matter, and to absolutely force myself to look the facts in the face as they were presented to me from Captain Ponsonby's point of view. Strange as it may seem, my whole nature became subjected to a sort of revulsion, and far now from being angry with Captain Ponsonby for his accusations, I could not but admire something chivalrous in him which made him come as he thought to my assistance. My only wonder now was, that the Erstfields and Lady Violet were not also convinced of my guilt.

"I remained silent, therefore, for a couple of minutes before I replied.

"'I understand,' I said then, slowly, 'you have explained the position of affairs. I see plainly how very black the circumstantial evidence is against me. I am not surprised at your suspicions, and my wonder is that they are not shared by the rest of the family. As it happens, I am not the thief you imagine me.'

"When I said this, he sighed heavily, shook his head, and, turning, began to walk slowly back with me towards the house.

"'I am not a thief,' I continued, 'for the simple reason that the temptation you spoke about did not exist. The beauty of the gems attracted me yesterday, and I looked at them with pleasure, as I like to look at all lovely things, but I never coveted them; the thought never even occurred to me to wish to possess them. I am not as other girls—my life is consecrated—consecrated to the cause of suffering and pain. I live to help people who are obliged to keep on the shady side of life. My whole mind and heart are occupied with these people and their concerns. I do not want money, for my profession supplies me with plenty, and if I had diamonds ten times as beautiful, when, as a professional nurse, could I wear them? I have listened to your side of the affair—I must beg of you to listen to mine. You must see for yourself that, the temptation not existing, it could not be acted upon. I believe you mean kindly by all that you have said, and I thank you for the kindness. Now I will go indoors.'

"I left him—he did not say another word, but I saw by the expression of his face that I had only puzzled without convincing him.

"I went straight up to my own room, and sitting down, thought over the queer turn of events. The horror of the thing grew greater and greater the more I thought it over. I felt torn in two — longing one moment to rush to Lady Erstfield and tell her everything, and the next being kept back by the thought that by so doing I might only put a suspicion into her head which did not exist.

"I was presently sent for to attend to Violet. She had awakened after a bad dream and was in a very uncomfortable and depressed condition. Notwithstanding my own great unhappiness, I could see that she had something on her mind, but although I did all in my power to break the ice, I could not get her to talk to me in a free and natural manner.

"That evening the detectives arrived from London, and the next day several visitors came to the house. Everything went on with outward smoothness, and the subject of the diamonds was by mutual consent never alluded to. Lady Violet grew worse, and the gay house party dispersed sooner than was intended. Captain Ponsonby stayed on, however. I met him occasionally, but we scarcely exchanged a word. I could see that he was anxious and haggard, but I set this down to his fears with regard to Lady Violet, who steadily refused to see him, and never left her bedroom and boudoir. I spent almost all my time with her, but as the days wore on I could not but feel the horror of my position more and more. I saw plainly that the suspicion which Captain Ponsonby harboured was shared by the two detectives, and also, in process of time, the poisonous thought was communicated to Lord and Lady Erstfield. Lady Erstfield's manner to me completely altered. Instead of treating me with almost the affection of a mother, she was cold and distant; she avoided meeting my eyes, and never spoke to me on any subject except what related to Violet's health. That is the position of affairs to-day, Dr. Halifax. I am suspected of the most horrible theft, and have not a chance of clearing myself. Lady Violet alone

"I FELT TORN IN TWO."

loves me as of old. She is my dear sister, and for her sake I——"

Here the poor girl completely broke down, and, covering her face with her hands, sobbed aloud.

"Take courage," I said to her. "I have, at least, one bit of comfort for you: I also fully believe in you. You no more stole the diamonds than I did."

"Oh, thank you—that is like you," she said. "God bless you for those words."

"I am glad I have come here, for every reason," I continued. "My presence here is necessary not only on account of Lady Violet, but also on your account. I introduced you to this house, and am responsible for your conduct; I shall therefore not leave a stone unturned to clear you, and now you must go back to your work with as brave a heart as you can."

She rose at once, wiping her eyes and trying to look cheerful.

"One word before you return to Lady Violet," I said. "Is it true that she has broken off her engagement?"

"Yes."

"Lady Erstfield told me that she gave you her confidence in this matter."

"Yes, she spoke to me this morning."

"Do you mind telling me what she said?"

"She was very weak and had a difficulty in using her voice, but she whispered to me. Her words were something like these:—

"'Tell my father and mother that I do not love Captain Ponsonby, and will never marry him. From the first he never attracted me, and now there is no inducement—not even the diamonds!'"

"Did she really say 'not even the diamonds'?"

"Yes, she certainly did. I thought it strange at the time."

"It was undoubtedly strange. Now go back to your patient and keep up all the courage you can. I shall remain at Beeches until to-morrow, and even longer if necessary. I wish to take care of Lady Violet myself to-night, in order to give you rest."

Miss Temple left the room, and after thinking matters over I went downstairs. Captain Ponsonby was still in the house. When I abruptly entered one of the drawing-rooms, I found him talking with Lady Erstfield.

"Can I speak to you?" I said to the lady.

"Certainly," she replied, starting up. "Is Violet worse? What is the matter?"

"There is no change in Lady Violet's condition," I replied. "What I have to speak about refers to Miss Temple."

Captain Ponsonby rose when I said this and prepared to leave the room.

I interrupted this movement.

"I beg of you not to go," I said. "I particularly want you to hear what I have come to say."

He turned and walked slowly back to one of the windows. I could see by the expression of his face that he was a good deal annoyed. He was a handsome, soldierly-looking man, of at least five-and-thirty years

"I BEG OF YOU NOT TO GO."

of age, with a somewhat overbearing manner. I could understand a child like Lady Violet shrinking from him in possible fear, and yet there was nothing underhand about him. I could see that he was scrupulously honourable, although his tact would probably not be of the finest.

"I should like you to hear what I have got to say," I continued, "for you seem to be mixed up in the matter. I refer to the loss of the diamonds."

"Oh, the diamonds!" exclaimed Lady Erstfield. "Do you suppose we, any of us, care about them in an hour of terrible sorrow like this?"

"Pardon me," I continued, "there is one person who cares a great deal about them. A young girl, who came here at my recommendation—I allude to Miss Temple. It seems that you, sir,"—here I turned to Captain Ponsonby—"have accused Miss Temple in the most unmistakable manner of having stolen the diamonds. You accused her of the theft nearly ten days ago, and since then she has reason to believe that you, Lady Erstfield, share the suspicion."

Lady Erstfield's face grew pale and troubled.

"Beryl has told you," she exclaimed. "Poor child, I feared that she would not fail to see the alteration in my manner. Try hard as I would to hide my feelings, I could not treat her as I did before.

"Well," she continued, "I am sorry, deeply sorry, to say that we all, with the exception of Violet, suspect her now. She alone had access to the safe—not a breath of suspicion falls on anyone else. Miss Temple has managed to hide the diamonds with wonderful skill for the time being—but in the end she must betray herself. We wish if possible to avoid having her arrested; she is closely watched, however, for there can be little doubt of her guilt."

"And believing this," I said, in a stern voice, "you allow this girl to continue to nurse your daughter?"

"Certainly," replied Lady Erstfield; "in Violet's present condition it would kill her to part with Miss Temple."

I had some difficulty in controlling my anger.

"I am glad I have come," I said, after a pause, "and that not only on Lady Violet's account. I cannot leave Beeches until this matter is satisfactorily cleared up. It is my firm conviction that Miss Temple no more stole the diamonds than you did, Lady Erstfield."

Lady Erstfield murmured something which I could not quite hear.

"I can say with the utmost truth that we are all only too anxious to clear Miss Temple from this horrible suspicion if it can be done," remarked Captain Ponsonby.

"Oh, certainly—most certainly," added Lady Erstfield. "Anything you can suggest, Dr. Halifax——"

Her words were interrupted—there came a hurried message from the sick room. Lady Violet had awakened in a high state of delirium. Lady Erstfield and I both hurried to her side. I saw that the case was truly one of life or death, and nothing further was said about the diamonds for the present.

Towards evening the sick girl seemed to grow a little easier; she sank into another heavy slumber, and I saw, with satisfaction, that the remedies I had employed were already getting the pneumonia under. I now arranged that Miss Temple was to have a night's rest, and that Lady Erstfield and I should watch by the patient for the night.

Lady Erstfield lay down on a sofa at the far end of the spacious bedroom, and I sat by Lady Violet. Her sleep was frequently broken by sharp cries of pain and distress, but I generally managed by a firm word or touch to control her wild fits of delirium. She did not know me, however, although she submitted immediately when I spoke to her. I had many anxious thoughts to occupy me during the night watches. These were chiefly centred round Beryl Temple. I could not help seeing that there was abundant ground for the suspicion which attached to her. She was, I knew well, innocent; but unless the diamonds were discovered, grave doubts would always arise when her name was mentioned. I did not think the Erstfields would prosecute her, but I almost wished them to do so, in order to bring the matter to an issue.

As the night wore on, I fell for a few moments into an uneasy sleep. In my sleep I dreamt of the diamonds. I saw them sparkling round the neck of Lady Violet, whose eyes shone with a strange, fierce fire, which made them look almost as bright as the glittering gems. I awoke with certain words on my lips. Lady Violet had said to Miss Temple: "Now there is no inducement to my marriage—not even the diamonds." I thought the words queer at the time—I pondered over them now.

Rising from my chair, I went over to the bed and looked at the sick girl. She was breathing more quietly. I laid my hand on her forehead, and knew at once that her temperature was less high.

I went across the room to Lady Erstfield. She had been asleep, but woke when I approached her.

"I think my patient is a shade easier," I said. The poor mother uttered a thankful exclamation.

"I will go and sit by her now for an hour or two," she answered. "I have had a long sleep and am refreshed. Won't you lie down, Dr. Halifax?—I will call you if Violet requires anything."

I told her that I would go into the outer room and lie on the sofa. I was by habit a light sleeper, and the least word from Lady Erstfield would bring me back to my patient. I lay down, and in a moment was asleep.

I had not slept long when the sound of conversation in the sick room aroused me.

I sprang to my feet, and went back there at once. Lady Erstfield did not hear me. She was standing, facing the bed. Lady Violet was sitting up and speaking in an eager voice.

"I am better," she said; "mother, I want the diamonds—mother, get them for me—I want to feel them and to look at them—they will comfort me—mother, do get them for me at once—the Ponsonby diamonds, you know what I mean—*do*, mother, dear, fetch me the Ponsonby diamonds."

"You must lie down," I said, going to the other side of the bed; "here, let me cover you up."

She turned to look at me. I forced her back on her pillow and put the bedclothes over her.

"Who are you?" she inquired, gazing at me with her bright, too bright, eyes.

"Your friend and doctor—my name is Halifax."

"Oh, have you come back again, Dr. Halifax? I like you very much. Thank you for sending me Beryl. I love Beryl. Where is she now?"

"Lying down, tired out; you must not disturb her: your mother and I will do anything for you that you want. Now you must not talk any more. Let me give you this drink."

She allowed me to put my hand under her head to raise her, and drank a little milk and soda-water, with a sigh of relief.

"That is nice," she said; "I am so thirsty."

"Turn on your side now and go to sleep," I said.

"I cannot; I cannot. Are you there, mother? Mother, don't leave me. Mother, won't you give me the diamonds? I shall sleep sound, very sound, if I may wear them round my neck! Do, mother, dear, give me the Ponsonby diamonds—you don't know how I long for them."

"My darling," said Lady Erstfield, falling suddenly on her knees by the bedside, and bursting into tears, "I would give them to you if I could; but they are lost, Violet, dear—the Ponsonby diamonds are lost."

"Oh! no, they aren't, mother," replied the girl, in a voice of astonishment; "they are in my jewel-case—in the lower drawer. The case

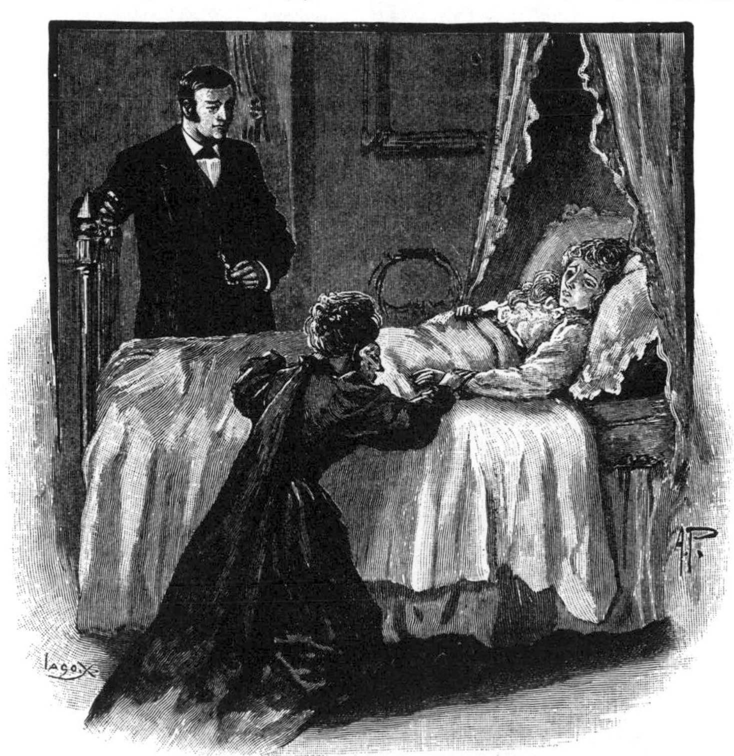

"THEY ARE LOST, VIOLET, DEAR."

which holds the diamonds just fits into the lower drawer of my jewel-case. You will find my keys on the dressing-table. Do, do fetch the diamonds, mother."

Lady Erstfield sprang to her feet and looked with a kind of horrified consternation at her child.

"No, my love," she said then, in a soothing voice, "you are dreaming—you are not well and have had a bad dream. Go to sleep, my sweet darling, go to sleep."

"But I am not dreaming," said Lady Violet—"the Ponsonby diamonds are in my dressing-case. I remember putting them there quite well—I had forgotten, but I remember now quite well. Dr. Halifax, won't you fetch them?"

"Certainly," I replied. "Lady Erstfield, will you direct me to Lady Violet's jewel-case?"

"Yes," replied Lady Erstfield.

The poor woman staggered rather than walked across the room. She gave me the key of the jewel-case. I opened it and lifted out the several compartments until I came to the bottom drawer. There lay an old-fashioned morocco case. I opened it, and the Ponsonby jewels in all their magnificence lay before me.

"My God, what does this mean?" gasped Lady Erstfield.

"Hush," I said, "don't say anything—take them to her."

"You must do it, I cannot," she moaned.

I took the case up to the bedside. Lady Violet gave a little cry of rapture when she saw it. In a twinkling, she had lifted the necklace from its bed of ruby velvet and had clasped it round her white throat.

"Oh, my beautiful, sparkling treasures!" she exclaimed; "how I love you—how you comfort me!"

She lay down at once and closed her eyes. In a moment she was in sound and dreamless sleep.

The case was one, without any doubt, of sudden and acute kleptomania. This strange nervous disorder had in all probability been developed in Lady Violet by the depression caused by her uncongenial engagement to Captain Ponsonby. The whole thing was now clear as daylight—poor Lady Violet was the unconscious thief. She had stolen the diamonds and then forgotten all about her theft. In her delirium memory returned to her, and in her desire to possess the gems she recalled where she had placed them. How she secured the keys of the safe was an unsolved mystery for some time, but Lady Erstfield, in thinking matters over, remembered how close Violet had sat by her side on the sofa in one of the drawing-rooms the evening before the loss was discovered.

"She was often fond of putting her hand into my pocket in play," said the lady; "it was a trick of hers as a child, and I used to be quite cross about it, sometimes. She must have transferred the keys from my pocket to her own on that occasion, gone upstairs and removed the diamonds from my jewel safe to her own jewel-case, and then once more slipped the keys back into my pocket."

This explanation seemed sufficiently likely to satisfy people; anyhow, no other was ever forthcoming. Poor Beryl was, of course, restored to higher favour than ever; indeed, Lord and Lady Erstfield felt that they could not possibly make enough of her. The finding of the diamonds was the turning-point in Lady Violet's illness. She slept for many hours with the sparkling gems round her neck, and when she awoke it was to consciousness and recovery.

The diamonds were returned to Captain Ponsonby on the following day, and the engagement between him and Lady Violet was at an end. There is only one strange thing to add to this strange story. Lady Violet has never, from the moment of her awakening to now, alluded to the Ponsonby diamonds. It is my belief that she has forgotten all about them, and, as far as I can tell, I do not think she will ever be visited by another attack of kleptomania.

IV

Martin Hewitt, Investigator

ARTHUR MORRISON

Martin Hewitt, Investigator.

BY ARTHUR MORRISON.

II.—THE LOSS OF SAMMY CROCKETT.

T was, of course, always a part of Martin Hewitt's business to be thoroughly at home among any and every class of people, and to be able to interest himself intelligently, or to appear to do so, in their various pursuits. In one of the most important cases ever placed in his hands, he could have gone but a short way toward success had he not displayed some knowledge of the more sordid aspects of professional sport, and a great interest in the undertakings of a certain dealer therein. The great case itself had nothing to do with sport, and, indeed, from a narrative point of view, was somewhat uninteresting, but the man who alone held the one piece of information wanted was a keeper, backer, or "gaffer" of professional pedestrians, and it was through the medium of his pecuniary interest in such matters that Hewitt was enabled to strike a bargain with him.

The man was a publican on the outskirts of Padfield, a northern town pretty famous for its sporting tastes, and to Padfield, therefore, Hewitt betook himself, and, arrayed in a way to indicate some inclination of his own toward sport, he began to frequent the bar of the "Hare and Hounds." Kentish, the landlord, was a stout, bull-necked man, of no great communicativeness at first; but after a little acquaintance he opened out wonderfully, became quite a jolly (and rather intelligent) companion, and came out with innumerable anecdotes of his sporting adventures. He could put a very decent dinner on the table, too, at the "Hare and Hounds," and Hewitt's frequent invitation to him to join therein and divide a bottle of the best in the cellar soon put the two on the very best of terms. Good terms with Mr. Kentish was Hewitt's great desire, for the information he wanted was of a sort that could never be extracted by casual questioning, but must be a matter of open communication by the publican, extracted in what way it might be.

"Look here," said Kentish one day, "I'll put you on to a good thing, my boy—a real good thing. Of course, you know all about the Padfield 135 Yards Handicap being run off now?"

"Well, I haven't looked into it much," Hewitt replied. "Ran the first round of heats last Saturday and Monday, didn't they?"

"They did. Well"—Kentish spoke in a stage whisper as he leaned over and rapped the table—"I've got the final winner in this house." He nodded his head, took a puff

"I'VE GOT THE WINNER IN THIS HOUSE."

at his cigar, and added, in his ordinary voice, "Don't say nothing."

"No, of course not. Got something on, of course?"

"Rather—what do *you* think? Got any price I liked. Been saving him up for this. Why, he's got twenty-one yards, and he can do even time all the way! Fact! Why, he could win runnin' back'ards. He won his heat on Monday like—like—like that!" The gaffer snapped his fingers, in default of a better illustration, and went on. "He might ha' took it a little easier, *I* think—it's shortened his price, of course, him jumpin' in by two yards. But you can get decent odds now, if you go about it right. You take my tip—back him for his heat next Saturday, in the second round, and for the final. You'll get a good price for the final, if you pop it down at once. But don't go makin' a song of it, will you, now? I'm givin' you a tip I wouldn't give anybody else."

"Thanks very much—it's awfully good of you. I'll do what you advise. But isn't there a dark horse anywhere else?"

"Not dark to me, my boy, not dark to me. I know every man runnin' like a book. Old Taylor—him over at the Cop—he's got a very good lad—eighteen yards, and a very good lad indeed; and he's a tryer this time, I know. But, bless you, my lad could give him ten, instead o' taking three, and beat him then! When I'm runnin' a real tryer, I'm generally runnin' something very near a winner, you bet; and this time, mind, *this* time, I'm runnin' the certainest winner I *ever* run—and I don't often make a mistake. You back him."

"I shall, if you're as sure as that. But who is he?"

"Oh, Crockett's his name—Sammy Crockett. He's quite a new lad. I've got young Steggles looking after him—sticks to him like wax. Takes his little breathers in my bit o' ground at the back here. I've got a cinder sprint path there, over behind the trees. I don't let him out o' sight much, I can tell you. He's a straight lad, and he knows it'll be worth his while to stick to me; but there's some 'ud poison him, if they thought he'd spoil their books."

Soon afterward the two strolled toward the tap-room. "I expect Sammy'll be there," the landlord said, "with Steggles. I don't hide him too much—they'd think I'd got something extra on, if I did."

In the tap-room sat a lean, wire-drawn-looking youth, with sloping shoulders and a thin face, and by his side was a rather short, thick-set man, who had an odd air, no matter

"IN THE TAP-ROOM."

what he did, of proprietorship and surveillance of the lean youth. Several other men sat about, and there was loud laughter, under which the lean youth looked sheepishly angry.

"'Tarn't no good, Sammy lad," someone was saying. "You a makin' after Nancy Webb—she'll ha' nowt to do with 'ee."

"Don' like 'em so thread-papery," added another. "No, Sammy, you aren't the lad for she. I see her——"

"What about Nancy Webb?" asked Kentish, pushing open the door. "Sammy's all right, anyway. You keep fit, my lad, an' go on improving, and some day you'll have as good a house as me. Never mind the lasses. Had his glass o' beer, has he?" This to Raggy Steggles, who, answering in the affirmative, viewed his charge as though he were a post, and the beer a recent coat of paint.

"Has two glasses of mild a-day," the landlord said to Hewitt. "Never puts on flesh, so he can stand it. Come out now." He nodded to Steggles, who rose, and marched Sammy Crockett away for exercise.

On the following afternoon (it was Thursday), as Hewitt and Kentish chatted in the landlord's own snuggery, Steggles burst into the room in a great state of agitation and spluttered out: "He—he's bolted; gone away!"

"What?"

"Sammy—gone. Hooked it. *I* can't find him."

The landlord stared blankly at the trainer, who stood with a sweater dangling from his hand, and stared blankly back. "What d'ye mean?" Kentish said, at last. "Don't be a fool. He's in the place somewhere; find him."

But this Steggles defied anybody to do. He had looked already. He had left Crockett at the cinder-path behind the trees, in his running-gear, with the addition of the long overcoat and cap he used in going between the path and the house, to guard against chill. "I was goin' to give him a bust or two with the pistol," the trainer explained, "but when we got over t'other side, 'Raggy,' ses he, 'it's blawin' a bit chilly. I think I'll ha' a sweater—there's one on my box, ain't there?' So in I coomes for the sweater, and it weren't on his box, and when I found it and got back—he weren't there. They'd seen nowt o' him in t' house, and he weren't nowhere."

Hewitt and the landlord, now thoroughly startled, searched everywhere, but to no purpose. "What should he go off the place for?" asked Kentish, in a sweat of apprehension. "'Tain't chilly a bit—it's warm—he didn't want no sweater; never wore one before. It was a piece of kid to be able to clear out. Nice thing, this is. I stand to win two years' takings over him. Here—you'll have to find him."

"Ah—but how?" exclaimed the disconcerted trainer, dancing about distractedly. "I've got all I could scrape on him myself; where can I look?"

Here was Hewitt's opportunity. He took Kentish aside and whispered. What he said startled the landlord considerably. "Yes, I'll tell you all about that," he said, "if that's all you want. It's no good or harm to me, whether I tell or no. But can you find him?"

"That I can't promise, of course. But you know who I am now, and what I'm here for. If you like to give me the information I want, I'll go into the case for you, and, of course, I sha'n't charge any fee. I may have luck, you know, but I can't promise, of course."

The landlord looked in Hewitt's face for a moment. Then he said, "Done! It's a deal."

"Very good," Hewitt replied; "get together the one or two papers you have, and we'll go into my business in the evening. As to Crockett, don't say a word to anybody. I'm afraid it must get out, since they all know about it in the house, but there's no use in making any unnecessary noise. Don't make hedging bets or do anything that will attract notice. Now we'll go over to the back and look at this cinder-path of yours."

Here Steggles, who was still standing near, was struck with an idea. "How about old Taylor, at the Cop, guv'nor, eh?" he said, meaningly. "His lad's good enough to win, with Sammy out, and Taylor is backing him plenty. Think he knows anything o' this?"

"That's likely," Hewitt observed, before Kentish could reply. "Yes. Look here—suppose Steggles goes and keeps his eye on the Cop for an hour or two, in case there's anything to be heard of? Don't show yourself, of course."

Kentish agreed, and the trainer went. When Hewitt and Kentish arrived at the path behind the trees, Hewitt at once began examining the ground. One or two rather large holes in the cinders were made, as the publican explained, by Crockett, in practising getting off his mark. Behind these were several fresh tracks of spiked shoes. The tracks led up to within a couple of yards of the high fence bounding the ground, and there stopped abruptly and entirely. In the fence, a little to the right of where the tracks stopped, there was a stout door. This Hewitt tried, and found ajar.

"That's always kept bolted," Kentish said; "he's gone out that way—he couldn't have gone any other without comin' through the house."

"But he isn't in the habit of making a step three yards long, is he?" Hewitt asked, pointing at the last footmark and then at the door, which was quite that distance away from it. Besides," he added, opening the door, "there's no footprint here nor outside."

The door opened on a lane, with another fence and a thick plantation of trees at the other side. Kentish looked at the footmarks, then at the door, then down the lane, and finally back towards the house. "That's a licker," he said.

"This is a quiet sort of lane," was Hewitt's next remark. "No houses in sight. Where does it lead?"

"THAT'S A LICKER!"

"That way it goes to the Old Kilns—disused. This way down to a turning off the Padfield and Catton Road."

Hewitt returned to the cinder-path again, and once more examined the footmarks. He traced them back over the grass toward the house. "Certainly," he said, "he hasn't gone back to the house. Here is the double line of tracks, side by side, from the house—Steggles's ordinary boots with iron tips and Crockett's running pumps—thus they came out. Here is Steggles's track in the opposite direction alone, made when he went back for the sweater. Crockett remained—you see various prints in those loose cinders at the end of the path where he moved this way and that, and then two or three paces toward the fence—not directly toward the door, you notice—and there they stop dead, and there are no more, either back or forward. Now, if he had wings, I should be tempted to the opinion that he flew straight away in the air from that spot—unless the earth swallowed him and closed again without leaving a wrinkle on its face."

Kentish stared gloomily at the tracks, and said nothing.

"However," Hewitt resumed, "I think I'll take a little walk now, and think over it. You go into the house and show yourself at the bar. If anybody wants to know how Crockett is, he's pretty well, thank you. By-the-bye, can I get to the Cop—this place of Taylor's—by this back lane?"

"Yes, down to the end leading to the Catton Road, turn to the left, and then first on the right. Anyone'll show you the Cop," and Kentish shut the door behind the detective, who straightway walked — toward the Old Kilns.

In little more than an hour he was back. It was now becoming dusk, and the landlord looked out papers from a box near the side window of his snuggery, for the sake of the extra light. "I've got these papers together for you," he said, as Hewitt entered. "Any news?"

"Nothing very great. Here's a bit of handwriting I want you to recognise, if you can. Get a light."

Kentish lit a lamp, and Hewitt laid upon the table half-a-dozen small pieces of torn paper, evidently fragments of a letter which had been torn up, here reproduced in facsimile.

The landlord turned the scraps over, regarding them dubiously. "These aren't much to recognise, anyhow. *I* don't know the writing. Where did you find 'em?"

"They were lying in the lane at the

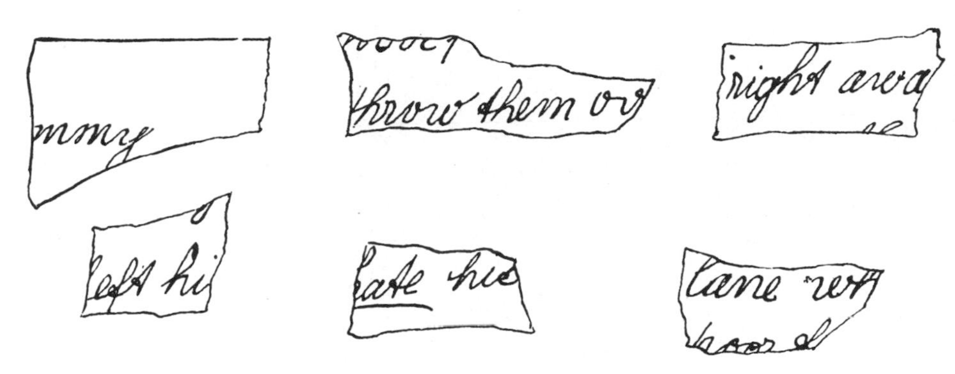

back, a little way down. Plainly they are pieces of a note addressed to someone called Sammy or something very like it. See the first piece with its 'mmy'? That is clearly from the beginning of the note, because there is no line between it and the smooth, straight edge of the paper above; also, nothing follows on the same line. Someone writes to Crockett—presuming it to be a letter addressed to him, as I do for other reasons—as Sammy. It is a pity that there is no more of the letter to be found than these pieces. I expect the person who tore it up put the rest in his pocket and dropped these by accident."

Kentish, who had been picking up and examining each piece in turn, now dolorously broke out:—

"Oh, it's plain he's sold us—bolted and done us; me as took him out o' the gutter, too. Look here—'throw them over'; that's plain enough—can't mean anything else. Means throw *me* over, and my friends—me, after what I've done for him. Then 'right away'—go right away, I s'pose, as he has done. Then," he was fiddling with the scraps and finally fitted two together, "why, look here, this one with 'lane' on it fits over the one about throwing over, and it says 'poor f' where it's torn; that means 'poor fool,' I s'pose—*me*, or 'fathead,' or something like that. That's nice. Why, I'd twist his neck if I could get hold of him; and I will!"

Hewitt smiled. "Perhaps it's not quite so uncomplimentary after all," he said. "If you can't recognise the writing, never mind. But if he's gone away to sell you, it isn't much use finding him, is it? He won't win if he doesn't want to."

"Why, he wouldn't dare to rope under my very eyes. I'd—I'd——"

"Well, well; perhaps we'll get him to run after all, and as well as he can. One thing is certain—he left this place of his own will. Further, I think he is in Padfield now—he went toward the town I believe. And I don't think he means to sell you."

"Well, he shouldn't. I've made it worth his while to stick to me. I've put a fifty on for him out of my own pocket, and told him so; and if he won, that would bring him a lump more than he'd probably get by going crooked, besides the prize money, and anything I might give him over. But it seems to me he's putting me in the cart altogether."

"That we shall see. Meantime, don't mention anything I've told you to anyone—not even to Steggles. He can't help us, and he might blurt things out inadvertently. Don't say anything about these pieces of paper, which I shall keep myself. By-the-bye, Steggles is indoors, isn't he? Very well, keep him in. Don't let him be seen hunting about this evening. I'll stay here to-night and we'll proceed with Crockett's business in the morning. And now we'll settle *my* business, please."

In the morning Hewitt took his breakfast in the snuggery, carefully listening to any conversation that might take place at the bar. Soon after nine o'clock a fast dog-cart stopped outside, and a red-faced, loud-voiced man swaggered in, greeting Kentish with boisterous cordiality. He had a drink with the landlord, and said: "How's things? Fancy any of 'em for the sprint handicap? Got a lad o' your own in, haven't you?"

"Oh, yes," Kentish replied. "Crockett. Only a young 'un—not got to his proper mark yet, I reckon. I think old Taylor's got No. 1 this time."

"Capital lad," the other replied, with a confidential nod. "Shouldn't wonder at all. Want to do anything yourself over it?"

"No—I don't think so. I'm not on at present. Might have a little flutter on the grounds just for fun; nothing else."

There were a few more casual remarks, and then the red-faced man drove away.

"'CAPITAL LAD,' THE OTHER REPLIED."

"Who was that?" asked Hewitt, who had watched the visitor through the snuggery window.

"That's Danby—bookmaker. Cute chap; he's been told Crockett's missing, I'll bet anything, and come here to pump me. No good though. As a matter of fact, I've worked Sammy Crockett into his books for about half I'm in for altogether—through third parties, of course."

Hewitt reached for his hat. "I'm going out for half an hour now," he said. "If Steggles wants to go out before I come back, don't let him. Let him go and smooth over all those tracks on the cinder-path, very carefully. And, by-the-bye, could you manage to have your son about the place to-day, in case I happen to want a little help out of doors?"

"Certainly; I'll get him to stay in. But what do you want the cinders smoothed for?"

Hewitt smiled and patted his host's shoulder. "I'll explain all my little tricks when the job's done," he said, and went out.

On the lane from Padfield to Sedby village stood the "Plough" beerhouse, wherein J. Webb was licensed to sell by retail beer to be consumed on the premises or off, as the thirsty list. Nancy Webb, with a very fine colour, a very curly fringe, and a wide-smiling mouth revealing a fine set of teeth, came to the bar at the summons of a stoutish old gentleman with spectacles, who walked with a stick.

The stoutish old gentleman had a glass of bitter beer and then said, in the peculiarly quiet voice of a very deaf man: "Can you tell me, if you please, the way into the main Catton Road?"

"Down the lane, turn to the right at the cross roads, then first to the left."

The old gentleman waited with his hand to his ear for some few seconds after she had finished speaking, and then resumed, in his whispering voice, "I'm afraid I'm very deaf this morning." He fumbled in his pocket and produced a note-book and pencil. "May I trouble you to write it down? I'm so very deaf at times, that I—thank you."

The girl wrote the direction, and the old gentleman bade her good morning and left. All down the lane he walked slowly with his stick. At the cross roads he turned, put the stick under his arm, thrust the spectacles into his pocket, and strode away in the ordinary guise of Martin Hewitt. He pulled out his note-book, examined Miss Webb's direction very carefully, and then went off another way altogether, toward the "Hare and Hounds."

Kentish lounged moodily in his bar. "Well, my boy," said Hewitt, "has Steggles wiped out the tracks?"

"Not yet—I haven't told him. But he's somewhere about—I'll tell him now."

"No, don't. I don't think we'll have that done, after all. I expect he'll want to go out soon—at any rate, some time during the day. Let him go whenever he likes. I'll sit upstairs a bit in the club room."

"Very well. But how do you know Steggles will be going out?"

"Well, he's pretty restless after his lost *protégé*, isn't he? I don't suppose he'll be able to remain idle long."

"And about Crockett. Do you give him up?"

"Oh, no. Don't you be impatient. I can't say I'm quite confident yet of laying hold of him—the time is so short, you see—

"NANCY WEBB."

but I think I shall at least have news for you by the evening."

Hewitt sat in the club-room until the afternoon, taking his lunch there. At length he saw, through the front window, Raggy Steggles walking down the road. In an instant Hewitt was downstairs and at the door. The road bent eighty yards away, and as soon as Steggles passed the bend the detective hurried after him.

All the way to Padfield town and more than half through it Hewitt dogged the trainer. In the end Steggles stopped at a corner and gave a note to a small boy who was playing near. The boy ran with the note to a bright, well-kept house at the opposite corner. Martin Hewitt was interested to observe the legend "H. Danby, Contractor," on a board over a gate in the side wall of the garden behind this house. In five minutes a door in the side gate opened, and the head and shoulders of the red-faced man emerged. Steggles immediately hurried across and disappeared through the gate.

This was both interesting and instructive. Hewitt took up a position in the side street and waited. In ten minutes the trainer reappeared and hurried off the way he had come, along the street Hewitt had considerately left clear for him. Then Hewitt strolled toward the smart house and took a good look at it. At one corner of the small piece of forecourt garden, near the railings, a small, baize-covered, glass-fronted notice-board stood on two posts. On its top edge appeared the words "H. Danby. Houses to be Sold or Let." But the only notice pinned to the green baize within was an old and dusty one, inviting tenants for three shops, which were suitable for any business, and which would be fitted to suit tenants. Apply within.

Hewitt pushed open the front gate and rang the door-bell. "There are some shops to let, I see," he said, when a maid appeared. "I should like to see them, if you will let me have the key."

"Master's out, sir. You can't see the shops till Monday."

"Dear me, that's unfortunate. I'm afraid I can't wait till Monday. Didn't Mr. Danby leave any instructions, in case anybody should inquire?"

"Yes, sir—as I've told you. He said anybody who called about 'em must come again on Monday."

"Oh, very well, then; I suppose I must try. One of the shops is in High Street, isn't it?"

"No, sir; they're all in the new part—Granville Road."

"Ah, I'm afraid that will scarcely do. But I'll see. Good day."

Martin Hewitt walked away a couple of streets' lengths before he inquired the way to Granville Road. When at last he found that thoroughfare, in a new and muddy suburb, crowded with brick-heaps and half-finished streets, he took a slow walk along its entire length. It was a melancholy example of baffled enterprise. A row of a dozen or more shops had been built before any population had arrived to demand goods. Would-be tradesmen had taken many of these shops, and failure and disappointment stared from the windows. Some were half covered by shutters, because the scanty stock scarce sufficed to fill the remaining half. Others were shut almost altogether, the inmates only keeping open the door for their own convenience, and, perhaps, keeping down a shutter for the sake of a little light. Others again had not yet fallen so low, but struggled bravely still to maintain a show of business and prosperity, with very little success. Opposite the shops there still remained a dusty, ill-treated hedge and a forlorn-looking field, which an old board offered on building leases. Altogether a most depressing spot.

There was little difficulty in identifying the three shops offered for letting by Mr. H. Danby. They were all together near the middle of the row, and were the only ones that appeared not yet to have been occupied. A dusty "To Let" bill hung in each window, with written directions to inquire of Mr. H. Danby or at No. 7. Now, No. 7 was a melancholy baker's shop, with a stock of three loaves and a plate of stale buns. The disappointed baker assured Hewitt that he usually kept the keys of the shops, but that the landlord, Mr. Danby, had taken them away the day before, to see how the ceilings were standing, and had not returned them. "But if you was thinking of taking a shop here," the poor baker added, with some hesitation, "I—I—if you'll excuse my advising you—I shouldn't recommend it. I've had a sickener of it myself."

"I'VE HAD A SICKENER OF IT MYSELF."

Hewitt thanked the baker for his advice, wished him better luck in future, and left. To the "Hare and Hounds" his pace was brisk. "Come," he said, as he met Kentish's inquiring glance, "this has been a very good day, on the whole. I know where our man is now, and I think we can get him, by a little management."

"Where is he?"

"Oh, down in Padfield. As a matter of fact, he's being kept there against his will, we shall find. I see that your friend, Mr. Danby, is a builder as well as a bookmaker."

"Not a regular builder. He speculates in a street of new houses now and again, that's all. But is he in it?"

"He's as deep in it as anybody, I think. Now, don't fly into a passion. There are a few others in it as well, but you'll do harm if you don't keep quiet."

"But go and get the police—come and fetch him, if you know where they're keeping him; why——"

"So we will, if we can't do it without them. But it's quite possible we can, and without all the disturbance and, perhaps, delay that calling in the police would involve. Consider, now, in reference to your own arrangements. Wouldn't it pay you better to get him back quietly, without a soul knowing — perhaps not even Danby knowing—till the heat is run to-morrow?"

"Well, yes, it would, of course."

"Very good, then, so be it. Remember what I have told you about keeping your mouth shut—say nothing to Steggles or anybody. Is there a cab or brougham your son and I can have for the evening?"

"There's an old hiring landau in the stables you can shut up into a cab, if that'll do."

"Excellent. We'll run down to the town in it as soon as it's ready. But, first, a word about Crockett. What sort of a lad is he? Likely to give them trouble, show fight, and make a disturbance?"

"No, I should say not. He's no plucked 'un, certainly—all his manhood's in his legs, I believe. You see, he ain't a big sort o' chap at best, and he'd be pretty easy put upon—at least, I guess so."

"Very good, so much the better, for then he won't have been damaged, and they will probably only have one man to guard him. Now the carriage, please."

Young Kentish was a six-foot sergeant of Grenadiers, home on furlough, and luxuriating in plain clothes. He and Hewitt walked a little way towards the town, allowing the landau to catch them up. They travelled in it to within a hundred yards of the empty shops and then alighted, bidding the driver wait.

"I shall show you three empty shops," Hewitt said, as he and young Kentish walked down Granville Road. "I am pretty sure that Sammy Crockett is in one of them, and I am pretty sure that that is the middle one. Take a look as we go past."

When the shops had been slowly passed, Hewitt resumed: "Now, did you see anything about those shops that told a tale of any sort?"

"No," Sergeant Kentish replied. "I can't say I noticed anything beyond the fact that they were empty—and likely to stay so, I should think."

"We'll stroll back, and look in at the windows, if nobody's watching us," Hewitt said. "You see, it's reasonable to suppose they've put him in the middle one, because that would suit their purpose best. The shops at each side of the three are occupied, and if the prisoner struggled, or shouted, or made an uproar, he might be heard if he were in one of the shops next those inhabited. So that the middle shop is the most likely. Now, see there," he went on, as they stopped before the window of the shop in question, "over at the back there's a staircase not yet partitioned off. It goes down below and up above; on the stairs and on the floor near them there are muddy footmarks. These must have been made to-day, else they would not be muddy, but dry and dusty, since there hasn't been a shower for a week till to-day. Move on again. Then you noticed that there were no other such marks in the shop. Consequently the man with the muddy feet did not come in by the front door, but by the back; otherwise he would have made a trail from the door. So we will go round to the back ourselves."

It was now growing dusk. The small pieces of ground behind the shops were bounded by a low fence, containing a door for each house.

"This door is bolted inside, of course," Hewitt said, "but there is no difficulty in climbing. I think we had better wait in the garden till dark. In the meantime, the gaoler, whoever he is, may come out; in which case we shall pounce on him as soon as he opens the door. You have that few yards of cord in your pocket, I think? And my handkerchief, properly rolled, will make a very good gag. Now over."

They climbed the fence and quietly approached the house, placing themselves in the angle of an outhouse out of sight from the windows. There was no sound, and no light appeared. Just above the ground about a foot of window was visible, with a grating over it, apparently lighting a basement. Suddenly Hewitt touched his companion's arm, and pointed toward the window. A faint rustling sound was perceptible, and as nearly as could be discerned in the darkness, some white blind or covering was placed over the glass from the inside. Then came the sound of a striking match, and at the side edge of the window there was a faint streak of light.

"That's the place," Hewitt whispered. "Come, we'll make a push for it. You stand against the wall at one side of the door and I'll stand at the other, and we'll have him as he comes out. Quietly, now, and I'll startle them."

He took a stone from among the rubbish littering the garden and flung it crashing through the window. There was a loud exclamation from within, the blind fell, and somebody rushed to the back door and flung it open. Instantly Kentish let fly a heavy right-hander, and the man went over like a skittle. In a moment Hewitt was upon him and the gag in his mouth.

"Hold him," Hewitt whispered, hurriedly. "I'll see if there are others."

He peered down through the low window. Within, Sammy Crockett, his bare legs dangling from beneath his long overcoat, sat on a packing-box, leaning with his head on his hand and his back towards the window. A guttering candle stood on the mantelpiece, and the newspaper which had been stretched across the window lay in scattered sheets on the floor. No other person besides Sammy was visible.

They led their prisoner indoors. Young Kentish recognised him as a public-house loafer and race-course ruffian well known in the neighbourhood.

"So it's you, is it, Browdie?" he said. "I've caught you one hard clump, and I've half a mind to make it a score more. But you'll get it pretty warm one way or another, before this job's forgotten."

Sammy Crockett was overjoyed at his rescue. He had not been ill-treated, he explained, but had been thoroughly cowed by Browdie, who had from time to time threatened him savagely with an iron bar, by way of persuading him to quietness and submission. He had been fed, and had taken no worse harm than a slight stiffness from his adventure, due to his light under-attire of jersey and knee-shorts.

Sergeant Kentish tied Browdie's elbows firmly together behind, and carried the line round the ankles, bracing all up tight. Then he ran a knot from one wrist to the other over the back of the neck, and left the prisoner, trussed and helpless, on the heap of straw that had been Sammy's bed.

"You won't be very jolly, I expect," Kentish said, "for some time. You can't

"THE PRISONER—TRUSSED AND HELPLESS."

shout and you can't walk, and I know you can't untie yourself. You'll get a bit hungry, too, perhaps, but that'll give you an appetite. I don't suppose you'll be disturbed till some time to-morrow, unless our friend Danby turns up in the meantime. But you can come along to gaol instead, if you prefer it."

They left him where he lay, and took Sammy to the old landau. Sammy walked in slippers, carrying his spiked shoes, hanging by the lace, in his hand.

"Ah," said Hewitt, "I think I know the name of the young lady who gave you those slippers."

Crockett looked ashamed and indignant. "Yes," he said; "they've done me nicely between 'em. But I'll pay her—I'll——"

"Hush, hush!" Hewitt said; "you mustn't talk unkindly of a lady, you know. Get into this carriage, and we'll take you home. We'll see if I can tell you your adventures without making a mistake. First, you had a note from Miss Webb, telling you that you were mistaken in supposing she had slighted you, and that as a matter of fact she had quite done with somebody else—left him—of whom you were jealous. Isn't that so?"

"Well, yes," young Crockett answered, blushing deeply under the carriage-lamp; "but I don't see how you come to know that."

"Then she went on to ask you to get rid of Steggles on Thursday afternoon for a few minutes, and speak to her in the back lane. Now, your running pumps, with their thin soles, almost like paper, no heels and long spikes, hurt your feet horribly if you walk on hard ground, don't they?"

"Ay, that they do — enough to cripple you. I'd never go on much hard ground with 'em."

"They're not like cricket shoes, I see."

"Not a bit. Cricket shoes you can walk anywhere in."

"Well, she knew this—I think I know who told her—and she promised to bring you a new pair of slippers, and to throw them over the fence for you to come out in."

"I s'pose she's been tellin' you all this?" Crockett said, mournfully. "You couldn't ha' seen the letter—I saw her tear it up and put the bits in her pocket. She asked me for it in the lane, in case Steggles saw it."

"Well, at any rate, you sent Steggles away, and the slippers did come over, and you went into the lane. You walked with her as far as the road at the end, and then you were seized and gagged, and put into a carriage."

"That was Browdie did that," said Crockett, "and another chap I don't know. But—why, this is Padfield High Street!" He looked through the window and regarded the familiar shops with astonishment.

"Of course it is. Where did you think it was?"

"Why, where was that place you found me in?"

"Granville Road, Padfield. I suppose they told you you were in another town?"

"Told me it was Newstead Hatch. They drove for about three or four hours, and kept me down on the floor between the seats so as I couldn't see where we was going."

"Done for two reasons," said Hewitt.

"First, to mystify you, and prevent any discovery of the people directing the conspiracy; and, second, to be able to put you indoors at night and unobserved. Well, I think I have told you all you know yourself now as far as the carriage.

"But there is the 'Hare and Hounds' just in front. We'll pull up here and I'll get out and see if the coast is clear. I fancy Mr. Kentish would rather you came in unnoticed."

In a few seconds Hewitt was back, and Crockett was conveyed indoors by a side entrance. Hewitt's instructions to the landlord were few but emphatic. "Don't tell Steggles about it," he said; "make an excuse to get rid of him, and send him out of the house. Take Crockett into some other bedroom, not his own, and let your son look after him. Then come here, and I'll tell you all about it."

Sammy Crockett was undergoing a heavy grooming with white embrocation at the hands of Sergeant Kentish, when the landlord returned to Hewitt. "Does Danby know you've got him?" he asked. "How did you do it?"

"Danby doesn't know yet, and with luck he won't know till he sees Crockett running to-morrow. The man who has sold you is Steggles."

"Steggles?"

"Steggles it is. At the very first, when Steggles rushed in to report Sammy Crockett missing, I suspected him. You didn't, I suppose?"

"No. He's always been considered a straight man, and he looked as startled as anybody."

"Yes, I must say he acted it very well. But there was something suspicious in his story. What did he say? Crockett had remarked a chilliness, and asked for a sweater, which Steggles went to fetch. Now, just think. You understand these things. Would any trainer who knew his business (as Steggles does) have gone to bring out a sweater for his man to change for his jersey in the open air, at the very time the man was complaining of chilliness? Of course not. He would have taken his man indoors again and let him change there under shelter. Then supposing Steggles had really been surprised at missing Crockett, wouldn't he have looked about, found the gate open, and *told* you it was open, when he first came in? He said nothing of that—we found the gate open for ourselves. So that from the beginning, I had a certain opinion of Steggles."

"What you say seems pretty plain now, although it didn't strike me at the time. But if Steggles was selling us, why couldn't he have drugged the lad? That would have been a deal simpler."

"Because Steggles is a good trainer and has a certain reputation to keep up. It would have done him no good to have had a runner drugged while under his care—certainly it would have cooked his goose with *you*. It was much the safer thing to connive at kidnapping. That put all the active work into other hands, and left him safe, even if the trick failed. Now you remember that we traced the prints of Crockett's spiked shoes to within a couple of yards of the fence, and that there they ceased suddenly?"

"Yes. You said it looked as though he had flown up into the air; and so it did."

"But I was sure that it was by that gate that Crockett had left, and by no other. He couldn't have got through the house without being seen, and there was no other way—let alone the evidence of the unbolted gate. Therefore, as the footprints ceased where they did, and were not repeated anywhere in the lane, I knew that he had taken his spiked shoes off—probably changed them for something else, because a runner anxious as to his chances would never risk walking on bare feet, with a chance of cutting them. Ordinary, broad, smooth-soled slippers would leave no impression on the coarse cinders bordering the track, and nothing short of spiked shoes would leave a mark on the hard path in the lane behind. The spike tracks were leading, not directly toward the door, but in the direction of the fence, when they stopped—somebody had handed, or thrown, the slippers over the fence and he had changed them on the spot. The enemy had calculated upon the spikes leaving a track in the lane that might lead us in our search, and had arranged accordingly.

"So far, so good. I could see no footprints near the gate in the lane. You will remember that I sent Steggles off to watch at the Cop before I went out to the back—merely, of course, to get him out of the way. I went out into the lane, leaving you behind, and walked its whole length, first toward the Old Kilns and then back toward the road. I found nothing to help me except these small pieces of paper—which are here in my pocket-book, by-the-bye. Of course, this 'mmy' might have meant 'Jimmy' or 'Tommy,' as possibly as 'Sammy,' but they were not to be rejected on that account. Certainly Crockett had been decoyed out of your ground, not taken by force, or there would have been marks of a scuffle in the cinders. And as his request for a sweater was probably ar excuse—because it was not at all a cold afternoon—he must have previously designed going out—inference, a letter received; and here were pieces of a letter. Now, in the light of what I have said, look at these pieces. First there is the 'mmy'—that I have dealt with. Then, see this 'throw them ov'—clearly a part of 'throw them over'; exactly what had probably been done with the slippers. Then the 'poor f,' coming just on the line before, and seen, by joining up with this other piece, might easily be a reference to 'poor feet.' These coincidences, one on the other, went far to establish the identity of the letter, and to confirm my previous impressions. But then there is something else. Two other pieces evidently mean 'left him,' and 'right away'—send Steggles 'right away,' perhaps; but there is another, containing almost all of the words 'hate his,' with the word 'hate' underlined. Now, who writes 'hate' with the emphasis of underscoring—who but a woman? The writing is large and not very regular; it might easily be that of a half-educated woman. Here was something more—Sammy had been enticed away by a woman.

"Now, I remembered that when we went into the tap-room on Wednesday, some of his companions were chaffing Crockett about a certain Nancy Webb, and the chaff went home, as was plain to see. The woman, then, who could most easily entice Sammy Crockett away was Nancy Webb. I resolved to find who Nancy Webb was and learn more of her.

"Meantime I took a look at the road at the end of the lane. It was damper than the lane, being lower, and overhung by trees. There were many wheel tracks, but only one set that turned in the road and went back the way it came—towards the town—and they were narrow wheels, carriage wheels. Crockett tells me now that they drove him about for a long time before shutting him up—probably the inconvenience of taking him straight to the hiding-place didn't strike them when they first drove off.

"A few inquiries soon set me in the direction of the 'Plough' and Miss Nancy Webb. I had the curiosity to look round the place as I approached, and there, in the garden behind the house, were Steggles and the young lady in earnest confabulation!

"Every conjecture became a certainty. Steggles was the lover of whom Crockett was jealous, and he had employed the girl to bring Sammy out. I watched Steggles home, and gave you a hint to keep him there.

"STEGGLES AND THE YOUNG LADY IN EARNEST CONFABULATION."

"But the thing that remained was to find Steggles's employer in this business. I was glad to be in when Danby called—he came, of course, to hear if you would blurt out anything, and to learn, if possible, what steps you were taking. He failed. By way of making assurance doubly sure, I took a short walk this morning in the character of a deaf gentleman, and got Miss Webb to write me a direction that comprised three of the words on these scraps of paper—'left,' 'right,' and 'lane'—see, they correspond, the peculiar 'f's,' 't's,' and all.

"Now, I felt perfectly sure that Steggles would go for his pay to-day. In the first place, I knew that people mixed up with shady transactions in professional pedestrianism are not apt to trust one another far—they know better. Therefore, Steggles wouldn't have had his bribe first. But he would take care to get it before the Saturday heats were run, because once they were over the thing was done, and the principal conspirator might have refused to pay up, and Steggles couldn't have helped himself. Again I hinted he should not go out till I could follow him, and this afternoon when he went, follow him I did. I saw him go into Danby's house by the side way and come away again. Danby it was, then, who had arranged the business; and nobody was more likely, considering his large pecuniary stake against Crockett's winning this race.

"But now, how to find Crockett? I made up my mind he wouldn't be in Danby's own house—that would be a deal too risky, with servants about, and so on. I saw that Danby was a builder, and had three shops to let—it was on a paper before his house. What more likely prison than an empty house? I knocked at Danby's door and asked for the keys of those shops. I couldn't have them. The servant told me Danby was out (a manifest lie, for I had just seen him), and that nobody could see the shops till Monday. But I got out of her the address of the shops, and that was all I wanted at the time.

"Now, why was nobody to see those shops till Monday? The interval was suspicious—just enough to enable Crockett to be sent away again and cast loose after the Saturday racing, supposing him to be kept in one of the empty buildings. I went off at once and looked at the shops, forming my conclusions as to which would be the most likely for Danby's purpose. Here I had another confirmation of my ideas. A poor, half-bankrupt baker in one of the shops had, by the bills, the custody of a set of keys; but *he*, too, told me I couldn't have them; Danby had taken them away—and on Thursday, the very day—with some trivial excuse, and hadn't brought them back. That was all I wanted, or could expect in the way of guidance; the whole thing was plain. The rest you know all about."

"Well, you're certainly as smart as they give you credit for, I must say. But suppose Danby had taken down his 'to let' notice, what would you have done then?"

"We had our course even then. We should have gone to Danby, astounded him by telling him all about his little games, terrorized him with threats of the law, and made him throw up his hand and send Crockett back. But as it is, you see, he doesn't know at this moment—probably won't know till to-morrow afternoon—that the lad is safe and sound here. You will probably use the interval to make him pay for losing the game—by some of the ingenious financial devices you are no doubt familiar with."

"Aye, that I will. He'll give any price against Crockett now, so long as the bet don't come direct from me."

"But about Crockett, now," Hewitt went on. "Won't this confinement be likely to have damaged his speed for a day or two?"

"Ah, perhaps," the landlord replied; "but, bless ye, that won't matter. There's four more in his heat to-morrow. Two I know aren't tryers, and the other two I can hold in at a couple of quid apiece any day. The third round and final won't be till to-morrow week, and he'll be as fit as ever by then. It's as safe as ever it was. How much are you going to have on? I'll lump it on for you safe enough. This is a chance not to be missed—it's picking money up."

"Thank you; I don't think I'll have anything to do with it. This professional pedestrian business doesn't seem a pretty one at all. I don't call myself a moralist, but, if you'll excuse my saying so, the thing is scarcely the game I care to pick up money at in any way."

"Oh! very well, if you think so, I won't persuade ye, though I don't think so much of your smartness as I did, after that. Still, we won't quarrel—you've done me a mighty good turn, that I must say, and I only feel I aren't level without doing something to pay the debt. Come, now, you've got your trade as I've got mine. Let me have the bill, and I'll pay it like a lord, and feel a deal more pleased than if you made a favour of it—not that I'm above a favour, of course. But I'd prefer paying, and that's a fact."

"My dear sir, you have paid," Hewitt said, with a smile. "You paid in advance. It was a bargain, wasn't it, that I should do your business if you would help me in mine? Very well, a bargain's a bargain, and we've both performed our parts. And you mustn't be offended at what I said just now."

"That I won't. But as to that Raggy Steggles, once those heats are over to-morrow, I'll——well——!"

It was on the following Sunday week that Martin Hewitt, in his rooms in London, turned over his paper and read, under the head "Padfield Annual 135 Yards Handicap," this announcement: "Final Heat: Crockett, first; Willis, second; Trewby, third; Owen, 0; Howell, 0. A runaway win by nearly three yards."

Martin Hewitt, Investigator.

BY ARTHUR MORRISON.

III.—THE CASE OF MR. FOGGATT.

ALMOST the only dogmatism that Martin Hewitt permitted himself in regard to his professional methods was one on the matter of accumulative probabilities. Often when I have remarked upon the apparently trivial nature of the clues by which he allowed himself to be guided—sometimes, to all seeming, in the very face of all likelihood—he has replied that two trivialities, pointing in the same direction, became at once, by their mere agreement, no trivialities at all, but enormously important considerations. "If I were in search of a man," he would say, "of whom I knew nothing but that he squinted, bore a birthmark on his right hand, and limped, and I observed a man who answered to the first peculiarity, so far the clue would be trivial, because thousands of men squint. Now, if that man presently moved and exhibited a birthmark on his right hand, the value of that squint and that mark would increase at once a hundred or a thousand fold. Apart they are little; together much. The weight of evidence is not doubled merely; it would be only doubled if half the men who squinted had right-hand birthmarks; whereas, the proportion, if it could be ascertained, would be perhaps more like one in ten thousand. The two trivialities, pointing in the same direction, become very strong evidence. And when the man is seen to walk with a limp, that limp (another triviality), reinforcing the others, brings the matter to the rank of a practical certainty. The Bertillon system of identification—what is it but a summary of trivialities? Thousands of men are of the same height, thousands of the same length of foot, thousands of the same girth of head—thousands correspond in any separate measurement you may name. It is when the measurements are taken *together* that you have your man identified for ever. Just consider how few, if any, of your friends correspond exactly in any two personal peculiarities." Hewitt's dogma received its illustration unexpectedly close at home.

MR. FOGGATT.

The old house wherein my chambers and Hewitt's office were situated contained, beside my own, two or three more bachelors' dens, in addition to the offices on the ground and first and second floors. At the very top of all, at the back, a fat, middle-aged man, named Foggatt, occupied a set of four rooms. It was only after long residence, by an accidental remark of the housekeeper's, that I learned the man's name, which was not painted on his door or displayed, with all the others, on the wall of the ground-floor porch.

Mr. Foggatt appeared to have few friends, but lived in something as nearly approaching luxury as an old bachelor in chambers can live An ascending case of champagne was a common phenomenon of the staircase, and I have more than once seen a picture, destined for the top floor, of a sort that went far to awaken green covetousness in the heart of a poor journalist.

The man himself was not altogether prepossessing. Fat as he was, he had a way of carrying his head forward on his extended neck and gazing widely about with a pair of the roundest and most prominent eyes I remember to have ever seen, except in a fish. On the whole, his appearance was rather vulgar, rather arrogant, and rather suspicious, without any very pronounced quality of any sort. But certainly he was not pretty. In the end, however, he was found shot dead in his sitting-room.

It was in this way: Hewitt and I had dined together at my club, and late in the evening had returned to my rooms to smoke and discuss whatever came uppermost. I had made a bargain that day with two speculative odd lots at a book sale, each of which contained a hidden prize. We sat talking and turning over these books while time went unperceived, when suddenly we were startled by a loud report. Clearly it was in the building. We listened for a moment, but heard nothing else, and then Hewitt expressed his opinion that the report was that of a gunshot. Gunshots in residential chambers are not common things, wherefore I got up and went to the landing, looking up the stairs and down.

At the top of the next flight I saw Mrs. Clayton, the housekeeper. She appeared to be frightened, and told me that the report came from Mr. Foggatt's room. She thought he might have had an accident with the pistol that usually lay on his mantelpiece. We went upstairs with her, and she knocked at Mr. Foggatt's door.

There was no reply. Through the ventilating fanlight over the door it could be seen that there were lights within, a sign, Mrs. Clayton maintained, that Mr. Foggatt was not out. We knocked again, much more loudly, and called, but still ineffectually. The door was locked, and an application of the housekeeper's key proved that the tenant's key had been left in the lock inside. Mrs. Clayton's conviction that "something had happened" became distressing, and in the end Hewitt prised open the door with a small poker.

Something *had* happened. In the sitting-room Mr. Foggatt sat with his head bowed over the table, quiet and still. The head was ill to look at, and by it lay a large revolver, of the full-sized Army pattern. Mrs. Clayton ran back toward the landing with faint screams.

"SOMETHING HAD HAPPENED.

"Run, Brett," said Hewitt; "a doctor and a policeman!"

I bounced down the stairs half a flight at a time. "First," I thought, "a doctor. He may not be dead." I could think of no doctor in the immediate neighbourhood, but ran up the street away from the Strand, as being the more likely direction for the doctor, although less so for the policeman. It took me a good five minutes to find the medico, after being led astray by a red lamp at a private hotel, and another five to get back, with a policeman.

Foggatt was dead, without a doubt. Probably had shot himself, the doctor thought, from the powder-blackening and other circumstances. Certainly nobody could have left the room by the door, or he must have passed my landing, while the fact of the door being found locked from the inside made the thing impossible. There were two windows to the room, both of which were shut, one being fastened by the catch, while the catch of the other was broken—an old fracture. Below these windows was a sheer drop of 50ft. or more, without a foot or hand-hold near. The windows in the other rooms were shut and fastened. Certainly it seemed suicide—unless it were one of those accidents that will occur to people who fiddle ignorantly with firearms. Soon the rooms were in possession of the police, and we were turned out.

We looked in at the housekeeper's kitchen, where her daughter was reviving and calming Mrs. Clayton with gin and water.

"You mustn't upset yourself, Mrs. Clayton," Hewitt said, "or what will become of us all? The doctor thinks it was an accident."

He took a small bottle of sewing-machine oil from his pocket and handed it to the daughter, thanking her for the loan.

There was little evidence at the inquest. The shot had been heard, the body had been found—that was the practical sum of the matter. No friends or relatives of the dead man came forward. The doctor gave his opinion as to the probability of suicide or an accident, and the police evidence tended in the same direction. Nothing had been found to indicate that any other person had been near the dead man's rooms on the night of the fatality. On the other hand, his papers, bank-book, etc., proved him to be a man of considerable substance, with no apparent motive for suicide. The police had been unable to trace any relatives, or, indeed, any nearer connections than casual acquaintances, fellow club-men, and so on. The jury found that Mr. Foggatt had died by accident.

"Well, Brett," Hewitt asked me afterwards, "what do you think of the verdict?"

I said that it seemed to be the most reasonable one possible, and to square with the common-sense view of the case.

"Yes," he replied, "perhaps it does. From the point of view of the jury, and on their information, their verdict was quite reasonable. Nevertheless, Mr. Foggatt did not shoot himself. He was shot by a rather tall, active young man, perhaps a sailor, but certainly a gymnast—a young man whom I think I could identify, if I saw him."

"But how do you know this?"

"By the simplest possible inferences, which you may easily guess, if you will but think."

"But, then, why didn't you say this at the inquest?"

"My dear fellow, they don't want my inferences and conjectures at an inquest, they only want evidence. If I had traced the murderer, of course then I should have communicated with the police. As a matter of fact, it is quite possible that the police have observed and know as much as I do—or more. They don't give everything away at an inquest, you know—it wouldn't do."

"But if you are right, how did the man get away?"

"Come, we are near home now. Let us take a look at the back of the house. He *couldn't* have left by Foggatt's landing-door, as we know; and as he *was* there (I am certain of that), and as the chimney is out of the question—for there was a good fire in the grate—he must have gone out by the window. Only one window is possible—that with the broken catch — for all the others were fastened inside. Out of that window, then, he went."

"But how? The window is 50ft. up."

"Of course it is. But why *will* you persist in assuming that the only way of escape by a window is downward? See, now, look up there. The window is at the top-floor, and it has a very broad sill. Over the window is nothing but the flat face of the gable-end; but to the right, and a foot or two above the level of the top of the window, an iron gutter ends. Observe, it is not of lead composition, but a strong iron gutter, supported, just at its end, by an iron bracket. If a tall man stood on the end of the window-sill, steadying himself by the left hand and leaning to the right, he could just touch the end of this gutter with his right hand—the full stretch, toe to finger, is 7ft. 3in.; I have measured it. An active gymnast, or a sailor, could catch the gutter with a slight spring, and by it draw himself upon the roof. You will say he would have to be *very* active, dexterous, and cool. So he would. And that very fact helps us, because it narrows the field of inquiry. We know the sort of man to look for. Because, being certain (as I am) that the man was in the room, I *know* that he left in the way I am telling you. He must have left in some way, and all the other ways being impossible, this alone remains, difficult as the feat may seem. The fact of his shutting the window behind him further proves his coolness and address at so great a height from the ground."

All this was very plain, but the main point was still dark.

"You say you *know* that another man was in the room," I said; "how do you know that?"

"As I said, by an obvious inference. Come now, you shall guess how I arrived at that inference. You often speak of your interest in my work, and the attention with which you follow it. This shall be a simple exercise for you. You saw everything in the room as plainly as I myself. Bring the scene back to your memory, and think over the various small objects littering about, and how they would affect the case. Quick observation is the first essential for my work. Did you see a newspaper, for instance?"

"Yes. There was an evening paper on the floor, but I didn't examine it."

"Anything else?"

"On the table there was a whisky decanter, taken from the tantalus stand on the sideboard, and one glass. That, by-the-bye," I added, "looked as though only one person were present."

"So it did, perhaps, although the inference wouldn't be very strong. Go on."

"There was a fruit-stand on the sideboard, with a plate beside it, containing a few nutshells, a piece of apple, a pair of nutcrackers, and, I think, some orange peel. There was, of course, all the ordinary furniture, but no chair pulled up to the table except that used by Foggatt himself. That's all I noticed, I think. Stay—there was an ash-tray on the table, and a partly-burned cigar near it—only one cigar, though."

"Excellent—excellent, indeed, as far as memory and simple observation go. You saw everything plainly, and you remember everything. Surely *now* you know how I found out that another man had just left?"

"No, I don't; unless there were different kinds of ash in the ash-tray."

"That is a fairly good suggestion, but there were not—there was only a single ash, corresponding in every way to that on the cigar. Don't you remember anything that I did as we went downstairs?"

"You returned a bottle of oil to the housekeeper's daughter, I think."

"I did. Doesn't that give you a hint? Come, you surely have it now?"

"I haven't."

"Then I shan't tell you; you don't deserve it. Think, and don't mention the subject again till you have at least one guess to make. The thing stares you in the face—you see it,

"DOESN'T THAT GIVE YOU A HINT?"

you remember it, and yet you *won't* see it. I won't encourage your slovenliness of thought, my boy, by telling you what you can know for yourself if you like. Good-bye—I'm off now. There is a case in hand I can't neglect."

"Don't you propose to go further into this, then?"

Hewitt shrugged his shoulders. "I'm not a policeman," he said. "The case is in very good hands. Of course, if anybody comes to me to do it as a matter of business, I'll take it up. It's very interesting, but I can't neglect my regular work for it. Naturally, I shall keep my eyes open and my memory in order. Sometimes these things come into the hands by themselves, as it were; in that case, of course, I am a loyal citizen, and ready to help the law. *Au revoir.*"

I am a busy man myself, and thought little more of Hewitt's conundrum for some time —indeed, when I did think, I saw no way to the answer. A week after the inquest I took a holiday (I had written my nightly leaders regularly every day for the past five years), and saw no more of Hewitt for six weeks. After my return, with still a few days of leave to run, one evening we together turned into Luzatti's, off Coventry Street, for dinner.

"I have been here several times lately," Hewitt said; "they feed you very well. No, not that table"—he seized my arm as I turned to an unoccupied corner—"I fancy it's draughty." He led the way to a longer table where a dark, lithe, and (as well as could be seen) tall young man already sat, and took chairs opposite him.

We had scarcely seated ourselves before Hewitt broke into a torrent of conversation on the subject of bicycling. As our previous conversation had been of a literary sort, and as I had never known Hewitt at any other time to show the slightest interest in bicycling, this rather surprised me. I had, however, such a general outsider's grasp of the subject as is usual in a journalist-of-all-work, and managed to keep the talk going from my side. As we went on I could see the face of the young man opposite brighten with interest. He was a rather fine-looking fellow, with a dark though very clear skin, but had a hard, angry look of eye, a prominence of cheek-bone, and a squareness of jaw that gave him a rather uninviting aspect. As Hewitt rattled on, however, our neighbour's expression became one of pleasant interest merely.

"Of course," Hewitt said, "we've a number of very capital men just now, but I believe a deal in the forgotten riders of five, ten, and fifteen years back. Osmond, I believe, was better than any man riding now, and I think it would puzzle some of them to beat Furnivall as he was at his best. But poor old Cortis—really, I believe he was as good as anybody. Nobody ever beat Cortis—except—let me see—I think somebody beat Cortis once—who was it, now? I can't remember."

"Liles," said the young man opposite, looking up quickly.

"Ah, yes—Liles it was; Charley Liles. Wasn't it a championship?"

"Mile championship, 1880; Cortis won the other three, though."

"Yes, so he did. I saw Cortis when he first broke the old 2.46 mile record." And straightway Hewitt plunged into a whirl of talk of bicycles, tricycles, records, racing cyclists, Hillier and Synyer and Noel Whiting, Taylerson and Appleyard; talk wherein the young man opposite bore an animated share, while I was left in the cold.

Our new friend, it seemed, had himself been a prominent racing bicyclist a few years back, and was presently, at Hewitt's request, exhibiting a neat gold medal that hung at his watch-guard. That was won, he explained, in the old tall bicycle days, the days of bad tracks, when every racing cyclist carried cinder scars on his face from numerous accidents. He pointed to a blue mark on his forehead, which, he told us, was a track scar, and described a bad fall that had cost him two teeth, and broken others. The gaps among his teeth were plain to see as he smiled.

Presently the waiter brought dessert, and the young man opposite took an apple. Nutcrackers and a fruit-knife lay on our side of the stand, and Hewitt turned the stand to offer him the knife.

"No, thanks," he said, "I only polish a good apple, never peel it. It's a mistake except with thick-skinned, foreign ones."

And he began to munch the apple as only a boy or a healthy athlete can. Presently he turned his head to order coffee. The waiter's back was turned, and he had to be called twice. To my unutterable amazement Hewitt reached swiftly across the table, snatched the half-eaten apple from the young man's plate and pocketed it; gazing immediately, with an abstracted air, at a painted Cupid on the ceiling.

Our neighbour turned again, looked doubtfully at his plate and the tablecloth about it, and then shot a keen glance in the direction of Hewitt. He said nothing, however, but took his coffee and his bill, deliberately drank the former, gazing quietly at Hewitt as he did it, paid the latter, and left.

Immediately Hewitt was on his feet and, taking an umbrella which stood near, followed. Just as he reached the door he met our late neighbour, who had turned suddenly back.

"Your umbrella, I think?" Hewitt asked, offering it.

"Yes, thanks." But the man's eye had more than its former hardness, and his jaw-muscles tightened as I looked. He turned and went. Hewitt came back to me. "Pay the bill," he said, "and go back to your rooms; I will come on later: I must follow this man—it's the Foggatt case." As he went out I heard a cab rattle away, and immediately after it another.

"HEWITT REACHED SWIFTLY ACROSS THE TABLE.'

I paid the bill and went home. It was ten o'clock before Hewitt turned up, calling in at his office below on his way up to me.

"Mr. Sidney Mason," he said, "is the gentleman the police will be wanting to-morrow, I expect, for the Foggatt murder. He is as smart a man as I remember ever meeting, and has done me rather neatly twice this evening."

"You mean the man we sat opposite at Luzatti's, of course?"

"Yes, I got his name, of course, from the reverse of that gold medal he was good enough to show me. But I fear he has bilked me over the address. He suspected me, that was plain, and left his umbrella by way of experiment, to see if I were watching him sharply enough to notice the circumstance, and to avail myself of it to follow him. I was hasty and fell into the trap. He cabbed it away from Luzatti's, and I cabbed it after him. He has led me a pretty dance up and down London to-night, and two cabbies have made quite a stroke of business out of us. In the end he entered a house of which, of course, I have taken the address, but I expect he doesn't live there. He is too smart a man to lead me to his den; but the police can certainly find something of him at the house he went in at—and, I expect, left by the back way. By the way, you never guessed that simple little puzzle as to how I found that this *was* a murder, did you? You see it now, of course?"

"Something to do with that apple you stole, I suppose?"

"Something to do with it? I should think so, you worthy innocent. Just ring your bell—we'll borrow Mrs. Clayton's sewing-machine oil again. On the night we broke into Foggatt's room you saw the nutshells and the bitten remains of an apple on the sideboard, and you remembered it; and yet you couldn't see that in that piece of apple possibly lay an important piece of evidence. Of course, I never expected you to have arrived at any conclusion, as I had, because I had ten minutes in which to examine that apple, and to do what I did with it. But at least you should have seen the possibility of evidence in it.

"First, now, the apple was white. A bitten apple, as you must have observed, turns of a reddish-brown colour if left to stand long. Different kinds of apples brown with different rapidities, and the browning always begins at the core. This is one of the twenty thousand tiny things that few people take the trouble to notice, but which it is useful for a man in my position to know. A russet will brown quite quickly. The apple on the sideboard was, as near as I could tell, a Newtown pippin or other apple of that kind, which will brown at the core in from twenty minutes to half an hour, and in other parts in a quarter of an hour more. When we saw it it was white, with barely a tinge of brown about the exposed core. Inference—somebody had been eating it fifteen or twenty minutes before—perhaps a little longer; an inference supported by the fact that it was only partly eaten.

"I examined that apple, and found it bore marks of very irregular teeth. While you were gone I oiled it over, and, rushing down to my rooms, where I always have a little plaster of Paris handy for such work, took a mould of the part where the teeth had left the clearest marks. I then returned the apple to its place, for the police to use if they thought fit. Looking at my mould, it was plain that the person who had bitten that apple had lost two teeth, one at top and one below, not exactly opposite, but nearly so. The other teeth, although they would appear to have been fairly sound, were irregular in size and line. Now the dead man had, as I saw, a very excellent set of false teeth, regular and sharp, with none missing. Therefore it was plain that *somebody else* had been eating that apple. Do I make myself clear?"

"Quite. Go on."

"There were other inferences to be made—slighter, but all pointing the same way. For instance, a man of Foggatt's age does not as a rule munch an unpeeled apple like a schoolboy—inference, a young man, and healthy. Why I came to the conclusion that he was tall, active, a gymnast, and perhaps a sailor, I have already told you, when we examined the outside of Foggatt's window. It was also pretty clear that robbery was not the motive, since nothing was disturbed, and that a friendly conversation had preceded the murder—witness the drinking and the eating of the apple. Whether or not the police noticed these things I can't say. If they had had their best men on they certainly would, I think; but the case, to a rough observer, looked so clearly one of accident or suicide, that possibly they didn't.

"As I said, after the inquest I was unable to devote any immediate time to the case, but I resolved to keep my eyes open. The man to look for was tall, young, strong and active, with a very irregular set of teeth, a tooth missing from the lower jaw just to the left of the centre, and another from the upper jaw a little further still toward the left. He might possibly be a person I had seen about the premises (I have a good memory for faces), or, of course, he possibly might not.

"Just before you returned from your holiday I noticed a young man at Luzatti's whom I remembered to have seen somewhere about the offices in this building. He was tall, young, and so on, but I had a client with me, and was unable to examine him more narrowly—indeed, as I was not exactly engaged on the case, and as there are several tall young men about, I took little trouble. But to-day, finding the same young man with a vacant seat opposite him, I took the opportunity of making a closer acquaintance."

"You certainly managed to draw him out."

"Oh, yes—the easiest person in the world to draw out is a cyclist. The easiest cyclist to draw out is, of course, the novice, but the next easiest is the veteran. When you see a healthy, well-trained looking man, who nevertheless has a slight stoop in the shoulders, and, maybe, a medal on his watch-guard, it is always a safe card to try him first with a little cycle-racing talk. I soon brought Mr. Mason out of his shell, read his name on his medal, and had a chance of observing his teeth—indeed, he spoke of them himself. Now, as I observed just now, there are several tall, athletic young men about, and also there are several men who have lost teeth. But now I saw that this tall and athletic young man had lost exactly *two* teeth — one from the lower jaw, just to the left of the centre, and another from the upper jaw, further still toward the left! Trivialities, pointing in the same direction, became important considerations. More, his teeth were irregular throughout, and, as nearly as I could remember it, looked remarkably like this little plaster mould of mine."

He produced from his pocket an irregular lump of plaster, about three inches long. On one side of this appeared in relief the likeness of two irregular rows of six or eight teeth, minus one in each row, where a deep gap was seen, in the position spoken of by my friend. He proceeded:—

"This was enough at least to set me after this young man. But he gave me the greatest chance of all when he turned and left his apple (eaten unpeeled, remember!—another important triviality) on his plate. I'm afraid I wasn't at all polite, and I ran the risk of arousing his suspicions, but I couldn't resist the temptation to steal it. I did, as you saw, and here it is."

He brought the apple from his coat-pocket. One bitten side, placed against the upper half of the mould, fitted precisely, a projection of apple filling exactly the deep gap. The other side similarly fitted the lower half.

"There's no getting behind that, you see," Hewitt remarked. "Merely observing the man's teeth was a guide, to some extent, but

"FITTED PRECISELY."

this is as plain as his signature or his thumb-impression. You'll never find two men *bite* exactly alike, no matter whether they leave distinct teeth-marks or not. Here, by-the-bye, is Mrs. Clayton's oil. We'll take another mould from this apple, and compare *them*."

He oiled the apple, heaped a little plaster in a newspaper, took my water-jug and rapidly pulled off a hard mould. The parts corresponding to the merely broken places in the apple were, of course, dissimilar; but as to the teeth-marks, the impressions were identical.

"That will do, I think," Hewitt said. "To-morrow morning, Brett, I shall put up these things in a small parcel, and take them round to Bow Street."

"But are they sufficient evidence?"

"Quite sufficient for the police purpose. There is the man, and all the rest—his movements on the day and so forth are simple matters of inquiry; at any rate, that is police business."

I had scarcely sat down to my breakfast on the following morning when Hewitt came into the room and put a long letter before me.

"From our friend of last night," he said; "read it."

This letter began abruptly, and undated, and was as follows:—

"TO MARTIN HEWITT, ESQ.

"SIR,—I must compliment you on the adroitness you exhibited this evening in extracting from me my name. The address I was able to balk you of for the time being, although by the time you read this you will probably have found it through the *Law List*, as I am an admitted solicitor. That, however, will be of little use to you, for I am removing myself, I think, beyond the reach even of your abilities of search. I knew you well by sight, and was, perhaps, foolish to allow myself to be drawn as I did. Still, I had no idea that it would be dangerous, especially after seeing you, as a witness with very little to say, at the inquest upon the scoundrel I shot. Your somewhat discourteous seizure of my apple at first amazed me—indeed, I was a little doubtful as to whether you had really taken it—but it was my first warning that you might be playing a deep game against me, incomprehensible as the action was to my mind. I subsequently reflected that I had been eating an apple, instead of taking the drink he first offered me, in the dead wretch's rooms on the night he came to his merited end. From this I assume that your design was in some way to compare what remained of the two apples—although I do not presume to fathom the depths of your detective system. Still, I have heard of many of your cases, and profoundly admire the keenness you exhibit. I am thought to be a keen man myself, but although I was able, to some extent, to hold my own to-night, I admit that your acumen in this case alone is something beyond me.

"I do not know by whom you are commissioned to hunt me, nor to what extent you may be acquainted with my connection with the creature I killed. I have sufficient respect for you, however, to wish that you should not regard me as a vicious criminal, and a couple of hours to spare in which to offer you an explanation that may persuade you that such is not altogether the case. A hasty and violent temper I admit possessing; but even now I cannot regret the one crime it has led me into—for it is, I suppose, strictly speaking, a crime. For it was the man Foggatt who made a felon of my father before the eyes of the world, and killed him with shame. It was he who murdered my mother, and none the less murdered her because she died of a broken heart. That he was also a thief and a hypocrite might have concerned me little, but for that.

"Of my father I remember very little. He must, I fear, have been a weak and incapable man in many respects. He had no business abilities—in fact, was quite unable to understand the complicated business matters in which he largely dealt. Foggatt was a consummate master of all those arts of financial jugglery that make so many fortunes, and ruin so many others, in matters of company promoting, stocks and shares. He was unable to exercise them, however, because of a great financial disaster in which he had been mixed up a few years before, and which made his name one to be avoided in future. In these circumstances he made a sort of secret and informal partnership with my father, who, ostensibly alone in the business, acted throughout on the directions of Foggatt, understanding as little of what he did, poor, simple man, as a schoolboy would have done. The transactions carried on went from small to large, and, unhappily, from honourable to dishonourable. My father relied on the superior abilities of Foggatt with an absolute trust, carrying out each day the directions given him privately the previous evening, buying, selling, printing prospectuses, signing whatever had to be signed, all with sole responsibility and as sole partner, while Foggatt, behind the scenes, absorbed the larger share of the profits. In brief, my unhappy and foolish father was a mere tool in the hands of the cunning scoundrel who pulled all the wires of the business, himself unseen and irresponsible. At last three companies, for the promotion of which my father was responsible, came to grief in a heap. Fraud was written large over all their history, and, while Foggatt retired with his plunder, my father was left to meet ruin, disgrace, and imprisonment. From beginning to end he, and he only, was responsible. There was no shred of evidence to connect Foggatt with the matter, and no means of escape from the net drawn about my father. He lived through three years of imprisonment and then, entirely abandoned by the man who had made use of his simplicity, he died—of nothing but shame and a broken heart.

"Of this I knew nothing at the time. Again and again, as a small boy, I remember asking of my mother why I had no father at home, as other boys had—unconscious of the stab I thus inflicted on her gentle heart. Of her my earliest, as well as my latest, memory is that of a pale, weeping woman, who grudged to let me out of her sight.

"Little by little I learnt the whole cause of my mother's grief, for she had no other confidant, and I fear my character developed early, for my first coherent remembrance of the matter is that of a childish design to take a table-knife and kill the bad man who had made my father die in prison and caused my mother to cry.

"One thing, however, I never knew: the name of that bad man. Again and again, as I grew older, I demanded to know, but my mother always withheld it from me, with a gentle reminder that vengeance was for a greater hand than mine.

"I was seventeen years of age when my mother died. I believe that nothing but her strong attachment to myself and her desire to see me safely started in life kept her alive so long. Then I found that through all those years of narrowed means she had contrived to scrape and save a little money—sufficient, as it afterwards proved, to see me through the examinations for entrance to my profession, with the generous assistance of my father's old legal advisers, who gave me my articles, and who have all along treated me with extreme kindness.

"For most of the succeeding years my life does not concern the matter in hand. I was a lawyer's clerk in my benefactors' service, and afterwards a qualified man among their assistants. All through, the firm were careful, in pursuance of my poor mother's wishes, that I should not learn the name or whereabouts of the man who had wrecked her life and my father's. I first met the man himself at the Clifton Club, where I had gone with an acquaintance who was a member. It was not till afterwards that I understood his curious awkwardness on that occasion. A week later I called (as I have frequently done) at the building in which your office is situated, on business with a solicitor who has an office on the floor above your own. On the stairs I almost ran against Mr. Foggatt. He started and turned pale, exhibiting signs of alarm that I could not understand, and asked me if I wished to see him.

"'No,' I replied; 'I didn't know you lived here. I am after somebody else just now. Aren't you well?'

"He looked at me rather doubtfully, and said he was *not* very well.

"I met him twice or thrice after that, and on each occasion his manner grew more friendly, in a servile, flattering, and mean sort of way—a thing unpleasant enough in anybody, but doubly so in the intercourse of a man with another young enough to be his own son. Still, of course, I treated the man civilly enough. On one occasion he asked me into his rooms to look at a rather fine picture he had lately bought, and observed casually, lifting a large revolver from the mantelpiece :—

"'You see I am prepared for any unwelcome visitors to my little den! He! he!'

"YOU SEE I AM PREPARED."

Conceiving him, of course, to refer to burglars, I could not help wondering at the forced and hollow character of his laugh. As we went down the stairs he said, 'I think we know one another pretty well now, Mr. Mason, eh? And if I could do anything to advance your professional prospects I should be glad of the chance, of course. I understand the struggles of a young professional man—he! he!' It was the forced laugh again, and the man spoke nervously. 'I think,' he added, 'that if you will drop in to-morrow evening, perhaps I may have a little proposal to make. Will you?'

"I assented, wondering what this proposal could be. Perhaps this eccentric old gentleman was a good fellow, after all, anxious to do me a good turn, and his awkwardness was nothing but a natural delicacy in breaking the ice. I was not so flush of good friends as to be willing to lose one. He might be desirous of putting business in my way.

"I went, and was received with a cordiality that even then seemed a little over-effusive. We sat and talked of one thing and another for a long while, and I began to wonder when Mr. Foggatt was coming to the point that most interested me. Several times he invited me to drink and smoke, but long usage to athletic training has given me a distaste for both practices, and I declined. At last he began to talk about myself. He was afraid that my professional prospects in this country were not great, but he had heard that in some of the Colonies — South Africa, for example—young lawyers had brilliant opportunities.

"'If you'd like to go there,' he said, 'I've no doubt, with a little capital, a clever man like you could get a grand practice together very soon. Or you might buy a share in some good established practice. I should be glad to let you have five hundred pounds, or even a little more if that wouldn't satisfy you, and——'

"I stood aghast. Why should this man, almost a stranger, offer me five hundred pounds, or even more—'if that wouldn't satisfy' me? What claim had I on him? It was very generous of him, of course, but out of the question. I was at least a gentleman, and had a gentleman's self-respect. Meanwhile he had gone maundering on, in a halting sort of way, and presently let slip a sentence that struck me like a blow between the eyes.

"'I shouldn't like you to bear ill-will because of what has happened in the past,' he said. 'Your late — your late lamented mother—I'm afraid—she had unworthy suspicions—I'm sure—it was best for all parties—your father always appreciated——'

"I set back my chair and stood erect before him. This grovelling wretch, forcing the words through his dry lips, was the thief who had made another of my father and had brought to miserable ends the lives of both my parents. Everything was clear. The creature went in fear of me, never imagining that I did not know him, and sought to buy me off; to buy me from the remembrance of my dead mother's broken heart for £500—£500 that he had made my father steal for him. I said not a word. But the memory of all my mother's bitter years, and a savage sense of this crowning insult to myself, took a hold upon me, and I was a tiger. Even then, I verily believe that one word of repentance, one tone of honest remorse, would have saved him. But he drooped his eyes, snuffled excuses, and stammered of 'unworthy suspicions' and 'no ill-will.' I let him stammer. Presently he looked up and saw my face; and fell back in his chair, sick with terror. I snatched the pistol from the mantelpiece, and, thrusting it in his face, shot him where he sat.

"My subsequent coolness and quietness surprise me now. I took my hat and stepped toward the door. But there were voices on the stairs. The door was locked on the inside, and I left it so. I went back and quietly opened a window. Below was a clear drop into darkness, and above was plain wall; but away to one side, where the slope of the gable sprang from the roof, an iron gutter ended, supported by a strong bracket. It was the only way. I got upon the sill and carefully shut the window behind me, for people were already knocking at the lobby door. From the end of the sill, holding on by the reveal of the window with one hand, leaning and stretching my utmost, I caught the gutter, swung myself clear, and scrambled on the roof. I climbed over many roofs before I found, in an adjoining street, a ladder lashed perpendicularly against the front of a house in course of repair. This, to me, was an easy opportunity of descent, notwithstanding the boards fastened over the face of the ladder, and I availed myself of it.

"I STOOD ERECT BEFORE HIM."

"I have taken some time and trouble in order that you (so far as I am aware the only human being beside myself who knows me to be the author of Foggatt's death) shall have at least the means of appraising my crime at its just value of culpability. How much you already know of what I have told you I cannot guess. I am wrong, hardened and flagitious, I make no doubt, but I speak of the facts as they are. You see the thing, of course, from your own point of view—I from mine. And I remember my mother.

"Trusting that you will forgive the odd freak of a man—a criminal, let us say—who makes a confidant of the man set to hunt him down, I beg leave to be, Sir, your obedient servant, "SIDNEY MASON."

I read the singular document through and handed it back to Hewitt.

"How does it strike you?" Hewitt asked.

"Mason would seem to be a man of very marked character," I said. "Certainly no fool. And, if his tale is true, Foggatt is no great loss to the world."

"Just so—if the tale is true. Personally, I am disposed to believe it is."

"Where was the letter posted?"

"It wasn't posted. It was handed in with the others from the front door letter-box this morning in an unstamped envelope. He must have dropped it in himself during the night. Paper," Hewitt proceeded, holding it up to the light, "Turkey mill, ruled foolscap. Envelope, blue official shape, Pirie's watermark. Both quite ordinary and no special marks."

"Where do you suppose he's gone?"

"Impossible to guess. Some might think he meant suicide by the expression 'beyond the reach even of your abilities of search,' but I scarcely think he is the sort of man to do that. No, there is no telling. Something may be got by inquiring at his late address, of course; but when such a man tells you he doesn't think you will find him, you may count upon its being a difficult job. His opinion is not to be despised"

"What shall you do?"

"Put the letter in the box with the casts for the police. *Fiat justitia*, you know, without any question of sentiment. As to the apple—I really think, if the police will let me, I'll make you a present of it. Keep it somewhere as a souvenir of your absolute deficiency in reflective observation in this case, and look at it whenever you feel yourself growing dangerously conceited. It should cure you."

"TURKEY MILL, RULED FOOLSCAP."

This is the history of the withered and almost petrified half-apple that stands in my cabinet among a number of flint implements and one or two rather fine old Roman vessels. Of Mr. Sidney Mason we never heard another word. The police did their best, but he had left not a track behind him. His rooms were left almost undisturbed, and he had gone without anything in the way of elaborate preparation for his journey, and yet without leaving a trace of his intentions.

Martin Hewitt, Investigator.

BY ARTHUR MORRISON.

IV.—THE CASE OF THE DIXON TORPEDO.

EWITT was very apt, in conversation, to dwell upon the many curious chances and coincidences that he had observed, not only in connection with his own cases, but also in matters dealt with by the official police, with whom he was on terms of pretty regular and, indeed, friendly acquaintanceship. He has told me many an anecdote of singular happenings to Scotland Yard officials with whom he has exchanged experiences. Of Inspector Nettings, for instance, who spent many weary months in a search for a man wanted by the American Government, and in the end found, by the merest accident (a misdirected call), that the man had been lodging next door to himself the whole of the time; just as ignorant, of course, as was the inspector himself as to the enemy at the other side of the party-wall. Also of another inspector, whose name I cannot recall, who, having been given rather meagre and insufficient details of a man whom he anticipated having great difficulty in finding, went straight down the stairs of the office where he had received instructions, and actually *fell over* the man near the door, where he had stooped down to tie his shoe-lace! There were cases, too, in which, when a great and notorious crime had been committed and various persons had been arrested on suspicion, some were found among them who had long been badly wanted for some other crime altogether. Many criminals had met their deserts by venturing out of their own particular line of crime into another: often a man who got into trouble over something comparatively small, found himself in for a startlingly larger trouble, the result of some previous misdeed that otherwise would have gone unpunished. The rouble note-forger, Mirsky, might never have been handed over to the Russian authorities had he confined his genius to forgery alone. It was generally supposed at the time of his extradition that he had communicated with the Russian Embassy, with a view to giving himself up—a foolish proceeding on his part, it would seem, since his whereabouts, indeed, even his identity as the forger, had not been suspected. He *had* communicated with the Russian Embassy, it is true, but for quite a different purpose, as Martin Hewitt well understood at the time. What that purpose was is now for the first time published.

The time was half-past one in the afternoon, and Hewitt sat in his inner office examining and comparing the handwriting of two letters by the aid of a large lens. He put down the lens and glanced at the clock on the mantelpiece with a premonition of lunch; and as he did so his clerk quietly entered the room with one of those printed slips which were kept for the announcement of unknown visitors. It was filled up in a hasty and almost illegible hand thus:—

Name of visitor: *F. Graham Dixon.*
Address: *Chancery Lane.*
Business: *Private and urgent.*

"Show Mr. Dixon in," said Martin Hewitt.

Mr. Dixon was a gaunt, worn-looking man of fifty or so, well although rather carelessly dressed, and carrying in his strong though drawn face and dullish eyes the look that characterizes the life-long strenuous brain-worker. He leaned forward anxiously in the chair which Hewitt offered him, and told his story with a great deal of very natural agitation.

"You may possibly have heard, Mr. Hewitt—I know there are rumours—of the new locomotive torpedo which the Government is about adopting; it is, in fact, the Dixon torpedo, my own invention; and in every respect—not merely in my own opinion, but in that of the Government experts—by far the most efficient and certain yet produced. It will travel at least four hundred yards farther than any torpedo now made, with perfect accuracy of aim (a very great desideratum, let me tell you), and will carry an unprecedentedly heavy charge. There are other advantages, speed, simple discharge, and so forth, that I needn't bother you about. The machine is the result of many years of work and disappointment, and its design has only been arrived at by a careful balancing of principles and means, which are expressed on the only four existing sets of drawings. The whole thing, I need hardly tell you, is a profound secret, and you may judge of my present state of mind when I tell you that one set of drawings has been stolen."

"From your house?"

"YOU WISH ME TO UNDERTAKE THE RECOVERY OF THESE DRAWINGS?"

"From my office, in Chancery Lane, this morning. The four sets of drawings were distributed thus: Two were at the Admiralty Office, one being a finished set on thick paper, and the other a set of tracings therefrom; and the other two were at my own office, one being a pencilled set, uncoloured —a sort of finished draft, you understand—and the other a set of tracings similar to those at the Admiralty. It is this last set that has gone. The two sets were kept together in one drawer in my room. Both were there at ten this morning, of that I am sure, for I had to go to that very drawer for something else, when I first arrived. But at twelve the tracings had vanished."

"You suspect somebody, probably?"

"I cannot. It is a most extraordinary thing. Nobody has left the office (except myself, and then only to come to you) since ten this morning, and there has been no visitor. And yet the drawings are gone!"

"But have you searched the place?"

"Of course I have. It was twelve o'clock when I first discovered my loss, and I have been turning the place upside down ever since—I and my assistants. Every drawer has been emptied, every desk and table turned over, the very carpet and linoleum have been taken up, but there is not a sign of the drawings. My men even insisted on turning all their pockets inside out, although I never for a moment suspected either of them, and it would take a pretty big pocket to hold the drawings, doubled up as small as they might be."

"You say your men—there are two, I understand—had neither left the office?"

"Neither; and they are both staying in now. Worsfold suggested that it would be more satisfactory if they did not leave till something was done towards clearing the mystery up, and although, as I have said, I don't suspect either in the least, I acquiesced."

"Just so. Now—I am assuming that you wish me to undertake the recovery of these drawings?"

The engineer nodded hastily.

"Very good; I will go round to your office. But first perhaps you can tell me something about your assistants; something it might be awkward to tell me in their presence, you know. Mr. Worsfold, for instance?"

"He is my draughtsman—a very excellent and intelligent man, a very smart man, indeed, and, I feel sure, quite beyond suspicion. He has prepared many important drawings for me (he has been with me nearly ten years now), and I have always found him trustworthy. But, of course, the temptation in this case would be enormous. Still, I cannot suspect Worsfold. Indeed, how can I suspect anybody in the circumstances?"

"The other, now?"

"His name's Ritter. He is merely a tracer, not a fully skilled draughtsman. He is quite a decent young fellow, and I have had him two years. I don't consider him particularly smart, or he would have learned a little more of his business by this time. But I don't see the least reason to suspect him. As I said before, I can't reasonably suspect anybody."

"Very well; we will get to Chancery Lane now, if you please, and you can tell me more as we go."

"I have a cab waiting. What else can I tell you?"

"I understand the position to be succinctly this: the drawings were in the office when you arrived. Nobody came out, and nobody went in; and *yet* they vanished. Is that so?"

"That is so. When I say that absolutely

nobody came in, of course I except the postman. He brought a couple of letters during the morning. I mean that absolutely nobody came past the barrier in the outer office—the usual thing, you know, like a counter, with a frame of ground glass over it."

"I quite understand that. But I think you said that the drawings were in a drawer in your *own* room—not the outer office, where the draughtsmen are, I presume?"

"That is the case. It is an inner room, or, rather, a room parallel with the other, and communicating with it; just as your own room is, which we have just left."

"But then, you say you never left your office, and yet the drawings vanished—apparently by some unseen agency—while you were there, in the room?"

"Let me explain more clearly." The cab was bowling smoothly along the Strand, and the engineer took out a pocket-book and pencil. "I fear," he proceeded, "that I am a little confused in my explanation—I am naturally rather agitated. As you will see presently, my offices consist of three rooms, two at one side of a corridor, and the other opposite: thus." He made a rapid pencil sketch.

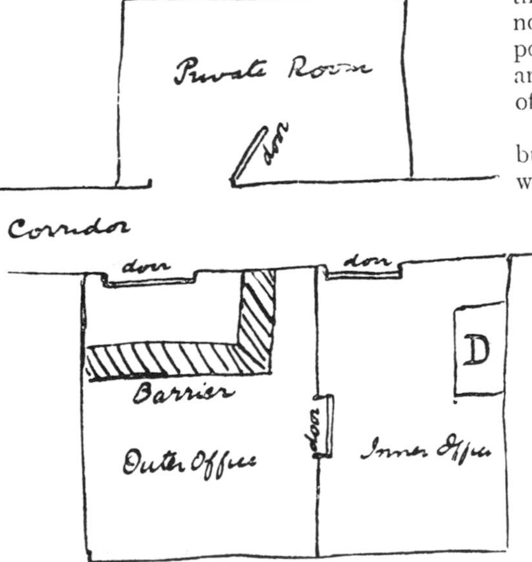

"In the outer office my men usually work. In the inner office I work myself. These rooms communicate, as you see, by a door. Our ordinary way in and out of the place is by the door of the outer office leading into the corridor, and we first pass through the usual lifting flap in the barrier. The door leading from the *inner* office to the corridor is always kept locked on the inside, and I don't suppose I unlock it once in three months. It has not been unlocked all the morning. The drawer in which the missing drawings were kept, and in which I saw them at ten o'clock this morning, is at the place marked D—it is a large chest of shallow drawers, in which the plans lie flat."

"I quite understand. Then there is the private room opposite. What of that?"

"That is a sort of private sitting-room that I rarely use, except for business interviews of a very private nature. When I said I never left my office I did not mean that I never stirred out of the inner office. I was about in one room and another, both the outer and the inner offices, and once I went into the private room for five minutes, but nobody came either in or out of any of the rooms at that time, for the door of the private room was wide open and I was standing at the book-case (I had gone to consult a book), just inside the door, with a full view of the doors opposite. Indeed, Worsfold was at the door of the outer office most of the short time. He came to ask me a question."

"Well," Hewitt replied, "it all comes to the simple first statement. You know that nobody left the place or arrived, except the postman, who couldn't get near the drawings, and yet the drawings went. Is this your office?"

The cab had stopped before a large stone building. Mr. Dixon alighted and led the way to the first floor. Hewitt took a casual glance round each of the three rooms. There was a sort of door in the frame of ground glass over the barrier, to admit of speech with visitors. This door Hewitt pushed wide open, and left so.

He and the engineer went into the inner office. "Would you like to ask Worsfold and Ritter any questions?" Mr. Dixon inquired.

"Presently. Those are their coats, I take it, hanging just to the right of the outer office door, over the umbrella stand?"

"Yes, those are all their things—coats, hats, stick, and umbrella."

"And those coats were searched, you say?"

"Yes."

"And this is the drawer—thoroughly searched, of course?"

"Oh, certainly, every drawer was taken out and turned over."

"Well, of course, I must assume you made no mistake in your hunt. Now tell me, did

"I WAS STANDING AT THE BOOK-CASE."

anybody know where these plans were beyond yourself and your two men?"

"As far as I can tell, not a soul."

"You don't keep an office-boy?"

"No. There would be nothing for him to do except to post a letter now and again, which Ritter does quite well for."

"As you are quite sure that the drawings were there at ten o'clock, perhaps the thing scarcely matters. But I may as well know if your men have keys of the office?"

"Neither. I have patent locks to each door and I keep all the keys myself. If Worsfold or Ritter arrive before me in the morning, they have to wait to be let in; and I am always present myself when the rooms are cleaned. I have not neglected precautions, you see."

"No. I suppose the object of the theft—assuming it is a theft—is pretty plain: the thief would offer the drawings for sale to some foreign Government?"

"Of course. They would probably command a great sum. I have been looking, as I need hardly tell you, to that invention to secure me a very large fortune, and I shall be ruined, indeed, if the design is taken abroad. I am under the strictest engagements to secrecy with the Admiralty, and not only should I lose all my labour, but I should lose all the confidence reposed in me at head-quarters—should, in fact, be subject to penalties for breach of contract, and my career stopped for ever. I cannot tell you what a serious business this is for me. If you cannot help me, the consequences will be terrible. Bad for the service of the country, too, of course."

"Of course. Now tell me this. It would, I take it, be necessary for the thief to *exhibit* these drawings to anybody anxious to buy the secret—I mean, he couldn't describe the invention by word of mouth?"

"Oh, no, that would be impossible. The drawings are of the most complicated description, and full of figures upon which the whole thing depends. Indeed, one would have to be a skilled expert properly to appreciate the design at all. Various principles of hydrostatics, chemistry, electricity, and pneumatics are most delicately manipulated and adjusted, and the smallest error or omission in any part would upset the whole. No, the drawings are necessary to the thing, and they are gone."

At this moment the door of the outer office was heard to open, and somebody entered. The door between the two offices was ajar, and Hewitt could see right through to the glass door left open over the barrier, and into the space beyond. A well-dressed, dark, bushy-bearded man stood there carrying a hand-bag, which he placed on the ledge before him. Hewitt raised his hand to enjoin silence. The man spoke in a rather high-pitched voice and with a slight accent. "Is Mr. Dixon now within?" he asked.

"He is engaged," answered one of the draughtsmen; "very particularly engaged. I'm afraid you won't be able to see him this afternoon. Can I give him any message?"

"This is two—the second time I have come to-day. Not two hours ago Mr. Dixon himself tells me to call again. I have a very important—very excellent steam-packing to show him that is very cheap and the best of the market." The man tapped his bag. "I have just taken orders from the largest railway companies. Cannot I see him, for one second only? I will not detain him."

"Really, I'm sure you can't this afternoon—he isn't seeing anybody. But if you'll leave your name——"

"My name is Hunter; but what the good of that? He ask me to call a little later and I come, and now he is engaged. It is a very great pity." And the man snatched up his bag and walking-stick and stalked off indignantly.

Hewitt stood still, gazing through the small aperture in the doorway.

"You'd scarcely expect a man with such a name as Hunter to talk with that accent, would you?" he observed, musingly. "It isn't a French accent, nor a German; but it seems foreign. You don't happen to know him, I suppose?"

"No, I don't. He called here about half-past twelve, just while we were in the middle of our search and I was frantic over the loss of the drawings. I was in the outer office myself, and told him to call later. I have lots of such agents here, anxious to sell all sorts of engineering appliances. But what will you do now? Shall you see my men?"

"I think," said Hewitt, rising, "I think I'll get you to question them yourself."

"Myself?"

"Yes, I have a reason. Will you trust me with the key of the private room opposite? I will go over there for a little, while you talk to your men in this room. Bring them in here and shut the door—I can look after the office from across the corridor, you know. Ask them each to detail his exact movements about the office this morning, and get them to recall each visitor who has been here from the beginning of the week. I'll let you know the reason of this later. Come across to me in a few minutes."

Hewitt took the key and passed through the outer office into the corridor.

Ten minutes later, Mr. Dixon, having questioned his draughtsmen, followed him. He found Hewitt standing before the table in the private room, on which lay several drawings on tracing-paper.

"See here, Mr. Dixon," said Hewitt, "I think these are the drawings you are anxious about?"

The engineer sprang toward them with a cry of delight. "Why, yes, yes," he exclaimed, turning them over, "every one of them. But where—how—they must have been in the place after all, then? What a fool I have been!"

"MY NAME IS HUNTER."

Hewitt shook his head. "I'm afraid you're not quite so lucky as you think, Mr. Dixon," he said. "These drawings have most certainly been out of the house for a little while. Never mind how—we'll talk of that after. There is no time to lose. Tell me, how long would it take a good draughtsman to copy them?"

"They couldn't possibly be traced over properly in less than two or two and a half long days of very hard work," Dixon replied, with eagerness.

"Ah! then, it is as I feared. These tracings have been photographed, Mr. Dixon, and our task is one of every possible difficulty. If they had been copied in the ordinary way, one might hope to get hold of the copy. But photography upsets everything. Copies can be multiplied with such amazing facility that, once the thief gets a decent start, it is almost hopeless to checkmate him. The only chance is to get at the negatives before copies are taken. I must act at once; and I fear, between ourselves, it may be necessary for me to step very distinctly over the line of the law in the matter. You see, to get at those negatives may involve something very like housebreaking. There must be no delay—no waiting for legal procedure—or the mischief is done. Indeed, I very much question whether you have any legal remedy, strictly speaking."

"Mr. Hewitt, I implore you, do what you can. I need not say that all I have is at your disposal. I will guarantee to hold you harmless for anything that may happen. But do, I entreat you, do everything possible. Think of what the consequences may be!"

"Well, yes, so I do," Hewitt remarked, with a smile. "The consequences to me, if I were charged with housebreaking, might be something that no amount of guarantee could mitigate. However, I will do what I can, if only from patriotic motives. Now, I must see your tracer, Ritter. He is the traitor in the camp."

"Ritter? But how?"

"Never mind that now. You are upset and agitated, and had better not know more than necessary for a little while, in case you say or do something unguarded. With Ritter I must take a deep course; what I don't know I must appear to know, and that will seem more likely to him if I disclaim acquaintance with what I do know. But first put these tracings safely away out of sight."

Dixon slipped them behind his book-case.

"Now," Hewitt pursued, "call Mr. Worsfold and give him something to do that will keep him in the inner office across the way, and tell him to send Ritter here."

Mr. Dixon called his chief draughtsman and requested him to put in order the drawings in the drawers of the inner room that had been disarranged by the search, and to send Ritter, as Hewitt had suggested.

Ritter walked into the private room, with an air of respectful attention. He was a puffy-faced, unhealthy-looking young man, with very small eyes and a loose, mobile mouth.

"Sit down, Mr. Ritter," Hewitt said, in a stern voice. "Your recent transactions with your friend, Mr. Hunter, are well known both to Mr. Dixon and myself."

Ritter, who had at first leaned easily back in his chair, started forward at this, and paled.

"You are surprised, I observe; but you should be more careful in your movements out of doors if you do not wish your acquaintances to be known. Mr. Hunter, I believe, has the drawings which Mr. Dixon has lost, and, if so, I am certain that you have given them to him. That, you know, is theft, for which the law provides a severe penalty."

Ritter broke down completely and turned appealingly to Mr. Dixon:—

"Oh, sir," he pleaded, "it isn't so bad, I assure you. I was tempted, I confess, and hid the drawings; but they are still in the office, and I can give them to you—really, I can."

"Indeed?" Hewitt went on. "Then, in that case, perhaps you'd better get them at once. Just go and fetch them in—we won't trouble to observe your hiding-place. I'll only keep this door open, to be sure you don't lose your way, you know—down the stairs, for instance."

The wretched Ritter, with hanging head, slunk into the office opposite. Presently he reappeared, looking, if possible, ghastlier than before. He looked irresolutely down the corridor, as if meditating a run for it, but Hewitt stepped toward him and motioned him back to the private room.

"You mustn't try any more of that sort of humbug," Hewitt said, with increased severity. "The drawings are gone, and you have stolen them — you know that well enough. Now attend to me. If you received your deserts, Mr. Dixon would send for a policeman this moment, and have you hauled off to the gaol that is your proper place. But, unfortunately, your accomplice, who calls himself Hunter—but who has other names beside that, as I happen to know—has the drawings, and it is absolutely

"SIT DOWN, MR. RITTER."

necessary that these should be recovered. I am afraid that it will be necessary, therefore, to come to some arrangement with this scoundrel—to square him, in fact. Now, just take that pen and paper, and write to your confederate as I dictate. You know the alternative if you cause any difficulty."

Ritter reached tremblingly for the pen.

"Address him in your usual way," Hewitt proceeded. "Say this: '*There has been an alteration in the plans.*' Have you got that? '*There has been an alteration in the plans. I shall be alone here at six o'clock. Please come, without fail.*' Have you got it? Very well, sign it, and address the envelope. He must come here, and then we may arrange matters. In the meantime, you will remain in the inner office opposite."

The note was written, and Martin Hewitt, without glancing at the address, thrust it into his pocket. When Ritter was safely in the inner office, however, he drew it out and read the address. "I see," he observed, "he uses the same name, Hunter; 27, Little Carton Street, Westminster, is the address, and there I shall go at once with the note. If the man comes here, I think you had better lock him in with Ritter, and send for a policeman—it may at least frighten him. My object is, of course, to get the man away, and then, if possible, to invade his house, in some way or another, and steal or smash his negatives if they are there and to be found. Stay here, in any case, till I return. And don't forget to lock up those tracings."

It was about six o'clock when Hewitt returned, alone, but with a smiling face that told of good fortune at first sight.

"First, Mr. Dixon," he said, as he dropped into an easy chair in the private room, "let me ease your mind by the information that I have been most extraordinarily lucky—in fact, I think you have no further cause for anxiety. Here are the negatives. They were not all quite dry when I—well, what?—stole them, I suppose I must say; so that they have stuck together a bit, and probably the films are damaged. But you don't mind that, I suppose?"

He laid a small parcel, wrapped in newspaper, on the table. The engineer hastily tore away the paper and took up five or six glass photographic negatives, of the half-plate size, which were damp, and stuck together by the gelatine films, in couples. He held them, one after another, up to the light of the window, and glanced through them. Then, with a great sigh of relief, he placed them on the hearth and pounded them to dust and fragments with the poker.

For a few seconds neither spoke. Then Dixon, flinging himself into a chair, said:—

"Mr. Hewitt, I can't express my obligation to you. What would have happened if you had failed I prefer not to think of. But what shall we do with Ritter now? The other man hasn't been here yet, by-the-bye."

"No—the fact is, I didn't deliver the letter. The worthy gentleman saved me a world of trouble by taking himself out of the way." Hewitt laughed. "I'm afraid he has rather got himself into a mess by trying two kinds of theft at once, and you may not be sorry to hear that his attempt on your torpedo plans is likely to bring him a dose of penal servitude for something else. I'll tell you what has happened.

"Little Carton Street, Westminster, I found to be a seedy sort of place—one of those old streets that have seen much better days. A good many people seem to live in each house—they are fairly large houses, by the way—and there is quite a company of bell-handles on each doorpost—all down the side, like organ-stops. A barber had possession of the ground-floor front of No. 27 for trade purposes, so to him I went. 'Can you tell me,' I said, 'where in this house I can find Mr. Hunter?' He looked doubtful, so I went on: 'His friend will do, you know—I can't think of his name; foreign gentleman, dark, with a bushy beard.'

"The barber understood at once. 'Oh, that's Mirsky, I expect,' he said. 'Now I come to think of it, he has had letters addressed to Hunter once or twice—I've took 'em in. Top floor back.'

"This was good, so far. I had got at 'Mr. Hunter's' other alias. So, by way of possessing him with the idea that I knew all about him, I determined to ask for him as Mirsky, before handing over the letter addressed to him as Hunter. A little bluff of that sort is invaluable at the right time. At the top floor back I stopped at the door and tried to open it at once, but it was locked. I could hear somebody scuttling about within, as though carrying things about, and I knocked again. In a little while the door opened about a foot, and there stood Mr. Hunter—or Mirsky, as you like—the man who, in the character of a traveller in steam-packing, came here twice to-day. He was in his shirt sleeves and cuddled something under his arm, hastily covered with a spotted pocket-handkerchief.

"'I have called to see M. Mirsky,' I said, 'with a confidential letter——'

"'Oh, yas, yas,' he answered, hastily; 'I know—I know. Excuse me one minute.' And he rushed off downstairs with his parcel.

"Here was a noble chance. For a moment I thought of following him, in case there might be anything interesting in the parcel. But I had to decide in a moment, and I decided on trying the room. I slipped inside the door, and, finding the key on the inside, locked it. It was a confused sort of room, with a little iron bedstead in one corner and a sort of rough boarded inclosure in another. This I rightly conjectured to be the photographic dark-room, and made for it at once.

"There was plenty of light within when the door was left open, and I made at once for the drying-rack that was fastened over the sink. There were a number of negatives in it, and I began hastily examining them one after another. In the middle of this, our friend Mirsky returned and tried the door. He rattled violently at the handle and pushed. Then he called.

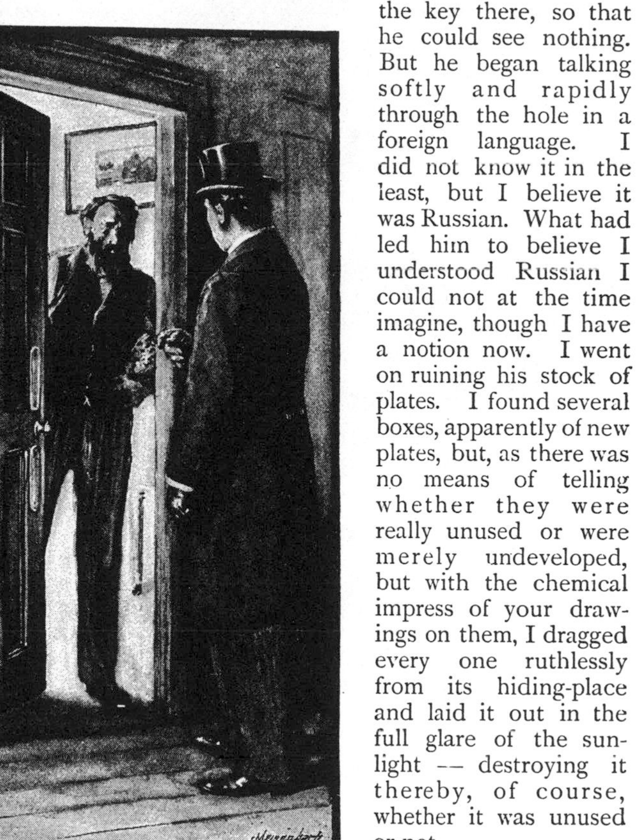
"I HAVE CALLED TO SEE M. MIRSKY."

"At this moment I had come upon the first of the negatives you have just smashed. The fixing and washing had evidently only lately been completed, and the negative was drying on the rack. I seized it, of course, and the others which stood by it.

"'Who are you, there, inside?' Mirsky shouted indignantly from the landing. 'Why for you go in my room like that? Open this door at once, or I call the police!'

"I took no notice. I had got the full number of negatives, one for each drawing, but I was not by any means sure that he had not taken an extra set; so I went on hunting down the rack. There were no more, so I set to work to turn out all the undeveloped plates. It was quite possible, you see, that the other set, if it existed, had not yet been developed.

"Mirsky changed his tune. After a little more banging and shouting, I could hear him kneel down and try the key-hole. I had left the key there, so that he could see nothing. But he began talking softly and rapidly through the hole in a foreign language. I did not know it in the least, but I believe it was Russian. What had led him to believe I understood Russian I could not at the time imagine, though I have a notion now. I went on ruining his stock of plates. I found several boxes, apparently of new plates, but, as there was no means of telling whether they were really unused or were merely undeveloped, but with the chemical impress of your drawings on them, I dragged every one ruthlessly from its hiding-place and laid it out in the full glare of the sunlight — destroying it thereby, of course, whether it was unused or not.

"Mirsky left off talking, and I heard him quietly sneaking off. Perhaps his conscience was not sufficiently clear to warrant an appeal to the police, but it seemed to me rather probable at the time that that was what he was going for. So I hurried on with my work. I found three dark slides—the parts that carry the plates in the back of the camera, you know—one of them fixed in the camera itself. These I opened, and exposed the plates to ruination as before. I suppose nobody ever did so much devastation in a photographic studio in ten minutes as I managed.

"I had spoilt every plate I could find and had the developed negatives safely in my pocket, when I happened to glance at a porcelain washing-well under the sink. There was one negative in that, and I took it up. It was *not* a negative of a drawing

"HE BEGAN TALKING SOFTLY AND RAPIDLY."

of yours, but of a Russian twenty-rouble note!

"This *was* a discovery. The only possible reason any man could have for photographing a bank-note was the manufacture of an etched plate for the production of forged copies. I was almost as pleased as I had been at the discovery of *your* negatives. He might bring the police now as soon as he liked; I could turn the tables on him completely. I began to hunt about for anything else relating to this negative.

"I found an inking-roller, some old pieces of blanket (used in printing from plates), and in a corner on the floor, heaped over with newspapers and rubbish, a small copying-press. There was also a dish of acid, but not an etched plate or a printed note to be seen. I was looking at the press, with the negative in one hand and the inking-roller in the other, when I became conscious of a shadow across the window. I looked up quickly, and there was Mirsky, hanging over from some ledge or projection to the side of the window, and staring straight at me, with a look of unmistakable terror and apprehension.

"The face vanished immediately. I had to move a table to get at the window, and by the time I had opened it, there was no sign or sound of the rightful tenant of the room. I had no doubt now of his reason for carrying a parcel downstairs. He probably mistook me for another visitor he was expecting, and, knowing he must take this visitor into his room, threw the papers and rubbish over the press, and put up his plates and papers in a bundle and secreted them somewhere downstairs, lest his occupation should be observed.

"Plainly, my duty now was to communicate with the police. So, by the help of my friend the barber downstairs, a messenger was found and a note sent over to Scotland Yard. I awaited, of course, for the arrival of the police, and occupied the interval in another look round—finding nothing important, however. When the official detective arrived he recognised at once the importance of the case. A large number of forged Russian notes have been put into circulation on the Continent lately, it seems, and it was suspected that they came from London. The Russian Government have been sending urgent messages to the police here on the subject.

"Of course I said nothing about your business; but while I was talking with the Scotland Yard man a letter was left by a messenger, addressed to Mirsky. The letter will be examined, of course, by the proper authorities, but I was not a little interested to perceive that the envelope bore the Russian Imperial arms above the words, 'Russian Embassy.' Now, why should Mirsky communicate with the Russian Embassy? Certainly not to let the officials know that he was carrying on a very extensive and lucrative business in the manufacture of spurious Russian notes. I think it is rather more than possible that he wrote—probably before he actually got your drawings—to say that he could sell information of the highest importance, and that this letter was a reply. Further, I think it quite possible that, when I asked for him by his Russian name and spoke of 'a confidential letter,' he at once concluded that *I* had come from the Embassy in answer to his letter. That would account for his addressing me in Russian through the keyhole; and, of course, an official from the Russian Embassy would be the very last person

"MIRSKY WAS STARING STRAIGHT AT ME."

in the world whom he would like to observe any indications of his little etching experiments. But anyhow, be that as it may," Hewitt concluded, "your drawings are safe now, and if once Mirsky is caught—and I think it likely, for a man in his shirt-sleeves, with scarcely any start and, perhaps, no money about him, hasn't a great chance to get away—if he is caught, I say, he will probably get something handsome at St. Petersburg in the way of imprisonment, or Siberia, or what-not; so that you will be amply avenged."

"Yes, but I don't at all understand this business of the drawings even now. How in the world were they taken out of the place, and how in the world did you find it out?"

"Nothing could be simpler; and yet the plan was rather ingenious. I'll tell you exactly how the thing revealed itself to me. From your original description of the case, many people would consider that an impossibility had been performed. Nobody had gone out and nobody had come in, and yet the drawings had been taken away. But an impossibility is an impossibility after all, and as drawings don't run away of themselves, plainly somebody had taken them, unaccountable as it might seem. Now, as they were in your inner office, the only people who could have got at them beside yourself were your assistants, so that it was pretty clear that one of them, at least, had something to do with the business. You told me that Worsfold was an excellent and intelligent draughtsman. Well, if such a man as that meditated treachery, he would probably be able to carry away the design in his head—at any rate, a little at a time—and would be under no necessity to run the risk of stealing a set of the drawings. But Ritter, you remarked, was an inferior sort of man, 'not particularly smart,' I think, were your words—only a mechanical sort of tracer. *He* would be unlikely to be able to carry in his head the complicated details of such designs as yours, and, being in a subordinate position, and continually overlooked, he would find it impossible to make copies of the plans in the office. So that, to begin with, I thought I saw the most probable path to start on.

"When I looked round the rooms I pushed open the glass door of the barrier and left the door to the inner office ajar, in order to be able to see anything that *might* happen in any part of the place, without actually expecting any definite development. While we were talking, as it happened, our friend Mirsky (or Hunter—as you please) came into the outer office, and my attention was instantly called to him by the first thing he did. Did you notice anything peculiar yourself?"

"No, really I can't say I did. He seemed to behave much as any traveller or agent might."

"Well, what I noticed was the fact that as soon as he entered the place he put his walking-stick into the umbrella stand, over there by the door, close by where he stood; a most unusual thing for a casual caller to do, before even knowing whether you were in. This made me watch him closely. I perceived, with increased interest, that the stick was exactly of the same kind and pattern as one already standing there; also a curious thing. I kept my eyes carefully on those sticks, and was all the more interested and edified to see, when he left, that he took the *other* stick—not the one he came with—from the stand, and carried it away, leaving his own behind. I might have followed him, but I decided that more could be learnt by staying—as, in fact, proved to be the case. This, by-the-bye, is the stick he carried away with him. I took the liberty of fetching it back from Westminster, because I conceive it to be Ritter's property."

Hewitt produced the stick. It was an ordinary, thick Malacca cane, with a buck-horn handle and a silver band. Hewitt bent it across his knee, and laid it on the table.

"Yes," Dixon answered, "that is Ritter's stick. I think I have often seen it in the stand. But what in the world——"

"One moment; I'll just fetch the stick Mirsky left behind." And Hewitt stepped across the corridor.

He returned with another stick, apparently an exact facsimile of the other, and placed it by the side of the other.

"When your assistants went into the inner room, I carried this stick off for a minute or two. I knew it was not Worsfold's, because there was an umbrella there with his initial on the handle. Look at this."

Martin Hewitt gave the handle a twist, and rapidly unscrewed it from the top. Then it was seen that the stick was a mere tube of very thin metal, painted to appear like a Malacca cane.

"It was plain at once that this was no Malacca cane—it wouldn't bend. Inside it I found your tracings, rolled up tightly. You can get a marvellous quantity of thin tracing-paper into a small compass by tight rolling."

"And this—this was the way they were

"HEWITT PRODUCED THE STICK."

brought back!" the engineer exclaimed. "I see that, clearly. But how did they get away? That's as mysterious as ever."

"Not a bit of it. See here. Mirsky gets hold of Ritter, and they agree to get your drawings and photograph them. Ritter is to let his confederate have the drawings, and Mirsky is to bring them back as soon as possible, so that they shan't be missed for a moment. Ritter habitually carries this Malacca cane, and the cunning of Mirsky at once suggests that this tube should be made in outward facsimile. This morning, Mirsky keeps the actual stick and Ritter comes to the office with the tube. He seizes the first opportunity—probably when you were in this private room, and Worsfold was talking to you from the corridor — to get at the tracings, roll them up tightly, and put them in the tube, putting the tube back into the umbrella stand. At half-past twelve, or whenever it was, Mirsky turns up for the first time with the actual stick and exchanges them, just as he afterwards did when he brought the drawings back."

"Yes, but Mirsky came half an hour after they were—oh, yes, I see. What a fool I was! I was forgetting. Of course, when I first missed the tracings they were in this walking-stick, safe enough, and I was tearing my hair out within arm's reach of them!"

"Precisely. And Mirsky took them away before your very eyes. I expect Ritter was in a rare funk when he found that the drawings were missed. He calculated, no doubt, on your not wanting them for the hour or two they would be out of the office."

"How lucky that it struck me to jot a pencil-note on one of them! I might easily have made my note somewhere else, and then I should never have known that they had been away."

"Yes, they didn't give you any too much time to miss them. Well, I think the rest's pretty clear. I brought the tracings in here, screwed up the sham stick and put it back. You identified the tracings and found none missing, and then my course was pretty clear, though it looked difficult. I knew you would be very naturally indignant with Ritter, so, as I wanted to manage him myself, I told you nothing of what he had actually done, for fear that, in your agitated state, you might burst out with something that would spoil my game. To Ritter I pretended to know nothing of the return of the drawings or *how* they had been stolen—the only things I did know with certainty. But I *did* pretend to know all about Mirsky—or Hunter—when, as a matter of fact, I knew nothing at all, except that he probably went under more than one name. That put Ritter into my hands completely. When he found the game was up he began with a lying confession. Believing that the tracings were still in the stick and that we knew nothing of their return, he said that they had not been away, and that he would fetch them—as I had expected he would. I let him go for them alone, and when he returned, utterly broken up by the discovery that they were not there, I had him altogether at my mercy. You see, if he had known that the drawings were all the time behind your book-case, he might have brazened it out, sworn that the drawings had been there all the time, and we could have done nothing with him. We couldn't have sufficiently frightened him by a threat of prosecution for theft, because there the things were, in your possession, to his knowledge.

"As it was, he answered the helm capitally: gave us Mirsky's address on the envelope, and wrote the letter that was to have got him out of the way while I committed burglary, if that disgraceful expedient had not been rendered unnecessary. On the whole, the case has gone very well."

"It has gone marvellously well, thanks to yourself. But what shall I do with Ritter?"

"Here's his stick—knock him downstairs with it, if you like. I should keep the tube, if I were you, as a memento. I don't suppose the respectable Mirsky will ever call to ask for it. But I should certainly kick Ritter out of doors—or out of window, if you like—without delay."

Mirsky was caught, and after two remands at the police-court was extradited on the charge of forging Russian notes. It came out that he had written to the Embassy, as Hewitt had surmised, stating that he had certain valuable information to offer, and the letter which Hewitt had seen delivered was an acknowledgment, and a request for more definite particulars. This was what gave rise to the impression that Mirsky had himself informed the Russian authorities of his forgeries. His real intent was very different, but was never guessed.

"I wonder," Hewitt has once or twice

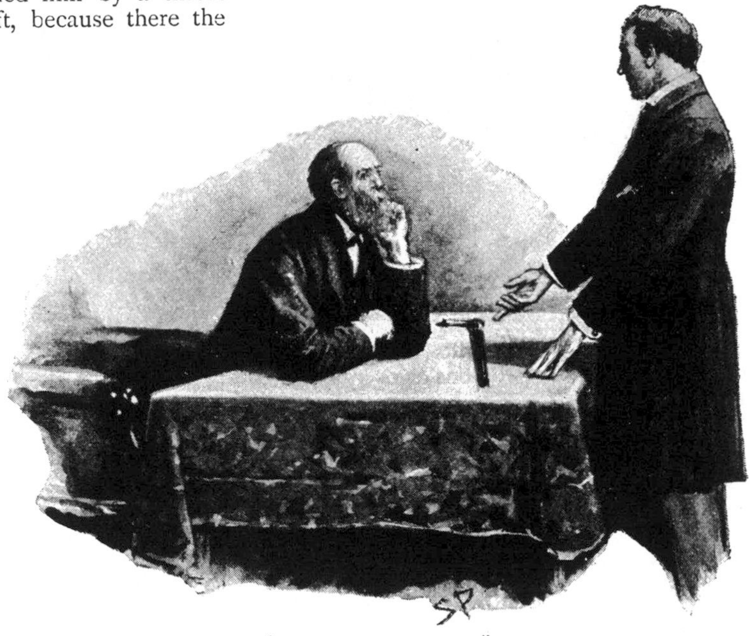

"KNOCK HIM DOWNSTAIRS."

observed, "whether, after all, it would not have paid the Russian authorities better on the whole if I had never investigated Mirsky's little note-factory. The Dixon torpedo was worth a good many twenty-rouble notes."

Martin Hewitt, Investigator.

By Arthur Morrison.

VI.—THE STANWAY CAMEO MYSTERY

IT is now a fair number of years back since the loss of the famous Stanway Cameo made its sensation, and the only person who had the least interest in keeping the real facts of the case secret has now been dead for some time, leaving neither relatives nor other representatives. Therefore no harm will be done in making the inner history of the case public; on the contrary, it will afford an opportunity of vindicating the professional reputation of Hewitt, who is supposed to have completely failed to make anything of the mystery surrounding the case. At the present time connoisseurs in ancient objects of art are often heard regretfully to wonder whether the wonderful cameo—so suddenly discovered and so quickly stolen—will ever again be visible to the public eye. Now this question need be asked no longer.

The cameo, as may be remembered from the many descriptions published at the time, was said to be absolutely the finest extant. It was a sardonyx of three strata—one of those rare sardonyx cameos in which it has been possible for the artist to avail himself of three different colours of superimposed stone—the lowest for the ground and the two others for the middle and high relief of the design. In size it was, for a cameo, immense, measuring seven and a half inches by nearly six. In subject it was similar to the renowned Gonzaga Cameo—now the property of the Czar of Russia—a male and a female head with Imperial insignia; but in this case supposed to represent Tiberius Claudius and Messalina. Experts considered it probably to be the work of Athenion, a famous gem-cutter of the first Christian century, whose most notable other work now extant is a smaller cameo, with a mythological subject, preserved in the Vatican.

The Stanway Cameo had been discovered in an obscure Italian village by one of those travelling agents who scour all Europe for valuable antiquities and objects of art. This man had hurried immediately to London with his prize and sold it to Mr. Claridge, of St. James's Street, eminent as a dealer in such objects. Mr. Claridge, recognising the importance and value of the article, lost no opportunity of making its existence known, and very soon the Claudius Cameo, as it was at first usually called, was as famous as any in the world. Many experts in ancient art examined it, and several large bids were made for its purchase. In the end it was bought

MR. CLARIDGE.

by the Marquis of Stanway for £5,000 for the purpose of presentation to the British Museum. The Marquis kept the cameo at his town house for a few days, showing it to his friends, and then returned it to Mr. Claridge to be finally and carefully cleaned before passing into the national collection. Two nights after, Mr. Claridge's premises were broken into and the cameo stolen.

Such, in outline, was the generally known history of the Stanway Cameo. The circumstances of the burglary in detail were these: Mr. Claridge had himself been the last to leave the premises at about eight in the evening, at dusk, and had locked the small side door as usual. His assistant, Mr. Cutler, had left an hour and a half earlier. When Mr. Claridge left everything was in order, and the policeman on fixed point duty just opposite, who bade Mr. Claridge good evening as he left, saw nothing suspicious during the rest of his term of duty, nor did his successors at the point throughout the night.

In the morning, however, Mr. Cutler, the assistant, who arrived first, soon after nine o'clock, at once perceived that something unlooked-for had happened. The door, of which he had a key, was still fastened, and had not been touched; but in the room behind the shop Mr. Claridge's private desk had been broken open, and the contents turned out in confusion. The door leading on to the staircase had also been forced. Proceeding up the stairs, Mr. Cutler found another door open, leading from the top landing to a small room—this door had been opened by the simple expedient of unscrewing and taking off the lock, which had been on the inside. In the ceiling of this room was a trap-door, and this was six or eight inches open, the edge resting on the half-wrenched-off bolt, which had been torn away when the trap was levered open from the outside.

LORD STANWAY.

Plainly, then, this was the path of the thief or thieves. Entrance had been made through the trap-door, two more doors had been opened, and then the desk had been ransacked. Mr. Cutler afterwards explained that at this time he had no precise idea what had been stolen, and did not know where the cameo had been left on the previous evening. Mr. Claridge had himself undertaken the cleaning and had been engaged on it, the assistant said, when he left.

There was no doubt, however, after Mr. Claridge's arrival at ten o'clock: the cameo was gone. Mr. Claridge, utterly confounded at his loss, explained incoherently, and with curses on his own carelessness, that he had locked the precious article in his desk on relinquishing work on it the previous evening, feeling rather tired and not taking the trouble to carry it as far as the safe in another part of the house.

The police were sent for at once, of course, and every investigation made, Mr. Claridge offering a reward of £500 for the recovery of the cameo. The affair was scribbled of at large in the earliest editions of the evening papers, and by noon all the world was aware of the extraordinary theft of the Stanway Cameo, and many people were discussing the probabilities of the case, with very indistinct ideas of what a sardonyx cameo precisely was.

It was in the afternoon of this day that Lord Stanway called on Martin Hewitt. The Marquis was a tall, upstanding man of spare figure and active habits, well known as a member of learned societies and a great patron of art. He hurried into Hewitt's private room as soon as his name had been announced, and, as soon as Hewitt had given him a chair, plunged into business.

"Probably you already guess my business with you, Mr. Hewitt—you have seen the early evening papers? Just so; then I needn't tell you again what you already know. My cameo is gone, and I badly want it back. Of course, the police are hard at work at Claridge's, but I'm not quite satisfied. I have been there myself for two or three hours, and can't see that they know any more about it than I do myself. Then, of course, the police, naturally and properly enough from their point of view, look first to find the criminal—regarding the recovery of the property almost as a secondary consideration. Now, from *my* point of view, the chief consideration is the property. Of course I want the thief caught, if possible, and properly punished; but still more, I want the cameo."

"Certainly it is a considerable loss. Five thousand pounds——"

"Ah, but don't misunderstand me. It isn't the monetary value of the thing that I regret. As a matter of fact, I am indemnified for that already. Claridge has behaved most honourably—more than honourably. Indeed, the first intimation I had of the loss was a cheque from him for £5,000, with a letter assuring me that the restoration to me of the amount I had paid was the least he could do to repair the result of what he called his unpardonable carelessness. Legally, I'm not sure that I could demand anything of him, unless I could prove very flagrant neglect indeed to guard against theft."

"Then I take it, Lord Stanway," Hewitt observed, "that you much prefer the cameo to the money?"

"Certainly. Else I should never have been willing to pay the money for the cameo. It was an enormous price—perhaps much above the market value, even for such a valuable thing; but I was particularly anxious that it should not go out of the country. Our public collections here are not so fortunate as they should be in the possession of the very finest examples of that class of work. In short, I had determined on the cameo, and, fortunately, happen to be able to carry out determinations of that sort without regarding an extra thousand pounds or so as an obstacle. So that, you see, what I want is not the value, but the thing itself. Indeed, I don't think I can possibly keep the money Claridge has sent me—the affair is more his misfortune than his fault. But I shall say nothing about returning it for a little while: it may possibly have the effect of sharpening everybody in the search."

"Just so. Do I understand that you would like me to look into the case independently, on your behalf?"

"Exactly. I want you, if you can, to approach the matter entirely from *my* point of view—your sole object being to find the cameo. Of course, if you happen on the thief as well, so much the better. Perhaps, after all, looking for the one is the same thing as looking for the other?"

"Not always; but usually it is, of course—even if they are not together, they certainly *have* been at one time, and to have one is a very long step toward having the other. Now, to begin with, is anybody suspected?"

"Well, the police are reserved, but I believe the fact is they've nothing to say Claridge won't admit that he suspects anyone, though he believes that whoever it was must have watched him yesterday evening through the back window of his room, and must have seen him put the cameo away in his desk; because the thief would seem to have gone straight to the place. But I half fancy that, in his inner mind, he is inclined to suspect one of two people. You see, a robbery of this sort is different from others. That cameo would never be stolen, I imagine, with the view of its being sold—it is much too famous a thing; a man might as well walk about offering to sell the Tower of London. There are only a very few people who buy such things, and every one of them knows all about it. No dealer would touch it—he could never even show it, much less sell it, without being called to account. So that it really seems more likely that it has been taken by somebody who wishes to keep it for mere love of the thing—a collector, in fact—who would then have to keep it secretly at home, and never let a soul beside himself see it, living in the consciousness that at his death it must be found and his theft known; unless, indeed, an ordinary vulgar burglar has taken it without knowing its value."

"That isn't likely," Hewitt replied. "An ordinary burglar, ignorant of its value, wouldn't have gone straight to the cameo and have taken it in preference to many other things of more apparent worth, which must be lying near in such a place as Claridge's."

"True—I suppose he wouldn't. Although the police seem to think that the breaking in is clearly the work of a regular criminal—from the jemmy marks, you know, and so on."

"Well, but what of the two people you think Mr. Claridge suspects?"

"Of course, I can't say that he does suspect them—I only fancied from his tone that it might be possible; he himself insists that he can't in justice suspect anybody. One of these men is Hahn, the travelling agent who sold him the cameo. This man's character does not appear to be absolutely irreproachable—no dealer trusts him very far. Of course, Claridge doesn't say what he paid him for the cameo—these dealers are very reticent about their profits, which I believe are as often something like 500 per cent. as not. But it seems Hahn bargained to have something extra, depending on the amount Claridge could sell the carving for. According to the appointment he should have turned up this morning, but he hasn't been seen, and nobody seems to know exactly where he is."

"Yes; and the other person?"

"Well, I scarcely like mentioning him, because he is certainly a gentleman, and I believe, in the ordinary way, quite incapable of anything in the least degree dishonourable; although, of course, they say a collector has no conscience in the matter of his own particular hobby, and certainly Mr. Woollett is as keen a collector as any man alive. He lives in chambers in the next turning past Claridge's premises—can, in fact, look into Claridge's back windows if he likes. He examined the cameo several times before I bought it, and made several high offers—appeared, in fact, very anxious indeed to get it. After I had bought it, he made, I understand, some rather strong remarks about people like myself 'spoiling the market' by paying extravagant prices, and altogether cut up 'crusty,' as they say, at losing the specimen." Lord Stanway paused for a few seconds, and then went on: "I'm not sure that I ought to mention Mr. Woollett's name for a moment in connection with such a matter—I am personally perfectly certain that he is as incapable of anything like theft as myself. But I am telling you all I know."

"Precisely. I can't know too much in a case like this. It can do no harm if I know all about fifty innocent people, and may save me from the risk of knowing nothing about the thief. Now, let me see: Mr. Woollett's rooms, you say, are near Mr. Claridge's place of business? Is there any means of communication between the roofs?"

"Yes, I am told that it is perfectly possible to get from one place to the other by walking along the leads."

"Very good. Then, unless you can think of any other information that may help me, I think, Lord Stanway, I will go at once and look at the place."

"Do, by all means. I think I'll come back with you. Somehow, I don't like to feel idle in the matter, though I suppose I can't do much. As to more information—I don't think there is any."

"In regard to Mr. Claridge's assistant, now: do you know anything of him?"

"Only that he has always seemed a very civil and decent sort of man. Honest, I should say, or Claridge wouldn't have kept him so many years — there are a good many valuable things about at Claridge's. Besides, the man has keys of the place himself, and even if he were a thief he wouldn't need to go breaking in through the roof."

"So that," said Hewitt, "we have, directly connected with this cameo, besides yourself, these people: Mr. Claridge, the dealer, Mr. Cutler, the assistant in Mr. Claridge's business, Hahn, who sold the article to Claridge, and Mr. Woollett, who made bids for it. These are all?"

"All that I know of. Other gentlemen made bids, I believe, but I don't know them."

"Take these people in their order. Mr. Claridge is out of the question, as a dealer with a reputation to keep up would be, even if he hadn't immediately sent you this £5,000—more than the market value, I understand, of the cameo. The assistant is a reputable man, against whom nothing is known, who would never need to break in, and who must understand his business well enough to know that he could never attempt to sell the missing stone without instant detection. Hahn is a man of shady antecedents, probably clever enough to know as well as anybody how to dispose of such plunder—if it be possible to dispose of it at all; also, Hahn hasn't been to Claridge's to-day, although he had an appointment to take money. Lastly, Mr. Woollett is a gentleman of the most honourable record, but a perfectly rabid collector, who had made every effort to secure the cameo before you bought it; who, moreover, could have seen Mr. Claridge working in his back room, and who has perfectly easy access to Mr. Claridge's roof. If we find it can be none of these, then we must look where circumstances indicate."

There was unwonted excitement at Mr. Claridge's place when Hewitt and his client arrived. It was a dull old building, and in the windows there was never more show than an odd blue china vase or two, or, mayhap, a few old silver shoe-buckles and a curious small-sword. Nine men out of ten would have passed it without a glance; but the tenth at least would probably know it for a place famous through the world for the number and value of the old and curious objects of art that had passed through it.

On this day two or three loiterers, having heard of the robbery, extracted what gratification they might from staring at nothing between the railings guarding the windows. Within, Mr. Claridge, a brisk, stout, little old man, was talking earnestly to a burly police inspector in uniform, and Mr. Cutler, who had seized the opportunity to attempt amateur detective work on his own account, was grovelling perseveringly about the floor among old porcelain and loose pieces of armour in the futile hope of finding any clue that the thieves might have considerately dropped.

"TALKING TO A BURLY POLICE-INSPECTOR."

Mr. Claridge came forward eagerly.

"The leather case has been found, I am pleased to be able to tell you, Lord Stanway, since you left."

"Empty, of course?"

"Unfortunately, yes. It had evidently been thrown away by the thief behind a chimney-stack a roof or two away, where the police have found it. But it is a clue, of course."

"Ah, then this gentleman will give me his opinion of it," Lord Stanway said, turning to Hewitt. "This, Mr. Claridge, is Mr. Martin Hewitt, who has been kind enough to come with me here at a moment's notice. With the police on the one hand, and Mr. Hewitt on the other, we shall certainly recover that cameo if it is to be recovered, I think."

Mr. Claridge bowed, and beamed on Hewitt through his spectacles. "I'm very glad Mr. Hewitt has come," he said. "Indeed, I had already decided to give the police till this time to-morrow, and then, if they had found nothing, to call in Mr. Hewitt myself."

Hewitt bowed in his turn, and then asked, "Will you let me see the various breakages? I hope they have not been disturbed."

"Nothing whatever has been disturbed. Do exactly as seems best — I need scarcely say that everything here is perfectly at your disposal. You know all the circumstances, of course?"

"In general, yes. I suppose I am right in the belief that you have no resident housekeeper?"

"No," Claridge replied, "I haven't. I had one housekeeper who sometimes pawned my property in the evening, and then another who used to break my most valuable china, till I could never sleep or take a moment's ease at home for fear my stock was being ruined here. So I gave up resident housekeepers. I felt some confidence in doing it, because of the policeman who is always on duty opposite."

"Can I see the broken desk?"

Mr. Claridge led the way into the room behind the shop. The desk was really a sort of work-table, with a lifting top and a lock. The top had been forced roughly open by some instrument which had been pushed in below it and used as a lever, so that the catch of the lock was torn away. Hewitt examined the damaged parts and the marks of the lever, and then looked out at the back window.

"There are several windows about here," he remarked, "from which it might be possible to see into this room. Do you know any of the people who live behind them?"

"Two or three I know," Mr. Claridge answered, "but there are two windows—the pair almost immediately before us—belonging to a room or office which is to let. Any stranger might get in there and watch."

"Do the roofs above any of those windows communicate in any way with yours?"

"None of those directly opposite. Those at the left do—you may walk all the way along the leads."

"And whose windows are they?"

Mr. Claridge hesitated. "Well," he said, "they're Mr. Woollett's—an excellent customer of mine. But he's a gentleman and—well, I really think it's absurd to suspect him."

"In a case like this," Hewitt answered, "one must disregard nothing but the impossible. Somebody—whether Mr. Woollett himself or another person—could possibly have seen into this room from those windows, and equally possibly could have reached this roof from that one. Therefore, we must not forget Mr. Woollett. Have any of your neighbours been burgled during the night? I mean that strangers anxious to get at your trap-door would probably have to begin by getting into some other house close by, so as to reach your roof."

"No," Mr. Claridge replied; "there has been nothing of that sort. It was the first thing the police ascertained."

Hewitt examined the broken door and then made his way up the stairs, with the others. The unscrewed lock of the door of the top back room required little examination. In the room, below the trap-door, was a dusty table on which stood a chair, and at the other side of the table sat Detective-Inspector Plummer, whom Hewitt knew very well, and who bade him "good day ' and then went on with his docket.

"This chair and table were found as they are now, I take it?" Hewitt asked.

"Yes," said Mr. Claridge; "the thieves, I should think, dropped in through the trap-door, after breaking it open, and had to place this chair where it is to be able to climb back."

Hewitt scrambled up through the trap-way and examined it from the top. The door was hung on long external barn-door hinges, and had been forced open in a similar manner to that practised on the desk. A jemmy had been pushed between the frame and the door near the bolt, and the door had been prised open, the bolt being torn away from the screws in the operation.

Presently, Inspector Plummer, having finished his docket, climbed up to the roof after Hewitt, and the two together went to the spot, close under a chimney-stack on the next roof but one, where the case had been found. Plummer produced the case, which

"THE TWO TOGETHER WENT TO THE SPOT."

he had in his coat-tail pocket, for Hewitt's inspection.

"I don't see anything particular about it; do you?" he said. "It shows us the way they went, though, being found just here."

"Well, yes," Hewitt said; "if we kept on in this direction we should be going towards Mr. Woollett's house, and *his* trap-door, shouldn't we?"

The inspector pursed his lips, smiled, and shrugged his shoulders. "Of course, we haven't waited till now to find that out," he said.

"No, of course. And, as you say, I don't think there is much to be learned from this leather case. It is almost new, and there isn't a mark on it." And Hewitt handed it back to the inspector.

"Well," said Plummer, as he returned the case to his pocket, "what's your opinion?"

"It's rather an awkward case."

"Yes, it is. Between ourselves, I don't mind telling you, I'm having a sharp look-out kept over there"—Plummer jerked his head in the direction of Mr. Woollett's chambers—"because the robbery's an unusual one. There's only two possible motives—the sale of the cameo or the keeping of it. The sale's out of the question, as you know—the thing's only saleable to those who would collar the thief at once, and who wouldn't have the thing in their places now for anything. So that it must be taken to keep—and that's a thing nobody but the maddest of collectors would do—just such persons as——" and the inspector nodded again towards Mr. Woollett's quarters. "Take that with the other circumstances," he added, "and I think you'll agree it's worth while looking a little farther that way. Of course, some of the work—taking off the lock and so on—looks rather like a regular burglar, but it's just possible that anyone badly wanting the cameo would hire a man who was up to the work."

"Yes, it's possible."

"Do you know anything of Hahn, the agent?" Plummer asked, a moment later.

"No, I don't. Have you found him yet?"

"I haven't yet, but I'm after him. I've found he was at Charing Cross a day or two ago, booking a ticket for the Continent. That and his failing to turn up to-day seem to make it worth while not to miss *him* if we can help it. He isn't the sort of man that lets a chance of drawing a bit of money go for nothing."

They returned to the room. "Well," said Lord Stanway, "what's the result of the consultation? We've been waiting here very patiently while you two clever men have been discussing the matter on the roof."

On the wall just beneath the trap-door a very dusty old tall hat hung on a peg. This Hewitt took down and examined very closely, smearing his fingers with the dust from the inside lining. "Is this one of your valuable and crusted old antiques?" he asked, with a smile, of Mr. Claridge.

"That's only an old hat that I used to keep here for use in bad weather," Mr. Claridge said, with some surprise at the question. "I haven't touched it for a year or more."

"Oh, then it couldn't have been left here by your last night's visitor," Hewitt replied, carelessly replacing it on the hook. "You left here at eight last night, I think?"

"Eight exactly—or within a minute or two."

"Just so. I think I'll look at the room on the opposite side of the landing, if you'll let me."

"Certainly, if you'd like to," Claridge replied; "but they haven't been there—it is exactly as it was left. Only a lumber-room, you see," he concluded, flinging the door open.

A number of partly broken-up packing-cases littered about this room, with much other rubbish. Hewitt took the lid of one of the newest-looking packing-cases, and glanced at the address label. Then he turned to a rusty old iron box that stood against a wall. "I should like to see behind this," he said, tugging at it with his hands. "It is heavy and dirty. Is there a small crowbar about the house, or some similar lever?"

Mr. Claridge shook his head. "Haven't such a thing in the place," he said.

"Never mind," Hewitt replied, "another time will do to shift that old box, and perhaps after all there's little reason for moving it. I will just walk round to the police-station, I think, and speak to the constables who were on duty opposite during the night. I think, Lord Stanway, I have seen all that is necessary here."

"I suppose," asked Mr. Claridge, "it is too soon yet to ask if you have formed any theory in the matter?"

"Well—yes, it is," Hewitt answered. "But perhaps I may be able to surprise you in an hour or two; but that I don't promise. By-the-bye," he added, suddenly, "I suppose you're sure the trap-door was bolted last night?"

"Certainly," Mr. Claridge answered,

smiling. "Else how could the bolt have been broken? As a matter of fact, I believe the trap hasn't been opened for months. Mr. Cutler, do you remember when the trap-door was last opened?"

Mr. Cutler shook his head. "Certainly not for six months," he said.

"Ah, very well—it's not very important," Hewitt replied.

As they reached the front shop, a fiery-faced old gentleman bounced in at the street door, stumbling over an umbrella that stood in a dark corner, and kicking it three yards away.

"What the deuce do you mean," he roared at Mr. Claridge, "by sending these police people smelling about my rooms and asking questions of my servants? What do you mean, sir, by treating me as a thief? Can't a gentleman come into this place to look at an article without being suspected of stealing it, when it disappears through your wretched carelessness? I'll ask my solicitor, sir, if there isn't a remedy for this sort of thing. And if I catch another of your spy fellows on my staircase, or crawling about my roof, I'll—I'll shoot him!"

"A FIERY-FACED OLD GENTLEMAN BOUNCED IN AT THE DOOR."

"Really, Mr. Woollett," began Mr. Claridge, somewhat abashed, but the angry old man would hear nothing.

"Don't talk to me, sir—you shall talk to my solicitor. And am I to understand, my lord"—turning to Lord Stanway—"that these things are being done with your approval?"

"Whatever is being done," Lord Stanway answered, "is being done by the police on their own responsibility, and entirely without prompting, I believe, by Mr. Claridge—certainly without a suggestion of any sort from myself. I think that the personal opinion of Mr. Claridge—certainly my own—is that anything like a suspicion of your position in this wretched matter is ridiculous. And if you will only consider the matter calmly——"

"Consider it calmly? Imagine yourself considering such a thing calmly, Lord Stanway. I *won't* consider it calmly. I'll—I'll—I won't have it. And if I find another man on my roof, I'll pitch him off." And Mr. Woollett bounced into the street again.

"Mr. Woollett is annoyed," Hewitt observed, with a smile. "I'm afraid Plummer has a clumsy assistant somewhere."

Mr. Claridge said nothing, but looked rather glum. For Mr. Woollett was a most excellent customer.

Lord Stanway and Hewitt walked slowly down the street, Hewitt staring at the pavement in profound thought. Once or twice Lord Stanway glanced at his face, but refrained from disturbing him. Presently, however, he observed, "You seem at least, Mr. Hewitt, to have noticed something that has set you thinking. Does it look like a clue?"

Hewitt came out of his cogitation at once. "A clue?" he said; "the case bristles with clues. The extraordinary thing to me is that Plummer, usually a smart man, doesn't seem to have seen one of them. He must be out of sorts, I'm afraid. But the case is decidedly a very remarkable one."

"Remarkable, in what particular way?"

"In regard to motive. Now it would seem, as Plummer was saying to me just now on the roof, that there were only two possible motives for such a robbery. Either the man who took all this trouble and risk to break into Claridge's place must have desired to sell the cameo at a good price, or he must have desired to keep it for himself, being a lover of such things. But neither of these has been the actual motive."

"Perhaps he thinks he can extort a good sum from me by way of ransom?"

"No, it isn't that. Nor is it jealousy, nor spite, nor anything of that kind. I know the motive, I *think*—but I wish we could get hold of Hahn. I will shut myself up alone and turn it over in my mind for half an hour presently."

"Meanwhile, what I want to know is, apart from all your professional subtleties—which I confess I can't understand—can you get back the cameo?"

"That," said Hewitt, stopping at the corner of the street, "I am rather afraid I cannot—nor anybody else. But I am pretty sure I know the thief."

"Then surely that will lead you to the cameo?"

"It *may*, of course; but then it is just possible that by this evening you may not want to have it back after all."

Lord Stanway stared in amazement.

"Not want to have it back!" he exclaimed. "Why, of course, I shall want to have it back. I don't understand you in the least; you talk in conundrums. Who is the thief you speak of?"

"I think, Lord Stanway," Hewitt said, "that perhaps I had better not say until I have quite finished my inquiries, in case of mistakes. The case is quite an extraordinary one, and of quite a different character from what one would at first naturally imagine, and I must be very careful to guard against the possibility of error. I have very little fear of a mistake, however, and I hope I may wait on you in a few hours at Piccadilly with news. I have only to see the policemen."

"Certainly, come whenever you please. But why see the policemen? They have already most positively stated that they saw nothing whatever suspicious in the house or near it."

"I shall not ask them anything at all about the house," Hewitt responded. "I shall just have a little chat with them—about the weather." And with a smiling bow, he turned away, while Lord Stanway stood and gazed after him, with an expression that implied a suspicion that his special detective was making a fool of him.

In rather more than an hour Hewitt was back in Mr. Claridge's shop. "Mr. Claridge," he said, "I think I must ask you one or two questions in private. May I see you in your own room?"

They went there at once, and Hewitt, pulling a chair before the window, sat down with his back to the light. The dealer shut

"CAN YOU GET BACK THE CAMEO?"

the door, and sat opposite him, with the light full in his face.

"Mr. Claridge," Hewitt proceeded, slowly, "*when did you first find that Lord Stanway's cameo was a forgery?*"

Claridge literally bounced in his chair. His face paled, but he managed to stammer, sharply, "What—what—what d'you mean? Forgery? Do you mean to say I sell forgeries? Forgery? It wasn't a forgery!"

"Then," continued Hewitt, in the same deliberate tone, watching the other's face the while, "if it wasn't a forgery, *why did you destroy it and burst your trap-door and desk to imitate a burglary?*"

The sweat stood thick on the dealer's face, and he gasped. But he struggled hard to keep his faculties together, and ejaculated, hoarsely: "Destroy it? What—what—I didn't—didn't destroy it!"

"Threw it into the river, then—don't prevaricate about details."

"No—no—it's a lie. Who says that? Go away. You're insulting me!" Claridge almost screamed.

"Come, come, Mr. Claridge," Hewitt said, more placably, for he had gained his point; "don't distress yourself, and don't attempt to deceive me—you can't, I assure you. I know everything you did before you left here last night—everything."

Claridge's face worked painfully. Once or twice he appeared to be on the point of returning an indignant reply, but hesitated, and finally broke down altogether.

"Don't expose me, Mr. Hewitt," he pleaded; "I beg you won't expose me. I haven't harmed a soul but myself. I've paid Lord Stanway every penny back, and I never knew the thing was a forgery till I began to clean it. I'm an old man, Mr. Hewitt, and my professional reputation has been spotless till now. I beg you won't expose me."

Hewitt's voice softened. "Don't make an unnecessary trouble of it," he said. "I see a decanter on your sideboard—let me give you a little brandy and water. Come, there's nothing criminal, I believe, in a man's breaking open his own desk, or his own trap-door, for that matter. Of course, I'm acting for Lord Stanway in this affair, and I must, in duty, report to him without reserve. But Lord Stanway is a gentleman, and I'll undertake he'll do nothing inconsiderate of your feelings, if you're disposed to be frank. Let us talk the affair over—tell me about it."

"It was that swindler Hahn who deceived me in the beginning," Claridge said. "I have never made a mistake with a cameo before, and I never thought so close an imitation was possible. I examined it most carefully, and was perfectly satisfied, and many experts examined it afterwards, and were all equally deceived. I felt as sure as I possibly could feel that I had bought one of the finest, if not actually the finest cameo known to exist. It was not until after it had come back from Lord Stanway's, and I was cleaning it, the evening before last, that in course of my work it became apparent that the thing was nothing but

"DON'T EXPOSE ME, MR. HEWITT."

a consummately clever forgery. It was made of three layers of moulded glass, nothing more or less. But the glass was treated in a way I had never before known of, and the surface had been cunningly worked on till it defied any ordinary examination. Some of the glass imitation cameos made in the latter part of the last century, I may tell you, are regarded as marvellous pieces of work, and, indeed, command very fair prices, but this was something quite beyond any of those.

"I was amazed and horrified. I put the thing away and went home. All that night I lay awake in a state of distraction, quite unable to decide what to do. To let the cameo go out of my possession was impossible. Sooner or later the forgery would be discovered, and my reputation—the highest in these matters in this country, I may safely claim, and the growth of nearly fifty years of honest application and good judgment—this reputation would be gone for ever. But without considering this, there was the fact that I had taken £5,000 of Lord Stanway's money for a mere piece of glass, and that money I must, in mere common honesty as well as for my own sake, return. But how? The name of the Stanway Cameo had become a household word, and to confess that the whole thing was a sham would ruin my reputation and destroy all confidence — past, present, and future — in me and in my transactions. Either way spelled ruin. Even if I confided in Lord Stanway privately, returned his money and destroyed the cameo, what then? The sudden disappearance of an article so famous would excite remark at once. It had been presented to the British Museum, and if it never appeared in that collection, and no news were to be got of it, people would guess at the truth at once. To make it known that I myself had been deceived would have availed nothing. It is my business *not* to be deceived; and to have it known that my most expensive specimens might be forgeries would equally mean ruin, whether I sold them cunningly as a rogue or ignorantly as a fool. Indeed, my pride, my reputation as a connoisseur is a thing near to my heart, and it would be an unspeakable humiliation to me to have it known that I had been imposed on by such a forgery. What could I do? Every expedient seemed useless, but one—the one I adopted. It was not straightforward, I admit; but, oh! Mr. Hewitt, consider the temptation—and remember that it couldn't do a soul any harm. No matter who might be suspected, I knew there could not possibly be evidence to make them suffer. All the next day—yesterday—I was anxiously worrying out the thing in my mind and carefully devising the—the trick, I'm afraid you'll call it—that you by some extraordinary means have seen through. It seemed the only thing—what else was there? More I needn't tell you—you know it. I have only now to beg that you will use your best influence with Lord Stanway to save me from public derision and exposure. I will do anything — pay anything — anything but exposure, at my age, and with my position."

"Well, you see," Hewitt replied, thoughtfully, "I've no doubt Lord Stanway will show you every consideration, and certainly I will do what I can to save you, in the circumstances; though you must remember that you *have* done some harm—you have caused suspicions to rest on at least one honest man. But as to reputation—I've a professional reputation of my own. If I help to conceal your professional failure, I shall appear to have failed in *my* part of the business."

"But the cases are different, Mr. Hewitt—consider. You are not expected—it would be impossible—to succeed invariably; and there are only two or three who know you have looked into the case. Then your other conspicuous successes——"

"Well, well—we shall see. One thing I don't know, though—whether you climbed out of a window to break open the trap-door, or whether you got up through the trap-door itself and pulled the bolt with a string through the jamb, so as to bolt it after you."

"There was no available window—I used the string, as you say. My poor little cunning must seem very transparent to you, I fear. I spent hours of thought over the question of the trap-door—how to break it open so as to leave a genuine appearance, and especially how to bolt it inside after I had reached the roof. I thought I had succeeded beyond the possibility of suspicion; how you penetrated the device surpasses my comprehension. How, to begin with, could you possibly know that the cameo was a forgery? Did you ever see it?"

"Never. And if I had seen it, I fear I should never have been able to express an opinion on it; I'm not a connoisseur. As a matter of fact, I *didn't* know that the thing was a forgery in the first place; what I knew in the first place was that it was *you* who had broken into the house. It was from that that I arrived at the conclusion—after a certain amount of thought—that the cameo must have been forged. Gain was out of the question—you, beyond all men, could never sell the Stanway Cameo again, and, besides, you had paid back Lord Stanway's money. I knew enough of your reputation to know that you would never incur the scandal of a great theft at your place for the sake of getting the cameo for yourself, when you might have kept it in the beginning, with no trouble and mystery. Consequently, I had to look for another motive, and at first another motive seemed an impossibility. Why should you wish to take all this trouble to lose £5,000? You had nothing to gain; perhaps you had something to save—your professional reputation, for instance. Looking at it so, it was plain that you were *suppressing* the cameo—burking it; since, once taken as you had taken it, it could never come to light again. That suggested the solution of the mystery at once—you had discovered, after the sale, that the cameo was not genuine."

"Yes, yes—I see; but you say you began with the knowledge that I broke into the place myself. How did you know that? I cannot imagine a trace——"

"My dear sir, you left traces everywhere. In the first place, it struck me as curious, before I came here, that you had sent off that cheque for £5,000 to Lord Stanway an hour or so after the robbery was discovered —it looked so much as though you were sure of the cameo never coming back, and were in a hurry to avert suspicion. Of course, I understood that, so far as I then knew the case, you were the most unlikely person in the world, and that your eagerness to repay Lord Stanway might be the most creditable thing possible. But the point was worth remembering, and I remembered it.

"When I came here I saw suspicious indications in many directions, but the conclusive piece of evidence was that old hat hanging below the trap-door."

"But I never touched it, I assure you, Mr. Hewitt, I never touched the hat—haven't touched it for months——"

"Of course. If you *had* touched it, I might never have got the clue. But we'll deal with the hat presently; that wasn't what struck me at first. The trap-door first took my attention. Consider, now: here was a trap-door, most insecurely hung on *external* hinges; the burglar had a screw-driver, for he took off the door-lock below with it. Why, then, didn't he take this trap off by the hinges, instead of making a noise and taking longer time and trouble to burst the bolt from its fastenings? And why, if he were a stranger, was he able to plant his jemmy from the outside just exactly opposite the interior bolt? There was only one mark on the frame, and that precisely in the proper place.

"After that, I saw the leather case. It had not been thrown away, or some corner would have shown signs of the fall. It had been put down carefully where it was found. These things, however, were of small importance compared with the hat. The hat, as you know, was exceedingly thick with dust—the accumulation of months. But, on the top side, presented toward the trap-door, were a score or so of *raindrop marks*. That was all. They were new marks, for there was no dust over them; they had merely had time to dry and cake the dust they had fallen on. *Now, there had been no rain since a sharp shower just after seven o'clock last night.* At that time you, by your own statement, were in the place. You left at eight, and the rain was all over at ten minutes or a quarter-past seven. The trap-door, you also told me, had not been opened for months. The thing was plain. You, or somebody who was here when you were, had opened that trap-door during, or just before, that shower. I said little then, but went, as soon as I had left, to the police-station. There I made perfectly certain that there had been no rain during the night by questioning the policemen who were on duty outside all the time. There had been none. I knew everything.

"The only other evidence there was pointed with all the rest. There were no rain-marks on the leather case; it had been put on the roof as an after-thought when there was no rain. A very poor after-thought, let me tell you, for no thief would throw away a useful case that concealed his booty and protected it from breakage, and throw it away just so as to leave a clue as to what direction he had gone in. I also saw, in the lumber-room, a number of packing-cases—one with a label dated two days back—which had been opened with an iron lever; and yet, when I made an excuse to ask for it, you said there was no such thing in the place. Inference: you didn't want me to compare it with the marks on the desks and doors. That is all, I think."

Mr. Claridge looked dolorously down at the floor. "I'm afraid," he said, "that I took an unsuitable *rôle* when I undertook to rely on my wits to deceive men like you. I thought there wasn't a single vulnerable spot in my defence, but you walk calmly through it at the first attempt. Why did I never think of those raindrops?"

"Come," said Hewitt, with a smile, "that sounds unrepentant. I am going, now, to Lord Stanway's. If I were you, I think I should apologize to Mr. Woollett in some way."

Lord Stanway, who, in the hour or two of reflection left him after parting with Hewitt, had come to the belief that he had employed a man whose mind was not always in order, received Hewitt's story with natural astonishment. For some time he was in doubt as to whether he would be doing right in acquiescing in anything but a straightforward public statement of the facts connected with the disappearance of the cameo, but in the end was persuaded to let the affair drop, on receiving an assurance from Mr. Woollett that he unreservedly accepted the apology offered him by Mr. Claridge.

"HAHN WALKED SMILINGLY INTO HIS OFFICE."

As for the latter, he was at least sufficiently punished in loss of money and personal humiliation for his escapade. But the bitterest and last blow he sustained when the unblushing Hahn walked smilingly into his office two days later to demand the extra payment agreed on in consideration of the sale. He had been called suddenly away, he explained, on the day he should have come, and hoped his missing the appointment had occasioned no inconvenience. As to the robbery of the cameo, of course he was very sorry, but "pishness was pishness," and he would be glad of a cheque for the sum agreed on. And the unhappy Claridge was obliged to pay it, knowing that the man had swindled him, but unable to open his mouth to say so.

The reward remained on offer for a long time—indeed, it was never publicly withdrawn, I believe, even at the time of Claridge's death. And several intelligent newspapers enlarged upon the fact that an ordinary burglar had completely baffled and defeated the boasted acumen of Mr. Martin Hewitt, the well-known private detective.

V

An African Millionaire

GRANT ALLEN

By Grant Allen.

I.—THE EPISODE OF THE MEXICAN SEER.

MY name is Seymour Wilbraham Wentworth. I am brother-in-law and secretary to Sir Charles Vandrift, the South African millionaire and famous financier. Many years ago, when Charlie Vandrift was a small lawyer in Cape Town, I had the (qualified) good fortune to marry his sister. Much later, when the Vandrift estate and farm near Kimberley developed by degrees into the Cloetedorp Golcondas, Limited, my brother-in-law offered me the not unremunerative post of secretary; in which capacity I have ever since been his constant and attached companion.

He is not a man whom any common sharper can take in, is Charles Vandrift. Middle height, square build, firm mouth, keen eyes—the very picture of a sharp and successful business genius. I have only known one rogue impose upon Sir Charles, and that one rogue, as the Commissary of Police at Nice remarked, would doubtless have imposed upon a syndicate of Vidocq, Robert Houdin, and Cagliostro.

We had run across to the Riviera for a few weeks in the season. Our object being strictly rest and recreation from the arduous duties of financial combination, we did not think it necessary to take our wives out with us. Indeed, Lady Vandrift is absolutely wedded to the joys of London, and does not appreciate the rural delights of the Mediterranean littoral. But Sir Charles and I, though immersed in affairs when at home, both thoroughly enjoy the complete change from the City to the charming vegetation and pellucid air on the terrace at Monte Carlo. We *are* so fond of scenery. That delicious view over the rocks of Monaco, with the Maritime Alps in the rear, and the blue sea in front, not to mention the imposing Casino in the foreground, appeals to me as one of the most beautiful prospects in all Europe. Sir Charles has a sentimental attachment for the place. He finds it restores and freshens him, after the turmoil of London, to win a few hundreds at roulette in the course of an afternoon, among the palms and cactuses and pure breezes of Monte Carlo. The country, say I, for a jaded intellect! However, we never on any account actually stop in the Principality itself. Sir Charles thinks Monte Carlo is not a sound address for a financier's letters. He prefers a comfortable hotel on the Promenade des Anglais at Nice, where he recovers health and renovates his nervous system by taking daily excursions along the coast to the Casino.

This particular season we were snugly ensconced at the Hôtel des Anglais. We had capital quarters on the first floor—salon, study, and bedrooms—and found on the spot a most agreeable cosmopolitan society. All Nice, just then, was ringing with talk about a curious impostor, known to his followers as the Great Mexican Seer, and supposed to be gifted with second sight, as well as with endless other supernatural powers. Now, it is a peculiarity of my able brother-in-law's that, when he meets with a quack, he burns to expose him; he is so keen a man of business himself that it gives him, so to speak, a disinterested pleasure to unmask and detect imposture in others. Many ladies at the hotel, some of whom had met and conversed with the Mexican Seer, were constantly telling us strange stories of his doings—he had disclosed to one the present whereabouts of a runaway husband; he had pointed out to another the numbers that would win at roulette next evening; he had shown a third the image on a screen of the man she had for years adored without his knowledge. Of course, Sir Charles didn't believe a word of it; but his curiosity was roused; he wished to see and judge for himself of the wonderful thought-reader.

"What would be his terms, do you think, for a private *séance?*" he asked of Madame Picardet, the lady to whom the Seer had successfully predicted the winning numbers.

"He does not work for money," Madame Picardet answered, "but for the good of humanity. I'm sure he would gladly come and exhibit for nothing his miraculous faculties."

"Nonsense!" Sir Charles answered. "The man must live. I'd pay him five guineas, though, to see him alone. What hotel is he stopping at?"

"The Cosmopolitan, I think," the lady answered. "Oh, no; I remember now, the Westminster."

Sir Charles turned to me quietly. "Look here, Seymour," he whispered. "Go round to this fellow's place immediately after dinner, and offer him five pounds to give a private *séance* at once in my rooms, without mentioning who I am to him; keep the name quite quiet. Bring him back with you, too, and come straight upstairs with him, so that there may be no collusion. We'll see just how much the fellow can tell us."

I went, as directed. I found the Seer a very remarkable and interesting person. He stood about Sir Charles's own height, but was slimmer and straighter, with an aquiline nose, strangely piercing eyes, very large, black pupils, and a finely-chiselled, close-shaven face like the bust of Antinous in our hall in Mayfair. What gave him his most characteristic touch, however, was his odd head of hair, curly and wavy like Paderewski's, standing out in a halo round his high white forehead and his delicate profile. I could see at a glance why he succeeded so well in impressing women: he had the look of a poet, a singer, a prophet.

"I have come round," I said, "to ask whether you will consent to give a *séance* at once in a friend's rooms; and my principal wishes me to add that he is prepared to pay five pounds as the price of the entertainment."

Señor Antonio Herrera—that was what he called himself—bowed to me with impressive Spanish politeness. His dusky olive cheeks were wrinkled with a smile of gentle contempt as he answered, gravely:—

"I do not sell my gifts; I bestow them freely. If your friend—your anonymous friend—desires to behold the cosmic wonders that are wrought through my hands, I am glad to show them to him. Fortunately, as often happens when it is necessary to convince and confound a sceptic (for that your friend is a sceptic I feel instinctively), I chance to have no engagements at all this evening." He ran his hand through his fine, long hair, reflectively. "Yes, I go," he continued, as if addressing some unknown presence that hovered about the ceiling; "I go; come with me!" Then he put on his broad sombrero, with its crimson ribbon, wrapped a cloak round his shoulders, lighted a cigarette, and strode forth by my side towards the Hôtel des Anglais.

He talked little by the way, and that little in curt sentences. He seemed buried in

"YES, I GO."

deep thought; indeed, when we reached the door and I turned in, he walked a step or two farther on, as if not noticing to what place I had brought him. Then he drew himself up short, and gazed around him for a moment. "Ha, the Anglais," he said—and I may mention in passing that his English, in spite of a slight southern accent, was idiomatic and excellent. "It is here, then; it is here!" He was addressing once more the unseen presence.

I smiled to think that these childish devices were intended to deceive Sir Charles Vandrift. Not quite the sort of man (as the City of London knows) to be taken in by hocus-pocus. And all this, I saw, was the cheapest and most commonplace conjurer's patter.

We went upstairs to our rooms. Charles had gathered together a few friends to watch the performance. The Seer entered, wrapt in thought. He was in evening dress, but a red sash round his waist gave a touch of picturesqueness and a dash of colour. He paused for a moment in the middle of the salon, without letting his eyes rest on anybody or anything. Then he walked straight up to Charles, and held out his dark hand. "Good evening," he said. "You are the host. My soul's sight tells me so."

"Good shot," Sir Charles answered. "These fellows have to be quick-witted, you know, Mrs. Mackenzie, or they'd never get on at it."

The Seer gazed about him, and smiled blankly at a person or two whose faces he seemed to recognise from a previous existence. Then Charles began to ask him a few simple questions, not about himself, but about me, just to test him. He answered most of them with surprising correctness. "His name? His name begins with an S—I think—You call him Seymour." He paused long between each clause, as if the facts were revealed to him slowly. "Seymour—Wilbraham—Earl of Strafford. No, not Earl of Strafford! Seymour Wilbraham Wentworth. There seems to be some connection in somebody's mind now present between Wentworth and Strafford. I am not English. I do not know what it means. But they are somehow the same name, Wentworth and Strafford."

He gazed around apparently for confirmation. A lady came to his rescue.

"Wentworth was the surname of the great Earl of Strafford," she murmured, gently; "and I was wondering, as you spoke, whether Mr. Wentworth might possibly be descended from him."

"He is," the Seer replied, instantly, with a flash of those dark eyes. And I thought this curious; for though my father always maintained the reality of the relationship, there was one link wanting to complete the pedigree. He could not make sure that the Hon. Thomas Wilbraham Wentworth was the father of Jonathan Wentworth, the Bristol horse-dealer, from whom we are descended.

"Where was I born?" Sir Charles interrupted, coming suddenly to his own case.

The Seer clapped his two hands to his forehead and held it between them, as if to prevent it from bursting. "Africa," he said, slowly, as the facts narrowed down, so to speak. "South Africa; Cape of Good Hope; Jansenville; De Witt Street. 1840."

"By Jove, he's correct," Sir Charles muttered. "He seems really to do it. Still, he may have found me out. He may have known where he was coming."

"I never gave a hint," I answered; "till he

reached the door, he didn't even know to what hotel I was piloting him."

The Seer stroked his chin softly. His eye appeared to me to have a furtive gleam in it. "Would you like me to tell you the number of a bank-note inclosed in an envelope?" he asked, casually.

"Go out of the room," Sir Charles said, "while I pass it round the company."

Señor Herrera disappeared. Sir Charles passed it round cautiously, holding it all the time in his own hand, but letting his guests see the number. Then he placed it in an envelope and gummed it down firmly.

The Seer returned. His keen eyes swept the company with a comprehensive glance. He shook his shaggy mane. Then he took the envelope in his hands and gazed at it fixedly. "AF, 73549," he answered, in a slow tone. "A Bank of England note for fifty pounds—exchanged at the Casino for gold won yesterday at Monte Carlo."

"I see how he did that," Sir Charles said, triumphantly. "He must have changed it there himself; and then I changed it back again. In point of fact, I remember seeing a fellow with long hair loafing about. Still, it's capital conjuring."

"He can see through matter," one of the ladies interposed. It was Madame Picardet. "He can see through a box." She drew a little gold vinaigrette, such as our grandmothers used, from her dress-pocket. "What is in this?" she inquired, holding it up to him.

Señor Herrera gazed through it. "Three gold coins," he replied, knitting his brows with the effort of seeing into the box: "one, an American five dollars; one, a French ten-franc piece; one, twenty marks, German, of the old Emperor William."

She opened the box and passed it round. Sir Charles smiled a quiet smile.

"Confederacy!" he muttered, half to himself. "Confederacy!"

The Seer turned to him with a sullen air. "You want a better sign?" he said, in a very impressive voice. "A sign that will convince you! Very well: you have a letter in your left waistcoat pocket—a crumpled-up letter. Do you wish me to read it out? I will, if you desire it."

It may seem to those who know Sir Charles incredible, but, I am bound to admit, my brother-in-law coloured. What that letter contained, I cannot say; he only answered, very testily and evasively, "No, thank you; I won't trouble you. The exhibition you have already given us of your skill in this kind more than amply suffices." And his fingers strayed nervously to his waistcoat pocket, as if he was half afraid, even then, Señor Herrera would read it.

I fancied, too, he glanced somewhat anxiously towards Madame Picardet.

The Seer bowed courteously. "Your will, señor, is law," he said. "I make it a principle, though I can see through all things, invariably to respect the secrecies and sanctities. If it were not so, I might dissolve society. For which of us is there who could bear the whole truth being told about him?" He gazed around the room. An unpleasant thrill supervened. Most of us felt this uncanny Spanish American knew really too much. And some of us were engaged in financial operations.

"For example," the Seer continued, blandly, "I happened a few weeks ago to travel down here from Paris by train with a very intelligent man, a company promoter. He had in his bag some documents — some confidential documents": he glanced at Sir Charles. "You know the kind of thing, my dear sir: reports from experts—from mining engineers. You may have seen some such; marked, *strictly private*."

"They form an element in high finance," Sir Charles admitted, coldly.

"Pre-cisely," the Seer murmured, his accent for a moment less Spanish than before. "And, as they were marked *strictly private*, I respect, of course, the seal of confidence. That's all I wish to say. I hold it a duty, being intrusted with such powers, not to use them in a manner which may annoy or incommode my fellow-creatures."

"Your feeling does you honour," Sir Charles answered, with some acerbity. Then he whispered in my ear: "Confounded clever scoundrel, Sey; rather wish we hadn't brought him here."

Señor Herrera seemed intuitively to divine this wish, for he interposed, in a lighter and gayer tone:—

"I will now show you a different and more interesting embodiment of occult power, for which we shall need a somewhat subdued arrangement of surrounding lights. Would you mind, señor host—for I have purposely abstained from reading your name on the brain of anyone present—would you mind my turning down this lamp just a little? . . . So! That will do. Now, this one; and this one. Exactly! that's right." He poured a few grains of powder out of a packet into a saucer. "Next, a match, if you please.

Thank you!" It burnt with a strange green light. He drew from his pocket a card, and produced a little ink-bottle. "Have you a pen?" he asked.

I instantly brought one. He handed it to Sir Charles. "Oblige me," he said, "by writing your name there." And he indicated a place in the centre of the card, which had an embossed edge, with a small middle square of a different colour.

The Seer strode forward. "Give me the envelope," he said. He took it in his hand, walked over towards the fire-place, and solemnly burnt it. "See—it crumbles into ashes," he cried. Then he came back to the middle of the room, close to the green light, rolled up his sleeve, and held his arm before Sir Charles. There, in blood-red letters, my brother-in-law read the name, "Charles Vandrift," in his own handwriting!

"IN BLOOD-RED LETTERS, MY BROTHER-IN-LAW READ THE NAME."

Sir Charles has a natural disinclination to signing his name without knowing why. "What do you want with it?" he asked. (A millionaire's signature has so many uses.)

"I want you to put the card in an envelope," the Seer replied, "and then to burn it. After that, I shall show you your own name written in letters of blood on my arm, in your own handwriting."

Sir Charles took the pen. If the signature was to be burned as soon as finished, he didn't mind giving it. He wrote his name in his usual firm, clear style — the writing of a man who knows his worth and is not afraid of drawing a cheque for five thousand.

"Look at it long," the Seer said, from the other side of the room. He had not watched him write it.

Sir Charles stared at it fixedly. The Seer was really beginning to produce an impression.

"Now, put it in that envelope," the Seer exclaimed.

Sir Charles, like a lamb, placed it as directed.

"I see how that's done," Sir Charles murmured, drawing back. "It's a clever delusion; but still, I see through it. It's like that ghost-book. Your ink was deep green; your light was green; you made me look at it long; and then I saw the same thing written on the skin of your arm in complementary colours."

"You think so?" the Seer replied, with a curious curl of the lip.

"I'm sure of it," Sir Charles answered.

Quick as lightning, the Seer again rolled up his sleeve. "That's your name," he cried, in a very clear voice, "but not your whole name. What do you say, then, to my right? Is this one also a complementary colour?" He held his other arm out. There, in sea-green letters, I read the name, "Charles O'Sullivan Vandrift." It is my brother-in-law's full baptismal designation; but he has dropped the O'Sullivan for many years past, and, to say the truth, doesn't like it. He is a little bit ashamed of his mother's family.

Charles glanced at it hurriedly. "Quite right," he said, "quite right!" But his voice was hollow. I could guess he didn't care to continue the *séance*. He could see through the man, of course: but it was clear the fellow knew too much about us to be entirely pleasant.

"Turn up the lights," I said, and a servant turned them. "Shall I say coffee and benedictine?" I whispered to Vandrift.

"By all means," he answered. "Anything to keep this fellow from further impertinences! And, I say, don't you think you'd better suggest at the same time that the men should smoke? Even these ladies are not above a cigarette—some of them."

There was a sigh of relief. The lights burned brightly. The Seer for the moment retired from business, so to speak. He accepted a partaga with a very good grace, sipped his coffee in a corner, and chatted to the lady who had suggested Strafford with marked politeness. He was a polished gentleman.

Next morning, in the hall of the hotel, I saw Madame Picardet again, in a neat tailor-made travelling dress; evidently bound for the railway-station.

"What, off, Madame Picardet?" I cried.

She smiled, and held out her prettily-gloved hand. "Yes, I'm off," she answered, archly. "Florence, or Rome, or somewhere. I've drained Nice dry—like a sucked orange. Got all the fun I can out of it. Now I'm away again to my beloved Italy."

But it struck me as odd that, if Italy was her game, she went by the omnibus which takes down to the *train de luxe* for Paris. However, a man of the world accepts what a lady tells him, no matter how improbable; and I confess, for ten days or so, I thought no more about her, or the Seer either.

At the end of that time, our fortnightly pass-book came in from the bank in London. It is part of my duty, as the millionaire's secretary, to make up this book once a fortnight, and to compare the cancelled cheques with Sir Charles's counterfoils. On this particular occasion, I happened to observe what I can only describe as a very grave discrepancy. In fact, a discrepancy of £5,000. On the wrong side, too. Sir Charles was debited with £5,000 more than the total amount that was shown on the counterfoils.

I examined the book with care. The source of the error was obvious. It lay in a cheque to Self or Bearer, for £5,000, signed by Sir Charles, and evidently paid across the counter in London, as it bore on its face no stamp or indication of any other office.

I called in my brother-in-law from the salon to the study. "Look here, Charles," I said, "there's a cheque in the book which you haven't entered." And I handed it to him without comment, for I thought it might have been drawn to settle some little loss on the turf or at cards, or to make up some other affair he didn't desire to mention to me. These things will happen.

He looked at it and stared hard. Then he pursed up his mouth and gave a long, low "Whew!" At last he turned it over and remarked, "I say, Sey, my boy, we've just been done jolly well brown, haven't we?"

I glanced at the cheque. "How do you mean?" I inquired.

"Why, the Seer," he replied, still staring at it ruefully. "I don't mind the five thou., but to think the fellow should have gammoned the pair of us like that—ignominious, I call it!"

"How do you know it's the Seer?" I asked.

"Look at the green ink," he answered. "Besides, I recollect the very shape of the last flourish. I flourished a bit like that in the excitement of the moment, which I don't always do with my regular signature."

"He's done us," I answered, recognising it. "But how the dickens did he manage to transfer it to the cheque? This looks like your own handwriting, Charles, not a clever forgery."

"It is," he said. "I admit it—I can't deny it. Only fancy his bamboozling me when I was most on my guard! I wasn't to be taken in by any of his silly occult tricks and catch-words; but it never occurred to me he was going to victimize me financially in this way. I expected attempts at a loan or an extortion; but to collar my signature to a blank cheque—atrocious!"

"How did he manage it?" I asked.

"I haven't the faintest conception. I only know those are the words I wrote. I could swear to them anywhere."

"Then you can't protest the cheque?"

"Unfortunately, no; it's my own true signature."

We went that afternoon without delay to see the Chief Commissary of Police at the office. He was a gentlemanly Frenchman, much less formal and red-tapey than usual, and he spoke excellent English, with an American accent, having acted, in fact, as a detective in New York for about ten years in his early manhood.

"I guess," he said slowly, after hearing our story, "you've been victimized right here by Colonel Clay, gentlemen."

"I GUESS YOU'VE BEEN VICTIMIZED."

"Who is Colonel Clay?" Sir Charles asked.

"That's just what I want to know," the Commissary answered, in his curious American-French-English. "He is a Colonel, because he occasionally gives himself a commission; he is called Colonel Clay, because he appears to possess an indiarubber face, and he can mould it like clay in the hands of the potter. Real name, unknown. Nationality, equally French and English. Address, usually Europe. Profession, former maker of wax figures to the Musée Grévin. Age, what he chooses. Employs his knowledge to mould his own nose and cheeks, with wax additions, to the character he desires to personate. Aquiline, this time, you say. *Hein!* Anything like these photographs?"

He rummaged in his desk and handed us two.

"Not in the least," Sir Charles answered; "except, perhaps, as to the neck, everything here is quite unlike him."

"Then that's the Colonel!" the Commissary answered, with decision, rubbing his hands in glee. "Look here," and he took out a pencil and rapidly sketched the outline of one of the two faces—that of a bland-looking young man, with no expression worth mentioning. "There's the Colonel in his simple disguise. Very good. Now watch me: figure to yourself that he adds here a tiny patch of wax to his nose—an aquiline bridge—just so; well, you have him right there; and the chin, ah, one touch: now, for hair, a wig: for complexion, nothing easier: that's the profile of your rascal, isn't it?"

"Exactly," we both murmured. By two curves of the pencil, and a shock of false hair, the face was transmuted.

"He had very large eyes, with very big pupils, though," I objected, looking close; "and the man in the photograph here has them small and boiled-fishy."

"That's so," the Commissary answered. "A drop of belladonna expands—and produces the Seer; five grains of opium contract—and give a dead-alive, stupidly-innocent appearance. Well, you leave this affair to me, gentlemen. I'll see the fun out. I don't say I'll catch him for you; nobody ever yet has caught Colonel Clay; but I'll explain how he did the trick; and that ought to be consolation enough to a man of your means for a trifle of five thousand!"

"You are not the conventional French office-holder, M. le Commissaire," I ventured to interpose.

"You bet!" the Commissary replied, and drew himself up like a captain of infantry. "Messieurs," he continued, in French, with the utmost dignity, "I shall devote the resources of this office to tracing out the crime, and, if possible, to effectuating the arrest of the culpable."

We telegraphed to London, of course, and we wrote to the bank, with a full description of the suspected person. But I need hardly add that nothing came of it.

Three days later, the Commissary called at our hotel. "Well, gentlemen," he said, "I am glad to say I have discovered everything!"

"What? Arrested the Seer?" Sir Charles cried.

The Commissary drew back, almost horrified at the suggestion.

"Arrested Colonel Clay?" he exclaimed. "*Mais*, monsieur, we are only human! Arrested him? No, not quite. But tracked out how he did it. That is already much—to unravel Colonel Clay, gentlemen!"

"Well, what do you make of it?" Sir Charles asked, crestfallen.

The Commissary sat down and gloated over his discovery. It was clear a well-planned crime amused him vastly. "In the first place, monsieur," he said, "disabuse your mind of the idea that when monsieur your secretary went out to fetch Señor Herrera that night, Señor Herrera didn't know to whose rooms he was coming. Quite otherwise, in point of fact. I do not doubt myself that Señor Herrera, or Colonel Clay (call him which you like), came to Nice this winter for no other purpose than just to rob you."

"But I sent for him," my brother-in-law interposed.

"Yes; he *meant* you to send for him. He forced a card, so to speak. If he couldn't do that, I guess he would be a pretty poor conjurer. He had a lady of his own—his wife, let us say, or his sister—stopping here at this hotel; a certain Madame Picardet. Through her, he induced several ladies of your circle to attend his *séances*. She and they spoke to you about him, and aroused your curiosity. You may bet your bottom dollar that when he came to this room, he came ready primed and prepared with endless facts about both of you."

"What fools we have been, Sey," my brother-in-law exclaimed. "I see it all now. That designing woman sent round before dinner to say I wanted to meet him; and by the time you got there, he was ready for bamboozling me."

"That's so," the Commissary answered. "He had your name ready painted on both his arms; and he had made other preparations of still greater importance."

"You mean the cheque. Well, how did he get it?"

The Commissary opened the door. "Come in," he said. And a young man entered whom we recognised at once as the chief clerk in the Foreign Department of the Crédit Marseillais, the principal bank all along the Riviera.

"State what you know of this cheque," the Commissary said, showing it to him, for we had handed it over to the police as a piece of evidence.

"About four weeks since——" the clerk began.

"Say ten days before your *séance*," the Commissary interposed.

"A gentleman with very long hair and an aquiline nose, dark, strange, and handsome, called in at my department and asked if I could tell him the name of Sir Charles Vandrift's London banker. He said he had a sum to pay in to your credit, and asked if we would forward it for him. I told him it was irregular for us to receive the money, as you had no account with us, but that your London bankers were Darby, Drummond, and Rothenberg, Limited."

"Quite right," Sir Charles murmured.

"Two days later a lady, Madame Picardet, who was a customer of ours, brought in a good cheque for three hundred pounds, signed by a first-rate name, and asked us to pay it in on her behalf to Darby, Drummond, and Rothenberg's, and to open a London account with them for her. We did so, and received in reply a cheque-book."

"From which this cheque was taken, as I learn from the number, by telegram from London," the Commissary put in. "Also, that on the same day on which your cheque was cashed, Madame Picardet, in London, withdrew her balance."

"But how did the fellow get me to sign the cheque?" Sir Charles cried. "How did he manage the card trick?"

The Commissary produced a similar card from his pocket. "Was that the sort of thing?" he asked.

"Precisely! A facsimile."

"I thought so. Well, our Colonel, I find, bought a packet of such cards, intended for admission to a religious function, at a shop in the Quai Masséna. He cut out the centre,

"MADAME PICARDET WITHDREW HER BALANCE."

and, see here——" The Commissary turned it over, and showed a piece of paper pasted neatly over the back; this he tore off, and there, concealed behind it, lay a folded cheque, with only the place where the signature should be written showing through on the face which the Seer had presented to us. "I call that a neat trick," the Commissary remarked, with professional enjoyment of a really good deception.

"But he burnt the envelope before my eyes," Sir Charles exclaimed.

"Pooh!" the Commissary answered. "What would he be worth as a conjurer, anyway, if he couldn't substitute one envelope for another between the table and the fire-place without your noticing it? And Colonel Clay, you must remember, is a prince among conjurers."

"Well, it's a comfort to know we've identified our man, and the woman who was with him," Sir Charles said, with a slight sigh of relief. "The next thing will be, of course, you'll follow them up on these clues in England and arrest them?"

The Commissary shrugged his shoulders. "Arrest them!" he exclaimed, much amused. "Ah, monsieur, but you are sanguine! No officer of justice has ever succeeded in arresting le Colonel Caoutchouc, as we call him in French. He is as slippery as an eel, that man. He wriggles through our fingers. Suppose even we caught him, what could we prove? I ask you. Nobody who has seen him once can ever swear to him again in his next impersonation. He is *impayable*, this good Colonel. On the day when I arrest him, I assure you, monsieur, I shall consider myself the smartest police-officer in Europe."

"Well, I shall catch him yet," Sir Charles answered, and relapsed into silence.

BY GRANT ALLEN.

"LET us take a trip to Switzerland," said Lady Vandrift. And anyone who knows Amelia will not be surprised to learn that we *did* take a trip to Switzerland accordingly. Nobody can drive Sir Charles except his wife. And nobody at all can drive Amelia.

There were difficulties at the outset, because we had not ordered rooms at the hotels beforehand, and it was well on in the season; but they were overcome at last by the usual application of a golden key; and we found ourselves in due time pleasantly quartered in Lucerne, at that most comfortable of European hostelries, the Schweitzerhof.

We were a square party of four — Sir Charles and Amelia, myself and Isabel. We had nice big rooms, on the first floor, overlooking the lake, and as none of us was possessed with the faintest symptom of that incipient mania which shows itself in the form of an insane desire to climb mountain heights of disagreeable steepness and unnecessary snowiness, I will venture to assert we all enjoyed ourselves. We spent most of our time sensibly in lounging about the lake on the jolly little steamers; and when we did a mountain climb, it was on the Rigi or Pilatus —where an engine undertook all the muscular work for us.

As usual, at the hotel, a great many miscellaneous people showed a burning desire to be specially nice to us. If you wish to see how friendly and charming humanity is, just try being a well-known millionaire for a week, and you'll learn a thing or two. Wherever Sir Charles goes, he is surrounded by charming and disinterested people, all eager to make his distinguished acquaintance, and all familiar with several excellent investments, or several deserving objects of Christian charity. It is my business in life, as his brother-in-law and secretary, to decline with thanks the excellent investments, and to throw judicious cold water on the objects of charity. Even I myself, as the great man's almoner, am very much sought after. People casually allude before me to artless stories of "poor curates in Cumberland, you know, Mr. Wentworth," or widows in Cornwall, penniless poets with epics in their desks, and young painters who need but the breath of a patron to open to them the doors of an admiring Academy. I smile and look wise, while I administer cold water in minute doses; but I never report one of these cases to Sir Charles, except in the rare or almost unheard-of event where I think there is really something in them.

Ever since our little adventure with the Seer at Nice, Sir Charles, who is constitutionally cautious, had been even more careful than usual about possible sharpers. And, as chance would have it, there sat just opposite us at *table d'hôte* at the Schweitzerhof—'tis a fad of Amelia's to dine at *table d'hôte ;* she says she can't bear to be boxed up all day in private rooms with "too much family"--a sinister-looking man with dark hair and eyes, conspicuous by his bushy, overhanging eyebrows. My attention was first called to the eyebrows in question by a nice little parson who sat at our side, and who observed that they were made up of certain large and bristly hairs, which (he told us) had been traced by Darwin to our monkey ancestors. Very pleasant little fellow, this fresh-faced young parson, on his honeymoon tour with a nice wee wife, a bonnie Scotch lassie with a charming accent.

I looked at the eyebrows close. Then a sudden thought struck me. "Do you believe they're his own?" I asked of the curate; "or are they only stuck on—a make-up disguise? They really almost look like it."

"You don't suppose——" Charles began, and checked himself suddenly.

"Yes, I do," I answered; "the Seer!" Then I recollected my blunder, and looked down sheepishly. For, to say the truth, Vandrift had straightly enjoined on me long before to say nothing of our painful little episode at Nice to Amelia; he was afraid if *she* once heard of it, *he* would hear of it for ever after.

"What Seer?" the little parson inquired, with parsonical curiosity.

I noticed the man with the overhanging eyebrows give a queer sort of start. Charles's glance was fixed upon me. I hardly knew what to answer.

"Oh, a man who was at Nice with us last year," I stammered out, trying hard to look unconcerned. "A fellow they talked about, that's all." And I turned the subject.

But the curate, like a donkey, wouldn't let me turn it.

"Had he eyebrows like that?" he inquired, in an undertone. I was really angry. If this *was* Colonel Clay, the curate was obviously giving him the cue, and making it much more difficult for us to catch him, now we might possibly have lighted on the chance of doing so.

"No, he hadn't," I answered, testily; "it was a passing expression. But this is not the man. I was mistaken, no doubt." And I nudged him gently.

The little curate was too innocent for anything. "Oh, I see," he replied, nodding hard and looking wise. Then he turned to his wife, and made an obvious face, which the man with the eyebrows couldn't fail to notice.

Fortunately, a political discussion going on a few places further down the table spread up to us and diverted attention for a moment. The magical name of Gladstone saved us. Sir Charles flared up. I was truly pleased, for I could see Amelia was boiling over with curiosity by this time.

"THE MAN WITH THE BIG EYEBROWS SIDLED UP."

After dinner, in the billiard-room, however, the man with the big eyebrows sidled up and began to talk to me. If he *was* Colonel Clay, it was evident he bore us no grudge at all for the five thousand pounds he had done us out of. On the contrary, he seemed quite prepared to do us out of five thousand more when opportunity offered; for he introduced himself at once as Dr. Hector Macpherson, the exclusive grantee of extensive concessions from the Brazilian Government on the Upper Amazons. He dived into conversation with me at once as to the splendid mineral resources of his Brazilian estate—the silver, the platinum, the actual rubies, the possible diamonds. I listened and smiled; I knew what was coming. All he needed to develop this magnificent concession was a little more capital. It was sad to see thousands of pounds' worth of platinum and car-loads of rubies just crumbling in the soil or carried away by the river, for want of a few hundreds to work them with properly. If he knew of anybody, now, with money to invest, he could recommend him — nay, offer him — a unique opportunity of earning, say, 40 per cent. on his capital, on unimpeachable security.

"I wouldn't do it for every man," Dr. Hector Macpherson remarked, drawing himself up; "but if I took a fancy to a fellow who had command of ready cash, I might choose to put him in the way of feathering his nest with unexampled rapidity."

"Exceedingly disinterested of you," I answered, drily, fixing my eyes on his eyebrows.

The little curate, meanwhile, was playing billiards with Sir Charles. His glance followed mine as it rested for a moment on the monkey-like hairs.

"False, obviously false," he remarked with his lips; and I'm bound to confess I never saw any man speak so well by movement alone; you could follow every word, though not a sound escaped him.

During the rest of that evening, Dr. Hector Macpherson stuck to me as close as a mustard-plaster. And he was almost as irritating. I got heartily sick of the Upper Amazons. I have positively waded in my time through ruby mines (in prospectuses, I mean) till the mere sight of a ruby absolutely sickens me. When Charles, in an unwonted fit of generosity, once gave his sister Isabel (whom I had the honour to marry) a ruby necklet (inferior stones), I made Isabel change it for sapphires and amethysts, on the judicious plea that they suited her complexion better. (I scored one, incidentally, for having considered Isabel's complexion.) By the time I went to bed I was prepared to sink the Upper Amazons in the sea, and to stab, shoot, poison, or otherwise seriously damage the man with the concession and the false eyebrows.

For the next three days, at intervals, he returned to the charge. He bored me to death with his platinum and his rubies. He didn't want a capitalist who would personally exploit the thing; he would prefer to do it all on his own account, giving the capitalist preference debentures of his bogus company, and a lien on the concession. I listened and smiled; I listened and yawned; I listened and was rude; I ceased to listen at all; but still, he droned on with it. I fell asleep on the steamer one day, and woke up in ten minutes to hear him droning yet: "And the yield of platinum per ton was certified to be——" I forget how many pounds, or ounces, or pennyweights. These details of assays have ceased to interest me; like the man who "didn't believe in ghosts," I have seen too many of them.

The fresh-faced little curate and his wife, however, were quite different people. He was a cricketing Oxford man; she was a breezy Scotch lass, with a wholesome breath of the Highlands about her. I called her "White Heather." Their name was Brabazon. Millionaires are so accustomed to being beset by harpies of every description, that when they come across a young couple who are simple and natural, they delight in the purely human relation. We picnicked and went excursions a great deal with the honeymooners. They were so frank in their young love, and so proof against chaff, that we all really liked them. But whenever I called the pretty girl "White Heather," she looked so shocked, and cried: "Oh, Mr. Wentworth!" Still, we were the best of friends. The curate offered to row us in a boat on the lake one day, while the Scotch lassie assured us she could take an oar almost as well as he did. However, we did not accept their offer, as row-boats exert an unfavourable influence upon Amelia's digestive organs.

"Nice young fellow, that man Brabazon," Sir Charles said to me one day, as we lounged together along the quay; "never talks about advowsons or next presentations. Doesn't seem to me to care two pins about promotion. Says he's quite content in his country curacy; enough to live upon, and needs no more; and his wife has a little, a very little, money. I asked him about his poor to-day, on purpose to test him: these parsons are always trying to screw something out of one for their poor; men in my position know the truth of the saying that we have that class of the population always with us. Would you believe it, he says he hasn't any poor at all in his parish! They're all well-to-do farmers or else able-bodied labourers, and his one terror is that somebody will come and try to pauperize them. 'If a philanthropist were to give me fifty pounds to-day for use at Empingham,' he said, 'I assure you, Sir Charles, I shouldn't know what to do with it. I think I should buy new dresses for Jessie, who wants them about as much as anybody else in the village--that is to say, not at all.' There's a parson for you, Sey, my boy. Only wish we had one of his sort at Seldon."

"He certainly doesn't want to get anything out of you," I answered.

That evening at dinner, a queer little episode happened. The man with the eyebrows began talking to me across the table in his usual fashion, full of his wearisome concession on the Upper Amazons. I was trying to squash him as politely as possible, when I caught Amelia's eye. Her look amused me. She was engaged in making signals to Charles at her side to observe the little curate's curious sleeve-links. I glanced at them, and saw at once they were a singular possession for so unobtrusive a person. They consisted each of a short gold bar for one arm of the link, fastened by a tiny chain of the same material to what seemed to my tolerably experienced eye — a first-rate diamond. Pretty big diamonds, too, and of remarkable shape, brilliancy, and cutting. In a moment, I knew what Amelia meant. She owned a diamond *rivière*, said to be of Indian origin, but short by two stones for the circumference of her tolerably ample neck. Now, she had long been wanting two diamonds like these to match her set; but owing to the unusual shape and antiquated cutting of her own gems, she had never been able to complete the necklet, at least without removing an extravagant amount from a much larger stone of the first water.

The Scotch lassie's eyes caught Amelia's at the same time, and she broke into a pretty smile of good-humoured amusement. "Taken in another person, Dick, dear!" she exclaimed, in her breezy way, turning to her husband. "Lady Vandrift is observing your diamond sleeve-links."

"They're very fine gems," Amelia observed, incautiously. (A most unwise admission, if she desired to buy them.)

But the pleasant little curate was too transparently simple a soul to take advantage of her slip of judgment. "They *are* good stones," he replied; "very good stones—considering. They're not diamonds at all, to tell you the truth. They're best old-fashioned Oriental paste. My great-grandfather bought them, after the siege of Seringapatam, for a few rupees, from a Sepoy who had looted them from Tippoo Sultan's palace. He thought, like you, he had got a good thing. But it turned out, when they came to be examined by experts, they were only paste — very wonderful paste; it is supposed they had even imposed upon Tippoo himself, so fine is the imitation. But they are worth—well, say, fifty shillings at the utmost."

While he spoke, Charles looked at Amelia, and Amelia looked at Charles. Their eyes spoke volumes. The *rivière* was also supposed to have come from Tippoo's collection. Both drew at once an identical conclusion. These were two of the same stones, very likely torn apart and disengaged from the rest in the *mêlée* at the capture of the Indian palace.

"Can you take them off?" Sir Charles asked, blandly. He spoke in the tone that indicates business.

"Certainly," the little curate answered, smiling. "I'm accustomed to taking them off. They're always noticed. They've been kept in the family ever since the siege, as a sort of valueless heirloom, for the sake of the picturesqueness of the story, you know; and nobody ever sees them without asking, as you do, to examine them closely. They deceive even experts at first. But they're paste, all the same; unmitigated Oriental paste, for all that."

He took them both off, and handed them to Charles. No man in England is a finer judge of gems than my brother-in-law. I watched him narrowly. He examined them close, first with the naked eye, then with the little pocket-lens which he always carries. "Admirable imitation," he muttered, passing them on to Amelia. "I'm not surprised they should impose upon inexperienced observers."

But from the tone in which he said it, I could see at once he had satisfied himself they were real gems of unusual value. I know Charles's way of doing business so well. His glance to Amelia meant, "These are the very stones you have so long been in search of."

The Scotch lassie laughed a merry laugh. "He sees through them now, Dick," she cried. "I felt sure Sir Charles would be a judge of diamonds."

Amelia turned them over. I know Amelia, too; and I knew from the way Amelia looked at them that she meant to have them. And when Amelia means to have anything, people who stand in the way may just as well spare themselves the trouble of opposing her.

They were beautiful diamonds. We found out afterwards the little curate's account was quite correct: these stones *had* come from the same necklet as Amelia's *rivière*, made for a favourite wife of Tippoo's, who had presumably as expansive personal charms as our beloved sister-in-law's. More perfect diamonds have seldom been seen. They have excited the universal admiration of thieves and connoisseurs. Amelia told me afterwards that, according to legend, a Sepoy stole the necklet at the sack of the palace, and then fought with another for it. It was believed that two stones got spilt in the scuffle, and were picked up and sold by a third person—a looker-on—who had no idea of the value of his booty. Amelia had been hunting for them for several years, to complete her necklet.

"They are excellent paste," Sir Charles observed, handing them back. "It takes a first-rate judge to detect them from the reality. Lady Vandrift has a necklet much the same in character, but composed of genuine stones; and as these are so much like them, and would complete her set, to all outer appearance, I wouldn't mind giving you, say, £10 for the pair of them."

Mrs. Brabazon looked delighted. "Oh, sell them to him, Dick," she cried, "and buy me a brooch with the money! A pair of common links would do for you just as well. Ten pounds for two paste stones! It's quite a lot of money."

She said it so sweetly, with her pretty Scotch accent, that I couldn't imagine how Dick had the heart to refuse her. But he did, all the same.

"No, Jess, darling," he answered. "They're worthless, I know; but they have for me a certain sentimental value, as I've often told you. My dear mother wore them, while she lived, as earrings; and as soon as she died, I had them set as links in order that I might always keep them about me. Besides, they have historical and family interest. Even a worthless heirloom, after all, *is* an heirloom."

Dr. Hector Macpherson looked across and intervened. "There is a part of my concession," he said, "where we have reason to believe a perfect new Kimberley will soon be discovered. If at any time you would care, Sir Charles, to look at my diamonds—when I get them—it would afford me the greatest pleasure in life to submit them to your consideration."

Sir Charles could stand it no longer. "Sir," he said, gazing across at him with his sternest air, "if your concession were as full of diamonds as Sindbad the Sailor's valley, I would not care to turn my head to look at them. I am acquainted with the nature and practice of salting." And he glared at the man with the overhanging eyebrows as if he would devour him raw. Poor Dr. Hector Macpherson subsided instantly. We learnt a little later that he was a harmless lunatic, who went about the world with successive concessions for ruby mines and platinum reefs, because he had been ruined and driven mad by speculations in the two, and now recouped himself by imaginary grants in Burmah and Brazil, or anywhere else that turned up handy. And his eyebrows, after all, were of Nature's handicraft. We were sorry for the incident; but a man in Sir Charles's position is such a mark for rogues

"CHARLES, I SHALL NEVER BE HAPPY AGAIN TILL I GET THEM."

that, if he did not take means to protect himself promptly, he would be for ever overrun by them.

When we went up to our *salon* that evening, Amelia flung herself on the sofa. "Charles," she broke out in the voice of a tragedy queen, "those are real diamonds, and I shall never be happy again till I get them."

"They are real diamonds," Charles echoed. "And you shall have them, Amelia. They're worth not less than three thousand pounds. But I shall bid them up gently."

So, next day, Charles set to work to higgle with the curate. Brabazon, however, didn't care to part with them. He was no money-grubber, he said. He cared more for his mother's gift and a family tradition than for a hundred pounds, if Sir Charles were to offer it. Charles's eye gleamed. "But if I give you *two* hundred!" he said, insinuatingly. "What opportunities for good! You could build a new wing to your village school-house!"

"We have ample accommodation," the curate answered. "No, I don't think I'll sell them."

Still, his voice faltered somewhat, and he looked down at them inquiringly.

Charles was too precipitate.

"A hundred pounds more or less matters little to me," he said; "and my wife has set her heart on them. It's every man's duty to please his wife—isn't it, Mrs. Brabazon?—I offer you three hundred."

The little Scotch girl clasped her hands.

"Three hundred pounds! Oh, Dick, just think what fun we could have, and what good we could do with it! Do let him have them."

Her accent was irresistible. But the curate shook his head.

"Impossible," he answered. "My dear mother's earrings! Uncle Aubrey would be so angry if he knew I'd sold them. I daren't face Uncle Aubrey."

"Has he expectations from Uncle Aubrey?" Sir Charles asked of White Heather.

Mrs. Brabazon laughed. "Uncle Aubrey! Oh, dear, no. Poor dear old Uncle Aubrey! Why, the darling old soul hasn't a penny to bless himself with, except his pension. He's a retired post captain." And she laughed melodiously. She was a charming woman.

"Then I should disregard Uncle Aubrey's feelings," Sir Charles said, decisively.

"No, no," the curate answered. "Poor dear old Uncle Aubrey! I wouldn't do anything for the world to annoy him. And he'd be sure to notice it."

We went back to Amelia. "Well, have you got them?" she asked.

"No," Sir Charles answered. "Not yet. But he's coming round, I think. He's hesitating now. Would rather like to sell them himself, but is afraid what 'Uncle Aubrey' would say about the matter. His wife will talk him out of his needless consideration for Uncle Aubrey's feelings; and to-morrow we'll finally clench the bargain."

Next morning we stayed late in our *salon*, where we always breakfasted, and did not come down to the public rooms till just before *déjeûner*, Sir Charles being busy with me over arrears of correspondence. When we *did* come down, the *concierge* stepped forward with a twisted little feminine note for Amelia. She took it and read it. Her countenance fell. "There, Charles," she

"THE CONCIERGE STEPPED FORWARD WITH A LITTLE NOTE FOR AMELIA."

cried, handing it to him, "you've let the chance slip. I shall *never* be happy now! They've gone off with the diamonds."

Charles seized the note and read it. Then he passed it on to me. It was short, but final:—

"Thursday, 6 a.m.

"Dear Lady Vandrift,

"*Will* you kindly excuse our having gone off hurriedly without bidding you good-bye? We have just had a horrid telegram to say that Dick's favourite sister is *dangerously* ill of fever in Paris. I wanted to shake hands with you before we left—you have all been so sweet to us—but we go by the morning train, absurdly early, and I wouldn't for worlds disturb you. Perhaps some day we may meet again—though, buried as we are in a North-country village, it isn't likely; but in any case, you have secured the grateful recollection of

"Yours very cordially,

"JESSIE BRABAZON.

"P.S.—Kindest regards to Sir Charles and those *dear* Wentworths, and a kiss for yourself, if I may venture to send you one."

"She doesn't even mention where they've gone," Amelia exclaimed, in a very bad humour.

"The *concierge* may know," Isabel suggested, looking over my shoulder.

We asked at his office.

Yes, the gentleman's address was the Rev. Richard Peploe Brabazon, Holme Bush Cottage, Empingham, Northumberland.

Any address where letters might be sent at once, in Paris?

For the next ten days, or till further notice, Hotel des Deux Mondes, Avenue de l'Opéra.

Amelia's mind was made up at once.

"Strike while the iron's hot," she cried. "This sudden illness, coming at the end of their honeymoon, and involving ten days' more stay at an expensive hotel, will probably upset the curate's budget. He'll be glad to sell now. You'll get them for three hundred. It was absurd of Charles to offer so much at first; but offered once, of course we must stick to it."

"What do you propose to do?" Charles asked. "Write, or telegraph?"

"Oh, how silly men are!" Amelia cried. "Is this the sort of business to be arranged by letter, still less by telegram? No. Seymour must start off at once, taking the night train to Paris; and the moment he gets there, he must interview the curate or Mrs. Brabazon. Mrs. Brabazon's the best. She has none of this stupid, sentimental nonsense about Uncle Aubrey."

It is no part of a secretary's duties to act as a diamond broker. But when Amelia puts her foot down, she puts her foot down—a fact which she is unnecessarily fond of emphasizing in that identical proposition. So the self-same evening saw me safe in the train on my way to Paris; and next morning I turned out of my comfortable sleeping-car at the Gare de Strasbourg. My orders were to bring back those diamonds, alive or dead, so to speak, in my pocket, to Lucerne; and to offer any needful sum, up to two thousand five hundred pounds, for their immediate purchase.

When I arrived at the Deux Mondes, I found the poor little curate and his wife both greatly agitated. They had sat up all night, they said, with their invalid sister; and the sleeplessness and suspense had certainly told upon them after their long railway journey. They were pale and tired; Mrs. Brabazon in particular looking ill and worried—too much like White Heather. I was more than half ashamed of bothering them about the diamonds at such a moment; but it occurred to me that Amelia was probably right; they would now have reached the end of the sum set apart for their Continental trip; and a little ready cash might be far from unwelcome.

I broached the subject delicately. It was a fad of Lady Vandrift's, I said. She had set her heart upon those useless trinkets. And she wouldn't go without them. She must and would have them. But the curate was obdurate. He threw Uncle Aubrey still in my teeth. Three hundred?—no, never! A mother's present; impossible, dear Jessie! Jessie begged and prayed; she had grown really attached to Lady Vandrift, she said; but the curate wouldn't hear of it. I went up tentatively to four hundred. He shook his head gloomily. It wasn't a question of money, he said. It was a question of affection. I saw it was no use trying that tack any longer. I struck out a new line. "These stones," I said, "I think I ought to inform you, are really diamonds. Sir Charles is certain of it. Now, is it right for a man of your profession and position to be wearing a pair of big gems like those, worth several hundred pounds, as ordinary sleeve-links? A woman? Yes, I grant you; but for a man, is it manly? And you a cricketer!"

He looked at me and laughed. "Will nothing convince you?" he cried. "They have been examined and tested by half-a-dozen jewellers, and we know them to be paste. It wouldn't be right of me to sell them to you under false pretences, however unwilling on my side. I *couldn't* do it."

"Well, then," I said, going up a bit in my bids to meet him; "I'll put it like this. These gems are paste. But Lady Vandrift has an unconquerable and unaccountable desire to possess them. Money doesn't matter to her. She is a friend of your wife's. As a personal favour, won't you sell them to her for a thousand?"

He shook his head. "It would be wrong," he said—"I might even add, criminal."

"But we take all risk," I cried.

He was absolute adamant. "As a clergyman," he answered, "I feel I cannot do it."

"Will *you* try, Mrs. Brabazon?" I asked.

The pretty little Scotchwoman leant over and whispered. She coaxed and cajoled him. Her ways were winsome. I couldn't hear what she said; but he seemed to give way at last. "I should love Lady Vandrift to have them," she murmured, turning to me.

The curate looked up as if ashamed of himself.

"I consent," he said, slowly, "since Jessie wishes it. But as a clergyman, and to prevent any future misunderstanding, I should like you to give me a statement in writing that you buy them on my distinct and positive declaration that they are made of paste—old Oriental paste—not genuine stones, and that I do not claim any other qualities for them."

I popped the gems into my purse, well pleased.

"Certainly," I said, pulling out a paper. Charles, with his unerring business instinct, had anticipated the request, and given me a signed agreement to that effect.

"You will take a cheque?" I inquired.

He hesitated.

"Notes of the Bank of France would suit me better," he answered.

"Very well," I replied. "I will go out and get them."

How very unsuspicious some people are!

"SHE TOOK OUT THE LINKS FROM HER HUSBAND'S CUFFS."

"She *is* such a dear!" And she took out the links from her husband's cuffs and handed them across to me.

"How much?" I asked.

"Two thousand?" she answered, interrogatively. It was a big rise, all at once; but such are the ways of women.

"Done!" I replied. "Do you consent?"

He allowed me to go off—with the stones in my pocket!

Sir Charles had given me a blank cheque, not exceeding two thousand five hundred pounds. I took it to our agents and cashed it for notes of the Bank of France. The curate clasped them with pleasure. And right glad I was to go back to Lucerne that night, feeling that I had got those diamonds

"HAVE YOU BOUGHT THEM, SEYMOUR?

into my hands for about a thousand pounds under their real value!

At Lucerne railway station Amelia met me. She was positively agitated.

"Have you bought them, Seymour?" she asked.

"Yes," I answered, producing my spoils in triumph.

"Oh, how dreadful!" she cried, drawing back. "Do you think they're real? Are you sure he hasn't cheated you?"

"Certain of it," I replied, examining them. "No one can take me in, in the matter of diamonds. Why on earth should you doubt them?"

"Because I've been talking to Mrs. O'Hagan, at the hotel, and she says there's a well-known trick just like that—she's read of it in a book. A swindler has two sets, one real, one false; and he makes you buy the false ones by showing you the real, and pretending he sells them as a special favour."

"You needn't be alarmed," I answered. "I am a judge of diamonds."

"I sha'n't be satisfied," Amelia murmured, "till Charles has seen them."

We went up to the hotel. For the first time in her life, I saw Amelia really nervous as I handed the stones to Charles to examine. Her doubt was contagious. I half feared, myself, he might break out into a deep monosyllabic interjection, losing his temper in haste, as he often does when things go wrong. But he looked at them with a smile, while I told him the price.

"Eight hundred pounds less than their value," he answered, well satisfied.

"You have no doubt of their reality?" I asked.

"Not the slightest," he replied, gazing at them. "They are genuine stones, precisely the same in quality and type as Amelia's necklet."

Amelia drew a sigh of relief. "I'll go upstairs," she said, slowly, "and bring down my own for you both to compare with them."

One minute later, she rushed down again, breathless. Amelia is far from slim, and I never before knew her exert herself so actively.

"Charles, Charles!" she cried, "do you know what dreadful thing has happened? Two of my own stones are gone. He's stolen a couple of diamonds from my necklet, and sold them back to me."

She held out the *rivière*. It was all too true. Two gems were missing—and these two just fitted the empty places!

A light broke in upon me. I clapped my hand to my head. "By Jove," I exclaimed, "the little curate is—Colonel Clay!"

Charles clapped his own hand to his brow in turn. "And Jessie," he cried, "White Heather—that innocent little Scotchwoman! I often detected a familiar ring in her voice, in spite of the charming Highland accent. Jessie is—Madame Picardet!"

We had absolutely no evidence; but, like the Commissary at Nice, we felt instinctively sure of it.

Sir Charles was determined to catch the rogue. This second deception put him on his mettle. "The worst of the man is," he said, "he has a method. He doesn't go out of his way to cheat us; he makes us go out of ours to be cheated. He lays a trap, and we tumble headlong into it. To-morrow, Sey, we must follow him on to Paris."

Amelia explained to him what Mrs.

O'Hagan had said. Charles took it all in at once, with his usual sagacity. "That explains," he said, "why the rascal used this particular trick to draw us on by. If we had suspected him, he could have shown the diamonds were real, and so escaped detection. It was a blind to draw us off from the fact of the robbery. He went to Paris to be out of the way when the discovery was made, and to get a clear day's start of us. What a consummate rogue! And to do me twice running!"

"How did he get at my jewel-case, though?" Amelia exclaimed.

"That's the question," Charles answered. "You *do* leave it about so!"

"And why didn't he steal the whole *rivière* at once, and sell the gems?" I inquired.

"Too cunning," Charles replied. "This was much better business. It isn't easy to dispose of a big thing like that. In the first place, the stones are large and valuable; in the second place, they're well known—every dealer has heard of the Vandrift *rivière*, and seen pictures of the shape of them. They're marked gems, so to speak. No, he played a better game—took a couple of them off, and offered them to the only one person on earth who was likely to buy them without suspicion. He came here, meaning to work this very trick; he had the links made right to the shape beforehand, and then he stole the stones and slipped them into their places. It's a wonderfully clever trick. Upon my soul, I almost admire the fellow."

For Charles is a business man himself, and can appreciate business capacity in others.

How Colonel Clay came to know about that necklet, and to appropriate two of the stones, we only discovered much later. I will not here anticipate that disclosure. One thing at a time is a good rule in life. For the moment, he succeeded in baffling us altogether.

However, we followed him on to Paris, telegraphing beforehand to the Bank of France to stop the notes. It was all in vain. They had been cashed within half an hour of my paying them. The curate and his wife, we found, quitted the Hotel des Deux Mondes for parts unknown that same afternoon. And, as usual with Colonel Clay, they vanished into space, leaving no clue behind them. In other words, they changed their disguise, no doubt, and reappeared somewhere else that night in altered characters. At any rate, no such person as the Reverend Richard Peploe Brabazon was ever afterwards heard of—and, for the matter of that, no such village exists as Empingham, Northumberland.

We communicated the matter to the Parisian police. They were *most* unsympathetic. "It is, no doubt, Colonel Clay," said the official whom we saw; "but you seem to have little just ground of complaint against him. As far as I can see, messieurs, there is not much to choose between you. You, Monsieur le Chevalier, desired to buy diamonds at the price of paste. You, madame, feared you had bought paste at the price of diamonds. You, monsieur the secretary, tried to get the stones from an unsuspecting person for half their value. He took you all in, that brave Colonel Caoutchouc—it was diamond cut diamond."

Which was true, no doubt, but by no means consoling.

We returned to the Grand Hotel. Charles was fuming with indignation. "This is really too much," he exclaimed. "What an audacious rascal! But he will never again take me in, my dear Sey. I only hope he'll try it on. I should love to catch him. I'd know him another time, I'm sure, in spite of his disguises. It's absurd my being tricked twice running like this. But never again while I live! Never again, I declare to you!"

"*Jamais de la vie!*" a courier in the hall close by murmured responsive. We stood under the veranda of the Grand Hotel, in the big glass courtyard. And I verily believe that courier was really Colonel Clay himself in one of his disguises.

But perhaps we were beginning to suspect him everywhere.

VI

Round the Fire

A. CONAN DOYLE

Round the Fire.

II.—THE STORY OF THE MAN WITH THE WATCHES.

By A. Conan Doyle.

HERE are many who will still bear in mind the singular circumstances which, under the heading of the Rugby Mystery, filled many columns of the daily Press in the spring of the year 1892. Coming as it did at a period of exceptional dulness, it attracted perhaps rather more attention than it deserved, but it offered to the public that mixture of the whimsical and the tragic which is most stimulating to the popular imagination. Interest drooped, however, when, after weeks of fruitless investigation, it was found that no final explanation of the facts was forthcoming, and the tragedy seemed from that time to the present to have finally taken its place in the dark catalogue of inexplicable and unexpiated crimes. A recent communication (the authenticity of which appears to be above question) has, however, thrown some new and clear light upon the matter. Before laying it before the public it would be as well, perhaps, that I should refresh their memories as to the singular facts upon which this commentary is founded. These facts were briefly as follows:—

At five o'clock upon the evening of the 18th of March in the year already mentioned a train left Euston Station for Manchester. It was a rainy, squally day, which grew wilder as it progressed, so it was by no means the weather in which anyone would travel who was not driven to do so by necessity. The train, however, is a favourite one among Manchester business men who are returning from town, for it does the journey in four hours and twenty minutes, with only three stoppages upon the way. In spite of the inclement evening it was, therefore, fairly well filled upon the occasion of which I speak. The guard of the train was a tried servant of the company—a man who had worked for twenty-two years without blemish or complaint. His name was John Palmer.

The station clock was upon the stroke of five, and the guard was about to give the customary signal to the engine-driver, when he observed two belated passengers hurrying down the platform. The one was an exceptionally tall man, dressed in a long black overcoat with an astrakhan collar and cuffs. I have already said that the evening was an inclement one, and the tall traveller had the high, warm collar turned up to protect his throat against the bitter March wind. He appeared, as far as the guard could judge by so hurried an inspection, to be a man between fifty and sixty years of age, who had retained a good deal of the vigour and activity of his youth. In one hand he carried a brown leather Gladstone bag. His companion was a lady, tall and erect, walking with a vigorous step which outpaced the gentleman beside her. She wore a long, fawn-coloured dust-cloak, a black, close-fitting toque, and a dark veil which concealed the greater part of her face. The two might very well have passed as father and daughter. They walked swiftly down the line of carriages, glancing in at the

"THE TWO MIGHT VERY WELL HAVE PASSED AS FATHER AND DAUGHTER."

windows, until the guard, John Palmer, overtook them.

"Now, then, sir, look sharp, the train is going," said he.

"First-class," the man answered.

The guard turned the handle of the nearest door. In the carriage, which he had opened, there sat a small man with a cigar in his mouth. His appearance seems to have impressed itself upon the guard's memory, for he was prepared, afterwards, to describe or to identify him. He was a man of thirty-four or thirty-five years of age, dressed in some grey material, sharp nosed, alert, with a ruddy, weather-beaten face, and a small, closely cropped black beard. He glanced up as the door was opened. The tall man paused with his foot upon the step.

"This is a smoking compartment. The lady dislikes smoke," said he, looking round at the guard.

"All right! Here you are, sir!" said John Palmer. He slammed the door of the smoking carriage, opened that of the next one, which was empty, and thrust the two travellers in. At the same moment he sounded his whistle, and the wheels of the train began to move. The man with the cigar was at the window of his carriage, and said something to the guard as he rolled past him, but the words were lost in the bustle of the departure. Palmer stepped into the guard's van as it came up to him, and thought no more of the incident.

Twelve minutes after its departure the train reached Willesden Junction, where it stopped for a very short interval. An examination of the tickets has made it certain that no one either joined or left it at this time, and no passenger was seen to alight upon the platform. At 5.14 the journey to Manchester was resumed, and Rugby was reached at 6.50, the express being five minutes late.

"HE GLANCED UP AS THE DOOR WAS OPENED."

At Rugby the attention of the station officials was drawn to the fact that the door of one of the first-class carriages was open. An examination of that compartment, and of its neighbour, disclosed a remarkable state of affairs.

The smoking carriage in which the short, red-faced man with the black beard had been seen was now empty. Save for a half-smoked cigar, there was no trace whatever of its recent occupant. The door of this carriage was fastened. In the next compartment, to which attention had been originally drawn, there was no sign either of the gentleman with the astrakhan collar or of the young lady who accompanied him. All three passengers had disappeared. On the other hand, there was found upon the floor of this carriage—the one in which the tall traveller and the lady had been—a young man, fashionably dressed and of elegant appearance. He lay with his knees drawn up, and his head resting against the further door, an elbow upon either seat. A bullet had penetrated his heart, and his death must have been instantaneous. No one had seen such a man enter the train, and no railway ticket was found in his pocket, nor were there any markings upon his linen, nor papers or personal property which might help to identify him. Who he was, whence he had come, and how he had met his end were each as great a mystery as what had occurred to the three people who had started an hour and a half before from Willesden in those two compartments.

"A BULLET HAD PENETRATED HIS HEART."

I have said that there was no personal property which might help to identify him, but it is true that there was one peculiarity about this unknown young man which was much commented upon at the time. In his pockets were found no fewer than six valuable gold watches, three in the various pockets of his waistcoat, one in his ticket-pocket, one in his breast-pocket, and one small one set in a leather strap and fastened round his left wrist. The obvious explanation that the man was a pick-pocket, and that this was his plunder, was discounted by the fact that all six were of American make, and of a type which is rare in England. Three of them bore the mark of the Rochester Watchmaking Company; one was by Mason, of Elmira; one was unmarked; and the small one, which was highly jewelled and ornamented, was from Tiffany, of New York. The other contents of his pocket consisted of an ivory knife with a corkscrew by Rodgers, of Sheffield; a small circular mirror, one inch in diameter; a re-admission slip to the Lyceum theatre; a silver box full of vesta matches, and a brown leather cigar-case containing two cheroots—also two pounds fourteen shillings in money. It was clear then that whatever motives may have led to his death, robbery was not among them. As already mentioned, there were no markings upon the man's linen, which appeared to be new, and no tailor's name upon his coat. In appearance he was young, short, smooth cheeked, and delicately featured. One of his front teeth was conspicuously stopped with gold.

On the discovery of the tragedy an examination was instantly made of the tickets of all passengers, and the number of the passengers themselves was counted. It was found that only three tickets were unaccounted for, corresponding to the three travellers who were missing. The express was then allowed to proceed, but a new guard was sent with it, and John Palmer was detained as a witness at Rugby. The carriage which included the two compartments in question was uncoupled and side-tracked. Then, on the arrival of Inspector Vane, of Scotland Yard, and of Mr. Henderson, a detective in the service of the railway company, an exhaustive inquiry was made into all the circumstances.

That crime had been committed was certain. The bullet, which appeared to have come from a small pistol or revolver, had been fired from some little distance, as there was no scorching of the clothes. No weapon was found in the compartment (which finally disposed of the theory of suicide), nor was there any sign of the brown leather bag which the guard had seen in the hand of the tall gentleman. A lady's parasol was found upon the rack, but no other trace was to be seen of the travellers in either of the sections. Apart from the crime, the question of how or why three passengers (one of them a lady) could get out of the train, and one other get in during the unbroken run between Willesden and Rugby, was one which excited the utmost curiosity among the general public, and gave rise to much speculation in the London Press.

John Palmer, the guard, was able at the inquest to give some evidence which threw a little light upon the matter. There was a spot between Tring and Cheddington, according to his statement, where, on account of some repairs to the line, the train had for a few minutes slowed down to a pace not exceeding eight or ten miles an hour. At that place it might be possible for a man, or even for an exceptionally active woman, to have left the train without serious injury. It was true that a gang of platelayers was there, and that they had seen nothing, but it was their custom to stand in the middle between the metals, and the open carriage door was upon the far side, so that it was conceivable that someone might have alighted unseen, as the darkness would by that time be drawing in. A steep embankment would instantly screen anyone who sprang out from the observation of the navvies.

The guard also deposed that there was a good deal of movement upon the platform at Willesden Junction, and that though it was certain that no one had either joined or left the train there, it was still quite possible that some of the passengers might have changed unseen from one compartment to another. It was by no means uncommon for a gentleman to finish his cigar in a smoking carriage and then to change to a clearer atmosphere. Supposing that the man with the black beard had done so at Willesden (and the half-smoked cigar upon the floor seemed to favour the supposition), he would naturally go into the nearest section, which would bring him into the company of the two other actors in this drama. Thus the first stage of the affair might be surmised without any great breach of probability. But what the second stage had been, or how the final one had been arrived at, neither the guard nor the experienced detective officers could suggest.

"A GANG OF PLATELAYERS WAS THERE."

A careful examination of the line between Willesden and Rugby resulted in one discovery which might or might not have a bearing upon the tragedy. Near Tring, at the very place where the train slowed down, there was found at the bottom of the embankment a small pocket Testament, very shabby and worn. It was printed by the Bible Society of London, and bore an inscription: "From John to Alice. Jan. 13th, 1856," upon the fly-leaf. Underneath was written: "James. July 4th, 1859," and beneath that again: "Edward. Nov. 1st, 1869," all the entries being in the same handwriting. This was the only clue, if it could be called a clue, which the police obtained, and the coroner's verdict of "Murder by a person or persons unknown" was the unsatisfactory ending of a singular case. Advertisement, rewards, and inquiries proved equally fruitless, and nothing could be found which was solid enough to form the basis for a profitable investigation.

It would be a mistake, however, to suppose that no theories were formed to account for the facts. On the contrary, the Press, both in England and in America, teemed with suggestions and suppositions, most of which were obviously absurd. The fact that the watches were of American make, and some peculiarities in connection with the gold stopping of his front tooth, appeared to indicate that the deceased was a citizen of the United States, though his linen, clothes, and boots were undoubtedly of British manufacture. It was surmised, by some, that he was concealed under the seat, and that, being discovered, he was for some reason, possibly because he had overheard their guilty secrets, put to death by his fellow-passengers. When coupled with generalities as to the ferocity and cunning of anarchical and other secret societies, this theory sounded as plausible as any.

The fact that he should be without a ticket would be consistent with the idea of concealment, and it was well known that women played a prominent part in the Nihilistic propaganda. On the other hand, it was clear, from the guard's statement, that the man must have been hidden there *before* the others arrived, and how unlikely the coincidence that conspirators should stray exactly into the very compartment in which a spy was already concealed! Besides, this explanation ignored the man in the smoking carriage, and gave no reason at all for his simultaneous disappearance. The police had little difficulty in showing that such a theory would not cover the facts, but they were unprepared in the absence of evidence to advance any alternative explanation.

There was a letter in the *Daily Gazette*, over the signature of a well-known criminal investigator, which gave rise to considerable discussion at the time. He had formed a hypothesis which had at least ingenuity to recommend it, and I cannot do better than append it in his own words.

"Whatever may be the truth," said he, "it must depend upon some bizarre and rare combination of events, so we need have no hesitation in postulating such events in our explanation. In the absence of data we must abandon the analytic or scientific method of investigation, and must approach it in the synthetic fashion. In a word, instead of taking known events and deducing from them what has occurred, we must build up a fanciful explanation if it will only be consistent with known events. We can then test this explanation by any fresh facts which may arise. If they all fit into their places, the probability is that we are upon the right track, and with each fresh fact this probability increases in a geometrical progression until the evidence becomes final and convincing.

"Now, there is one most remarkable and suggestive fact which has not met with the attention which it deserves. There is a local train running through Harrow and King's Langley, which is timed in such a way that the express must have overtaken it at or about the period when it eased down its speed to eight miles an hour on account of the repairs of the line. The two trains would at that time be travelling in the same direction at a similar rate of speed and upon parallel lines. It is within everyone's experience how, under such circumstances, the occupant of each carriage can see very plainly the passengers in the other carriages opposite to him. The lamps of the express had been lit at Willesden, so that each compartment was brightly illuminated, and most visible to an observer from outside.

"Now, the sequence of events as I reconstruct them would be after this fashion. This young man with the abnormal number of watches was alone in the carriage of the slow train. His ticket, with his papers and gloves and other things, was, we will suppose, on the seat beside him. He was probably an American, and also probably a man of weak intellect. The excessive wearing of jewellery is an early symptom in some forms of mania.

"As he sat watching the carriages of the express which were (on account of the state of the line) going at the same pace as himself, he suddenly saw some people in it whom he knew. We will suppose for the sake of our theory that these people were a woman whom he loved and a man whom he hated—and who in return hated him. The young man was excitable and impulsive. He opened the door of his carriage, stepped from the footboard of the local train to the footboard of the express, opened the other door, and made his way into the presence of these two people. The feat (on the supposition that the trains were going at the same pace) is by no means so perilous as it might appear.

"Having now got our young man without his ticket into the carriage in which the elder man and the young woman are travelling, it is not difficult to imagine that a violent scene ensued. It is possible that the pair were also Americans, which is the more probable as the man carried a weapon—an unusual thing in England. If our supposition of incipient mania is correct, the young man is likely to have assaulted the other. As the upshot of the quarrel the elder man shot the intruder, and then made his escape from the carriage, taking the young lady with him. We will suppose that all this happened very rapidly, and that the train was still going at so slow a pace that it was not difficult for them to leave it. A woman might leave a train going at eight miles an hour. As a matter of fact, we know that this woman *did* do so.

"And now we have to fit in the man in the smoking carriage. Presuming that we have, up to this point, reconstructed the tragedy correctly, we shall find nothing in this other man to cause us to reconsider our conclusions. According to my theory, this man saw the young fellow cross from one train to the other, saw him open the door, heard the pistol-shot, saw the two fugitives spring out on to the line, realized that murder had been done, and sprang out himself in pursuit. Why he has never been heard of since—whether he met his own death in the pursuit, or whether, as is more likely, he was made to realize that it was not a case for his interference—is a detail which we have at present no means of explaining. I acknowledge that there are some difficulties in the way. At first sight, it might seem improbable that at such a moment a murderer would burden himself in his flight with a brown leather bag. My answer is that he was well aware that if the bag were found his identity would be established. It was absolutely necessary for him to take it with him. My theory stands or falls upon one point, and I call upon the railway company to make strict inquiry as to whether a ticket was found unclaimed in the local train through Harrow and King's Langley upon the 18th of March. If such a ticket were found my case is proved. If not, my theory may still be the correct one, for it is conceivable either that he travelled without a ticket or that his ticket was lost."

To this elaborate and plausible hypothesis the answer of the police and of the company was, first, that no such ticket was found; secondly, that the slow train would never run parallel to the express; and, thirdly, that the local train had been stationary in King's Langley Station when the express, going at fifty miles an hour, had flashed past it. So perished the only satisfying explanation, and five years have elapsed without supplying a new one. Now, at last, there comes a statement which covers all the facts, and which must be regarded as authentic. It took the shape of a letter dated from New York, and addressed to the same criminal investigator whose theory I have quoted. It is given here in extenso, with the exception of the two opening paragraphs, which are personal in their nature:—

"You'll excuse me if I am not very free with names. There's less reason now than there was five years ago when mother was still living. But for all that, I had rather cover up our tracks all I can. But I owe you an explanation, for if your idea of it was wrong, it was a mighty ingenious one all the same. I'll have to go back a little so as you may understand all about it.

"My people came from Bucks, England, and emigrated to the States in the early fifties. They settled in Rochester, in the State of New York, where my father ran a large dry goods store. There were only two sons: myself, James, and my brother, Edward. I was ten years older than my brother, and after my father died I sort of took the place of a father to him, as an elder brother would. He was a bright, spirited boy, and just one of the most beautiful creatures that ever lived. But there was always a soft spot in him, and it was like mold in cheese, for it spread and spread, and nothing that you could do would stop it. Mother saw it just as clearly as I did, but she went on spoiling him all the same, for he had such a way with him that you could refuse him nothing. I did all I could to hold him in, and he hated me for my pains.

"At last he fairly got his head, and nothing that we could do would stop him. He got off into New York, and went rapidly from bad to worse. At first he was only fast, and then he was criminal; and then, at the end of a year or two, he was one of the most notorious young crooks in the city. He had formed a friendship with Sparrow MacCoy, who was at the head of his profession as a bunco-steerer, green-goodsman, and general rascal. They took to card-sharping, and frequented some of the best hotels in New York. My brother was an excellent actor (he might have made an honest name for himself if he had chosen), and he would take the parts of a young Englishman of title, of a simple lad from the West, or of a college undergraduate, whichever suited Sparrow MacCoy's purpose. And then one day he dressed himself as a girl, and he carried it off so well, and made himself such a valuable decoy, that it was their favorite game afterwards. They had made it right with Tammany and with the police, so it seemed as if nothing could ever stop them, for those were in the days before the Lexow Commission, and if you only had a pull, you could do pretty nearly anything you wanted.

"HE FORMED A FRIENDSHIP WITH SPARROW MACCOY."

"And nothing would have stopped them if they had only stuck to cards and New York, but they must needs come up Rochester way, and forge a name upon a check. It was my brother that did it, though every-one knew that it was under the influence of Sparrow MacCoy. I bought up that check, and a pretty sum it cost me. Then I went to my brother, laid it before him on the table, and swore to him that I would prosecute if he did not clear out of the country. At first he simply laughed. I could not prosecute, he said, without breaking our mother's heart, and he knew that I would not do that. I made him understand, however, that our mother's heart was being broken in any case, and that I had set firm on the point that I would rather see him in a Rochester gaol than in a New York hotel. So at last he gave in, and he made me a solemn promise that he would see Sparrow MacCoy no more, that he would go to Europe, and that he would turn his hand to any honest trade that I helped him to get. I took him down right away to an old family friend, Joe Willson, who is an exporter of American watches and clocks, and I got him to give Edward an agency in London, with a small salary and a 5 per cent. commission on all business. His manner and appearance were so good that he won the old man over at once, and within a week he was sent off to London with a case full of samples.

"It seemed to me that this business of the check had really given my brother a fright, and that there was some chance of his settling down into an honest line of life. My mother had spoken with him, and what she said had touched him, for she had always been the best of mothers to him, and he had been the great sorrow of her life. But I knew that this man Sparrow MacCoy had a great influence over Edward, and my chance of keeping the lad straight lay in breaking the connection between them. I had a friend in the New York detective force, and through him I kept a watch upon MacCoy. When within a fortnight of my brother's sailing I heard that MacCoy had taken a berth in the *Etruria*, I was as certain as if he had told me that he was going over to

England for the purpose of coaxing Edward back again into the ways that he had left. In an instant I had resolved to go also, and to put my influence against MacCoy's. I knew it was a losing fight, but I thought, and my mother thought, that it was my duty. We passed the last night together in prayer for my success, and she gave me her own Testament that my father had given her on the day of their marriage in the Old Country, so that I might always wear it next my heart.

"'Who is it, anyway?' asked one of the dudes.

"'He's Sparrow MacCoy, the most notorious card-sharper in the States.'

"Up he jumped with a bottle in his hand, but he remembered that he was under the flag of the effete Old Country, where law and order run, and Tammany has no pull. Gaol and the gallows wait for violence and murder, and there's no slipping out by the back door on board an ocean liner.

"UP HE JUMPED WITH A BOTTLE IN HIS HAND."

"I was a fellow-traveller, on the steamship, with Sparrow MacCoy, and at least I had the satisfaction of spoiling his little game for the voyage. The very first night I went into the smoking-room, and found him at the head of a card table, with half-a-dozen young fellows who were carrying their full purses and their empty skulls over to Europe. He was settling down for his harvest, and a rich one it would have been. But I soon changed all that.

"'Gentlemen,' said I, 'are you aware whom you are playing with?'

"'What's that to you? You mind your own business!' said he, with an oath.

"'Prove your words, you——!' said he.

"'I will!' said I. 'If you will turn up your right shirt-sleeve to the shoulder, I will either prove my words or I will eat them.'

"He turned white and said not a word. You see, I knew something of his ways, and I was aware that part of the mechanism which he and all such sharpers use consists of an elastic down the arm with a clip just above the wrist. Is is by means of this clip that they withdraw from their hands the cards which they do not want, while they substitute other cards from another hiding-place. I reckoned on it being there, and it was. He cursed me, slunk out of the saloon, and was hardly seen again during the voyage. For once, at any rate, I got level with Mister Sparrow MacCoy.

"But he soon had his revenge upon me, for when it came to influencing my brother he outweighed me every time. Edward had kept himself straight in London for the first few weeks, and had done some business with his American watches, until this villain came across his path once more. I did my best, but the best was little enough. The next thing I heard there had been a scandal at one of the Northumberland Avenue hotels: a traveller had been fleeced of a large sum by two confederate card-sharpers, and the matter was in the hands of Scotland Yard. The first I learned of it was in the evening paper, and I was at once certain that my brother and MacCoy were back at their old games. I hurried at once to Edward's lodgings. They told me that he and a tall gentleman (whom I recognised as MacCoy) had gone off together, and that he had left the lodgings and taken his things with him. The landlady had heard them give several directions to the cabman, ending with Euston Station, and she had accidentally overheard the tall gentleman saying something about Manchester. She believed that that was their destination.

"A glance at the time-table showed me that the most likely train was at five, though there was another at 4.35 which they might have caught. I had only time to get the later one, but found no sign of them either at the depôt or in the train. They must have gone on by the earlier one, so I determined to follow them to Manchester and search for them in the hotels there. One last appeal to my brother by all that he owed to my mother might even now be the salvation of him. My nerves were overstrung, and I lit a cigar to steady them. At that moment, just as the train was moving off, the door of my compartment was flung open, and there were MacCoy and my brother on the platform.

"They were both disguised, and with good reason, for they knew that the London police were after them. MacCoy had a great astrakhan collar drawn up, so that only his eyes and nose were showing. My brother was dressed like a woman, with a black veil half down his face, but of course it did not deceive me for an instant, nor would it have done so even if I had not known that he had often used such a dress before. I started up, and as I did so MacCoy recognised me. He said something, the conductor slammed the door, and they were shown into the next compartment. I tried to stop the train so as to follow them, but the wheels were already moving, and it was too late.

"When we stopped at Willesden, I instantly changed my carriage. It appears that I was not seen to do so, which is not surprising, as the station was crowded with people. MacCoy, of course, was expecting me, and he had spent the time between Euston and Willesden in saying all he could to harden my brother's heart and set him against me. That is what I fancy, for I had never found him so impossible to soften or to move. I tried this way and I tried that; I pictured his future in an English gaol; I described the sorrow of his mother when I came back with the news; I said everything to touch his heart, but all to no purpose. He sat there with a fixed sneer upon his handsome face, while every now and then Sparrow MacCoy would throw in a taunt at me, or some word of encouragement to hold my brother to his resolutions.

"'Why don't you run a Sunday-school?' he would say to me, and then, in the same breath: 'He thinks you have no will of your own. He thinks you are just the baby brother and that he can lead you where he likes. He's only just finding out that you are a man as well as he.'

"It was those words of his which set me talking bitterly. We had left Willesden, you understand, for all this took some time. My temper got the better of me, and for the first time in my life I let my brother see the rough side of me. Perhaps it would have been better had I done so earlier and more often.

"'A man!' said I. 'Well, I'm glad to have your friend's assurance of it, for no one would suspect it to see you like a boarding-school missy. I don't suppose in all this country there is a more contemptible-looking creature than you are as you sit there with that Dolly pinafore upon you.' He coloured up at that, for he was a vain man, and he winced from ridicule.

"'It's only a dust-cloak,' said he, and he slipped it off. 'One has to throw the coppers off one's scent, and I had no other way to do it.' He took his toque off with the veil attached, and he put both it and the cloak into his brown bag. 'Anyway, I don't need to wear it until the conductor comes round,' said he.

"'Nor then, either,' said I, and taking the bag I slung it with all my force out of the window. 'Now,' said I, 'you'll never make a Mary Jane of yourself while I can help it. If nothing but that disguise stands between you and a gaol, then to gaol you shall go.'

"That was the way to manage him. I felt my advantage at once. His supple nature was one which yielded to roughness far more readily than to entreaty. He flushed with shame, and his eyes filled with tears. But MacCoy saw my advantage also, and was determined that I should not pursue it.

"'He's my pard, and you shall not bully him,' he cried.

"'He's my brother, and you shall not ruin him,' said I. 'I believe a spell of prison is the very best way of keeping you apart, and you shall have it, or it will be no fault of mine.'

"'Oh, you would squeal, would you?' he cried, and in an instant he whipped out his revolver. I sprang for his hand, but saw that I was too late, and jumped aside. At the same instant he fired, and the bullet which would have struck me passed through the heart of my unfortunate brother.

"He dropped without a groan upon the floor of the compartment, and MacCoy and I, equally horrified, knelt at each side of him, trying to bring back some signs of life. MacCoy still held the loaded revolver in his hand, but his anger against me and my resentment towards him had both for the moment been swallowed up in this sudden tragedy. It was he who first realized the situation. The train was for some reason going very slowly at the moment, and he saw his opportunity for escape. In an instant he had the door open, but I was as quick as he, and jumping upon him the two of us fell off the foot-board and rolled in each other's arms down a steep embankment. At the bottom I struck my head against a stone, and I remembered nothing more. When I came to myself I was lying among some low bushes, not far from the railroad track, and somebody was bathing my head with a wet handkerchief. It was Sparrow MacCoy.

"'I guess I couldn't leave you,' said he. 'I didn't want to have the blood of two of you on my hands in one day. You loved your brother, I've no doubt; but you didn't love him a cent more than I loved him, though you'll say that I took a queer way to show it. Anyhow, it seems a mighty empty world now that he is gone, and I don't care a continental whether you give me over to the hangman or not.'

"'I GUESS I COULDN'T LEAVE YOU,' SAID HE."

"He had turned his ankle in the fall, and there we sat, he with his useless foot, and I with my throbbing head, and we talked and talked until gradually my bitterness began to soften and to turn into something like sympathy. What was the use of revenging his death upon a man who was as much stricken by that death as I was? And then, as my wits gradually returned, I began to realize also that I could do nothing against MacCoy which would not recoil upon my mother and myself. How could we convict him without a full account of my brother's career being made public—the very thing which of all others we had to avoid? It was really as much our interest as his to cover the matter up, and from being an avenger of crime I found myself changed to a conspirator against Justice. The place in which we found ourselves was one of those pheasant preserves which are so common in the Old Country, and as we groped our way through it I found myself consulting the slayer of my brother as to how far it would be possible to hush it up.

"I soon realized from what he said that unless there were some papers of which we knew nothing in my brother's pockets, there was really no possible means by which the police could identify him or learn how he had got there. His ticket was in MacCoy's pocket, and so was the ticket for some baggage which they had left at the depôt. Like most Americans, he had found it cheaper and easier to buy an outfit in London than to bring one from New York, so that all his linen and clothes were new and unmarked. The bag, containing the dust cloak, which I had thrown out of the window, may have fallen among some bramble patch where it is still concealed, or may have been carried off by some tramp, or may have come into the possession of the police, who kept the incident to themselves. Anyhow, I have seen nothing about it in the London papers. As to the watches, they were a selection from those which had been intrusted to him for business purposes. It may have been for the same business purposes that he was taking them to Manchester, but—well, it's too late to enter into that.

"I don't blame the police for being at fault. I don't see how it could have been otherwise. There was just one little clew that they might have followed up, but it was a small one. I mean that small circular mirror which was found in my brother's pocket. It isn't a very common thing for a young man to carry about with him, is it? But a gambler might have told you what such a mirror may mean to a card-sharper. If you sit back a little from the table, and lay the mirror, face upwards, upon your lap, you can see, as you deal, every card that you give to your adversary. It is not hard to say whether you see a man or raise him when you know his cards as well as your own. It was as much a part of a sharper's outfit as the elastic clip upon Sparrow MacCoy's arm. Taking that, in connection with the recent frauds at the hotels, the police might have got hold of one end of the string.

"I don't think there is much more for me to explain. We got to a village called Amersham that night in the character of two gentlemen upon a walking tour, and afterwards we made our way quietly to London, whence MacCoy went on to Cairo and I returned to New York. My mother died six months afterwards, and I am glad to say that to the day of her death she never knew what had happened. She was always under the delusion that Edward was earning an honest living in London, and I never had the heart to tell her the truth. He never wrote; but, then, he never did write at any time, so that made no difference. His name was the last upon her lips.

"There's just one other thing that I have to ask you, sir, and I should take it as a kind return for all this explanation, if you could do it for me. You remember that Testament that was picked up. I always carried it in my inside pocket, and it must have come out in my fall. I value it very highly, for it was the family book with my birth and my brother's marked by my father in the beginning of it. I wish you would apply at the proper place and have it sent to me. It can be of no possible value to anyone else. If you address it to X, Bassano's Library, Broadway, New York, it is sure to come to hand."

Round the Fire.

By A. Conan Doyle.

III.—THE STORY OF THE LOST SPECIAL.

HE confession of Herbert de Lernac, now lying under sentence of death at Marseilles, has thrown a light upon one of the most inexplicable crimes of the century — an incident which is, I believe, absolutely unprecedented in the criminal annals of any country. Although there is a reluctance to discuss the matter in official circles, and little information has been given to the Press, there are still indications that the statement of this arch-criminal is corroborated by the facts, and that we have at last found a solution for a most astounding business. As the matter is eight years old, and as its importance was somewhat obscured by a political crisis which was engaging the public attention at the time, it may be as well to state the facts as far as we have been able to ascertain them. They are collated from the Liverpool papers of that date, from the proceedings at the inquest upon John Slater, the engine-driver, and from the records of the London and West Coast Railway Company, which have been courteously put at my disposal. Briefly, they are as follows.

On the 3rd of June, 1890, a gentleman, who gave his name as Monsieur Louis Caratal, desired an interview with Mr. James Bland, the superintendent of the Central London and West Coast Station in Liverpool. He was a small man, middle-aged and dark, with a stoop which was so marked that it suggested some deformity of the spine. He was accompanied by a friend, a man of imposing physique, whose deferential manner and constant attention suggested that his position was one of dependence. This friend or companion, whose name did not transpire, was certainly a foreigner, and probably, from his swarthy complexion, either a Spaniard or a South American. One peculiarity was observed in him. He carried in his left hand a small black leather despatch-box, and it was noticed by a sharp-eyed clerk in the Central office that this box was fastened to his wrist by a strap. No importance was attached to the fact at the time, but subsequent events endowed it with some significance. Monsieur Caratal was shown up to Mr. Bland's office, while his companion remained outside.

Monsieur Caratal's business was quickly dispatched. He had arrived that afternoon from Central America. Affairs of the utmost importance demanded that he should be in Paris without the loss of an unnecessary hour. He had missed the London express. A special must be provided. Money was of no importance. Time was everything. If the company would speed him on his way, they might make their own terms.

MONSIEUR LOUIS CARATAL AND HIS FRIEND.

Mr. Bland struck the electric bell, summoned Mr. Potter Hood, the traffic manager, and had the matter arranged in five minutes. The train would start in three-quarters of an hour. It would take that time to insure that the line should be clear. The powerful engine called Rochdale (No. 247 on the company's register) was attached to two carriages, with a guard's van behind. The first carriage was solely for the purpose of decreasing the inconvenience arising from the oscillation. The second was divided, as usual, into four compartments, a first-class, a first-class smoking, a second-class, and a second-class smoking. The first compartment, which was the nearest to the engine, was the one allotted to the travellers. The other three were empty. The guard of the special train was James McPherson, who had been some years in the service of the company. The stoker, William Smith, was a new hand.

Monsieur Caratal, upon leaving the superintendent's office, rejoined his companion, and both of them manifested extreme impatience to be off. Having paid the money asked, which amounted to fifty pounds five shillings, at the usual special rate of five shillings a mile, they demanded to be shown the carriage, and at once took their seats in it, although they were assured that the better part of an hour must elapse before the line could be cleared. In the meantime a singular coincidence had occurred in the office which Monsieur Caratal had just quitted.

A request for a special is not a very uncommon circumstance in a rich commercial centre, but that two should be required upon the same afternoon was most unusual. It so happened, however, that Mr. Bland had hardly dismissed the first traveller before a second entered with a similar request. This was a Mr. Horace Moore, a gentlemanly man of military appearance, who alleged that the sudden serious illness of his wife in London made it absolutely imperative that he should not lose an instant in starting upon the journey. His distress and anxiety were so evident that Mr. Bland did all that was possible to meet his wishes. A second special was out of the question, as the ordinary local service was already somewhat deranged by the first. There was the alternative, however, that Mr. Moore should share the expense of Monsieur Caratal's train, and should travel in the other empty first-class compartment, if Monsieur Caratal objected to having him in the one which he occupied. It was difficult to see any objection to such an arrangement, and yet Monsieur Caratal, upon the suggestion being made to him by Mr. Potter Hood, absolutely refused to consider it for an instant. The train was his, he said, and he would insist upon the exclusive use of it. All argument failed to overcome his ungracious objections, and finally the plan had to be abandoned. Mr. Horace Moore left the station in great distress, after learning that his only course was to take the ordinary slow train which leaves Liverpool at six o'clock. At four thirty-one exactly by the station clock the special train, containing the crippled Monsieur Caratal and his gigantic companion, steamed out of the Liverpool station. The line was at that time clear, and there should have been no stoppage before Manchester.

MR. HORACE MOORE.

The trains of the London and West Coast Railway run over the lines of another company as far as this town, which should have been reached by the special rather before six o'clock. At a quarter after six considerable surprise and some consternation were caused amongst the officials at Liverpool by the receipt of a telegram from Manchester to say that it had not yet arrived. An inquiry directed to St. Helens, which is a third of the way between the two cities, elicited the following reply:

"To James Bland, Superintendent, Central L. & W. C., Liverpool. — Special passed here at 4.52, well up to time. —Dowser, St. Helens."

This telegram was received at 6.40. At 6.50 a second message was received from Manchester:—

"No sign of special as advised by you."

And then ten minutes later a third, more bewildering:—

"Presume some mistake as to proposed running of special. Local train from St. Helens timed to follow it has just arrived and has seen nothing of it. Kindly wire advices.—Manchester."

The matter was assuming a most amazing aspect, although in some respects the last telegram was a relief to the authorities at Liverpool. If an accident had occurred to the special, it seemed hardly possible that the local train could have passed down the same line without observing it. And yet, what was the alternative? Where could the train be? Had it possibly been side-tracked for some reason in order to allow the slower train to go past? Such an explanation was possible if some small repair had to be effected. A telegram was dispatched to each of the stations between St. Helens and Manchester, and the superintendent and traffic manager waited in the utmost suspense at the instrument for the series of replies which would enable them to say for certain what had become of the missing train. The answers came back in the order of questions, which was the order of the stations beginning at the St. Helens end :—

"Special passed here five o'clock. —Collins Green."

"Special passed here six past five. —Earlestown."

"Special passed here 5.10. — Newton."

"Special passed here 5.20. — Kenyon Junction."

"No special train has passed here.—Barton Moss."

The two officials stared at each other in amazement.

"This is unique in my thirty years of experience," said Mr. Bland.

"Absolutely unprecedented and inexplicable, sir. The special has gone wrong between Kenyon Junction and Barton Moss."

"And yet there is no siding, as far as my memory serves me, between the two stations. The special must have run off the metals."

"But how could the four-fifty parliamentary pass over the same line without observing it?"

"There's no alternative, Mr. Hood. It *must* be so. Possibly the local train may have observed something which may throw some light upon the matter. We will wire to Manchester for more information, and to Kenyon Junction with instructions that the line be examined instantly as far as Barton Moss."

The answer from Manchester came within a few minutes.

"No news of missing special. Driver and guard of slow train positive that no accident between Kenyon Junction and Barton Moss. Line quite clear, and no sign of anything unusual.—Manchester."

"That driver and guard will have to go," said Mr. Bland, grimly. "There has been a wreck and they have missed it. The special has obviously run off the metals without disturbing the line—how it could have done so passes my comprehension—but so it must be, and we shall have a wire from Kenyon or Barton Moss presently to say that they have found her at the bottom of an embankment."

But Mr. Bland's prophecy was not destined to be fulfilled. A half-hour passed, and then there arrived the following message from the station-master of Kenyon Junction :—

"There are no traces of the missing special. It is quite certain that she passed here, and that she did not arrive at Barton Moss. We have detached engine from goods train, and I have myself ridden down the line, but all is clear, and there is no sign of any accident."

"THE TWO OFFICIALS STARED AT EACH OTHER IN AMAZEMENT."

Mr. Bland tore his hair in his perplexity.

"This is rank lunacy, Hood!" he cried. "Does a train vanish into thin air in England in broad daylight? The thing is preposterous. An engine, a tender, two carriages, a van, five human beings—and all lost on a straight line of railway! Unless we get something positive within the next hour I'll take Inspector Collins, and go down myself."

And then at last something positive did occur. It took the shape of another telegram from Kenyon Junction.

"Regret to report that the dead body of

John Slater, driver of the special train, has just been found among the gorse bushes at a point two and a quarter miles from the Junction. Had fallen from his engine, pitched down the embankment, and rolled among bushes. Injuries to his head, from the fall, appear to be cause of death. Ground has now been carefully examined, and there is no trace of the missing train."

The country was, as has already been stated, in the throes of a political crisis, and the attention of the public was further distracted by the important and sensational developments in Paris, where a huge scandal threatened to destroy the Government and to wreck the reputations of many of the leading men in France. The papers were full of these events, and the singular disappearance of the special train attracted less attention than would have been the case in more peaceful times. The grotesque nature of the event helped to detract from its importance, for the papers were disinclined to believe the facts as reported to them. More than one of the London journals treated the matter as an ingenious hoax, until the coroner's inquest upon the unfortunate driver (an inquest which elicited nothing of importance) convinced them of the tragedy of the incident.

"MR. BLAND AND INSPECTOR COLLINS WENT DOWN TO KENYON JUNCTION."

Mr. Bland, accompanied by Inspector Collins, the senior detective officer in the service of the company, went down to Kenyon Junction the same evening, and their research lasted throughout the following day, but was attended with purely negative results. Not only was no trace found of the missing train, but no conjecture could be put forward which could possibly explain the facts. At the same time, Inspector Collins's official report (which lies before me as I write) served to show that the possibilities were more numerous than might have been expected.

"In the stretch of railway between these two points," said he, "the country is dotted with ironworks and collieries. Of these, some are being worked and some have been abandoned. There are no fewer than twelve which have small gauge lines which run trolly-cars down to the main line. These can, of course, be disregarded. Besides these, however, there are seven which have or have had proper lines running down and connecting with points to the main line, so as to convey their produce from the mouth of the mine to the great centres of distribution. In every case these lines are only a few miles in length. Out of the seven, four belong to collieries which are worked out, or at least to shafts which are no longer used. These are the Redgauntlet, Hero, Slough of Despond, and Heartsease mines, the latter having ten years ago been one of the principal mines in Lancashire. These four side lines may be eliminated from our inquiry, for, to prevent possible accidents, the rails nearest to the main line have been taken up, and there is no longer any connection. There remain three other side lines leading

(a) to the Carnstock Iron Works;
(b) to the Big Ben Colliery;
(c) to the Perseverance Colliery.

Of these the Big Ben line is not more than a quarter of a mile long, and ends at a dead wall of of coal waiting removal from the mouth of the mine. Nothing had been seen or heard there of any special. The Carnstock Iron Works line was blocked all day upon the 3rd of June by sixteen truck-loads of hematite. It is a single line, and nothing could have passed. As to the Perseverance line, it is a large double line, which does a considerable traffic, for the output of the mine is very large. On the 3rd of June this traffic proceeded as usual; hundreds of men, including a gang of railway platelayers, were working along the two miles and a quarter which constitute the total length of the line, and it is inconceivable that an unexpected train could have come down there without attracting universal attention. It may be remarked in conclusion that this branch line is nearer to St. Helens than the point at which the engine-driver was discovered, so that we have every reason to believe that the train was past that point before misfortune overtook her.

"As to John Slater, there is no clue to be gathered from his appearance or injuries. We can only say that, as far as we can see, he met his end by falling off his engine, though why he fell, or what became of the engine after his fall, is a question upon which I do not feel qualified to offer an opinion." In conclusion, the inspector offered his resignation to the Board, being much nettled by an accusation of incompetence in the London papers.

A month elapsed, during which both the police and the company prosecuted their inquiries without the slightest success. A reward was offered and a pardon promised in case of crime, but they were both unclaimed. Every day the public opened their papers with the conviction that so grotesque a mystery would at last be solved, but week after week passed by, and a solution remained as far off as ever. In broad daylight, upon a June afternoon in the most thickly inhabited portion of England, a train with its occupants had disappeared as completely as if some master of subtle chemistry had volatilized it into gas. Indeed, among the various conjectures which were put forward in the public Press there were some which seriously asserted that supernatural, or, at least, preternatural, agencies had been at work, and that the deformed Monsieur Caratal was probably a person who was better known under a less polite name. Others fixed upon his swarthy companion as being the author of the mischief, but what it was exactly which he had done could never be clearly formulated in words.

Amongst the many suggestions put forward by various newspapers or private individuals, there were one or two which were feasible enough to attract the attention of the public. One which appeared in the *Times*, over the signature of an amateur reasoner of some celebrity at that date, attempted to deal with the matter in a critical and semi-scientific manner. An extract must suffice, although the curious can see the whole letter in the issue of the 3rd of July.

"It is one of the elementary principles of practical reasoning," he remarked, "that when the impossible has been eliminated the residuum, *however improbable*, must contain the truth. It is certain that the train left Kenyon Junction. It is certain that it did not reach Barton Moss. It is in the highest degree unlikely, but still possible, that it may have taken one of the seven available side lines. It is obviously impossible for a train to run where there are no rails, and, therefore, we may reduce our improbables to the three open lines, namely, the Carnstock Iron Works, the Big Ben, and the Perseverance. Is there a secret society of colliers, an English *camorra*, which is capable of destroying both train and passengers? It is improbable, but it is not impossible. I confess that I am unable to suggest any other solution. I should certainly advise the company to direct all their energies towards the observation of those three lines, and of the workmen at the end of them. A careful supervision of the pawnbrokers' shops of the district might possibly bring some suggestive facts to light."

The suggestion coming from a recognised authority upon such matters created considerable interest, and a fierce opposition from those who considered such a statement to be a preposterous libel upon an honest and deserving set of men. The only answer to this criticism was a challenge to the objectors to lay any more feasible explanation before the public. In reply to this two others were forthcoming (*Times*, July 7th and 9th). The first suggested that the train might have run off the metals and be lying submerged in the Lancashire and Staffordshire Canal, which runs parallel to the railway for some hundreds of yards. This suggestion was thrown out of court by the published depth of the canal, which was entirely insufficient to conceal so large an object. The second correspondent wrote calling attention to the bag which appeared to be the sole luggage which the travellers had brought with them, and suggesting that some novel explosive of immense and pulverizing power might have been concealed in it. The obvious absurdity, however, of supposing that the whole train might be blown to dust while the metals remained uninjured reduced any such explanation to a farce. The investigation had drifted into this hopeless position when a new and most unexpected incident occurred, which raised hopes never destined to be fulfilled.

This was nothing less than the receipt by Mrs. McPherson of a letter from her husband, James McPherson, who had been the guard of the missing train. The letter, which was dated July 5th, 1890, was dispatched from New York, and came to hand upon July

"A LETTER FROM JAMES MCPHERSON."

14th. Some doubts were expressed as to its genuine character, but Mrs. McPherson was positive as to the writing, and the fact that it contained a remittance of a hundred dollars in five-dollar notes was enough in itself to discount the idea of a hoax. No address was given in the letter, which ran in this way:—

"MY DEAR WIFE,—I have been thinking a great deal, and I find it very hard to give you up. The same with Lizzie. I try to fight against it, but it will always come back to me. I send you some money which will change into twenty English pounds. This should be enough to bring both Lizzie and you across the Atlantic, and you will find the Hamburg boats which stop at Southampton very good boats, and cheaper than Liverpool. If you could come here and stop at the Johnston House I would try and send you word how to meet, but things are very difficult with me at present, and I am not very happy, finding it hard to give you both up. So no more at present, from your loving husband,

"JAMES MCPHERSON."

For a time it was confidently anticipated that this letter would lead to the clearing up of the whole matter, the more so as it was ascertained that a passenger who bore a close resemblance to the missing guard had travelled from Southampton under the name of Summers in the Hamburg and New York liner *Vistula*, which started upon the 7th of June. Mrs. McPherson and her sister Lizzie Dolton went across to New York as directed, and stayed for three weeks at the Johnston House, without hearing anything from the missing man. It is probable that some injudicious comments in the Press may have warned him that the police were using them as a bait. However this may be, it is certain that he neither wrote nor came, and the women were eventually compelled to return to Liverpool.

And so the matter stood, and has continued to stand up to the present year of 1898. Incredible as it may seem, nothing has transpired during these eight years which has shed the least light upon the extraordinary disappearance of the special train which contained Monsieur Caratal and his companion. Careful inquiries into the antecedents of the two travellers have only established the fact that Monsieur Caratal was well known as a financier and political agent in Central America, and that during his voyage to Europe he had betrayed extraordinary anxiety to reach Paris. His companion, whose name was entered upon the passenger lists as Eduardo Gomez, was a man whose record was a violent one, and whose reputation was that of a bravo and a bully. There was evidence to show, however, that he was honestly devoted to the interests of Monsieur Caratal, and that the latter, being a man of puny physique, employed the other as a guard and protector. It may be added that no information came from Paris as to what the objects of Monsieur Caratal's hurried journey may have been. This comprises all the facts of the case up to the publication in the Marseilles papers of the recent confession of Herbert de Lernac, now under sentence of death for the murder of a merchant named Bonvalot. This statement may be literally translated as follows:—

"It is not out of mere pride or boasting that I give this information, for, if that were my object, I could tell a dozen actions of mine which are quite as splendid; but I do it in order that certain gentlemen in Paris may understand that I, who am able here to tell about the fate of Monsieur Caratal, can also tell in whose interest and at whose request the deed was done, unless the reprieve which I am awaiting comes to me very quickly. Take warning, messieurs, before it is too late! You know Herbert de Lernac, and you are aware that his deeds are as ready as his words. Hasten then, or you are lost!

"At present I shall mention no names—if you only heard the names, what would you not think!—but I shall merely tell you how cleverly I did it. I was true to my employers then, and no doubt they will be true to me now. I hope so, and until I am convinced that they have betrayed me, these names, which would convulse Europe, shall not be divulged. But on that day . . . . well, I say no more!

"In a word, then, there was a famous trial in Paris, in the year 1890, in connection with a monstrous scandal in politics and finance. How monstrous that scandal was can never be known save by such confidential agents as myself. The honour and careers of many of the chief men in France were at stake. You have seen a group of nine-pins standing, all so rigid, and prim, and unbending. Then there comes the ball from far away and pop, pop, pop—there are your nine-pins on the floor. Well, imagine some of the greatest men in France as these nine-pins, and then this Monsieur Caratal was the ball which could be seen coming from far away. If he arrived, then it was pop, pop, pop for all of them. It was determined that he should not arrive.

"I do not accuse them all of being conscious of what was to happen. There were, as I have said, great financial as well as political interests at stake, and a syndicate was formed to manage the business. Some subscribed to the syndicate who hardly understood what were its objects. But others understood very well, and they can rely upon it that I have not forgotten their names. They had ample warning that Monsieur Caratal was coming long before he left South America, and they knew that the evidence which he held would certainly mean ruin to all of them. The syndicate had the command of an unlimited amount of money—absolutely unlimited, you understand. They looked round for an agent who was capable of wielding this gigantic power. The man chosen must be inventive, resolute, adaptive—a man in a million. They chose Herbert de Lernac, and I admit that they were right.

"My duties were to choose my subordinates, to use freely the power which money gives, and to make certain that Monsieur Caratal should never arrive in Paris. With characteristic energy I set about my commission within an hour of receiving my instructions, and the steps which I took were the very best for the purpose which could possibly be devised.

"A man whom I could trust was dispatched instantly to South America to travel home with Monsieur Caratal. Had he arrived in time the ship would never have reached Liverpool; but, alas, it had already started before my agent could reach it. I fitted out a small armed brig to intercept it, but again I was unfortunate. Like all great organizers I was, however, prepared for failure, and had a series of alternatives prepared, one or the other of which must succeed. You must not underrate the difficulties of my undertaking, or imagine that a mere commonplace assassination would meet the case. We must destroy not only Monsieur Caratal, but Monsieur Caratal's documents, and Monsieur Caratal's companions also, if we had reason to believe that he had communicated his secrets to them. And you must remember that they were on the alert, and keenly suspicious of any such attempt. It was a task which was in every way worthy of me, for I am always most masterful where another would be appalled.

"I was all ready for Monsieur Caratal's reception in Liverpool, and I was the more eager because I had reason to believe that he had made arrangements by which he would have a considerable guard from the moment that he arrived in London. Anything which was to be done must be done between the moment of his setting foot upon the Liverpool quay and that of his arrival at the London and West Coast terminus in London. We prepared six plans, each more elaborate than the last; which plan would be used would depend upon his own movements. Do what he would, we were ready for him. If he had stayed in Liverpool, we were ready. If he took an ordinary train, an express, or a special, all was ready. Everything had been foreseen and provided for.

"You may imagine that I could not do all this myself. What could I know of the English railway lines? But money can procure willing agents all the world over, and I soon had one of the acutest brains in England to assist me. I will mention no names, but it would be unjust to claim all the credit for myself. My English ally was worthy of such an alliance. He knew the London and

West Coast line thoroughly, and he had the command of a band of workers who were trustworthy and intelligent. The idea was his, and my own judgment was only required in the details. We bought over several officials, amongst whom the most important was James McPherson, whom we had ascertained to be the guard most likely to be employed upon a special train. Smith, the stoker, was also in our employ. John Slater, the engine-driver, had been approached, but had been found to be obstinate and dangerous, so we desisted. We had no certainty that Monsieur Caratal would take a special, but we thought it very probable, for it was of the utmost importance to him that he should reach Paris without delay. It was for this contingency, therefore, that we made special preparations — preparations which were complete down to the last detail long before his steamer had sighted the shores of England. You will be amused to learn that there was one of my agents in the pilot-boat which brought that steamer to its moorings.

"The moment that Caratal arrived in Liverpool we knew that he suspected danger and was on his guard. He had brought with him as an escort a dangerous fellow, named Gomez, a man who carried weapons, and was prepared to use them. This fellow carried Caratal's confidential papers for him, and was ready to protect either them or his master. The probability was that Caratal had taken him into his counsels, and that to remove Caratal without removing Gomez would be a mere waste of energy. It was necessary that they should be involved in a common fate, and our plans to that end were much facilitated by their request for a special train. On that special train you will understand that two out of the three servants of the company were really in our employ, at a price which would make them independent for a lifetime. I do not go so far as to say that the English are more honest than any other nation, but I have found them more expensive to buy.

"I have already spoken of my English agent—who is a man with a considerable future before him, unless some complaint of the throat carries him off before his time. He had charge of all arrangements at Liverpool, whilst I was stationed at the inn at Kenyon, where I awaited a cipher signal to act. When the special was arranged for, my agent instantly telegraphed to me and warned me how soon I should have everything ready. He himself under the name of Horace Moore applied immediately for a special also, in the hope that he would be sent down with Monsieur Caratal, which might under certain circumstances have been helpful to us. If, for example, our great *coup* had failed, it would then have become the duty of my agent to have shot them both and destroyed their papers. Caratal was on his guard, however, and refused to admit any other traveller. My agent then left the station, returned by another entrance, entered the guard's van on the side farthest from the platform, and travelled down with McPherson, the guard.

"A DANGEROUS FELLOW, NAMED GOMEZ."

"In the meantime you will be interested to know what my own movements were. Everything had been prepared for days before, and only the finishing touches were needed. The side line which we had chosen had once joined the main line, but it had been disconnected. We had only to replace a few rails to connect it once more. These rails had been laid down as far as could be done without danger of attracting attention, and now it was merely a case of completing a juncture with the line, and arranging the points as they had been before. The sleepers had never been removed, and the rails, fish-plates, and rivets were all ready, for we had taken them from a siding on the abandoned portion of the line. With my small but competent band of workers, we had everything ready long before the special arrived. When it did arrive, it ran off upon the small side line so easily that the jolting of the points appears to have been entirely unnoticed by the two travellers.

"Our plan had been that Smith the stoker should chloroform John Slater the driver, and so that he should vanish with the others. In this respect, and in this respect only, our plans miscarried—I except the criminal folly of McPherson in writing home to his wife. Our stoker did his business so clumsily that Slater in his struggles fell off the engine, and though fortune was with us so far that he broke his neck in the fall, still he remained as a blot upon that which would otherwise have been one of those complete masterpieces which are only to be contemplated in silent admiration. The criminal expert will find in John Slater the one flaw in all our admirable combinations. A man who has had as many triumphs as I can afford to be frank, and I therefore lay my finger upon John Slater, and I proclaim him to be a flaw.

"But now I have got our special train upon the small line two kilomètres, or rather more than one mile in length, which leads, or rather used to lead, to the abandoned Heartsease mine, once one of the largest coal mines in England. You will ask how it is that no one saw the train upon this unused line. I answer that along its entire length it runs through a deep cutting, and that, unless someone had been on the edge of that cutting, he could not have seen it. There *was* someone on the edge of that cutting. I was there. And now I will tell you what I saw.

"My assistant had remained at the points in order that he might superintend the switching off of the train. He had four armed men with him, so that if the train ran off the line — we thought it probable, because the points were very rusty —we might still have resources to fall back upon. Having once seen it safely on the side line, he handed over the responsibility to me. I was waiting at a point which overlooks the mouth of the mine, and I was also armed, as were my two companions. Come what might, you see, I was always ready.

"The moment that the train was fairly on the side line, Smith, the stoker, slowed-down the engine, and then, having turned it on to the fullest speed again, he and McPherson, with my English lieutenant, sprang off before it was too late. It may be that it was this slowing-down which first attracted the attention of the travellers, but the train was running at full speed again before their heads appeared at the open window. It makes me smile to think how bewildered they must have been. Picture to yourself your own feelings if, on looking out of your luxurious carriage, you suddenly perceived that the lines upon which you ran were rusted and corroded, red and yellow with disuse and decay! What a catch must have come in their breath as in a second it flashed upon them that it was not Manchester but Death which was waiting for them at the end of that sinister line. But the train was running with frantic speed, rolling and rocking over the rotten line, while the wheels made a frightful screaming sound upon the rusted

"I WAS WAITING AT A POINT WHICH OVERLOOKS THE MOUTH OF THE MINE."

surface. I was close to them, and could see their faces. Caratal was praying, I think—there was something like a rosary dangling out of his hand. The other roared like a bull who smells the blood of the slaughter-house. He saw us standing on the bank, and he beckoned to us like a madman. Then he tore at his wrist and threw his despatch-box out of the window in our direction. Of course, his meaning was obvious. Here was the evidence, and they would promise to be silent if their lives were spared. It would have been very agreeable if we could have done so, but business is business. Besides, the train was now as much beyond our control as theirs.

"He ceased howling when the train rattled round the curve and they saw the black mouth of the mine yawning before them. We had removed the boards which had covered it, and we had cleared the square entrance. The rails had formerly run very close to the shaft for the convenience of loading the coal, and we had only to add two or three lengths of rail in order to lead to the very brink of the shaft. In fact, as the lengths would not quite fit, our line projected about three feet over the edge. We saw the two heads at the window: Caratal below, Gomez above; but they had both been struck silent by what they saw. And yet they could not withdraw their heads. The sight seemed to have paralyzed them.

"I had wondered how the train running at a great speed would take the pit into which I had guided it, and I was much interested in watching it. One of my colleagues thought that it would actually jump it, and indeed it was not very far from doing so. Fortunately, however, it fell short, and the buffers of the engine struck the other lip of the shaft with a tremendous crash. The funnel flew off into the air. The tender, carriages, and van were all mashed into one jumble, which, with the remains of the engine, choked for a minute or so the mouth of the pit. Then something gave way in the middle, and the whole mass of green iron, smoking coals, brass fittings, wheels, woodwork, and cushions all crumbled together and crashed down into the mine. We heard the rattle, rattle, rattle, as the *débris* struck against the walls, and then quite a long time afterwards there came a deep roar as the remains of the train struck the bottom. The boiler may have burst, for a sharp crash came after the roar, and then a dense cloud of steam and smoke swirled up out of the black depths, falling in a spray as thick as rain all round us. Then the vapour shredded off into thin wisps, which floated away in the summer sunshine, and all was quiet again in the Heartsease mine.

"And now, having carried out our plans so successfully, it only remained to leave no trace behind us. Our little band of workers at the other end had already ripped up the rails and disconnected the side line, replacing everything as it had been before. We were equally busy at the mine. The funnel and other fragments were thrown in, the shaft was planked over as it used to be, and the lines which led to it were torn up and taken away. Then, without flurry, but without delay, we all made our way out of the country, most of us to Paris, my English colleague to Manchester, and McPherson to Southampton, whence he emigrated to America. Let the English papers of that date tell how thoroughly we had done our work, and how completely we had thrown the cleverest of their detectives off our track.

"You will remember that Gomez threw his bag of papers out of the window, and I need not say that I secured that bag and brought them to my employers. It may interest my employers now, however, to learn that out of that bag I took one or two little papers as a souvenir of the occasion. I have no wish to publish these papers; but, still, it is every man for himself in this world, and what else can I do if my friends will not come to my aid when I want them? Messieurs, you may believe that Herbert de Lernac is quite as formidable when he is against you as when he is with you, and that he is not a man to go to the guillotine until he has seen that every one of you is *en route* for New Caledonia. For your own sake, if not for mine, make haste, Monsieur de ——, and General ——, and Baron —— (you can fill up the blanks for yourselves as you read this). I promise you that in the next edition there will be no blanks to fill.

"P.S.—As I look over my statement there is only one omission which I can see. It concerns the unfortunate man McPherson, who was foolish enough to write to his wife and to make an appointment with her in New York. It can be imagined that when interests like ours were at stake, we could not leave them to the chance of whether a man in that class of life would or would not give away his secrets to a woman. Having once broken his oath by writing to his wife, we could not trust him any more. We took steps therefore to insure that he should not see his wife. I have sometimes thought that it would be a kindness to write to her and to assure her that there is no impediment to her marrying again."

Round the Fire.

BY A. CONAN DOYLE.

V.—THE STORY OF THE BLACK DOCTOR.

BISHOP'S CROSSING is a small village lying ten miles in a south-westerly direction from Liverpool. Here in the early seventies there settled a doctor named Aloysius Lana. Nothing was known locally either of his antecedents or of the reasons which had prompted him to come to this Lancashire hamlet. Two facts only were certain about him: the one that he had gained his medical qualification with some distinction at Glasgow; the other that he came undoubtedly of a tropical race, and was so dark that he might almost have had a strain of the Indian in his composition. His predominant features were, however, European, and he possessed a stately courtesy and carriage which suggested a Spanish extraction. A swarthy skin, raven-black hair, and dark, sparkling eyes under a pair of heavily-tufted brows made a strange contrast to the flaxen or chestnut rustics of England, and the new-comer was soon known as "The Black Doctor of Bishop's Crossing." At first it was a term of ridicule and reproach; as the years went on it became a title of honour which was familiar to the whole country-side, and extended far beyond the narrow confines of the village.

" THE BLACK DOCTOR."

For the new-comer proved himself to be a capable surgeon and an accomplished physician. The practice of that district had been in the hands of Edward Rowe, the son of Sir William Rowe, the Liverpool consultant, but he had not inherited the talents of his father, and Dr. Lana, with his advantages of presence and of manner, soon beat him out of the field. Dr. Lana's social success was as rapid as his professional. A remarkable surgical cure in the case of the Hon. James Lowry, the second son of Lord Belton, was the means of introducing him to county society, where he became a favourite through the charm of his conversation and the elegance of his manners. An absence of antecedents and of relatives is sometimes an aid rather than an impediment to social advancement, and the distinguished individuality of the handsome doctor was its own recommendation.

His patients had one fault—and one fault only—to find with him. He appeared to be a confirmed bachelor. This was the more remarkable since the house which he occupied was a large one, and it was known that his success in practice had enabled him to save considerable sums. At first the local match-makers were continually coupling his name with one or other of the eligible ladies, but as years passed and Doctor Lana remained unmarried, it came to be generally understood that for some reason he must remain a bachelor. Some even went so far as to assert that he was already married, and that it was in order to escape the consequence of an early misalliance that he had buried himself at Bishop's Crossing. And then, just as the match-makers had finally given him up in despair, his engagement was suddenly announced to Miss Frances Morton, of Leigh Hall.

Miss Morton was a young lady who was well known upon the country-side, her father, James Haldane Morton, having been the Squire of Bishop's Crossing. Both her parents were, however, dead, and she lived with her only brother, Arthur Morton, who had inherited the family estate. In person Miss Morton was tall and stately, and she was famous for her quick, impetuous nature and for her strength of character. She met Dr. Lana at a garden-party, and a friendship, which quickly ripened into love, sprang up between them. Nothing could exceed their devotion to each other. There was some discrepancy in age, he being thirty-seven, and she twenty-four; but, save in that one respect, there was no possible objection to be found with the match. The engagement was in February, and it was arranged that the marriage should take place in August.

Upon the 3rd of June Dr. Lana received a letter from abroad. In a small village the postmaster is also in a position to be the gossip-master, and Mr. Bankley, of Bishop's Crossing, had many of the secrets of his neighbours in his possession. Of this particular letter he remarked only that it was in a curious envelope, that it was in a man's handwriting, that the postscript was Buenos Ayres, and the stamp of the Argentine Republic. It was the first letter which he had ever known Dr. Lana have from abroad, and this was the reason why his attention was particularly called to it before he handed it to the local postman. It was delivered by the evening delivery of that date.

Next morning—that is, upon the 4th of June—Dr. Lana called upon Miss Morton, and a long interview followed, from which he was observed to return in a state of great agitation. Miss Morton remained in her room all that day, and her maid found her several times in tears. In the course of a week it was an open secret to the whole village that the engagement was at an end, that Dr. Lana had behaved shamefully to the young lady, and that Arthur Morton, her brother, was talking of horse-whipping him. In what particular respect the doctor had behaved badly was unknown—some surmised one thing and some another; but it was observed, and taken as the obvious sign of a guilty conscience, that he would go for miles round rather than pass the windows of Leigh Hall, and that he gave up attending morning service upon Sundays where he might have met the young lady. There was an advertisement also in the *Lancet* as to the sale of a practice which mentioned no names, but which was thought by some to refer to Bishop's Crossing, and to mean that Dr. Lana was thinking of abandoning the scene of his success. Such was the position of affairs when, upon the evening of Monday, June 21st, there came a fresh development which changed what had been a mere village scandal into a tragedy which arrested the attention of the whole nation. Some detail is necessary to cause the facts of that evening to present their full significance.

The sole occupants of the doctor's house were his housekeeper, an elderly and most respectable woman, named Martha Woods, and a young servant—Mary Pilling. The coachman and the surgery-boy slept out. It was the custom of the doctor to sit at night in his study, which was next the surgery in the wing of the house which was farthest from the servants' quarters. This side of the house had a door of its own for the convenience of patients, so that it was possible for the doctor to admit and receive a visitor there without the knowledge of anyone. As a matter of fact, when patients came late it was quite usual for him to let them in and out by the surgery entrance, for the maid and the housekeeper were in the habit of retiring early.

On this particular night Martha Woods went into the doctor's study at half-past nine, and found him writing at his desk. She bade him good-night, sent the maid to bed, and then occupied herself until a quarter to eleven in household matters. It was striking eleven upon the hall clock when she went to her own room. She had been there about a quarter of an hour or twenty minutes when she heard a cry or call, which appeared to come from within the house. She waited some time, but it was not repeated. Much alarmed, for the sound was loud and urgent, she put on a dressing-gown, and ran at the top of her speed to the doctor's study.

"Who's there?" cried a voice, as she tapped at the door.

"I am here, sir—Mrs. Woods."

"I beg that you will leave me in peace. Go back to your room this instant!" cried the voice, which was, to the best of her belief, that of her master. The tone was so harsh and so unlike her master's usual manner, that she was surprised and hurt.

"I thought I heard you calling, sir," she explained, but no answer was given to her. Mrs. Woods looked at the clock as she returned to her room, and it was then half-past eleven.

At some period between eleven and twelve (she could not be positive as to the exact hour) a patient called upon the doctor and was unable to get any reply from him. This late visitor was Mrs. Madding, the wife of the village grocer, who was dangerously ill of

"I AM HERE, SIR—MRS. WOODS."

typhoid fever. Dr. Lana had asked her to look in the last thing and let him know how her husband was progressing. She observed that the light was burning in the study, but having knocked several times at the surgery door without response, she concluded that the doctor had been called out, and so returned home.

There is a short, winding drive with a lamp at the end of it leading down from the house to the road. As Mrs. Madding emerged from the gate a man was coming along the footpath. Thinking that it might be Dr. Lana returning from some professional visit, she waited for him, and was surprised to see that it was Mr. Arthur Morton, the young squire. In the light of the lamp she observed that his manner was excited, and that he carried in his hand a heavy hunting-crop. He was turning in at the gate when she addressed him.

"The doctor is not in, sir," said she.

"How do you know that?" he asked, harshly.

"I have been to the surgery door, sir."

"I see a light," said the young squire, looking up the drive. "That is in his study, is it not?"

"Yes, sir; but I am sure that he is out."

"Well, he must come in again," said young Morton, and passed through the gate while Mrs. Madding went upon her homeward way.

At three o'clock that morning her husband suffered a sharp relapse, and she was so alarmed by his symptoms that she determined to call the doctor without delay. As she passed through the gate she was surprised to see someone lurking among the laurel bushes. It was certainly a man, and to the best of her belief Mr. Arthur Morton. Preoccupied with her own troubles, she gave no particular attention to the incident, but hurried on upon her errand.

When she reached the house she perceived to her surprise that the light was still burning in the study. She therefore tapped at the surgery door. There was no answer. She repeated the knocking several times without effect. It appeared to her to be unlikely that the doctor would either go to bed or go out leaving so brilliant a light behind him, and it struck Mrs. Madding that it was possible that he might have dropped asleep in his chair. She tapped at the study window, therefore, but without result. Then, finding that there was an opening between the curtain and the woodwork, she looked through.

The small room was brilliantly lighted from a large lamp on the central table, which was littered with the doctor's books and instruments. No one was visible, nor did she see anything unusual, except that in the further shadow thrown by the table a dingy white glove was lying upon the carpet. And then suddenly, as her eyes became more accustomed to the light, a boot emerged from the other end of the shadow, and she realized, with a thrill of horror, that what she had taken to be a glove was the hand of a man, who was prostrate upon the floor. Understanding that something terrible had occurred, she rang at the front door, roused Mrs. Woods, the housekeeper, and the two women made their way into the study, having first

"IT WAS MR. ARTHUR MORTON, THE YOUNG SQUIRE."

dispatched the maidservant to the police-station.

At the side of the table, away from the window, Dr. Lana was discovered stretched upon his back and quite dead. It was evident that he had been subjected to violence, for one of his eyes was blackened, and there were marks of bruises about his face and neck. A slight thickening and swelling of his features appeared to suggest that the cause of his death had been strangulation. He was dressed in his usual professional clothes, but wore cloth slippers, the soles of which were perfectly clean. The carpet was marked all over, especially on the side of the door, with traces of dirty boots, which were presumably left by the murderer. It was evident that someone had entered by the surgery door, had killed the doctor, and had then made his escape unseen. That the assailant was a man was certain, from the size of the footprints and from the nature of the injuries. But beyond that point the police found it very difficult to go.

There were no signs of robbery, and the doctor's gold watch was safe in his pocket. He kept a heavy cash-box in the room, and this was discovered to be locked but empty. Mrs. Woods had an impression that a large sum was usually kept there, but the doctor had paid a heavy corn bill in cash only that very day, and it was conjectured that it was to this and not to a robber that the emptiness of the box was due. One thing in the room was missing—but that one thing was suggestive. The portrait of Miss Morton, which had always stood upon the side-table, had been taken from its frame and carried off. Mrs. Woods had observed it there when she waited upon her employer that evening, and now it was gone. On the other hand, there was picked up from the floor a green eye-patch, which the housekeeper could not remember to have seen before. Such a patch might, however, be in the possession of a doctor, and there was nothing to indicate that it was in any way connected with the crime.

Suspicion could only turn in one direction, and Arthur Morton, the young squire, was immediately arrested. The evidence against him was circumstantial, but damning. He was devoted to his sister, and it was shown that since the rupture between her and Dr. Lana he had been heard again and again to express himself in the most vindictive terms towards her former lover. He had, as stated, been seen somewhere about eleven o'clock entering the doctor's drive with a hunting-crop in his hand. He had then, according to the theory of the police, broken in upon the doctor, whose exclamation of fear or of anger had been loud enough to attract the attention of Mrs. Woods. When Mrs. Woods descended, Dr. Lana had made up his mind to talk it over with his visitor, and had, therefore, sent his housekeeper back to her room. This conversation had lasted a long time, had become more and more fiery, and had ended by a personal struggle, in which the doctor lost his life. The fact, revealed by a *post-mortem*, that his heart was much diseased—an ailment quite unsuspected during his life—would make it possible that death might in his case ensue from injuries which would not be fatal to a healthy man. Arthur Morton had then removed his sister's photograph, and had made his way homeward, stepping aside into the laurel bushes to avoid Mrs. Madding at the gate. This was the theory of the prosecution, and the case which they presented was a formidable one.

On the other hand, there were some strong points for the defence. Morton was high-spirited and impetuous, like his sister, but he was respected and liked by everyone, and his frank and honest nature seemed to be incapable of such a crime. His own explanation was that he was anxious to have a conversation with Dr. Lana about some urgent family matters (from first to last he refused even to mention the name of his sister). He did not attempt to deny that this conversation would probably have been of an unpleasant nature. He heard from a patient that the doctor was out, and he therefore waited until about three in the morning for his return, but as he had seen nothing of him up to that hour, he had given it up and had returned home. As to his death, he knew no more about it than the constable who arrested him. He had formerly been an intimate friend of the deceased man; but circumstances, which he would prefer not to mention, had brought about a change in his sentiments.

There were several facts which supported his innocence. It was certain that Dr. Lana was alive and in his study at half-past eleven o'clock. Mrs. Woods was prepared to swear that it was at that hour that she had heard his voice. The friends of the prisoner contended that it was probable that at that time Dr. Lana was not alone. The sound which had originally attracted the attention of the housekeeper, and her master's unusual impatience that she should leave him in peace, seemed to point to that. If this were so, then it appeared to be probable that he had met his end between the moment when the housekeeper heard his voice and the time when Mrs. Madding made her first call and found it impossible to attract his attention. But if this were the time of his death, then it was certain that Mr. Arthur Morton could not be guilty, as it was *after* this that she had met the young squire at the gate.

If this hypothesis were correct, and someone was with Dr. Lana before Mrs. Madding met Mr. Arthur Morton, then who was this someone, and what motives had he for wishing evil to the doctor? It was universally admitted that if the friends of the accused could throw light upon this, they would have gone a long way towards establishing his innocence. But in the meanwhile it was open to the public to say—as they did say—that there was no proof that anyone had been there at all except the young squire; while, on the other hand, there was ample proof that his motives in going were of a sinister kind. When Mrs. Madding called, the doctor might have retired to his room, or he might, as she thought at the time, have gone out and returned afterwards to find Mr. Arthur Morton waiting for him. Some of the supporters of the accused laid stress upon the fact that the photograph of his sister Frances, which had been removed from the doctor's room, had not been found in her brother's possession. This argument, however, did not count for much, as he had ample time before his arrest to burn it or to destroy it. As to the only positive evidence in the case—the muddy footmarks upon the floor—they were so blurred by the softness of the carpet that it was impossible to make any trustworthy deduction from them. The most that could be said was that their appearance was not inconsistent with the theory that they were made by the accused, and it was further shown that his boots were very muddy upon that night. There had been a heavy shower in the afternoon, and all boots were probably in the same condition.

Such is a bald statement of the singular and romantic series of events which centred public attention upon this Lancashire tragedy. The unknown origin of the doctor, his curious and distinguished personality, the position of the man who was accused of the murder, and the love affair which had preceded the crime, all combined to make the affair one of those dramas which absorb the whole interest of a nation. Throughout the three kingdoms men discussed the case of the Black Doctor of Bishop's Crossing, and many were the theories put forward to explain the facts; but it may safely be said that among them all there was not one which prepared the minds of the public for the extraordinary sequel, which caused so much excitement upon the first day of the trial, and came to a climax upon the second. The long files of the *Lancaster Weekly* with their report of the case lie before me as I write, but I must content myself with a synopsis of the case up to the point when, upon the evening of the first day, the evidence of Miss Frances Morton threw a singular new light upon the case.

Mr. Porlock Carr, the counsel for the prosecution, had marshalled his facts with his usual skill, and as the day wore on, it became more and more evident how difficult was the task which Mr. Humphrey, who had been retained for the defence, had before him. Several witnesses were put up to swear to the intemperate expressions which the young squire had been heard to utter about the doctor, and the fiery manner in which he resented the alleged ill-treatment of his sister. Mrs. Madding repeated her evidence as to the visit which had been paid late at night by the prisoner to the deceased, and it was shown by another witness that the prisoner was aware that the doctor was in the habit of sitting up alone in this isolated wing of the house, and that he had chosen this very late hour to call because he knew that his victim would then be at his mercy. A servant at the squire's house was compelled to admit that he had heard his master return about three that morning, which corroborated Mrs. Madding's statement that she had seen him among the laurel bushes near the gate upon the occasion of her second visit. The muddy boots and an alleged similarity in the footprints were duly dwelt upon, and it was felt when the case for the prosecution had been presented that, however circumstantial it might be, it was none the less so complete and so convincing, that the fate of the prisoner was sealed, unless something quite unexpected should be disclosed by the defence. It was three o'clock when the prosecution closed. At half-past four, when the Court rose, a new and unlooked-for development had occurred. I extract the incident, or part of it, from the journal which I have already mentioned, omitting the preliminary observations of the counsel.

Considerable sensation was caused in the crowded court when the first witness called for the defence proved to be Miss Frances Morton, the sister of the prisoner. Our readers will remember that the young lady had been engaged to Dr. Lana, and that it was his anger over the sudden termination of this engagement which was thought to have driven her brother to the perpetration of this crime. Miss Morton had not, however, been directly implicated in the case in any way, either at the inquest or at the police-court proceedings, and her appearance as the leading witness for the defence came as a surprise upon the public.

"THE FIRST WITNESS FOR THE DEFENCE."

Miss Frances Morton, who was a tall and handsome brunette, gave her evidence in a low but clear voice, though it was evident throughout that she was suffering from extreme emotion. She alluded to her engagement to the doctor, touched briefly upon its termination, which was due, she said, to personal matters connected with his family, and surprised the Court by asserting that she had always considered her brother's resentment to be unreasonable and intemperate. In answer to a direct question from her counsel, she replied that she did not feel that she had any grievance whatever against Dr. Lana, and that in her opinion he had acted in a perfectly honourable manner. Her brother, on an insufficient knowledge of the facts, had taken another view, and she was compelled to acknowledge that, in spite of her entreaties, he had uttered threats of personal violence against the doctor, and had, upon the evening of the tragedy, announced his intention of "having it out with him." She had done her best to bring him to a more reasonable frame of mind, but he was very headstrong where his emotions or prejudices were concerned.

Up to this point the young lady's evidence had appeared to make against the prisoner rather than in his favour. The questions of her counsel, however, soon put a very different light upon the matter, and disclosed an unexpected line of defence.

Mr. Humphrey: Do you believe your brother to be guilty of this crime?

The Judge: I cannot permit that question, Mr. Humphrey. We are here to decide upon questions of fact—not of belief.

Mr. Humphrey: Do you know that your brother is not guilty of the death of Doctor Lana?

Miss Morton: Yes.

Mr. Humphrey: How do you know it?

Miss Morton: Because Dr. Lana is not dead.

There followed a prolonged sensation in court, which interrupted the cross examination of the witness.

Mr. Humphrey: And how do you know, Miss Morton, that Dr. Lana is not dead?

Miss Morton: Because I have received a letter from him since the date of his supposed death.

Mr. Humphrey: Have you this letter?

Miss Morton: Yes, but I should prefer not to show it.

Mr. Humphrey: Have you the envelope?

Miss Morton: Yes, it is here.

Mr. Humphrey: What is the post-mark?

Miss Morton: Liverpool.

Mr. Humphrey: And the date?

Miss Morton: June the 22nd.

Mr. Humphrey: That being the day after his alleged death. Are you prepared to swear to this handwriting, Miss Morton?

Miss Morton: Certainly.

Mr. Humphrey: I am prepared to call six other witnesses, my lord, to testify that this letter is in the writing of Doctor Lana.

The Judge: Then you must call them to-morrow.

Mr. Porlock Carr (counsel for the prosecution): In the meantime, my lord, we claim possession of this document, so that we may obtain expert evidence as to how far it is an imitation of the handwriting of the gentleman whom we still confidently assert to be deceased. I need not point out that the theory so unexpectedly sprung upon us may prove to be a very obvious device adopted by the friends of the prisoner in order to divert this inquiry. I would draw attention to the fact that the young lady must, according to her own account, have possessed this letter during the proceedings at the inquest and at the police-court. She desires us to believe that she permitted these to proceed, although she held in her pocket evidence which would at any moment have brought them to an end.

Mr. Humphrey: Can you explain this, Miss Morton?

Miss Morton: Dr. Lana desired his secret to be preserved.

Mr. Porlock Carr: Then why have you now made this public?

Miss Morton: To save my brother.

A murmur of sympathy broke out in court, which was instantly suppressed by the Judge.

The Judge: Admitting this line of defence, it lies with you, Mr. Humphrey, to throw a light upon who this man is whose body has been recognised by so many friends and patients of Dr. Lana as being that of the doctor himself.

A Juryman: Has anyone up to now expressed any doubt about the matter?

Mr. Porlock Carr: Not to my knowledge.

Mr. Humphrey: We hope to make the matter clear.

The Judge: Then the Court adjourns until to-morrow.

This new development of the case excited the utmost interest among the general public. Press comment was prevented by the fact that the trial was still undecided, but the question was everywhere argued as to how far there could be truth in Miss Morton's declaration, and how far it might be a daring ruse for the purpose of saving her brother. The obvious dilemma in which the missing doctor stood was that if by any extraordinary chance he was not dead, then he must be held responsible for the death of this unknown man, who resembled him so exactly, and who was found in his study. This letter which Miss Morton refused to produce was possibly a confession of guilt, and she might find herself in the terrible position of only being able to save her brother from the gallows by the sacrifice of her former lover. The court next morning was crammed to overflowing, and a murmur of excitement passed over it when Mr. Humphrey was observed to enter in a state of emotion, which even his trained nerves could not conceal, and to confer with the opposing counsel. A few hurried words —words which left a look of amazement upon Mr. Porlock Carr's face — passed between them, and then the counsel for the defence, addressing the judge, announced that, with the consent of the prosecution, the young lady who had given evidence upon the sitting before would not be recalled.

The Judge: But you appear, Mr. Humphrey, to have left matters in a very unsatisfactory state.

Mr. Humphrey: Perhaps, my lord, my next witness may help to clear them up.

The Judge: Then call your next witness.

Mr. Humphrey: I call Dr. Aloysius Lana.

The learned counsel has made many telling remarks in his day, but he has certainly never produced such a sensation with so short a sentence. The Court was simply stunned with amazement as the very man whose fate had been the subject of so much contention appeared bodily before them in the witness-box. Those among the spectators who had known him at Bishop's Crossing saw him now, gaunt and thin, with deep lines of care upon his face. But in spite of his melancholy bearing and despondent expression, there were few who could say that they had ever seen a man of more distinguished presence. Bowing to the judge, he asked if he might be allowed to make a statement, and having been duly informed that whatever he said might be used against him, he bowed once more, and proceeded :—

"My wish," said he, "is to hold nothing back, but to tell with perfect frankness all that occurred upon the night of the 21st of June. Had I known that the innocent had suffered, and that so much trouble had been brought upon those whom I love best in the world, I should have come forward long ago; but there were reasons which prevented these things from coming to my ears. It was my desire that an unhappy man should vanish from the world which had known him, but I had not foreseen that others would be affected by my actions. Let me to the best of my ability repair the evil which I have done.

"To anyone who is acquainted with the history of the Argentine Republic the name of Lana is well known. My father, who came of the best blood of old Spain, filled all the highest offices of the State, and would have been President but for his death in the riots at San Juan. A brilliant career might have been open to my twin brother Ernest and myself had it not been for financial losses which made it necessary that we should earn

"HE BOWED TO THE JUDGE."

our own living. I apologize, sir, if these details appear to be irrelevant, but they are a necessary introduction to that which is to follow.

"I had, as I have said, a twin brother

named Ernest, whose resemblance to me was so great that even when we were together people could see no difference between us. Down to the smallest detail we were exactly the same. As we grew older this likeness became less marked because our expression was not the same, but with our features in repose the points of difference were very slight.

"It does not become me to say too much of one who is dead, the more so as he is my only brother, but I leave his character to those who knew him best. I will only say—for I *have* to say it—that in my early manhood I conceived a horror of him, and that I had good reason for the aversion which filled me. My own reputation suffered from his actions, for our close resemblance caused me to be credited with many of them. Eventually, in a peculiarly disgraceful business, he contrived to throw the whole odium upon me in such a way that I was forced to leave the Argentine for ever, and to seek a career in Europe. The freedom from his hated presence more than compensated me for the loss of my native land. I had enough money to defray my medical studies at Glasgow, and I finally settled in practice at Bishop's Crossing, in the firm conviction that in that remote Lancashire hamlet I should never hear of him again.

"For years my hopes were fulfilled, and then at last he discovered me. Some Liverpool man who visited Buenos Ayres put him upon my track. He had lost all his money, and he thought that he would come over and share mine. Knowing my horror of him, he rightly thought that I would be willing to buy him off. I received a letter from him saying that he was coming. It was at a crisis in my own affairs, and his arrival might conceivably bring trouble, and even disgrace, upon some whom I was especially bound to shield from anything of the kind. I took steps to insure that any evil which might come should fall on me only, and that"—here he turned and looked at the prisoner—"was the cause of conduct upon my part which has been too harshly judged. My only motive was to screen those who were dear to me from any possible connection with scandal or disgrace. That scandal and disgrace would come with my brother was only to say that what had been would be again.

"I HEARD A FOOTSTEP UPON THE GRAVEL OUTSIDE."

"My brother arrived himself one night not very long after my receipt of the letter. I was sitting in my study after the servants had gone to bed, when I heard a footstep upon the gravel outside, and an instant later I saw his face looking in at me through the window. He was a clean-shaven man like myself, and the resemblance between us was still so great that, for an instant, I thought it was my own reflection in the glass. He had a dark patch over his eye, but our features were absolutely the same. Then he smiled in a sardonic way which had been a trick of his from his boyhood, and I knew that he was the same brother who had driven me from my native land, and brought disgrace upon what had been an honourable name.

I went to the door and I admitted him. That would be about ten o'clock that night.

"When he came into the glare of the lamp, I saw at once that he had fallen upon very evil days. He had walked from Liverpool, and he was tired and ill. I was quite shocked by the expression upon his face. My medical knowledge told me that there was some serious internal malady. He had been drinking also, and his face was bruised as the result of a scuffle which he had had with some sailors. It was to cover his injured eye that he wore this patch, which he removed when he entered the room. He was himself dressed in a pea-jacket and flannel shirt, and his feet were bursting through his boots. But his poverty had only made him more savagely vindictive towards me. His hatred rose to the height of a mania. I had been rolling in money in England, according to his account, while he had been starving in South America. I cannot describe to you the threats which he uttered or the insults which he poured upon me. My impression is, that hardships and debauchery had unhinged his reason. He paced about the room like a wild beast, demanding drink, demanding money, and all in the foulest language. I am a hot-tempered man, but I thank God that I am able to say that I remained master of myself, and that I never raised a hand against him. My coolness only irritated him the more. He raved, he cursed, he shook his fists in my face, and then suddenly a horrible spasm passed over his features, he clapped his hand to his side, and with a loud cry he fell in a heap at my feet. I raised him up and stretched him upon the sofa, but no answer came to my exclamations, and the hand which I held in mine was cold and clammy. His diseased heart had broken down. His own violence had killed him.

"For a long time I sat as if I were in some dreadful dream, staring at the body of my brother. I was aroused by the knocking of Mrs. Woods, who had been disturbed by that dying cry. I sent her away to bed. Shortly afterwards a patient tapped at the surgery door, but as I took no notice, he or she went off again. Slowly and gradually as I sat there a plan was forming itself in my head in the curious automatic way in which plans do form. When I rose from my chair my future movements were finally decided upon without my having been conscious of any process of thought. It was an instinct which irresistibly inclined me towards one course.

"Ever since that change in my affairs to which I have alluded, Bishop's Crossing had become hateful to me. My plans of life had been ruined, and I had met with hasty judgments and unkind treatment where I had expected sympathy. It is true that any danger of scandal from my brother had passed away with his life; but still, I was sore about the past, and felt that things could never be as they had been. It may be that I was unduly sensitive, and that I had not made sufficient allowance for others, but my feelings were as I describe. Any chance of getting away from Bishop's Crossing and of everyone in it would be most welcome to me. And here was such a chance as I could never have dared to hope for, a chance which would enable me to make a clean break with the past.

"There was this dead man lying upon the sofa, so like me that save for some little thickness and coarseness of the features there was no difference at all. No one had seen him come and no one would miss him. We were both clean shaven, and his hair was about the same length as my own. If I changed clothes with him, then Dr. Aloysius Lana would be found lying dead in his study, and there would be an end of an unfortunate fellow, and of a blighted career. There was plenty of ready money in the room, and this I could carry away with me to help me to start once more in some other land. In my brother's clothes I could walk by night unobserved as far as Liverpool, and in that great seaport I would soon find some means of leaving the country. After my lost hopes, the humblest existence where I was unknown was far preferable in my estimation to a practice, however successful, in Bishop's Crossing, where at any moment I might come face to face with those whom I should wish, if it were possible, to forget. I determined to effect the change.

"And I did so. I will not go into particulars, for the recollection is as painful as the experience; but in an hour my brother lay, dressed down to the smallest detail in my clothes, while I slunk out by the surgery door, and taking the back path which led across some fields, I started off to make the best of my way to Liverpool, where I arrived the same night. My bag of money and a certain portrait were all I carried out of the house, and I left behind me in my hurry the shade which my brother had been wearing over his eye. Everything else of his I took with me.

"I give you my word, sir, that never for

one instant did the idea occur to me that people might think that I had been murdered, nor did I imagine that anyone might be caused serious danger through this stratagem by which I endeavoured to gain a fresh start in the world. On the contrary, it was the thought of relieving others from the burden of my presence which was always uppermost in my mind. A sailing vessel was leaving Liverpool that very day for Corunna, and in this I took my passage, thinking that the voyage would give me time to recover my balance, and to consider the future. But before I left my resolution softened. I bethought me that there was one person in the world to whom I would not cause an hour of sadness. She would mourn me in her heart, however harsh and unsympathetic her relatives might be. She understood and appreciated the motives upon which I had acted, and if the rest of her family condemned me, she, at least, would not forget. And so I sent her a note under the seal of secrecy to save her from a baseless grief. If under the pressure of events she broke that seal, she has my entire sympathy and forgiveness.

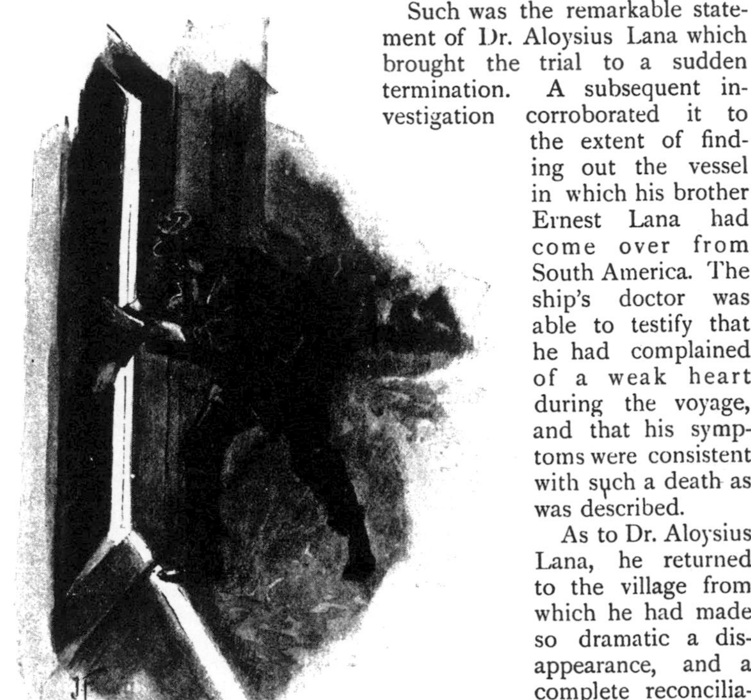

"I SLUNK OUT BY THE SURGERY DOOR."

"It was only last night that I returned to England, and during all this time I have heard nothing of the sensation which my supposed death had caused, nor of the accusation that Mr. Arthur Morton had been concerned in it. It was in a late evening paper that I read an account of the proceedings of yesterday, and I have come this morning as fast as an express train could bring me to testify to the truth."

Such was the remarkable statement of Dr. Aloysius Lana which brought the trial to a sudden termination. A subsequent investigation corroborated it to the extent of finding out the vessel in which his brother Ernest Lana had come over from South America. The ship's doctor was able to testify that he had complained of a weak heart during the voyage, and that his symptoms were consistent with such a death as was described.

As to Dr. Aloysius Lana, he returned to the village from which he had made so dramatic a disappearance, and a complete reconciliation was effected between him and the young squire, the latter having acknowledged that he had entirely misunderstood the other's motives in withdrawing from his engagement. That another reconciliation followed may be judged from a notice extracted from a prominent column in the *Morning Post*:—

"A marriage was solemnized upon September 19th, by the Rev. Stephen Johnson, at the parish church of Bishop's Crossing, between Aloysius Xavier Lana, son of Don Alfredo Lana, formerly Foreign Minister of the Argentine Republic, and Frances Morton, only daughter of the late James Morton, J.P., of Leigh Hall, Bishop's Crossing, Lancashire."

Round the Fire.

IX.—THE STORY OF THE JEW'S BREAST-PLATE.

BY A. CONAN DOYLE.

MY particular friend Ward Mortimer was one of the best men of his day at everything connected with Oriental archæology. He had written largely upon the subject, he had lived two years in a tomb at Thebes, while he had excavated in the Valley of the Kings, and finally he had created a considerable sensation by his exhumation of the alleged mummy of Cleopatra in the inner room of the Temple of Horus, at Philæ. With such a record at the age of thirty-one, it was felt that a considerable career lay before him, and no one was surprised when he was elected to the curatorship of the Belmore Street Museum, which carries with it the lectureship at the Oriental College, and an income which has sunk with the fall in land, but which still remains at that ideal sum which is large enough to encourage an investigator, and not so large as to enervate him.

There was only one reason which made Ward Mortimer's position a little difficult at the Belmore Street Museum, and that was the extreme eminence of the man whom he had to succeed. Professor Andreas was a profound scholar and a man of European reputation. His lectures were frequented by students from every part of the world, and his admirable management of the collection intrusted to his care was a commonplace in all learned societies. There was, therefore, considerable surprise when, at the age of fifty-five, he suddenly resigned his position and retired from those duties which had been both his livelihood and his pleasure. He and his daughter left the comfortable suite of rooms which had formed his official residence in connection with the museum, and my friend, Mortimer, who was a bachelor, took up his quarters there.

On hearing of Mortimer's appointment Professor Andreas had written him a very kindly and flattering congratulatory letter, but I was actually present at their first meeting, and I went with Mortimer round the museum when the Professor showed us the admirable collection which he had cherished so long. The Professor's beautiful daughter and a young man, Captain Wilson, who was, as I understood, soon to be her husband, accompanied us in our inspection. There were fifteen rooms in all, but the Babylonian, the Syrian, and the central hall, which contained the Jewish and Egyptian collection, were the finest of all. Professor Andreas was a quiet, dry, elderly man, with a clean-shaven face and an impassive manner, but his dark eyes sparkled and his features quickened into enthusiastic life as he pointed out to us the rarity and the beauty of some of his specimens. His hand lingered so fondly over them, that one could read his pride in them and the grief in his heart now that they were passing from his care into that of another.

He had shown us in turn his mummies, his papyri, his rare scarabs, his inscriptions, his Jewish relics, and his duplication of the famous seven-branched candlestick of the Temple, which was brought to Rome by Titus, and which is supposed by some to be lying at this instant in the bed of the Tiber. Then he approached a case which stood in the very centre of the hall, and he looked down through the glass with reverence in his attitude and manner.

"This is no novelty to an expert like yourself, Mr. Mortimer," said he; "but I daresay that your friend, Mr. Jackson, will be interested to see it."

Leaning over the case I saw an object, some five inches square, which consisted of twelve precious stones in a framework of gold, with golden hooks at two of the corners. The stones were all varying in sort and colour, but they were of the same size.

Their shapes, arrangement, and gradation of tint made me think of a box of water-colour paints. Each stone had some hieroglyphic scratched upon its surface.

"You have heard, Mr. Jackson, of the urim and thummim?"

I had heard the term, but my idea of its meaning was exceedingly vague.

"The urim and thummim was a name given to the jewelled plate which lay upon the breast of the high priest of the Jews. They had a very special feeling of reverence for it—something of the feeling which an ancient Roman might have for the Sibylline books in the Capitol. There are, as you see, twelve magnificent stones, inscribed with mystical characters. Counting from the left-hand top corner, the stones are carnelian, peridot, emerald, ruby, lapis lazuli, onyx, sapphire, agate, amethyst, topaz, beryl, and jasper."

I was amazed at the variety and beauty of the stones.

"Has the breast-plate any particular history?" I asked.

"It is of great age and of immense value," said Professor Andreas. "Without being able to make an absolute assertion, we have many reasons to think that it is possible that it may be the original urim and thummim of Solomon's Temple. There is certainly nothing so fine in any collection in Europe. My friend, Captain Wilson here, is a practical authority upon precious stones, and he would tell you how pure these are."

Captain Wilson, a man with a dark, hard, incisive face, was standing beside his *fiancée* at the other side of the case.

"Yes," said he, curtly, "I have never seen finer stones."

"And the gold-work is also worthy of attention. The ancients excelled in——"—he was apparently about to indicate the setting of the stones, when Captain Wilson interrupted him.

"You will see a finer example of their gold-work in this candlestick," said he, turning to another table, and we all joined him in his admiration of its embossed stem and delicately ornamented branches. Altogether it was an interesting and a novel experience to have objects of such rarity explained by so great an expert; and when, finally, Professor Andreas finished our inspection by formally handing over the precious collection to the care of my friend, I could not help pitying him and envying his successor whose life was to pass in so pleasant a duty. Within a week, Ward Mortimer was duly installed in his new set of rooms, and had become the autocrat of the Belmore Street Museum.

"'IT IS OF GREAT AGE AND OF IMMENSE VALUE,' SAID PROFESSOR ANDREAS."

About a fortnight afterwards my friend gave a small dinner to half-a-dozen bachelor friends to celebrate his promotion. When his guests were departing he pulled my sleeve and signalled to me that he wished me to remain.

"You have only a few hundred yards to go," said he—I was living in chambers in the Albany. "You may as well stay and have a quiet cigar with me. I very much want your advice."

I relapsed into an arm-chair and lit one of his excellent Matronas. When he had returned from seeing the last of his guests out, he drew a letter from his dress-jacket and sat down opposite to me.

"This is an anonymous letter which I received this morning," said he. "I want to read it to you and to have your advice."

"You are very welcome to it for what it is worth."

"This is how the note runs: 'Sir,—I should strongly advise you to keep a very careful watch over the many valuable things which are committed to your charge. I do not think that the present system of a single watchman is sufficient. Be upon your guard, or an irreparable misfortune may occur.'"

"Is that all?"

"Yes, that is all."

"Well," said I, "it is at least obvious that it was written by one of the limited number of people who are aware that you have only one watchman at night."

Ward Mortimer handed me the note, with a curious smile. "Have you an eye for handwriting?" said he. "Now, look at this!" He put another letter in front of me. "Look at the *c* in 'congratulate' and the *c* in 'committed.' Look at the capital *I*. Look at the trick of putting in a dash instead of a stop!"

"They are undoubtedly from the same hand—with some attempt at disguise in the case of this first one."

"The second," said Ward Mortimer, "is the letter of congratulation which was written to me by Professor Andreas upon my obtaining my appointment."

I stared at him in amazement. Then I turned over the letter in my hand, and there, sure enough, was "Martin Andreas" signed upon the other side. There could be no doubt, in the mind of anyone who had the slightest knowledge of the science of graphology, that the Professor had written an anonymous letter, warning his successor against thieves. It was inexplicable, but it was certain.

"Why should he do it?" I asked.

"Precisely what I should wish to ask you. If he had any such misgivings, why could he not come and tell me direct?"

"Will you speak to him about it?"

"There again I am in doubt. He might choose to deny that he wrote it."

"At any rate," said I, "this warning is meant in a friendly spirit, and I should certainly act upon it. Are the present precautions enough to insure you against robbery?"

"I should have thought so. The public are only admitted from ten till five, and there is a guardian to every two rooms. He stands at the door between them, and so commands them both."

"But at night?"

"When the public are gone, we at once put up the great iron shutters, which are absolutely burglar-proof. The watchman is a capable fellow. He sits in the lodge, but he walks round every three hours. We keep one electric light burning in each room all night."

"It is difficult to suggest anything more—short of keeping your day watchers all night."

"We could not afford that."

"THIS WARNING IS MEANT IN A FRIENDLY SPIRIT."

"At least, I should communicate with the police, and have a special constable put on outside in Belmore Street," said I. "As to the letter, if the writer wishes to be anonymous, I think he has a right to remain so. We must trust to the future to show some reason for the curious course which he has adopted."

So we dismissed the subject, but all that night after my return to my chambers I was puzzling my brain as to what possible motive Professor Andreas could have for writing an anonymous warning letter to his successor—for that the writing was his was as certain to me as if I had seen him actually doing it. He foresaw some danger to the collection. Was it because he foresaw it that he abandoned his charge of it? But if so, why should he hesitate to warn Mortimer in his own name? I puzzled and puzzled until at last I fell into a troubled sleep, which carried me beyond my usual hour of rising.

I was aroused in a singular and effective method, for about nine o'clock my friend Mortimer rushed into my room with an expression of consternation upon his face. He was usually one of the most tidy men of my acquaintance, but now his collar was undone at one end, his tie was flying, and his hat at the back of his head. I read his whole story in his frantic eyes.

"The museum has been robbed!" I cried, springing up in bed.

"I fear so! Those jewels! The jewels of the urim and thummim!" he gasped, for he was out of breath with running. "I'm going on to the police-station. Come to the museum as soon as you can, Jackson! Good-bye!" He rushed distractedly out of the room, and I heard him clatter down the stairs.

I was not long in following his directions, but I found when I arrived that he had already returned with a police inspector, and another elderly gentleman, who proved to be Mr. Purvis, one of the partners of Morson and Company, the well-known diamond merchants. As an expert in stones he was always prepared to advise the police. They were grouped round the case in which the breast-plate of the Jewish priest had been exposed. The plate had been taken out and laid upon the glass top of the case, and the three heads were bent over it.

"It is obvious that it has been tampered with," said Mortimer. "It caught my eye the moment that I passed through the room this morning. I examined it yesterday evening, so that it is certain that this has happened during the night."

It was, as he had said, obvious that someone had been at work upon it. The settings of the uppermost row of four stones—the carnelian, peridot, emerald, and ruby—were rough and jagged as if someone had scraped all round them. The stones were in their places, but the beautiful gold work which we had admired only a few days before had been very clumsily pulled about.

"It looks to me," said the police inspector, "as if someone had been trying to take out the stones."

"My fear is," said Mortimer, "that he not only tried, but succeeded. I believe these four stones to be skilful imitations which have been put in the place of the originals."

The same suspicion had evidently been in the mind of the expert, for he had been carefully examining the four stones with the aid of a lens. He now submitted them to several tests, and finally turned cheerfully to Mortimer.

"I congratulate you, sir," said he, heartily. "I will pledge my reputation that all four of these stones are genuine, and of a most unusual degree of purity."

The colour began to come back to my poor friend's frightened face, and he drew a long breath of relief.

"Thank God!" he cried, "Then what in the world did the thief want?"

"Probably he meant to take the stones, but was interrupted."

"In that case one would expect him to take them out one at a time, but the setting of each of these has been loosened, and yet the stones are all here."

"It is certainly most extraordinary," said the inspector. "I never remember a case like it. Let us see the watchman."

The commissionaire was called—a soldierly, honest-faced man, who seemed as concerned as Ward Mortimer at the incident.

"No, sir, I never heard a sound," he answered, in reply to the questions of the inspector. "I made my rounds four times, as usual, but I saw nothing suspicious. I've been in my position ten years, but nothing of the kind has ever occurred before."

"No thief could have come through the windows?"

"Impossible, sir."

"Or passed you at the door?"

"No, sir; I never left my post except when I walked my rounds."

"What other openings are there into the museum?"

"There is the door into Mr. Ward Mortimer's private rooms."

"That is locked at night," my friend explained, "and in order to reach it anyone from the street would have to open the outside door as well."

"Your servants?"

"Their quarters are entirely separate."

"Well, well," said the inspector, "this is certainly very obscure. However, there has been no harm done, according to Mr. Purvis."

"I will swear that those stones are genuine."

"So that the case appears to be merely one of malicious damage. But none the less, I should be very glad to go carefully round the premises, and to see if we can find any trace to show us who your visitor may have been."

"I WILL SWEAR THAT THOSE STONES ARE GENUINE."

His investigation, which lasted all the morning, was careful and intelligent, but it led in the end to nothing. He pointed out to us that there were two possible entrances to the museum which we had not considered. The one was from the cellars by a trap-door opening in the passage. The other through a skylight from the lumber-room, overlooking that very chamber to which the intruder had penetrated. As neither the cellar nor the lumber-room could be entered unless the thief was already within the locked doors, the matter was not of any practical importance, and the dust of cellar and attic assured us that no one had used either one or the other. Finally, we ended as we began, without the slightest clue as to how, why, or by whom the setting of these four jewels had been tampered with.

There remained one course for Mortimer to take, and he took it. Leaving the police to continue their fruitless researches, he asked me to accompany him that afternoon in a visit to Professor Andreas. He took with him the two letters, and it was his intention to openly tax his predecessor with having written the anonymous warning, and to ask him to explain the fact that he should have anticipated so exactly that which had actually occurred. The Professor was living in a small villa in Upper Norwood, but we were informed by the servant that he was away from home. Seeing our disappointment, she asked us if we should like to see Miss Andreas, and showed us into the modest drawing-room.

I have mentioned incidentally that the Professor's daughter was a very beautiful girl. She was a blonde, tall and graceful, with a skin of that delicate tint which the French call "mat," the colour of old ivory or of the lighter petals of the sulphur rose. I was shocked, however, as she entered the room to see how much she had changed in the last fortnight. Her young face was haggard and her bright eyes heavy with trouble.

"Father has gone to Scotland," she said. "He seems to be tired, and has had a good deal to worry him. He only left us yesterday."

"You look a little tired yourself, Miss Andreas," said my friend.

"I have been so anxious about father."

"Can you give me his Scotch address?"

"Yes, he is with his brother, the Rev. David Andreas, 1, Arran Villas, Ardrossan."

Ward Mortimer made a note of the address, and we left without saying anything as to the object of our visit. We found ourselves in Belmore Street in the evening in exactly the same position in which we had been in the morning. Our only clue was the Professor's letter, and my friend had made up his mind to start for Ardrossan next day, and to get to the bottom of the anonymous letter, when a new development came to alter our plans.

Very early upon the following morning I was aroused from my sleep by a tap upon my bedroom door. It was a messenger with a note from Mortimer.

"Do come round," it said; "the matter is becoming more and more extraordinary."

When I obeyed his summons I found him pacing excitedly up and down the central room, while the old soldier who guarded the premises stood with military stiffness in a corner.

"My dear Jackson," he cried, "I am so delighted that you have come, for this is a most inexplicable business."

"What has happened, then?"

He waved his hand towards the case which contained the breastplate.

"Look at it," said he.

I did so, and could not restrain a cry of surprise. The setting of the middle row of precious stones had been profaned in the same manner as the upper ones. Of the twelve jewels, eight had been now tampered with in this singular fashion. The setting of the lower four was still neat and smooth. The others jagged and irregular.

"Have the stones been altered?" I asked.

"No, I am certain that these upper four are the same which the expert pronounced to be genuine, for I observed yesterday that little discoloration on the edge of the emerald. Since they have not extracted the upper stones, there is no reason to think that the lower have been transposed. You say that you heard nothing, Simpson?"

"No, sir," the commissionaire answered. "But when I made my round after daylight I had a special look at these stones, and I saw at once that someone had been meddling with them. Then I called you, sir, and told you. I was backwards and forwards all the night, and I never saw a soul or heard a sound."

"Come up and have some breakfast with me," said Mortimer, and he took me into his own chambers.

"Now, what *do* you think of this, Jackson?" he asked.

"It is the most objectless, futile, idiotic business that ever I heard of. It can only be the work of a monomaniac."

"Can you put forward any theory?"

"I NEVER SAW A SOUL OR HEARD A SOUND."

A curious idea came into my head. "This object is a Jewish relic of great antiquity and sanctity," said I. "How about the anti-Semitic movement? Could one conceive that a fanatic of that way of thinking might desecrate——"

"No, no, no!" cried Mortimer. "That will never do! Such a man might push his lunacy to the length of destroying a Jewish relic, but why on earth should he nibble round every stone so carefully that he can only do four stones in a night? We must have a better solution than that, and we must find it for ourselves, for I do not think that our inspector is likely to help us. First of all, what do you think of Simpson, the porter?"

"Have you any reason to suspect him?"

"Only that he is the one person on the premises."

"But why should he indulge in such wanton destruction? Nothing has been taken away. He has no motive."

"Mania?"

"No, I will swear to his sanity."

"Have you any other theory?"

"Well, yourself, for example. You are not a somnambulist, by any chance?"

"Nothing of the sort, I assure you."

"Then I give it up."

"But I don't—and I have a plan by which we will make it all clear."

"To visit Professor Andreas?"

"No, we shall find our solution nearer than Scotland. I will tell you what we shall do. You know that skylight which overlooks the central hall? We will leave the electric lights in the hall, and we will keep watch in the lumber-room, you and I, and solve the mystery for ourselves. If our mysterious visitor is doing four stones at a time, he has four still to do, and there is every reason to think that he will return to-night and complete the job."

"Excellent!" I cried.

"We shall keep our own secret, and say nothing either to the police or to Simpson. Will you join me?"

"With the utmost pleasure," said I, and so it was agreed.

It was ten o'clock that night when I returned to the Belmore Street Museum. Mortimer was, as I could see, in a state of suppressed nervous excitement, but it was still too early to begin our vigil, so we remained for an hour or so in his chambers, discussing all the possibilities of the singular business which we had met to solve. At last the roaring stream of hansom cabs and the rush of hurrying feet became lower and more intermittent as the pleasure-seekers passed on their way to their stations or their homes. It was nearly twelve when Mortimer led the way to the lumber-room which overlooked the central hall of the museum.

He had visited it during the day, and had spread some sacking so that we could lie at our ease, and look straight down into the museum. The skylight was of unfrosted glass, but was so covered with dust that it would be impossible for anyone looking up from below to detect that he was overlooked. We cleared a small piece at each corner, which gave us a complete view of the room beneath us. In the cold, white light of the electric lamps everything stood out hard and clear, and I could see the smallest detail of the contents of the various cases.

Such a vigil is an excellent lesson, since one has no choice but to look hard at those objects which we usually pass with such half-hearted interest. Through my little peep-hole I employed the hours in studying every specimen, from the huge mummy-case which leaned against the wall to those very jewels which had brought us there, which gleamed and sparkled in their glass case immediately beneath us. There was much precious gold-work and many valuable stones scattered through the numerous cases, but those wonderful twelve which made up the urim and thummim glowed and burned with a radiance which far eclipsed the others. I studied in turn the tomb-pictures of Sicara, the friezes from Karnak, the statues of Memphis, and the inscriptions of Thebes, but my eyes would always come back to that wonderful Jewish relic, and my mind to the singular mystery which surrounded it. I was lost in the thought of it when my companion suddenly drew his breath sharply in, and seized my arm in a convulsive grip. At the same instant I saw what it was which had excited him.

I have said that against the wall—on the right-hand side of the doorway (the right-hand side as we looked at it, but the left as one entered)—there stood a large mummy-case. To our unutterable amazement it was slowly opening. Gradually, gradually, the lid was swinging back, and the black slit which marked the opening was becoming wider and wider. So gently and carefully was it done that the movement was quite imperceptible. Then, as we breathlessly watched it, a white, thin hand appeared at the opening, pushing back the painted lid, then another hand, and finally a face—a face which was familiar to us both, that of Professor Andreas. Stealthily he slunk out of the mummy-case, like a fox stealing from its burrow, his head turning incessantly to left and to right, stepping, then pausing, then stepping again, the very image of craft and of caution. Once some sound in the street struck him motionless, and he stood listening, with his ear turned, ready to dart back to the shelter behind him. Then he crept onwards again upon tiptoe, very, very softly and slowly, until he had reached the case in the centre of the room. Then he took a bunch of keys from his pocket, unlocked the case, took out the Jewish breast-plate, and, laying it upon the glass in front of him, began to work upon it with some sort of small, glistening tool. He was so directly underneath us that his bent head covered his work, but we could guess from the movement of his hand that he was engaged in finishing the strange disfigurement which he had begun.

I could realize from the heavy breathing of my companion, and the twitchings of the hand which still clutched my wrist, the furious indignation which filled his heart as he saw this vandalism in the very quarter of all others where he could least have expected it. He, the very man who a fortnight before had reverently bent over this unique relic, and who had impressed its antiquity and its sanctity upon us, was now engaged in this outrageous profanation. It was impossible, unthinkable—and yet there, in the white glare of the electric light beneath us, was that dark figure with the bent, grey head, and the twitching elbow. What inhuman hypocrisy, what hateful depth of malice against his successor must underlie these sinister nocturnal labours. It was painful to think of and dreadful to watch. Even I, who had none of the acute feelings of a virtuoso, could not bear to look on and see this deliberate mutilation of so ancient a relic. It was a relief to me when my companion tugged at my sleeve as a signal that I was to follow him as he softly crept out of the room. It was not until we were within his own quarters that he opened his lips, and then I saw by his agitated face how deep was his consternation.

"THIS HE OPENED SOFTLY WITH HIS KEY."

"The abominable Goth!" he cried. "Could you have believed it?"

"It is amazing."

"He is a villain or a lunatic — one or the other. We shall very soon see which. Come with me, Jackson, and we shall get to the bottom of this black business."

A door opened out of the passage which was the private entrance from his rooms into the museum. This he opened softly with his key, having first kicked off his shoes, an example which I followed. We crept together through room after room, until the large hall lay before us, with that dark figure still stooping and working at the central case. With an advance as cautious as his own we closed in upon him, but softly as we went we could not take him entirely unawares. We were still a dozen yards from him when he looked round with a start, and uttering a husky cry of terror, ran frantically down the museum.

"Simpson! Simpson!" roared Mortimer,

and far away down the vista of electric-lighted doors we saw the stiff figure of the old soldier suddenly appear. Professor Andreas saw him also, and stopped running, with a gesture of despair. At the same instant we each laid a hand upon his shoulder.

"Yes, yes, gentlemen," he panted, "I will come with you. To your room, Mr. Ward Mortimer, if you please! I feel that I owe you an explanation."

My companion's indignation was so great that I could see that he dared not trust himself to reply. We walked on each side of the old Professor, the astonished commissionaire bringing up the rear. When we reached the violated case, Mortimer stopped and examined the breast-plate. Already one of the stones of the lower row had had its setting turned back in the same manner as the others. My friend held it up and glanced furiously at his prisoner.

"How could you!" he cried. "How could you!"

"It is horrible — horrible!" said the Professor. "I don't wonder at your feelings. Take me to your room."

"But this shall not be left exposed!" cried Mortimer. He picked the breast-plate up and carried it tenderly in his hand, while I walked beside the Professor, like a policeman with a malefactor. We passed into Mortimer's chambers, leaving the amazed old soldier to understand matters as best he could. The Professor sat down in Mortimer's arm-chair, and turned so ghastly a colour that, for the instant, all our resentment was changed to concern. A stiff glass of brandy brought the life back to him once more.

"There, I am better now!" said he. "These last few days have been too much for me. I am convinced that I could not stand it any longer. It is a nightmare — a horrible nightmare—that I should be arrested as a burglar in what has been for so long my own museum. And yet I cannot blame you. You could not have done otherwise. My hope always was that I should get it all over before I was detected. This would have been my last night's work."

"How did you get in?" asked Mortimer.

"By taking a very great liberty with your private door. But the object justified it. The object justified everything. You will not be angry when you know everything—at least, you will not be angry with me. I had a key to your side door and also to the museum door. I did not give them up when I left. And so you see it was not difficult for me to let myself into the museum. I used to come in early before the crowd had cleared from the street. Then I hid myself in the mummy-case, and took refuge there whenever Simpson came round. I could always hear him coming. I used to leave in the same way as I came."

"You ran a risk."

"I had to."

"But why? What on earth was your object—*you* to do a thing like that!" Mortimer pointed reproachfully at the plate which lay before him on the table.

"I could devise no other means. I thought and thought, but there was no alter-

"MORTIMER POINTED REPROACHFULLY AT THE PLATE."

native except a hideous public scandal, and a private sorrow which would have clouded our lives. I acted for the best, incredible as it may seem to you, and I only ask your attention to enable me to prove it."

"I will hear what you have to say before I take any further steps," said Mortimer, grimly.

"I am determined to hold back nothing, and to take you both completely into my confidence. I will leave it to your own generosity how far you will use the facts with which I supply you."

"We have the essential facts already."

"And yet you understand nothing. Let me go back to what passed a few weeks ago, and I will make it all clear to you. Believe me that what I say is the absolute and exact truth.

"You have met the person who calls himself Captain Wilson. I say 'calls himself' because I have reason now to believe that it is not his correct name. It would take me too long if I were to describe all the means by which he obtained an introduction to me and ingratiated himself into my friendship and the affection of my daughter. He brought letters from foreign colleagues which compelled me to show him some attention. And then, by his own attainments, which are considerable, he succeeded in making himself a very welcome visitor at my rooms. When I learned that my daughter's affections had been gained by him, I may have thought it premature, but I certainly was not surprised, for he had a charm of manner and of conversation which would have made him conspicuous in any society.

"He was much interested in Oriental antiquities, and his knowledge of the subject justified his interest. Often when he spent the evening with us he would ask permission to go down into the museum and have an opportunity of privately inspecting the various specimens. You can imagine that I, as an enthusiast, was in sympathy with such a request, and that I felt no surprise at the constancy of his visits. After his actual engagement to Elise, there was hardly an evening which he did not pass with us, and an hour or two were generally devoted to the museum. He had the free run of the place, and when I have been away for the evening I had no objection to his doing whatever he wished here. This state of things was only terminated by the fact of my resignation of my official duties and my retirement to Norwood, where I hoped to have the leisure to write a considerable work which I had planned.

"It was immediately after this—within a week or so—that I first realized the true nature and character of the man whom I had so imprudently introduced into my family. The discovery came to me through letters from my friends abroad, which showed me that his introductions to me had been forgeries. Aghast at the revelation, I asked myself what motive this man could originally have had in practising this elaborate deception upon me. I was too poor a man for any fortune-hunter to have marked me down. Why, then, had he come? I remembered that some of the most precious gems in Europe had been under my charge, and I remembered also the ingenious excuses by which this man had made himself familiar with the cases in which they were kept. He was a rascal who was planning some gigantic robbery. How could I, without striking my own daughter, who was infatuated about him, prevent him from carrying out any plan which he might have formed? My device was a clumsy one, and yet I could think of nothing more effective. If I had written a letter under my own name, you would naturally have turned to me for details which I did not wish to give. I resorted to an anonymous letter begging you to be upon your guard.

"I may tell you that my change from Belmore Street to Norwood had not affected the visits of this man, who had, I believe, a real and overpowering affection for my daughter. As to her, I could not have believed that any woman could be so completely under the influence of a man as she was. His stronger nature seemed to entirely dominate her. I had not realized how far this was the case, or the extent of the confidence which existed between them, until that very evening when his true character for the first time was made clear to me. I had given orders that when he called he should be shown into my study instead of to the drawing-room. There I told him bluntly that I knew all about him, that I had taken steps to defeat his designs, and that neither I nor my daughter desired ever to see him again. I added that I thanked God that I had found him out before he had time to harm those precious objects which it had been the work of my life-time to protect.

"He was certainly a man of iron nerve. He took my remarks without a sign either of surprise or of defiance, but listened gravely and attentively until I had finished. Then he walked across the room without a word and struck the bell.

"'Ask Miss Andreas to be so kind as to step this way,' said he to the servant.

"My daughter entered, and the man closed the door behind her. Then he took her hand in his.

"'Elise,' said he, 'your father has just discovered that I am a villain. He knows now what you knew before.'

"She stood in silence, listening.

"'He says that we are to part for ever,' said he.

"She did not withdraw her hand.

"'Will you be true to me, or will you remove the last good influence which is ever likely to come into my life?'

"'John,' she cried, passionately, 'I will never abandon you! Never, never, not if the whole world were against you.'

"In vain I argued and pleaded with her. It was absolutely useless. Her whole life was bound up in this man before me. My daughter, gentlemen, is all that I have left to love, and it filled me with agony when I saw how powerless I was to save her from her ruin. My helplessness seemed to touch this man who was the cause of my trouble.

"'It may not be as bad as you think, sir,' said he, in his quiet, inflexible way. 'I love Elise with a love which is strong enough to rescue even one who has such a record as I have. It was but yesterday that I promised her that never again in my whole life would I do a thing of which she should be ashamed. I have made up my mind to it, and never yet did I make up my mind to a thing which I did not do.'

"He spoke with an air which carried conviction with it. As he concluded he put his hand into his pocket and he drew out a small cardboard box.

"'I am about to give you a proof of my determination,' said he. 'This, Elise, shall be the first-fruits of your redeeming influence over me. You are right, sir, in thinking that I had designs upon the jewels in your possession. Such ventures have had a charm for me, which depended as much upon the risk run as upon the value of the prize. Those famous and antique stones of the Jewish priest were a challenge to my daring and my ingenuity. I determined to get them.'

"'I guessed as much.'

"'There was only one thing that you did not guess.'

"'And what is that?'

"HE TILTED OUT THE CONTENTS."

"'That I got them. They are in this box.'

"He opened the box, and tilted out the contents upon the corner of my desk. My hair rose and my flesh grew cold as I looked. There were twelve magnificent square stones engraved with mystical characters. There could be no doubt that they were the jewels of the urim and thummim.

"'Good God!' I cried. 'How have you escaped discovery?'

"'By the substitution of twelve others, made especially to my order in which the

"'JOHN,' SHE CRIED, PASSIONATELY, 'I WILL NEVER ABANDON YOU!'"

originals are so carefully imitated that I defy the eye to detect the difference.'

"'Then the present stones are false?' I cried.

"'They have been for some weeks.'

"We all stood in silence, my daughter white with emotion, but still holding this man by the hand.

"'You see what I am capable of, Elise,' said he.

"'I see that you are capable of repentance and restitution,' she answered.

"'Yes, thanks to your influence! I leave the stones in your hands, sir. Do what you like about it. But remember that whatever you do against me, is done against the future husband of your only daughter. You will hear from me soon again, Elise. It is the last time that I will ever cause pain to your tender heart,' and with these words he left both the room and the house.

"My position was a dreadful one. Here I was with these precious relics in my possession, and how could I return them without a scandal and an exposure? I knew the depth of my daughter's nature too well to suppose that I would ever be able to detach her from this man now that she had entirely given him her heart. I was not even sure how far it was right to detach her if she had such an ameliorating influence over him. How could I expose him without injuring her—and how far was I justified in exposing him when he had voluntarily put himself into my power? I thought and thought, until at last I formed a resolution which may seem to you to be a foolish one, and yet, if I had to do it again, I believe it would be the best course open to me.

"My idea was to return the stones without anyone being the wiser. With my keys I could get into the museum at any time, and I was confident that I could avoid Simpson, whose hours and methods were familiar to me. I determined to take no one into my confidence—not even my daughter—whom I told that I was about to visit my brother in Scotland. I wanted a free hand for a few nights, without inquiry as to my comings and goings. To this end I took a room in Harding Street that very night, with an intimation that I was a Pressman, and that I should keep very late hours.

"That night I made my way into the museum, and I replaced four of the stones. It was hard work, and took me all night. When Simpson came round I always heard his footsteps, and concealed myself in the mummy-case. I had some knowledge of gold-work, but was far less skilful than the thief had been. He had replaced the setting so exactly that I defy anyone to see the difference. My work was rude and clumsy. However, I hoped that the plate might not be carefully examined, or the roughness of the setting observed, until my task was done. Next night I replaced four more stones. And to-night I should have finished my task had it not been for the unfortunate circumstance which has caused me to reveal so much which I should have wished to keep concealed. I appeal to you, gentlemen, to your sense of honour and of compassion, whether what I have told you should go any farther or not. My own happiness, my daughter's future, the hopes of this man's regeneration, all depend upon your decision."

"Which is," said my friend, "that all is well that ends well, and that the whole matter ends here and at once. To-morrow the loose settings shall be tightened by an expert goldsmith, and so passes the greatest danger to which, since the destruction of the Temple, the urim and thummim have been exposed. Here is my hand, Professor Andreas, and I can only hope that under such difficult circumstances I should have carried myself as unselfishly and as well."

Just one footnote to this narrative. Within a month Elise Andreas was married to a man whose name, had I the indiscretion to mention it, would appeal to my readers as one who is now widely and deservedly honoured. But if the truth were known, that honour is due not to him but to the gentle girl who plucked him back when he had gone so far down that dark road along which few return.

VII

The Stir Outside the Cafe Royal

CLARENCE ROOK

THE STIR OUTSIDE THE CAFÉ ROYAL.

A STORY OF MISS VAN SNOOP, DETECTIVE.

By Clarence Rook.

Illustrated by Hal Hurst.

COLONEL MATHURIN was one of the aristocrats of crime; at least Mathurin was the name under which he had accomplished a daring bank robbery in Detroit which had involved the violent death of the manager, though it was generally believed by the police that the Rossiter who was at the bottom of some long firm frauds in Melbourne was none other than Mathurin under another name, and that the designer and chief gainer in a sensational murder case in the Midlands was the same mysterious and ubiquitous personage.

But Mathurin had for some years successfully eluded pursuit; indeed, it was generally known that he was the most desperate among criminals, and was determined never to be taken alive. Moreover, as he invariably worked through subordinates who knew nothing of his whereabouts and were scarcely acquainted with his appearance, the police had but a slender clue to his identity.

As a matter of fact, only two people beyond his immediate associates in crime could have sworn to Mathurin if they had met him face to face. One of them was the Detroit bank manager whom he had shot with his own hand before the eyes of his fiancée. It was through the other that Mathurin was arrested, extradited to the States, and finally made to atone for his life of crime. It all happened in a distressingly common-place way, so far as the average spectator was concerned. But the story, which I have pieced together from the details supplied—firstly, by a certain detective sergeant whom I met in a tavern hard by Westminster; and secondly, by a certain young woman named Miss Van Snoop—has an element of romance, if you look below the surface.

"HE SHOT THE BANK MANAGER BEFORE THE EYES OF HIS FIANCÉE."

It was about half-past one o'clock, on a bright and pleasant day, that a young lady was driving down Regent Street in a hansom which she had picked up outside her boarding-house near Portland Road Station. She had told the cabman to drive slowly, as she was nervous behind a horse; and so she had leisure to scan, with the curiosity of a stranger, the strolling crowd that at nearly all hours of the day throngs Regent Street. It was a sunny morning, and everybody looked cheerful. Ladies were shopping, or looking in at the shop windows. Men about town were collecting an appetite for lunch; flower girls were selling "nice vi'lets, sweet vi'lets, penny a bunch"; and the girl in the cab leaned one arm on the apron and regarded the scene with alert attention. She was not exactly pretty, for the symmetry of her features was discounted by a certain hardness in the set of the mouth. But her hair, so dark as to be almost black, and her eyes of greyish blue set her beyond comparison with the commonplace.

"THERE WAS A SLIGHT STIR OUTSIDE THE CAFÉ ROYAL."

Just outside the Café Royal there was a slight stir, and a temporary block in the foot traffic. A brougham was setting down, behind it was a victoria, and behind that a hansom; and as the girl glanced round the heads of the pair in the brougham, she saw several men standing on the steps. Leaning back suddenly, she opened the trap-door in the roof.

"Stop here," she said, "I've changed my mind."

The driver drew up by the kerb, and the girl skipped out.

"You shan't lose by the change," she said, handing him half-a-crown.

There was a tinge of American accent in the voice; and the cabman, pocketing the half-crown with thanks, smiled.

"They may talk about that McKinley tariff," he soliloquised as he crawled along the kerb towards Piccadilly Circus, "but it's better 'n free trade—lumps!"

Meanwhile the girl walked slowly back towards the Café Royal, and, with a quick glance at the men who were standing there, entered. One or two of the men raised their eyebrows; but the girl was quite unconscious, and went on her way to the luncheon-room.

"American, you bet," said one of the loungers. "They'll go anywhere and do anything."

Just in front of her as she entered was a tall, clean-shaven man, faultlessly dressed in glossy silk hat and frock coat, with a flower in his button-hole. He looked around for a moment in search of a convenient table. As he hesitated, the girl hesitated; but when the waiter waved him to a small table laid for two, the girl immediately sat down behind him at the next table.

"Excuse me, madam," said the waiter, "this table is set for four; would you mind——"

"I guess," said the girl, "I'll stay where I am." And the look in her eyes, as well as a certain sensation in the waiter's palm, ensured her against further disturbance.

The restaurant was full of people lunching, singly or in twos, in threes and even larger parties; and many curious glances were directed to the girl who sat at a table alone and pursued her way calmly through the menu. But the girl appeared to notice no one. When her eyes were off her plate they were fixed straight ahead—on the back of the man who had entered in front of her. The man, who had drunk a half-bottle of champagne with his lunch, ordered a liqueur to accompany his coffee. The girl, who had drunk an aerated water, leaned back in her chair and wrinkled her brows. They were very straight brows, that seemed to meet over her nose when she wrinkled them in perplexity. Then she called a waiter.

"Bring me a sheet of note-paper, please," she said, "and my bill."

The waiter laid the sheet of paper before her, and the girl proceeded, after a few moments' thought, to write a few lines in pencil upon it. When this was done, she folded the sheet carefully, and laid it in her purse. Then, having paid her bill, she returned her purse to her dress pocket, and waited patiently.

"SHE WAS LOOKING INTO THE MIRROR AND PATTING HER HAIR."

In a few minutes the clean-shaven man at the next table settled his bill and made preparations for departure. The girl at the same time drew on her gloves, keeping her eyes immovably upon her neighbour's back. As the man rose to depart, and passed the table at which the girl had been sitting, the girl was looking into the mirror upon the wall, and patting her hair. Then she turned and followed the man out of the restaurant, while a pair at an adjacent table remarked to one another that it was a rather curious coincidence for a man and woman to enter and leave at the same moment when they had no apparent connection.

But what happened outside was even more curious.

The man halted for a moment upon the steps at the entrance. The porter, who was in conversation with a policeman, turned, whistle in hand.

"Hansom, sir?" he asked.

"Yes," said the clean-shaven man.

The porter was raising his whistle to his lips when he noticed the girl behind.

"Do you wish for a cab, madam?" he asked, and blew upon his whistle.

As he turned again for an answer, he plainly saw the girl, who was standing close behind the clean-shaven man, slip her hand under his coat, and snatch from his hip pocket something which she quickly transferred to her own.

"Well, I'm ——" began the clean-shaven man, swinging round and feeling in his pocket.

"Have you missed anything, sir?" said the porter, standing full in front of the girl to bar her exit.

"My cigarette-case is gone," said the man, looking from one side to another.

"What's this?" said the policeman, stepping forward.

"I saw the woman's hand in the gentleman's pocket, plain as a pikestaff," said the porter.

"Oh, that's it, is it?" said the policeman, coming close to the girl. "I thought as much."

"Come now," said the clean-shaven man, "I don't want to make a fuss. Just hand back that cigarette-case, and we'll say no more about it."

"I haven't got it," said the girl. "How dare you? I never touched your pocket."

The man's face darkened.

"Oh, come now!" said the porter.

"Look here, that won't do," said the policeman, "you'll have to come along of me. Better take a four-wheeler, eh, sir?"

For a knot of loafers, seeing something interesting in the wind, had collected round the entrance.

A four-wheeler was called, and the girl entered, closely followed by the policeman and the clean-shaven man.

"I was never so insulted in my life," said the girl.

Nevertheless, she sat back quite calmly in the cab, as though she was perfectly ready to face this or any other situation, while the policeman watched her closely to make sure that she did not dispose in any surreptitious way of the stolen article.

At the police-station hard by, the usual formalities were gone through, and the clean-shaven man was constituted prosecutor. But the girl stoutly denied having been guilty of any offence.

The inspector in charge looked doubtful.

"Better search her," he said.

And the girl was led off to a room for an interview with the female searcher.

The moment the door closed the girl put her hand into her pocket, pulled out the cigarette-case, and laid it upon the table.

"'HAVE YOU MISSED ANYTHING?' SAID THE PORTER."

"There you are," she said. "That will fix matters so far."

The woman looked rather surprised.

"Now," said the girl, holding out her arms, "feel in this other pocket, and find my purse."

The woman picked out the purse.

"Open it and read the note on the bit of paper inside."

On the sheet of paper which the waiter had given her, the girl had written these words, which the searcher read in a muttered undertone—

"I am going to pick this man's pocket as the best way of getting him into a police-station without violence. He is Colonel Mathurin, alias Rossiter, alias Connell, and he is wanted in Detroit, New York, Melbourne, Colombo, and London. Get four men to pin him unawares, for he is armed and desperate. I am a member of the New York detective force—Nora Van Snoop."

"It's all right," said Miss Van Snoop, quickly, as the searcher looked up at her after reading the note. "Show that to the boss—right away."

The searcher opened the door. After whispered consultation the inspector appeared, holding the note in his hand.

"Now then, be spry," said Miss Van Snoop. "Oh, you needn't worry! I've got my credentials right here," and she dived into another pocket.

"But do you know—can you be sure," said the inspector, "that this is the man who shot the Detroit bank manager?"

"Great heavens! Didn't I see him shoot Will Stevens with my own eyes! And didn't I take service with the police to hunt him out?"

The girl stamped her foot, and the inspector left. For two, three, four minutes, she stood listening intently. Then a muffled shout reached her ears. Two minutes later the inspector returned.

"I think you're right," he said. "We have found enough evidence on him to identify him. But why didn't you give him in charge before to the police?"

"I wanted to arrest him myself," said Miss Van Snoop, "and I have. Oh, Will! Will!"

Miss Van Snoop sank into a cane-bottomed chair, laid her head upon the table, and cried. She had earned the luxury of hysterics. In half an hour she left the station, and, proceeding to a post-office, cabled her resignation to the head of the detective force in New York.

An Unposted Letter

NEWTON MacTAVISH

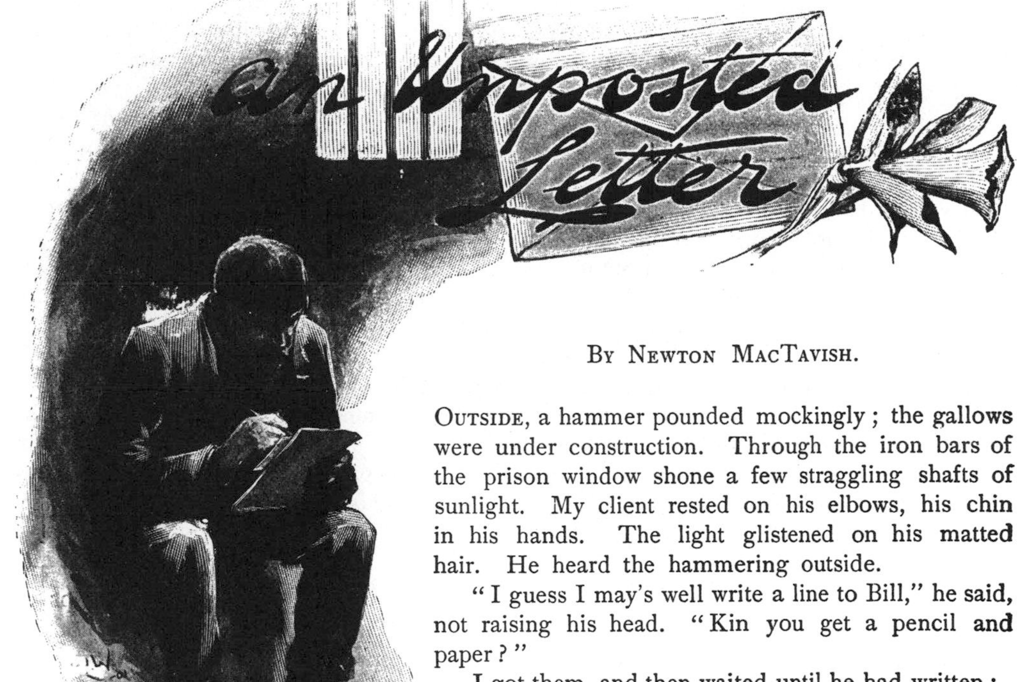

By Newton MacTavish.

Outside, a hammer pounded mockingly; the gallows were under construction. Through the iron bars of the prison window shone a few straggling shafts of sunlight. My client rested on his elbows, his chin in his hands. The light glistened on his matted hair. He heard the hammering outside.

"I guess I may's well write a line to Bill," he said, not raising his head. "Kin you get a pencil and paper?"

I got them, and then waited until he had written:

"Dear Bill,—By the sound of things, I reckon I've got to swing this trip. I've had a hope all along that they might git scent on the right track; but I see that Six-Eye'll be 'bliged to kick the bucket, with head up—the galleys is goin' up mighty fast.

"I say, Bill, there ain't no good in burglarin'. I swore once I'd quit it, and wish I had. But a feller can't allus do just as he fancies; I guess he can't allus do it, kin he, Bill? You never knew how I got into this scrape, did you?

"One day I was standin' around, just standin' around, nothin' doin', when I saw a pair of runaway horses a-comin' down the street like mad. I jumped out and caught the nigh one by the bridle. I hauled 'em up mighty sudden, but somethin' swung me round, and I struck my head agin the neck-yoke, kersmash.

"When I come to, I was sittin' back in the carriage with the sweetest faced girl bendin over me, and wipin' my face with cool water. She asked where she would drive me home; and, do you know, Bill, for the first time, I was ashamed to say where. But I told her, and, so help me, she came clear down in there with me, and made Emily put me to bed. She left money, and every day till I got well she come out and sat and read the Bible and all them things. Do you know, Bill, it wasn't long afore things seemed different. I couldn't look at her pure, sweet face and plan a job. The last day she came I made up my mind I'd try somethin' else—quit burglarin'.

"I started out to get work. One man asked me what I'd served my time at. I said I'd served most of it in jail, and then he wouldn't have anythin' to do with me. A chap gave me a couple of days breakin' stones in a cellar. He said I did it so good he guessed I must have been in jail. After that I couldn't get nothin' to do, because no one wouldn't have nothin' to do with a jail-bird, and I had made up my mind to tell the truth.

"At last Emily began to kick and little Bob to cry for grub. I got sick of huntin' for work, and it seemed as if everybody was pushin' me back to my old job. I got disgusted. I had to do somethin', so I sat down and planned to do a big house in the suburbs. I'd sized it up before.

"The moon was high that night, so I waited till it went down, long after midnight. I found the back door already open, so it was a snap to git in.

"I went upstairs and picked on a side room near the front. I eased the door and looked in. A candle flickered low, and flames danced from a few coals in the fireplace.

"I entered noiselessly.

"A high-backed chair was in front of the hearth. I sneaked up and looked over the top. A young girl, all dressed in white, with low neck and bare arms, laid there asleep. Her hair hung over her shoulders; she looked like as if she'd come home from a dance, and just threw herself there tired out.

"Just as I was goin' to turn away, the flames in the fireplace flickered, and I caught the glow of rubies at the girl's throat. How they shone and gleamed and shot fire from their blood-red depths! The candle burned low and sputtered; but the coals on the hearth flickered, the rubies glowed, and the girl breathed soft in her sleep.

"'It's an easy trick,' I said to myself, and I leaned over the back of the chair, my breath fanning the light hair that fell over marble shoulders. I took out my knife and reached over. Just then the fire burned up a bit. As I leaned over I saw her sweet, girlish face, and, so h'lp me, Bill, it was her, her whose face I couldn't look into and plan a job.

"Hardly knowing it, I bared my head, and stood there knife in hand, the blood rushin' to my face, and my feelin's someway seemin' to go agin me.

"I looked at her, and gradually closed my knife and straightened up from that sneakin' shape a feller gets into. I remembered a verse that she used to read to me, 'Ye shall not go forth empty-handed,' so I said to myself I'd try again. But just as I was turnin' to go, I heard a shot in the next room; then a heavy thud. I stood stock-still for a jiffy, and then ran out in time to see someone dart down the stairs. At the bottom I heard a stumble. I hurried along the hall and ran straight into the arms of the butler.

"I guess someone else was doin' that job that night. But they had me slicker'n a whistle. 'Twas no use; everythin' went agin me. I had on my big revolver, the mate to the one you got. As it happened, one chamber was empty, and the ball they took from the old man's head was the same size. I had a bad record; it was all up with me. The only thing they brought up in court to the contrary was the top of an ear they found in the hall, where someone must have hit agin somethin' sharp. But they wouldn't listen to my lawyer.

"Give up burglarin', Bill; see what I've come to. But I hope you'll do a turn for Emily if ever she's in need, and don't learn little Bob filchin'. Do this for an old pal's sake, Bill."

The doomed man stopped writing, as the last shaft of sunlight passed beyond the iron bars of the prison window. Outside the hammering had ceased; the scaffold was finished.

"You'll find Emily, my wife, in the back room of the basement at 126, River Street," said my client, handing me the letter. "She'll tell you where to find Bill."

I took the letter, but did not then know its contents. I started, but he called me back.

"You have a flower in your button-hole," he said. "I'd like to wrap it up and send it to Emily."

Next day, after the sentence of the law had been executed, I went to find Emily. I descended the musty old stairway at 126, River Street, where all was filth and squalor. At the back room I stopped and rapped. A towzy head was thrust out of the next door.

"They're gone," it said.

"Where?"

"Don't know. The woman went with some man."

"Did you know him?"

"I saw him here before sometimes, but the top of his ear wasn't cut off then. They called him Bill—sort of pal."

"And where's the little boy?"

"He's gone to the Shelter."

I went out into the pure air, and, standing on the kerbstone, read the letter:

". . . The only thing they brought up in court to the contrary was the top of an ear. . . ."

When I had finished, I remembered the flower in my hand. I didn't throw it away; I took it to my office and have it there still, wrapped in the paper as he gave it me.

IX

The Black Narcissus

FRED M. WHITE

THE BLACK NARCISSUS.

BY FRED M. WHITE

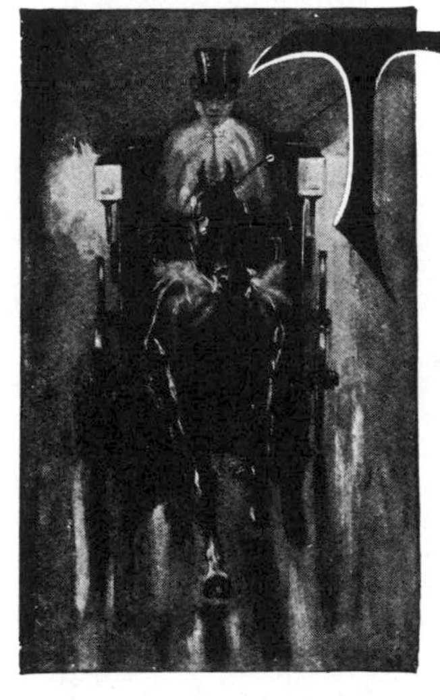

TWISTING the card in his fingers, Lancaster Vane stood, impatient. He had all the novelist's scarring, lightning flash of passion for puerile interruption.

"Didn't I tell you—?" he growled. Then he paused, with the surging sense of humour uppermost. The black and white starched parlourmaid was wilting before his scathing indignation. "Don't you know that I once murdered a maid who disobeyed my orders like this? Show the man in."

The girl gurgled and vanished. Then followed a man with a gliding step and a moist grey eye, that took the whole room and the trim garden beyond and eke the novelist in like the flash of a camera, and held the picture on the mental gelatine for all time.

"I am afraid I am intruding upon you, sir," the stranger suggested.

"Oh, you are," Vane said quietly. "Don't let that trouble you, though. I always work in the mornings, and I play golf all the afternoon. I make this arrangement so that if people waste my time in the mornings I can make up for it by sacrificing my pleasure after luncheon."

Inspector Darch, of Scotland Yard, ventured upon a smile.

"I come upon business of importance," he said.

"I guessed that from your card. Had you not been a policeman I should have declined to see you. In search of copy I have spent a deal of time in police and criminal courts, and I am bound to say I have a certain affection for the average constable. He has imagination—the way he generally gives his evidence shows that. He is a novelist in the nut."

Inspector Darch looked searchingly at the speaker. He was just a little disappointing. He was not tall and pale, with flashing eyes and long hair; on the contrary, his hair was that of the athlete, and he might have passed for a pugilist of the better class. The sensitive mouth and fine grey eyes saved the countenance from the commonplace. Thus it was that, after a second searching gaze, Darch seemed to see a face kaleidoscope from broad commonplace into the rugged suggestion of a young Gladstone. Here was no ordinary man. But then everybody who had studied Lancaster Vane's novels knew that.

"My complaint is, that we all lack imagination," the inspector said. "Of course, what you so playfully allude to is inventiveness. Young policemen always invent—they fancy that their first duty is to get a conviction. But they have no imagination. I've got a name and a good reputation, but no imagination."

"You have come to a deadlock in some case you have on hand?"

"That's it, sir. And I've made so bold as to come and ask for your assistance."

"Come out into the garden and smoke a cigar, then," Vane said suddenly.

Darch complied willingly. Vane's thatched cottage was on the river—a tiny place consisting of a large study, a smoking-room, and a dining-room, with quarters at the back for bachelor friends. Hither he had come earlier in the season than usual, with the intention of finishing a novel, before turning from "his beans and bacon," as he phrased it, to the butterfly delights of the London Season. For Vane's books were satires for the most part, and he knew his world as well as any man living. Audacity and insight were the jewels in the wheel of his style. He had a marvellous faculty for seeing through a thing, a faculty that made him both respected and feared.

The garden was a riotous delight of daffodils and tulips, primulas and narcissus. There was no finer show of those pure spring flowers to be seen anywhere. Vane had a perfect passion for flowers, especially the Spring varieties. He could name a bulb as a savant can locate the flint or the sandstone. With an eye for detail, Darch did not fail to notice that there were no less than sixteen varieties of daffodils.

"Here I live for my work and my flowers," said Vane. "When down here, I smoke a pipe and live more or less on fish and bacon. When I am in town, I am nice over my wine and critical to rudeness over my friend's cigarettes. You are fond of flowers, Mr. Darch?"

"At present I am deeply interested in them," Darch replied.

"And thereby hangs a tale," said Vane. "Go on."

"There! I knew you were the man for me," Darch said admiringly.

Vane smiled; for even a novelist is only a man in disguise.

"Heavens! If I'd only got that insight of yours! It's a murder case, sir."

"You have a murder case on hand that utterly puzzles you?" Vane had dropped into a rustic garden seat, where he was thoughtfully pulling at his pipe. "And the matter is not remotely connected with flowers," he concluded.

"Got it again, sir!" the delighted Darch exclaimed. "You see, it's like this. I've read all your books—indeed, I have read most novels that make for the study of humanity, and I don't deny that I've learnt a lot that way."

"Have you, really?" Vane said quietly.

"I don't mind your little joke, sir. I've learnt that an innocent man can show exactly the same terror as the guilty caught red-handed; I've learnt—— But no matter. And many a time it has struck me what a wonderful detective a first class novelist would make. I don't mean in little things, such as tracking criminals and the like—I mean in elucidating big problems. When we exhaust every avenue, his imagination would find a score of others, especially if he had a good psychological knowledge of his man. Now, I've got a case on hand that I believe you can solve for me, sir."

"Possibly," said Vane. "But where does my psychological knowledge come in? Seeing that there is no suspect, and that the victim is a stranger to me——"

"The victim is no stranger to you, Mr. Vane; I've found that out. And because you know him, and because of your novels, I am here to-day."

"This is getting interesting," Vane murmured. "The victim?"

"Ernst Van Noop. He was found dead in his cottage at Pinner last night, and there is not the slightest trace of the murderer. Van Noop lived in his house quite alone, and he seemed to have no hobby or occupation beyond his little garden and greenhouses."

"Except when he was spouting sedition in Hyde Park on Sundays," said Vane. "I'm sorry to hear about this. Really, Van Noop was a perfectly harmless creature, and at heart as gentle as a child. A little eccentric, but that was all."

Darch dissented mildly. He was bound to regard the doings of the dead Dutchman with an official eye. The man had been an Anarchist of the worst type; his Sunday orations would never have been tolerated in any other country; his doctrines were, to say the least, inflammatory.

"You are quite wrong," said Vane. "Poor Van Noop would not have injured a fly. In his way the man was a genius, and genius must have an outlet, or it is apt to become chargeable upon the rates. Anarchy was Van Noop's safety valve. He and I came together over the common table of flowers—bulbs especially. He could have worked wonders in the way of hybrids and new varieties had he lived. Your dangerous character theory won't hold water. I defy you to prove to me that the poor old Dutchman consorted with notoriously dangerous characters."

"Then why did he ask for police protection?" Darch demanded. "What was he afraid of? He had no money or valuables, he never went near any of the Soho clubs; so far as we can tell, nobody suspicious ever went near him. Yet for the last few days that man has been frightened out of his life—afraid of being murdered, he said. At the same time he refused to give any account of the party or parties who held him in terror, and he point-blank declined to open his mouth as to the reason for any threats or danger."

"You fancy he was a Nihilist who had fallen under the ban of the Order?"

"I feel practically certain of it, sir," Darch replied. "He has been murdered by those

"He glanced at Darch with mingled contempt and pity."

people, and they have left no trace behind. That is why I am here."

Vane smiled in a manner calculated to annoy anybody but a detective.

"I don't fancy you are far wrong to appeal to the imagination of a novelist," he said, "especially to a novelist who knows the victim. I don't know the murderer, any more than you do, but I'll prophesy for once. Within a week you shall have the assassin within your hands. Come, isn't that assertion enough even for a writer of fiction?"

"You can put your hand upon the Nihilist?" Darch cried. "You know him?"

"I don't know him, and he isn't a Nihilist," Vane replied. "I haven't the remotest idea who the murderer is, and yet I stick to my opinion. I am going entirely on a theory, which theory is built upon some knowledge of the dead man's past. You will, perhaps, be glad to hear that it is a theory that would only occur to a novelist; therefore you were perfectly right in the line of policy that brought you here. Now, perhaps you will be so good as to tell me all the details."

"The details are *nil*, practically," Darch replied. "The policeman on duty near Van Noop's cottage had certain special orders. He noticed that the door was not open late in the afternoon, and he could not make anybody hear. Then he burst open the door and found Van Noop lying dead in the kitchen with a wound in his side. There were no signs of violence; indeed, Van Noop must have been taken quite by surprise, for just under his heel, as if he had slipped upon it, was a small smashed onion."

"Onion!" Vane cried. "An onion! Great Scott!"

The mention of that homely yet pungent vegetable seemed to have the strangest effect on the novelist. He glanced at Darch with mingled contempt and pity, a great agitation possessed him as he restlessly strode to and fro. Then he dropped into his seat again, and his shoulders shook in a fit of uncontrollable laughter.

"You will pardon me," he said, after a pause; "but your apparently commonplace words swept all the strings of emotion at once. And yet you say there is no clue. Now, *could* you have any clue stronger than an onion?"

"You are slightly too subtle for me, sir," Darch said, not without heat.

"I beg your pardon," Vain said contritely. "But I should very much like to see that onion."

Darch replied that the request might be complied with. He would have permitted himself the luxury of satire with anybody else but Vane over the matter. But then Vane had made him a cold, concrete promise that he should handle the quarry within seven days. From a novelist who had consistently refused to be interviewed, the promise carried weight.

"Was there anything else?" Vane asked.

"Nothing so prominent as the onion," Darch replied. "I, of course, made a close examination of the body, and in the right hand I found a flower. It looks to me like a periwinkle. Of course, it is much faded, and perhaps you may attach some importance to it. Being an ordinary man, it conveys nothing to me."

Vane's eyes were gleaming. The lines of his sensitive mouth twitched. If he was moved to laughter any more, he laughed inside.

"I don't suppose it would," he said thoughtfully, "seeing that Van Noop was a lover of flowers. He might have been looking at the bloom at the moment when the fatal blow was struck. It would be quite natural for him to keep the flower in his grasp. You have it, of course?"

"Yes, sir," said Darch. "One never quite knows. Didn't some great man once say that there are no such things as small details?"

"Details are the cog-wheels of great actions," Vane said sententiously. "Give me the flower."

Darch took the withered bloom from his pocket-book. It was wilted and lank, with a grass green stem and some dank velvet tassels hanging forlornly to the head. Had it been some precious treasure of the storied ages Vane could not have examined it more tenderly.

"What do you make of it?" Darch asked carelessly.

Vane shook his head. "The bloom is too far gone at present," he said. "It might be possible to revive it by plunging the whole into tepid water, with a little salt added." And yet, in spite of his assumed indifference, Vane's voice shook a little as he spoke.

"You had better leave this with me," he said. "In any case, it will be quite safe in my hands, and as the inquest on Van Noop's body is over, you will not need it for the present. At the same time, I am quite in earnest over my prophecy. If you will come here this day week at 6 p.m., I will go with you and assist you, if necessary, in arresting the murderer."

Darch departed, somewhat dazed at the result of his interview. But there was no smile on the face of the novelist, nothing but eager, palpitating curiosity, as he proceeded to plunge the wilted flower into water, to which a little salt was added.

"I'll go for a long pull on the river," he murmured. "I can't stay here by that thing. I should get an attack of nerves watching it expand. I wonder if it is possible that——"

He came back at length, two hours later, and proceeded to the study. Then he drew the flower from the water, and, behold! a glorious and pleasing transformation. The dead, crape-like petals had filled out to a

"Held it where the sun might play upon the velvety lustre."

velvety, glossy softness, black as night and lustrous as ebony. There were five of these black petals, and in the centre a calyx of deep purple with a heart of gold. Vane's hand shook as if with wine as he examined the perfect flowers, his eyes were glowing with admiration.

He flicked the water from it and dried it carefully. Then he held it where the sun might play upon the velvety lustre and shine upon the perfect dead blackness. Vane's eyes were like those of a mother gazing at a child back from the gates of death.

"Now I know what Van Noop was hinting at," he said. "He said he had a fortune in his pocket, and he was right. And I am the only living man who has been as yet permitted to look upon a *black narcissus*."

II.

It was characteristic of Lancaster Vane that he should throw himself heart and soul into his undertaking. It had occurred to him more than once that the typical detective officer was lacking in imagination, and crime in the abstract interested him, as it must interest all writers of fiction; and more than once he had found his theories of some great case not only at variance with the police, but absolutely right when they had been as absolutely wrong.

That marvellous audacity and insight had rarely failed Vane when dealing with living, breathing humanity. And he had no fear of failure here.

All the same, Inspector Darch began to grow uneasy when the sixth day came and nothing had transpired—at least, nothing of a tangible nature. He came down to the cottage late in the evening with a sufficiently flimsy excuse for seeing the man of letters.

Vane was seated in his study, reading by the light of a shaded lamp. The vivid blood-red line of the fringed silk was but one crimson spot in a dim, shimmering blackness. The novelist half sighed, and then smiled as he laid down his book.

"I had forgotten all about you, Darch," he said.

"You don't mean to say you have done nothing, sir?" the inspector cried.

"On the contrary, I have done a great deal, my friend," Vane replied. "I meant that I had forgotten you for a moment. I am reading a novel here which in my humble opinion is the best that Dumas ever wrote."

"'Monte Cristo'?" Darch murmured. "Hear, hear!"

"No, it is not 'Monte Cristo,'" Vane replied. "I am alluding to 'The Black Tulip.' Later on you will appreciate the value of the work. Imagination and education do a good deal for a man, but a judicious system of novel-reading does more. Some day our prophet shall arise and tell the world what an influence for good the best novels have wielded. Do you know the book?"

Darch admitted having skimmed it. He had found the characterisation feeble—at least, from a detective's point of view. Vane smiled.

"I shall change your opinion presently," he said. "Have you discovered anything?"

"As to Van Noop, you mean? No, sir. Have you?"

"No," Vane replied. "I am still quite as much in the dark as yourself."

"But you promised me that within a week——"

"I would show you the man. Well, I am going to do so. I haven't the remotest idea who he is yet, but I am going to meet him to-morrow afternoon. When I have done so, I shall send you a telegram to Scotland Yard giving you the man's address and the hour you are meet me there. Does that satisfy you?"

Darch expressed his thanks but feebly. All this was very irregular. Also, though it had an element of Gasconade about it, it was impossible to look into Vane's strong, grave face and doubt that he believed every word that he uttered. If this were detective's work, why, then, it amounted to genius. And thus Darch departed, with a strong feeling of uncertainty.

It was a little after twelve the next day that Vane set out to walk from Pinner Station on the Metropolitan to the cottage recently inhabited by the unhappy Van Noop. Nearing his destination he felt in his pocket-book for certain news-cuttings and a printed circular he had there. And this printed circular was to the effect that on this same date the whole of the garden produce and plants and flowers, bulbs and apparatus generally, belonging to the late Ernst Van Noop, were to be sold by auction, by order of the landlord, under a distress for rent. By the time Vane came to the cottage a free sprinkling of gardeners and florists had arrived, for, though the sale was a small one, Van Noop had been fairly well known amongst the brotherhood, and there was just the chance of picking up an odd parcel or so of hybrid bulbs which might become worth their weight in gold later on.

A lover of flowers and a man keen on anything new in that direction, Vane was respectfully recognised. Most of the dealers present were gathered in the kitchen of the cottage, where the bulbs were set out in little coarse blue paper bags. Most of them were properly labelled and catalogued, but there were three packets, of four bulbs each, to which the most trained florist present would have found it hard to give a name.

Vane pushed his way through a little knot of dealers. One of them touched his hat.

"Anything new here, Harris?" he asked.

"Well, sir," was the reply. "Van Noop was a close sort of party. I did hear something—in fact, I read it in the *Garden Herald* to-day—as Van Noop had some wonderful black bulbs here, but maybe it's all nonsense. I can't make head or tail of those little packets yonder, and I should be sorry to risk a sovereign on the chance of them turning out anything beyond the common. The other bulbs look good, but we could all show as fine a variety."

"I'll speculate," said Vane. "There's a commission for you, Harris. You can go up to five pounds each for those particular packets, but not a penny beyond. Of course, it will be throwing money away; but nothing venture, nothing win. And it may be possible that the *Garden Herald* was right, and Van Noop had invented the black tulip, after all."

Vane had spoken loud enough for everybody to hear. Then he left the cottage and strode down with the air of a man who has important business before him. He came back later and lounged into the cottage unconcernedly with a pipe in his mouth. The small knot of buyers were still lingering there. Vane came up to Harris languidly.

"Well," he asked. "Do you want my cheque for those mysterious bulbs?"

"No, sir," Harris replied, "and in my opinion you're quite well out of it. I bid up to five pounds, and then a stranger raised me a sovereign a bag, and I dropped it, of course. There he is, sir. You don't often get a chance to see the amateur enthusiast at his best; but he's only a foreigner."

This with the finest insular contempt. Vane glanced carelessly at the slight, stooping figure and thin, pinched features of the man who had incurred the florist's displeasure. The eyes he could not see, for they were behind glasses.

"Evidently an enthusiast, like myself," Vane said. "We all have our philosopher's stone, Harris."

"I dare say we do," Harris replied sententiously.

Vane smiled again. He passed over to the auctioneer and, after a few minutes with that worthy, scribbled out a telegram in pencil. When he looked round again, the foreign connoisseur had disappeared. Harris was busily engaged in directing the package of his own small purchase.

"I am coming over to-morrow to see that salmon auricula of yours," said Vane. "I am sorry to say that mine are doing indifferently. Not enough shade, perhaps."

"That's it, sir," Harris responded. "Aristocratic flower, naturally, is the auricula. Put 'em in an old garden along the borders under apple trees, and you can grow 'em like peonies. It's only county people who can grow auriculas."

"I'll put a coat-of-arms over mine," Vane laughed. "By the way, as you are passing a station, will you be good enough to send this telegram for me?"

The telegram merely contained an address, followed by a single figure, and was directed to Darch's registered address at Scotland Yard. To the casual reader it conveyed nothing. Then Vane made his way into the road.

He walked on for a mile or more until he came, at length, to a pretty little cottage, a double-fronted one-storey affair, covered with creepers. There was a long garden in front, a garden deep sunken between trim, thick hedges, the black soil of which was studded with thousands of flowers—hyacinths, tulips, narcissus, nothing was wanting.

Vane's artistic eye revelled in the lovely sight.

He stood thus feasting his soul on the mass of beautiful colours before him. The more important mission was forgotten for the moment. There was something of envy in Vane's glance, too, for with all his lavish outlay he could not produce blooms like these. And the owner of the place was obviously a poor man.

"A better soil, perhaps," Vane muttered, "or perhaps it's because these beauties get the whole attention of the grower. Flowers want more attention than most women. When those gladiolas come into bloom——"

Vane paused in his ruminations as the owner of the cottage came out. He had a black velvet skull cap on the back of his head, around which grey hairs straggled like a thatch. As he stood in the path of the setting sun Vane noticed the long, slender hands and a heavy signet ring on

"'There he is, sir. You don't often get a chance to see the amateur enthusiast at his best.'"

the right little finger. They were not the hands of the toiler or workman, and yet to Vane they indicated both strength and resolution.

"I am admiring your flowers," he said. "They are absolutely perfect. I am an enthusiast myself, but I have nothing like this."

"Nothing so perfect?" the old man said. "Won't you come in, sir?"

The question was asked with a certain mixture of humility and high courtesy that seemed to take Vane back over the bridge of the centuries. The man before him was bent and shaken by the palsy of old age, and yet his eyes were full of fire and determination. His English was thin and foreign, yet he spoke with the easy fluency of the scholar. Again Vane forgot his mission. An hour or more passed, the sun had flamed down behind the fragrant hawthorn, and Vane was still listening.

He had met a man with an enthusiasm greater than his own. Vane was standing in the presence of a master, and he knew it. The man was talking excitedly.

"I was a rich man once," he said. "The Van Eykes were a power in Holland at one time. And I have ruined myself over flowers as Orientals ruin themselves over their harems, and as the visionary in seeking for the elixir of life. Flowers have ever been my mistress—I have given my all for them, my life to the study of the secrets of Nature. If I could only go down to posterity as the inventor of something new——"

"A black tulip, for instance," Vane suggested.

The dark eyes behind the glasses flashed. Vane looked at his watch.

"Oh, yes!" Van Eyke cried. "It was that fascinating romance that first set me thinking. Perhaps you, too, have had your dreams, sir?"

"I confess it," Vane smiled. "You see, I am a novelist as well as a florist. I am still sanguine of seeing a black, a velvety black, flower. It will be soft-stemmed when it comes, and, as you know, it will be a bulbous plant."

"Perhaps I shall be able to show it to you."

Van Eyke spoke quietly, yet with a thrill in his voice. His hand trembled with something more than the weight of years. His glance wandered towards the house.

"I had it almost within my grasp five years ago," he said. "I was living near Amsterdam then. You should have seen my hybrids—black, and white, and patches, and the black predominating. Heavens! how I longed and waited for the next springtime!"

"You are speaking of tulips, of course?" Vane asked carelessly.

"Oh, no," said Van Eyke. He paused in confusion, the red thread of his lips paled. "Yes, yes, of course I meant tulips. The black tulip. Ah, ah!"

His gaiety was not a pleasant thing. It was too suggestive of the butterfly on the skeleton.

"Oh! I waited for the springtime," he went on. "Aye, I waited as a prisoner for freedom. And they all came pink! My children had been stolen! Sir, you are a novelist. You can understand the frame of mind in which one commits murder."

"Did you track the man who had robbed you?" Vane asked.

"After a time I did; but it was years. Sir, I am talking nonsense."

"You may have said too much in the excitement of the moment," Vane said coolly, "but certainly you are not talking nonsense. You tracked your man, and you killed him. Why?"

Van Eyke's hands went up with an almost mechanical gesture. At the same moment a step was heard, crunching the gravel outside, and Darch appeared. Vane made a motion with his hand in the direction of Van Eyke's bent, quivering figure.

"You have come in time,' he said. "This is Mr. Darch, of Scotland Yard. And this is Mr. Van Eyke, the man who killed Van Noop a few days ago."

Darch was too astonished to speak for a moment. The dramatic force of the situation had almost overpowered him. For crime as a rule is sordid enough, and the heroic in the life of a detective is only for the pages of fiction.

"This is a poor return for all my courtesy," Van Eyke said, not without dignity. "I have never even heard of the gentleman you mention."

Darch looked helplessly at Vane. The suggestion that he was about to be fooled was painful. Never had the mantle of the majesty of the law lain more awkwardly on his shoulders.

"It is quite possible," Vane said, "that you never heard of Van Noop by that name. But assuredly you knew all about the man at Pinner, the man who was murdered, and some of whose bulbs to-day fetched over five

"In the lapel of his coat he wore Van Noop's black narcissus."

pounds a packet, or nearly two pounds per bulb."

"I have not heard of that," said Van Eyke.

"Strange, seeing that you purchased them," Vane went on. "This is nonsense, Mr. Van Eyke. I saw you at the sale, and I am surprised that you did not see me. However, all this is beside the point. You bought those bulbs at an extravagant price because you believed that they were the bulbs of the black——"

"There is not a black—a black tulip in the world."

"Who said anything about a black tulip?" Vane retorted. "What you were after was a black narcissus. Perhaps you will deny the existence of that?"

"I should like to see it, above all things."

The sneer passed over Vane's head. He stepped close to Van Eyke and opened his overcoat. In the lapel of his coat, the stem carefully preserved in water, he wore Van Noop's black narcissus. The flower was slightly ragged at the edges, but it was all there, like a lovely woman past her prime.

The effect was staggering. Van Eyke fell, as if some unseen power had beaten him to his knees.

"Where did you get it?" he asked hoarsely. "Where did you get it?"

"Surely you need not ask the question," said Vane. "It was the one Van Noop was holding in his hand at the time you murdered him."

Van Eyke rose slowly to his feet. He made no further denial of the grave charge, he seemed to be absolutely unconscious of the danger hanging over his head. He had only eyes for the flower in Vane's coat. Darch watched the scene with lively admiration.

"Let me see it, let me hold it," said Van Eyke. He spoke like a man in a dream. "I don't care what you do, I don't care what happens to me, so long as I can hold that flower in my hand. You need not be afraid. I will not injure it. Injure it? Bah! Would a mother injure her firstborn? I have sold my soul for it, as Faust sold his for Marguerite."

His eyes had grown soft and pleading. It seemed impossible to believe that the gentle, quivering creature could have the blood of a fellow creature on his hands. Vane passed the flower over, in spite of a glance of disapproval from Darch. It seemed like madness to hand over to the prisoner's custody the strongest link of evidence against him; and how frail that link was!

Van Eyke bent over the flower and pressed it to his lips.

"This is mine," he said, "mine! For twenty years I have laboured to attain this result. Another hand grew it, another hand tended it and fostered it, but the child is mine. Van Noop stole my black and white hybrids two years ago, and from them he has developed this. He has been no more than the clod who has made the frame and varnished the canvas, for the picture is mine. And I killed him."

The confession was out at last. Darch stepped forward. The man was merged in the official. For the moment he forgot to admire Vane and the wonderful way in which he had elucidated the mystery. He became a mere detective again.

"I must warn you," he said, "that all you say will be taken in evidence against you."

Van Eyke smiled. Then he handed the black narcissus back to Vane. "What does it matter?" he said. "What does anything matter? I have seen all the fond hopes of years gratified, and I can die happy. I care nothing whatever whether Van Noop or myself gets the credit for the black narcissus, so long as it is there. He robbed me—I found him—and I killed him—killed him with the very thing I coveted in his hand. He died with it in his hand, and I never knew it.

"It is two years since I tracked Van Noop to England, after he robbed me. Then I settled down in this cottage, waiting my time; and for two years he lived within a mile of me, and I never knew it—never found it out. A month last Sunday I was in London. I was passing through Hyde Park when I heard an Anarchist addressing a mob. Something in his voice impelled me to draw near. It was my man, the man who had robbed me of the best part of my life.

"I followed him home. I found where he lived, and I waited my opportunity. It came. I slipped into the cottage when the door was open, and there he was, bending over a pot with a flower growing in it. I made a noise, and he turned and saw me. I fancied that it was his fear that caused him to break off the flower in the pot, but I had only eyes for my foe. Then with a knife I had I struck him to the heart, and he died without a murmur. For an hour I remained there, searching the house, but I could not find what I was searching for. I was looking for the black narcissus. Gentlemen, that is all."

"One question," said Vane. "Had you been hanging about Van Noop's cottage?"

"For three or four weeks, yes," Van Eyke replied. "I was seeking for my opportunity."

"Is it possible that he might have discovered this?"

"Oh, it is possible all these things are possible. Why?"

"I was merely asking for my own information," said Vane. "There was a point to be cleared up, and you have done it for us. I am sorry for this, very sorry. It seems a pity that so fine and innocent and beautiful a place should be mixed up in a sordid crime like this."

Van Eyke shrugged his shoulders. There was no trace of fear in his eyes now; indeed, it seemed to Vane that those eyes were blazing with a fire beyond the bright glow of reason.

"Most of the brightest jewels in the world are stained with blood," Van Eyke said, "and if the orchids in your millionaires' houses could speak, what tragedies they might tell! Sir, I am in your hands. Sir, I wish you good-night."

The Dutchman turned from Darch to Vane with a stately courtesy. He might have been a lordly host bowing out two objectionable visitors. A little later, and the prisoner found himself with a stolid policeman in the back of a dog-cart. Darch lingered a moment before he took his seat.

"Mr. Vane," he said, "this is really wonderful."

"It is exceedingly painful and squalid to me," Vane replied. "But I see you are puzzled. You have seen the problem finished, and naturally you are anxious to have the moves all explained. If you will come to the Lotus Club after dinner to-morrow night, I will make everything clear. Say nine o'clock."

"Mr. Vane," Darch said emphatically, "I will be there."

III.

"And now, Darch," said Vane, as he finished his coffee daintily, "I am going to be egoistical. I am going to talk about myself to the extent of some one thousand words. As a rule, I get some twenty guineas per thousand for my words—but that is another story.

"The other night you came to me with a story of an Anarchist who asked for police protection, because—so you imagined—he had done something wrong in the eyes of other Nihilists, and feared for his life. You came to me, in the first place, to obtain inspiration from a novelist, and, secondly, because the victim was, like myself, an ardent lover of flowers.

"Now, in the first place, permit me to correct a wrong impression of yours. From your point of view I should never make a good detective. I decline to believe in the theory of obvious deduction. Dupin and Sherlock Holmes were steeped to the lips in it. My word! what blunders they would have made had they reduced those theories to practice! Holmes takes a watch, and from a keyhole, by the scratches, deduces that the owner is a man of dissipated habits. But suppose he had been partially blind or suffering from paralysis, eh? No, that's no good save in fiction.

"Now, I knew Van Noop. I knew him to be incapable of injuring a fly. His socialism was merely a safety valve. The man might have been a visionary, but what he didn't know about flowers wasn't worth knowing. And more than once he had hinted to me that he was on the verge of a great discovery. As bulbs were his hobby, and as he was a Dutchman, also, as he was a great admirer of Dumas, I guessed he was after a black flower. They are all after it. And it was not to be a tulip, because Van Noop didn't care much for tulips.

"Then you came to me and told me he had been murdered. You told me about the mysterious way in which he had asked for police protection, and instantly it flashed across my mind that somebody had discovered his secret and was trying to get it from him. When you brought me that withered flower, I was sure of my argument; and when you spoke of that smashed onion, I was positive. You made me laugh over that onion, you remember. That probably was a bulb of the black narcissus, though as a layman you were quite justified in taking it for that succulent vegetable.

"After you were gone I developed the black narcissus. There before me was a motive for the murder. It seemed to me that there had been a struggle for it, and that Van Noop had destroyed the flower and crushed the bulb just before he was killed. Then, as a natural sequence to this important discovery, the story of 'The Black Tulip' came into my mind. I had to find the man who committed the crime for the sake of the narcissus. And this is where the novelist comes in. It was not a case for obvious deduction, it was a case of introspection. *You* would have gone on blundering your head against Nihilist revenge and the like. I simply had to weave a romance round that flower, a romance with blood in it. And gradually my art and my imagination led me to the true and only possible solution of the mystery. Van Noop had been murdered for the sake of the black narcissus beyond question, and the assassin must be an enthusiast and a madman, like himself. You will call all this intuition.

"Then I had to draw my man. I found out when the sale was coming off, and a man who knows the address of every amateur gardener in London posted a special circular I had printed hinting that Van Noop's collection held rare things to buyers. When I reached Van Noop's cottage on the day of the sale I had no idea who the murderer was, but I felt absolutely certain that he would be present, whether he had my circular or no. Then, in a stage whisper, I asked a florist to purchase a parcel or two of bulbs for me at a fancy price. As I expected, on my return I found they had been bought over my head by somebody else. And then, my dear Darch, I knew the man who had murdered Van Noop. I had only to go over to the auctioneer and obtain the address of the man who had given a large sum for a parcel of bulbs which he fondly hoped contained the black narcissus. I obtained that address and followed Van Eyke to his cottage."

"Wonderful!" Darch cried. "I should never have thought of it."

"Of course you wouldn't," Vane replied. "Crime for crime's sake would be the only motive that appealed to you. And why? Because it is impossible for the detective trained in the ordinary way to appreciate or understand the poetic side of crime. And yet I defy you to find anything sordid in the case. The whole thing is absolutely mediæval. In this prosaic age it seems extraordinary that a man should commit murder for the sake of a flower. And yet in Van Eyke you have a man who would not have shed a drop of blood for all the mines of Golconda."

"You are right, sir," said Darch thoughtfully; "and I was right also. I knew that a man of imagination would be required here, and I found him. And I don't mind confessing that I should never have dreamt of connecting that crime with a simple flower."

"You might," Vane replied. "When everything else failed, you would probably have started to look out for the owner of the flower, going on the theory that the dead man had snatched it from the coat of the murderer. Another time, perhaps, I may show you how my detective theory can be worked out in another fashion. And the next time you find an onion, be quite sure it is an onion, and not a priceless bulb worth a king's ransom."

X

The Mysteries of Great Cities

BARONESS E. ORCZY

By
BARONESS E. ORCZY.

Illustrated by
P. B. Hickling.

THE GLASGOW MYSTERY.

DRAMATIS PERSONÆ.

THE MAN IN THE CORNER, *who tells the story to*
THE LADY JOURNALIST.
MRS. CARMICHAEL—*The landlady who was murdered.*
MR. YARDLEY—*A poet living in her house.*
MR. JAMES LUCAS—*Another of her boarders.*
UPTON—*Her manservant.*
EMMA—*Her cook.*

I.

"IT has often been declared," remarked the man in the corner, "that a murder—a successful murder, I mean—can never be committed single-handed in a busy city, and that on the other hand, once a murder *is* committed by more than one person, one of the accomplices is sure to betray the other, and that is the reason why comparatively so few crimes remain undetected. Now I must say I quite agree with this latter theory."

It was some few weeks after my first introduction to the man in the corner and the inevitable bit of string he always played with when unravelling his mysteries, and some time before he recounted to me his grim version of the tragedy in Percy-street, which I have already retold in the ROYAL.

Now I had made it a hard and fast rule whenever he made an assertion of that kind to disagree with it. This invariably irritated him; he became comically excited, produced his bit of string, and started off at rattling speed, after a few rude remarks directed at lady journalists in general and myself in particular, on one of his madly bewildering, true cock-and-bull stories.

"What about the Glasgow murder, then?" I remarked sceptically.

"Ah, the Glasgow murder," he repeated "Yes, what about the Glasgow murder? I see you are one of those people who, like the police, believe that Yardley was an accomplice to that murder, and you still continue to hope, as they do, that sooner or later he, and the other man, Upton, will meet, divide the spoils, and throw themselves into the expectant arms of the Glasgow police."

"Do you mean to tell me that you don't think Yardley had anything to do with that murder?"

"What does it matter what a humble amateur like myself thinks of that or any other case? Pshaw!" he added, breaking his bit of string between his bony fingers in his comical excitement. "Why, think a moment how simple is the whole thing! There was Mrs. Carmichael, the widow of a medical officer, young, good-looking, and fairly well-off, who for the sake of company, more than for actual profit-making, rents one of the fine houses in Woodbine Crescent with a view to taking in 'paying guests.' Her house is beautifully furnished—I told you she was fairly well-off. She has no difficulty in getting boarders.

"The house is soon full. At the time of which I am speaking she had ten or eleven 'guests'—mostly men out at business all day, also a married couple, an officer's widow with her daughter, and two journalists. At first she kept four female servants; then one day there was a complaint among the gentlemen boarders that their boots were insufficiently polished and their clothes very sketchily brushed. Chief among these complainants was Mr. Yardley, a young man who wrote verses for magazines, called himself a poet, and, in consequence, indulged in sundry eccentric habits which furnished food for gossip both in the kitchen and in the drawing-room over the coffee-cups.

"As I said before, it was he who was loudest in his complaint on the subject of his boots; it was he, again, who, when Mrs. Carmichael expressed herself willing to do anything to please her boarders, recommended her a quiet, respectable man named Upton to come in for a couple of hours daily, clean boots, knives, windows, and what-nots, and make himself 'generally useful'—I believe that is the technical expression. Upton, it appears, had been known to Mr. Yardley for some time, had often run errands and delivered messages for him, and had even been intrusted with valuable poetical MSS. to be left at various editorial offices.

"It was in July of last year, was it not, that Glasgow—honest, stodgy, busy Glasgow—was thrilled to its very marrow by the recital in its evening papers of one of the most ghastly and most dastardly crimes?

"At two o'clock that afternoon, namely, Mrs. Carmichael, of Woodbine Crescent, was found murdered in her room. Her safe had been opened, and all its contents—which were presumed to include a good deal of jewellery and money—had vanished. The evening papers had also added that the murderer was known to the police, and that no doubt was entertained as to his speedy arrest.

"It appears that in the household at Woodbine Crescent it was the duty of Mary, one of the maids, to take up a cup of tea to Mrs. Carmichael every morning at seven o'clock. The girl was not supposed to go into the room, but merely to knock at the door, wait for a response from her mistress, and then leave the tray outside on the mat.

"Usually Mrs. Carmichael took the tray in immediately, and was down to breakfast with her boarders at half-past eight. But on that eventful morning Mary seems to have been in a hurry. She could not positively state afterwards whether she had heard her mistress's answer to her knock or not; against that, she was quite sure that she had taken up the tray at seven o'clock precisely.

"When everybody went down to breakfast a couple of hours or so later, it was noticed that Mrs. Carmichael had not taken in her tea-tray as usual. A few anxious comments were made as to the genial hostess being unwell, and then the matter was dropped. The servants did not seem to have been really anxious about their mistress during the morning. Mary, who had been in the house two years, said that once before Mrs. Carmichael had stayed in bed with a bad headache until one o'clock.

"However, when the lunch hour came and went, Mrs. Tyrrell, one of the older lady boarders, became alarmed. She went up to her hostess's door and knocked at it loudly and repeatedly, but received no reply. The door, mind you, was locked or bolted, presumably, of course, from the inside. After consultation with her fellow boarders, Mrs. Tyrrell at last, feeling that something must be very wrong, took it upon herself to call in the police. Constable Rae came in; he too knocked and called, shook the door, and finally burst it open.

"It is not for me," continued the man in the corner, "to give you a description of that room as it appeared before the horrified eyes of the constable, the servants, and lady boarders; that lies more in your province than in mine.

"Suffice it to say that the unfortunate lady lay in her bed with her throat cut.

"No key or bolt was found on the inside of the door; the murderer, therefore, having accomplished his ghastly deed, must have locked his victim in, and probably taken the key away with him. Hardly had the terrible discovery been made than Emma the cook, half hysterical with fear and horror, rushed up to Constable Rae, and, clutching him wildly by the arm, whispered under her breath, 'Upton, Upton; he did it, I know . . . My poor mistress; he cut her throat with that fowl carver this morning. I saw it in his hand . . . It is him, constable!'

"'Where is he?' asked the constable peremptorily. 'See that no one leaves the house. Who has seen this man?'

"But neither the constable, nor anyone else for that matter, was much surprised to find that on searching the house throughout, the man Upton had disappeared."

II.

"At first, of course, the case seemed simplicity itself. No doubt existed, either in the public mind or that of the police, as to Upton being the author of the grim and horrible tragedy. The only difficulty, so far, was the fact that Upton had managed not only to get away on the day of the murder, but also had contrived to evade the rigorous search instituted throughout the city after him by the police—a search, I assure you, in which many an amateur detective readily joined.

"The inquest had been put off for a day or two in the hope that Upton might be found before it occurred. However, three days had now elapsed, and it could not be put off any longer. Little did the public expect the sensational developments which the case suddenly began to assume.

"The medical evidence revealed nothing new. On the contrary, it added its usual quota of vague indefiniteness which so often helps to puzzle the police. The medical officer had been called in by Constable Rae, directly after his discovery of the murder. That was

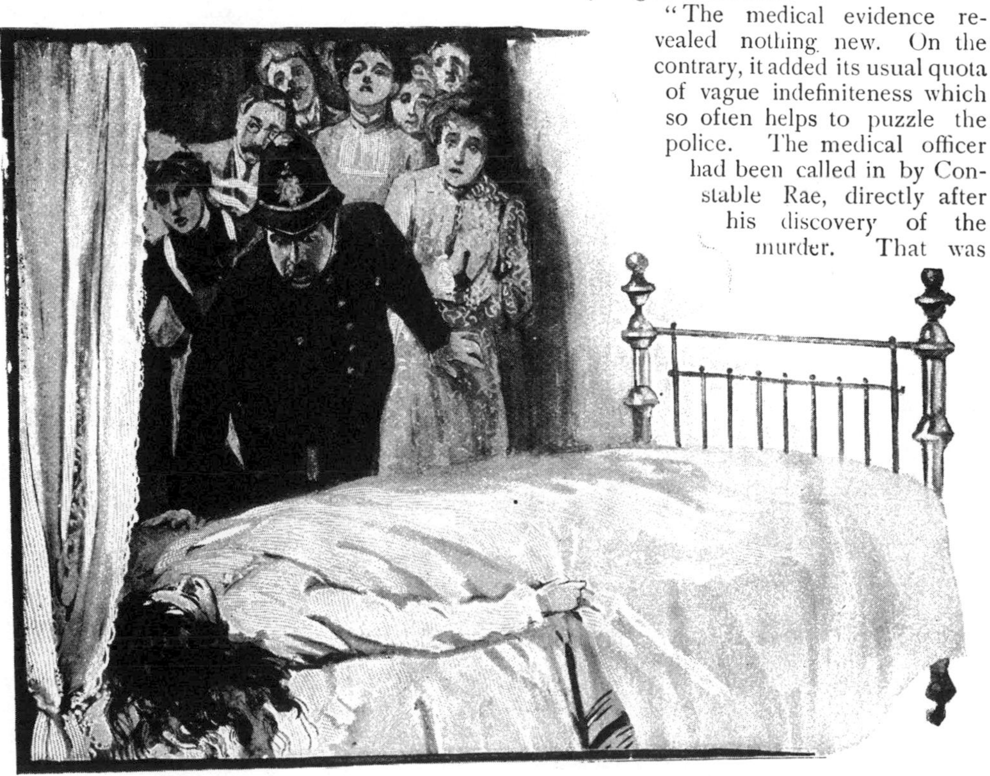

"Mrs. Carmichael was found murdered in her room."

"This fowl carver is awful blunt."

of course, in the dining-room," and he goes off with the fowl carver in his hand, and that is the last I ever saw of that carver and of Upton himself.'

"'Have you known Upton long?' asked the coroner.

"'No, sir, he had only been in the house two days. Mr. Yardley gave him a character, and the mistress took him on, to clean boots and knives. His hours were half-past six to ten, but he used to turn up about a quarter to seven. He seemed obliging and willing, but not much up to his work, and didn't say much. But I hadn't seen him so funny except that morning when the poor missus was murdered.'

"'Is this the carver you speak of?' asked the coroner, directing a constable to show one he held in his hand to the witness.

about two o'clock in the afternoon. Death had occurred a good many hours before that time, stated Dr. Dawlish—possibly nine or ten hours; but it might also have been eleven or twelve hours previously.

"Then Emma the cook was called. Her evidence was, of course, most important, as she had noticed and talked to the man Upton the very morning of the crime. He came as usual to his work, about a quarter to seven, but the cook immediately noticed that he seemed very strange and excited.

"'What do you mean by strange?' asked the coroner.

"'Well, it was strange of him, sir, to start first thing in the morning cleaning knives when we had as many knives as we wanted clean for breakfast.'

"'Yes? He started cleaning knives, and then what did he do?'

"'Oh, he turned and turned that there knife machine so as I told him he would be turning all the edges. Then he suddenly took up the fowl carver and said to me; "This fowl carver is awful blunt—where's the steel?" I says to him: "In the sideboard,

"With renewed hysterical weeping Emma identified the carver as the one she had last seen in Upton's hand. It appears that Detective McMurdoch had found the knife, together with the key of Mrs. Carmichael's bedroom door, under the hall mat. Sensational, wasn't it?" laughed the man in the corner; "quite in the style of the penny novelette — sensational, but not very mysterious.

"Then Mrs. Tyrrell had to be examined, as it was she who had first been alarmed about Mrs. Carmichael, and who had taken it upon herself to call in the police. Whether through spite or merely accidentally Mrs. Tyrrell insisted in her evidence on the fact that it was Mr. Yardley who was indirectly responsible for the awful tragedy, since it was he who had introduced the man Upton into the house.

"The coroner felt more interested. He thought he would like to put a few questions to Mr. Yardley. Now Mr. Yardley when called up did not certainly look prepossessing; and from the first most persons present were prejudiced against him. He was, as I think I said before, that *rara avis*, a successful poet: he wrote dainty scraps for magazines and weekly journals.

"In appearance he was a short, sallow, thin man, with no body and long limbs, and carried his head so much to one side as to almost appear deformed. Here is a snapshot I got of him some time subsequently. He is no beauty, is he?

"Still his manner, his small shapely hands, and quiet voice undoubtedly proclaimed him a gentleman.

"It was very well known throughout the household that Mr. Yardley was very eccentric; being a poet he would enjoy the privilege with impunity. It appears that his most eccentric habit was to get up at unearthly hours in the morning—four o'clock sometimes—and wander about the streets of Glasgow.

"'I have written my best pieces,' he stated in response to the coroner's astonished remark upon this strange custom of his, 'leaning against a lamp post in Sauchiehall Street at five o'clock in the morning. I spend my afternoons in the various public libraries, reading. I have only boarded and lodged in this house for two or three months, but, as the servants will tell you, I leave it long before they are up in the morning. I am never in to breakfast or luncheon, but always in to dinner. I go to bed early, naturally, as I require several hours sleep.'

"Mr. Yardley was then very closely questioned as to his knowledge of the man Upton.

"'I first met the man,' replied Mr. Yardley, 'about a year ago. He was loafing in Buchanan Street, outside the *Herald* office, and spoke to me, telling me a most pitiable tale—namely, that he was an ex-compositor, had had to give up his work owing to failing eyesight, that he had striven for weeks and months to get some other kind of employment, spending in the meanwhile the hard-earned savings of many years' toil; that he had come to his last shilling two days ago, and had been reduced to begging, not for money, but for some kind of job—anything to earn a few honest coins.

"'Well, I somehow liked the look of the man; moreover, as I just happened to want to send a message to the other end of the city, I sent Upton. Since then I have seen him almost every day. He takes my manuscripts for me to the editorial offices, and runs various errands. I have recommended him to one or two of my friends, and they have always found him honest and sober. He has eked out a very meagre livelihood in this way, and when Mrs. Carmichael thought of having a man in the house to do odd jobs, I thought I should be doing a kind act by recommending Upton to her. Little did I dream then what terrible consequences such a kind act would bring in its trail. I can only account for the man's awful crime by thinking that perhaps his mind had become suddenly unhinged.'

"All this seemed plain and straightforward enough. Mr. Yardley spoke quietly, without the slightest nervousness or agitation. The coroner and jury both pressed him with questions on the subject of Upton, but his attitude remained equally self-possessed throughout. Perhaps he felt, after a somewhat severe cross-examination on the part of the coroner, who prided himself on his talent in that direction, that a certain amount of doubt might lurk in the minds of the jury and consequently the public. Be that as it may, he certainly begged that two or three of the servants might be recalled in order to enable them to state definitely that he was out of the house, as usual, when they came downstairs that morning.

"One of the housemaids, recalled, fully corroborated that statement. Mr. Yardley's room, she said, was on the ground floor, next to the dining-room. She went into it soon after half-past six, turned down the bed, and began tidying it up generally.

"There was only one other witness of any importance to examine. One other boarder—Mr. James Lucas, a young journalist, employed on the editorial staff of the *Glasgow Banner*.

"The reason why he had been called specially was because he was well known to be one of the privileged guests of the house, and had been more intimate with the deceased than any of her other boarders. This privilege, it appears, chiefly consisted in being admitted to coffee, and possibly whiskey and soda after dinner, in Mrs. Carmichael's special private sitting-room. Moreover, there was a generally accepted theory among the other boarders that Mr. James Lucas entertained certain secret hopes with regard to his amiable hostess, and that, but for the fact that he was several years her junior, she might have encouraged these hopes.

"Now, Mr. James Lucas was the exact opposite of Mr. Yardley, the poet; tall, fair, athletic, his appearance would certainly prepossess everyone in his favour. He seemed very much upset, and recounted with much, evidently genuine, feeling, his last interview with the unfortunate lady—the evening before the murder.

"'I saw Mr. Yardley descending the stairs.'"

"'I spent about an hour with Mrs. Carmichael in her sitting-room,' he concluded, and parted from her about ten o'clock. I then went to my club, where I stayed pretty late, until closing time, in fact. After that I went for a stroll, and it was a quarter past two by my watch when I came in. I let myself in with my latch-key.

"'It was pitch dark in the outer hall, and I was groping for my candle, when I heard the sound of a door opening and shutting on one of the floors above, and directly after someone coming down the stairs. As you have seen yourself, the outer hall is divided from the inner one by a glass door, which on this occasion stood open. In the inner hall there was a faint glimmer of light, which worked its way down from a skylight on one of the landings, and by this glimmer I saw Mr. Yardley descending the stairs, cross the hall, and go into his room. He did not see me, and I did not speak.'

"An extraordinary, almost breathless, hush had descended over all those assembled there. The coroner sat with his chin buried in his hand, his eyes resting searchingly on the witness who had just spoken. The jury had not uttered a sound. At last the coroner queried:

"'Is the jury to understand, Mr. Lucas, that you can swear positively that at a quarter-past two in the morning, or thereabouts, you saw Mr. Yardley come down the stairs from one of the floors above and go into his own room, which is on the ground floor?'

"'Positively.'

"That was enough. Mr. Lucas was dismissed and Mr. Yardley was recalled. As he once more stood before the coroner, his curious one-sided stoop, his sallowness, and length of limb seemed even more marked than before. Perhaps he was a shade or two paler, but certainly neither his hands nor his voice trembled in the slightest degree.

"Questioned by the coroner, he replied quietly:

"'Mr. Lucas was obviously mistaken. At the hour he names I was in bed and asleep.'

"There had been excitement and breathless interest when Mr. James Lucas had made his statement, but that excitement and breathlessness was as nothing compared with the absolutely dumbfounded awe which fell over everyone there, as the sallow, half-deformed, little poet, gave the former witness so completely, so emphatically the lie.

"The coroner himself hardly knew how to

keep up his professional dignity as he almost gasped the query:

"'Then is the jury to understand that you can swear positively that at a quarter-past two o'clock on that particular morning you were in bed and asleep?'

"'Positively.'

"It seemed as if Mr. Yardley had repeated purposely the other man's emphatic and laconic assertion. Certainly his voice was as steady, his eye as clear, his manner as calm as that of Mr. Lucas. The coroner and jury were silent, and Mr. Yardley turned to where young Lucas had retired in a further corner of the room. The eyes of the two met, almost like the swords of two duellists before the great attack; neither flinched. One or the other was telling a lie. A terrible lie since it might entail loss of honour, or life perhaps to the other, yet *neither* flinched. One was telling a lie, remember, and in everyone's mind there arose at once the great all absorbing queries 'Which?' and 'Wherefore!'"

III.

I HAD been so absorbed in listening to the thrilling narrative of that highly dramatic inquest that I really had not noticed until then that the man in the corner was recounting it as if he had been present at it himself.

"That is because I heard it all from an eye-witness," he suddenly replied with that eerie knack he seemed to possess of reading my thoughts, "but it must have been very dramatic, and, above all, terribly puzzling. You see there were two men swearing against one another, both in good positions, both educated men; it was impossible for any jury to take either evidence as absolutely convincing, and it could not be proved that either of them lied. Mr. Lucas might have done so from misapprehension. There was just a possibility that he had had more whiskey at his club than was good for him. Mr. Yardley, on the other hand, if he lied, lied because he had something to hide, something to hide in that case which might have been terrible.

"Of course Dr. Dawlish was recalled, and with wonderful learning and wonderful precision he repeated his vague medical statements:

"'When I examined the body with my colleague, Dr. Swanton, death had evidently supervened several hours ago. Personally, I believe that it must have occurred certainly more like twelve hours ago than seven.

"More than that he could not say. After all, medical science has its limits.

"Then Emma, the cook, was again called. There was an important point which, oddly enough, had been overlooked up to this moment. The question, namely, of the doormat under which the knife (which, by the way, was blood-stained) and also the key of Mrs. Carmichael's bedroom door was found. Emma, however, could make a very clear and very definite statement on that point. She had cleaned the hall and shaken the mat at half-past six that morning. At that hour the housemaid was making Mr. Yardley's bed; he had left the house already. There certainly was neither key nor knife under the mat then.

"The balance of evidence, which perhaps for one brief moment had inclined oh, ever so slightly, against Mr. Yardley, returned to its original heavy weight against the man Upton. Of course there was practically nothing to implicate Mr. Yardley seriously The coroner made a resumé of the case before his jury worthy of a judge in the High Courts.

"He recapitulated all the evidence. It was very strong, undeniable, damning against Upton, and the jury could arrive but at one conclusion with regard to him. Then there was the medical evidence. That certainly favoured Upton a very little, if at all. Remember that both the medical gentlemen refused to make a positive statement as to the time; their evidence could not, therefore, be said to weigh either for or against anyone.

"There was then the strange and unaccountably conflicting evidence between two gentlemen of the house—Mr. Lucas and Mr. Yardley. That was a matter which for the present must rest between either of these gentlemen and their conscience. There was also the fact that the man Upton—the evident actual murderer—had been introduced into the house by Mr. Yardley. The jury knew best themselves if this fact should or should not weigh with them in their decision.

"That was the sum total of the evidence. The jury held but a very brief consultation. Their foreman pronounced their verdict of 'Wilful murder against Upton.' Not a word about Mr. Yardley. What could they have said? There was really no evidence against him—not enough, certainly, to taint his name for ever with so hideous a blight.

"In a case like that, remember, the jury are fully aware that the police would never for a moment lose sight of a man who had so narrowly escaped a warrant as Yardley had done. Relying on the certainty that very soon Upton would be arrested, it was not to be doubted for a moment but that he would betray his accomplice, if he had one. Criminals in such a plight nearly always do. In the meanwhile, every step of Yardley's would be dogged, unbeknown to himself, even if he attempted to leave the country. As for Upton——"

The man in the corner paused. He was eyeing me through his great bone-rimmed spectacles, watching with ironical delight my evident breathless interest in his narrative. I remembered that Glasgow murder so well. I remember the talks, the arguments, the quarrels that would arise in every household. Was Yardley an accomplice? Did he kill Mrs. Carmichael at two in the morning? Did he tell a lie? If so, why? Did Mr. James Lucas tell a lie? Many people, I remember, held this latter theory, more particularly as Mrs. Carmichael's will was proved some days later, and it was found that she had left all her money to him.

For a little while public opinion veered dead against him. Some people thought that if he were innocent he would refuse to touch a penny of her money; others, of a more practical turn of mind, did not see why he should not. He was a struggling young journalist; the lady had obviously been in love with him, and intended to marry him; she had a perfect right—as she had no children or any near relative—to leave her money to whom she choose, and it would indeed be hard on him, if, through the act of some miscreant, he should at one fell swoop be deprived both of wife and fortune.

Then, of course, there was Upton—Upton! Upton! whom the police could not find! who must be guilty, seeing that he so hid himself, who never would have acted the hideous comedy with the carver. Why should he have wilfully drawn attention to himself, and left, as it were, his visiting card on the scene of the murder?

Why? why? why?

"Ah, yes, why?" came as a funny, shrill echo from my eccentric *vis-a-vis*. "I see that in spite of my earnest endeavour to teach you to think out a case logically and clearly, you start off with a preconceived notion, which naturally leads you astray *because* it is preconceived, just like any blundering detective in these benighted islands."

"Preconceived?" I retorted indignantly. "There is no question of preconception. Whether Mr. Yardley knew of the contemplated murder or not, whether he was an accomplice or Mr. Lucas, there is one thing very clear—namely, that Upton was not innocent in the matter."

"What makes you say that?" he asked blandly.

"Obviously, because if he were innocent he would not have acted the hideous tragic comedy with the carver; he would not, above all, have absolutely damned himself by disappearing out of the house and out of sight at the very moment when the discovery of Mrs. Carmichael's murdered body had become imminent."

"It never struck you, I suppose," retorted the man in the corner with quiet sarcasm, "how *very* damning Upton's actions were on that particular morning?"

"Of course they were *very* damning. That is just my contention."

"And you have never then studied my methods of reasoning sufficiently to understand that when a criminal—a clever criminal, mind you—appears to be damning himself in the most brainless fashion, that is the time to guard against the clever pitfalls he is laying up for the police?"

"Exactly. That is why I, as well as many people connected with journalism, believe that Upton was acting a comedy in order to save his accomplice. The question only remains as to who the accomplice was."

"He must have been singularly unselfish and self-sacrificing, then."

"How do you mean?"

"According to your argument, Upton heaped up every conceivable circumstantial evidence against himself in order to shield his accomplice. Firstly he acts the part of strange, unnatural excitement, he loudly proclaims the fact that he leaves the kitchen with the fowl carver in his hand, thirdly he deposits that same blood-stained knife and the key of Mrs. Carmichael's room under the mat a few moments before he leaves the house. You must own that the man must have been singularly unselfish since, if he is ever caught, nothing would save him from the gallows, whilst, unless a great deal more evidence can be brought up, his accomplice could continue to go free."

"Yes, that might be," I said thoughtfully; "it was of course a part of the given plan. Many people held that Upton and Yardley were great friends—they might have been brothers, who knows?"

"Yes, who knows?" he repeated scornfully, as getting more and more excited his long thin fingers wound and unwound his bit of string, making curious complicated knots, and then undoing them feverishly.

"Do brothers usually so dote on each other, that they are content to swing for one another? And have you never wondered why the police never found Upton? How did he get away? Where is he? Has the earth swallowed him up?

"Surely a clumsy brute like that, who gives himself hopelessly away on the very day when he commits a murder, cannot have brains enough to hide altogether away from the police—a man who before a witness selects the weapon with which he means to kill his victim, and who then deliberately leaves it blood-stained there where it is sure to be found at once? Why imagine such a consummate fool evading the police, not a day, not a week, not a month, but nearly two years now, which means altogether? Why, such a fool as you, the public, and the police have branded him would have fallen into a trap within twenty-four hours of his attempt at evasion; whereas the man who planned and accomplished that murder was a genius before he became a blackguard."

"That's just what I said. He was doing it to shield his accomplice."

"His accomplice!" gasped the funny creature, with ever increasing excitement. "Yes, the accomplice he loved and cherished above all—his brother you say, perhaps. No, someone he would love ten thousand times more than any brother."

"Then you mean——"

"*Himself*, of course! Didn't you see it all along? Lord bless my soul! The young man—poet or blackguard, what you will—who comes into a boarding-house, then realises that its mistress is wealthy. He studies the rules of the house, the habits of its mistress, finds out about her money, her safe, her jewels, and then makes his plans. Oh, they were magnificently laid! That man ought to have been a great diplomatist, a great general—he was only a great scoundrel.

"The sort of disguise he assumed is so easy to manage. Only remember one thing: When a fool wishes to sink his identity he does so *after* he has committed a crime and is wanted by the police; he is bound, therefore, for the best part of the remainder of his life, to keep up the disguise he has selected at all times, every hour, every minute of the day; to alter his voice, his walk, his manners. On the other hand, how does a clever man like Yardley proceed?

"He chooses his disguise and assumes it *before* the execution of his crime; it is then only a matter of a few days, and when all is over, the individual, the known criminal, disappears; and, mind you, he takes great care that the criminal shall be known. Now in this case Upton is introduced into the house; say he calls one evening on Mr. Yardley's recommendation; Mrs. Carmichael sees him in the hall for a few moments, arranges the question of work and wages, and after that he comes every morning, with a dirty face, towzled hair, false beard and moustache—the usual type of odd job man very much down in his luck—his work lies in the kitchen, no one sees him upstairs, whilst the cook and kitchen folk never see Mr. Yardley.

"After a little while something—carelessness perhaps—might reveal the trick, but the deception is only carried on two days. Then the murder is accomplished and Upton disappears. In the meanwhile Mr. Yardley continues his eccentric habits. He goes out at unearthly hours; he is a poet; he is out of the house while Upton carries on the comedy with the carving knife. He knows that there never will be any evidence against him as Yardley; he has taken every care that all should be against Upton, all; hopeless, complete, absolute, damning!

"Then he leaves the police to hunt for Upton. He 'lies low' for a time, after a little while he will go abroad, I dare say he has done so already. A jeweller in Vienna, or perhaps St. Petersburg, will buy some loose stones of him, the stones he has picked out of Mrs. Carmichael's brooches and rings, the gold he will melt down and sell, the notes he can cash at any foreign watering-place, without a single question being asked of him. English banknotes find a very ready market abroad, and 'no questions asked.'

"After that he will come back to his friends in Glasgow and write dainty bits of poetry for magazines; the only difference being that he will write them at more reasonable hours. And during all the time the police will hunt for Upton.

"It was clever, was it not? You have his photo? I gave it you just now. Clever-looking, isn't he? As Upton he wore a beard and dyed his hair very black; it must have been a great trouble every morning, mustn't it?"

THE YORK MYSTERY.

Being the Second of a Series of Stories entitled "The Mysteries of Great Cities."

Illustrated by P. B. Hickling.

BY
BARONESS E. ORCZY.

DRAMATIS PERSONÆ.

THE MAN IN THE CORNER *of the A.B.C. shop who tells the story to*
THE LADY JOURNALIST.
LORD ARTHUR SKELMERTON.
LADY ARTHUR SKELMERTON.
COLONEL MCINTOSH.
CHIPPS (*Butler*).
JAMES TERRY.
CHARLES LAVENDER. } *Bookmakers.*
GEORGE HIGGINS.

I.

THE man in the corner looked quite cheerful this morning; he had had two glasses of milk and had even gone to the extravagance of an extra cheese-cake. He was itching to talk police and murders I knew, for he cast furtive glances at me from time to time, produced a bit of string, tied and untied it into scores of complicated knots, and finally, bringing out his pocket-book, he placed before me two or three photographs.

"Do you know who that is?" he asked, pointing to one of these.

I looked at the face on the picture. It was that of a woman, not exactly pretty, but very gentle and childlike, with a strange pathetic look in the large eyes which was wonderfully appealing.

"That was Lady Arthur Skelmerton," he said, and in a flash there flitted before my mind the weird and tragic history which had broken this loving woman's heart. Lady Arthur Skelmerton! That name recalled to me one of the most bewildering, most mysterious passages in the annals of undiscovered crimes.

"Yes. It was sad, wasn't it?" he commented, in answer to my thoughts. "Another case which, but for idiotic blunders on the part of the police, must have stood clear as daylight before the public and satisfied general anxiety. Would you object to my recapitulating its preliminary details?"

I said nothing, so he continued without waiting for a reply.

"It all occurred during the York racing week, a time which brings to the quietest cathedral city its quota of shady characters, who congregate wherever money and wits happen to fly away from their owners. Lord Arthur Skelmerton, a very well-known figure in London society and in racing circles, had rented one of the fine houses which overlook the racecourse. He had entered Peppercorn by St. Armand—Notre Dame, for the Great Ebor Handicap. Peppercorn was the winner of the Newmarket and his chances for the Ebor were considered a practical certainty.

"If you have ever been to York you will have noticed the fine houses which have their drive and front entrances in the road called 'The Mount,' and the gardens of which extend as far as the racecourse, commanding a lovely view over the entire track. It was one of these houses called 'The Elms' which Lord Arthur Skelmerton had rented for the summer.

"Lady Arthur came down some little time before the racing week with her servants—she had no children; but she had many relatives and friends in York, since she was the daughter of old Sir John Etty, the cocoa manufacturer, a rigid Quaker, who, it was generally said, kept the tightest possible hold on his own purse-strings and looked with marked disfavour upon his aristocratic son-in-law's fondness for gaming tables and betting books.

"As a matter of fact, Maud Etty had married the handsome young lieutenant in the ——th Hussars, quite against her father's wishes. But she was an only child, and after a good deal of demur and grumbling, Sir John, who idolised his daughter, gave way to her whim, and a reluctant consent to the marriage was wrung from him.

"But as a Yorkshireman, he was far too shrewd a man of the world not to know that love played but a very small part in persuading a Duke's son to marry the daughter of a cocoa manufacturer, and as long as he lived he determined that since his daughter was being wed because of her wealth, that wealth should at least secure her own happiness. He refused to give Lady Arthur any capital, which in spite of the most carefully-worded settlements would inevitably, sooner or later, have found its way into the pockets of Lord Arthur's racing friends. But he made his daughter a very handsome allowance, amounting to over £3000 a year, which enabled her to keep up an establishment befitting her new rank.

"A great many of these facts, intimate enough as they are, leaked out, you see, during that period of intense excitement which followed the murder of Charles Lavender, and when the public eye was fixed searchingly upon Lord Arthur Skelmerton, probing all the inner details of his idle, useless life.

"It soon became a matter of common gossip that poor little Lady Arthur continued to worship her handsome husband in spite of his obvious neglect, and not having as yet presented him with an heir, she settled herself down into a life of humble apology for her plebeian existence, atoning for it by condoning all his faults and forgiving all his vices, even to the extent of cloaking them before the prying eyes of Sir John, who was persuaded to look upon his son-in-law as a paragon of all the domestic virtues and a perfect model of a husband.

"Among Lord Arthur Skelmerton's many expensive tastes, there was certainly that for horseflesh and cards. After some successful betting at the beginning of his married life, he had started a racing-stable which it was generally believed—as he was very lucky—was a regular source of income to him.

"Peppercorn, however, after his brilliant performances at Newmarket did not continue to fulfil his master's expectations. His collapse at York was attributed to the hardness of the course, and to various other causes, but its immediate effect was to put Lord Arthur Skelmerton in what is popularly called a tight place for he had backed his horse for all he was worth, and must have stood to lose considerably over £5000 on that one day.

"The collapse of the favourite and the grand victory of 'King Cole,' a rank outsider, on the other hand had proved a golden harvest for the bookmakers, and all the York hotels were busy with dinners and suppers given by the confraternity of the turf to celebrate the happy occasion. The next day was Friday, one of few important racing events, after which the brilliant and the shady throng which had flocked into the venerable city for the week would fly to more congenial climes, and leave it, with its fine old Minster and its ancient walls, as sleepy, as quiet as before.

"Lord Arthur Skelmerton also intended to leave York on the Saturday, and on the Friday night he gave a farewell bachelor dinner party at 'The Elms,' at which Lady Arthur did not appear. After dinner, the gentlemen settled down to 'bridge,' with pretty stiff points, you may be sure. It had just struck eleven at the Minster Tower, when constables McNaught and Murphy, who were patrolling the racecourse, were startled by loud cries of 'murder' and 'police.'

"Quickly ascertaining whence these cries proceeded, they hurried on at a gallop, and came up—quite close to the boundary of Lord Arthur Skelmerton's grounds—upon a group of three men, two of whom seemed to be wrestling vigorously with one another, whilst the third was lying face downwards on the ground. As soon as the constables drew near, one of the wrestlers shouted more vigorously, and with a certain tone of authority:

"'Here, you fellows, hurry up, sharp; the brute is giving me the slip!'

"But the brute did not seem inclined to do anything of the sort; he certainly extricated himself with a violent jerk from his assailant's grasp, but made no attempt to run away. The constables had quickly dismounted, whilst he, who had shouted for help originally, added more quietly:

"'My name is Skelmerton. This is the boundary of my property. I was smoking a cigar at the pavilion over there with a friend when I heard loud voices, followed by a cry and a groan. I hurried down the steps, and saw this poor fellow lying on the ground, with a knife sticking between his shoulder-blades, and his murderer,' he added, pointing to the man who stood quietly by with constable McNaught's firm grip upon his shoulder, 'still stooping over the body of his victim. I was too late, I fear, to save the latter, but just in time to grapple with the assassin——'

"'It's a lie!' here interrupted the man hoarsely. 'I didn't do it, constable; I swear I didn't do it. I saw him fall—I was coming along a couple of hundred yards away, and I tried to see if the poor fellow was dead. I swear I didn't do it.'

"'You'll have to explain that to the inspector presently, my man,' was constable McNaught's quiet comment, and, still vigorously protesting his innocence, the accused allowed himself to be led away, and the body was conveyed to the station, pending fuller identification.

"The next morning the papers were full of the tragedy; a column and a half of the *York Herald* was devoted to an account of Lord Arthur Skelmerton's plucky capture of the assassin. The latter had continued to declare his innocence, but had remarked, it appears, with grim humour, that he quite saw he was in a tight place, out of which, however, he would find it easy to extricate himself. He had stated to the police that the deceased's name was Charles Lavender, a well-known bookmaker, which fact was soon verified, for many of the murdered man's 'pals' were still in the city.

"So far the most pushing of newspaper reporters had been unable to glean further information from the police; no one doubted, however, but that the man in charge, who gave his name as George Higgins, had killed the bookmaker for purposes of robbery. The inquest had been fixed for the Tuesday after the murder.

"Lord Arthur had been obliged to stay in York a few days, as his evidence would be needed. That fact gave the case, perhaps, a

"Two seemed to be wrestling vigorously with one another, whilst a third was lying face downwards on the ground."

certain amount of interest as far as York and London 'society' were concerned. Charles Lavender, moreover, was well known on the turf; but no bombshell exploding beneath the walls of the ancient cathedral city could more have astonished its inhabitants than the news which, at about five in the afternoon on the day of the inquest, spread like wildfire throughout the town. That news was that the inquest had concluded at three o'clock with a verdict of 'Wilful murder against some person or persons unknown,' and that two hours later the police had arrested Lord Arthur Skelmerton at his private residence, 'The Elms,' and charged him on a warrant with the murder of Charles Lavender, the bookmaker."

II.

"THE police, it appears, instinctively feeling that some mystery lurked round the death of the bookmaker and his supposed murderer's quiet protestations of innocence, had taken a very considerable amount of trouble in collecting all the evidence they could for the inquest, which might throw some light upon Charles Lavender's life, previous to his tragic end. Thus it was that a very large array of witnesses was brought before the coroner, chief among whom was, of course, Lord Arthur Skelmerton.

"The first witnesses called were the two constables, who deposed that, just as the church clocks in the neighbourhood were striking eleven, they had heard the cries for help, had ridden to the spot whence the sounds proceeded, and had found the prisoner in the tight grasp of Lord Arthur Skelmerton, who at once accused the man of murder, and gave him in charge. Both constables gave the same version of the incident, and both were positive as to the time when it occurred.

"Medical evidence went to prove that the deceased had been stabbed from behind between the shoulder blades whilst he was walking, that the wound was inflicted by a large hunting knife, which was produced, and which had been left sticking in the wound.

"Lord Arthur Skelmerton was then called and substantially repeated what he had already told the constables. He stated, namely, that on the night in question he had some gentlemen friends to dinner, and afterwards 'bridge' was played. He himself was not playing much, and at a few minutes before eleven he strolled out with a cigar as far as the pavilion at the end of his garden; he then heard the voices, the cry and the groan previously described by him, and managed to hold the murderer down until the arrival of the constables.

"At this point the police proposed to call a witness, James Terry by name and a bookmaker by profession, who had been chiefly instrumental in identifying the deceased, a 'pal' of his. It was his evidence which first introduced that element of sensation into the case which culminated in the wildly exciting arrest of a Duke's son upon a capital charge.

"It appears that on the evening after the Ebor, Terry and Lavender were in the bar of the Black Swan Hotel having drinks.

"'I had done pretty well over Peppercorn's fiasco,' he explained, 'but poor old Lavender was very much down in the dumps; he had held only a very few small bets against the favourite, and the rest of the day had been a poor one with him. I asked him if he had any bets with the owner of Peppercorn, and he told me that he only held one for less than £500.

"'I laughed and said that if he held one for £5000 it would make no difference, as from what I had heard from the other fellows, Lord Arthur Skelmerton must be about stumped. Lavender seemed terribly put out at this, and swore he would get that £500 out of Lord Arthur, if no one else got another penny from him.

"'"It's the only money I've made to-day,' he says to me. "I mean to get it."

"'"You won't," I says.

"'"I will," he says.

"'"You will have to look pretty sharp about it then," I says, "for everyone will be wanting to get something, and first come first served."

"'"Oh! He'll serve me right enough, never you mind!" says Lavender to me with a laugh. "If he don't pay up willingly, I've got that in my pocket which will make him sit up and open my lady's eyes and Sir John Etty's too about their precious noble lord."

"'Then he seemed to think he had gone too far and wouldn't say anything more to me about that affair. I saw him on the course the next day. I asked him if he had got his £500. He said: "No, but I shall get it to-day."'

"Lord Arthur Skelmerton, after having given his own evidence, had left the court; it was therefore impossible to know how he would take this account which threw so serious a light upon an association with the dead man, of which he himself had said nothing.

"Nothing could shake James Terry's account of the facts he had placed before the jury, and when the police informed the coroner that they proposed to place George Higgins himself in the witness box, as his evidence would prove, as it were, a complement and corollary of that of Terry, the jury very eagerly assented.

"If James Terry, the bookmaker, loud, florid, vulgar, was an unprepossessing individual, certainly George Higgins, who was still under the accusation of murder, was ten thousand times more so.

"None too clean, slouchy, obsequious yet insolent, he was the very personification of the cad who haunts the racecourse and who lives not so much by his own wits as by the lack of them in others. He described himself as a turf commission agent, whatever that may be.

"He stated that at about six o'clock on the Friday afternoon, when the racecourse was still full of people, all hurrying after the day's excitements, he himself happened to be standing close to the hedge which marks the boundary of Lord Arthur Skelmerton's grounds. There is a pavilion there at the end of the garden, he explained, on slightly elevated ground, and he could hear and see a group of ladies and gentlemen having tea. Some steps lead down a little to the left of the garden, on to the course, and presently he noticed at the bottom of these steps Lord Arthur Skelmerton and Charles Lavender standing talking together. He knew both gentlemen by sight, but he could not see them very well as they were both partly hidden by the hedge. He was quite sure that the gentlemen had not seen him, and he could not help overhearing some of their conversation.

"'That's my last word, Lavender,' Lord Arthur was saying very quietly. 'I haven't got the money and I can't pay you now. You'll have to wait.'

"'Wait? I can't wait,' said old Lavender in reply. 'I've got my engagements to meet, same as you. I'm not going to risk being posted up as a defaulter while you hold £500

"If he don't pay up willingly I've got that in my pocket which will make him sit up.

of my money. You'd better give it me now or—'

"But Lord Arthur interrupted him very quietly, and said:

"'Yes, my good man . . . . or?'

"'Or I'll let Sir John have a good look at that little bill I had of yours a couple of years ago. If you'll remember, my lord, it has got at the bottom of it Sir John's signature in *your* handwriting. Perhaps Sir John, or perhaps my lady, would pay me something for that little bill. If not the police can have a squint at it. I've held my tongue long enough, and—'

"'Look here, Lavender,' said Lord Arthur, 'do you know what this little game of yours is called in law?'

"'Yes, and I don't care,' says Lavender. 'If I don't have that £500 I am a ruined man. If you ruin me I'll do for you, and we shall be quits. That's my last word.'

"He was talking very loudly, and I thought some of Lord Arthur's friends up in the pavilion must have heard. He thought so, too, I think, for he said quickly:

"'If you don't hold your confounded tongue, I'll give you in charge for blackmail, this instant.'

"'You wouldn't dare,' says Lavender, and he began to laugh. But just then a lady from the top of the steps said: 'Your tea is getting cold,' and Lord Arthur turned to go; but just before he went, Lavender says to him: 'I'll come back to-night. You'll have the money then.'

"George Higgins, it appears, after he had heard this interesting conversation, pondered as to whether he could not turn what he knew into some sort of profit. Being a gentleman who lives entirely by his wits, this type of knowledge forms his chief source of income. As a preliminary to future moves, he decided not to lose sight of Lavender for the rest of the day.

"'He went and had dinner at The Black Swan,' he explained, 'and I, after I had had a bite myself, waited outside till I saw him come out. At about ten o'clock I was rewarded for my trouble. He told the hall porter to get him a fly and he jumped into it. I could not hear what direction he gave the driver, but the fly certainly drove off towards the racecourse.

"'Now, I was interested in this little affair,' continued the witness, 'and I couldn't afford a fly. I started to run. Of course I couldn't keep up with it, but I thought I knew which way my gentleman had gone. I made straight for the racecourse, and for the hedge at the bottom of Lord Arthur Skelmerton's grounds.

"'It was rather a dark night and there was a slight drizzle. I couldn't see more than about a hundred yards before me. All at once it seemed to me as if I heard Lavender's voice talking loudly in the distance. I hurried forward, and suddenly saw a group of two figures—mere blurs in the darkness—for one instant, at a distance of about fifty yards from where I was.

"'The next moment, one figure had fallen forward and the other had disappeared. I ran to the spot, only to find the body of the murdered man lying on the ground. I stooped to see if I could be of any use to him, and immediately I was collared from behind by Lord Arthur himself.'

"You may imagine," said the man in the corner, "how keen was the excitement at that moment in court. Coroner and jury alike literally hung breathless on every word that shabby vulgar individual uttered. You see, by itself his evidence would have been worth very little, but coming on the top of that given by James Terry, its significance—more, its truth—had become glaringly apparent. Closely cross-examined, he adhered strictly to his statement; and having finished his evidence, George Higgins remained in charge of the constables, and the next witness of importance was called up.

"This was Mr. Chipps, the senior footman in the employment of Lord Arthur Skelmerton. He deposed that at about 10.30 on the Friday evening a 'party' drove up to 'The Elms' in a fly, and asked to see Lord Arthur. On being told that his lordship had company he seemed terribly put out.

"'I hasked the party to give me 'is card,' continued Mr. Chipps, 'as I didn't know, perhaps, that 'is lordship might wish to see 'im, but I kept 'im standing at the 'all door, as I didn't altogether like his looks. I took the card in. His lordship and the gentlemen was playin' cards in the smoking-room, and as soon as I could do so without disturbing 'is lordship, I give him the party's card.'

"'What name was there on the card?' here interrupted the coroner.

"'I couldn't say now, sir,' replied Mr. Chipps; 'I don't really remember. It was a name I had never seen before. But I see so many visiting cards one way and the other in 'is lordship's 'all that I can't remember all the names.'

"'Then, after a few minutes waiting, you gave his lordship the card? What happened then?'

"'Is lordship didn't seem at all pleased,' said Mr. Chipps with much guarded dignity; 'but finally he said: "show him into the library, Chipps, I'll see him," and he got up from the card table, saying to the gentlemen: "Go on without me; I'll be back in a minute or two."

"'I was about to open the door for 'is lordship when my lady came into the room, and then his lordship suddenly changed his mind like, and said to me: "Tell that man I'm busy and can't see him," and 'e sat down again at the card table. I went back to the 'all, and told the party 'is lordship wouldn't see 'im. 'E said: "Oh! it doesn't matter," and went away quite quiet like.'

"'Do you recollect at all at what time that was?' asked one of the jury.

"'Yes, sir, while I was waiting to speak to 'is lordship I looked at the clock, sir; it was twenty past ten, sir.'

"There was one more significant fact in connection with the case, which tended still more to excite the curiosity of the public at the time, and still further to bewilder the police later on, and that fact was mentioned by Chipps in his evidence. The knife, namely, with which Charles Lavender had been stabbed, and which, remember, had been left in the wound, was now produced in court. After a little hesitation Chipps identified it as the property of his master, Lord Arthur Skelmerton.

"Tell the man I'm busy and can't see him."

"Can you wonder, then, that the jury absolutely refused to bring in a verdict against George Higgins? There was really, beyond Lord Arthur Skelmerton's testimony, not one particle of evidence against him, whilst, as the day wore on and witness after witness was called up, suspicion ripened in the minds of all those present that the murderer could be no other than Lord Arthur Skelmerton himself.

"The knife was of course the strongest piece of circumstantial evidence, and no doubt the police hoped to collect a great deal more now that they held a clue in their hands. Directly after the verdict, therefore, which was guardedly directed against some person unknown, the police obtained a warrant and later on arrested Lord Arthur in his own house.

III.

"The sensation, of course, was tremendous. Hours before he was brought up before the magistrate the approach to the court was thronged. His friends, mostly ladies, were all eager, you see, to watch the dashing society man in so terrible a position. There was universal sympathy for Lady Arthur, who was in a very precarious state of health. Her worship of her worthless husband was well known; small wonder that his final and awful misdeed had practically broken her heart.

"At last the prisoner was brought in. He looked very pale, perhaps, but otherwise kept up the bearing of a high-bred gentleman.

He was accompanied by his solicitor, Sir Marmaduke Ingersoll, who was evidently talking to him in quiet, reassuring tones.

"Mr. Buçhanan prosecuted for the Treasury, and certainly his indictment was terrific. According to him but one decision could be arrived at, namely, that the accused in the dock had, in a moment of passion, and perhaps of fear, killed the blackmailer who threatened him with disclosures which might for ever have ruined him socially, and, having committed the deed and fearing its consequences, probably realising that the patrolling constables might catch sight of his retreating figure, he had availed himself of George Higgins's presence on the spot to loudly accuse him of the murder.

"Having concluded his able speech, Mr. Buchanan called his witnesses, and the evidence, which on second hearing seemed more damning than ever, was all gone through again.

"Sir Marmaduke had no question to ask of the witnesses for the prosecution; he stared at them placidly through his gold rimmed spectacles. Then he was ready to call his own for the defence. Colonel McIntosh, R.A., was the first. He was present at the bachelor's party given by Lord Arthur the night of the murder. His evidence tended at first to corroborate that of Chipps the footman with regard to Lord Arthur's orders to show the visitor into the library, and his counter-order as soon as his wife came into the room.

"'Did you not think it strange, Colonel?' asked Mr. Buchanan, 'that Lord Arthur should so suddenly have changed his mind about seeing his visitor?'

"'Well, not exactly strange,' said the Colonel, a fine, manly, soldierly figure who looked curiously out of his element in the witness-box. 'I don't think that it is a very rare occurrence for racing men to have certain acquaintances whom they would not wish their wives to know anything about?'

"'Then it did not strike you that Lord Arthur Skelmerton had some reason for not wishing his wife to know of that particular visitor's presence in his house?'

"'I don't think that I gave the matter the slightest serious consideration,' was the Colonel's guarded reply.

"Mr. Buchanan did not press the point, and allowed the witness to conclude his statements.

"'I had finished my turn at "bridge," he said, 'and went out into the garden to smoke a cigar. Lord Arthur Skelmerton joined me a few minutes later, and we were sitting in the pavilion when I heard a loud, and as I thought, threatening voice from the other side of the hedge.

"'I did not catch the words, but Lord Arthur said to me: "There seems to be a row down there. I'll go and have a look and see what it is." I tried to dissuade him, and certainly made no attempt to follow him, but not more than half a minute could have elapsed before I heard a cry and a groan, then Lord Arthur's footsteps hurrying down the wooden stairs which lead on to the racecourse.'

"You may imagine," said the man in the corner, "what severe cross-examination the gallant Colonel had to undergo in order that his assertions might in some way be shaken by the prosecution, but with military precision and frigid calm he repeated his important statements amidst a general silence, through which you could have heard the proverbial pin.

"He had heard the threatening voice *while* sitting with Lord Arthur Skelmerton; then came the cry and groan, and, *after that*, Lord Arthur's steps down the stairs. He himself thought of following to see what had happened, but it was a very dark night and he did not know the grounds very well. While trying to find his way to the garden steps he heard Lord Arthur's cry for help, the tramp of the patrolling constables' horses, and subsequently the whole scene between Lord Arthur, the man Higgins, and the constables. When he finally found his way to the stairs, Lord Arthur was returning in order to send a groom for police assistance.

"The witness stuck to his points as he had to his guns at Beckfontein a year ago; nothing could shake him, and Sir Marmaduke looked triumphantly across at his opposing colleague.

"With the gallant Colonel's statements, the edifice of the prosecution certainly began to collapse. You see, there was not a particle of evidence to show that the accused had met and spoken to the deceased, after the latter's visit at the front door of 'The Elms.' He told Chipps that he wouldn't see the visitor, and Chipps went into the hall directly and showed Lavender out the way he came. No assignation could have been made, no hint could have been given by the murdered man to Lord Arthur that he would go round to the back entrance and wished to see him there.

"Two other guests of Lord Arthur's swore positively that after Chipps had announced the visitor, their host stayed at the card-table until a quarter to eleven, when evidently he went out to join Colonel McIntosh in the garden. Sir Marmaduke's speech was clever in the extreme. Bit by bit he demolished that tower of strength, the case against the accused, basing his defence entirely upon the evidence of Lord Arthur Skelmerton's guests that night.

"'Until 10.45 Lord Arthur was playing cards; a quarter of an hour later the police were on the scene, and the murder had been committed. In the meanwhile Colonel McIntosh's evidence proved conclusively that the accused had been sitting with him, smoking a cigar. It was obvious, therefore, clear as daylight,' concluded the great lawyer, 'that his client was entitled to a full discharge; nay, more, he thought that the police should have been more careful before they harrowed up public feeling by arresting a high-born gentleman on such insufficient evidence as they had brought forward.'

"The question of the knife remained certainly, but Sir Marmaduke passed over it with guarded eloquence, placing that strange question in the category of those inexplicable coincidences which tend to puzzle the ablest detectives, and cause them to commit such unpardonable blunders as the present one had been. After all, the footman may have been mistaken. The pattern of that knife was not an exclusive one, and he, on behalf of his client, flatly denied that it had ever belonged to him.

"Well," continued the man in the corner, with the chuckle peculiar to him in moments of excitement, "the noble prisoner was discharged. Perhaps it would be invidious to say that he left the court without a stain on his character, for I daresay you know from experience that the crime known as the York Mystery has never been satisfactorily cleared up.

"Many people shook their heads dubiously when they remembered that after all Charles Lavender was killed with a knife which one witness had sworn belonged to Lord Arthur; others, again, reverted to the original theory that George Higgins was the murderer, that he and James Terry had concocted the story of Lavender's attempt at blackmail on Lord Arthur, and that the murder had been committed for the sole purpose of robbery.

"Be that as it may, the police have not so far been able to collect sufficient evidence against Higgins or Terry, and the crime has been classed by press and public alike in the category of so-called impenetrable mysteries."

IV.

The man in the corner called for another glass of milk, and drank it down slowly before he resumed:

"Now Lord Arthur lives mostly abroad," he said. "His poor, suffering wife died the day after he was liberated by the magistrate. She never recovered consciousness even sufficiently to hear the joyful news that the man she loved so well was innocent after all.

"Mystery!" he added as if in answer to my own thoughts. "The murder of that man was never a mystery to me. I cannot understand how the police could have been so blind when every one of the witnesses, both for the prosecution and defence, practically pointed all the time to the one guilty person. What do you think of it all yourself?"

"I think the whole case so bewildering," I replied, "that I do not see one single clear point in it."

"You don't?" he said excitedly, while the bony fingers fidgeted again with that inevitable bit of string. "You don't see that there is one point clear which to me was the key of the whole thing.

"Lavender was murdered, wasn't he? Lord Arthur did not kill him. He had at least in Colonel McIntosh an unimpeachable witness to prove that he could not have committed that murder—and yet," he added with slow, excited emphasis, marking each sentence with a knot, "and yet he deliberately tries to throw the guilt upon a man who obviously was also innocent. Now why?"

"He may have thought him guilty."

"Or wished to shield or cover the retreat of *one he knew to be guilty*."

"I don't understand."

"Think of someone," he said excitedly, "someone whose desire would be as great as that of Lord Arthur to silence a scandal round that gentleman's name. Someone who, unknown perhaps to Lord Arthur, had overheard the same conversation which George Higgins related to the police and the magistrate, someone who, whilst Chipps was taking Lavender's card in to his master had a few minutes' time wherein to make an assignation with Lavender, promising him money, no doubt, in exchange for the compromising bills."

"Surely you don't mean—" I gasped.

"Point No. 1," he interrupted quietly, "utterly missed by the police. George Higgins in his deposition stated that at the most animated stage of Lavender's conversation with Lord Arthur, and when the bookmaker's tone of voice became loud and threatening, a voice from the top of the steps interrupted that conversation, saying: 'Your tea is getting cold.'"

"Yes—but—" I argued.

"Wait a moment, for there is point No. 2. That voice was a lady's voice. Now I did exactly what the police should have done but did not do. I went to have a look from the racecourse side at those garden steps which to my mind are such important factors in the discovery of this crime. I found only about a dozen rather low steps; anyone standing on the top must have heard every word Charles Lavender uttered the moment he raised his voice."

"Even then——"

"Very well, you grant that," he said excitedly. "Then there was the great, the all-important point which, oddly enough, the prosecution never for a moment took into consideration. When Chipps, the footman, first told Lavender that Lord Arthur could not see him the bookmaker was terribly put out; Chipps then goes to speak to his master; a few minutes elapse, and when the footman once again tells Lavender that his lordship won't see him, the latter says 'Very well' and seems to treat the matter with complete indifference.

"Obviously, therefore, something must have happened in between to alter the bookmaker's frame of mind. Well! What had happened? Think over all the evidence and you will see that one thing only had occurred in the interval, namely, Lady Arthur's advent into the room.

"In order to go into the smoking-room she must have crossed the hall; she must have seen Lavender. In that brief interval she must have realised that the man was persistent and therefore a living danger to her husband. Remember, women have done strange things, they are a far greater puzzle to the student of human nature than the sterner, less complex sex has ever been. As I argued before—as the police should have argued all along—why did Lord Arthur deliberately accuse an innocent man of murder if not to shield the guilty one?

"Remember Lady Arthur may have been discovered; the man, George Higgins, may have caught sight of her before she had time to make good her retreat. His attention as well as that of the constables had to be diverted. Lord Arthur acted on the blind impulse of saving his wife at any cost."

"She may have been met by Colonel McIntosh," I argued.

"Perhaps she was," he said. "Who knows? The gallant colonel had to swear to his friend's innocence. He could do that in all conscience—after that his duty was accomplished. No innocent man was suffering for the guilty. The knife which had belonged to Lord Arthur would always save George Higgins. For a time it had pointed to the husband; fortunately never to the wife. Poor thing, she died probably of a broken heart, but women when they love think only of one object on earth—the one who is beloved.

"To me the whole thing was clear from the very first. When I read the account of the murder—the knife! stabbing!—bah! Don't I know enough of *English* crime not to be certain at once that no English*man*, be he ruffian from the gutter or be he Duke's son, ever stabs his victim in the back. Italians, French, Spaniards do it, if you will, and women of most nations. An Englishman's instinct is to strike and not to stab. George Higgins or Lord Arthur Skelmerton would have knocked their victim down; the woman only would lie in wait till the enemy's back was turned. She knows her weakness, and she does not mean to miss.

"Think it over. There is not one flaw in my argument, but the police never thought the matter out—perhaps in this case it was as well."

He had gone and left me still staring at the photograph of a pretty, gentle-looking woman, with a decided wilful curve round the mouth, and a strange unaccountable look in the large pathetic eyes; and I felt quite thankful that in this case, the murder of Charles Lavender the bookmaker—cowardly, wicked as it was—had remained a mystery to the police and the public.

By

Baroness E. Orczy.

Illustrated by

P. B.

Hickling.

THE LIVERPOOL MYSTERY.

Being the Third of a Series of Stories, "The Mysteries of Great Cities," told by the famous Man in the Corner.

DRAMATIS PERSONÆ.

The Man *in the corner, who tells the story to the* Lady Journalist.
Prince Semionicz.
His French Secretary.
Messrs. Winslow & Vassall (*Jewellers in Liverpool*).
Schwarz (*German assistant at Winslow & Vassall's*).

CHAPTER I.

"A title—a foreign title, I mean—is always very useful for purposes of swindles and frauds," remarked the man in the corner to me one day. "The cleverest robberies of modern times were perpetrated lately in Vienna by a man who dubbed himself Lord Seymour; whilst over here the same class of thief calls himself Count Something ending in 'o,' or Prince the other, ending in 'off.'"

"Fortunately for our hotel and lodging-house keepers over here," I replied, "they are beginning to be more alive to the ways of foreign swindlers, and look upon all titled gentry who speak broken English as possible swindlers or thieves."

"The result sometimes being exceedingly unpleasant to the real 'grands seigneurs' who honour this country at times with their visits," replied the man in the corner "Now, take the case of Prince Semionicz, a man whose sixteen quarterings are duly recorded in Gotha, who carried enough luggage with him to pay for the use of every room in a hotel for at least a week, whose gold cigarette case with diamond and turquoise ornament was actually stolen without his taking the slightest trouble in trying to recover it; that same man was undoubtedly looked upon with suspicion by the manager of the Liverpool North-Western Hotel from the moment that his secretary—a dapper, somewhat vulgar little Frenchman—bespoke on behalf of his employer, with himself and a valet, the best suite of rooms the hotel contained.

"Obviously those suspicions were unfounded, for the little secretary, as soon as Prince Semionicz had arrived, deposited with the manager a pile of bank notes, also papers and bonds, the value of which would exceed tenfold the most outrageous bill that could possibly be placed before the noble visitor. Moreover, M. Albert Lambert explained that the Prince, who only meant to stay in Liverpool a few days, was on his way to Chicago, where he wished to visit Princess Anna Semionicz, his sister, who was married to Mr. Girwan, the great copper king and multi-millionaire.

"Yet, as I told you before, in spite of all

these undoubted securities, suspicion of the wealthy Russian Prince lurked in the minds of most Liverpudlians who came in business contact with him. He had been at the North-Western two days when he sent his secretary to Winslow and Vassall, the jewellers of Bold Street, with a request that they would kindly send a representative round to the hotel with some nice pieces of jewellery, diamonds and pearls chiefly, which he was desirous of taking as a present to his sister in Chicago.

"Mr. Winslow took the order from M. Albert with a pleasant bow. Then he went to his inner office and consulted with his partner, Mr. Vassall, as to the best course to adopt. Both the gentlemen were desirous of doing business, for business had been very slack lately: neither wished to refuse a possible customer, or to offend Mr. Pettitt, the manager of the North-Western, who had recommended them to the Prince. But that foreign title and the vulgar little French secretary stuck in the throats of the two pompous and worthy Liverpool jewellers, and together they agreed, firstly, that no credit should be given; and, secondly, that if a cheque or even a banker's draft were tendered, the jewels were not to be given up until that cheque or draft was cashed.

"Then came the question as to who should take the jewels to the hotel. It was altogether against business etiquette for the senior partners to do such errands themselves; moreover it was thought that it would be easier for a clerk to explain without giving undue offence that he could not take the responsibility of a cheque or draft without having cashed it previously to giving up the jewels.

"Then there was the question of the probable necessity of conferring in a foreign tongue. The head assistant, Charles Needham, who had been in the employ of Winslow and Vassall for over twelve years, was, in true British fashion, ignorant of any language save his own; it was therefore decided to dispatch Mr. Schwarz, a young German clerk lately arrived.

"Mr. Schwarz was Mr. Winslow's nephew and godson, a sister of that gentleman having married the head of the great German firm of Schwarz & Co., silversmiths, of Hamburg and Berlin.

"The young man had soon become a great favourite with his uncle, whose heir he would presumably be, as Mr. Winslow had no children.

"At first Mr. Vassall made some demur about sending Mr. Schwarz with so many valuable jewels alone in a city which he had not yet had the time to study thoroughly; but finally he allowed himself to be persuaded by his senior partner, and a fine selection of necklaces, pendants, bracelets, and rings, amounting in value to over £16,000, having been made, it was decided that Mr. Schwarz should go to the North-Western in a cab the next day at about three o'clock in the afternoon. This he accordingly did, the following day being a Thursday.

"Business went on in the shop as usual under the direction of the head assistant, until about five o'clock Mr. Winslow returned from his club, where he usually spent an hour over the papers every afternoon, and asked for his nephew. To his astonishment Mr. Needham informed him that Mr. Schwarz had not yet returned. This seemed a little strange, and Mr. Winslow, with a slightly anxious look in his face, went in to consult his junior partner. Mr. Vassall offered to go round to the hotel and interview Mr. Pettitt.

"'I was beginning to get anxious myself," he said, 'but did not quite like to say so. I have been in over half-an-hour, hoping every moment that you would come in, and that perhaps you could give me some reassuring news. I thought that perhaps you had met Mr. Schwarz, and were coming back together.'

"However Mr. Vassall walked round to the hotel and interviewed the hall porter. The latter perfectly well remembered Mr. Schwarz sending in his card to Prince Semionicz.

"'At what time was that?' asked Mr. Vassall.

"'About ten minutes past three, sir, when he came; it was about an hour later when he left.'

"'When he left?' gasped, more than said, Mr. Vassall.

"'Yes, sir. Mr. Schwarz left here about a quarter before four, sir.'

"'Are you quite sure?'

"'Quite sure. Mr. Pettitt was in the hall when he left, and he asked him something about business. Mr. Schwarz laughed and said, "not bad." I hope there's nothing wrong, sir,' added the man.

"'Oh—er—nothing—thank you. Can I see Mr. Pettitt?'

"'Certainly, sir.'

"Mr. Pettitt, the manager of the hotel, shared Mr. Vassall's anxiety immediately when he heard that the young German had not yet returned home.

"'I spoke to him a little before four o'clock

We had just switched on the electric light, which we always do these winter months at that hour. But I shouldn't worry myself, Mr. Vassall; the young man may have seen to some business on his way home. You'll probably find him in when you go back.'

"Apparently somewhat reassured, Mr. Vassall thanked Mr. Pettitt and hurried back to the shop, only to find that Mr. Schwarz had not returned, though it was now close on eight o'clock.

"Mr. Winslow looked so haggard and upset that it would have been cruel to heap reproaches upon his other troubles or to utter so much as the faintest suspicion that young Schwarz's permanent disappearance with £16,000 in jewels and money was within the bounds of probability.

"When he left?" gasped, more than said, Mr. Vassall.

"There was one chance left, but under the circumstances a very slight one indeed. The Winslows' private house was up the Birkenhead end of the town. Young Schwarz had been living with them ever since his arrival in Liverpool, and he may have—either not feeling well or for some other reason—gone straight home without calling at the shop. It was unlikely as valuable jewellery was never kept at the private house, but—it just might have happened.

"It would be useless," continued the man in the corner, "and decidedly uninteresting were I to relate to you Messrs. Winslow's and Vassall's further anxieties with regard to the missing young man. Suffice it to say that on reaching his private house Mr. Winslow found that his godson had neither returned nor sent any telegraphic message of any kind.

"Not wishing to needlessly alarm his wife, Mr. Winslow made an attempt at eating his dinner, but directly after he hurried back to the North-Western Hotel, and asked to see Prince Semionicz. The Prince was at the theatre with his secretary, and probably would not be home until nearly midnight.

"Mr. Winslow, then, not knowing what to think, nor yet what to fear, and in spite of the horror he felt of giving publicity to his nephew's disappearance, thought it his duty to go round to the police station and interview the inspector. It is wonderful how news of that type travels in a large city like Liverpool. Already the morning papers of the following day were full of the latest sensation: 'Mysterious disappearance of a well-known tradesman.'

"Mr. Winslow found a copy of the paper containing the sensational announcement on his breakfast-table. It lay side by side with a letter addressed to him in his nephew's hand writing, which had been posted in Liverpool.

II.

"Mr. Winslow placed that letter, written to him by his nephew, into the hands of the police. Its contents, therefore, quickly became public property. The astounding statements made therein by Mr. Schwarz created, in quiet, business-like Liverpool, a sensation which has seldom been equalled.

"It appears that the young fellow did call on Prince Semionicz at a quarter past three on Wednesday, December 10th, with a bag full of jewels, amounting in value to some £16,000. The prince duly admired, and finally selected from among the ornaments, a necklace, pendant and bracelet, the whole being priced by Mr. Schwarz, according to his instructions, at £10,500. Prince Semionicz was most prompt and business-like in his dealings.

"'You will require immediate payment for these, of course,' he said in perfect English, 'and I know you business men prefer solid cash to cheques, especially when dealing with foreigners. I always provide myself with plenty of Bank of England notes in consequence,' he added with a pleasant smile, 'as £10,500 in gold would perhaps be a little inconvenient to carry. If you will kindly make out the receipt my secretary, M. Lambert, will settle all business matters with you.'

"He thereupon took the jewels he had selected and locked them up in his dressing case, the beautiful silver fittings of which Mr. Schwarz just caught a short glimpse of. Then, having been accommodated with paper and ink, the young jeweller made out the account and receipt whilst M. Lambert, the secretary, counted out before him 105 crisp Bank of England notes of £100 each. Then, with a final bow to his exceedingly urbane and eminently satisfactory customer, Mr. Schwarz took his leave. In the hall he saw and spoke to Mr. Pettitt, and then he went out into the street.

"He had just left the hotel and was about to cross towards St. George's Hall when a gentleman, in a magnificent fur coat, stepped quickly out of a cab which had been stationed near the kerb, and touching him lightly upon the shoulder said with an unmistakable air of authority, at the same time handing him a card:

"'That is my name. I must speak with you immediately.

"Schwarz glanced at the card and by the light of the arc lamps above his head read on it the name of 'Dimitri Slaviansky Burgreneff, De la IIIe Section Police Imperial de S. M. le Czar.'

"Quickly the owner of the unpronounceable name and the significant titles, pointed to the cab from which he had just alighted, and Schwarz, whose every suspicion with regard to his princely customer bristled up in one moment, clutched his bag and followed his imposing interlocutor; as soon as they were both comfortably seated in the cab the latter began with courteous apology in broken but fluent English:

"'I must ask your pardon, sir, for thus trespassing upon your valuable time, and I certainly should not have done so but for the certainty that our interests in a certain matter which I have in hand are practically identical, in so far that we both should wish to outwit a clever rogue.'

"Instinctively, and his mind full of terrible apprehension, Mr. Schwarz's hand wandered to his pocket-book filled to overflowing with the bank-notes which he had so lately received from the Prince.

"'Ah, I see,' interposed the courteous Russian with a smile, 'he has played the confidence trick on you, with the usual addition of so many so-called bank-notes.'

"'So-called,' gasped the unfortunate young man.

"'I don't think I often err in my estimate of my own countrymen,' continued M. Burgreneff; 'I have vast experience, you must remember. Therefore, I doubt if I am doing M.—er—what does he call himself?—Prince something—an injustice if I assert, even without handling those crisp bits of paper you have in your pocket-book, that no bank would exchange them for gold.'

"Remembering his uncle's suspicion and his own, Mr. Schwarz cursed himself for his blindness and folly in accepting notes so easily without for a moment imagining that they might be false. Now, with everyone of those suspicions fully on the alert, he felt the bits of paper with nervous, anxious fingers, while the imperturbable Russian calmly struck a match.

"'See here,' he said, pointing to one of the notes, 'the shape of that "w" in the signature of the chief cashier. I am not an English police officer, but I could pick out that spurious "w" among a thousand genuine ones. You see, I have seen a good many.'

"Now, of course, poor young Schwarz had not seen very many Bank of England notes. He could not have told whether one 'w' in Mr. Bowen's signature is better than another, but, though he did not speak English nearly as fluently as his pompous interlocutor, he understood every word of the appalling statement the latter had just made.

"'Then that Prince,' he said, 'at the hotel?——'

"'Is no more Prince than you and I, my dear sir,' concluded the gentleman of His Imperial Majesty's police, calmly.

When a gentleman, in a magnificent fur coat, stepped quickly out of a cab which had been stationed near the kerb.

"'And the jewels? Mr. Winslow's jewels?'

"'With the jewels there may be a chance—oh! a mere chance. These forged bank notes, which you accepted so trustingly, may prove the means of recovering your property.'

"'How?'

"'The penalty of forging and circulating spurious bank notes is very heavy. You know that. The fear of seven years' penal servitude will act as a wonderful sedative upon the—er—Prince's joyful mood. He will give up the jewels to me all right enough, never you fear. He knows,' added the Russian officer grimly, 'that there are plenty of old scores to settle up, without the additional one of forged bank notes. Our interests, you see, are identical. May I rely on your cooperation?'

"'Oh, I will do as you wish,' said the delighted young German. 'Mr. Winslow and Mr. Vassall, they trusted me, and I have been such a fool. I hope it is not too late.'

"'I think not,' said M. Burgreneff, his hand already on the door of the cab. 'Though I have been talking to you I have kept an eye on the hotel, and our friend the Prince has not yet gone out. We are accustomed, you know, to have eyes everywhere, we of the Russian secret police. I don't think that I will ask you to be present at the confrontation. Perhaps you will wait for me in the cab. There is a nasty fog outside, and you

He showed him the jewels, the receipt he held, and also a large bundle of bank notes.

too late, Schwarz cursed himself once again for the double-dyed idiot that he was. He had been only too ready to believe that Prince Semionicz was a liar and a rogue, and under these unjust suspicions he had fallen an all too easy prey to one of the most cunning rascals he had ever come across.

"An inquiry from the hall porter at the North-Western elicited the fact that no such personage as Mr. Schwarz described had entered the hotel. The young man asked to see Prince Semionicz, hoping against hope that all was not yet lost. The Prince received him most courteously; he was dictating some letters to his secretary, while the valet was in the next room preparing his master's evening

will be more private. Will you give me those beautiful banknotes? Thank you! Don't be anxious. I won't be long.'

"He lifted his hat, and slipped the notes into the inner pocket of his magnificent fur coat. As he did so, Mr. Schwarz caught sight of a rich uniform and a wide sash, which no doubt was destined to carry additional moral weight with the clever rogue upstairs.

"Then His Imperial Majesty's police officer stepped quickly out of the cab, and Mr. Schwarz was left alone.

III.

"Yes, left severely alone," continued the man in the corner with a sarcastic chuckle. "So severely alone in fact that one quarter of an hour after another passed by and still the magnificent police officer in the gorgeous uniform did not return. Then, when it was

clothes. Mr. Schwarz found it very difficult to explain what he actually did want.

"There stood the dressing-case in which the Prince had locked up the jewels, and there the bag from which the secretary had taken the bank-notes. After much hesitation on Schwarz's part and much impatience on that of the Prince, the young man blurted out the whole story of the so-called Russian police officer whose card he still held in his hand.

"The Prince, it appears, took the whole thing wonderfully good-naturedly; no doubt he thought the jeweller a hopeless fool. He showed him the jewels, the receipt he held, and also a large bundle of bank-notes similar to those Schwarz had with such culpable folly given up to the clever rascal in the cab.

"'I pay all my bills with Bank of England notes, Mr. Schwarz. It would have been wiser, perhaps, if you had spoken to the manager of the hotel about me before you were so ready to believe any cock-and-bull story about my supposed rogueries.'

"Finally he placed a small 16mo volume before the young jeweller, and said with a pleasant smile:

"'If people in this country who are in a large way of business, and are therefore likely to come in contact with people of foreign nationality, were to study these little volumes before doing business with any foreigner who claims a title, much disappointment and a great loss would often be saved. Now in this case had you looked up page 797 of this little volume of Gotha's Almanac you would have seen my name in it and known from the first that the so-called Russian detective was a liar.'

"There was nothing more to be said, and Mr. Schwarz left the hotel. No doubt now that he had been hopelessly duped; he dared not go home and half hoped by communicating with the police that they might succeed in arresting the thief before he had time to leave Liverpool. He interviewed Detective-Inspector Watson, and was at once confronted with the awful difficulty which would make the recovery of the bank-notes practically hopeless. He had never had the time or opportunity of jotting down the numbers of the notes.

"Mr. Winslow, though terribly wrathful against his nephew, did not wish to keep him out of his home. As soon as he had received Schwarz's letter, he traced him, with Inspector Watson's help, to his lodgings in North Street, where the unfortunate young man meant to remain hidden until the terrible storm had blown over, or perhaps until the thief had been caught red-handed with the booty still in his hands.

"This happy event, needless to say, never did occur, though the police made every effort to trace the man who had decoyed Schwarz into the cab. His appearance was such an uncommon one; it seemed most unlikely that no one in Liverpool should have noticed him after he left that cab. The wonderful fur coat, the long beard, all must have been noticeable, even though it was past four o'clock on a somewhat foggy December afternoon.

"But every investigation proved futile; no one answering Schwarz's description of the man had been seen anywhere. The papers continued to refer to the case as "the Liverpool Mystery." Scotland Yard sent Mr. Fairburn down—the celebrated detective—at the request of the Liverpool police, to help in the investigations, but nothing availed.

"Prince Semionicz with his suite left Liverpool, and he who had attempted to blacken his character, and had succeeded in robbing Messrs. Winslow and Vassall of £10,500, had completely disappeared."

IV.

The man in the corner re-adjusted his collar and necktie, which, during the narrative of this interesting mystery, had worked its way up his long, crane-like neck under his large flappy ears. His costume of checked tweed of a peculiarly loud pattern had tickled the fancy of some of the waitresses who were standing gazing at him and giggling in one corner. This evidently made him nervous. He gazed up very meekly at me, looking for all the world like a bald-headed adjutant dressed for a holiday.

"Of course, at first all sorts of theories of the theft got about. One of the most popular, and at the same time most quickly exploded, being that young Schwarz had told a cock-and-bull story, and was the actual thief himself.

"However, as I said before that was very quickly exploded, as Mr. Schwarz, senior, a very wealthy merchant, never allowed his son's carelessness to be a serious loss to his kind employers. As soon as he thoroughly grasped all the circumstances of the extraordinary case, he drew a cheque for £10,500 and remitted it to Messrs. Winslow and Vassall. It was just, but it was also high-minded.

"All Liverpool knew of the generous action, as Mr. Winslow took care that it should; and any evil suspicion regarding young Mr. Schwarz vanished as quickly as it had come.

"Then, of course, there was the theory about the Prince and his suite, and to this day I fancy there are plenty of people in Liverpool, and also in London, who declare that the so-called Russian police officer was a confederate. No doubt that theory was very plausible, and Messrs. Winslow and Vassall spent a good deal of money in trying to prove a case against the Russian Prince.

"Very soon, however, that theory was also bound to collapse. Mr. Fairburn, whose reputation as an investigator of crime waxes in direct inverted ratio to his capacities, did hit upon the obvious course of interviewing the managers of the larger London and Liverpool *agents-de-change*. He soon found that Prince Semionicz had converted a great deal of Russian and French money into English banknotes since his arrival in this country a few days ago. More than £30,000 in good, solid honest money, was traced to the pockets of the gentleman with the sixteen quarterings. It seemed, therefore, more than improbable, that a man who was obviously fairly wealthy would risk imprisonment and hard labour, if not worse, for the sake of increasing his fortune by £10,000.

"However, the theory of the Prince's guilt has taken firm root in the dull minds of our police authorities. They have had every information with regard to Prince Semionicz's antecedents from Russia; his position, his wealth, have been placed above suspicion, and yet they suspect and go on suspecting him or his secretary. They have communicated with the police of every European capital; and while they still hope to obtain sufficient evidence against those they suspect, they calmly allow the guilty to enjoy the fruit of his clever roguery."

"The guilty?" I said. "Who do you think—?"

"Who do I think knew at that moment that young Schwarz had money in his possession?" he said excitedly, wriggling in his chair like a jack in the box. "Obviously someone was guilty of that theft who knew that Schwarz had gone to interview a rich Russian and would in all probability return with a large sum of money in his possession?"

"Who, indeed, but the Prince and his secretary?" I argued. "But just now you said—"

"Just now I said that the police were determined to find the Prince and his secretary guilty; they did not look further than their own stumpy noses. Messrs. Winslow and Vassall spent money with a free hand in those investigations. Mr. Winslow, as the senior partner, stood to lose over £9000 by that robbery. Now with Mr. Vassall it was different.

"When I saw how the police went on blundering in this case I took the trouble to make certain inquiries, the whole thing interested me so much, and I learnt all that I wished to know. I found out, namely, that Mr. Vassall was very much a junior partner in the firm, that he only drew ten per cent. of the profits, having been promoted lately to a partnership from having been senior assistant.

"Now the police did not take the trouble to find that out."

"But you don't mean that—"

"I mean that in all cases where robbery affects more than one person the first thing to find out is whether it affects the second party equally with the first. I proved that to you, didn't I, over that robbery in Phillimore Terrace. There, as here, one of the two parties stood to lose very little in comparison with the other—

"Even then—" I began.

"Wait a moment, for I found out something more. The moment I had ascertained that Mr. Vassall was not drawing more than about £500 a year from the business profits I tried to ascertain at what rate he lived and what were his chief vices. I found that he kept a fine house in Albert Terrace. Now the rents of those houses are £250 a year. Therefore speculation, horse-racing or some sort of gambling, must help to keep up that establishment. Speculation and most forms of gambling are synonymous with debt and ruin. It is only a question of time. Whether Mr. Vassall was in debt or not at the time that I cannot say, but this I do know that ever since that unfortunate loss to him of about £1000 he has kept his house in nicer style than before, and he now has a good banking account at the Lancashire and Liverpool bank, which he opened a year after his 'heavy loss.'"

"But it must have been very difficult—" I argued.

"What?" he said. "To have planned out the whole thing? For carrying it out was mere child's play. He had twenty-four hours in which to put his plan into execution. Why, what was there to do? Firstly, to go to a local printer in some out of the way part of the town and get him to print a few cards with the high-sounding name. That, of course, is done 'while you wait.' Beyond that there was the purchase of a good second-hand uniform, fur coat, and a beard and a wig from a costumier's.

"No, no, the execution was not difficult; it was the planning of it all, the daring that was so fine. Schwarz, of course, was a foreigner; he had only been in England a little over a fortnight. Vassall's broken English misled him; probably he did not know the junior partner very intimately. I have no doubt that but for his uncle's absurd British prejudice and suspicions against the Russian Prince, Schwarz would not have been so ready to believe in the latter's roguery. As I said, it would be a great boon if English tradesmen studied Gotha more; but it was clever, wasn't it? I couldn't have done it much better myself."

That last sentence was so characteristic. I wished I could render its supreme overwhelming self-conceit. Before I could think of some plausible argument against his theory he was gone, and I was trying vainly to find another solution to the Liverpool mystery.

THE . . BRIGHTON MYSTERY.

Being the Fourth of a Series of Stories entitled "The Mysteries of Great Cities."

Illustrated by P. B. Hickling.

BY
BARONESS E. ORCZY.

DRAMATIS PERSONÆ.

THE MAN IN THE CORNER *of the A.B.C. shop who tells the story to*
THE LADY JOURNALIST.
MR. FRANCIS MORTON (*City man*).
MRS. FRANCIS MORTON.
MR. EDWARD SKINNER.
INSPECTOR BUCKLE.
MRS. CHAPMAN

I.

"Do you care for the seaside?" asked the man in the corner, when he had finished his lunch. "I don't mean the seaside at Ostend or Trouville, but honest English seaside with minstrels, three shilling excursionists, and dirty, expensive, furnished apartments, where they charge you a shilling for lighting the hall gas on Sundays and sixpence on other evenings. Do you care for that?"

"I prefer the country."

"Ah! perhaps it is preferable. Personally I only liked one of our English seaside resorts once, and that was for a week, when Edward Skinner was up before the magistrate, charged with what was known as the 'Brighton Outrage.' I don't know if you remember the memorable day in Brighton, memorable for that elegant town which deals more in amusements than mysteries, when Mr. Francis Morton, one of its most noted residents disappeared. Yes! disappeared as completely as any vanishing lady in a music hall. He was wealthy, had a fine house, servants, a wife and children, and he disappeared. There was no getting away from that.

"Mr. Francis Morton lived with his wife in one of the large houses in Sussex Square at the Kemp Town end of Brighton. Mrs. Morton was well known for her Americanisms, her swagger dinner parties and beautiful Paris gowns. She was the daughter of one of the many American millionaires, (I think her father was a Chicago porkbutcher,) who conveniently provide wealthy wives for English gentlemen; and she had married Mr. Francis Morton a few years ago and brought him her quarter of a million, for no other reason but that she fell in love with him. He was neither good-looking nor distinguished, in fact, he was one of those men who seem to have CITY stamped all over their person.

"He was a gentleman of very regular habits, going up to London every morning on business and returning every afternoon by the 'husband's train.' So regular was he in these habits that all the servants at the Sussex Square house were betrayed into actual gossip over the fact that on Wednesday, March 17th, the master was not home for dinner. Hales, the butler, remarked that the mistress seemed a bit anxious and didn't eat much food. The evening wore on and Mr. Morton did not appear. At nine o'clock the young footman was dispatched to the station to make inquiries whether his master had been seen there in the afternoon, or whether—which Heaven forbid—there had been an accident on the line. The young man interviewed two or three porters, the bookstall boy and ticket clerk; all were agreed that Mr. Morton did not go up to London during the day; no

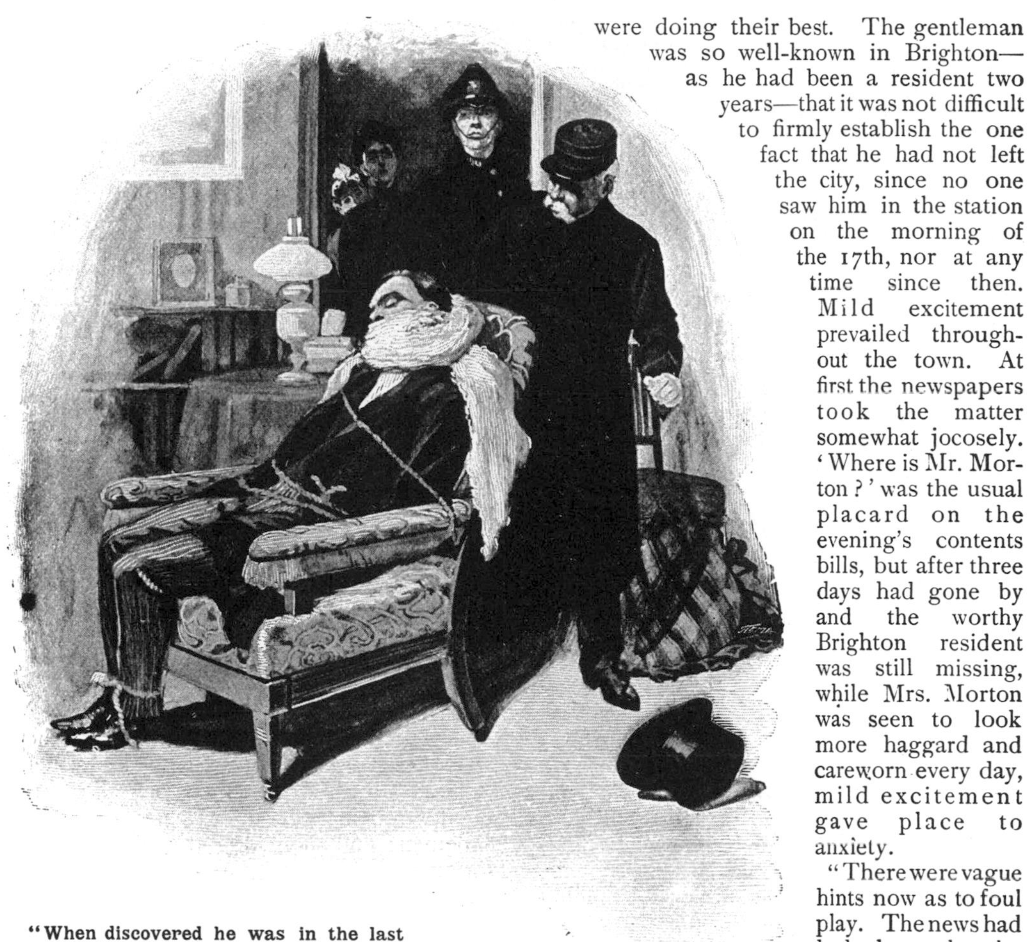

"When discovered he was in the last stage of inanition; he was tied into an armchair with ropes, a thick wool shawl had been wound round his mouth."

one had seen him within the precincts of the station. There certainly had been no accident reported either on the up or down line.

"But the morning of the 18th came, with its usual postman's knock, but neither Mr. Morton nor any sign or news from him. Mrs. Morton, who evidently had spent a sleepless night, for she looked sadly changed and haggard, sent a wire to the hall porter at the large building in Cannon Street, where her husband had his office. An hour later she had the reply: 'Not seen Mr. Morton all day yesterday, not here to-day.' By the afternoon everyone in Brighton knew that a fellow resident had mysteriously disappeared from or in the city.

"A couple of days, then another, elapsed, and still no sign of Mr. Morton. The police were doing their best. The gentleman was so well-known in Brighton—as he had been a resident two years—that it was not difficult to firmly establish the one fact that he had not left the city, since no one saw him in the station on the morning of the 17th, nor at any time since then. Mild excitement prevailed throughout the town. At first the newspapers took the matter somewhat jocosely. 'Where is Mr. Morton?' was the usual placard on the evening's contents bills, but after three days had gone by and the worthy Brighton resident was still missing, while Mrs. Morton was seen to look more haggard and careworn every day, mild excitement gave place to anxiety.

"There were vague hints now as to foul play. The news had leaked out that the missing gentleman was carrying a large sum of money on the day of his disappearance. There were also vague rumours of a scandal not unconnected with Mrs. Morton herself and her own past history, which in her anxiety for her husband she had been forced to reveal to the detective-inspector in charge of the case.

"Then on Saturday the news the late evening papers contained was this:

"'Acting on certain information received, the police to-day forced an entrance into one of the rooms of Russells House, a high class furnished apartment on the King's Parade, and there they discovered our missing distinguished townsman Mr. Francis Morton, who had been robbed and subsequently locked up in that room since Wednesday the 17th. When discovered he was in the last stages of inanition; he was tied into an armchair with ropes, a thick wool shawl had been wound round his mouth, and it is a positive marvel that, left thus without food and very little air, the unfortunate gentleman survived the horrors of these four days of incarceration.

"'He has been conveyed to his residence in Sussex Square, and we are pleased to say that Doctor Mellish, who is in attendance, has declared his patient to be out of serious danger, and that with care and rest will be soon quite himself again.

"'At the same time our readers will learn with unmixed satisfaction that the police of our city, with their usual acuteness and activity, have already discovered the identity and whereabouts of the cowardly ruffian who committed this unparalleled outrage'

II.

"I really don't know," continued the man in the corner blandly, "what it was that interested me in the case from the very first. Certainly it had nothing very out of the way or mysterious about it, but I journeyed down to Brighton nevertheless, as I felt that something deeper and more subtle lay behind that extraordinary assault, following a robbery no doubt.

"I must tell you that the police had allowed it to be freely circulated abroad that they held a clue. It had been easy enough to ascertain who the lodger was who had rented the furnished room in Russells House. His name was supposed to be Edward Skinner, and he had taken the room about a fortnight ago, but had gone away ostensibly for two or three days on the very day of Mr. Morton's mysterious disappearance. It was on the 20th that Mr. Morton was found, and thirty-six hours later the public were gratified to hear that Mr. Edward Skinner had been traced to London and arrested on the charge of assault upon the person of Mr. Francis Morton and of robbing him of the sum of £10,000.

"Then a further sensation was added to the already bewildering case by the startling announcement that Mr. Francis Morton refused to prosecute.

"Of course, the Treasury took up the case and subpœnaed Mr. Morton as a witness, so that gentleman—if he wished to hush the matter up, or had been in any way terrorised into a promise of doing so—gained nothing by his refusal, except an additional amount of curiosity in the public mind and further sensation around the mysterious case.

"It was all this, you see, which had interested me and brought me down to Brighton on March 23rd to see the prisoner Edward Skinner arraigned before the beak. I must say that he was a very ordinary-looking individual. Fair, of ruddy complexion, with snub nose and the beginning of a bald place on the top of his head, he, too, looked the embodiment of a prosperous, stodgy 'city gent.'

"I took a quick survey of the witnesses present, and guessed that the handsome, stylish woman sitting next to Mr. Reginald Pepys, the noted lawyer for the Crown, was Mrs. Morton.

"There was a large crowd in court, and I heard whispered comments among the feminine portion thereof as to the beauty of Mrs. Morton's gown, the value of her large picture hat, and the magnificence of her diamond rings.

"The police gave all the evidence required with regard to the finding of Mr. Morton in the room at Russells House and also to the arrest of Skinner at the Lingham Hotel in London. It appears that the prisoner seemed completely taken aback at the charge preferred against him and declared that though he knew Mr. Francis Morton slightly in business he knew nothing as to his private life.

"'Prisoner stated,' continued Inspector Buckle, 'that he was not even aware Mr. Morton lived in Brighton, but I have evidence here which I will place before your Honour, to prove that the prisoner was seen in the company of Mr. Morton at 9.30 o'clock on the morning of the assault.'

"Cross-examined by Mr. Matthew Quiller, the detective inspector admitted that prisoner merely said that he did not know that Mr. Morton was a *resident* of Brighton, he never denied having met him there.

"The witness or rather witnesses referred to by the police were two Brighton tradesmen who knew Mr. Morton by sight and had seen him on the morning of the 17th walking with the accused.

"In this instance Mr. Quiller had no question to ask of the witnesses and it was generally understood that the prisoner did not wish to contradict their statement.

"Constable Hartrick told the story of the finding of the unfortunate Mr. Morton after his four days' incarceration. The constable had been sent round by the chief inspector after certain information given by Mrs. Chapman, the landlady of Russells House. He had found the door locked and forced it open. Mr. Morton was in an armchair, with several yards of rope wound loosely round him; he was almost unconscious and there was a thick wool shawl tied round his mouth which must have deadened any cry or groan the poor gentleman might have uttered. But, as a matter of fact, the constable was under the impression that Mr. Morton had been either drugged or stunned in some way at first, which had left him weak and faint and prevented him from making himself heard, or extricating himself from his bonds, which were very clumsily, evidently very hastily, wound round his body.

"The medical officer who was called in, and also Dr. Mellish who attended Mr. Morton, both said that he seemed dazed by some stupefying drug, and also, of course, terribly weak and faint with the want of food.

"The first witness of real importance was Mrs. Chapman, the proprietress of Russells House, whose original information to the police led to the discovery of Mr. Morton. In answer to Mr. Pepys she said that on March 1 the accused called at her house and gave his name as Mr. Edward Skinner.

"'He required, he said, a furnished room at a moderate rental for a permanency with full attendance when he was in, but he added that he would often be away for two or three days, or even longer, at a time.

"'He told me that he was a traveller for a tea-house,' continued Mrs. Chapman, 'and I showed him the front room on the third floor, as he did not want to pay more than twelve shillings a week. I asked him for a reference, but he put three sovereigns in my hand and said with a laugh that he supposed paying for his room a month in advance was sufficient reference; if I didn't like him after that, I could give him a week's notice to quit.'

"'You did not think of asking him the name of the firm for which he travelled?' asked Mr. Pepys.

"'No, I was quite satisfied as he paid me for the room. The next day he sent in his luggage and took possession of the room. He went out most mornings on business, but was always in Brighton for Saturday and Sunday. On the 16th he told me that he was going to Liverpool for a couple of days; he slept in the house that night, and went off early on the 17th, taking his portmanteau with him.'

"'At what time did he leave?' asked Mr. Pepys.

"'I couldn't say exactly,' replied Mrs. Chapman with some hesitation. 'You see this is the off season here. None of my rooms are let, except the one to Mr. Skinner, and I only have one servant. I keep four during the summer, autumn and winter season,' she added with conscious pride, fearing that her former statement might prejudice the reputation of Russells House. 'I thought I had heard Mr. Skinner go out about nine o'clock, but about an hour later the girl and I were both in the basement, and we heard the front door open and shut with a bang, and then a step in the hall.

"'"That's Mr. Skinner," said Mary. "So it is," I said, "why, I thought he had gone an hour ago." "He did go out then," said Mary, "for he left his bedroom door open and I went in to do his bed and tidy his room." "Just go and see if that's him, Mary," I said, and Mary ran up to the hall, and up the stairs, and came back to tell me that that was Mr. Skinner all right enough, he had gone straight up to his room. Mary didn't see him, but he had another gentleman with him, as she could hear them talking in Mr. Skinner's room.'

"The very embodiment of a prosperous, stodgy 'city gent.'"

"'Then you can't tell us at what time the prisoner left the house finally?'

"'No, that I can't. I went out shopping soon after that. When I came in it was twelve o'clock. I went up to the third floor and found that Mr. Skinner had locked his door and taken the key with him. As I knew Mary had already done the room I did not trouble more about it, though I did think it strange for a gentleman to lock up his room and not leave the key with me.'

"'And, of course, you heard no noise of any kind in the room then?'

"'No. Not that day or the next, but on the third day Mary and I both thought we heard a funny sound. I said that Mr. Skinner had left his window open and it was the blind flapping against the window-pane; but when we heard that funny noise again I put my ear to the keyhole and I thought I could hear a groan.

I was very frightened and sent Mary for the police.'

"Mrs. Chapman had nothing more of interest to say. The prisoner certainly was her lodger. She had last seen him on the evening of the 16th going up to his room with his candle. Mary the servant had much the same story to relate as her mistress.

"'I think it was 'im, right enough,' said Mary guardedly. 'I didn't see 'im, but I went up to 'is landing and stopped a moment outside 'is door. I could 'ear loud voices in the room—gentlemen talking.'

"'I suppose you would not do such a thing as to listen, Mary?' queried Mr. Pepys with a smile.

"'No, sir,' said Mary with a bland smile, 'I didn't catch what the gentlemen said, but one of them spoke so loud, I thought they must be quarrelling.'

"'Mr. Skinner was the only person in possession of a latch-key I presume. No one else could have come in without ringing at the door?'

"'Oh no, sir.'

"That was all. So far, you see, the case was progressing splendidly for the Crown against the prisoner. The contention of course was that Skinner had met Mr. Morton, brought him home with him, assaulted, drugged, then gagged and bound him and finally robbed him of whatever money he had in his possession, which according to certain affidavits which presently would be placed before the magistrate, amounted to £10,000 in notes.

"But in all this there still remained the great element of mystery for which the public and the magistrate would demand an explanation: namely, what were the relationships between Mr. Morton and Skinner, which had induced the former to refuse the prosecution of the man who had not only robbed him, but had so nearly succeeded in leaving him to die a terrible and lingering death. Mr. Morton was too ill as yet to appear in person. Dr. Mellish had absolutely forbidden his patient to undergo the fatigue and excitement of giving evidence himself in court that day. But his depositions had been taken at his bedside, were sworn to by him, and were now placed before the magistrate by the prosecuting counsel, and the facts they revealed were certainly as remarkable as they were brief and enigmatical.

"As they were read by Mr. Pepys, an awed and expectant hush seemed to descend over the large crowd gathered there, and all necks were strained eagerly forward to catch a glimpse of a tall, elegant woman, faultlessly dressed and wearing exquisite jewellery, but whose handsome face wore, as the prosecuting counsel read her husband's deposition, a more and more ashen hue.

"'This, your Honour, is the statement made upon oath by Mr. Francis Morton,' commenced Mr. Pepys in that loud, sonorous voice of his which sounds so impressive in a crowded and hushed court. '"I was obliged for certain reasons which I refuse to disclose to make a payment of a large sum of money to a man whom I did not know and have never seen. It was in a matter of which my wife was cognisant and which had entirely to do with her own affairs. I was merely the go-between, as I thought it was not fit that she should see to this matter herself. The individual in question had made certain demands, of which she kept me in ignorance as long as she could, not wishing to unnecessarily worry me. At last she decided to place the whole matter before me, and I agreed with her that it would be best to satisfy the man's demands.

"'"I then wrote to that individual whose name I do not wish to disclose, addressing the letter, as my wife directed me to do, to the Brighton post office, saying that I was ready to pay the £10,000 to him, at any place or time and in what manner he might appoint. I received a reply which bore the Brighton postmark, and which desired me to be outside Furnival's, the drapers in West Street, at 9.30 on the morning of March 17th, and to bring the money (£10,000) in Bank of England notes.

"'"On the 16th, my wife gave me a cheque for the amount and I cashed it at her bank—Bird's in Fleet Street. At half past nine the following morning I was at the appointed place. An individual wearing a grey overcoat, bowler hat, and red tie accosted me by name and requested me to walk as far as his lodgings in the King's Parade. I followed him. Neither of us spoke. He stopped at a house which bore the name 'Russells House,' and which I shall be able to swear to as soon as I am able to go out. He let himself in with a latch-key and asked me to follow him up to his room on the third floor. I thought I noticed when we were in the room that he locked the door; however I had nothing of any value about me except the £10,000, which I was ready to give him. We had not exchanged the slightest word.

"'"I gave him the notes and he folded them and put them in his pocket-book. Then I turned towards the door, and without the slightest warning I felt myself suddenly gripped by the shoulder while a handkerchief was pressed to my nose and mouth. I struggled as best I could, but the handkerchief was saturated with chloroform, and I soon lost consciousness. I hazily remember the man saying to me in short, jerky sentences spoken at intervals while I was still weakly struggling:

"'"'What a fool you must think me, my dear sir! did you really think that I was going to let you quietly walk out of here, straight to the police-station, eh? Such dodges have been done before, I know, when a man's silence has to be bought for money. Find out who he is, see where he lives, give him the money, then inform against him. No you don't! not this time. I am off to the Continong with this £10,000 and I can get to Newhaven in time for the mid-day boat, so you'll have to keep quiet until I am the other side of the Channel, my friend. You won't be much inconvenienced, my landlady will hear your groans presently and release you, so you'll be all right. There, now, drink this—that's better.' He forced something bitter down my throat then I remember nothing more.

"'"When I regained consciousness I was sitting in an armchair with some rope tied round me and a wool shawl round my mouth. I hadn't the strength to make the slightest effort to disentangle myself or to utter a scream. I felt terribly sick and faint."'

"Mr. Reginald Pepys had finished reading and no one in that crowded court had thought of uttering a sound, the magistrate's eyes were fixed upon the handsome lady in the magnificent gown, who was mopping her eyes with a dainty lace handkerchief.

"The extraordinary narrative of the victim of so daring an outrage, had kept everyone in suspense; one thing was still expected to make the measure of sensation as full as it had ever been over any criminal case, and that was Mrs. Morton's evidence. She was called by the prosecuting counsel, and slowly, gracefully, she entered the witness-box. There was no doubt that she had felt keenly the tortures which her husband had undergone, and also the humiliation of seeing her name dragged forcibly into this ugly, blackmailing scandal.

"Closely questioned by Mr. Reginald Pepys, she was forced to admit that the man who blackmailed her was connected with her early life in a way which would have brought terrible disgrace upon her and upon her children. The story she told, amidst many tears and sobs, and much use of her beautiful lace handkerchief and beringed hands, was exceedingly pathetic.

"It appears that when she was barely seventeen she was inveigled into a secret marriage with one of those foreign adventurers who swarm in every country, and who styled himself Comte Armand de la Tremouille. He seems to have been a blackguard of unusually low pattern, for, after he had extracted from her some £200 of her pin money and a few diamond brooches, he left her one fine day with a laconic word to say that he was sailing for Europe by the *Argentina*, and would not be back for some time. She was in love with the brute, poor young soul, for when, a week later, she read that the *Argentina* was wrecked, and presumably every soul on board had perished, she wept very many bitter tears over her early widowhood.

"Fortunately her father, a very wealthy pork butcher of Chicago, had known nothing of his daughter's culpable foolishness. Four years later he took her to London, where she met Mr. Francis Morton and married him. She led six or seven years of very happy married life when one day, like a thunderbolt from a clear, blue sky, she received a typewritten letter, signed 'Armand de la Tremouille,' full of protestations of undying love, telling a long and pathetic tale of years of suffering in a foreign land, whither he had drifted after having been rescued almost miraculously from the wreck of the *Argentina*, and where he never had been able to scrape a sufficient amount of money to pay for his passage home. At last fate had favoured him. He had after many vicissitudes found the whereabouts of his dear wife, and was now ready to forgive all that was past and take her to his loving arms once again.

"What followed was the usual course of events when there is a blackguard and a fool of a woman. She was terrorised and did not dare to tell her husband for some time; she corresponded with the Comte de la Tremouille, begging him for her sake and in memory of the past not to attempt to see her. She found him amenable to reason in the shape of several hundred pounds which passed through the Brighton post office into his hands. At last one day, by accident, Mr. Morton came across one of the Comte de la Tremouille's interesting letters. She confessed everything, throwing herself upon her husband's mercy.

"Now Mr. Francis Morton was a business

man who viewed life practically and soberly. He liked his wife who kept him in luxury, and wished to keep her, whereas the Comte de la Tremouille seemed willing enough to give her up for a consideration. Mrs. Morton, who had the sole and absolute control of her fortune on the other hand, was willing enough to pay the price and hush up the scandal, which she believed—since she was a bit of a fool—would land her in prison for bigamy. Mr. Francis Morton wrote to the Comte de la Tremouille that his wife was ready to pay him the sum of £10,000 which he demanded in payment for her absolute liberty and his own complete disappearance out of her life now and for ever. The appointment was made and Mr. Morton left his house at 9 a.m. on March 17th, with the £10,000 in his pocket.

"The public and the magistrate had hung breathless upon her words. There was nothing but sympathy felt for this handsome woman, who throughout had been more sinned against than sinning, and whose gravest fault seems to have been a total lack of intelligence in dealing with her own life. But I can assure you of one thing, that in no case within my recollection was there ever such a sensation in a court, as when the magistrate, after a few minutes' silence, said gently to Mrs. Morton:

"'And now, Mrs. Morton, will you kindly look at the prisoner, and tell me if in him you recognise your former husband?'

"And she, without even turning to look at the accused, said quietly:

"'Oh no! your honour! of course that man is *not* the Comte de la Tremouille.'

"'She confessed everything, throwing herself upon her husband's mercy."

III.

"I can assure you that the situation was quite dramatic," continued the man in the corner, whilst his funny, claw-like hands took up a bit of string with renewed feverishness.

"In answer to further questions from the magistrate, she declared that she had never seen the accused; he might have been the go-between, however, that she could not say. The letters she received were all typewritten, but signed 'Armand de la Tremouille,' and certainly the signature was identical with that on the letters she used to receive from him years ago, all of which she had kept.

"'And did it *never* strike you,' asked the magistrate with a smile, 'that the letters you received might be forgeries?'

"'How could they be?' she replied decisively; 'no one knew of my marriage to the Comte de la Tremouille, no one in England certainly. And besides, if some one did know the Comte intimately enough to forge his handwriting and to blackmail me, why should that some one have waited all these years? I have been married seven years, your honour.'

"That was true enough, and there the matter rested as far as she was concerned. But the identity of Mr. Francis Morton's assailant had to be finally established, of course, before the prisoner was committed for trial. Dr. Mellish promised that Mr. Morton would be allowed to come to court for half-an-hour and identify the accused on the following day, and the case was adjourned until then. The accused was led away between two constables, bail being refused, and Brighton had perforce to moderate its impatience until the Wednesday.

"The court was crowded to overflowing; actors, playwrights, literary men of all sorts had fought for admission to study for themselves the various phases and faces in connection with the case. Mrs. Morton was not present when the prisoner, quiet and self-possessed, was brought in and placed in the dock. His solicitor was with him and a sensational defence was expected.

"Presently there was a stir in the court, and that certain sound, half rustle, half sigh, which preludes an expected palpitating event. Mr. Morton, pale, thin, wearing yet in his hollow eyes the stamp of those five days of suffering, walked into court leaning on the arm of his doctor—Mrs. Morton was not with him.

"He was at once accommodated with a chair in the witness-box, and the magistrate, after a few words of kindly sympathy, asked him if he had anything to add to his written statement. On Mr. Morton replying in the negative, the magistrate added—

"'And now, Mr. Morton, will you kindly look at the accused in the dock and tell me whether you recognise the person who took you to the room in Russells House and then assaulted you?'

"Slowly the sick man turned towards the prisoner and looked at him; then he shook his head and replied quietly:

"'No, sir, that certainly was not the man.'

"'You are quite sure?' asked the magistrate in amazement, while the crowd literally gasped with wonder.

"'I swear it,' asserted Mr. Morton.

"'Can you describe the man who assaulted you?'

"'Certainly. He was dark, of swarthy complexion, tall, thin, with bushy eyebrows and thick black hair and short beard. He spoke English with just the faintest suspicion of a foreign accent.'

"The prisoner, as I told you before, was English in every feature. English in his ruddy complexion, and absolutely English in his speech.

"After that the case for the prosecution began to collapse. Everyone had expected a sensational defence, and Mr. Matthew Quiller, counsel for Skinner, fully justified all these expectations. He had no fewer than four witnesses present who swore positively that at 9.45 a.m. on the morning of Wednesday, March 17, the prisoner was in the express train leaving Brighton for Victoria.

"Not being endowed with the gift of being in two places at once, and Mr. Morton having added the whole weight of his own evidence in Mr. Edward Skinner's favour, that gentleman was once more remanded by the magistrate, pending further investigation by the police, bail being allowed this time in two sureties of £50 each.

IV.

"Tell me what you think of it," said the man in the corner, seeing that I remained silent and puzzled.

"Well," I said dubiously, "I suppose that the so-called Armand de la Tremouille's story was true in substance. That he did not perish on the *Argentina*, but drifted home, and blackmailed his former wife."

"Doesn't it strike you that there are at least two very strong points against that theory?" he asked, making two gigantic knots in his piece of string.

"Two?"

"Yes. In the first place, if the blackmailer was the 'Comte de la Tremouille' returned to life, why should he have been content to take £10,000 from a lady who was his lawful wife, and who could keep him in luxury for the rest of his natural life upon her large fortune, which was close upon a quarter of a million. The real Comte de la Tremouille, remember, had never found it difficult to get money out of his wife during their brief married life, whatever Mr. Morton's subsequent experience in the same direction might have been. And, secondly, why should he have type-written his letters to his wife?"

"Because——"

"That was a point which, to my mind, the police never made the most of. Now, my experience in criminal cases has invariably been that when a typewritten letter figures in one, that letter is a forgery. It is not very difficult to imitate a signature, but it is a jolly sight more difficult to imitate a handwriting throughout an entire letter."

"Then, do you think——"

"I think, if you will allow me," he interrupted excitedly, "that we will go through the points—the sensible, tangible points of the case. Firstly: Mr. Morton disappears with £10,000 in his pocket, for four entire days; at the end of that time he is discovered loosely tied to an arm-chair, and a wool shawl round his mouth. Secondly: A man named Skinner is accused of the outrage. Mr. Morton, although he himself is able—mind you—to furnish the best defence possible for Skinner, by denying his identity with the man who assaulted him, refuses to prosecute. Why?"

"He did not wish to drag his wife's name into the case."

"He must have known that the Crown would take up the case. Then again, how is it no one saw him in the company of the swarthy foreigner he described?"

"Two witnesses did see Mr. Morton in company with Skinner," I argued.

"Yes, at 9.20 in West Street; that would give Edward Skinner time to catch the 9.45 at the station, and to intrust Mr. Morton with the latchkey of Russells House," remarked my companion dryly.

"What nonsense!" I ejaculated.

"Nonsense, is it?" he said, tugging wildly at his bit of string; "is it nonsense to affirm that if a man wants to make sure that his victim shall not escape, he does not usually wind rope 'loosely' round his figure, nor does he throw a wool shawl lightly round his mouth. The police were idiotic beyond words; they themselves discovered that Morton was so 'loosely' fastened to his chair that very little movement would have disentangled him, and yet it never struck them that nothing was easier for that particular type of scoundrel to sit down in an armchair and wind a few yards of rope round himself, then, having wrapped a wool shawl round his throat, to slip his two arms inside the ropes."

"But what object would a man in Mr. Morton's position have for playing such extraordinary pranks?"

"Ah, the motive! There you are! What do I always tell you? Seek the motive! Now what was Mr. Morton's position? He was the husband of a lady who owned a quarter of a million of money, not one penny of which he could touch without her consent, as it was settled on herself, and who, after the terrible way in which she had been plundered and then abandoned in her early youth, no doubt kept a very tight hold upon the purse-strings. Mr. Morton's subsequent life has proved that he had certain expensive, not altogether avowable, tastes. One day he discovers the old love letters of the 'Comte Armand de la Tremouille.'

"Then he lays his plans: He typewrites a letter, forges the signature of the erstwhile Count, and awaits events. The fish does rise to the bait. He gets sundry bits of money, and his success makes him daring. He looks round him for an accomplice—clever, unscrupulous, greedy—and selects Mr. Edward Skinner, probably some former pal of his wild oats days.

"The plan was very neat you must confess. Mr. Skinner takes the room in Russells House, and studies all the manners and customs of his landlady and her servant. He then draws the full attention of the police upon himself. He meets Morton in West Street, then disappears ostensibly after the 'assault.' In the meanwhile, Morton goes to Russells House. He goes upstairs, talks loudly in the room, then makes elaborate preparations for his comedy."

"Why! he nearly died of starvation!"

"That, I daresay, was not a part of his reckoning. He thought, no doubt, that Mrs. Chapman or the servant would discover and rescue him pretty soon. He meant to appear just a little faint, and endured quietly the first twenty-four hours of inanition. But the excitement and want of food told on him more than he expected. After twenty-four hours he turned very giddy and sick, and, falling from one fainting fit into another, was unable to give the alarm.

"However, he is all right again now, and concludes his part of a downright blackguard to perfection. Under the plea that his conscience does not allow him to live with a lady whose first husband is still alive, he has taken a bachelor flat in London, and only pays afternoon calls on his wife in Brighton. But presently he will tire of his bachelor life, and will return to his wife. And I'll guarantee that the Comte de la Tremouille will never be heard of again."

And he left me alone with a couple of photos of two uninteresting, stodgy, quiet-looking men—Morton and Skinner—who, if the man in the corner was right in his theories, were a pair of the finest blackguards unhung.

THE EDINBURGH MYSTERY.

Being the Fifth of a Series of Stories entitled "The Mysteries of Great Cities."

Illustrated by P. B. Hickling.

By
Baroness E. Orczy.

DRAMATIS PERSONÆ.

The Man in the Corner *who tells the story to the*	Lady Donaldson.
Lady Journalist.	Miss Crawford
Mr. Graham.	Tremlett (*maid*).
David Graham.	Sir James Fenwick.

I.

The man in the corner had not enjoyed his lunch. I could see that he had something on his mind, for, even before he began to talk that morning, he was fidgeting with his bit of string, and setting all my nerves on the jar.

"Have you ever felt real sympathy with a criminal or a thief?" he asked after a while.

"Only once, I think," I replied, "and then I am not quite sure that the unfortunate woman who did enlist my sympathies was the criminal you make her out to be."

"You mean the heroine of the York mystery?" he replied blandly. "I know that you tried very hard that time to discredit the only possible version of that mysterious murder, the version which is my own. Now, I am equally sure that you have at the present moment no more notion as to who killed and robbed poor Lady Donaldson in Charlotte Square, Edinburgh, than the police have themselves, and yet you are fully prepared to pooh-pooh my arguments, and to disbelieve my version of the mystery. Such is the lady journalist's mind."

"If you have some cock and bull story to explain that extraordinary case," I retorted, "of course I shall disbelieve it. Certainly, if you are going to try and enlist my sympathies on behalf of Edith Crawford, I can assure you you won't succeed."

"Well, I don't know that that is altogether my intention. I see you are interested in the case, but I dare say you don't remember all the circumstances. You must forgive me if I repeat that which you know already. If you have ever been to Edinburgh at all, you will have heard of Graham's bank, and Mr. Andrew Graham, the present head of the firm, is undoubtedly one of the most prominent notabilities of 'modern Athens.'"

The man in the corner took two or three photos from his pocket-book and placed them before me; then pointing at them with his long bony finger—

"That," he said, "is Mr. Elphinstone Graham, the eldest son, a typical young Scotchman, as you see, and this is David Graham, the second son."

I looked more closely at this last photo, and saw before me a young face, upon which some lasting sorrow seemed already to have left its mark. The face was delicate and thin, the features pinched, and the eyes seemed almost unnaturally large and prominent.

"He was deformed," commented the man in the corner in answer to my thoughts, "and, as such, an object of pity and even of repugnance to most of his friends. There was also a good deal of talk in Edinburgh society as to his mental condition, his mind, according to many intimate friends of the Grahams, being at times decidedly unhinged. Be that as it may, I fancy that his life must have been a very sad one; he had lost his mother when quite a baby, and his father seemed, strangely enough, to have an almost unconquerable dislike towards him.

"Everyone got to know presently of David Graham's sad position in his father's own house, and also of the great affection lavished upon him by his godmother, Lady Donaldson, who was a sister of Mr. Graham's.

"She was a lady of considerable wealth, being the widow of Sir George Donaldson, the great distiller, but she seems to have been decidedly eccentric. Latterly she had astonished all her family—who were rigid Presbyterians—by announcing her intention of embracing the Roman Catholic faith, and then retiring to the convent of St. Augustine's at Newton Abbot in Devonshire.

"She had sole and absolute control of the vast fortune a doting husband had bequeathed to her. Clearly, therefore, she was at liberty to bestow it upon a Devonshire convent if she chose. But this evidently was not altogether her intention.

"I told you how fond she was of her deformed godson, did I not? Being a bundle of eccentricities, she had many hobbies, none more pronounced than the fixed determination to see—before retiring from the world altogether—David Graham happily married.

"Now, it appears that David Graham, ugly, deformed, half-demented as he was, had fallen desperately in love with Miss Edith Crawford, daughter of the late Dr. Crawford of Prince's Gardens. The young lady, however—very naturally, perhaps—fought shy of David Graham, who, about this time, certainly seemed very queer and morose, but Lady Donaldson, with characteristic determination, seems to have made up her mind to melt Miss Crawford's heart towards her unfortunate nephew.

"On October the 2nd, at a family party given by Mr. Graham in his fine mansion in Charlotte Square, Lady Donaldson openly announced her intention of making over, by deed of gift, to her nephew, David Graham, certain property, money and shares, amounting in total value to the sum of £100,000, and also her magnificent diamonds, which were worth £50,000, for the use of the said David's wife. Keith Macfinlay, a lawyer of Prince's Street, received the next day instructions for drawing up the necessary deed of gift, which she pledged herself to sign the day of her godson's wedding.

"A week later *The Scotsman* contained the following paragraph:

"A marriage is arranged and will shortly take place between David, younger son of Andrew Graham, Esq., of Charlotte Square, Edinburgh and Dochnakirk, Perthshire, and Edith Lillian, only surviving daughter of the late Dr. Kenneth Crawford, of Prince's Gardens.

"In Edinburgh society comments were loud and various upon the forthcoming marriage, and, on the whole, these comments were far from complimentary to the families concerned. I do not think that the Scotch are a particularly sentimental race, but there was such obvious buying, selling, and bargaining about this marriage that Scottish chivalry rose in revolt at the thought.

"Against that the three people most concerned seemed perfectly satisfied. David Graham was positively transformed; his moroseness was gone from him, he lost his queer ways and wild manners, and became gentle and affectionate in the midst of this great and unexpected happiness. Miss Edith Crawford ordered her trousseau, and talked of the diamonds to her friends, and Lady Donaldson was only waiting for the consummation of this marriage—her heart's desire—before she finally retired from the world, at peace with it and with herself.

"The deed of gift was ready for signature on the wedding day, which was fixed for November 7th, and Lady Donaldson took up her abode temporarily in her brother's house in Charlotte Square.

"Mr. Graham gave a large ball on October 23rd. Special interest is attached to this ball, from the fact that for this occasion Lady Donaldson insisted that David's future wife should wear the magnificent diamonds which were soon to be hers.

"They were, it seems, superb, and became Miss Crawford's stately beauty to perfection. The ball was a brilliant success, the last guest leaving at four a.m. The next day it was the universal topic of conversation, and the day after that, when Edinburgh unfolded the late editions of its morning papers, it learned with horror and dismay that Lady Donaldson had been found murdered in her room, and that the celebrated diamonds had been stolen.

"Hardly had the beautiful little city, however, recovered from this awful shock than its newspapers had another thrilling sensation ready for their readers.

"Already all Scotch and English papers had mysteriously hinted at 'startling information' obtained by the Procurator Fiscal, and at an 'impending sensational arrest.'

"Then the announcement came, and everyone in Edinburgh read, horror-struck and aghast, that the 'sensational arrest' was none other than that of Miss Edith Crawford, for murder and robbery, both so daring and horrible that reason refused to believe that a young lady, born and bred in the best social circle, could have conceived, much less executed, so heinous a crime. She had been arrested in London at the Midland Hotel, and brought to Edinburgh, where she was judicially examined, bail being refused."

II.

"Little more than a fortnight after that, Edith Crawford was duly committed to stand her trial before the High Court of Justiciary. She had pleaded 'Not Guilty' at the pleading diet, and her defence was intrusted to Sir James Fenwick, one of the most eminent advocates at the Criminal Bar.

"Strange to say," continued the man in the corner after awhile, "public opinion from the first went dead against the accused. The public is absolutely like a child, perfectly irresponsible and wholly illogical; it argued that since Miss Crawford had been ready to contract a marriage with a half-demented, deformed creature for the sake of his £100,000, she must have been equally ready to murder and rob an old lady for the sake of £50,000 worth of jewellery, without the incumbrance of so undesirable a husband.

"Perhaps the great sympathy aroused in the popular mind for David Graham had much to do with this ill-feeling against the accused. David Graham had, by this cruel and dastardly murder, lost the best—if not the only—friend he possessed. He had also lost at one fell swoop the large fortune which Lady Donaldson had been about to assign to him.

"The deed of gift had never been signed, and the old lady's vast wealth, instead of enriching her favourite nephew, was distributed—since she had made no will—amongst her heirs-at-law. And now to crown this long chapter of sorrow David Graham saw the girl he loved accused of the awful crime which had robbed him of friend and fortune.

"It was, therefore, with an unmistakable thrill of righteous satisfaction that

'Lady Donaldson had been found murdered in her room.'

Edinburgh society saw this 'mercenary girl' in so terrible a plight.

"I was immensely interested in the case, and journeyed down to Edinburgh in order to get a good view of the chief actors in the thrilling drama which was about to be unfolded there.

"I succeeded—I generally do—in securing one of the front seats among the audience, and was already comfortably installed in my place in court when through the trap door I saw the head of the prisoner emerge. She was very becomingly dressed in deep black, and, led by two policemen, she took her place in the dock. Sir James Fenwick shook hands with her very warmly, and I could almost hear him instilling words of comfort into her.

"The trial lasted six clear days, during which time more than forty persons were examined for the prosecution, and as many for the defence. But the most interesting witnesses were certainly the two doctors, the maid Tremlett, Campbell, the High Street jeweller, and David Graham.

"There was, of course, a great deal of medical evidence to go through. Poor Lady Donaldson had been found with a silk scarf tied tightly round her neck, her face showing even to the inexperienced eye every symptom of strangulation.

"Then Tremlett, Lady Donaldson's confidential maid was called. Closely examined by Crown Counsel she gave an account of the ball at Charlotte Square on the 23rd, and the wearing of the jewels by Miss Crawford on that occasion.

"'I helped Miss Crawford on with the tiara over her hair,' she said; 'and my lady put the two necklaces round Miss Crawford's neck herself. There were also some beautiful brooches, bracelets and earrings. At four o'clock in the morning when the ball was over, Miss Crawford brought the jewels back to my lady's room. My lady had already gone to bed, and I had put out the electric light, as I was going, too. There was only one candle left in the room, close to the bed.

"'Miss Crawford took all the jewels off, and asked Lady Donaldson for the key of the safe, so that she might put them away. My lady gave her the key, and said to me: "You can go to bed, Tremlett, you must be dead tired." I was glad to go, for I could hardly stand up—I was so tired. I said "Good-night!" to my lady and also to Miss Crawford, who was busy putting the jewels away. As I was going out of the room, I heard Lady Donaldson saying: "Have you managed it, my dear?" Miss Crawford said: "I have put everything away very nicely."'

"In answer to Sir James Fenwick, Tremlett said that Lady Donaldson always carried the key of her jewel safe on a ribbon round her neck, and had done so the whole day preceding her death.

"'On the night of the 24th,' she continued, 'Lady Donaldson still seemed rather tired, and went up to her room directly after dinner, and while the family were still sitting in the dining room. She made me dress her hair, then she slipped on her dressing gown, and sat in the armchair with a book. She told me then that she felt strangely uncomfortable and nervous and could not account for it.

"'However, she did not want me to sit with her, so I thought that the best thing I could do was to tell Mr. David Graham that her Ladyship did not seem very cheerful. Her Ladyship was so fond of Mr. David; it always made her happy to have him with her. I then went to my room, and at half-past eight Mr. David called me. He said: "Your mistress does seem a little restless to-night. If I were you I would just go and listen at her door in about an hour's time, and if she has not gone to bed I would go in and stay with her until she has." At about ten o'clock I did as Mr. David suggested, and listened at her Ladyship's door. However, all was quiet in the room, and, thinking her Ladyship had gone to sleep, I went back to bed.

"'The next morning at eight o'clock, when I took in my mistress's cup of tea, I saw her lying on the floor, her poor dear face all purple and distorted. I screamed, and the other servants came rushing along. Then Mr. Graham had the door locked and sent for the doctor and the police.'

"The poor woman seemed to find it very difficult not to break down. She was closely questioned by Sir James Fenwick, but had nothing further to say. She had last seen her mistress alive at eight o'clock on the evening of the 24th.

"'And when you listened at her door at ten o'clock,' asked Sir James, 'did you try to open it?'

"'I did, but it was locked,' she replied.

"'Did Lady Donaldson usually lock her bedroom at night?'

"'Nearly always.'

"'And in the morning when you took in the tea?'

"'The door was open. I walked straight in.'

"'You are quite sure?' insisted Sir James.

"'I swear it,' solemnly asserted the woman.

"After that we were informed by several members of Mr. Graham's establishment that Miss Crawford had been in to tea at Charlotte Square in the afternoon of the 24th, that she told everyone she was going to London by the night mail, as she had some special shopping she wished to do there. It appears that Mr. Graham and David both tried to persuade her to stay to dinner, and then to go by the 9.10 p.m. from the Caledonian Station. Miss Crawford, however, had refused, saying she always preferred to go from the Waverley Station. It was nearer to her own rooms, and she still had a good deal of writing to do.

"In spite of this, two witnesses saw the accused in Charlotte Square later on in the evening. She was carrying a bag which seemed heavy, and was walking towards the Caledonian Railway Station.

"But the most thrilling moment in that sensational trial was reached on the second day, when David Graham, looking wretchedly ill, unkempt, and haggard, stepped into the witness-box. A murmur of sympathy went round the audience at sight of him, who was the second, perhaps, most deeply stricken victim of the Charlotte Square tragedy.

"David Graham, in answer to Crown Counsel, gave an account of his last interview with Lady Donaldson.

"'Tremlett had told me that she seemed anxious and upset, and I went to have a chat with her; she soon cheered up and . . . .'

"There the unfortunate young man hesitated visibly, but after a while resumed with an obvious effort.

"'She spoke of my marriage, and of the gift she was about to bestow upon me. She said the diamonds would be for my wife, and after that for my daughter if I had one. She also complained that Mr. Macfinlay had been so punctilious about preparing the deed of gift, and that it was a

"My lady put the two necklaces round Miss Crawford's neck herself."

great pity the £100,000 could not just pass from her hands to mine, without so much fuss.

"'I stayed talking with her for about half an hour; then I left her as she seemed ready to go to bed, but I told her maid to listen at the door in about an hour's time.'

"There was deep silence in the court for a few moments, a silence which to me seemed almost electrical. It was as if, some time before it was uttered, the next question put by Crown Counsel to the witness—had hovered in the air.

"'You were engaged to Miss Edith Crawford at one time, were you not?'

"One felt, rather than heard, the almost inaudible 'Yes,' which escaped from David Graham's compressed lips.

"'Under what circumstances was that engagement broken off?'

"Sir James Fenwick had already risen in protest, but David Graham had been the first to speak.

"'I do not think that I need answer that question.'

"'I will put it in a different form then,' said Crown Counsel urbanely—'one to which my learned friend cannot possibly take exception. Did you or did you not on October 27th receive a letter from the accused, in which she desired to be released from her promise of marriage to you?'

"Again David Graham would have refused to answer, and he certainly gave no audible reply to the learned counsel's question; but every one in the audience there present—aye, every member of the jury and of the bar—read upon David Graham's pale countenance and large, sorrowful eyes that ominous 'Yes!' which had failed to reach his trembling lips."

III.

"There is no doubt," continued the man in the corner, "that what little sympathy the young girl's terrible position had aroused in the public mind, had died out the moment that David Graham left the witness box on the second day of the trial. Whether Edith Crawford was guilty of murder or not, the callous way, in which she had accepted a deformed lover, and then thrown him over, had set every one's mind against her.

"It was Mr. Graham himself who had been the first to put the Procurator Fiscal in possession of the fact that the accused had written to David from London. breaking off her engagement. This information had, no doubt, directed the attention of the Fiscal to Miss Crawford, and the police soon brought forward the evidence which had led to her arrest.

"We had a final sensation on the third day, when Mr. Campbell, jeweller, of High Street, gave his evidence. He said that on October 25th a lady came to his shop, and offered to sell him a pair of diamond earrings. Trade had been very bad, and he had refused the bargain, although the lady seemed ready to part with the earrings for an extraordinarily low sum considering the beauty of the stones.

"In fact it was because of this evident desire on the lady's part to sell at *any* cost that he had looked at her more keenly than he otherwise would have done. He was now ready to swear that the lady that offered him the diamond earrings was the prisoner in the dock.

"I can assure you that as we all listened to this apparently damnatory evidence you might have heard a pin drop amongst the audience in that crowded court. The girl alone, there in the dock, remained calm and unmoved. Remember that for two days we had heard evidence to prove that old Dr. Crawford had died leaving his daughter penniless, that having no mother she had been brought up by a maiden aunt, who had trained her to be a governess, which occupation she had followed for years, and that certainly she had never been known by any of her friends to be in possession of solitaire diamond earrings.

"The prosecution had certainly secured an ace of trumps, but Sir James Fenwick, who during the whole of that day, had seemed to take little interest in the proceedings, here rose from his seat, and I knew at once that he had got a tit-bit in the way of a 'point' up his sleeve. Gaunt, and unusually tall, and with his beak-like nose, he always looks strangely impressive when he seriously tackles a witness. He did it this time with a vengeance, I can tell you. He was all over the pompous little jeweller in a moment.

"'Had Mr. Campbell made a special entry in his book, as to the visit of the lady in question?'

"'No.'

"'Had he any special means of ascertaining when that visit did actually take place?'

"'No—but——'

"'What record had he of the visit?'

"Mr. Campbell had none. In fact, after about twenty minutes of cross-examination, he had to admit that he had given but little thought to the interview with the lady at the time, and certainly not in connection with the murder of Lady Donaldson, until he had read in the papers that a young lady had been arrested.

"Then he and his clerk talked the matter over, it appears, and together they had certainly recollected that a lady had brought some beautiful earrings for sale on a day which *must have been* the very morning after the murder. If Sir James Fenwick's object was to discredit this special witness, he certainly gained his point.

"All the pomposity went out of Mr. Campbell; he became flurried, then excited, then he lost his temper. After that he was allowed to leave the court, and Sir James Fenwick resumed his seat, and waited like a vulture for its prey.

"It presented itself in the person of Mr. Campbell's clerk, who, before the Procurator Fiscal, had corroborated his employer's evidence in every respect. In Scotland no witness in any one case is present in court during the examination of another, and Mr. Macfarlane, the clerk, was, therefore, quite unprepared for the pitfalls which Sir James Fenwick had prepared for him. He tumbled into them, head foremost, and the eminent advocate turned him inside out like a glove.

"Mr. Macfarlane did not lose his temper, he was of too humble a frame of mind to do that, but he got into a hopeless quagmire of mixed recollections, and he too left the witness-box quite unprepared to swear as to the day of the interview with the lady with the diamond earrings.

"I dare say, mind you," continued the man in the corner, with a chuckle, "that to most people present, Sir James Fenwick's cross-questioning seemed completely irrelevant. Both Mr. Campbell and his clerk were quite ready to swear that they had had an interview concerning some diamond earrings with a lady, of whose identity with the accused they were perfectly convinced, and to the casual observer the question as to the time or even the day when that interview took place could make but little difference in the ultimate issue.

"Now I took in, in a moment, the entire drift of Sir James Fenwick's defence of Edith Crawford. When Mr. Macfarlane left the witness box, the second victim of the eminent advocate's caustic tongue, I could read as in a book the whole history of that crime, its investigation and the mistakes made by the police first and the public prosecution afterwards.

"Sir James Fenwick knew them, too, of course, and he placed a finger upon each one, demolishing—like a child who blows upon a house of cards—the entire scaffolding erected by the prosecution.

"Mr. Campbell's and Mr. Macfarlane's identification of the accused with the lady who, on some date—admitted to be uncertain—had tried to sell a pair of diamond earrings, was the first point. Sir James had plenty of witnesses to prove that on the 25th, the day after the murder, the accused was in London, whilst, the day before, Mr. Campbell's shop had been closed long before the family circle had seen the last of Lady Donaldson. Clearly the jeweller and his clerk must have seen some other lady, whom their vivid imagination had pictured as being identical with the accused.

"Then came the great question of time. Mr. David Graham had been evidently the last to see Lady Donaldson alive. He had spoken to her as late as 8.30 p.m. Sir James Fenwick had called two porters at the Caledonian Railway Station who testified to Miss Crawford having taken her seat in a first class carriage of the 9.10 train, some minutes before it started.

"'Was it conceivable therefore,' argued Sir James, 'that in the space of half-an-hour the accused—a young girl—could have found her way surreptitiously into the house, at a time when the entire household was still astir, that she should have strangled Lady Donaldson, forced open the safe, and made away with the jewels? A man—an experienced burglar might have done it, but I contend that the accused is physically incapable of accomplishing such a feat.

"'With regard to the broken engagement,' continued the eminent counsel with a smile, 'it may have seemed a little heartless, certainly, but heartlessness is no crime in the eyes of the law. The accused has stated in her declaration that at the time she wrote to Mr. David Graham, breaking off her engagement, she had heard nothing of the Edinburgh tragedy.

"'The London papers had reported the crime very briefly: the accused was busy shopping, she knew nothing of Mr. David Graham's altered position. In no case was the breaking off of the engagement a proof that the accused had obtained possession of the jewels by so foul a deed.'

"It is, of course, impossible for me," continued the man in the corner apologetically, "to give you any idea of the eminent advocate's eloquence and masterful logic. It struck every one, I think, just as it did me, that he chiefly directed his attention to the fact that there was absolutely no *proof* against the accused.

"Be that as it may, the result of that remarkable trial, was a verdict of 'Non Proven.' The jury were absent forty minutes, and it appears that in the mind of all of them there remained, in spite of Sir James' arguments, a firmly rooted conviction—call it instinct, if you like—that Edith Crawford had done away with Lady Donaldson in order to become possessed of those jewels, and that in spite of the pompous jeweller's many contradictions, she had offered him some of those diamonds for sale. But there was not enough proof to convict, and she was given the benefit of the doubt.

"I have heard English people argue that in England she would have been hanged. Personally I doubt that. I think that an English jury—not having the judicial loophole of 'Non Proven' would have been bound to acquit her. What do you think?"

IV.

There was silence between us for a few moments, for I did not reply immediately, and he went on making impossible knots in his bit of string. Then I said:

"I think that I agree with those English people who say that an English jury would have condemned her. . . I have no doubt that she was guilty. She may not have committed that awful deed herself. Someone in the Charlotte Square house may have been her accomplice and killed and robbed Lady Donaldson while Edith Crawford waited outside for the jewels. David Graham left his godmother at 8.30 p.m. If the accomplice was one of the servants in the house, he or she would have had plenty of time for any amount of villainy, and Edith Crawford could have yet caught the 9.10 p.m. train from the Caledonian Station."

"Then who, in your opinion," he asked sarcastically and cocking his funny birdlike head on one side, "tried to sell diamond earrings to Mr. Campbell the jeweller?"

"Edith Crawford, of course," I retorted triumphantly; "he and his clerk both recognised her."

"When did she try to sell them the earrings?"

"Ah! that is what I cannot quite make out, and there to my mind lies the only mystery in this case. On the 25th she was certainly in London, and it is not very likely that she would go back

David Graham.

to Edinburgh in order to dispose of the jewels there, where they could most easily be traced."

"Not very likely, certainly," he assented drily.

"And," I added, "on the day before she left for London, Lady Donaldson was alive."

"And pray," he said suddenly, as with comic complacency he surveyed a beautiful knot, he had just twisted up between his long fingers, "what has that fact got to do with it?"

"But it has everything to do with it!" I retorted.

"Ah! there you go," he sighed with comic emphasis. "My teachings don't seem to have improved your powers of reasoning. You are as bad as the police. Lady Donaldson has been robbed and murdered, and you immediately argue that she was robbed and murdered by the same person."

"But——" I argued.

"There is no but," he said, getting more and more excited. "See how simple it is. Edith Crawford wears the diamonds one night, then she brings them back to Lady Donaldson's room. Remember the maid's statement: 'My lady said: "Have you put them back, my dear?"'—a simple statement, utterly ignored by the prosecution. But what did it mean? That Lady Donaldson could not see for herself whether Edith Crawford had put back the jewels or not, *since she asked the question*."

"Then you argue——"

"I never argue," he interrupted excitedly, "I state undeniable facts. Edith Crawford, who wanted to steal the jewels, took them then and there, when she had the opportunity. Why in the world should she have waited? Lady Donaldson was in bed, and Tremlett, the maid, had gone.

"The next day—namely, the 25th—she tries to dispose of a pair of earrings to Mr. Campbell, she fails, and decides to go to London, where she has a better chance. Sir James Fenwick did not think it desirable to bring forward witnesses to prove what I have since ascertained is a fact, namely, that on the 27th of October, three days before her arrest, Miss Crawford crossed over to Belgium, and came back to London the next day. In Belgium, no doubt, Lady Donaldson's diamonds, taken out of their settings, calmly repose at this moment, while the money derived from their sale is safely deposited in a Belgian bank."

"But then who murdered Lady Donaldson, and why?" I gasped

"It was a daring, brutal murder, remember. Think of one who, not being the thief himself, would, nevertheless, have the strongest of all motives to shield the thief from the consequences of her own misdeed—since it would be absolutely illogical, nay, impossible, that he should be an accomplice."

"Surely——" I gasped.

"Think of a curious nature, warped morally, as well as physically—do you know how those natures feel? A thousand times more strongly than the even, straight natures in everyday life. Then think of such a nature brought face to face with this awful problem.

"Do you think that such a nature would hesitate a moment before committing a crime to save the loved one from the consequences of that deed? Mind you, I don't assert for a moment that David Graham had any *intention* of murdering Lady Donaldson. Tremlett tells him that she seems strangely upset, he goes to her room and finds that she has discovered that she has been robbed. She naturally suspects Edith Crawford, recollects the incidents of the other night, and probably expresses her feelings to David Graham, and threatens immediate prosecution, scandal, what you will, I repeat it again.

"I dare say he had no wish to kill her, probably he merely threatened to. A medical gentleman who spoke of sudden heart failure was no doubt right. hen imagine David Graham's remorse, his horror and his fears. The empty safe probably is the first object that suggested to him the grim tableau of robbery and murder, which he arranges, in order to insure his own safety.

"But remember one thing: no miscreant was seen to enter or leave the house surreptitiously, the murderer left no signs of entrance, and none of exit. An armed burglar would have left some trace—*someone* would have heard *something*. Then who locked and unlocked Lady Donaldson's door that night while she herself lay dead?

"Someone in the house, I tell you—Someone who left no trace—Someone against whom there could be no suspicion—Someone who killed without apparently the slightest premeditation, and without the slightest motive. Think of it. I know I am right, and then tell me if I have at all enlisted your sympathies in the author of the Edinburgh Mystery."

He was gone. I looked again at the photo of David Graham. Did a crooked mind really dwell in that crooked body, and were there in the world such crimes that were great enough to be deemed sublime?

THE DUBLIN MYSTERY.

Being the Sixth of a Series of Stories entitled "The Mysteries of Great Cities."

Illustrated by P. B. Hickling.

By

BARONESS E. ORCZY.

DRAMATIS PERSONÆ.

THE MAN IN THE CORNER *of the A. B. C. shop who tells the story to*
THE LADY JOURNALIST.
PERCIVAL BROOKS.
MURRAY BROOKS (*his younger brother*).
HENRY ORANMORE, K.C. } *Barristers.*
WALTER HIBBERT. }
JOHN O'NEIL (*Butler to the Brooks*).

I.

"I ALWAYS thought that the history of that forged will was about as interesting as any I had read," said the man in the corner that day. He had been silent for some time, and was meditatively sorting and looking through a packet of small photographs in his pocket-book. I guessed that some of these would presently be placed before me for my inspec tion, and I had not long to wait.

"That is old Brooks," he said, pointing to one of the photographs, "Millionaire Brooks as he was called, and these are his two sons, Percival and Murray. It was a curious case, wasn't it? Personally I don't wonder that the police were completely at sea. If a member of that highly estimable force happened to be as clever as the clever author of that forged will, we should have very few undetected crimes in this country."

"That is why I always try to persuade you to give our poor ignorant police the benefit of your great insight and wisdom," I said.

"I know," he said blandly, "you have been most kind in that way, but I am only an amateur. Crime interests me only when it resembles a clever game of chess, with many intricate moves which all tend to one solution, the checkmating of the antagonist—the detective force of the country. Now confess that, in the Dublin mystery, the clever police there were absolutely checkmated."

"Absolutely."

"Just as the public was. There were actually two crimes there which have completely baffled detection. The murder of Patrick Wethered the lawyer, and the forged will of Millionaire Brooks. There are not many millionaires in Ireland; no wonder old Brooks was a notability in his way, since his business—bacon-curing, I believe it is —is said to be worth over £2,000,000 of solid money.

"His younger son Murray was a refined, highly-educated man, and was moreover the apple of his father's eye, as he was the spoilt darling of Dublin society; good looking, a splendid dancer, and a perfect rider, he was the acknowledged 'catch' of the matrimonial market of Ireland, and many a very aristocratic house was opened hospitably to the favourite son of the millionaire.

"Of course Percival Brooks, the eldest son, would inherit the bulk of the old man's property and also probably the larger share in the business; he, too, was good-looking, more so than his brother, he, too, rode, danced, and talked well, but it was many years ago that mammas with marriageable daughters had given up all hopes of Percival

Brooks as a probable son-in-law. That young man's infatuation for Maisie Fortescue, a lady of undoubted charm but very doubtful antecedents, who had astonished the London and Dublin music-halls with her extravagant dances—was too well known and too old-established to encourage any hopes in other quarters.

"Whether Percival Brooks would ever marry Maisie Fortescue was thought to be very doubtful. Old Brooks had the full disposal of all his wealth, and it would have fared ill with Percival if he introduced an undesirable wife into the magnificent Fitzwilliam Place establishment.

"That is how matters stood," continued the man in the corner, "when Dublin society one morning learnt with deep regret and dismay that old Brooks had died very suddenly at his residence after only a few hours' illness. At first it was generally understood that he had had an apoplectic stroke; anyway, he had been at business hale and hearty as ever the day before his death, which occurred late on the evening of December 1st.

"It was the morning papers of December 2nd which told the sad news to their readers, and it was those self-same papers which on that eventful morning contained another, even more startling piece of news, which proved the prelude to a series of sensations, such as tranquil, placid Dublin had not experienced for many years. This was, that on that very afternoon which saw the death of Dublin's greatest millionaire, Mr. Patrick Wethered, his solicitor, was murdered in Phœnix Park at five o'clock in the afternoon, while actually walking to his own house from his visit to his client in Fitzwilliam Place.

"Patrick Wethered was as well known as the proverbial town pump; his mysterious and tragic death filled all Dublin with dismay. The lawyer, who was a man sixty years of age, had been struck on the back of his head by a heavy stick, garrotted, and subsequently robbed, for neither money, watch, or pocket-book were found upon his person, whilst the police soon gathered from Patrick Wethered's household that he had left home at two o'clock that afternoon, carrying both watch and pocket-book, and undoubtedly money as well.

"An inquest was held, and a verdict of wilful murder was found against some person or persons unknown.

"But Dublin had not exhausted its stock of sensations yet. Millionaire Brooks had been buried with due pomp and magnificence and his will had been proved (his business and personalty being estimated at £2,500,000), by Percival Gordon Brooks, his eldest son and sole executor. The younger son, Murray, who had devoted the best years of his life to being a friend and companion to his father, while Percival ran after ballet dancers and music-hall stars—Murray who had avowedly been the apple of his father's eye in consequence—was left with a miserly pittance of £300 a year, and no share whatever in the gigantic business of Brooks & Sons, bacon curers of Dublin.

"Something had evidently happened within the precincts of the Brooks' town mansion, which the public and Dublin society tried in vain to fathom. Elderly mammas and blushing *débutantes* were already thinking of the best means whereby next season they might more easily show the cold shoulder to young Murray Brooks, who had so suddenly become a hopeless 'detrimental' in the marriage market, when all these sensations terminated in one gigantic, overwhelming bit of scandal, which for the next three months furnished food for gossip in every drawing room in Dublin.

"Mr. Murray Brooks, namely, had entered a claim for probate of a will made by his father in 1891, declaring that the later will made the very day of his father's death and proved by his brother as sole executor was null and void, that will being a forgery."

II.

"The facts that transpired in connection with this extraordinary case were sufficiently mysterious to puzzle everybody. As I told you before, all Mr. Brooks' friends never quite grasped the idea that the old man should so completely have cut off his favourite son with the proverbial shilling.

"You see Percival had always been a thorn in the old man's flesh. Horse-racing, gambling, theatres, and music-halls were, in the old pork-butcher's eyes, so many deadly sins which his son committed every day of his life, and all the Fitzwilliam Place household could testify to the many and bitter quarrels which had arisen between father and son over the latter's gambling or racing debts. Many people asserted that Brooks would sooner have left his money to charitable institutions than seen it squandered upon the brightest stars that adorned the music-hall stage.

"The case came up for hearing early in the spring. In the meanwhile Percival Brooks had given up his racecourse associates, settled down in the Fitzwilliam Place mansion and conducted his father's business, without a manager, but with all the energy and forethought which he had previously devoted to more unworthy causes.

"Murray had elected not to stay on in the old house; no doubt associations were of too painful and recent a nature ; he was boarding with the family of a Mr. Wilson Hibbert, who was the late Patrick Wethered's, the murdered lawyer's, partner. They were quiet, homely people, who lived in a very pokey little house in Kilkenny Street, and poor Murray must, in spite of his grief, have felt very bitterly the change from his luxurious quarters in his father's mansion to his present tiny room and homely meals.

"The lawyer . . . had been struck on the back of his head by a heavy stick."

"Percival Brooks, who was now drawing an income of over a hundred thousand a year was very severely criticised for adhering so strictly to the letter of his father's will, and only paying his brother that paltry £300 a year, which was very literally but the crumbs off his own magnificent dinner table.

"The issue of that contested will case was therefore awaited with eager interest. In the meanwhile the police, who had at first seemed fairly loquacious on the subject of the murder of Mr. Patrick Wethered, suddenly became strangely reticent and by their very reticence aroused a certain amount of uneasiness in the public mind, until one day the *Irish Times* published the following extraordinary, enigmatic paragraph.

"'We hear on authority, which cannot be questioned, that certain extraordinary developments are expected in connection with the brutal murder of our distinguished townsman Mr. Wethered ; the police, in fact, are vainly trying to keep it secret that they hold a clue which is as important as it is sensational, and that they only await the impending issue of a well known litigation in the probate court to effect an arrest.'

"The Dublin public flocked to the court to hear the arguments in the great will case. I myself journeyed down to Dublin. As soon as I succeeded in fighting my way to the densely crowded court, I took stock of the various actors in the drama, which I as a spectator was prepared to enjoy. There were Percival Brooks and Murray his brother, the two litigants, both good-looking and well dressed, and both striving, by keeping up a running conversation with their lawyer, to appear unconcerned and confident of the issue. With Percival Brooks was Henry Oranmore, the eminent Irish K.C., whilst Walter Hibbert, a rising young barrister, the son of Wilson Hibbert, appeared for Murray.

"The will of which the latter claimed probate was one dated 1891, and had been made by Mr. Brooks during a severe illness which threatened to end his days. This will had been deposited in the hands of Messrs. Wethered & Hibbert, solicitors to the deceased, and by it Mr. Brooks left his personalty equally divided between his two sons, but had left his business entirely to his youngest son, with a charge of £2000 a year upon it, payable to Percival. You see that Murray Brooks therefore had a very deep interest in that second will being found null and void.

"Old Mr. Hibbert had very ably instructed his son, and Walter Hibbert's opening speech was exceedingly clever. He would show, he said, on behalf of his client, that the will dated December 1st, 1900 could never have been made by the the late Mr. Brooks as it was absolutely contrary to his avowed intentions, and that if the late Mr. Brooks did on the day in question make any fresh will at all, it certainly was *not* the one proved by Mr. Percival Brooks, for that was absolutely a forgery from beginning to end. Mr. Walter Hibbert proposed to call several witnesses in support of both these points.

"On the other hand Mr. Henry Oranmore, K.C., very ably and courteously replied that he too had several witnesses to prove that Mr. Brooks certainly did make a will on the day in question, and that whatever his intentions may have been in the past, he must have modified them on the day of his death, for the will proved by Mr. Percival Brooks was found after his death under his pillow, duly signed and witnessed and in every way legal.

"Then the battle began in sober earnest. It chiefly centred round the prosaic figure of John O'Neill, the butler at Fitzwilliam Place, who had been in Mr. Brooks' family for thirty years.

"'I was clearing away my breakfast things,' said John, 'when I heard the master's voice in the study close by. Oh my, he was that angry! I could hear the words "disgrace," and "villain," and "liar," and "ballet-dancer," and one or two other ugly words as applied to some female lady, which I would not like to repeat. At first I did not take much notice, as I was quite used to hearing my poor dear master having words with Mr. Percival. So I went downstairs carrying my breakfast things; but I had just started cleaning my silver when the study bell goes ringing violently, and I hear Mr. Percival's voice shouting in the hall: "John! quick! Send for Dr. Mulligan at once. Your master is not well! Send one of the men, and you come up and help me to get Mr. Brooks to bed."

"'I sent one of the grooms for the doctor,' continued John, who seemed still affected at the recollection of his poor master, to whom he had evidently been very much attached, 'and I went up to see Mr. Brooks. I found him lying on the study floor, his head supported in Mr. Percival's arms. "My father has fallen in a faint," said the young master; "help me to get him up to his room before Dr. Mulligan comes."

"'Mr. Percival looked very white and upset, which was only natural; and when we had got my poor master to bed, I asked if I should not go and break the news to Mr. Murray, who had gone to business an hour ago. However, before Mr. Percival had time to give me an order, the doctor came. I thought I had seen death plainly writ in my master's face, and when I showed the doctor out an hour later, and he told me that he would be back directly, I knew that the end was near.

"'Mr. Brooks rang for me a minute or two later. He told me to send at once for Mr. Wethered, or else for Mr. Hibbert, if Mr. Wethered could not come. "I haven't many hours to live, John," he says to me—"my heart is broke, the doctor says my heart is broke. A man shouldn't marry and have children, John, for they will sooner or later break his heart." I was so upset I couldn't speak; but I sent round at once for Mr. Wethered, who came himself just about three o'clock that afternoon.

"'After he had been with my master about an hour, I was called in, and Mr. Wethered said to me that Mr. Brooks wished me and one other of us servants to witness that he had signed a paper which was on a table by his bedside. I called Pat Mooney, the head footman, and before us both Mr. Brooks put his name at the bottom of that paper. Then Mr. Wethered give me the pen and told me to write my name as a witness, and that Pat Mooney was to do the same. After that we were both told that we could go.'

"He was present on the following day when the undertakers, who had come to lay his master out, found a paper underneath his pillow. John O'Neill, who recognised the paper as the one to which he had appended his signature the day before, took it to Mr. Percival, and gave it into his hands.

"In answer to Mr. Walter Hibbert, John asserted positively that he took the paper from the undertaker's hand and went straight with it to Mr. Percival's room.

"'He was alone,' said John, 'I gave him the paper. He just glanced at it, and I thought he looked rather astonished, but he said nothing, and I at once left the room.'

"'When you say that you recognised the paper as the one which you had seen your master sign the day before, how did you actually recognise that it was the same paper?' asked Mr. Hibbert amidst breathless interest on the part of the spectators. I narrowly observed the witness's face.

"'It looked exactly the same paper to me, sir,' replied John somewhat vaguely.

"'Did you look at the contents, then?'

"'No, sir; certainly not.'

"'Had you done so the day before?'

"'No, sir, only at my master's signature.'

"'Then you only thought by the *outside* look of the paper that it was the same.'

"'It looked the same thing, sir,' persisted John obstinately.

"You see," continued the man in the corner, leaning eagerly forward across the narrow marble table, "the contention of Murray Brooks' adviser was that Mr. Brooks, having made a will and hidden it—for some reason or other under his pillow—that will had fallen, through the means related by John O'Neill, into the hands of Mr. Percival Brooks, who had destroyed it and substituted a forged one in its place, which adjudged the whole of Mr. Brooks' millions to himself. It was a terrible and very daring accusation directed against a gentleman who, in spite of his many wild oats sowed in early youth, was a prominent and important figure in Irish high-life.

"'I found him lying on the study floor, his head supported in Mr. Percival's arms.'"

"All those present were aghast at what they heard, and the whispered comments I could hear around me showed me that public opinion at least did not uphold Mr. Murray Brooks' daring accusation against his brother.

"But John O'Neill had not finished his evidence, and Mr. Walter Hibbert had a bit of sensation still up his sleeve. He had, namely, produced a paper, the will proved by Mr. Percival Brooks, and had asked John O'Neill if once again he recognised the paper.

"'Certainly, sir,' said John unhesitatingly, 'that is the one the undertaker found under my poor dead master's pillow, and which I took to Mr. Percival's room immediately.'

"Then the paper was unfolded and placed before the witness.

"'Now, Mr. O'Neill, will you tell me if that is your signature?'

"John looked at it for a moment; then he said: 'Excuse me, sir,' and produced pair of spectacles which he carefully adjusted before he again examined the paper. Then he thoughtfully shook his head.

"'It don't look much like my writing, sir,' he said at last. 'That is to say,' he added, by way of elucidating the matter, 'it does look like my writing, but then I don't think it is.'

"There was at that moment a look in Mr. Percival Brooks' face," continued the man in the corner quietly, "which then and there gave me the whole history of that quarrel, that illness of Mr. Brooks, of the will, aye! and of the murder of Patrick Wethered too.

"All I wondered at was how every one of those learned counsel on both sides did not get the clue just the same as I did, but went on arguing, speechifying, cross-examining for nearly a week, until they arrived at the one conclusion which was inevitable from the very first, namely, that the will *was* a forgery—a gross, clumsy, idiotic forgery, since both John O'Neill and Pat Mooney, the two witnesses, absolutely repudiated the signatures as their own. The only successful bit of caligraphy the forger had done was the signature of old Mr. Brooks.

"'It don't look much like my writing, sir,' he said at last. 'That is to say,' he added, ... 'it does look like my writing, but then I don't think it is.'"

"It was a very curious fact, and one which had undoubtedly aided the forger in accomplishing his work quickly, that Mr. Wethered the lawyer having, no doubt, realised that Mr. Brooks had not many moments in life to spare, had not drawn up the usual engrossed, magnificent document dear to the lawyer heart, but had used for his client's will one of those regular printed forms which can be purchased at any stationer's.

"Mr. Percival Brooks, of course, flatly denied the serious allegation brought against him. He admitted that the butler had brought him the document the morning after his father's death, and that he certainly, on glancing at it, had been very much astonished to see that that document was his father's will. Against that he declared that its contents did not astonish him in the slightest degree, that he himself knew of the testator's intentions, but that he certainly thought his father had intrusted the will to the care of Mr. Wethered, who did all his business for him.

"'I only very cursorily glanced at the signature,' he concluded, speaking in a perfectly calm, clear voice, 'you must understand that the thought of forgery was very far from my mind, and that my father's signature is exceedingly well imitated, if, indeed, it is not his own, which I am not at all prepared to believe. As for the two witnesses' signatures, I don't think I had ever seen them before. I took the document to Messrs. Barkston & Maud, who had often done business for me before, and they assured me that the will was in perfect form and order.'

"Asked why he had not intrusted the will to his father's solicitors, he replied:

"'For the very simple reason, that exactly half an hour before the will was placed in my hands, I had read that Mr. Patrick Wethered had been murdered the night before. Mr. Hibbert, the junior partner, was not personally known to me.'

"After that, for form's sake, a good deal of expert evidence was heard on the subject of the dead man's signature. But that was quite unanimous, and merely went to corroborate what had already been established beyond a doubt, namely, that the will dated December 1st, 1900 was a forgery, and probate of the will dated 1891 was therefore granted to Mr. Murray Brooks, the sole executor mentioned therein."

III.

"Two days later the police applied for a warrant for the arrest of Mr. Percival Brooks on a charge of forgery.

"The Crown prosecuted, and Mr. Brooks had again the support of Mr. Oranmore, the eminent K.C. Perfectly calm, like a man conscious of his own innocence and unable to grasp the idea that justice does sometimes miscarry, Mr. Brooks, the son of the millionaire, himself still the possessor of a very large fortune, under the former will, stood up in the dock on that memorable day in May, 1902, which still no doubt lives in the memory of his many friends.

"All the evidence with regard to Mr. Brooks' last moments and the forged will was gone through over again. That will, it was the contention of the Crown, had been forged so entirely in favour of the accused, cutting out everyone else, that obviously no one but the beneficiary under that false will would have had any motive in forging it.

"Very pale, and with a frown between his deep set handsome Irish eyes, Percival Brooks listened to this large volume of evidence piled up against him by the Crown.

"At times he held brief consultations with Mr. Oranmore, who seemed as cool as a cucumber. Have you ever seen Oranmore in court? He is a character worthy of Dickens. His pronounced brogue, his fat, podgy clean-shaven face, his not always immaculately clean large hands, have often delighted the caricaturist. As it very soon transpired during that memorable magisterial inquiry he relied for a verdict in favour of his client upon two main points, and he had concentrated all his skill upon making these two points as telling as he possibly could.

"The first point was the question of time. John O'Neill, cross-examined by Oranmore, stated without hesitation that he had given the will to Mr. Percival at eleven o'clock in the morning. And now the eminent K.C. brought forward and placed in the witness box the very lawyers into whose hands the accused had then immediately placed the will. Now Mr. Barkston, a very well-known solicitor of King Street, declared positively that Mr. Percival Brooks was in his office at a quarter before twelve; two of his clerks testified to the same time exactly, and it was *impossible*, contended Mr. Oranmore, that within three-quarters of an hour Mr. Brooks could have gone to a stationer's, bought a will form, copied Mr. Wethered's writing, his father's signature, and that of John O'Neill and Pat Mooney.

"Such a thing might have been planned, arranged, practised, and ultimately after a great deal of trouble, successfully carried out, but human intelligence could not grasp the other as a possibility.

"Still the judge wavered. The eminent K.C. had shaken but not shattered his belief in the prisoner's guilt. But there was one point more, and this Oranmore, with the skill of a dramatist, had reserved for the fall of the curtain.

"He noted every sign in the judge's face, he guessed that his client was not yet absolutely safe, then only did he produce his last two witnesses.

"One of them was Mary Sullivan, one of the housemaids in the Fitzwilliam Mansion. She had been sent up by the cook at a quarter past four o'clock on the afternoon of December 1st with some hot water, which the nurse had ordered for the master's room. Just as she was about to knock at the door, Mr. Wethered was coming out of the room. Mary stopped with the tray in her hand, and at the door Mr. Wethered turned and said quite loud; 'Now, don't fret, don't be anxious; do try and be calm. Your will is safe in my pocket, nothing can change it, or alter one word of it but yourself.'

"It was of course a very ticklish point in law whether the housemaid's evidence could be accepted. You see she was quoting the words of a man since dead, spoken to another man also dead. There is no doubt that had there been very strong evidence on the other side against Percival Brooks, Mary Sullivan's would have counted for nothing, but as I told you before the judge's belief in the prisoner's guilt was already very seriously shaken, and now the final blow aimed at it by Mr. Oranmore shattered his last lingering doubts.

"Dr. Mulligan, namely, had been placed by Mr. Oranmore into the witness box. He was a medical man of unimpeachable authority, in fact absolutely at the head of his profession in Dublin. What he said practically corroborated Mary Sullivan's testimony. He had gone in to see Mr. Brooks at half-past

"Just as she was about to knock at the door, Mr. Wethered was coming out of the room."

four, and understood from him that his lawyer had just left him.

"Mr. Brooks certainly, though terribly weak, was calm and more composed. He was dying from a sudden heart attack, and Dr. Mulligan foresaw the almost immediate end. But he was still conscious and managed to murmur feebly, 'I feel much easier in my mind now, doctor—I have made my will—Wethered has been—he's got it in his pocket—it is safe there—safe from that ——' but the words died on his lips, and after that he spoke but little. He saw his two sons before he died, but hardly knew them or even looked at them."

IV.

"You see," concluded the man in the corner, "you see that the prosecution was bound to collapse. Oranmore did not give it a leg to stand upon. The will was forged, it is true, forged in the favour of Percival Brooks and of no one else, forged for him and for his benefit. Whether he knew and connived at the forgery, was never proved or, as far as I know, even hinted, but it was impossible to go against all the evidence, which pointed that, as far as the act itself was concerned, he at least was most innocent. You see Dr. Mulligan's evidence was not to be shaken. Mary Sullivan's was equally strong.

"There were two witnesses swearing positively that old Brooks' will was in Mr. Wethered's keeping when that gentleman left Fitzwilliam Mansion at a quarter-past-four. At five o'clock in the afternoon, the lawyer was found dead in Phœnix Park. Between a quarter-past-four and eight o'clock in the evening Percival Brooks never left the house,—that was subsequently proved by Oranmore beyond a doubt. Since the will found under old Brooks' pillow was a forged will, where then was the will he did make, and which Wethered carried away with him in his pocket?"

"Stolen, of course," I said, "by those who murdered and robbed him; it may have been of no value to them, but they naturally would destroy it, lest it might prove a clue against them."

"Then you think it was mere coincidence?" he asked excitedly.

"What?"

"That Wethered was murdered and robbed at the very moment that he carried the will in his pocket, whilst another was being forged in its place?"

"It certainly would be very curious, if it *were* a coincidence," I said musingly.

"Very," he repeated with biting sarcasm, whilst nervously his bony fingers played with the inevitable bit of string. "Very curious indeed. Just think of the whole thing. There was the old man with all his wealth, and two sons, one to whom he is devoted, and the other with whom he does nothing but quarrel. One day there is another of these quarrels, but more violent, more terrible than any that have previously occurred, with the result that the father, heart-broken by it all, has an attack of the heart—practically dies of a broken heart. After that he alters his will, and subsequently a will is proved which turns out to be a forgery.

"Now everybody, police, press, and public alike, at once jump to the conclusion that, as Percival Brooks benefits by that forged will, Percival Brooks must be the forger."

"Seek for him whom the crime benefits, is your own axiom," I argued.

"I beg your pardon?"

"Percival Brooks benefited to the tune of £2,000,000."

"I beg your pardon. He did nothing of the sort. He was left with less than half the share that his younger brother inherited."

"Now, yes; but that was a former will and——"

"And that forged will was so clumsily executed, the signature so carelessly imitated, that the forgery was bound to come to light. Did *that* never strike you?"

"Yes, but——"

"There is no but." he interrupted. "It was all as clear as daylight to me, from the very first. The quarrel with the old man, which broke his heart was not with his eldest son, with whom he was used to quarrelling, but with the second son whom he idolised, in whom he believed. Don't you remember how John O'Neill heard the words 'liar' and 'deceit'? Percival Brooks had never deceived his father. His sins were all on the surface. Murray had led a quiet life, had pandered to his father, and fawned upon him, until, like most hypocrites, he at last got found out. Who knows what ugly gambling debt or debt of honour, suddenly revealed to old Brooks, was the cause of that last and deadly quarrel?

"You remember that it was Percival who remained beside his father and carried him up to his room. Where was Murray throughout that long and painful day, when his father lay dying—he, the idolised son, the apple of the old man's eye? You never hear his name mentioned as being present there all that day. But he knew that he had offended his father mortally, and that his father meant to cut him off with a shilling. He knew that Mr. Wethered had been sent for, that Wethered left the house soon after four o'clock.

"And here the cleverness of the man comes in. Having lain in wait for Wethered and knocked him on the back of the head with a stick, he could not very well make that will disappear altogether. There remained the faint chance of some other witnesses knowing that Mr. Brooks had made a fresh will, Mr. Wethered's partner, his clerk, or one of the confidential servants in the house. Therefore *a* will must be discovered after the old man's death.

"Now Murray Brooks was not an expert forger, it takes years of training to become that. A forged will executed by himself would be sure to be found out—yes, that's it, sure to be found out. The forgery will be palpable—let it be palpable, and then it will be found out, branded as such, and the original will of 1891, so favourable to the young blackguard's interests, will be held as valid. Was it devilry or merely additional caution which prompted Murray to pen that forged will so glaringly in Percival's favour? It is impossible to say.

"Anyhow, it was the cleverest touch in that marvellously-devised crime. To plan that evil deed was great, to execute it was easy enough. He had several hours' leisure in which to do it. Then at night it was simplicity itself to slip the document under the dead man's pillow. Sacrilege causes no shudder to such natures as Murray Brooks. The rest of the drama you know already—"

"But Percival Brooks?"

"The jury returned a verdict of 'Not guilty.' There was no evidence against him."

"But the money? Surely the scoundrel does not have the enjoyment of it still?"

"No; he enjoyed it for a time, but he died about three months ago, and forgot to take the precaution of making a will, so his brother Percival has got the business after all. If you ever go to Dublin I should order some of Brooks' bacon if I were you. It is very good."

THE BIRMINGHAM MYSTERY.

Being the Seventh of a Series of Stories entitled "The Mysteries of Great Cities."

Illustrated by P. B. Hickling.

BY BARONESS E. ORCZY.

DRAMATIS PERSONÆ.

THE MAN IN THE CORNER *who tells the story to the*
LADY JOURNALIST.
THE EARL OF BROCKELSBY.
THE HON. ROBERT INGRAM DE GENNEVILLE *(his brother).*
TIMOTHY BEDDINGFIELD *(lawyer).*
CORONER.
PETER TYRREL *(night porter).*
MR. TREMLETT *(cashier at the Castle Hotel, Birmingham).*

I.

THE man in the corner rubbed his chin thoughtfully, and looked out upon the busy street below.

"I suppose," he said, "there is some truth in the saying that Providence watches over bankrupts, kittens, and lawyers."

"I didn't know there was such a saying," I replied, with guarded dignity.

"Isn't there? Perhaps I am misquoting; anyway, there should be. Kittens, it seems, live and thrive through social and domestic upheavals which would annihilate a self-supporting tom-cat, and to-day I read in the morning papers the account of a noble lord's bankruptcy, and in the society ones that of his visit at the house of a Cabinet minister, where he is the most honoured guest. As for lawyers, when Providence had exhausted all other means of securing their welfare, it brought forth the peerage cases."

"I believe, as a matter of fact, that this special dispensation of Providence, as you call it, requires more technical knowledge than any other legal complication that comes before the law courts," I said.

"And also a great deal more money in the client's pocket than any other complication. Now, take the Brockelsby peerage case. Have you any idea how much money was spent over that soap bubble, which only burst after many hundreds, if not thousands, of pounds went in lawyers' and counsels' fees?"

"I suppose a great deal of money was spent on both sides," I said, "until that sudden, awful issue——"

"Which settled the dispute effectually," he interrupted with a dry chuckle. "Of course, it is very doubtful if any reputable solicitor would have taken up the case. Timothy Beddingfield, the Birmingham lawyer, is a gentleman, who—well—has had some misfortunes, shall we say? He is still on the Rolls, mind you, but I doubt if any case would have its chances improved by his conducting it. Against that there is just this to be said, that some of these old peerages have such peculiar histories, and own such wonderful archives, that a claim is always worth investigating—you never know what may be the rights of it.

"I believe that—at first—everyone laughed over the pretensions of the Hon. Robert Ingram De Genneville to the joint title and part revenues of the old barony of Genneville, but, obviously, he *might* have got his case. It certainly sounded almost like a fairy tale, this claim based upon the supposed validity of an ancient document over 400 years old. It was *then* that a mediæval Lord De Genneville, more endowed with muscle than common sense, became during his turbulent existence much embarrassed and hopelessly puzzled through the presentation made to him by his lady of twin-born sons.

"His embarrassment chiefly arose from the fact that my lady's attendants, while ministering to the comforts of the mother, had, in a moment of absent-mindedness, so placed the two infants in their cot that subsequently no one, not even—perhaps least of all—the mother, could tell which was the one who had been the first to make his appearance into this troublesome and puzzling world.

"After many years of cogitation, during which the Lord De Genneville approached nearer to the grave and his sons to man's estate, he gave up trying to solve the riddle as to which of the twins should succeed to his title and revenues; he appealed to his liege lord and King Edward, fourth of that name, and with the latter's august sanction he drew up a certain document wherein he enacted that both his sons should, after his death, share his titles and goodly revenues, and that the first son born in wedlock of *either* father should subsequently be the sole heir.

"In this document was also added that if in future times should any Lords de Genneville be similarly afflicted with twin sons, who had equal rights to be considered the eldest born, the same rule should apply as to the succession.

"Subsequently a Lord De Genneville was created Earl of Brockelsby by one of the Stuart kings, but for four hundred years after its enactment the extraordinary deed of succession remained a mere tradition, the Countesses of Brockelsby having, seemingly, no predilection for twins. But in 1878 the mistress of Brockelsby Castle presented her lord with twin-born sons.

"Fortunately, in modern times, science is more wide-awake, and attendants more careful. The twin brothers did not get mixed up, and one of them was styled Viscount Tirlemont, and was heir to the earldom, whilst the other, born two hours later, was that fascinating, dashing young Guardsman, well known at Hurlingham, Goodwood, London, and in his own county—the Hon. Robert Ingram De Genneville.

"It certainly was an evil day for this brilliant young scion of the ancient race when he lent an ear to Timothy Beddingfield. This man, and his family before him, had been solicitors to the Earls of Brockelsby for many generations, but Timothy, owing to certain 'irregularities,' had forfeited the confidence of his client, the late earl.

"He was still in practice in Birmingham, however, and, of course, knew the ancient family tradition anent the twin succession. Whether he was prompted by revenge or merely self-advertisement no one knows.

"Certain it is that he did advise the Hon. Robert De Genneville—who apparently had more debts than he conveniently could pay, and more extravagant tastes than he could gratify on a younger son's portion—to lay a claim on his father's death to the joint title and a moiety of the revenues of the ancient barony of Genneville, that claim being based upon the validity of the fifteenth century document.

"You may gather how extensive were the pretensions of the Hon. Robert from the fact that the greater part of Edgbaston is now built upon land belonging to the old barony. Anyway, it was the last straw in an ocean of debt and difficulties, and I have no doubt that Beddingfield had not much trouble in persuading the Hon. Robert to commence litigation at once.

"The young Earl of Brockelsby's attitude, however, remained one of absolute quietude in his nine points of the law. He was in possession both of the title and of the document. It was for the other side to force him to produce the one or to share the other.

"It was at this stage of the proceedings that the Hon. Robert was advised to marry, in order to secure, if possible, the first male heir of the next generation, since the young earl himself was still a bachelor. A suitable *fiancée* was found for him by his friends in the person of Miss Mabel Brandon, the daughter of a rich Birmingham manufacturer, and the marriage was fixed to take place at Birmingham on Thursday, September 15th.

"On the 13th, the Hon. Robert Ingram De Genneville arrived at the Castle Hotel in New Street for his wedding, and on the 14th, at eight o'clock in the morning, he was discovered lying on the floor of his bedroom—murdered.

"The sensation which the awful and unexpected sequel to the De Genneville peerage case caused in the minds of the friends of both litigants was quite unparalleled. I don't think any crime of modern times created quite so much stir in all classes of society. Birmingham was wild with excitement, and the employees of the

Castle Hotel had real difficulty in keeping off the eager and inquisitive crowd who thronged daily to the hall, vainly hoping to gather details of news relating to the terrible tragedy.

"At present there was but little to tell. The shrieks of the chambermaid, who had gone into the Hon. Robert's room with his shaving water at eight o'clock, had attracted some of the waiters. Soon the manager and his secretary came up and immediately sent for the police.

"It seemed at first sight as if the young man had been the victim of a homicidal maniac, so brutal had been the way in which he had been assassinated. The head and body were battered and bruised by some heavy stick or poker, almost past human shape, as if the murderer had wished to wreak some awful vengeance upon the body of his victim. In fact, it would be impossible to recount the gruesome aspect of that room and of the murdered man's body such as the police and the medical officer took notes of that day.

"It was supposed that the murder had been committed the evening before, as the victim was dressed in his evening clothes, and all the lights in the room had been left fully turned on. Robbery, also, must have had a large share in the miscreant's motives, for the drawers and cupboards, the portmanteau and dressing bag had been ransacked as if in search of valuables. On the floor there lay a pocket-book torn in half and only containing a few letters addressed to the Hon. Robert De Genneville.

"The Earl of Brockelsby, next of kin to the deceased, was also telegraphed for. He drove over from Brockelsby Castle, which is about seven miles from Birmingham. He was terribly affected by the awfulness of the tragedy and offered a liberal reward to stimulate the activity of the police in search of the miscreant.

"The inquest was fixed for the 17th, three days later, and the public was left wondering where the solution lay of the terrible and gruesome murder at the Castle Hotel."

II.

"THE central figure in the coroner's court that day was undoubtedly the Earl of Brockelsby in deep black, which contrasted strongly with his florid complexion and fair hair. Sir Marmaduke Ingersoll, his solicitor, was with him, and he had already performed the

The shrieks of the chambermaid . . . . had attracted some of the waiters.

painful duty of identifying the deceased as his brother. This had been an exceedingly painful duty owing to the terribly mutilated state of the body and face; but the clothes and various trinkets he wore, including a signet ring, had fortunately not tempted the brutal assassin, and it was through them chiefly that Lord Brockelsby was able to swear to the identity of his brother.

"The various employees at the hotel gave evidence as to the discovery of the body, and the medical officer gave his opinion as to the immediate cause of death. Deceased had evidently been struck at the back of the head with a poker or heavy stick, the murderer then venting his blind fury upon the body by battering in the face and bruising it in a way that certainly suggested the work of a maniac.

"Then the Earl of Brockelsby was called, and was requested by the coroner to state when he had last seen his brother alive.

"'The morning before his death,' replied his lordship, 'he came up to Birmingham by an early train, and I drove up from Brockelsby to see him. I got to the hotel at eleven o'clock and stayed with him for about an hour.'

"'And that is the last you saw of the deceased?'

"'That is the last I saw of him,' replied Lord Brockelsby.

"He seemed to hesitate for a moment or two as if in thought whether he should speak or not, and then to suddenly make up his mind to speak, for he added, 'I stayed in town the whole of that day, and only drove back to Brockelsby late in the evening. I had some business to transact, and put up at the Grand, as I usually do, and dined with some friends.'

"'Would you tell us at what time you returned to Brockelsby Castle?'

"'I think it must have been about eleven o'clock. It is a seven mile drive from here.'

"'I believe,' said the coroner after a slight pause, during which the attention of all the spectators was rivetted upon the handsome figure of the young man as he stood in the witness-box, the very personification of a high-bred gentleman, 'I believe that I am right in stating that there was an unfortunate legal dispute between your lordship and your brother?'

"'That is so.'

"The coroner stroked his chin thoughtfully for a moment or two, then he added:

"'In the event of the deceased's claim to the joint title and revenues of De Genneville being held good in the courts of law, there would be a great importance, would there not, attached to his marriage which was to have taken place on the 15th?'

"'In that event, there certainly would be.'

"'Is the jury to understand, then, that you and the deceased parted on amicable terms after your interview wi h him in the morning.'

"The Earl of Brockelsby hesitated again for a minute or two, while the crowd and the jury hung breathless upon his lips.

"'There was no enmity between us,' he replied at last.

"'From which we may gather that there may have been—shall I say? a slight disagreement at that interview?'

"'My brother had unfortunately been misled by the misrepresentations or perhaps the too optimistic views of his lawyer. He had been dragged into litigation on the strength of an old family document which he had never seen, which moreover is antiquated, and, owing to certain wording in it, invalid. I thought that it would be kinder and more considerate if I were to let my brother judge of the document for himself. I knew that when he had seen it, he would be convinced of the absolutely futile basis of his claim, and that it would be a terrible disappointment to him. That is the reason why I wished to see him myself about it, rather than to do it through the more formal—perhaps more correct—medium of our respective lawyers. I placed the facts before him, with, on my part, a perfectly amicable spirit.'

"The young Earl of Brockelsby had made this somewhat lengthy perfectly voluntary explanation of the state of affairs, in a calm, quiet voice, with much dignity and perfect simplicity, but the coroner did not seem impressed by it, for he asked very drily:

"'Did you part good friends?'

"'On my side absolutely so.'

"'But not on his?' insisted the coroner.

"'I think he felt naturally annoyed that he had been so ill-advised by his solicitors.'

"'And you made no attempt later on in the day to adjust any ill-feeling that may have existed between you and him?' asked the coroner, marking with strange, earnest emphasis every word he uttered.

"'If you mean did I go and see my brother again that day—no, I did not.'

"'And your lordship can give us no further information which might throw some light upon the mystery which surrounds the Hon. Robert De Genneville's death?' still persisted the coroner.

"'I am sorry to say I cannot,' replied the Earl of Brockelsby with firm decision.

"The coroner still looked puzzled and thoughtful. It seemed at first as if he wished to press his point further; every one felt that some deep import had lain behind his examination of the witness, and all were on tenterhooks as to what the next evidence might bring forth. The Earl of Brockelsby had waited a minute or two, then at a sign from the coroner had left the witness box in order to have a talk with his solicitor.

"At first he paid no attention to the depositions of the cashier and hall porter of the Castle Hotel, but gradually it seemed to strike him that curious statements were being made by these witnesses, and a frown of anxious wonder settled between his brows, whilst his young face lost some of its florid hue.

"Mr. Tremlett, the cashier at the hotel, had been holding the attention of the court. He stated that the Hon. Robert Ingram De Genneville had arrived at the hotel at eight o'clock on the morning of the 13th; he had the room which he usually occupied when he came to the 'Castle,' namely, No. 21, and he went up to it immediately on his arrival, ordering some breakfast to be brought up to him.

"At eleven o'clock the Earl of Brockelsby called to see his brother and remained with him until about twelve. In the afternoon deceased went out, and returned for his dinner at seven o'clock in company with a gentleman whom the cashier knew well by sight, Mr. Timothy Beddingfield, the lawyer of Paradise Street. The gentlemen had their dinner downstairs, and after that they went up to the Hon. Mr. De Genneville's room for coffee and cigars.

"'I could not say at what time Mr. Beddingfield left,' continued the cashier, 'but I rather fancy I saw him in the hall at about 9.15 p.m. He was wearing an Inverness cape over his dress clothes and a Glengarry cap. It was just at the hour when the visitors who had come down for the night from London were arriving thick and fast; the hall was very full, and there was a large party of Americans monopolising most of our *personnel*, so I could not swear positively whether I did see Mr. Beddingfield or not then, though I am quite sure that it was Mr. Timothy Beddingfield who dined and spent the evening with the Hon. Mr. De Genneville, as I know him quite well by sight. At ten o'clock I am off duty, and the night porter remains alone in the hall.'

"Mr. Tremlett's evidence was corroborated in most respects by a waiter and by the hall porter. They had both seen the deceased come in at seven o'clock in company with a gentleman, and their description of the latter coincided with that of the appearance of Mr. Timothy Beddingfield, whom, however, they did not actually know.

"At this point of the proceedings the foreman of the jury wished to know why Mr. Timothy Beddingfield's evidence had not been obtained, and was informed by the detective-inspector in charge of the case that that gentleman had seemingly left Birmingham, but was expected home shortly. The coroner suggested an adjournment pending Mr. Beddingfield's appearance, but at the earnest request of the detective he consented to hear the evidence of Peter Tyrrell, the night porter at the Castle Hotel, who, if you remember the case at all, succeeded in creating the biggest sensation of any which had been made through this extraordinary and weirdly gruesome case.

"'It was the first time I had been on duty at "The Castle," he said, 'for I used to be night porter at "Bright's," in Wolverhampton, but just after I had come on duty at ten o'clock, a gentleman came and asked if he could see the Hon. Robert De Genneville. I said that I thought he was in, but would send up and see. The gentleman said: "It doesn't matter. Don't trouble; I know his room. Twenty-one, isn't it?" And up he went before I could say another word.'

"'Did he give you any name?' asked the coroner.

"'No, sir,'

"'What was he like?'

"'A young gentleman, sir, as far as I can remember, in an Inverness cape and Glengarry cap, but I could not see his face very well as he stood with his back to the light, and the cap shaded his eyes, and he only spoke to me for a minute.'

"'Look all round you,' said the coroner quietly, 'is there anyone in this court at all like the gentleman you speak of?'

"An awed hush fell over the many spectators there present as Peter Tyrrell, the night porter of the Castle Hotel, turned his head towards the body of the court and slowly scanned the many faces there present; for a moment he seemed to hesitate—only for a moment though, then as if vaguely conscious of the terrible importance his next words might have, he shook his head gravely and said:

"'I wouldn't like to swear.'

"The coroner tried to press him, but with

"I wouldn't like to swear."

true British stolidity he repeated : 'I wouldn't like to say.'

"'Well, then, what happened?' asked the coroner, who had perforce to abandon his point.

"'The gentleman went upstairs, sir, and about a quarter of an hour later he come down again, and I let him out. He was in a great hurry then, he threw me a half-crown, and said: "Good-night."'

"'And though you saw him again then, you cannot tell us if you would know him again?'

"Once more the hall porter's eyes wandered as if instinctively to a certain face in the court; once more he hesitated for many seconds which seemed like so many hours during which a man's honour, a man's life, hung perhaps in the balance.

"Then Peter Tyrrell repeated slowly: 'I wouldn't swear.'

"But coroner and jury alike, aye and every spectator in that crowded court had seen that the man's eyes had rested during that one moment of hesitation upon the face of the Earl of Brockelsby."

III.

THE man in the corner blinked at me with his funny mild blue eyes.

"No wonder you are puzzled," he continued, "so was everybody in the court that day, everyone save myself. I alone could see in my mind's eye that gruesome murder such as it had been committed, with all its details, and, above all, its motive, and such as you will see it presently, when I place it all clearly before you.

"But before you see daylight in this strange case, I must plunge you into further darkness, in the same manner as the coroner and jury were plunged on the following day, the second day of that remarkable inquest. It had to be adjourned, since the appearance of Mr. Timothy Beddingfield had now become of vital importance. The public had come to regard his absence from Birmingham at this critical moment as decidedly remarkable, to say the least of it, and all those who did not know the lawyer by sight, wished to see him in his Inverness cape and Glengarry cap such as he had appeared before the several witnesses on the night of the awful murder

"When the coroner and jury were seated, the first piece of information which the police placed before them was the astounding statement that Mr. Timothy Beddingfield's whereabouts had not been ascertained, though it was confidently expected that he had not gone far and could easily be traced. There was a witness present who, the police thought, might throw some light as to the lawyer's probable destination, for obviously he had left Birmingham directly after his interview with the deceased.

"This witness was Mrs. Higgins, who was Mr. Beddingfield's housekeeper. She stated that her master was in the constant habit—especially latterly—of going up to London on business. He usually left by a late evening train on those occasions, and mostly was only absent thirty-six hours. He kept a portmanteau always ready packed for the purpose, for he often left at a few moments' notice. Mrs. Higgins added that her master stayed at the Great Western Hotel in

London, for it was there that she was instructed to wire, if anything urgent required his presence back in Birmingham.

"'On the night of the 14th,' she continued, 'at nine o'clock or thereabouts, a messenger came to the door with the master's card, and said that he was instructed to fetch Mr. Beddingfield's portmanteau, and then to meet him at the station in time to catch the 9.35 p.m. up train. I gave him the portmanteau, of course, as he had brought the card, and I had no idea there could be anything wrong; but since then I have heard nothing of my master, and I don't know when he will return.'

"Questioned by the coroner, she added that Mr. Beddingfield had never stayed away quite so long, without having his letters forwarded to him. There was a large pile waiting for him now; she had written to the Great Western Hotel, London, asking what she should do about the letters, but had received no reply. She did not know the messenger by sight who had called for the portmanteau. Once or twice before, Mr. Beddingfield had sent for his things in that manner when he had been dining out.

"Mr. Beddingfield certainly wore his Inverness cape over his dress clothes when he went out at about six o'clock in the afternoon. He also wore a Glengarry cap.

"The messenger had so far not yet been found, and from this point—namely, the sending for the portmanteau—all traces of Mr. Timothy Beddingfield seem to have been lost. Whether he went up to London by that 9.35 train or not could not be definitely ascertained. The police had questioned at least a dozen porters at the railway, as well as ticket-collectors; but no one had any special recollection of a gentleman in an Inverness cape and Glengarry cap, a costume worn by more than one first-class passenger on a cold night in September.

"There was the hitch, you see; it all lay in this. Mr. Timothy Beddingfield, the lawyer, had undoubtedly made himself scarce. He was last seen in company with the deceased, and wearing an Inverness cape and Glengarry cap; two or three witnesses saw him leaving the hotel at about 9.15. Then the messenger calls at the lawyer's house for the portmanteau, after which Mr. Timothy Beddingfield seems to vanish into thin air; but—and that is a great 'but'—the night porter at the 'Castle' seems to have seen someone wearing the momentous Inverness and Glengarry half-an-hour or so later on, and going up to deceased's room, where he stayed about a quarter of an hour.

"Undoubtedly you will say, as everyone said to themselves that day after the night porter and Mrs. Higgins had been heard, that there was a very ugly and very black finger which pointed unpleasantly at Mr. Timothy Beddingfield, especially as that gentleman, for some reason which still required an explanation, was not there to put matters right for himself. But there was just one little thing—a mere trifle, perhaps—which neither the coroner nor the jury dared to overlook, though strictly speaking it was not evidence.

"You will remember that when the night porter was asked if he could, among the persons present in court, recognise the Hon. Robert De Genneville's belated visitor, everyone had noticed his hesitation, and marked that the man's eyes had rested doubtingly upon the face and figure of the young Earl of Brockelsby.

"Now, if that belated visitor had been Mr. Timothy Beddingfield—tall, lean, dry as dust, with a bird-like beak and clean-shaven chin—no one could for a moment have mistaken his face—even if they only saw it very casually and recollected it but very dimly—with that of young Lord Brockelsby, who was florid and rather short—the only point in common between them was their Saxon hair.

"You see that it was a curious point, don't you?" added the man in the corner, who now had become so excited that his fingers worked like long thin tentacles round and round his bit of string. "It weighed very heavily in favour of Timothy Beddingfield. Added to which you must also remember that as far as he was concerned, the Hon. Robert De Genneville was to him the goose with the golden eggs.

"The 'De Genneville peerage case' had brought Beddingfield's name in great prominence. With the death of the claimant all hopes of prolonging the litigation came to an end. There was a total lack of motive as far as Beddingfield was concerned."

"Not so with the Earl of Brockelsby," I said, "and I've often maintained—"

"What?" he interrupted. "That the Earl of Brockelsby changed clothes with Beddingfield in order more conveniently to murder his own brother? Where and when could the exchange of costume have been effected, considering that the Inverness cape and Glengarry cap were in the hall of the Castle Hotel at 9.15, and at that hour and until ten o'clock Lord Brockelsby was at the Grand Hotel finishing dinner with some friends.

That was subsequently proved, remember, and also that he was back at Brockelsby Castle, which is seven miles from Birmingham, at eleven o'clock sharp. Now, the visit of the individual in the Glengarry occurred some time after 10 p.m."

"Then there was the disappearance of Beddingfield," I said musingly. "That certainly points very strongly to him. He was a man in good practice, I believe, and fairly well-known."

"And yet see how simple it is!" cried my friend. "Only the police would not look further than these two men—Lord Brockelsby with a strong motive and the night-porter's hesitation against him, and Beddingfield without a motive, but with strong circumstantial evidence and his own disappearance as condemnatory signs.

"If only they would look at the case as I did and think a little about the dead as well as about the living. If they had remembered that peerage case, the Hon. Robert's debts, his last straw which proved a futile claim.

"Only that very day the Earl of Brockelsby had, by quietly showing the original ancient document to his brother, persuaded him how futile were all his hopes. Who knows how many were the debts contracted, the promises made, the money borrowed and obtained on the strength of that claim which was mere romance? Ahead nothing but ruin, enmity with his brother, his marriage probably broken off, a wasted life, in fact.

"Is it small wonder that, though ill-feeling against the Earl of Brockelsby may have been deep, there was hatred, bitter deadly hatred against the man who with false promises had led him into so hopeless a quagmire? Probably the Hon. Robert owed a great deal of money to Beddingfield, which the latter hoped to recoup at usurious interest, with threats of scandal and what not.

"Think of all that," he added, "and then tell me if you believe that a stronger motive for the murder of such an enemy could well be found."

He slips out unrecognised.

"But what you suggest is impossible," I said aghast.

"Allow me," he said, "it is more than possible—it is very easy and simple. The two men were alone together in the Hon. Robert De Genneville's room after dinner. You, as representing the public, and the police say that Beddingfield went away and returned half an hour later in order to kill his client. I say that it was the lawyer who was murdered at nine o'clock that evening, and that Robert De Genneville, the ruined man, the hopeless bankrupt, was the assassin."

"Then——"

"Yes, of course, now you remember, for I have put you on the track. The face and the body were so battered and bruised that they were past recognition. Both men were of equal height. The hair which alone could not be disfigured or obliterated was in both men similar in colour.

"Then the murderer proceeds to dress his victim in his own clothes. With the utmost care he places his own rings on the fingers of the dead man, his own watch in the pocket; a gruesome task, but an important one, and it is thoroughly well done. Then he himself puts on the clothes of his victim, with finally the Inverness cape and Glengarry, and when the hall is full of visitors he slips out unperceived. He sends the messenger for Beddingfield's portmanteau and starts off by the night express."

"But then his visit at the Castle Hotel at ten o'clock—" I urged. "How dangerous!"

"Dangerous? Yes! but oh, how clever. You see he was the Earl of Brockelsby's twin brother, and twin brothers are always somewhat alike. He wished to appear dead, murdered by someone, he cared not whom, but what he did care about was to throw clouds of dust in the eyes of the police, and he succeeded with a vengeance. Perhaps, who knows? he wished to assure himself that he had forgotten nothing in the *mise-en-scène*, that the body, battered and bruised past all semblance of any human shape save for its clothes, really would appear to everyone as that of the Hon. Robert De Genneville, while the latter disappeared for ever from the old world and started life again in the new.

"Then you must always reckon with the practically invariable rule that a murderer always revisits, if only once, the scene of his crime.

"Two years have elapsed since the crime; no trace of Timothy Beddingfield, the lawyer, has ever been found, and I can assure you that it will never be, for his plebeian body lies buried in the aristocratic family vault of the Earls of Brockelsby."

He was gone before I could say another word. The faces of Timothy Beddingfield, of the Earl of Brockelsby, of the Hon. Robert De Genneville seemed to dance before my eyes and to mock me for the hopeless bewilderment in which I found myself plunged because of them; then all the faces vanished, or, rather, were merged in one long, thin, birdlike one, with bone-rimmed spectacles on the top of its beak, and a wide, rude grin beneath it, and, still puzzled, still doubtful, I too paid for my scanty luncheon and went my way.

XI

The Sorceress of the Strand

L.T. MEADE & ROBERT EUSTACE

The Sorceress of the Strand.

BY L. T. MEADE AND ROBERT EUSTACE.

STORY I.—MADAME SARA.

EVERYONE in trade and a good many who are not have heard of Werner's Agency, the Solvency Inquiry Agency of all British trade. Its business is to know the financial condition of all wholesale and retail firms, from Rothschild's to the smallest sweetstuff shop in Whitechapel. I do not say that every firm figures on its books, but by methods of secret inquiry it can discover the status of any firm or individual. It is the great safeguard to British trade and prevents much fraudulent dealing.

Of this agency I, Dixon Druce, was appointed manager in 1890. Since then I have met queer people and seen strange sights, for men do curious things for money in this world.

It so happened that in June, 1899, my business took me to Madeira on an inquiry of some importance. I left the island on the 14th of the month by the *Norham Castle* for Southampton. I got on board after dinner. It was a lovely night, and the strains of the band in the public gardens of Funchal came floating across the star-powdered bay through the warm, balmy air. Then the engine bells rang to "Full speed ahead," and, flinging a farewell to the fairest island on earth, I turned to the smoking-room in order to light my cheroot.

"DO YOU WANT A MATCH, SIR?

"Do you want a match, sir?"

The voice came from a slender, young-looking man who stood near the taffrail. Before I could reply he had struck one and held it out to me.

"Excuse me," he said, as he tossed it overboard, "but surely I am addressing Mr. Dixon Druce?"

"You are, sir," I said, glancing keenly back at him, "but you have the advantage of me."

"Don't you know me?" he responded. "Jack Selby, Hayward's House, Harrow, 1879."

"By Jove! so it is," I cried.

Our hands met in a warm clasp, and a moment later I found myself sitting close to my old friend, who had fagged for me in the bygone days, and whom I had not seen from the moment when I said good-bye to the "Hill" in the grey mist of a December morning twenty years ago. He was a boy of fourteen then, but nevertheless I recognised him. His face was bronzed and good-looking, his features refined. As a boy Selby had been noted for his grace, his well-shaped head, his clean-cut features; these characteristics still were his, and although he was now slightly past his first youth he was decidedly handsome. He gave me a quick sketch of his history.

"My father left me plenty of money," he said, "and The Meadows, our old family place, is now mine. I have a taste for natural history; that taste took me two years ago to South America. I have had my share of strange adventures, and have collected valuable specimens and trophies. I am now on my way home from Para, on the Amazon, having come by a Booth boat to Madeira and changed there to the Castle Line. But why all this talk about myself?" he added, bringing his deck-chair a little nearer to mine. "What about your history, old chap? Are you settled down with a wife and kiddies of your own, or is that dream of your school days fulfilled, and are you the owner of the best private laboratory in London?"

"As to the laboratory," I said, with a

smile, "you must come and see it. For the rest I am unmarried. Are you?"

"I was married the day before I left Para, and my wife is on board with me."

"Capital," I answered. "Let me hear all about it."

"You shall. Her maiden name was Dallas; Beatrice Dallas. She is just twenty now. Her father was an Englishman and her mother a Spaniard; neither parent is living. She has an elder sister, Edith, nearly thirty years of age, unmarried, who is on board with us. There is also a step-brother, considerably older than either Edith or Beatrice. I met my wife last year in Para, and at once fell in love. I am the happiest man on earth. It goes without saying that I think her beautiful, and she is also very well off. The story of her wealth is a curious one. Her uncle on the mother's side was an extremely wealthy Spaniard, who made an enormous fortune in Brazil out of diamonds and minerals; he owned several mines. But it is supposed that his wealth turned his brain. At any rate, it seems to have done so as far as the disposal of his money went. He divided the yearly profits and interest between his nephew and his two nieces, but declared that the property itself should never be split up. He has left the whole of it to that one of the three who should survive the others. A perfectly insane arrangement, but not, I believe, unprecedented in Brazil."

"Very insane," I echoed. "What was he worth?"

"Over two million sterling."

"By Jove!" I cried, "what a sum! But what about the half-brother?"

"He must be over forty years of age, and is evidently a bad lot. I have never seen him. His sisters won't speak to him or have anything to do with him. I understand that he is a great gambler; I am further told that he is at present in England, and, as there are certain technicalities to be gone through before the girls can fully enjoy their incomes, one of the first things I must do when I get home is to find him out. He has to sign certain papers, for we sha'n't be able to put things straight until we get his whereabouts. Some time ago my wife and Edith heard that he was ill, but dead or alive we must know all about him, and as quickly as possible."

I made no answer, and he continued:—

"I'll introduce you to my wife and sister-in-law to-morrow. Beatrice is quite a child compared to Edith, who acts towards her almost like a mother. Bee is a little beauty, so fresh and round and young-looking. But Edith is handsome, too, although I sometimes think she is as vain as a peacock. By the way, Druce, this brings me to another part of my story. The sisters have an acquaintance on board, one of the most remarkable women I have ever met. She goes by the name of Madame Sara, and knows London well. In fact, she confesses to having a shop in the Strand. What she has been doing in Brazil I do not know, for she keeps all her affairs strictly private. But you will be amazed when I tell you what her calling is."

"What?" I asked.

"A professional beautifier. She claims the privilege of restoring youth to those who consult her. She also declares that she can make quite ugly people handsome. There is no doubt that she is very clever. She knows a little bit of everything, and has wonderful recipes with regard to medicines, surgery, and dentistry. She is a most lovely woman herself, very fair, with blue eyes, an innocent, childlike manner, and quantities of rippling gold hair. She openly confesses that she is very much older than she appears. She looks about five-and-twenty. She seems to have travelled all over the world, and says that by birth she is a mixture of Indian and Italian, her father having been Italian and her mother Indian. Accompanying her is an Arab, a handsome, picturesque sort of fellow, who gives her the most absolute devotion, and she is also bringing back to England two Brazilians from Para. This woman deals in all sorts of curious secrets, but principally in cosmetics. Her shop in the Strand could, I fancy, tell many a strange history. Her clients go to her there, and she does what is necessary for them. It is a fact that she occasionally performs small surgical operations, and there is not a dentist in London who can vie with her. She confesses quite naïvely that she holds some secrets for making false teeth cling to the palate that no one knows of. Edith Dallas is devoted to her—in fact, her adoration amounts to idolatry."

"You give a very brilliant account of this woman," I said. "You must introduce me to-morrow."

"I will," answered Jack, with a smile. "I should like your opinion of her. I am right glad I have met you, Druce, it is like old times. When we get to London I mean to put up at my town house in Eaton Square for the remainder of the season. The Meadows shall be re-furnished, and Bee and

I will take up our quarters some time in August; then you must come and see us. But I am afraid before I give myself up to mere pleasure I must find that precious brother-in-law, Henry Joachim Silva."

"If you have any difficulty apply to me," I said. "I can put at your disposal, in an unofficial way, of course, agents who would find almost any man in England, dead or alive."

I then proceeded to give Selby a short account of my own business.

"Thanks," he said, presently, "that is capital. You are the very man we want."

The next morning after breakfast Jack introduced me to his wife and sister-in-law. They were both foreign-looking, but very handsome, and the wife in particular had a graceful and uncommon appearance.

We had been chatting about five minutes when I saw coming down the deck a slight, rather small woman, wearing a big sun hat.

"Ah, Madame," cried Selby, "here you are. I had the luck to meet an old friend on board—Mr. Dixon Druce—and I have been telling him all about you. I should like you to know each other. Druce, this lady is Madame Sara, of whom I have spoken to you. Mr. Dixon Druce—Madame Sara."

She bowed gracefully and then looked at me earnestly. I had seldom seen a more lovely woman. By her side both Mrs. Selby and her sister seemed to fade into insignificance. Her complexion was almost dazzlingly fair, her face refined in expression, her eyes penetrating, clever, and yet with the innocent, frank gaze of a child. Her dress was very simple; she looked altogether like a young, fresh, and natural girl.

As we sat chatting lightly and about commonplace topics, I instinctively felt that she took an interest in me even greater than might be evinced from an ordinary introduction. By slow degrees she so turned the conversation as to leave Selby and his wife and sister out, and then as they moved away she came a little nearer, and said in a low voice:—

"I am very glad we have met, and yet how odd this meeting is! Was it really accidental?"

"I do not understand you," I answered.

"I know who you are," she said, lightly. "You are the manager of Werner's Agency; its business is to know the private affairs of those people who would rather keep their own secrets. Now, Mr. Druce, I am going to be absolutely frank with you. I own a small shop in the Strand—it is a perfumery shop—and behind those innocent-looking doors I conduct that business which brings me in gold of the realm. Have you, Mr. Druce, any objection to my continuing to make a livelihood in perfectly innocent ways?"

"None whatever," I answered. "You puzzle me by alluding to the subject."

"I want you to pay my shop a visit when you come to London. I have been away for three or four months. I do wonders for my clients, and they pay me largely for my services. I hold some perfectly innocent secrets which I cannot confide to anybody. I have obtained them partly from the Indians and partly from the natives of Brazil. I have lately been in Para to inquire into certain methods by which my trade can be improved."

"And your trade is——?" I said, looking at her with amusement and some surprise.

"'I AM A BEAUTIFIER,' SHE SAID."

"I am a beautifier," she said, lightly. She looked at me with a smile. "You don't want me yet, Mr. Druce, but the time may come when even you will wish to keep back the infirmities of years. In the meantime can you guess my age?"

"I will not hazard a guess," I answered.

"And I will not tell you. Let it remain a secret. Meanwhile, understand that my calling is quite an open one, and I do hold secrets. I should advise you, Mr. Druce, even in your professional capacity, not to interfere with them."

The childlike expression faded from her face as she uttered the last words. There seemed to ring a sort of challenge in her tone. She turned away after a few moments and I rejoined my friends.

"You have been making acquaintance with Madame Sara, Mr. Druce," said Mrs. Selby. "Don't you think she is lovely?"

"She is one of the most beautiful women I have ever seen," I answered, "but there seems to be a mystery about her."

"Oh, indeed there is," said Edith Dallas, gravely.

"She asked me if I could guess her age," I continued. "I did not try, but surely she cannot be more than five-and-twenty."

"No one knows her age," said Mrs. Selby, "but I will tell you a curious fact, which, perhaps, you will not believe. She was bridesmaid at my mother's wedding thirty years ago. She declares that she never changes, and has no fear of old age."

"You mean that seriously?" I cried. "But surely it is impossible?"

"Her name is on the register, and my mother knew her well. She was mysterious then, and I think my mother got into her power, but of that I am not certain. Anyhow, Edith and I adore her, don't we, Edie?"

She laid her hand affectionately on her sister's arm. Edith Dallas did not speak, but her face was careworn. After a time she said, slowly:—

"Madame Sara is uncanny and terrible."

There is, perhaps, no business imaginable—not even a lawyer's—that engenders suspicions more than mine. I hate all mysteries—both in persons and things. Mysteries are my natural enemies; I felt now that this woman was a distinct mystery. That she was interested in me I did not doubt, perhaps because she was afraid of me.

The rest of our voyage passed pleasantly enough. The more I saw of Mrs. Selby and her sister the more I liked them. They were quiet, simple, and straightforward. I felt sure that they were both as good as gold.

We parted at Waterloo, Jack and his wife and her sister going to Jack's house in Eaton Square, and I returning to my quarters in St. John's Wood. I had a house there, with a long garden, at the bottom of which was my laboratory, the laboratory that was the pride of my life, it being, I fondly considered, the best private laboratory in London. There I spent all my spare time making experiments and trying this chemical combination and the other, living in hopes of doing great things some day, for Werner's Agency was not to be the end of my career. Nevertheless, it interested me thoroughly, and I was not sorry to get back to my commercial conundrums.

The next day, just before I started to go to my place of business, Jack Selby was announced.

"I want you to help me," he said. "I have been already trying in a sort of general way to get information about my brother-in-law, but all in vain. There is no such person in any of the directories. Can you put me on the road to discovery?"

I said I could and would if he would leave the matter in my hands.

"With pleasure," he replied. "You see how we are fixed up. Neither Edith nor Bee can get money with any regularity until the man is found. I cannot imagine why he hides himself."

"I will insert advertisements in the personal columns of the newspapers," I said, "and request anyone who can give information to communicate with me at my office. I will also give instructions to all the branches of my firm, as well as to my head assistants in London, to keep their eyes open for any news. You may be quite certain that in a week or two we shall know all about him."

Selby appeared cheered at this proposal, and, having begged of me to call upon his wife and her sister as soon as possible, took his leave.

On that very day advertisements were drawn up and sent to several newspapers and inquiry agents; but week after week passed without the slightest result. Selby got very fidgety at the delay. He was never happy except in my presence, and insisted on my coming, whenever I had time, to his house. I was glad to do so, for I took an interest both in him and his belongings, and as to Madame Sara I could not get her out of my head. One day Mrs. Selby said to me:—

"Have you ever been to see Madame? I know she would like to show you her shop and general surroundings."

"I did promise to call upon her," I answered, "but have not had time to do so yet."

"Will you come with me to-morrow morning?" asked Edith Dallas, suddenly.

She turned red as she spoke, and the worried, uneasy expression became more marked on her face. I had noticed for some time that she had been looking both nervous and depressed. I had first observed this peculiarity about her on board the *Norham Castle*, but, as time went on, instead of lessening it grew worse. Her face for so young a woman was haggard; she started at each sound, and Madame Sara's name was never spoken in her presence without her evincing almost undue emotion.

"Will you come with me?" she said, with great eagerness.

I immediately promised, and the next day, about eleven o'clock, Edith Dallas and I found ourselves in a hansom driving to Madame Sara's shop. We reached it in a few minutes, and found an unpretentious little place wedged in between a hosier's on one side and a cheap print-seller's on the other. In the windows of the shop were pyramids of perfume bottles, with scintillating facet stoppers tied with coloured ribbons. We stepped out of the hansom and went indoors. Inside the shop were a couple of steps, which led to a door of solid mahogany.

"This is the entrance to her private house," said Edith, and she pointed to a small brass plate, on which was engraved the name—"Madame Sara, Parfumeuse."

Edith touched an electric bell and the door was immediately opened by a smartly-dressed page-boy. He looked at Miss Dallas as if he knew her very well, and said:—

"Madame is within, and is expecting you, miss."

He ushered us both into a quiet-looking room, soberly but handsomely furnished. He left us, closing the door. Edith turned to me.

"Do you know where we are?" she asked.

"We are standing at present in a small room just behind Madame Sara's shop," I answered. "Why are you so excited, Miss Dallas? What is the matter with you?"

"We are on the threshold of a magician's cave," she replied. "We shall soon be face to face with the most marvellous woman in the whole of London. There is no one like her."

"And you—fear her?" I said, dropping my voice to a whisper.

She started, stepped back, and with great difficulty recovered her composure. At that moment the page-boy returned to conduct us through a series of small waiting-rooms, and we soon found ourselves in the presence of Madame herself.

"Ah!" she said, with a smile. "This is delightful. You have kept your word, Edith, and I am greatly obliged to you. I will now show Mr. Druce some of the mysteries of my trade. But understand, sir," she added, "that I shall not tell you any of my real secrets, only as you would like to know something about me you shall."

"THIS IS MY SANCTUM SANCTORUM."

"How can you tell I should like to know about you?" I asked.

She gave me an earnest glance which somewhat astonished me, and then she said:—

"Knowledge is power; don't refuse what. I am willing to give. Edith, you will not object to waiting here while I show Mr. Druce through my rooms. First observe this room, Mr. Druce. It is lighted only from the roof. When the door shuts it automatically locks itself, so that any intrusion from without is impossible. This is my sanctum sanctorum—a faint odour of perfumes pervades the room. This is a hot day, but the room itself is cool. What do you think of it all?"

I made no answer. She walked to the other end and motioned to me to accompany her. There stood a polished oak square table, on which lay an array of extraordinary-looking articles and implements—stoppered bottles full of strange medicaments, mirrors, plane and concave, brushes, sprays, sponges, delicate needle-pointed instruments of bright steel, tiny lancets, and forceps. Facing this table was a chair, like those used by dentists. Above the chair hung electric lights in powerful reflectors, and lenses like bull's-eye lanterns. Another chair, supported on a glass pedestal, was kept there, Madame Sara informed me, for administering static electricity. There were dry-cell batteries for the continuous currents and induction coils for Faradic currents. There were also platinum needles for burning out the roots of hairs.

Madame took me from this room into another, where a still more formidable array of instruments were to be found. Here were a wooden operating table and chloroform and ether apparatus. When I had looked at everything, she turned to me.

"Now you know," she said. "I am a doctor—perhaps a quack. These are my secrets. By means of these I live and flourish."

She turned her back on me and walked into the other room with the light, springy step of youth. Edith Dallas, white as a ghost, was waiting for us.

"You have done your duty, my child," said Madame. "Mr. Druce has seen just what I want him to see. I am very much obliged to you both. We shall meet to-night at Lady Farringdon's 'At-home.' Until then, farewell."

When we got into the street and were driving back again to Eaton Square, I turned to Edith.

"Many things puzzle me about your friend," I said, "but perhaps none more than this. By what possible means can a woman who owns to being the possessor of a shop obtain the *entrée* to some of the best houses in London? Why does Society open her doors to this woman, Miss Dallas?"

"I cannot quite tell you," was her reply. "I only know the fact that wherever she goes she is welcomed and treated with consideration, and wherever she fails to appear there is a universally expressed feeling of regret."

I had also been invited to Lady Farringdon's reception that evening, and I went there in a state of great curiosity. There was no doubt that Madame interested me. I was not sure of her. Beyond doubt there was a mystery attached to her, and also, for some unaccountable reason, she wished both to propitiate and defy me. Why was this?

I arrived early, and was standing in the crush near the head of the staircase when Madame was announced. She wore the richest white satin and quantities of diamonds. I saw her hostess bend towards her and talk eagerly. I noticed Madame reply and the pleased expression that crossed Lady Farringdon's face. A few minutes later a man with a foreign-looking face and long beard sat down before the grand piano. He played a light prelude and Madame Sara began to sing. Her voice was sweet and low, with an extraordinary pathos in it. It was the sort of voice that penetrates to the heart. There was an instant pause in the gay chatter. She sang amidst perfect silence, and when the song had come to an end there followed a *furore* of applause. I was just turning to say something to my nearest neighbour when I observed Edith Dallas, who was standing close by. Her eyes met mine; she laid her hand on my sleeve.

"The room is hot," she said, half panting as she spoke. "Take me out on the balcony."

I did so. The atmosphere of the reception-rooms was almost intolerable, but it was comparatively cool in the open air.

"I must not lose sight of her," she said, suddenly.

"Of whom?" I asked, somewhat astonished at her words.

"Of Sara."

"She is there," I said. "You can see her from where you stand."

We happened to be alone. I came a little closer.

"Why are you afraid of her?" I asked.

"Are you sure that we shall not be heard?" was her answer.

"Certain."

"She terrifies me," were her next words.

"I will not betray your confidence, Miss Dallas. Will you not trust me? You ought to give me a reason for your fears."

"I cannot—I dare not; I have said far too much already. Don't keep me, Mr. Druce. She must not find us together."

As she spoke she pushed her way through the crowd, and before I could stop her was standing by Madame Sara's side.

The reception in Portland Place was, I remember, on the 26th of July. Two days later the Selbys were to give their final "At-home" before leaving for the country. I was, of course, invited to be present, and Madame was also there. She had never been dressed more splendidly, nor had she ever before looked younger or more beautiful. Wherever she went all eyes followed her. As a rule her dress was simple, almost like what a girl would wear, but to-night she chose rich Oriental stuffs made of many colours, and absolutely glittering with gems. Her golden hair was studded with diamonds. Round her neck she wore turquoise and diamonds mixed. There were many younger women in the room, but not the youngest nor the fairest had a chance beside Madame. It was not mere beauty of appearance, it was charm — charm which carries all before it.

"WHY ARE YOU AFRAID OF HER?"

I saw Miss Dallas, looking slim and tall and pale, standing at a little distance. I made my way to her side. Before I had time to speak she bent towards me.

"Is she not divine?" she whispered. "She bewilders and delights everyone. She is taking London by storm."

"Then you are not afraid of her to-night?" I said.

"I fear her more than ever. She has cast a spell over me. But listen, she is going to sing again."

I had not forgotten the song that Madame had given us at the Farringdons', and stood still to listen. There was a complete hush in the room. Her voice floated over the heads of the assembled guests in a dreamy Spanish song. Edith told me that it was a slumber song, and that Madame boasted of her power of putting almost anyone to sleep who listened to her rendering of it.

"She has many patients who suffer from insomnia," whispered the girl, "and she generally cures them with that song, and that alone. Ah! we must not talk; she will hear us."

Before I could reply Selby came hurrying up. He had not noticed Edith. He caught me by the arm.

"Come just for a minute into this window, Dixon," he said. "I must speak to you. I suppose you have no news with regard to my brother-in-law?"

"Not a word," I answered.

"To tell you the truth, I am getting terribly put out over the matter. We cannot settle any of our money affairs just because this man chooses to lose himself. My wife's lawyers wired to Brazil yesterday, but even his bankers do not know anything about him."

"The whole thing is a question of time," was my answer. "When are you off to Hampshire?"

"On Saturday."

As Selby said the last words he looked around him, then he dropped his voice.

"I want to say something else. The more I see"—he nodded towards Madame Sara—"the less I like her. Edith is getting into a very strange state. Have you not noticed it? And the worst of it is my wife is also infected. I suppose it is that dodge of the woman's for patching people up and making them beautiful. Doubtless the temptation is overpowering in the case of a plain woman, but Beatrice is beautiful herself and young. What can she have to do with cosmetics and complexion pills?"

"You don't mean to tell me that your wife has consulted Madame Sara as a doctor?"

"Not exactly, but she has gone to her about her teeth. She complained of toothache lately, and Madame's dentistry is renowned. Edith is constantly going to her for one thing or another, but then Edith is infatuated."

As Jack said the last words he went over to speak to someone else, and before I could leave the seclusion of the window I perceived Edith Dallas and Madame Sara in earnest conversation together. I could not help overhearing the following words:—

"Don't come to me to-morrow. Get into the country as soon as you can. It is far and away the best thing to do."

As Madame spoke she turned swiftly and caught my eye. She bowed, and the peculiar look, the sort of challenge, she had before given me flashed over her face. It made me uncomfortable, and during the night that followed I could not get it out of my head. I remembered what Selby had said with regard to his wife and her money affairs. Beyond doubt he had married into a mystery—a mystery that Madame Sara knew all about. There was a very big money interest, and strange things happen when millions are concerned.

The next morning I had just risen and was sitting at breakfast when a note was handed to me. It came by special messenger, and was marked "Urgent." I tore it open. These were its contents:—

"MY DEAR DRUCE,—A terrible blow has fallen on us. My sister-in-law, Edith, was taken suddenly ill this morning at breakfast. The nearest doctor was sent for, but he could do nothing, as she died half an hour ago. Do come and see me, and if you know any very clever specialist bring him with you. My wife is utterly stunned by the shock.—Yours, JACK SELBY."

I read the note twice before I could realize what it meant. Then I rushed out and, hailing the first hansom I met, said to the man:—

"Drive to No. 192, Victoria Street, as quickly as you can."

Here lived a certain Mr. Eric Vandeleur, an old friend of mine and the police surgeon for the Westminster district, which included

"SHE BOWED, AND THE PECULIAR LOOK SHE HAD BEFORE GIVEN ME FLASHED OVER HER FACE."

Eaton Square. No shrewder or sharper fellow existed than Vandeleur, and the present case was essentially in his province, both legally and professionally. He was not at his flat when I arrived, having already gone down to the court. Here I accordingly hurried, and was informed that he was in the mortuary.

For a man who, as it seemed to me, lived in a perpetual atmosphere of crime and violence, of death and coroners' courts, his habitual cheerfulness and brightness of manner were remarkable. Perhaps it was only the reaction from his work, for he had the reputation of being one of the most astute experts of the day in medical jurisprudence, and the most skilled analyst in toxicological cases on the Metropolitan Police staff. Before I could send him word that I wanted to see him I heard a door bang, and Vandeleur came hurrying down the passage, putting on his coat as he rushed along.

"Halloa!" he cried. "I haven't seen you for ages. Do you want me?"

"Yes, very urgently," I answered. "Are you busy?"

"Head over ears, my dear chap. I cannot give you a moment now, but perhaps later on."

"What is it? You look excited."

"I have got to go to Eaton Square like the wind, but come along, if you like, and tell me on the way."

"Capital," I cried. "The thing has been reported, then? You are going to Mr. Selby's, No. 34A; then I am going with you."

He looked at me in amazement.

"But the case has only just been reported. What can you possibly know about it?"

"Everything. Let us take this hansom, and I will tell you as we go along."

As we drove to Eaton Square I quickly explained the situation, glancing now and then at Vandeleur's bright, clean-shaven face. He was no longer Eric Vandeleur, the man with the latest club story and the merry twinkle in his blue eyes: he was Vandeleur the medical jurist, with a face like a mask, his lower jaw slightly protruding and features very fixed.

"This thing promises to be serious," he replied, as I finished, "but I can do nothing until after the autopsy. Here we are, and there is my man waiting for me; he has been smart."

On the steps stood an official-looking man in uniform, who saluted.

"Coroner's officer," explained Vandeleur.

We entered the silent, darkened house. Selby was standing in the hall. He came to meet us. I introduced him to Vandeleur, and he at once led us into the dining-room, where we found Dr. Osborne, whom Selby had called in when the alarm of Edith's illness had been first given. Dr. Osborne was a pale, under-sized, very young man. His face expressed considerable alarm. Vandeleur, however, managed to put him completely at his ease.

"I will have a chat with you in a few minutes, Dr. Osborne," he said; "but first I must get Mr. Selby's report. Will you please tell us, sir, exactly what occurred?"

"Certainly," he answered. "We had a reception here last night, and my sister-in-law did not go to bed until early morning; she was in bad spirits, but otherwise in her usual health. My wife went into her room after she was in bed, and told me later on that she had found Edith in hysterics, and could not get her to explain anything. We both talked about taking her to the country without delay. Indeed, our intention was to get off this afternoon."

"Well?" said Vandeleur.

"We had breakfast about half-past nine, and Miss Dallas came down, looking quite in her usual health, and in apparently good spirits. She ate with appetite, and, as it happened, she and my wife were both helped from the same dish. The meal had nearly come to an end when she jumped up from the table, uttered a sharp cry, turned very pale, pressed her hand to her side, and ran out of the room. My wife immediately followed her. She came back again in a minute or two, and said that Edith was in violent pain, and begged of me to send for a doctor. Dr. Osborne lives just round the corner. He came at once, but she died almost immediately after his arrival."

"You were in the room?" asked Vandeleur, turning to Osborne.

"Yes," he replied. "She was conscious to the last moment, and died suddenly."

"Did she tell you anything?"

"No, except to assure me that she had not eaten any food that day until she had come down to breakfast. After the death occurred I sent immediately to report the case, locked the door of the room where the poor girl's body is, and saw also that nobody touched anything on this table."

Vandeleur rang the bell and a servant appeared. He gave quick orders. The entire remains of the meal were collected and taken charge of, and then he and the coroner's officer went upstairs.

When we were alone Selby sank into a chair. His face was quite drawn and haggard.

"It is the horrible suddenness of the thing which is so appalling," he cried. "As to

Beatrice, I don't believe she will ever be the same again. She was deeply attached to Edith. Edith was nearly ten years her senior, and always acted the part of mother to her. This is a sad beginning to our life. I can scarcely think collectedly."

"SHE JUMPED UP FROM THE TABLE AND UTTERED A SHARP CRY."

I remained with him a little longer, and then, as Vandeleur did not return, went back to my own house. There I could settle to nothing, and when Vandeleur rang me up on the telephone about six o'clock I hurried off to his rooms. As soon as I arrived I saw that Selby was with him, and the expression on both their faces told me the truth.

"This is a bad business," said Vandeleur. "Miss Dallas has died from swallowing poison. An exhaustive analysis and examination have been made, and a powerful poison, unknown to European toxicologists, has been found. This is strange enough, but how it has been administered is a puzzle. I confess, at the present moment, we are all nonplussed. It certainly was not in the remains of the breakfast, and we have her dying evidence that she took nothing else. Now, a poison with such appalling potency would take effect quickly. It is evident that she was quite well when she came to breakfast, and that the poison began to work towards the close of the meal. But how did she get it? This question, however, I shall deal with later on. The more immediate point is this. The situation is a serious one in view of the monetary issues and the value of the lady's life. From the aspects of the case, her undoubted sanity and her affection for her sister, we may almost exclude the idea of suicide. We must, therefore, call it murder. This harmless, innocent lady is struck down by the hand of an assassin, and with such devilish cunning that no trace or clue is left behind For such an act there must have been some very powerful motive, and the person who designed and executed it must be a criminal of the highest order of scientific ability. Mr. Selby has been telling me the exact financial position of the poor lady, and also of his own young wife. The absolute disappearance of the step-brother, in view of his previous character, is in the highest degree strange. Knowing, as we do, that between him and two million sterling there stood two lives—*one is taken!*"

A deadly sensation of cold seized me as Vandeleur uttered these last words. I glanced at Selby. His face was colourless and the pupils of his eyes were contracted, as though he saw something which terrified him.

"What has happened once may happen again," continued Vandeleur. "We are in the presence of a great mystery, and I counsel you, Mr. Selby, to guard your wife with the utmost care."

These words, falling from a man of Vandeleur's position and authority on such matters, were sufficiently shocking for me to hear, but for Selby to be given such a solemn warning about his young and beautiful and newly-married wife, who was all the world to

"I COUNSEL YOU, MR. SELBY, TO GUARD YOUR WIFE.

before I heard a clatter alongside the kerb, and turning round I saw a smart open carriage, drawn by a pair of horses, standing there. I also heard my own name. I turned. Bending out of the carriage was Madame Sara.

"I saw you going by, Mr. Druce. I have only just heard the news about poor Edith Dallas. I am terribly shocked and upset. I have been to the house, but they would not admit me. Have you heard what was the cause of her death?"

Madame's blue eyes filled with tears as she spoke.

"I am not at liberty to disclose what I have heard, Madame," I answered, "since I am officially connected with the affair."

him, was terrible indeed. He leant his head on his hands.

"Mercy on us!" he muttered. "Is this a civilized country when death can walk abroad like this, invisible, not to be avoided? Tell me, Mr. Vandeleur, what I must do."

"You must be guided by me," said Vandeleur, "and, believe me, there is no witchcraft in the world. I shall place a detective in your household immediately. Don't be alarmed; he will come to you in plain clothes and will simply act as a servant. Nevertheless, nothing can be done to your wife without his knowledge. As to you, Druce," he continued, turning to me, "the police are doing all they can to find this man Silva, and I ask you to help them with your big agency, and to begin at once. Leave your friend to me. Wire instantly if you hear news."

"You may rely on me," I said, and a moment later I had left the room.

As I walked rapidly down the street the thought of Madame Sara, her shop and its mysterious background, its surgical instruments, its operating-table, its induction coils, came back to me. And yet what could Madame Sara have to do with the present strange, inexplicable mystery?

The thought had scarcely crossed my mind

Her eyes narrowed. The brimming tears dried as though by magic. Her glance became scornful.

"Thank you," she answered; "your reply tells me that she did not die naturally. How very appalling! But I must not keep you. Can I drive you anywhere?"

"No, thank you."

"Good-bye, then."

She made a sign to the coachman, and as the carriage rolled away turned to look back at me. Her face wore the defiant expression I had seen there more than once. Could she be connected with the affair? The thought came upon me with a violence that seemed almost conviction. Yet I had no reason for it—none.

To find Henry Joachim Silva was now my principal thought. Advertisements were widely circulated. My staff had instructions to make every possible inquiry, with large money rewards as incitements. The collateral branches of other agencies throughout Brazil were communicated with by cable, and all the Scotland Yard channels were used. Still there was no result. The newspapers took up the case; there were paragraphs in most of them with regard to the missing step-brother and the mysterious death of Edith Dallas. Then someone got hold of the story of the will, and this was retailed with many additions for the benefit of the public. At the inquest the jury returned the following verdict:—

"*We find that Miss Edith Dallas died from taking poison of unknown name, but by whom or how administered there is no evidence to say.*"

This unsatisfactory state of things was destined to change quite suddenly. On the 6th of August, as I was seated in my office, a note was brought me by a private messenger. It ran as follows:—

"Norfolk Hotel, Strand.

"DEAR SIR,—I have just arrived in London from Brazil, and have seen your advertisements. I was about to insert one myself in order to find the whereabouts of my sisters. I am a great invalid and unable to leave my room. Can you come to see me at the earliest possible moment?—Yours,

"HENRY JOACHIM SILVA."

In uncontrollable excitement I hastily dispatched two telegrams, one to Selby and the other to Vandeleur, begging of them to be with me, without fail, as soon as possible. So the man had never been in England at all. The situation was more bewildering than ever. One thing, at least, was probable—Edith Dallas's death was not due to her step-brother. Soon after half-past six Selby arrived, and Vandeleur walked in ten minutes later. I told them what had occurred and showed them the letter. In half an hour's time we reached the hotel, and on stating who I was we were shown into a room on the first floor by Silva's private servant. Resting in an arm-chair, as we entered, sat a man; his face was terribly thin. The eyes and cheeks were so sunken that the face had almost the appearance of a skull. He made no effort to rise when we entered, and glanced from one of us to the other with the utmost astonishment. I at once introduced myself and explained who we were. He then waved his hand for his man to retire.

"You have heard the news, of course, Mr. Silva?" I said.

"News! What?" He glanced up to me and seemed to read something in my face. He started back in his chair.

"Good heavens!" he replied. "Do you allude to my sisters? Tell me, quickly, are they alive?"

"Your elder sister died on the 29th of July, and there is every reason to believe that her death was caused by foul play."

As I uttered these words the change that passed over his face was fearful to witness. He did not speak, but remained motionless. His claw-like hands clutched the arms of the chair, his eyes were fixed and staring, as though they would start from their hollow sockets, the colour of his skin was like clay. I heard Selby breathe quickly behind me, and Vandeleur stepped towards the man and laid his hand on his shoulder.

"Tell us what you know of this matter," he said, sharply.

Recovering himself with an effort, the invalid began in a tremulous voice:—

"Listen closely, for you must act quickly. I am indirectly responsible for this fearful thing. My life has been a wild and wasted one, and now I am dying. The doctors tell me I cannot live a month, for I have a large aneurism of the heart. Eighteen months ago I was in Rio. I was living fast and gambled heavily. Among my fellow-gamblers was a man much older than myself. His name was José Aranjo. He was, if anything, a greater gambler than I. One night we played alone. The stakes ran high until they reached a big figure. By daylight I had lost to him nearly £200,000. Though I am a rich man in point of income under my uncle's will, I could not pay a twentieth part of that sum. This man knew my financial position, and, in addition to a sum of £5,000 paid down, I gave him a document. I must have been mad to do so. The document was this—it was duly witnessed and attested by a lawyer—that, in the event of my surviving my two sisters and thus inheriting the whole of my uncle's vast wealth, half a million should go to José Aranjo. I felt I was breaking up at the time, and the chances of my inheriting the money were small. Immediately after the completion of the document this man left Rio, and I then heard a great deal about him that I had not previously known. He was a man of the queerest antecedents, partly Indian, partly Italian. He had spent many years of his life amongst the Indians. I heard also that he was as cruel as he was clever, and possessed some wonderful secrets of poisoning unknown to the West. I thought a great deal about this, for I knew that by signing that document I had placed the lives of my two sisters between him and a fortune. I came to Para six weeks ago, only to learn that one of my sisters was married and that both had gone to England. Ill as I was, I determined to follow them in order to warn them. I also wanted to arrange matters with you, Mr. Selby."

"One moment, sir," I broke in, suddenly.

"Do you happen to be aware if this man, José Aranjo, knew a woman calling herself Madame Sara?"

"Knew her?" cried Silva. "Very well indeed, and so, for that matter, did I. Aranjo and Madame Sara were the best friends, and constantly met. She called herself a professional beautifier—was very handsome, and had secrets for the pursuing of her trade unknown even to Aranjo."

"Good heavens!" I cried, "and the woman is now in London. She returned here with Mrs. Selby and Miss Dallas. Edith was very much influenced by her, and was constantly with her. There is no doubt in my mind that she is guilty. I have suspected her for some time, but I could not find a motive. Now the motive appears. You surely can have her arrested?"

Vandeleur made no reply. He gave me a strange look, then he turned to Selby.

"Has your wife also consulted Madame Sara?" he asked, sharply.

"Yes, she went to her once about her teeth, but has not been to the shop since Edith's death. I begged of her not to see the woman, and she promised me faithfully she would not do so."

"Has she any medicines or lotions given to her by Madame Sara—does she follow any line of treatment advised by her?"

"No, I am certain on that point."

"Very well, I will see your wife to-night in order to ask her some questions. You must both leave town at once. Go to your country house and settle there. I am quite serious when I say that Mrs. Selby is in the utmost possible danger until after the death of her brother. We must leave you now, Mr. Silva. All business affairs must wait for the present. It is absolutely necessary that Mrs. Selby should leave London at once. Good-night, sir. I shall give myself the pleasure of calling on you to-morrow morning."

"I HAD LOST TO HIM NEARLY £200,000!"

We took leave of the sick man. As soon as we got into the street Vandeleur stopped.

"I must leave it to you, Selby," he said, "to judge how much of this matter you will tell to your wife. Were I you I would explain everything. The time for immediate action has arrived, and she is a brave and sensible woman. From this moment you must watch all the foods and liquids that she takes. She must never be out of your sight or out of the sight of some other trustworthy companion."

"I shall, of course, watch my wife myself," said Selby. "But the thing is enough to drive one mad."

"I will go with you to the country, Selby," I said, suddenly.

"Ah!" cried Vandeleur, "that is the best thing possible, and what I wanted to propose. Go, all of you, by an early train to-morrow."

"Then I will be off home at once, to make arrangements," I said. "I will meet you, Selby, at Waterloo for the first train to Cronsmoor to-morrow."

As I was turning away Vandeleur caught my arm.

"I am glad you are going with them," he said. "I shall write to you to-night *re* instructions. Never be without a loaded revolver. Good-night."

By 6.15 the next morning Selby, his wife, and I were in a reserved, locked, first-class compartment, speeding rapidly west. The servants and Mrs. Selby's own special maid were in a separate carriage. Selby's face showed signs of a sleepless night, and presented a striking contrast to the fair, fresh face of the girl round whom this strange battle raged. Her husband had told her everything, and, though still suffering terribly from the shock and grief of her sister's death, her face was calm and full of repose.

A carriage was waiting for us at Cronsmoor, and by half-past nine we arrived at the old home of the Selbys, nestling amid its oaks and elms. Everything was done to make the home-coming of the bride as cheerful as circumstances would permit, but a gloom, impossible to lift, overshadowed Selby himself. He could scarcely rouse himself to take the slightest interest in anything.

The following morning I received a letter from Vandeleur. It was very short, and once more impressed on me the necessity of caution. He said that two eminent physicians had examined Silva, and the verdict was that he could not live a month. Until his death precautions must be strictly observed.

The day was cloudless, and after breakfast I was just starting out for a stroll when the butler brought me a telegram. I tore it open; it was from Vandeleur.

"Prohibit all food until I arrive. Am coming down," were the words. I hurried into the study and gave it to Selby. He read it and looked up at me.

"Find out the first train and go and meet him, old chap," he said. "Let us hope that this means an end of the hideous affair."

I went into the hall and looked up the trains. The next arrived at Cronsmoor at 10.45. I then strolled round to the stables and ordered a carriage, after which I walked up and down on the drive. There was no doubt that something strange had happened. Vandeleur coming down so suddenly must mean a final clearing up of the mystery. I had just turned round at the lodge gates to wait for the carriage when the sound of wheels and of horses galloping struck on my ears. The gates were swung open, and Vandeleur in an open fly dashed through them. Before I could recover from my surprise he was out of the vehicle and at my side. He carried a small black bag in his hand.

"VANDELEUR IN AN OPEN FLY DASHED THROUGH."

"I came down by special train," he said, speaking quickly. "There is not a moment to lose. Come at once. Is Mrs. Selby all right?"

"What do you mean?" I replied. "Of course she is. Do you suppose that she is in danger?"

"Deadly," was his answer. "Come."

We dashed up to the house together. Selby, who had heard our steps, came to meet us.

"Mr. Vandeleur!" he cried. "What is it? How did you come?"

"By special train, Mr. Selby. And I want to see your wife at once. It will be necessary to perform a very trifling operation."

"Operation!" he exclaimed.

"Yes; at once."

We made our way through the hall and into the morning-room, where Mrs. Selby was busily engaged reading and answering letters. She started up when she saw Vandeleur and uttered an exclamation of surprise.

"What has happened?" she asked.

Vandeleur went up to her and took her hand.

"Do not be alarmed," he said, "for I have come to put all your fears to rest. Now, please, listen to me. When you visited Madame Sara with your sister, did you go for medical advice?"

The colour rushed into her face.

"One of my teeth ached," she answered. "I went to her about that. She is, as I suppose you know, a most wonderful dentist. She examined the tooth, found that it required stopping, and got an assistant, a Brazilian, I think, to do it."

"And your tooth has been comfortable ever since?"

"Yes, quite. She had one of Edith's stopped at the same time."

"Will you kindly sit down and show me which was the tooth into which the stopping was put?"

She did so.

"This was the one," she said, pointing with her finger to one in the lower jaw. "What do you mean? Is there anything wrong?"

Vandeleur examined the tooth long and carefully. There was a sudden rapid movement of his hand, and a sharp cry from Mrs. Selby. With the deftness of long practice, and a powerful wrist, he had extracted the tooth with one wrench. The suddenness of the whole thing, startling as it was, was not so strange as his next movement.

"Send Mrs. Selby's maid to her," he said, turning to her husband; "then come, both of you, into the next room."

The maid was summoned. Poor Mrs. Selby had sunk back in her chair, terrified and half fainting. A moment later Selby joined us in the dining-room.

"That's right," said Vandeleur; "close the door, will you?"

He opened his black bag and brought out several instruments. With one he removed the stopping from the tooth. It was quite soft and came away easily. Then from the bag he produced a small guinea-pig, which he requested me to hold. He pressed the sharp instrument into the tooth, and opening the mouth of the little animal placed the point on the tongue. The effect was instantaneous. The little head fell on to one of my hands—the guinea-pig was dead. Vandeleur was white as a sheet. He hurried up to Selby and wrung his hand.

"Thank Heaven!" he said, "I've been in time, but only just. Your wife is safe. This stopping would hardly have held another hour. I have been thinking all night over the mystery of your sister-in-law's death, and over every minute detail of evidence as to how the poison could have been administered. Suddenly the coincidence of both sisters having had their teeth stopped struck me as remarkable. Like a flash the solution came to me. The more I considered it the more I felt that I was right; but by what fiendish cunning such a scheme could have been conceived and executed is still beyond my power to explain. The poison is very like hyoscine, one of the worst toxic-alkaloids known, so violent in its deadly proportions that the amount that would go into a tooth would cause almost instant death. It has been kept in by a gutta-percha stopping, certain to come out within a month, probably earlier, and most probably during mastication of food. The person would die either immediately or after a very few minutes, and no one would connect a visit to the dentist with a death a month afterwards."

What followed can be told in a very few words. Madame Sara was arrested on suspicion. She appeared before the magistrate, looking innocent and beautiful, and managed during her evidence completely to baffle that acute individual. She denied nothing, but declared that the poison must have been put into the tooth by one of the two Brazilians whom she had lately engaged to help her with her dentistry. She had her suspicions with regard to these men soon afterwards, and had dismissed them. She believed that they were in the pay of José Aranjo, but she could not tell anything for certain. Thus Madame escaped conviction. I was certain that she was guilty, but there was not a shadow of real proof. A month later Silva died, and Selby is now a double millionaire.

The Sorceress of the Strand.

By L. T. Meade and Robert Eustace.

II.—THE BLOOD-RED CROSS.

IN the month of November in the year 1899 I found myself a guest in the house of one of my oldest friends — George Rowland. His beautiful place in Yorkshire was an ideal holiday resort. It went by the name of Rowland's Folly, and had been built on the site of a former dwelling in the reign of the first George. The house was now replete with every modern luxury. It, however, very nearly cost its first owner, if not the whole of his fortune, yet the most precious heirloom of the family. This was a pearl necklace of almost fabulous value. It had been secured as booty by a certain Geoffrey Rowland at the time of the Battle of Agincourt, had originally been the property of one of the Dukes of Genoa, and had even for a short time been in the keeping of the Pope. From the moment that Geoffrey Rowland took possession of the necklace there had been several attempts made to deprive him of it. Sword, fire, water, poison, had all been used, but ineffectually. The necklace with its eighty pearls, smooth, symmetrical, pear-shaped, of a translucent white colour and with a subdued iridescent sheen, was still in the possession of the family, and was likely to remain there, as George Rowland told me, until the end of time. Each bride wore the necklace on her wedding-day, after which it was put into the strong-room and, as a rule, never seen again until the next bridal occasion. The pearls were roughly estimated as worth from two to three thousand pounds each, but the historical value of the necklace put the price almost beyond the dreams of avarice.

It was reported that in the autumn of that same year an American millionaire had offered to buy it from the family at their own price, but as no terms would be listened to the negotiations fell through.

George Rowland belonged to the oldest and proudest family in the West Riding, and no man looked a better gentleman or more fit to uphold ancient dignities than he. He was proud to boast that from the earliest days no stain of dishonour had touched his house, that the women of the family were as good as the men, their blood pure, their morals irreproachable, their ideas lofty.

I went to Rowland's Folly in November, and found a pleasant, hospitable, and cheerful hostess in Lady Kennedy, Rowland's only sister. Antonia Ripley was, however, the centre of all interest. Rowland was engaged to Antonia, and the history was romantic. Lady Kennedy told me all about it.

"LADY KENNEDY TOLD ME ALL ABOUT IT."

"She is a penniless girl without family," remarked the good woman, somewhat snappishly. "I can't imagine what George was thinking of."

"How did your brother meet her?" I asked.

"We were both in Italy last autumn; we were staying in Naples, at the Vesuve. An English lady was staying there of the name of Studley. She died while we were at the hotel. She had under her charge a young girl, the same Antonia who is now engaged to my brother. Before her death she begged of us to befriend her, saying that the child was without money and without friends. All Mrs. Studley's money died with her. We promised, not being able to do otherwise. George fell in love almost at first sight. Little Antonia was provided for by becoming engaged to my brother. I have nothing to say against the girl, but I dislike this sort of match very much. Besides, she is more foreign than English."

"Cannot Miss Ripley tell you anything about her history?"

"Nothing, except that Mrs. Studley adopted her when she was a tiny child. She says, also, that she has a dim recollection of a large building crowded with people, and a man who stretched out his arms to her and was taken forcibly away. That is all. She is quite a nice child, and amiable, with touching ways and a pathetic face; but no one knows what her ancestry was. Ah, there you are, Antonia! What is the matter now?"

The girl tripped across the room. She was like a young fawn; of a smooth, olive complexion—dark of eye and mysteriously beautiful, with the graceful step which is seldom granted to an English girl.

"My lace dress has come," she said. "Markham is unpacking it—but the bodice is made with a low neck."

Lady Kennedy frowned.

"You are too absurd, Antonia," she said. "Why won't you dress like other girls? I assure you that peculiarity of yours of always wearing your dress high in the evening annoys George."

"Does it?" she answered, and she stepped back and put her hand to her neck just below the throat—a constant habit of hers, as I afterwards had occasion to observe.

"It disturbs him very much," said Lady Kennedy. "He spoke to me about it only yesterday. Please understand, Antonia, that at the ball you cannot possibly wear a dress high to your throat. It cannot be permitted."

"I shall be properly dressed on the night of the ball," replied the girl.

Her face grew crimson, then deadly pale.

"It only wants a fortnight to that time, but I shall be ready."

There was a solemnity about her words. She turned and left the room.

"Antonia is a very trying character," said Lady Kennedy. "Why won't she act like other girls? She makes such a fuss about wearing a proper evening dress that she tries my patience—but she is all crotchets."

"A sweet little girl for all that," was my answer.

"Yes; men like her."

Soon afterwards, as I was strolling on the terrace, I met Miss Ripley. She was sitting in a low chair. I noticed how small, and slim, and young she looked, and how pathetic was the expression of her little face. When she saw me she seemed to hesitate; then she came to my side.

"May I walk with you, Mr. Druce?" she asked.

"I am quite at your service," I answered. "Where shall we go?"

"It doesn't matter. I want to know if you will help me."

"Certainly, if I can, Miss Ripley."

"It is most important. I want to go to London."

"Surely that is not very difficult?"

"They won't allow me to go alone, and they are both very busy. I have just sent a telegram to a friend. I want to see her. I know she will receive me. I want to go to-morrow. May I venture to ask that you should be my escort?"

"My dear Miss Ripley, certainly," I said. "I will help you with pleasure."

"It must be done," she said, in a low voice. "I have put it off too long. When I marry him he shall not be disappointed."

"I do not understand you," I said, "but I will go with you with the greatest willingness."

She smiled; and the next day, much to my own amazement, I found myself travelling first-class up to London, with little Miss Ripley as my companion. Neither Rowland nor his sister had approved; but Antonia had her own way, and the fact that I would escort her cleared off some difficulties.

During our journey she bent towards me and said, in a low tone:—

"Have you ever heard of that most wonderful, that great woman, Madame Sara?"

I looked at her intently.

"'IT MUST BE DONE,' SHE SAID."

"I have certainly heard of Madame Sara," I said, with emphasis, "but I sincerely trust that you have nothing to do with her."

"I have known her almost all my life," said the girl. "Mrs. Studley knew her also. I love her very much. I trust her. I am going to see her now."

"What do you mean?"

"It was to her I wired yesterday. She will receive me; she will help me. I am returning to the Folly to-night. Will you add to your kindness by escorting me home?"

"Certainly."

At Euston I put my charge into a hansom, arranging to meet her on the departure platform at twenty minutes to six that evening, and then taking another hansom drove as fast as I could to Vandeleur's address. During the latter part of my journey to town a sudden, almost unaccountable, desire to consult Vandeleur had taken possession of me. I was lucky enough to find this busiest of men at home and at leisure. He gave an exclamation of delight when my name was announced, and then came towards me with outstretched hand.

"I was just about to wire to you, Druce," he said. "From where have you sprung?"

"From no less a place than Rowland's Folly," was my answer.

"More and more amazing. Then you have met Miss Ripley, George Rowland's *fiancée*?"

"You have heard of the engagement, Vandeleur?"

"Who has not? What sort is the young lady?"

"I can tell you all you want to know, for I have travelled up to town with her."

"Ah!"

He was silent for a minute, evidently thinking hard; then drawing a chair near mine he seated himself.

"How long have you been at Rowland's Folly?" he asked.

"Nearly a week. I am to remain until after the wedding. I consider Rowland a lucky man. He is marrying a sweet little girl."

"You think so? By the way, have you ever noticed any peculiarity about her?"

"Only that she is singularly amiable and attractive."

"But any habit—pray think carefully before you answer me."

"Really, Vandeleur, your questions surprise me. Little Miss Ripley is a person with ideas and is not ashamed to stick to her principles. You know, of course, that in a house like Rowland's Folly it is the custom for the ladies to come to dinner in full dress. Now, Miss Ripley won't accommodate herself to this fashion, but *will* wear her dress high to the throat, however gay and festive the occasion."

"Ah! there doesn't seem to be much in that, does there?"

"I don't quite agree with you. Pressure has been brought to bear on the girl to make her conform to the usual regulations, and Lady Kennedy, a woman old enough to be her mother, is quite disagreeable on the point."

"But the girl sticks to her determination?"

"Absolutely, although she promises to yield and to wear the conventional dress at the ball given in her honour a week before the wedding."

Vandeleur was silent for nearly a minute; then dropping his voice he said, slowly:—

"Did Miss Ripley ever mention in your

presence the name of our mutual foe—Madame Sara?"

"How strange that you should ask! On our journey to town to-day she told me that she knew the woman—she has known her for the greater part of her life — poor child, she even loves her. Vandeleur, that young girl is with Madame Sara now."

"Don't be alarmed, Druce; there is no immediate danger; but I may as well tell you that through my secret agents I have made discoveries which show that Madame has another iron in the fire, that once again she is preparing to convulse Society, and that little Miss Ripley is the victim."

"SHE IS PREPARING TO CONVULSE SOCIETY."

"You must be mistaken."

"So sure am I, that I want your help. You are returning to Rowland's Folly?"

"To-night."

"And Miss Ripley?"

"She goes with me. We meet at Euston for the six o'clock train."

"So far, good. By the way, has Rowland spoken to you lately about the pearl necklace?"

"No; why do you ask?"

"Because I understand that it was his intention to have the pearls slightly altered and reset in order to fit Miss Ripley's slender throat; also to have a diamond clasp affixed in place of the somewhat insecure one at present attached to the string of pearls. Messrs. Theodore and Mark, of Bond Street, were to undertake the commission. All was in preparation, and a messenger, accompanied by two detectives, was to go to Rowland's Folly to fetch the treasure, when the whole thing was countermanded, Rowland having changed his mind and having decided that the strong-room at the Folly was the best place in which to keep the necklace."

"He has not mentioned the subject to me," I said. "How do you know?"

"I have my emissaries. One thing is certain — little Miss Ripley is to wear the pearls on her wedding-day — and the Italian family, distant relatives of the present Duke of Genoa, to whom the pearls belonged, and from whom they were stolen shortly before the Battle of Agincourt, are again taking active steps to secure them. You have heard the story of the American millionaire? Well, that was a blind—the necklace was in reality to be delivered into the hands of the old family as soon as he had purchased it. Now, Druce, this is the state of things: Madame Sara is an adventuress, and the cleverest woman in the world — Miss Ripley is very young and ignorant. Miss Ripley is to wear the pearls on her wedding-day—and Madame wants them. You can infer the rest."

"What do you want me to do?" I asked.

"Go back and watch. If you see anything to arouse suspicion, wire to me."

"What about telling Rowland?"

"I would rather not consult him. I want to protect Miss Ripley, and at the same time to get Madame into my power. She managed to elude us last time, but she shall not this. My idea is to inveigle her to her ruin. Why, Druce, the woman is being more trusted and run after and admired day by day. She appeals to the greatest foibles of the world. She knows some valuable secrets, and is an adept in the art of restoring beauty and to a certain extent conquering the ravages of time. She is at present aided by an Arab, one of the most dangerous men I have ever seen, with the subtlety of a serpent, and legerdemain in every one of his ten fingers. It is not an easy thing to entrap her."

"And yet you mean to do it?"

"Some day—some day. Perhaps now."

His eyes were bright. I had seldom seen him look more excited.

After a short time I left him. Miss Ripley met me at Euston. She was silent and unresponsive and looked depressed. Once I saw her put her hand to her neck.

"Are you in pain?" I asked.

"You might be a doctor, Mr. Druce, from your question."

"But answer me," I said.

She was silent for a minute; then she said, slowly:—

"You are good, and I think I ought to tell you. But will you regard it as a secret? You wonder, perhaps, how it is that I don't wear a low dress in the evening. I will tell you why. On my neck, just below the throat, there grew a wart or mole—large, brown, and ugly. The Italian doctors would not remove it on account of the position. It lies just over what they said was an *aberrant* artery, and the removal might cause very dangerous hæmorrhage. One day Madame saw it; she said the doctors were wrong, and that she could easily take it away and leave no mark behind. I hesitated for a long time, but yesterday, when Lady Kennedy spoke to me as she did, I made up my mind. I wired to Madame and went to her to-day. She gave me chloroform and removed the mole. My neck is bandaged up and it smarts a little. I am not to remove the bandage until she sees me again. She is very pleased with the result, and says that my neck will now be beautiful like other women's, and that I can on the night of the ball wear the lovely Brussels lace dress that Lady Kennedy has given me. That is my secret. Will you respect it?"

I promised, and soon afterwards we reached the end of our journey.

A few days went by. One morning at breakfast I noticed that the little signora only played with her food. An open letter lay by her plate. Rowland, by whose side she always sat, turned to her.

"What is the matter, Antonia?" he said. "Have you had an unpleasant letter?"

"It is from——"

"From whom, dear?"

"Madame Sara."

"What did I hear you say?" cried Lady Kennedy.

"I have had a letter from Madame Sara, Lady Kennedy."

"That shocking woman in the Strand—that adventuress? My dear, is it possible that you know her? Her name is in the mouth of everyone. She is quite notorious."

Instantly the room became full of voices, some talking loudly, some gently, but all praising Madame Sara. Even the men took her part; as to the women, they were unanimous about her charms and her genius.

In the midst of the commotion little Antonia burst into a flood of tears and left the room. Rowland followed her. What next occurred I cannot tell, but in the course of the morning I met Lady Kennedy.

"Well," she said, "that child has won, as I knew she would. Madame Sara wishes to come here, and George says that Antonia's friend is to be invited. I shall be glad when the marriage is over and I can get out of this. It is really detestable that in the last days of my reign I should have to give that woman the *entrée* to the house."

She left me, and I wandered into the entrance hall. There I saw Rowland. He had a telegraph form in his hands, on which some words were written.

"Ah, Druce!" he said. "I am just sending a telegram to the station. What! do you want to send one too?"

For I had seated myself by the table which held the telegraph forms.

"If you don't think I am taking too great a liberty, Rowland," I said, suddenly, "I should like to ask a friend of mine here for a day or two."

"Twenty friends, if you like, my dear Druce. What a man you are to apologize about such a trifle! Who is the special friend?"

"No less a person than Eric Vandeleur, the police-surgeon for Westminster."

"What! Vandeleur—the gayest, jolliest man I have ever met! Would he care to come?"

Rowland's eyes were sparkling with excitement.

"I think so; more especially if you will give me leave to say that you would welcome him."

"Tell him he shall have a thousand welcomes, the best room in the house, the best horse. Get him to come by all means, Druce."

Our two telegrams were sent off. In the course of the morning replies in the affirmative came to each.

That evening Madame Sara arrived. She came by the last train. The brougham was sent to meet her. She entered the house shortly before midnight. I was standing in the hall when she arrived, and I felt a momentary sense of pleasure when I saw her start as her eyes met mine. But she was not a woman to be caught off her guard. She approached me at once with outstretched hand and an eager voice.

"This is charming, Mr. Druce," she said. "I do not think anything pleases me more." Then she added, turning to Rowland, "Mr. Dixon Druce is a very old friend of mine."

Rowland gave me a bewildered glance. Madame turned and began to talk to her hostess. Antonia was standing near one of the open drawing-rooms. She had on a soft dress of pale green silk. I had seldom seen a more graceful little creature. But the expression of her face disturbed me. It wore now the fascinated look of a bird when a snake attracts it. Could Madame Sara be the snake? Was Antonia afraid of this woman?

The next day Lady Kennedy came to me with a confidence.

"I am glad your police friend is coming," she said. "It will be safer."

"Vandeleur arrives at twelve o'clock," was my answer.

"Well, I am pleased. I like that woman less and less. I was amazed when she dared to call you her friend."

"Oh, we have met before on business," I answered, guardedly.

"You won't tell me anything further, Mr. Druce?"

"You must excuse me, Lady Kennedy."

"Her assurance is unbounded," continued the good lady. "She has brought a maid or nurse with her—a most extraordinary-looking woman. That, perhaps, is allowable; but she has also brought her black servant, an Arabian, who goes by the name of Achmed. I must say he is a picturesque creature with his quaint Oriental dress. He was all in flaming yellow this morning, and the embroidery on his jacket was worth a small fortune. But it is the daring of the woman that annoys me. She goes on as though she were somebody."

"She is a very emphatic somebody," I could not help replying. "London Society is at her feet."

"I only hope that Antonia will take her remedies and let her go. The woman has no welcome from me," said the indignant mistress of Rowland's Folly.

I did not see anything of Antonia that morning, and at the appointed time I went down to the station to meet Vandeleur. He arrived in high spirits, did not ask a question with regard to Antonia, received the information that Madame Sara was in the house with stolid silence, and seemed intent on the pleasures of the moment.

"Rowland's Folly!" he said, looking round him as we approached one of the finest houses in the whole of Yorkshire. "A folly, truly, and yet a pleasant one, Druce, eh? I fancy," he added, with a slight smile, "that I am going to have a good time here."

"I hope you will disentangle a most tangled skein," was my reply.

He shrugged his shoulders. Suddenly his manner altered.

"Who is that woman?" he said, with a strain of anxiety quite apparent in his voice.

"Who?" I asked.

"That woman on the terrace in nurse's dress."

"I don't know. She has been brought here by Madame Sara—a sort of maid and nurse as well. I suppose poor little Antonia will be put under her charge."

"Don't let her see me, Druce, that's all. Ah, here is our host."

Vandeleur quickened his movements, and the next instant was shaking hands with Rowland.

The rest of the day passed without adventure. I did not see Antonia. She did not even appear at dinner. Rowland, however, assured me that she was taking necessary rest and would be all right on the morrow. He seemed inclined to be gracious to Madame Sara, and was annoyed at his sister's manner to their guest.

Soon after dinner, as I was standing in one of the smoking-rooms, I felt a light hand on my arm, and, turning, encountered the splendid pose and audacious, bright, defiant glance of Madame herself.

"Mr. Druce," she said, "just one moment. It is quite right that you and I should be plain with each other. I know the reason why you are here. You have come for the express purpose of spying upon me and spoiling what you consider my game. But understand, Mr. Druce, that there is danger to yourself when you interfere with the schemes of one like me. Forewarned is forearmed."

Someone came into the room and Madame left it.

The ball was but a week off, and preparations for the great event were taking place. Attached to the house at the left was a great room built for this purpose.

Rowland and I were walking down this room on a special morning; he was commenting on its architectural merits and telling me what band he intended to have in the musicians' gallery, when Antonia glided into the room.

"How pale you are, little Tonia!" he said.

This was his favourite name for her. He put his hand under her chin, raised her sweet, blushing face, and looked into her eyes.

"Ah, you want my answer. What a persistent little puss it is! You shall have your way, Tonia —yes, certainly. For you I will grant what has never been granted before. All the same, what will my lady say?"

"FOREWARNED IS FOREARMED."

He shrugged his shoulders.

"But you will let me wear them whether she is angry or not?" persisted Antonia.

"Yes, child, I have said it."

She took his hand and raised it to her lips, then, with a curtsy, tripped out of the room.

"A rare, bright little bird," he said, turning to me. "Do you know, I feel that I have done an extraordinarily good thing for myself in securing little Antonia. No troublesome mamma-in-law—no brothers and sisters, not my own and yet emphatically mine to consider—just the child herself. I am very happy and a very lucky fellow. I am glad my little girl has no past history. She is just her dear little, dainty self, no more and no less."

"What did she want with you now?" I asked.

"Little witch," he said, with a laugh. "The pearls—*the* pearls. She insists on wearing the great necklace on the night of the ball. Dear little girl. I can fancy how the baubles will gleam and shine on her fair throat."

I made no answer, but I was certain that little Antonia's request did not emanate from herself. I thought that I would search for Vandeleur and tell him of the circumstance, but the next remark of Rowland's nipped my project in the bud.

"By the way, your friend has promised to be back for dinner. He left here early this morning."

"Vandeleur?" I cried.

"Yes, he has gone to town. What a first-rate fellow he is!"

"He tells a good story," I answered.

"Capital. Who would suspect him of being the greatest criminal expert of the day? But, thank goodness, we have no need of his services at Rowland's Folly."

Late in the evening Vandeleur returned. He entered the house just before dinner. I observed by the brightness of his eyes and the intense gravity of his manner that he was satisfied with himself. This in his case was always a good sign. At dinner he was his brightest self, courteous to everyone, and to Madame Sara in particular.

Late that night, as I was preparing to go to bed, he entered my room without knocking.

"Well, Druce," he said, "it is all right."

"All right!" I cried; "what do you mean?"

"You will soon know. The moment I saw that woman I had my suspicions. I was in town to-day making some very interesting inquiries. I am primed now on every point. Expect a *dénouement* of a startling character very soon, but be sure of one thing—however black appearances may be the little bride is safe, and so are the pearls."

He left me without waiting for my reply.

The next day passed, and the next. I seemed to live on tenter-hooks. Little Antonia was gay and bright like a bird. Madame's invitation had been extended by Lady Kennedy at Rowland's command to the day after the ball—little Antonia skipped when she heard it.

"I love her," said the girl.

More and more guests arrived—the days flew on wings—the evenings were lively. Madame was a power in herself. Vandeleur was another. These two, sworn foes at heart, aided and abetted each other to make things go brilliantly for the rest of the guests. Rowland was in the highest spirits.

At last the evening before the ball came and went. Vandeleur's *grand coup* had not come off. I retired to bed as usual. The night was a stormy one—rain rattled against the window-panes, the wind sighed and shuddered. I had just put out my candle and was about to seek forgetfulness in sleep when once again in his unceremonious fashion Vandeleur burst into my room.

"I want you at once, Druce, in the bedroom of Madame Sara's servant. Get into your clothes as fast as you possibly can and join me there."

He left the room as abruptly as he had entered it. I hastily dressed, and with stealthy steps, in the dead of night, to the accompaniment of the ever-increasing tempest, sought the room in question.

I found it brightly lighted; Vandeleur pacing the floor as though he himself were the very spirit of the storm; and, most astonishing sight of all, the nurse whom Madame Sara had brought to Rowland's Folly, and whose name I had never happened to hear, gagged and bound in a chair drawn into the centre of the room.

"So I think that is all, nurse," said Vandeleur, as I entered. "Pray take a chair, Druce. We quite understand each other, don't we, nurse, and the facts are wonderfully simple. Your name as entered in the archives of crime at Westminster is not as you have given out, Mary Jessop, but Rebecca Curt. You escaped from Portland prison on the night of November 30th, just a year ago. You could not have managed your escape but for the connivance of the lady in whose service you are now. Your crime was forgery, with a strong and very daring attempt at poisoning. Your victim was a harmless invalid lady. Your knowledge of crime, therefore, is what may be called extensive. There are yet eleven years of your sentence to run. You have doubtless served Madame Sara well—but perhaps you can serve me better. You know the consequence if you refuse, for I explained that to you frankly and clearly before this gentleman came into the room. Druce, will you oblige me—will you lock the door while I remove the gag from the prisoner's mouth?"

I hurried to obey. The woman breathed more freely when the gag was removed. Her face was a swarthy red all over. Her crooked eyes favoured us with many shifty glances.

"Now, then, have the goodness to begin, Rebecca Curt," said Vandeleur. "Tell us everything you can."

She swallowed hard, and said:—

"You have forced me——"

"We won't mind that part," interrupted Vandeleur. "The story, please, Mrs. Curt."

If looks could kill, Rebecca Curt would have killed Vandeleur then. He gave her in return a gentle, bland glance, and she started on her narrative.

"Madame knows a secret about Antonia Ripley."

"Of what nature?"

"It concerns her parentage."

"And that is——?"

The woman hesitated and writhed.

"The names of her parents, please," said Vandeleur, in a voice cold as ice and hard as iron.

"Her father was Italian by birth."

"His name?"

"Count Gioletti. He was unhappily

"WE QUITE UNDERSTAND EACH OTHER, DON'T WE, NURSE?"

married, and stabbed his English wife in an access of jealousy when Antonia was three years old. He was executed for the crime on the 20th of June, 18—. The child was adopted and taken out of the country by an English lady who was present in court—her name was Mrs. Studley. Madame Sara was also present. She was much interested in the trial, and had an interview afterwards with Mrs. Studley. It was arranged that Antonia should be called by the surname of Ripley—the name of an old relative of Mrs. Studley's—and that her real name and history were never to be told to her."

"I understand," said Vandeleur, gently. "This is of deep interest, is it not, Druce?"

I nodded, too much absorbed in watching the face of the woman to have time for words.

"But now," continued Vandeleur, "there are reasons why Madame should change her mind with regard to keeping the matter a close secret—is that not so, Mrs. Curt?"

"Yes," said Mrs. Curt.

"You will have the kindness to continue."

"Madame has an object—she blackmails the signora. She wants to get the signora completely into her power."

"Indeed! Is she succeeding?"

"Yes."

"How has she managed? Be very careful what you say, please."

"The mode is subtle—the young lady had a disfiguring mole or wart on her neck, just below the throat. Madame removed the mole."

"Quite a simple process, I doubt not," said Vandeleur, in a careless tone.

"Yes, it was done easily—I was present. The young lady was conducted into a chamber with a red light."

Vandeleur's extraordinary eyes suddenly leapt into fire. He took a chair and drew it so close to Mrs. Curt's that his face was within a foot or two of hers.

"Now, you will be very careful what you say," he remarked. "You know the consequence to yourself unless this narrative is absolutely reliable."

She began to tremble, but continued:—

"I was present at the operation. Not a single ray of ordinary light was allowed to penetrate. The patient was put under chloroform. The mole was removed. Afterwards Madame wrote something on her neck. The words were very small and neatly done—they formed a cross on the young lady's neck. Afterwards I heard what they were."

"Repeat them."

"I can't. You will know in the moment of victory."

"I choose to know now. A detective from my division at Westminster comes here early to-morrow morning—he brings hand-cuffs—and——"

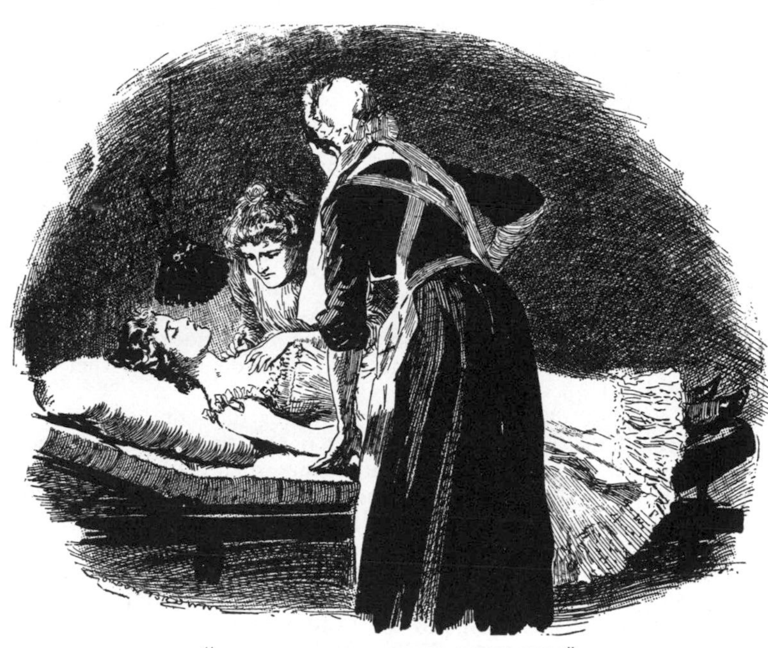

"MADAME WROTE SOMETHING ON HER NECK."

"I will tell you," interrupted the woman. "The words were these:—

"'I AM THE DAUGHTER OF PAOLO GIOLETTI, WHO WAS EXECUTED FOR THE MURDER OF MY MOTHER, JUNE 20TH, 18—.'"

"How were the words written?"

"With nitrate of silver."

"Fiend!" muttered Vandeleur.

He jumped up and began to pace the room. I had never seen his face so black with ungovernable rage.

"You know what this means?" he said at last to me. "Nitrate of silver eats into the flesh and is permanent. Once exposed to the light the case is hopeless, and the help-less child becomes her own executioner."

The nurse looked up restlessly.

"The operation was performed in a room with a red light," she said, "and up to the present the words have not been seen. Unless the young lady exposes her neck to the blue rays of ordinary light they never will be. In order to give her a chance to keep her deadly secret Madame has had a large carbuncle of the deepest red cut and prepared. It is in the shape of a cross, and is suspended to a fine gold, almost invisible, thread. This the signora is to wear when in full evening dress. It will keep in its place, for the back of the cross will be dusted with gum."

"But it cannot be Madame's aim to hide the fateful words," said Vandeleur. "You are concealing something, nurse."

Her face grew an ugly red. After a pause the following words came out with great reluctance:—

"The young lady wears the carbuncle as a reward."

"Ah," said Vandeleur, "now we are beginning to see daylight. As a reward for what?"

"Madame wants something which the signora can give her. It is a case of exchange; the carbuncle which hides the fatal secret is given in exchange for that which the signora can transfer to Madame."

"I understand at last," said Vandeleur. "Really, Druce, I feel myself privileged to say that of all the malevolent——" he broke off abruptly. "Never mind," he said, "we are keeping nurse. Nurse, you have answered all my questions with praiseworthy exactitude, but before you return to your well-earned slumbers I have one more piece of information to seek from you. Was it entirely by Miss Ripley's desire, or was it in any respect owing to Madame Sara's instigations, that the young lady is permitted to wear the pearl necklace on the night of the dance? You have, of course, nurse, heard of the pearl necklace?"

Rebecca Curt's face showed that she undoubtedly had.

"I see you are acquainted with that most interesting story. Now, answer my question. The request to wear the necklace to-morrow night was suggested by Madame, was it not?"

"Ah, yes—yes!" cried the woman, carried out of herself by sudden excitement. "It was to that point all else tended—all, all!"

"Thank you, that will do. You understand that from this day you are absolutely in my service. As long as you serve me faithfully you are safe."

"I will do my best, sir," she replied, in a modest tone, her eyes seeking the ground.

The moment we were alone Vandeleur turned to me.

"Things are simplifying themselves," he said.

"I fail to understand," was my answer. "I should say that complications, and alarming ones, abound."

"Nevertheless, I see my way clear. Druce, it is not good for you to be so long out of bed, but in order that you may repose soundly when you return to your room I will tell you frankly what my mode of operations will be to-morrow. The simplest plan would be to tell Rowland everything, but for various reasons that does not suit me. I take an interest in the little girl, and if she chooses to conceal her secret (at present, remember, she does not know it, but the poor child will certainly be told everything to-morrow) I don't intend to interfere. In the second place, I am anxious to lay a trap for Madame. Now, two things are evident. Madame Sara's object in coming here is to steal the pearls. Her plan is to terrify the little signora into giving them to her in order that the fiendish words written on the child's neck may not be seen. As the signora must wear a dress with a low neck to-morrow night, she can only hide the words by means of the red carbuncle. Madame will only give her the carbuncle if she, in exchange, gives Madame the pearls. You see?"

"I do," I answered, slowly.

He drew himself up to his slender height, and his eyes became full of suppressed laughter.

"The child's neck has been injured with nitrate of silver. Nevertheless, until it is exposed to the blue rays of light the ominous, fiendish words will not appear on her white throat. Once they do appear they will be indelible. Now, listen! Madame, with all her cunning, forgot something. To the action of nitrate of silver there is an antidote. This is nothing more or less than our old friend cyanide of potassium. To-morrow nurse, under my instructions, will take the little patient into a room carefully prepared with the hateful red light, and will bathe the neck just where the baleful words are written with a solution of cyanide of potassium. The nitrate of silver will then become neutralized and the letters will never come out."

"But the child will not know that. The terror of Madame's cruel story will be upon her, and she will exchange the pearls for the cross."

"I think not, for I shall be there to prevent it. Now, Druce, I have told you all that is necessary. Go to bed and sleep comfortably."

The next morning dawned dull and sullen, but the fierce storm of the night before was over. The ravages which had taken place, however, in the stately old park were very manifest, for trees had been torn up by their roots and some of the stateliest and largest of the oaks had been deprived of their best branches.

Little Miss Ripley did not appear at all that day. I was not surprised at her absence. The time had come when doubtless Madame found it necessary to divulge her awful scheme to the unhappy child. In the midst of that gay houseful of people no one specially missed her; even Rowland was engaged with many necessary matters, and had little time to devote to his future wife. The ball-room, decorated with real flowers, was a beautiful sight.

Vandeleur, our host, and I paced up and down the long room. Rowland was in great excitement, making many suggestions, altering this decoration and the other. The flowers were too profuse in one place, too scanty in another. The lights, too, were not bright enough.

"By all means have the ball-room well lighted," said Vandeleur. "In a room like this, so large, and with so many doors leading into passages and sitting-out rooms, it is well to have the light as brilliant as possible. You will forgive my suggestion, Mr. Rowland, when I say I speak entirely from the point of view of a man who has some acquaintance with the treacherous dealings of crime."

Rowland started.

"Are you afraid that an attempt will be made here to-night to steal the necklace?" he asked, suddenly.

"We won't talk of it," replied Vandeleur. "Act on my suggestion and you have nothing to fear."

Rowland shrugged his shoulders, and crossing the room gave some directions to several men who were putting in the final touches.

Nearly a hundred guests were expected to arrive from the surrounding country, and the house was as full as it could possibly hold. Rowland was to open the ball with little Antonia.

There was no late dinner that day, and as evening approached Vandeleur sought me.

"I say, Druce, dress as early as you can, and come down and meet me in our host's study."

I looked at him in astonishment, but did not question him. I saw that he was intensely excited. His face was cold and stern; it invariably wore that expression when he was most moved.

I hurried into my evening clothes and came down again. Vandeleur was standing in the study talking to Rowland. The guests were beginning to arrive. The musicians were tuning-up in the adjacent ball-room, and signs of hurry and festival pervaded the entire place. Rowland was in high spirits and looked very handsome. He and Vandeleur talked together, and I stood a little apart. Vandeleur was just about to make a light reply to one of our host's questions when we heard the swish of drapery in the passage outside, and little Antonia, dressed for her first ball, entered. She was in soft white lace, and her neck and arms were bare. The effect of her entrance was somewhat startling, and would have arrested attention even were we not all specially interested in her. Her face, neck, and arms were nearly as white as her dress, her dark eyes were much dilated, and her soft black hair surrounded her small face like a shadow. In the midst of the whiteness a large red cross sparkled on her throat like living fire. Rowland uttered an exclamation and then stood still; as for Vandeleur and myself, we held our breath in

"WHAT IS IT, LITTLE ONE?"

suspense. What might not the next few minutes reveal?

It was the look on Antonia's face that aroused our fears. What ailed her? She came forward like one blind, or as one who walks in her sleep. One hand was held out slightly in advance, as though she meant to guide herself by the sense of touch. She certainly saw neither Vandeleur nor me, but when she got close to Rowland the blind expression left her eyes. She gave a sudden and exceedingly bitter cry, and ran forward, flinging herself into his arms.

"Kiss me once before we part for ever. Kiss me just once before we part," she said.

"My dear little one," I heard him answer,

"what is the meaning of this? You are not well. There, Antonia, cease trembling. Before we part, my dear? But there is no thought of parting. Let me look at you, darling. Ah!"

He held her at arm's length and gazed at her critically.

"No girl could look sweeter, Antonia," he said, "and you have come now for the finishing touch—the beautiful pearls. But what is this, my dear? Why should you spoil your white neck with anything so incongruous? Let me remove it."

She put up her hand to her neck, thus covering the crimson cross. Then her wild eyes met Vandeleur's. She seemed to recognise his presence for the first time.

"You can safely remove it," he said to her, speaking in a semi-whisper.

Rowland gave him an astonished glance. His look seemed to say, "Leave us," but Vandeleur did not move.

"We must see this thing out," he said to me.

Meanwhile Rowland's arm encircled Antonia's neck, and his hand sought for the clasp of the narrow gold thread that held the cross in place.

"One moment," said Antonia.

She stepped back a pace; the trembling in her voice left it, it gathered strength, her fear gave way to dignity. This was the hour of her deepest humiliation, and yet she looked noble.

"My dearest," she said, "my kindest and best of friends. I had yielded to temptation, terror made me weak, the dread of losing you unnerved me, but I won't come to you charged with a sin on my conscience; I won't conceal anything from you. I know you won't wish me *now* to become your wife; nevertheless, you shall know the truth."

"What do you mean, Antonia? What do your strange words signify? Are you mad?" said George Rowland.

"No, I wish I were; but I am no mate for you; I cannot bring dishonour to your honour. Madame said it could be hidden, that this"—she touched the cross—"would hide it. For this I was to pay—yes, to pay a shameful price. I consented, for the terror was so cruel. But I—I came here and looked into your face and I could not do it. Madame shall have her blood-red cross back and you shall know all. You shall see."

With a fierce gesture she tore the cross from her neck and flung it on the floor.

"The pearls for this," she cried; "the pearls were the price; but I would rather you knew. Take me up to the brightest light and you will see for yourself."

Rowland's face wore an expression impossible to fathom. The red cross lay on the floor; Antonia's eyes were fixed on his. She was no child to be humoured; she was a woman and despair was driving her wild. When she said, "Take me up to the brightest light," he took her hand without a word and led her to where the full rays of a powerful electric light turned the place into day.

"Look!" cried Antonia, "look! Madame wrote it here—here."

She pointed to her throat.

"The words are hidden, but this light will soon cause them to appear. You will see for yourself, you will know the truth. At last you will understand who I really am."

There was silence for a few minutes. Antonia kept pointing to her neck. Rowland's eyes were fixed upon it. After a breathless period of agony Vandeleur stepped forward.

"Miss Antonia," he cried, "you have suffered enough. I am in a position to relieve your terrors. You little guessed, Rowland, that for the last few days I have taken an extreme liberty with regard to you. I have been in your house simply and solely in the exercise of my professional qualities. In the exercise of my manifest duties I came across a ghastly secret. Miss Antonia was to be subjected to a cruel ordeal. Madame Sara, for reasons of her own, had invented one of the most fiendish plots it has ever been my unhappy lot to come across. But I have been in time. Miss Antonia, you need fear nothing. Your neck contains no ghastly secret. Listen! I have saved you. The nurse whom Madame believed to be devoted to her service considered it best for prudential reasons to transfer herself to me. Under my directions she bathed your neck today with a preparation of cyanide of potassium. You do not know what that is, but it is a chemical preparation which neutralizes the effect of what that horrible woman has done. You have nothing to fear—your secret lies buried beneath your white skin."

"But what is the mystery?" said Rowland. "Your actions, Antonia, and your words, Vandeleur, are enough to drive a man mad. What is it all about? I will know."

"Miss Ripley can tell you or not, as she pleases," replied Vandeleur. "The unhappy child was to be blackmailed, Madame Sara's object being to secure the pearl necklace worth a King's ransom. The cross was to be given in exchange for the necklace. That was her aim, but she is defeated. Ask me no questions, sir. If this young lady chooses to tell you, well and good, but if not the secret is her own."

Vandeleur bowed and backed towards me.

"The secret is mine," cried Antonia, "but it also shall be yours, George. I will not be your wife with this ghastly thing between us. You may never speak to me again, but you shall know all the truth."

"Upon my word, a brave girl, and I respect her," whispered Vandeleur. "Come, Druce, our work so far as Miss Antonia is concerned is finished."

We left the room.

"Now to see Madame Sara," continued my friend. "We will go to her rooms. Walls have ears in her case; she doubtless knows the whole *dénouement* already; but we will find her at once, she can scarcely have escaped yet."

He flew upstairs. I followed him. We went from one corridor to another. At last we found Madame's apartments. Her bedroom door stood wide open. Rebecca Curt was standing in the middle of the room. Madame herself was nowhere to be seen, but there was every sign of hurried departure.

"Where is Madame Sara?" inquired Vandeleur, in a peremptory voice.

Rebecca Curt shrugged her shoulders.

"Has she gone down? Is she in the ball-room? Speak!" said Vandeleur.

The nurse gave another shrug.

"I only know that Achmed the Arabian rushed in here a few minutes ago," was her answer. "He was excited. He said something to Madame. I think he had been listening—eavesdropping, you call it. Madame was convulsed with rage. She thrust a few things together and she's gone. Perhaps you can catch her."

Vandeleur's face turned white.

"I'll have a try," he said. "Don't keep me, Druce."

He rushed away. I don't know what immediate steps he took, but he did not return to Rowland's Folly. Neither was Madame Sara captured.

But notwithstanding her escape and her meditated crime, notwithstanding little Antonia's hour of terror, the ball went on merrily, and the bride-elect opened it with her future husband. On her fair neck gleamed the pearls, lovely in their soft lustre. What she told Rowland was never known; how he took the news is a secret between Antonia and himself. But one thing is certain: no one was more gallant in his conduct, more ardent in his glances of love, than was the master of Rowland's Folly that night. They were married on the day fixed, and Madame Sara was defeated.

"REBECCA CURT WAS STANDING IN THE MIDDLE OF THE ROOM."

The Sorceress of the Strand.

By L. T. Meade and Robert Eustace.

III.—THE FACE OF THE ABBOT.

IF Madame Sara had one prerogative more than another it was that of taking people unawares. When least expected she would spring a mine at your feet, engulf you in a most horrible danger, stab you in the dark, or injure you through your best friend; in short, this dangerous woman was likely to become the terror of London if steps were not soon taken to place her in such confinement that her genius could no longer assert itself.

Months went by after my last adventure. Once again my fears slumbered. Madame Sara's was not the first name that I thought of when I awoke in the morning, nor the last to visit my dreams at night. Absorbed in my profession, I had little time to waste upon her. After all, I made up my mind, she might have left London; she might have carried her machinations, her cruelties, and her genius elsewhere.

That such was not the case this story quickly shows.

The matter which brought Madame Sara once again to the fore began in the following way.

On the 17th of July, 1900, I received a letter; it ran as follows:—

"23, West Terrace,
"Charlton Road, Putney.

"Dear Mr. Druce,—I am in considerable difficulty and am writing to beg for your advice. My father died a fortnight ago at his castle in Portugal, leaving me his heiress. His brother-in-law, who lived there with him, arrived in London yesterday and came to see me, bringing me full details of my father's death. These are in the last degree mysterious and terrifying. There are also a lot of business affairs to arrange. I know little about business and should greatly value your advice on the whole situation. Can you come here and see me to-morrow at three o'clock? Senhor de Castro, my uncle, my mother's brother, will be here, and I should like you to meet him. If you can come I shall be very grateful.—Yours sincerely,

"Helen Sherwood."

I replied to this letter by telegram:—

"Will be with you at three to-morrow."

Helen Sherwood was an old friend of mine; that is, I had known her since she was a child. She was now about twenty-three years of age, and was engaged to a certain Godfrey Despard, one of the best fellows I ever met. Despard was employed in a merchant's office in Shanghai, and the chance of immediate marriage was small. Nevertheless, the young people were determined to be true to each other and to wait that turn in the tide which comes to most people who watch for it.

Helen's life had been a sad one. Her mother, a Portuguese lady of good family, had died at her birth; her father, Henry Sherwood, had gone to Lisbon in 1860 as one of the Under-Secretaries to the Embassy and never cared to return to England. After the death of his wife he had lived as an eccentric recluse. When Helen was three years old he had sent her home, and she had been brought up by a maiden aunt of her father's, who had never understood the impulsive, eager girl, and had treated her with a rare want of sympathy. This woman had died when her young charge was sixteen

"SHE TREATED HER WITH A RARE WANT OF SYMPATHY."

years of age. She had left no money behind her, and, as her father declined to devote one penny to his daughter's maintenance, Helen had to face the world before her education was finished. But her character was full of spirit and determination. She stayed on at school as pupil teacher, and afterwards supported herself by her attainments. She was a good linguist, a clever musician, and had one of the most charming voices I ever heard in an amateur. When this story opens she was earning a comfortable independence, and was even saving a little money for that distant date when she would marry the man she loved.

Meanwhile Sherwood's career was an extraordinary one. He had an extreme stroke of fortune in drawing the first prize of the Grand Christmas State Lottery in Lisbon, amounting to one hundred and fifty million reis, representing in English money thirty thousand pounds. With this sum he bought an old castle in the Estrella Mountains, and, accompanied by his wife's brother, a certain Petro de Castro, went there to live. He was hated by his fellow-men and, with the exception of De Castro, he had no friends. The old castle was said to be of extraordinary beauty, and was known as Castello Mondego. It was situated some twenty miles beyond the old Portuguese town of Coimbra. The historical accounts of the place were full of interest, and its situation was marvellously romantic, being built on the heights above the Mondego River. The castle dated from the twelfth century, and had seen brave and violent deeds. It was supposed to be haunted by an old monk who was said to have been murdered there, but within living memory no one had seen him. At least, so Helen had informed me.

Punctually at three o'clock on the following day I found myself at West Terrace, and was shown into my young friend's pretty little sitting-room.

"How kind of you to come, Mr. Druce!" she said. "May I introduce you to my uncle, Senhor de Castro?"

The Senhor, a fine-looking man, who spoke English remarkably well, bowed, gave a

"'HOW KIND OF YOU TO COME, MR. DRUCE, SHE SAID.'"

gracious smile, and immediately entered into conversation. His face had strong features; his beard was iron-grey, so also were his hair and moustache. He was slightly bald about the temples. I imagined him to be a man about forty-five years of age.

"Now," said Helen, after we had talked to each other for a few minutes, "perhaps, Uncle Petro, you will explain to Mr. Druce what has happened."

As she spoke I noticed that her face was very pale and that her lips slightly trembled.

"It is a painful story," said the Portuguese, "most horrible and inexplicable."

I prepared myself to listen, and he continued :—

"For the last few months my dear friend had been troubled in his mind. The reason appeared to me extraordinary. I knew that Sherwood was eccentric, but he was also matter-of-fact, and I should have thought him the last man who would be likely to be a prey to nervous terrors. Nevertheless, such was the case. The old castle has the reputation of being haunted, and the apparition that is supposed to trouble Mondego is that of a ghastly white face that is now and then seen at night peering out through some of the windows or one of the embrasures of the battlements surrounding the courtyard. It is said to be the shade of an abbot who was foully murdered there by a Castilian nobleman who owned the castle a hundred years ago.

"It was late in April of this year when my brother-in-law first declared that he saw the apparition. I shall never forget his terror. He came to me in my room, woke me, and pointed out the embrasure where he had seen it. He described it as a black figure leaning out of a window, with an appallingly horrible white face, with wide-open eyes apparently staring at nothing. I argued with him and tried to appeal to his common sense, and did everything in my power to bring him to reason, but without avail. The terror grew worse and worse. He could think and talk of nothing else, and, to make matters worse, he collected all the old literature he could find bearing on the legend. This he would read, and repeat the ghastly information to me at meal times. I began to fear that his mind would become affected, and three weeks ago I persuaded him to come away with me for a change to Lisbon. He agreed, but the very night before we were to leave I was awakened in the small hours by hearing an awful cry, followed by another, and then the sound of my own name. I ran out into the courtyard and looked up at the battlements. There I saw, to my horror, my brother-in-law rushing along the edge, screaming as though in extreme terror, and evidently imagining that he was pursued by something. The next moment he dashed headlong down a hundred feet on to the flagstones by my side, dying instantaneously. Now comes the most horrible part. As I glanced up I saw, and I swear it with as much certainty as I am now speaking to you, a black figure leaning out over the battlement exactly at the spot from which he had fallen—a figure with a ghastly white face, which stared straight down at me. The moon was full, and gave the face a clearness that was unmistakable. It was large, round, and smooth, white with a whiteness I had never seen on human face, with eyes widely open, and a fixed stare; the face was rigid and tense; the mouth shut and drawn at the corners. Fleeting as the glance was, for it vanished almost the next moment, I shall never forget it. It is indelibly imprinted on my memory."

"HE DASHED HEADLONG DOWN."

He ceased speaking.

From my long and constant contact with men and their affairs, I knew at once that what De Castro had just said instantly raised the whole matter out of the commonplace; true or untrue, real or false, serious issues were at stake.

"Who else was in the castle that night?" I asked.

"No one," was his instant reply. "Not even old Gonsalves, our one man-servant. He had gone to visit his people in the mountains about ten miles off. We were absolutely alone."

"You know Mr. Sherwood's affairs pretty well?" I went on. "On the supposition of trickery, could there be any motive that you know of for anyone to play such a ghastly trick?"

"Absolutely none."

"You never saw the apparition before this occasion?"

"Never."

"And what were your next steps?"

"There was nothing to be done except to carry poor Sherwood indoors. He was buried on the following day. I made every effort to have a systematic inquiry set on foot, but the castle is in a remote spot and the authorities are slow to move. The Portuguese doctor gave his sanction to the burial after a formal inquiry. Deceased was testified as having committed suicide while temporarily insane, but to investigate the apparition they absolutely declined."

"And now," I said, "will you tell me what you can with regard to the disposition of the property?"

"The will is a very remarkable one," replied De Castro. "Senhor Sousa, my brother-in-law's lawyer, holds it. Sherwood died a much richer man than I had any idea of. This was owing to some very successful speculations. The real and personal estate amounts to seventy thousand pounds, but the terms of the will are eccentric. Henry Sherwood's passionate affection for the old castle was quite morbid, and the gist of the conditions of the will is this: Helen is to live on the property, and if she does, and as long as she does, she is to receive the full interest on forty thousand pounds, which is now invested in good English securities. Failing this condition, the property is to be sold, and the said forty thousand pounds is to go to a Portuguese charity in Lisbon. I also have a personal interest in the will. This I knew from Sherwood himself. He told me that his firm intention was to retain the castle in the family for his daughter, and for her son if she married. He earnestly begged of me to promote his wishes in the event of his dying. I was not to leave a stone unturned to persuade Helen to live at the castle, and in order to ensure my carrying out his wishes he bequeathed to me the sum of ten thousand pounds provided Helen lives at Castello Mondego. If she does not do so I lose the money. Hence my presence here and my own personal anxiety to clear up the mystery of my friend's death, and to see my niece installed as owner of the most lovely and romantic property in the Peninsula. It has, of course, been my duty to give a true account of the mystery surrounding my unhappy brother-in-law's death, and I sincerely trust that a solution to this terrible mystery will be found, and that Helen will enter into her beautiful possessions with all confidence."

"The terms of the will are truly eccentric," I said. Then turning to Helen I added:—

"Surely you can have no fear in living at Castello Mondego when it would be the means of bringing about the desire of your heart?"

"Does that mean that you are engaged to be married, Helen?" asked De Castro.

"It does," she replied. Then she turned to me. "I am only human, and a woman. I could not live at Castello Mondego with this mystery unexplained; but I am willing to take every step—yes, *every* step, to find out the truth."

"Let me think over the case," I said, after a pause. "Perhaps I may be able to devise some plan for clearing up this unaccountable matter. There is no man in the whole of London better fitted to grapple with the mystery than I, for it is, so to speak, my profession."

"You will please see in me your hearty collaborator, Mr. Druce," said Senhor de Castro.

"When do you propose to return to Portugal?" I asked.

"As soon as I possibly can."

"Where are you staying now?"

"At the Cecil."

He stood up as he spoke.

"I am sorry to have to run away," he said. "I promised to meet a friend, a lady, in half an hour from now. She is a very busy woman, and I must not keep her waiting."

His words were commonplace enough, but I noticed a queer change in his face. His eyes grew full of eagerness, and yet—was it possible?—a curious fear seemed also to fill them. He shook hands with Helen, bowed to me, and hurriedly left the room.

"I wonder whom he is going to meet," she said, glancing out of the window and watching his figure as he walked down the street. "He told me when he first came that he had an interview pending of a very important character. But, there, I must not keep you, Mr. Druce; you are also a very busy man. Before you go, however, do tell me what you think of the whole thing. I certainly cannot live at the castle while that ghastly face is unexplained; but at the same time I do not wish to give up the property."

"You shall live there, enjoy the property, and be happy," I answered. "I will think over everything; I am certain we shall see a way out of the mystery."

I wrung her hand and hurried away.

During the remainder of the evening this extraordinary case occupied my thoughts to the exclusion of almost everything else. I made up my mind to take it up, to set every inquiry on foot, and, above all things, to ascertain if there was a physical reason for the apparition's appearance; in short, if Mr. Sherwood's awful death was for the benefit of any living person. But I must confess that, think as I would, I could not see the slightest daylight until I remembered the curious expression of De Castro's face when he spoke of his appointment with a lady. The man had undoubtedly his weak point; he had his own private personal fear. What was its nature?

I made a note of the circumstance and determined to speak to Vandeleur about it when I had a chance.

The next morning one of the directors of our agency called. He and I had a long talk over business matters, and when he was leaving he asked me when I wished to take my holiday.

"If you like to go away for a fortnight or three weeks, now is your time," was his final remark.

I answered without a moment's hesitation that I should wish to go to Portugal, and would take advantage of the leave of absence which he offered me.

Now, it had never occurred to me to think of visiting Portugal until that moment; but so strongly did the idea now take possession of me that I went at once to the Cecil and had an interview with De Castro. I told him that I could not fulfil my promise to Miss Sherwood without being on the spot, and I should therefore accompany him when he returned to Lisbon. His face expressed genuine delight, and before we parted we arranged to meet at Charing Cross on the morning after the morrow. I then hastened to Putney to inform Helen Sherwood of my intention.

To my surprise I saw her busy placing different articles of her wardrobe in a large trunk which occupied the place of honour in the centre of the little sitting-room.

"What are you doing?" I cried.

She coloured.

"You must not scold me," she said. "There is only one thing to do, and I made up my mind this morning to do it. The day after to-morrow I am going to Lisbon. I mean to investigate the mystery for myself."

"You are a good, brave girl," I cried. "But listen, Helen; it is not necessary."

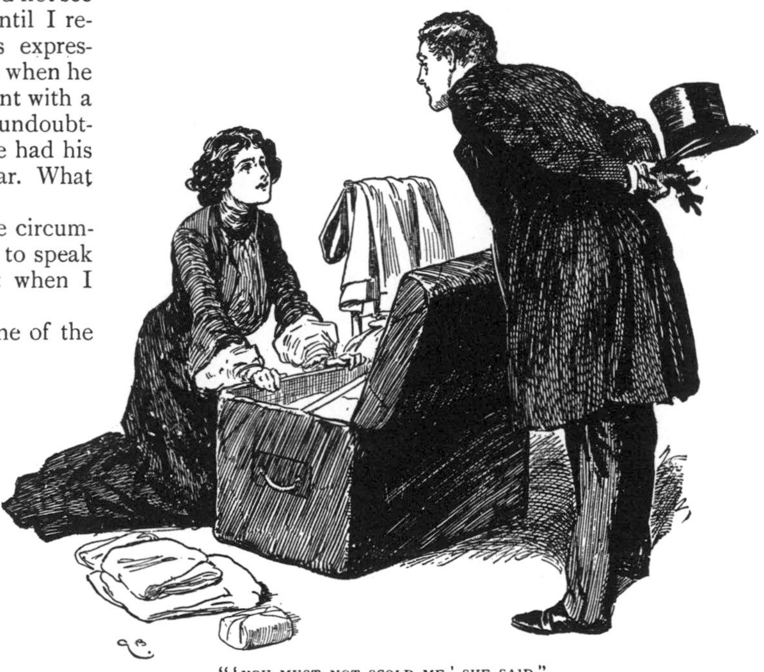

"'YOU MUST NOT SCOLD ME,' SHE SAID."

I then told her that I had unexpectedly obtained a few weeks' holiday, and that I intended to devote the time to her service.

"Better and better," she cried. "I go with you. Nothing could have been planned more advantageously for me."

"What put the idea into your head?" I asked.

"It isn't my own," she said. "I spent a dreadful night, and this morning, soon after ten o'clock, I had an unexpected visitor. She is not a stranger to me, although I have never mentioned her name. She is known as Madame Sara, and is——"

"My dear Helen!" I cried. "You don't mean to tell me you know that woman? She is one of the most unscrupulous in the whole of London. You must have nothing to do with her—nothing whatever."

Helen opened her eyes to their widest extent.

"You misjudge Madame Sara," she said. "I have known her for the last few years, and she has been a most kind friend to me. She has got me more than one good post as teacher, and I have always felt a warm admiration for her. She is, beyond doubt, the most unselfish woman I ever met."

I shook my head.

"You will not get me to alter my opinion of her," continued Helen. "Think of her kindness in calling to see me to-day. She drove here this morning just because she happened to see my uncle, Petro de Castro, yesterday. She has known him, too, for some time. She had a talk with him about me, and he told her all about the strange will. She was immensely interested, and said that it was imperative for me to investigate the matter myself. She spoke in the most sensible way, and said finally that she would not leave me until I had promised to go to Portugal to visit the castle, and in my own person to unearth the mystery. I promised her and felt she was right. I am keeping my word."

When Helen had done speaking I remained silent. I could scarcely describe the strange sensation which visited me. Was it possible that the fear which I had seen so strongly depicted on De Castro's face was caused by Madame Sara? Was the mystery in the old Portuguese castle also connected with this terrible woman? If so, what dreadful revelations might not be before us! Helen was not the first innocent girl who believed in Madame, and not the first whose life was threatened.

"Why don't you speak, Mr. Druce?" she asked me at last. "What are you thinking of?"

"I would rather not say what I am thinking of," I answered; "but I am very glad of one thing, and that is that I am going with you."

"You are my kindest, best friend," she said; "and now I will tell you one thing more. Madame said that the fact of your being one of the party put all danger out of the case so far as I was concerned, for she knew you to be the cleverest man she ever met."

"Ah!" I replied, slowly, "there is a cleverer man than I, and his name is Eric Vandeleur. Did she happen to speak of him?"

"No. Who is he? I have never heard of him."

"I will tell you some day," I replied, "but not now."

I rose, bade her a hasty good-bye, and went straight to Vandeleur's rooms.

Whatever happened, I had made up my mind to consult him in the matter. He was out when I called, but I left a note, and he came round to my place in the course of the evening.

In less than a quarter of an hour I put him in possession of all the facts. He received my story in silence.

"Well!" I cried at last. "What do you think?"

"There is but one conclusion, Druce," was his reply. "There is a motive in this mystery—method in this madness. Madame is mixed up in it. That being the case, anything supernatural is out of the question. I am sorry Miss Sherwood is going to Lisbon, but the fact that you are going too may be her protection. Beyond doubt her life is in danger. Well, you must do your best, and forewarned is forearmed. I should like to go with you, but I cannot. Perhaps I may do more good here watching the arch-fiend who is pulling the strings."

De Castro took the information quietly that his niece was about to accompany us.

"Women are strange creatures," he said. "Who would suppose that a delicate girl would subject herself to the nervous terrors she must undergo in the castle? Well, let her come—it may be best, and my friend, the lady about whom I spoke to you, recommended it."

"You mean Madame Sara?" I said.

"Ah!" he answered, with a start. "Do you know her?"

"Slightly," I replied, in a guarded tone. Then I turned the conversation.

Our journey took place without adventure, and when we got to Lisbon we put up at Durrand's Hotel.

On the afternoon of that same day we went to interview Manuel Sousa, the lawyer who had charge of Mr. Sherwood's affairs. His office was in the Rue do Rio Janeiro. He was a short, bright-eyed little man, having every appearance of honesty and ability. He received us affably and looked with much interest at Helen Sherwood, whose calm, brave face and English appearance impressed him favourably.

"So you have come all this long way,

"'YOU MEAN MADAME SARA?' I SAID."

Senhora," he said, "to investigate the mystery of your poor father's death? Be assured I will do everything in my power to help you. And now you would all like to see the documents and papers. Here they are at your service."

He opened a tin box and lifted out a pile of papers. Helen went up to one of the windows.

"I don't understand Portuguese," she said. "You will examine them for me, won't you, Uncle Petro, and you also, Mr. Druce?"

I had a sufficient knowledge of Portuguese to be able to read the will, and I quickly discovered that De Castro's account of it was quite correct.

"Is it your intention to go to Castello Mondego?" asked the lawyer, when our interview was coming to an end.

"I can answer for myself that I intend to go," I replied.

"It will give me great pleasure to take Mr. Druce to that romantic spot," said De Castro.

"And I go with you," cried Helen.

"My dear, dear young lady," said the lawyer, a flicker of concern crossing his bright eyes, "is that necessary? You will find the castle very lonely and not prepared for the reception of a lady."

"Even so, I have come all this long way to visit it," replied Helen. "I go with my friend, Mr. Druce, and with my uncle, and so far as I am concerned the sooner we get there the better."

The lawyer held up his hands.

"I wouldn't sleep in that place," he exclaimed, "for twenty contos of reis."

"Then you really believe in the apparition?" I said. "You think it is supernatural?"

He involuntarily crossed himself.

"The tale is an old one," he said. "It has been known for a hundred years that the castle is haunted by a monk who was treacherously murdered there. That is the reason, Miss Sherwood, why your father got it so cheap."

"Supernatural or not, I must get to the bottom of the thing," she said, in a low voice.

De Castro jumped up, an impatient expression crossing his face.

"If you don't want me for the present, Druce," he said, "I have some business of my own that I wish to attend to."

He left the office, and Helen and I were about to follow him when Senhor Sousa suddenly addressed me.

"By the way, Mr. Druce, I am given to understand that you are from the Solvency Inquiry Agency of London. I know that great business well; I presume, therefore, that matters of much interest depend upon this inquiry?"

"The interests are great," I replied, "but are in no way connected with my business. My motive in coming here is due to friendship. This young lady is engaged to be married to a special friend of mine, and I have known her personally from her childhood. If we can clear up the present mystery, Helen Sherwood's marriage can take place at once. If, on the other hand, that terror which hangs over Castello Mondego is so overpowering that Miss Sherwood cannot make up her mind to live there, a long separation awaits the young pair. I have answered your question, Senhor Sousa; will you, on your part, answer mine?"

"Certainly," he replied. His face looked keenly interested, and from time to time he glanced from Helen to me.

"Are you aware of the existence of any motive which would induce someone to personate the apparition and so bring about Mr. Sherwood's death?"

"I know of no such motive, my dear sir. Senhor de Castro will come into ten thousand pounds provided, and only provided, Miss Sherwood takes possession of the property. He is the one and only person who benefits under the will, except Miss Sherwood herself."

"We must, of course, exclude Senhor de Castro," I answered. "His conduct has been most honourable in the matter throughout; he might have been tempted to suppress the story of the ghost, which would have been to his obvious advantage. Is there no one else whom you can possibly suspect?"

"No one—absolutely no one."

"Very well; my course is clear. I have come here to get an explanation of the mystery. When it is explained Miss Sherwood will take possession of the castle."

"And should you fail, sir? Ghosts have a way of suppressing themselves when most earnestly desired to put in an appearance."

"I don't anticipate failure, Senhor Sousa, and I mean to go to the castle immediately."

"We are a superstitious race," he replied, "and I would not go there for any money you liked to offer me."

"I am an Englishman, and this lady is English on her father's side. We do not easily abandon a problem when we set to work to solve it."

"What do you think of it all?" asked Helen of me, when we found ourselves soon afterwards in the quaint, old-world streets.

"Think!" I answered. "Our course is clear. We have got to discover the motive. There must be a motive. There was someone who had a grudge against the old man, and who wished to terrify him out of the world. As to believing that the apparition is supernatural, I decline even to allow myself to consider it."

"Heaven grant that you may be right," she answered; "but I must say a strange and most unaccountable terror oppresses me whenever I conjure up that ghastly face."

"And yet you have the courage to go to the castle!"

"It is a case of duty, not of courage, Mr. Druce."

For the rest of that day I thought over the whole problem, looking at it from every point of view, trying to gaze at it with fresh eyes, endeavouring to discover the indiscoverable —the motive. There must be a motive. We should find it at the castle. We would go there on the morrow. But, no; undue haste was unnecessary. It might be well for me, helped as I should be by my own agency, a branch of which was to be found in Lisbon, to discover amongst the late Mr. Sherwood's acquaintances, friends, or relatives the motive that I wanted. My agents set to work for me, but though they did their utmost no discovery of the least value was found, and at the end of a week I told De Castro and Helen that I was ready to start.

"We will go early to-morrow morning," I said. "You must make all your preparations, Helen. It will take us the day to reach Castello Mondego. I hope that our work may be completed there, and that we may be back again in Lisbon within the week."

Helen's face lit up with a smile of genuine delight.

"The inaction of the last week has been terribly trying," she said. "But now that we are really going to get near the thing I feel quite cheerful."

"Your courage fills me with admiration," I could not help saying, and then I went out to make certain purchases. Amongst these were three revolvers—one for Helen, one for De Castro, and one for myself.

Afterwards I had an interview with Sousa, and took him as far as I could into my confidence.

"The danger of the supernatural is not worth considering," I said, "but the danger of treachery, of unknown motives, is considerable. I do not deny this fact for a moment. In case you get no tidings of us, come yourself or send some one to the castle within a week."

"This letter came for you by the last post," said Sousa, and he handed me one from Vandeleur.

I opened it and read as follows:—

"I met Madame Sara a week ago at the house of a friend. I spoke to her about Castello Mondego. She admitted that she was interested in it, that she knew Miss Sherwood, and hoped when she had taken possession to visit her in that romantic spot. I inquired further if she was aware of the contents of the strange will. She said she had heard of it. Her manner was perfectly frank, but I saw that she was uneasy. She took the first opportunity of leaving the house, and on making inquiries I hear that she left London by the first train this morning, *en route* for the Continent. These facts may mean a great deal, and I should advise you to be more than ever on your guard."

I put the letter into my pocket, got Sousa to promise all that was necessary, and went away.

At an early hour the following morning we left Rocio Station for Coimbra, and it was nearly seven in the evening when we finally came to the end of our railway journey and entered a light wagonette drawn by two powerful bay stallions for our twenty-mile drive to the castle.

The scenery as we approached the spurs of the Estrella was magnificent beyond description, and as I gazed up at the great peaks, now bathed in the purples and golds of the sunset, the magic and mystery of our strange mission became tenfold intensified. Presently the steep ascent began along a winding road between high walls that shut out our view, and by the time we reached the castle it was too dark to form any idea of its special features.

"A PHLEGMATIC-LOOKING MAN OPENED THE DOOR FOR US."

De Castro had already sent word of our probable arrival, and when we rang the bell at the old castle a phlegmatic-looking man opened the door for us.

"Ah, Gonsalves," cried De Castro, "here we are! I trust you have provided comfortable beds and a good meal, for we are all as hungry as hawks."

The old man shrugged his shoulders, raised his beetle-brows a trifle, and fixed his eyes on Helen with some astonishment. He muttered, in a Portuguese dialect which I did not in the least comprehend, something to De Castro, who professed himself satisfied. Then he said something further, and I noticed the face of my Portuguese friend turn pale.

"Gonsalves saw the spectre three nights ago," he remarked, turning to me. "It was leaning as usual out of one of the windows of the north-west turret. But, come; we must not terrify ourselves the moment we enter your future home, Niece Helen. You are doubtless hungry. Shall we go to the banqueting-hall?"

The supper prepared for us was not appetizing, consisting of some miserable goat-chops, and in the great hall, dimly lighted by a few candles in silver sconces, we could scarcely see each other's faces. As supper was coming to an end I made a suggestion.

"We have come here," I said, "on a serious matter. We propose to start an investigation of a very grave character. It is well known that ghosts prefer to reveal themselves to one man or woman alone, and not to a company. I propose, therefore, that we three should occupy rooms as far as possible each from the other in the castle, and that the windows of our three bedrooms should command the centre square."

De Castro shrugged his shoulders and a look of dismay spread for a moment over his face; but Helen fixed her great eyes on mine, her lips moved slightly as though she would speak, then she pulled herself together.

"You are right, Mr. Druce," she said. "Having come on this inquiry, we must fear nothing."

"Well, come at once, and we will choose

our bedrooms. You as the lady shall have the first choice."

De Castro called Gonsalves, who appeared holding a lantern in his hand. A few words were said to the man in his own dialect, and he led the way, going up many stone stairs, down many others, and at last he flung open a huge oak door and we found ourselves in a vast chamber with five windows, all mullioned and sunk in deep recesses. On the floor was a heavy carpet. A four-post bedstead with velvet hangings was in a recess. The rest of the furniture was antique and massive, nearly black with age, but relieved by brass mountings, which, strange to say, were bright as though they had recently been rubbed.

"This was poor Sherwood's own bedroom," said De Castro. "Do you mind sleeping here?"

He turned to Helen.

"No, I should like it," she replied, emphatically.

"I am glad that this is your choice," he said, "for I don't believe, although I am a man and you are a woman, that I could myself endure this room. It was here I watched by his dead body. Ah, poor fellow, I loved him well."

"We won't talk of memories to-night," said Helen. "I am very tired, and I believe I shall sleep. Strange as it may sound, I am not afraid. Mr. Druce, where will you locate yourself? I should like, at least, to know what room you will be in."

I smiled at her. Her bravery astonished me. I selected a room at right angles to Helen's. Standing in one of her windows she could, if necessary, get a glimpse of me if I were to stand in one of mine.

De Castro chose a room equally far away from Helen's on the other side. We then both bade the girl good-night.

"I hate to leave her so far from help," I said, glancing at De Castro.

"Nothing will happen," he replied. "I can guarantee that. I am dead tired; the moment I lay my head on my pillow, ghost or no ghost, I shall sleep till morning."

He hurried off to his own room.

The chamber that I had selected was vast, lofty, and might have accommodated twenty people. I must have been more tired even than I knew, for I fell asleep when my head touched the pillow.

When I awoke it was dawn, and, eager to see my surroundings by the light of day, I sprang up, dressed, and went down to the courtyard. Three sides of this court were formed by the castle buildings, but along the fourth ran a low balustrade of stone. I sauntered towards it. I shall never forget the loveliness of the scene that met my eyes. I stood upon what was practically a terrace—a mere shelf on the scarping of rock on the side of a dizzy cliff that went down below me a sheer two thousand feet. The Mondego River ran with a swift rushing noise at the foot of the gorge, although at the height at which I stood it looked more like a thread of silver than anything else. Towering straight in front of me, solemnly up into the heavens, stood the great peak of the Serra da Estrella, from which in the rosy sunrise the morning clouds were rolling into gigantic white wreaths. Behind me was the great irregular pile of the castle, with its battlements, turrets, and cupolas, hoar and grey with the weight of centuries, but now transfigured and bathed in the golden light. I had just turned to glance at them when I saw De Castro approaching me.

"Surely," I said, "there never was such a beautiful place in the world before! We can never let it go out of the family. Helen shall live here."

De Castro came close to me; he took my arm, and pointed to a spot on the stone flags.

"On this very spot her father fell from the battlements above," he said, slowly.

I shuddered, and all pleasant thoughts were instantly dispelled by the memory of that hideous tragedy and the work we had still to do. It seemed impossible in this radiant, living sunlight to realize the horror that these walls had contained, and might still contain. At some of these very windows the ghastly face had appeared.

Helen, De Castro, and I spent the whole day exploring the castle. We went from dungeons to turrets, and made elaborate plans for alternate nightly vigils. One of the first things that I insisted on was that Gonsalves should not sleep in the castle at night. This was easily arranged, the old man having friends in the neighbouring village. Thus the only people in the castle after nightfall would be De Castro, Helen, and myself.

After we had locked old Gonsalves out and had raised the portcullis, we again went the complete round of the entire place. Thus we ensured that no one else could be hiding in the precincts. Finally we placed across every entrance thin silken threads, which would be broken if anyone attempted to pass them.

Helen was extremely anxious that the night should be divided into three portions, and that she should share the vigils; but this both De Castro and I prohibited.

"At least for to-night," I said. "Sleep soundly; trust the matter to us. Believe me, this will be best. All arrangements are made. Your uncle will patrol until one o'clock in the morning, then I will go on duty."

This plan was evidently most repugnant to her, and when De Castro left the room she came up and began to plead with me.

"I have a strange and overpowering sensation of terror," she said. "Fight as I will, I cannot get rid of it. I would much rather be up than in that terrible room. I slept last night because I was too weary to do anything else, but I am wakeful to-night, and I shall not close my eyes. Let me share your watch at least. Let us pace the courtyard side by side."

"No," I answered, "that would not do. If two of us are together the ghost, or whatever human being poses as the ghost, will not dare to put in an appearance. We must abide by our terrible mission, Helen; each must watch alone. You will go to bed now, like a good girl, and to-morrow night, if we have not then discovered anything, you will be allowed to take your share in the night watch."

"Very well," she answered.

She sighed impatiently, and after a moment she said:—

"I have a premonition that something will happen to-night. As a rule my premonitions come right."

I made no answer, but I could not help giving her a startled glance. It is one thing to be devoid of ghostly terrors when living in practical London, surrounded by the world and the ways of men, but it is another thing to be proof against the strange terror which visits all human beings more or less when they are alone, when it is night, when the heart beats low. Then we are apt to have distorted visions, our mental equilibrium is upset, and we fear we know not what.

Helen and I knew that there was something to fear, and as our eyes met we dared not speak of what was uppermost in our thoughts. I could not find De Castro, and presumed that he had taken up his watch without further ado. I therefore retired to my own room and prepared to sleep. But the wakefulness which had seized Helen was also mine, for when the Portuguese entered my bedroom at one o'clock I was wide awake.

"You have seen nothing?" I said to him.

"Nothing," he answered, cheerfully. "The moon is bright, the night is glorious. It is my opinion that the apparition will not appear."

"I will take the precaution to put this in my pocket," I said, and I took up my revolver, which was loaded.

As I stepped out into the courtyard I found that the brilliant moonlight had lit up the north-west wall and the turrets; but the sharp black shadow of the south wall lay diagonally across the yard. Absolute stillness reigned, broken only by the croaking of thousands of frogs from the valley below. I sat down on a stone bench by the balustrade and tried to analyze my feelings. For a time the cheerfulness which I had seen so marked on De Castro's face seemed to have communicated itself to me; my late fears vanished, I was not even nervous, I found it difficult to concentrate my thoughts on the object which had brought me so far from England. My mind wandered back to London and to my work there. But by degrees, as the chill stole over me and the stillness of night began to embrace me, I found myself glancing ever and again at those countless windows and deep embrasures, while a queer, overpowering tension began to be felt, and against my own will a terror, strange and humiliating, overpowered me. I knew that it was stronger than I, and, fight against it as I would, I could not overcome it. The instinctive dread of the unknown that is at the bottom of the bravest man's courage was over me. Each moment it increased, and I felt that if the hideous face were to appear at one of the windows I would not be answerable for my self-control. Suddenly, as I sat motionless, my eyes riveted on the windows of the old castle, I felt, or fancied I felt, that I was not alone. It seemed to me that a shadow moved down in the courtyard and close to me. I looked again; it was coming towards me. It was with difficulty I could suppress the scream which almost rose to my lips. The next instant I was glad that I had not lost my self-control, when the slim, cold hand of Helen Sherwood touched mine.

"Come," she said, softly.

She took my hand and, without a word, led me across the courtyard.

"Look up," she said.

I did look up, and then my heart seemed to stop and every muscle in my body grew rigid as though from extreme cold. At one of the first-floor windows in the north-west tower, there in the moonlight leant the apparition itself: a black, solemn figure—its arms crossed on the sill—a large, round face of waxy whiteness, features immobile and fixed in a hideous, unwinking stare right across the courtyard.

"THERE IN THE MOONLIGHT LEANT THE APPARITION ITSELF."

My heart gave a stab of terror, then I remained absolutely rigid—I forgot the girl by my side in the wild beating of my pulse. It seemed to me that it must beat itself to death.

"Call my uncle," whispered Helen, and when I heard her voice I knew that the girl was more self-possessed than I was.

"Call him," she said again, "loudly—at once."

I shouted his name:—

"De Castro, De Castro; it is here!"

The figure vanished at my voice.

"Go," said Helen again. "Go; I will wait for you here. Follow it at once."

I rushed up the stairs towards the room where De Castro slept. I burst open his door. The room was empty. The next instant I heard his voice.

"I am here—here," he said. "Come at once—quick!"

In a moment I was at his side.

"This is the very room where it stood," I said.

I ran to the window and looked down. De Castro followed me. Helen had not moved. She was still gazing up—the moonlight fell full on her white face.

"You saw it too?" gasped De Castro.

"Yes," I said, "and so did Helen. It stood by this window."

"I was awake," he said, "and heard your shout. I rushed to my window; I saw the spectre distinctly, and followed it to this room. You swear you saw it? It was the face of the abbot."

My brain was working quickly, my courage was returning. The unfathomable terror of the night scene was leaving me. I took De Castro suddenly by both his arms and turned him round so that the moonlight should fall upon him.

"You and I are alone in this tower. Helen Sherwood is in the courtyard. There is not another living being in the whole castle. Now listen. There are only two possible explanations of what has just occurred. Either you are the spectre, or it is supernatural."

"I?" he cried. "Are you mad?"

"I well might be," I answered, bitterly. "But f this I am certain: you must prove to me whether you are the apparition or not. I make this suggestion now in order to clear you from all possible blame; I make it that we may have

"EITHER YOU ARE THE SPECTRE, OR IT IS SUPERNATURAL."

absolute evidence that could not be upset before the most searching tribunal. Will you now strip before me?—yes, before you leave the room, and prove that you have no mask hidden anywhere on you. If you do this I shall be satisfied. Pardon my insistence, but in a case like the present there must be no loophole."

"Of course, I understand you," he said. "I will remove my clothes."

In five minutes he had undressed and dressed again. There was no treachery on his part. There was no mask nor any possible means of his simulating that face on his person.

"There is no suspicion about you," I said, almost with bitterness. "By heavens, I wish there were. The awfulness of this thing will drive me mad. Look at that girl standing by herself in the courtyard. I must return to her. Think of the courage of a woman who would stand there alone."

He made no answer. I saw that he was shivering.

"Why do you tremble?" I said, suddenly.

"Because of the nameless fear," he replied. "Remember I saw her father—I saw him with the terror on him—he ran along the battlements; he threw himself over—he died. He was dashed to pieces on the very spot where she is standing. Get her to come in, Druce."

"I will go and speak to her," I said.

I went back to the courtyard. I rejoined Helen, and in a few words told her what had occurred.

"You must come in now," I said. "You will catch your death of cold standing here."

She smiled, a slow, enigmatic sort of smile.

"I have not given up the solution yet," she said, "nor do I mean to."

As she spoke she took her revolver from her belt, and I saw that she was strangely excited. Her manner showed intense excitement, but no fear.

"I suspect foul play," she said. "As I stood here and watched you and Uncle Petro talking to each other by that window I felt convinced—I am more than ever convinced——"

She broke off suddenly.

"Look! — oh, Heaven, look! What is that?"

She had scarcely uttered the words before the same face appeared at another window to the right. Helen gave a sharp cry, and the next instant she covered the awful face with her revolver and fired. A shrill scream rang out on the night air.

"It is human after all," said Helen; "I thought it was. Come."

She rushed up the winding stairs; I followed. The door of the room where we had seen the spectre was open. We both dashed in. Beneath the window lay a dark, huddled heap with the moonlight shining on it, and staring up with the same wide-open eyes was the face of the abbot. Just for a moment neither Helen nor I dared to approach it, but after a time we cautiously drew near the dark mass. The figure never moved. I ran forward and stretched out my hand. Closer and closer I bent until my hand touched the face. It was human flesh and was still warm.

"Helen," I said, turning to the girl, "go at once and find your uncle."

But I had scarcely uttered the words before Helen burst into a low, choking laugh—the most fearful laugh I had ever heard.

"Look, look!" she said.

For before our eyes the face tilted, foreshortened, and vanished. We were both

"BENEATH THE WINDOW LAY A DARK, HUDDLED HEAP."

gazing into the countenance of the man whom we knew as Petro de Castro. His face was bathed in blood and convulsed with pain. I lit the lantern, and as I once more approached I saw, lying on the ground by his side, something hairy which for an instant I did not recognise. The next moment I saw what it was—it explained everything. It was a wig. I bent still nearer, and the whole horrible deception became plain as daylight. For, painted upon the back of the man's perfectly bald head, painted with the most consummate skill, giving the startling illusion of depth and relief, and all the hideous expression that had terrified one man at least out of the world, was the face of the abbot. The wig had completely covered it, and so skilfully was it made that the keenest observer would never have suspected it was one, it being itself slightly bald in order to add to the deception.

There in that dim, bare room, in broken sentences, in a voice that failed as his life passed, De Castro faltered out the story of his sin.

"Yes," he said, "I have tried to deceive you, and Gonsalves aided me. I was mad to risk one more appearance. Bend nearer, both of you; I am dying. Listen.

"Upon this estate, not a league across the valley, I found six months ago alluvial gold in great quantities in the bed of the gully. In the 'Bibliotheca Publica' in Lisbon I had years before got accounts of mines worked by the Phœnicians, and was firmly persuaded that some of the gold still remained. I found it, and to get the full benefit of it I devised the ghastly scheme which you have just discovered. I knew that the castle was supposed to be haunted by the face of an old monk. Sherwood with all his peculiarities was superstitious. Very gradually I worked upon his fears, and then, when I thought the time ripe for my experiment, personated the apparition. It was I who flung him from the battlements with my own hand. I knew that the terms of the will would divert all suspicion from me, and had not your shot, Helen, been so true you would never have come here to live. Well, you have avenged your father and saved yourself at the same time. You will find in the safe in a corner of the banqueting-hall plans and maps of the exact spot where the gold is to be found. I could have worked there for years unsuspected. It is true that I should have lost ten thousand pounds, but I should have gained five times the amount. Between four and five months ago I went to see a special friend of mine in London. She is a woman who stands alone as one of the greatest criminals of her day. She promised at once to aid me, and she suggested, devised, and executed the whole scheme. She made the wig herself, with its strangely-bald appearance so deceptive to the ordinary eye, and she painted the awful face on my bald skull. When you searched me just now you suspected a mask, but I was safe from your detection. To remove or replace the wig was the work of an instant. The woman who had done all this was to share my spoils."

"Her name?" I cried.

"Sara, the Great, the Invincible," he murmured.

As he spoke the words he died.

In the Fog

RICHARD HARDING DAVIS

IN THE FOG.

BY RICHARD HARDING DAVIS.

THE Grill is the club most difficult of access in the world. To be placed on its rolls distinguishes the new member as greatly as though he had received a vacant Garter or had been caricatured in *Vanity Fair*.

Men who belong to the Grill Club never mention that fact. If you ask one of them which club he frequents, he will name all save that particular one. He is afraid if he told you he belonged to the Grill that it would sound like boasting.

The Grill Club dates back to the days when Shakespeare's Theatre stood on the present site of the *Times* office. It has a golden grill which Charles the Second presented to the Club, and the original manuscript of "Tom and Jerry in London," which was bequeathed to it by Pierce Egan himself. The members when they write letters at the Club still use sand to blot the ink.

The Grill enjoys the distinction of having without political prejudice blackballed a Prime Minister of each party. At the same sitting at which one of these fell, it elected, on account of his brogue and his bulls, Quiller, the Queen's Counsellor, who was then a penniless barrister.

When Paul Preval, the French artist who came to London by royal command to paint the portrait of the Prince of Wales, was made an honorary member—only foreigners may be honorary members—he said, as he signed his first wine card, "I would rather see my name on that than a picture in the Louvre."

At which Quiller remarked, "That is a devil of a compliment, because the only men who can read their names in the Louvre to-day have been dead fifty years."

On the night after the great fog of 1897 there were five members in the Club, four of them busy with supper, and one reading in front of the fireplace. There is only one room to the Club and one long table. At the far end of the room the fire of the grill glows red, and, when the fat falls, blazes into flame, and at the other there is a broad bow window of diamond panes, which looks down upon the street. The four men at the table were strangers to each other, but as they picked at the grilled bones, and sipped their Scotch-and-soda, they conversed with such charming animation that a visitor to the Club —which does not tolerate visitors—would have counted them as friends of long acquaintance, certainly not as Englishmen who had met without the form of an introduction and for the first time. But it is the etiquette and tradition of the Grill that whoever enters it must speak with whomever he finds there. It is to enforce this rule that there is but one long table, and whether there are twenty men at it, or two, the waiters, supporting the rule, will place them side by side.

For this reason the four strangers at supper were seated together, with the candles grouped about them and the long length of the table cutting a white path through the outer gloom of the room.

"I repeat," said the gentleman with the black pearl stud, "that the days for romantic adventure and deeds of foolish daring have passed, and that the fault lies with ourselves. Voyages to the Pole I do not catalogue as adventures. That African explorer, young Chetney, who turned up yesterday after he was supposed to have died in Uganda, did nothing adventurous. He made maps and explored the sources of rivers. He was in constant danger, but the presence of danger does not constitute adventure. Were that so, the chemist who studies high explosives or who investigates deadly poisons passes through adventures daily. No, 'adventures are for the adventurous.' But one no longer ventures. The spirit of it died of inertia. We are grown too practical, too just—above all, too sensible. In this room, for instance,

"The four strangers at supper."

members of this Club have, at the sword's point, disputed the proper scanning of one of Pope's couplets. Over so weighty a matter as spilled Burgundy on a gentleman's cuff ten men fought across this table, each with his rapier in one hand and a candle in the other. All ten were wounded. The question of the spilled Burgundy concerned but two of them. The other eight engaged because they were men of 'spirit.' They were, indeed, the first gentlemen of their day. To-night, were you to spill Burgundy on my cuff, were you even to insult me grossly, these gentlemen would not consider it incumbent upon them to kill each other. They would separate us and appear as witnesses against us at Bow Street to-morrow morning. We have here to-night, in the persons of Sir Andrew and myself, an illustration of how the ways have changed."

The men around the table turned and glanced toward the gentleman in front of the fireplace. He was an elderly and somewhat portly person, with a kindly wrinkled countenance, which wore continually a smile of almost childish confidence and good nature. It was a face which the illustrated prints had made intimately familiar. He held a book from him at arm's-length, as though to adjust it to his eyesight, and his brows were knit with interest.

"Now, were this the eighteenth century," continued the gentleman with the black pearl, "when Sir Andrew left the Club to-night I would have him bound and gagged and thrown into a sedan chair. The watch would not interfere, the passers-by would take to their heels, my hired bullies and ruffians would convey him to some lonely spot where we would guard him until morning. Nothing would come of it, except added reputation to myself as a gentleman of adventurous spirit, and possibly an essay in the *Tatler*, with stars for names, entitled, let us say, 'The Budget and the Baronet.'"

"But to what end, sir?" inquired the youngest of the members. "And why Sir Andrew, of all persons—why should you select him for this adventure?"

The gentleman with the black pearl shrugged his shoulders.

"It would prevent him speaking in the House to-night. The Navy Increase Bill," he added gloomily. "It is a Government measure, and Sir Andrew speaks for it. And so great is his influence and so large his following, that if he does"—the gentleman laughed ruefully—"if he does, it will go through. Now, had I the spirit of our ancestors," he exclaimed, "I would bring chloroform from the nearest chemist and drug him in that chair. I would tumble his unconscious form into a hansom cab and hold him prisoner until daylight. If I did, I would save the British taxpayer the cost of five more battleships, some many millions of pounds."

All the gentlemen again turned and surveyed the Baronet with freshened interest. The honorary member of the Grill, whose accent had already betrayed him as an American, laughed softly.

"To look at him now," he said, "one would not guess he was deeply concerned with the affairs of State."

The others nodded silently.

"He has not lifted his eyes from that book since we first entered," added the youngest member. "He surely cannot mean to speak to-night."

"Oh, yes, he will speak," muttered the one with the black pearl moodily. "During these last hours of the session the House sits late, but when the Navy Bill comes up on its third reading he will be in his place—and he will pass it."

The fourth member, a stout and florid gentleman of a somewhat sporting appearance, in a short smoking-jacket and black tie, sighed enviously.

"Fancy one of us being as cool as that, if he knew he had to stand up within an hour and rattle off a speech in Parliament. I'd be in a devil of a funk myself. And yet he is as keen over that book he's reading as though he had nothing before him until bedtime."

"Yes, see how eager he is," whispered the youngest member. "He does not lift his eyes even now when he cuts the pages. It is probably an Admiralty Report, or some other weighty work of statistics which bears upon his speech."

The gentleman with the black pearl laughed morosely.

"The weighty work in which the eminent statesman is so deeply engrossed," he said, "is called 'The Great Rand Robbery.' It is a detective novel for sale at all bookstalls."

The American raised his eyebrows in disbelief.

"'The Great Rand Robbery'?" he re-repeated incredulously. "What an odd taste!"

"It is not a taste, it is his vice," returned the gentleman with the pearl stud. "It is his one dissipation. He is noted for it. You, as a stranger, could hardly be expected to know of this idiosyncrasy. Mr. Gladstone sought relaxation in the Greek poets, Sir Andrew finds his in Gaboriau. Since I have been a member of Parliament I have never seen him in the library without a shilling shocker in his hands. He brings them even into the sacred precincts of the House, and from the Government benches reads them concealed inside his hat. Once started on a tale of murder, robbery, and sudden death, nothing can tear him from it, not even the call of the division bell, nor of hunger, nor the prayers of the party Whip. He gave up his country house because when he journeyed to it in the train he would become so absorbed in his detective stories that he was invariably carried past his station." The member of Parliament twisted his pearl stud nervously and bit at the edge of his moustache. "If it only were the first pages of 'The Rand Robbery' that he were reading now," he murmured bitterly, "instead of the last! With such another book as that, I swear I could hold him here until morning. There would be no need of chloroform then to keep him from the House."

The eyes of all were fastened upon Sir Andrew, and they saw with fascination that with his forefinger he was now separating the last two pages of the book. The member of Parliament struck the table softly with his open palm.

"I would give a hundred pounds," he whispered, "if I could place in his hands at this moment a new story of Sherlock Holmes —a thousand pounds!" he added wildly. "Five thousand pounds!"

The American observed the speaker sharply, as though the words bore to him some special application, and then, at an idea which apparently had but just come to him, smiled in great embarrassment.

Sir Andrew ceased reading, but, as though still under the influence of the book, sat looking blankly into the open fire. For a brief space no one moved, until the baronet withdrew his eyes and, with a sudden start of recollection, felt anxiously for his watch. He scanned its face eagerly and scrambled briskly to his feet.

The voice of the American instantly broke the silence in a high, nervous accent.

"And yet Sherlock Holmes himself," he cried, "could not decipher the mystery which to-night baffles the police of London."

At these unexpected words, which carried in them something of the tone of a challenge, the gentlemen about the table started as suddenly as though the American had fired a pistol in the air, and Sir Andrew halted abruptly and stood observing him with grave surprise.

The gentleman with the black pearl was the first to recover.

"Yes, yes," he said eagerly, throwing himself across the table. "A mystery that baffles the police of London? I had heard nothing of it. Tell us at once, pray do— tell us at once."

The American flushed uncomfortably and picked uneasily at the tablecloth.

"No one but the police has heard of it," he murmured, "and they only through me. It is a remarkable crime, to which, unfortunately, I am the only person who can bear witness. Because I am the only witness, I am, in spite of my immunity as a diplomat, detained in London by the authorities of Scotland Yard. My name," he said, inclining his head politely, "is Sears—Lieutenant Ripley Sears, of the United States Navy, at present Naval Attaché to the Court of Russia. Had I not been detained to-day by the police, I would have started this morning for Petersburg."

The gentleman with the black pearl interrupted with so pronounced an exclamation of excitement and delight that the American stammered and ceased speaking.

"Do you hear, Sir Andrew?" cried the member of Parliament jubilantly. "An American diplomat halted by our police because he is the only witness of a most remarkable crime—*the* most remarkable crime, I believe you said, sir," he added, bending eagerly toward the naval officer, "which has occurred in London in many years."

The American moved his head in assent and glanced at the two other members. They were looking doubtfully at him, and the face of each showed that he was greatly perplexed.

Sir Andrew advanced to within the light of the candles and drew a chair toward him.

"The crime must be exceptional indeed," he said, "to justify the police in interfering with a representative of a friendly Power. If I were not forced to leave at once, I should take the liberty of asking you to tell us the details."

The gentleman with the pearl pushed the chair toward Sir Andrew and motioned him to be seated.

"You cannot leave us now," he exclaimed. "Mr. Sears is just about to tell us of this remarkable crime."

He nodded vigorously at the naval officer and the American, after first glancing doubtfully toward the servants at the far end of the room, and leaned forward across the table. The others drew their chairs nearer and bent toward him. The baronet glanced irresolutely at his watch, and with an exclamation of annoyance snapped down the lid. "They can wait," he muttered. He seated himself quickly and nodded at Lieutenant Sears.

"If you will be so kind as to begin, sir," he said impatiently.

"Of course," said the American, "you understand that I understand that I am speaking to gentlemen. The confidences of this Club are inviolate. Until the police

"'At the first glance I saw that he was quite dead.'"

give the facts to the public press, I must consider you my confederates. You have heard nothing and you know no one connected with this mystery. Even I must remain anonymous."

The gentlemen seated around him nodded gravely.

"Of course," the Baronet assented with eagerness, "of course."

"We will refer to it," said the gentleman with the black pearl, "as 'The Story of the Naval Attaché.'"

"I arrived in London two days ago," said the American, "and I engaged a room at the Bath Hotel. I know very few people in London, and even the members of our Embassy were strangers to me. But in Hong Kong I had become great pals with an officer in your Navy, who has since retired, and who is now living in a small house in Rutland Gardens, opposite the Knightsbridge Barracks. I telegraphed him that I was in London, and yesterday morning I received a most hearty invitation to dine with him the same evening at his house. He is a bachelor, so we dined alone and talked over all our old days on the Asiatic Station, and of the changes which had come to us since we had last met there. As I was leaving the next morning for my post at Petersburg, and had many letters to write, I told him, about ten o'clock, that I must get back to the hotel, and he sent out his servant to call a hansom.

"For the next quarter of an hour, as we sat talking, we could hear the cab-whistle sounding violently from the doorstep, but apparently with no result.

"'It cannot be that the cabmen are on strike,' my friend said, as he rose and walked to the window.

"He pulled back the curtains and at once called to me.

"'You have never seen a London fog, have you?' he asked. 'Well, come here. This is one of the best, or, rather, one of the worst, of them.' I joined him at the window, but I could see nothing. Had I not known that the house looked out upon the street, I would have believed that I was facing a dead wall. I raised the sash and stretched out my head, but still I could see nothing. Even the light of the street lamps opposite, and in the upper windows of the barracks, had been smothered in the yellow mist. The lights of the room in which I stood penetrated the fog only to the distance of a few inches from my eyes.

"Below me the servant was still sounding his whistle, but I could afford to wait no longer, and told my friend that I would try and find the way to my hotel on foot. He objected, but the letters I had to write were for the Navy Department, and, besides, I had always heard that to be out in a London fog was the most wonderful experience, and I was curious to investigate one for myself.

"My friend went with me to his front door and laid down a course for me to follow. I was first to walk straight across the street to the brick wall of the Knightsbridge Barracks. I was then to feel my way along the wall until I came to a row of houses set back from the sidewalk. They would bring me to a cross street. On the other side of this street was a row of shops which I was to follow until they joined the iron railings of Hyde Park. I was to keep to the railings until I reached the gates at Hyde Park Corner, where I was to lay a diagonal course across Piccadilly and tack in toward the railings of Green Park. At the end of these railings, going east, I would find the Walsingham and my own hotel.

"To a sailor the course did not seem difficult, so I bade my friend good-night and walked forward until my feet touched the wooden paving. I continued upon it until I reached the kerbing of the sidewalk. A few steps further my hands struck the wall of the barracks. I turned in the direction from which I had just come, and saw a square of faint light cut into the yellow fog. I shouted 'All right!' and my friend's voice answered, 'Good luck to you!' The light from his open door disappeared with a bang, and I was left alone in a dripping, yellow darkness. I have been in the Navy for ten years, but I have never known such a fog as that of last night, not even among the icebergs of Behring Sea. There one could at least see the light of the binnacle, but last night I could not even distinguish the hand by which I guided myself along the barrack wall. At sea, a fog is a natural phenomenon. It is as familiar as the rainbow which follows a storm, it is as proper that a fog should spread upon the waters as that steam shall rise from a kettle. But a fog which springs from the paved streets, that rolls between solid house-fronts, that forces cabs to move at half speed, that drowns policemen and extinguishes the electric lights of the music-hall, that is to me incomprehensible. It is as out of place as a tidal wave on Broadway.

"As I felt my way along the wall, I encountered other men who were coming from the opposite direction, and each time when we hailed each other I stepped away from the wall to make room for them to pass. But the third time I did this, when I reached out my hand, the wall had disappeared, and the further I moved to find it the further I seemed to be sinking into space. I had the unpleasant conviction that at any moment I might step over a precipice. Since I had set out I had heard no traffic in the street, and now, although I listened some minutes, I could only distinguish the occasional footfalls of pedestrians. Several times I called aloud, and once a jocular gentleman answered me, but only to ask me where I thought he was, and then even he was swallowed up in the silence. Just above me I could make out a jet of gas which I guessed came from a street lamp, and I moved over to that, and, while I tried to recover my bearings, kept my hand on the iron post. Except for this flicker of gas, no larger than the tip of my finger, I could distinguish nothing about me. For the rest, the mist hung between me and the world like a damp and heavy blanket.

"I could hear voices, but I could not tell whence they came, and the scrape of a foot moving cautiously or a muffled cry as someone stumbled were the only sounds that reached me.

"I decided that I had best remain where I was until someone took me in tow, and it must have been for ten minutes that I waited, straining my ears and hailing distant footfalls. In a house near me some people were dancing to the music of a Hungarian band. I even fancied I could hear the windows shake to the rhythm of their feet, but I could not make out from which part of the compass the sounds came. And sometimes, as the music rose, it seemed close at my hand, and again, to be floating high in the air above my head. Although I was surrounded by thousands of householders—thirteen—I was as completely lost as though I had been set down by night in the Sahara Desert. There seemed to be no use in waiting longer for an escort, so I again set out and at once bumped against a low iron fence. At first I believed this to be an area railing, but on following it I found that it stretched for a long distance, and that it was pierced at regular intervals with gates. I was standing uncertainly, with my hand on one of these, when a square of light suddenly opened in the night, and in it I saw, as you see a picture thrown by a biograph in a darkened theatre, a young gentleman in evening dress, and at the back of him the lights of a hall. I guessed from its elevation and distance from the sidewalk that this light must come from the door of a house set back from the street, and I determined to approach it and ask the young man to tell me where I was. But in fumbling with the lock of the gate I instinctively bent my head, and when I raised it again the door had partly closed, leaving only a narrow shaft of light. Whether the young man had re-entered the house or had left it, I could not tell, but I hastened to open the gate, and as I stepped forward I found myself upon an asphalt walk. At the same instant there was the sound of quick steps upon the path and someone rushed past me. I called to him, but he made no reply, and I heard the gate click and the footsteps hurrying away upon the sidewalk.

"Under other circumstances the young man's rudeness, and his recklessness in dashing so hurriedly through the mist, would have struck me as peculiar, but everything was so distorted by the fog that at the moment I did not consider it. The door was still as he had left it, partly open. I went up the path, and after much fumbling found the knob of the door-bell and gave it a sharp pull. The bell answered me from a great depth and distance, but no movement followed from inside the house, and although I pulled the bell again and again I could hear nothing save the dripping of the mist about me. I was anxious to be on my way, but unless I knew my way there was little chance of my making any speed, and I was determined that until I learned my bearings I would not venture back into the fog. So I pushed the door open and stepped into the house.

"I found myself in a long and narrow hall upon which doors opened from either side. At the end of the hall was a staircase with a balustrade which ended in a sweeping curve. The balustrade was covered with heavy Persian rugs, and the walls of the hall were also hung with them. The door on my left was closed, but the one nearer me on the right was open, and as I stepped opposite to it I saw that it was a sort of reception or waiting room, and that it was empty. The door below it was also open, and with the idea that I would surely find someone there I walked on up the hall. I was in evening dress, and I felt I did not look like a burglar, so I had no great fear that, should I encounter one of the inmates of the house, he would shoot me on sight. The second door in the hall opened into a dining-room. This was also empty. One person had been dining at the table, but the cloth had not been cleared away, and a flickering candle showed half-filled wine-glasses and the ashes of cigarettes. The greater part of the room was in complete darkness.

"By this time I had grown conscious of the fact that I was wandering about in a strange house, and that apparently I was alone in it. The silence of the place began to try my nerves, and in a sudden, unexplainable panic I started for the open street. As I turned, I saw a man sitting on a bench which the curve of the balustrade had hidden from me. His eyes were shut and he was sleeping soundly.

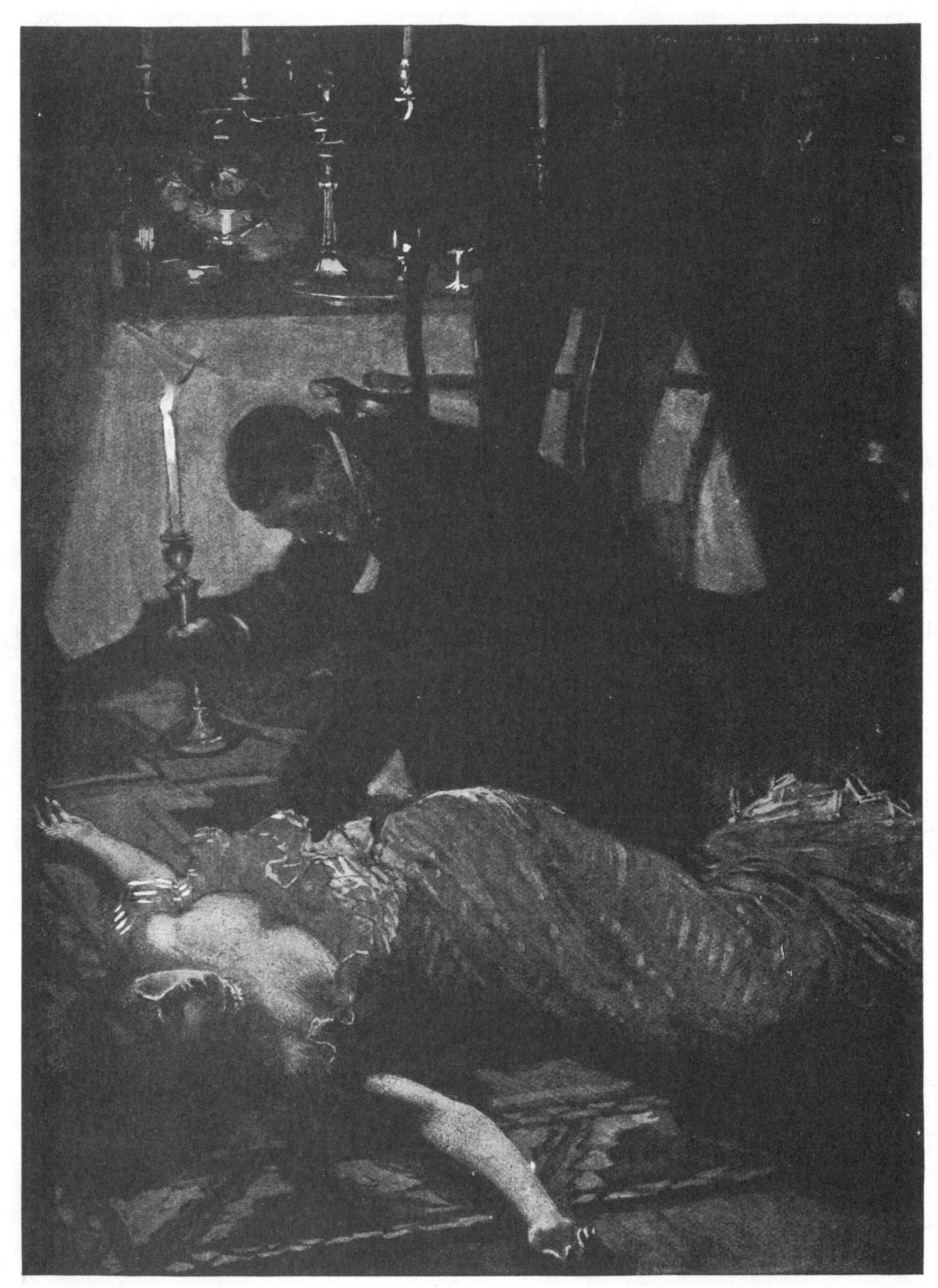

"'I dropped on my knees beside her and placed my hand above her heart.'"

"The moment before I had been bewildered because I could see no one, but at sight of this man I was much more bewildered.

"He was a very large man, a giant in height, with long, yellow hair which hung below his shoulders. He was dressed in a red silk shirt that was belted at the waist and hung outside black velvet trousers which, in turn, were stuffed into high, black boots. I recognised the costume at once as that of a Russian servant in his native livery, but what he could be doing in a private house in Knightsbridge was incomprehensible.

"I advanced and touched the man on the shoulder, and, after an effort, he awoke and, on seeing me, sprang to his feet and began bowing rapidly and making deprecatory gestures. I had picked up enough Russian in Petersburg to make out that the man was apologising for having fallen asleep, and I also was able to explain to him that I desired to see his master.

"He nodded vigorously and said, 'Will the Excellency come this way? The Princess is here.'

"I distinctly made out the word 'Princess,' and I was a good deal embarrassed. I had thought it would be easy enough to explain my intrusion to a man; but how a woman would look at it was another matter, and as I followed him down the hall I was somewhat puzzled.

"As we advanced he noticed that the front door was standing open, and, giving an exclamation of surprise, hastened toward it and closed it. Then he rapped twice on the door of what was apparently the drawing-room. There was no reply to his knock, and he tapped again, and then timidly, and cringing subserviently, opened the door and stepped inside. He withdrew himself almost at once and stared stupidly at me, shaking his head.

"'She is not there,' he said. He stood for a moment gazing blankly through the open door and then hastened toward the dining-room. The solitary candle which still burned there seemed to assure him that the room also was empty. He came back and bowed me toward the drawing-room. 'She is above,' he said; 'I will inform the Princess of the Excellency's presence.'

"Before I could stop him he had turned and was running up the staircase, leaving me alone at the open door of the drawing-room. I decided that the adventure had gone quite far enough, and if I had been able to explain to the Russian that I had lost my way in the fog, and now only wanted to get back into the street again, I would have left the house on the instant.

"Of course, when I first rang the bell of the house I had no other expectation than that it would be answered by a parlourmaid who would direct me on my way. I certainly could not then foresee that I would disturb a Russian princess in her boudoir, or that I might be thrown out by her athletic bodyguard. Still, I thought I ought not now to leave the house without making some apology, and, if the worst should come, I could show my card. They could hardly believe that a member of an embassy had any designs upon the hat-rack.

"The room in which I stood was dimly lighted, but I could see that, like the hall, it was hung with heavy Persian rugs. The corners were filled with palms, and there was the unmistakable odour in the air of Russian cigarettes and strange, dry scents that carried me back to the bazaars of Vladivostock. Near the front windows was a grand piano, and at the other end of the room a heavily carved screen of some black wood, picked out with ivory. The screen was overhung with a canopy of silken draperies and formed a sort of alcove. In front of the alcove was spread the white skin of a polar bear, and set on that was one of those low Turkish coffee tables. It held a lighted spirit-lamp and two gold coffee-cups. I had heard no movement from above stairs, and it must have been fully three minutes that I stood waiting, noting these details of the room and wondering at the delay and at the strange silence.

"And then, suddenly, as my eye grew more used to the half-light, I saw, projecting from behind the screen as though it were stretched along the back of a divan, the hand of a man and the lower part of his arm. I was as startled as though I had come across a footprint on a deserted island. Evidently the man had been sitting there ever since I had come into the room, even since I had entered the house, and he had heard the servant knocking upon the door. Why he had not declared himself I could not understand, but I supposed that possibly he was a guest, with no reason to interest himself in the Princess's other visitors, or perhaps, for some reason, he did not wish to be observed. I could see nothing of him except his hand, but I had an unpleasant feeling that he had been peering at me through the carving in the screen, and that he was still doing so. I moved my feet noisily on the floor and said tentatively, 'I beg your pardon.'

"There was no reply, and the hand did not stir. Apparently the man was bent upon ignoring me, but as all I wished was to apologise for my intrusion and to leave the house, I walked up to the alcove and peered around it. Inside the screen was a divan piled with cushions, and on the end of it nearer me the man was sitting. He was a young Englishman with light yellow hair and a deeply bronzed face. He was seated with his arms stretched out along the back of the divan, and with his head resting against a cushion. His attitude was one of complete ease. But his mouth had fallen open, and his eyes were set with an expression of utter horror. At the first glance I saw that he was quite dead.

"For a flash of time I was too startled to act, but in the same flash I was convinced that the man had met his death from no accident, that he had not died through any ordinary failure of the laws of Nature. The expression on his face was much too terrible to be misinterpreted. It spoke as eloquently as words. It told me that before the end had come he had watched his death approach and threaten him.

"I was so sure he had been murdered that I instinctively looked on the floor for the weapon, and, at the same moment, out of concern for my own safety, quickly behind me; but the silence of the house continued unbroken.

"I have seen a great number of dead men; I was on the Asiatic Station during the Japanese-Chinese war. I was in Port Arthur after the massacre. So a dead man for the single reason that he is dead does not repel me, and, though I knew that there was no hope that this man was alive, still, for decency's sake, I felt his pulse, and while I kept my ears alert for any sound from the floors above me, I pulled open his shirt and placed my hand upon his heart. My fingers instantly touched upon the opening of a wound, and as I withdrew them I found them wet with blood. He was in evening dress, and in the wide bosom of his shirt I found a narrow slit, so narrow that in the dim light it was scarcely discernible. The wound was no wider than the smallest blade of a pocket-knife, but when I stripped the shirt away from the chest and left it bare, I found that the weapon, narrow as it was, had been long enough to reach his heart. There is no need to tell you how I felt as I stood by the body of this boy (for he was hardly older than a boy), or of the thoughts that came into my head. I was bitterly sorry for this stranger, bitterly indignant at his murderer, and, at the same time, selfishly concerned for my own safety and for the notoriety which I saw was sure to follow. My instinct was to leave the body where it lay and to hide myself in the fog, but I also felt that since a succession of accidents had made me the only witness to a crime, my duty was to make myself a good witness and to assist to establish the facts of this murder.

That it might possibly be a suicide, and not a murder, did not disturb me for a moment. The fact that the weapon had disappeared and the expression on the boy's face were enough to convince at least me that he had had no hand in his own death. I judged it, therefore, of the first importance to discover who was in the house, or, if they had escaped from it, who had been in the house before I entered it. I had seen one man leave it; but all I could tell of him was that he was a young man, that he was in evening dress, and that he had fled in such haste that he had not stopped to close the door behind him.

"The Russian servant I had found apparently asleep, and, unless he acted a part with supreme skill, he was a stupid and ignorant boor and as innocent of the murder as myself. There was still the Russian Princess whom he had expected to find, or had pretended to expect to find, in the same room with the murdered man. I judged that she must now be either upstairs with the servant, or that she had, without his knowledge, already fled from the house. When I recalled his apparently genuine surprise at not finding her in the drawing-room, this latter supposition seemed the more probable. Nevertheless, I decided that it was my duty to make a search, and after a second hurried look for the weapon among the cushions of the divan and upon the floor, I cautiously crossed the hall and entered the dining-room.

"The single candle was still flickering in the draught, and showed only the white cloth. The rest of the room was draped in shadows. I picked up the candle and, lifting it high above my head, moved round the corner of the table. Either my nerves were on such a stretch that no shock could strain them further, or my mind was inoculated to horrors; for I did not cry out at what I saw nor retreat from it. Immediately at my feet was the body of a beautiful woman, lying at full length upon the floor, her arms flung out on either side of her, and her white face and shoulders gleaming dully in the unsteady light of the candle. Around her throat was a great chain of diamonds, and the light played upon these and made them flash and blaze in tiny flames. But the woman who wore them was dead, and I was so certain as to how she had died that without an instant's hesitation I dropped on my knees beside her and placed my hand above her heart. My fingers again touched the thin slit of a wound. I had no doubt in my mind but that this was the Russian Princess, and when I lowered the candle to her face I was assured that this was so. Her features showed the finest lines of both the Slav and the Jewess, the eyes were black, the hair blue-black and wonderfully heavy, and her skin, even in death, was rich in colour. She was a surpassingly beautiful woman.

"I rose and tried to light another candle with the one I held, but I found that my hand was so unsteady that I could not keep the wicks together. It was my intention to again search for this strange dagger which had been used to kill both the English boy and the beautiful Princess, but before I could light the second candle I heard footsteps descending the stairs, and the Russian servant appeared in the doorway.

"My face was in darkness, or I am sure that at the sight of it he would have taken alarm, for at that moment I was not sure but that this man himself was the murderer. His own face was plainly visible to me in the light from the hall, and I could see that it wore an expression of dull bewilderment. I stepped quickly toward him and took a firm hold upon his wrist.

"'She is not there,' he said. 'The Princess has gone. They have all gone.'

"'Who have gone?' I demanded. 'Who else has been here?'

"'The two Englishmen.'

"'What two Englishmen?' I demanded. 'What are their names?'

"The man now saw by my manner that some question of great moment hung upon his answer, and he began to protest that he did not know the names of the visitors, and that until the evening he had never seen them.

"I guessed that it was my tone which frightened him, so I took my hand off his wrist and spoke less eagerly.

"'How long have they been here?' I asked, 'and when did they go?'

"He pointed behind him toward the drawing-room.

"'One sat there with the Princess,' he said; 'the other came after I had placed the coffee in the drawing-room. The two Englishmen talked together, and the Princess returned here to the table. She sat there in that chair, and I brought her cognac and cigarettes. Then I sat outside upon the bench. It was a feast day and I had been drinking. Pardon, Excellency, but I fell asleep. When I woke, your Excellency was standing by me, but the Princess and the two Englishmen had gone. That is all I know.'

"I believed that the man was telling me the truth. His fright had passed, and he was now apparently puzzled, but not alarmed.

"'You must remember the names of the Englishmen,' I urged. 'Try to think. When you announced them to the Princess, what name did you give?'

"At this question he exclaimed with pleasure, and, beckoning to me, ran hurriedly down the hall and into the drawing-room. In the corner furthest from the screen was the piano, and on it was a silver tray. He picked this up and, smiling with pride at his own intelligence, pointed at two cards that lay upon it. I took them up and read the names engraved upon them."

The American paused abruptly and glanced at the faces about him. "I read the names," he repeated. He spoke with great reluctance.

"Continue!" cried the Baronet sharply.

"I read the names," said the American, with evident distaste, "and the family name of each was the same. They were the names of two brothers. One is well known to you. It is that of the African explorer of whom this gentleman was just speaking. I mean the Earl of Chetney. The other was the name of his brother, Lord Arthur Chetney."

The men at the table fell back as though a trapdoor had fallen open at their feet.

"Lord Chetney!" they exclaimed in chorus. They glanced at each other and back to the American with every expression of concern and disbelief.

"It is impossible!" cried the Baronet. "Why, my dear sir, young Chetney only arrived from Africa yesterday. It was so stated in the evening papers."

The jaw of the American set in a resolute square and he pressed his lips together.

"You are perfectly right, sir," he said,

"'I was still on my knees when I heard a cry behind me.'"

"Lord Chetney did arrive in London yesterday morning, and yesterday night I found his dead body."

The youngest member present was the first to recover. He seemed much less concerned over the identity of the murdered man than at the interruption of the narrative.

"Oh! please let him go on!" he cried. "What happened then? You say you found two visiting cards. How do you know which card was that of the murdered man?"

The American, before he answered, waited until the chorus of exclamations had ceased. Then he continued as though he had not been interrupted.

"The instant I read the names upon the cards," he said, "I ran to the screen and, kneeling beside the dead man, began a search through his pockets. My hand at once fell upon a card-case, and I found on all the cards it contained the title of the Earl of Chetney. His watch and cigarette-case also bore his name. These evidences, and the fact of his bronzed skin, and that his cheek-bones were worn with fever, convinced me that the dead man was the African explorer, and the boy who had fled past me in the night was Arthur, his younger brother.

"I was so intent upon my search that I had forgotten the servant, and I was still on my knees when I heard a cry behind me. I turned and saw the man gazing down at the body in abject and unspeakable horror.

"Before I could rise, he gave another cry of terror and, flinging himself into the hall, raced toward the door to the street. I leaped after him, shouting to him to halt, but before I could reach the hall he had torn open the door and I saw him spring out into the yellow fog. I cleared the steps in a jump and ran down the garden walk, but just as the gate clicked in front of me. I had it open on the instant, and, following the sound of the man's footsteps, I raced after him across the open street. He, also, could hear me, and he instantly stopped running, and there was absolute silence. He was so near that I almost fancied I could hear him panting, and I held my own breath to listen. But I could distinguish nothing but the dripping of the mist about us, and from far off the music of the Hungarian band, which I had heard when I first lost myself.

"All I could see was the square of light from the door I had left open behind me and a lamp in the hall beyond it flickering in the draught. But even as I watched it the flame of the lamp was blown violently to and fro, and the door, caught in the same current of air, closed slowly. I knew if it shut I could not again enter the house, and I rushed madly toward it. I believe I even shouted out, as though it were something human which I could compel to obey me, and then I caught my foot against the kerb and smashed into the sidewalk. When I rose to my feet I was dizzy and half stunned, and though I thought then that I was moving toward the door, I know now that I probably turned directly from it; for, as I groped about in the night, calling frantically for the police, my fingers touched nothing but the dripping fog, and the iron railings for which I sought seemed to have melted away. For many minutes I beat the mist with my arms like a man at blind man's buff, turning sharply in circles, cursing aloud at my stupidity, and crying continually for help. At last a voice answered me from the fog, and I found myself held in the circle of a policeman's lantern.

"That is the end of my adventure. What I have to tell you now is what I learned from the police.

"At the station-house to which the man guided me I related what you have just heard. I told them that the house they must at once find was one set back with others from the street within a radius of two hundred yards from the Knightsbridge Barracks, that within fifty yards of it someone was giving a dance to the music of a Hungarian band, and that the railings in front of it were about as high as a man's waist and filed to a point. With that to work upon, twenty men were at once ordered out into the fog to search for the house, and Inspector Lyle himself was despatched to the home of Lord Edam, Chetney's father, with a warrant for Lord Arthur's arrest. I was thanked and dismissed on my own recognisance.

"This morning, Inspector Lyle called on me, and from him I learned the police theory of the scene I have just described.

"Apparently I had wandered very far in the fog, for up to noon to-day the house had not been found, nor had they been able to arrest Lord Arthur. He did not return to his father's house last night, and there is no trace of him; but from what the police knew of the past lives of the people I found in that lost house they have evolved a theory, and their theory is that the murders were committed by Lord Arthur.

"The infatuation of his elder brother,

Lord Chetney, for a Russian Princess, so Inspector Lyle tells me, is well known to everyone. About two years ago the Princess Zichy, as she calls herself, and he were constantly together, and Chetney informed his friends that they were about to be married. The woman was notorious in two continents, and when Lord Edam heard of his son's infatuation he appealed to the police for her record.

"It is through his having applied to them that they know so much concerning her and her relations with the Chetneys. From the police Lord Edam learned that Madame Zichy had once been a spy in the employ of the Russian Third Section, but that lately she had been repudiated by her own Government and was living by her wits, by blackmail, and by her beauty. Lord Edam laid this record before his son, but Chetney either knew it already, or the woman persuaded him not to believe in it, and the father and son parted in great anger. Two days later the Marquis altered his will, leaving all his money to the younger brother, Arthur.

"The title and some of the landed property he could not keep from Chetney, but he swore if his son saw the woman again, that the will should stand as it was and he would be left without a penny.

"This was about eighteen months ago, when apparently Chetney tired of the Princess and suddenly went off to shoot and explore in Central Africa. No word came from him, except that twice he was reported as having died of fever in the jungle, and finally two traders reached the coast who said they had seen his body. This was accepted by all as conclusive, and young Arthur was recognised as the heir to the Edam millions. On the strength of this supposition he at once began to borrow enormous sums from the moneylenders. This is of great importance, as the police believe it was these debts which drove him to the murder of his brother. Yesterday, as you know, Lord Chetney suddenly returned from the grave, and it was the fact that for two years he had been considered as dead which lent such importance to his return, and which gave rise to those columns of detail concerning him which appeared in all the afternoon papers. But, obviously, during his absence he had not tired of the Princess Zichy, for we know that a few hours after he reached London he sought her out. His brother, who had also learned of his reappearance through the papers, probably suspected which would be the house he would first visit, and followed him there, arriving, so the Russian servant tells us, while the two were at coffee in the drawing-room. The Princess then, we also learn from the servant, withdrew to the dining-room, leaving the brothers together. What happened one can only guess.

"Lord Arthur knew now that when it was discovered he was no longer the heir the moneylenders would come down upon him. The police believe that he at once sought out his brother to beg for money to cover the *post obits*, but that, considering the sum he needed was several hundreds of thousands of pounds, Chetney refused to give it to him. No one knew that Arthur had gone to seek out his brother. They were alone. It is possible, then, that in a passion of disappointment, and crazed with the disgrace which he saw before him, young Arthur made himself the heir beyond further question. The death of his brother would have availed nothing if the woman remained alive. It is then possible that he crossed the hall and, with the same weapon which made him Lord Edam's heir, destroyed the solitary witness to the murder. The only other person who could have seen it was sleeping in a drunken stupor, to which fact undoubtedly he owed his life. And yet," concluded the Naval Attaché, leaning forward and marking each word with his finger, "Lord Arthur blundered fatally. In his haste he left the door of the house open, so giving access to the first passer-by, and he forgot that when he entered it he had handed his card to the servant. That piece of paper may yet send him to the gallows. In the meantime he has disappeared completely, and somewhere, in one of the millions of streets of this great capital, in a locked and empty house, lies the body of his brother, and of the woman his brother loved, undiscovered, unburied, and with their murder unavenged."

In the discussion which followed the conclusion of the story of the Naval Attaché the gentleman with the pearl took no part. Instead, he arose and, beckoning a servant to a far corner of the room, whispered earnestly to him until a sudden movement on the part of Sir Andrew caused him to return hurriedly to the table.

"There are several points in Mr. Sears' story I want explained," he cried. "Be seated, Sir Andrew," he begged. "Let us have the opinion of an expert. I do not care what the police think, I want to know what you think."

But Sir Andrew rose reluctantly from his chair.

"I should like nothing better than to discuss this," he said. "But it is most important that I should proceed to the House. I should have been there some time ago." He turned toward the servant and directed him to call a hansom.

The gentleman with the pearl stud looked appealingly at the Naval Attaché. "There are surely many details that you have not told us," he urged—"some you have forgotten?"

The Baronet interrupted quickly.

"I trust not," he said, "for I could not possibly stop to hear them."

"The story is finished," declared the Naval Attaché. "Until Lord Arthur is arrested or the bodies are found there is nothing more to tell of either Chetney or the Princess Zichy."

"Of Lord Chetney, perhaps not," interrupted the sporting-looking gentleman with the black tie; "but there'll always be something to tell of the Princess Zichy. I know enough stories about her to fill a book. She was a most remarkable woman." The speaker dropped the end of his cigar into his coffee-cup and, taking his case from his pocket, selected a fresh one. As he did so he laughed and held up the case that the others could see it. It was an ordinary cigar-case of well-worn pigskin, with a silver clasp.

"The only time I ever met her," he said, "she tried to rob me of this."

The Baronet regarded him closely.

"She tried to rob you?" he repeated.

"Tried to rob me of this," continued the gentleman in the black tie, "and of the Czarina's diamonds." His tone was one of mingled admiration and injury.

"The Czarina's diamonds!" exclaimed the Baronet. He glanced quickly and suspiciously at the speaker and then at the others about the table. But their faces gave evidence of no other emotion than that of ordinary interest.

"Yes, the Czarina's diamonds," repeated the man with the black tie. "It was a necklace of diamonds. I was told to take them to the Russian Ambassador in Paris, who was to deliver them at Moscow. I am a Queen's Messenger," he added.

"Oh! I see!" exclaimed Sir Andrew in a tone of relief. "And you say that this same Princess Zichy, one of the victims of this double murder, endeavoured to rob you of—of—that cigar-case?"

"And the Czarina's diamonds," answered the Queen's Messenger imperturbably. "It's not much of a story, but it gives you an idea of the woman's character. The robbery took place between Paris and Marseilles."

The Baronet interrupted him with an abrupt movement.

"No, no!" he cried, shaking his arms in protest, "don't tempt me! I really cannot listen. I must be at the House in ten minutes."

"I am sorry," said the Queen's Messenger. He turned to those seated about him. "I wonder if the other gentlemen——?" he inquired tentatively. There was a chorus of polite murmurs, and the Queen's Messenger, bowing his head in acknowledgment, took a preparatory sip from his glass. At the same moment the servant to whom the man with the black pearl had spoken slipped a piece of paper into his hand. He glanced at it, frowned, and threw it under the table.

The servant bowed to the Baronet.

"Your hansom is waiting, Sir Andrew," he said.

"The necklace was worth twenty thousand pounds," began the Queen's Messenger. "It was a present from the Queen of England to celebrate——"

The Baronet gave an exclamation of angry annoyance.

"Upon my word, this is most provoking!" he interrupted. "I really ought not to stay. But I certainly mean to hear this." He turned irritably to the servant. "Tell the hansom to wait," he commanded; and, with an air of a boy who is playing truant, slipped guiltily into his chair.

The gentleman with the black pearl smiled blandly and rapped upon the table.

"Order, gentlemen," he said. "Order for the story of the Queen's Messenger and the Czarina's diamonds."

IN THE FOG.

By RICHARD HARDING DAVIS.

No. II.—THE STORY OF THE QUEEN'S MESSENGER.

HE necklace was a present from the Queen of England to the Czarina of Russia," began the Queen's Messenger. "It was to celebrate the occasion of the Czar's coronation. Our Foreign Office knew that the Russian Ambassador in Paris was to proceed to Moscow for that ceremony, and I was directed to go to Paris and turn over the necklace to him. But when I reached Paris I found he had not expected me for a week later, and was taking a few day's vacation at Nice. His people asked me to leave the necklace with them at the Embassy, but I had been charged to get a receipt for it from the Ambassador himself, so I started at once for Nice. The fact that Monte Carlo is not two thousand miles from Nice may have had something to do with making me carry out my instructions so carefully.

"Now, how the Princess Zichy came to find out about the necklace, I don't know, but I can guess. As you have just heard, she was at one time a spy in the service of the Russian Government. And after they dismissed her she kept up her acquaintance with many of the Russian agents in London. It was probably through one of them that she learned that the necklace was to be sent to Moscow, and which of the Queen's Messengers had been detailed to take it there. Still, I doubt if even that knowledge would have helped her if she had not also known something which I supposed no one else in the world knew but myself and one other man. And, curiously enough, the other man was a Queen's Messenger, too, and a friend of mine. You must know that up to the time of this robbery I had always concealed my despatches in a manner peculiarly my own. I got the idea from that play called 'A Scrap of Paper.' In it a man wants to hide a certain compromising document. He knows that all his rooms will be secretly searched for it, so he puts it in a torn envelope and sticks it up where anyone can see it on his mantelshelf. The result is that the woman who is ransacking the house to find it looks in all the unlikely places, but passes over the scrap of paper that is just under her nose. Sometimes the papers and packages they give us to carry about Europe are of very great value, and sometimes they are special makes of cigarettes and orders to Court dressmakers. Sometimes we know what we are carrying, and sometimes we do not. If it is a large sum of money or a treaty, they generally tell us. But as a rule we have no knowledge of what the package contains; so, to be on the safe side, we naturally take just as great care of it as though we knew it held the terms of an ultimatum or the Crown jewels. As a rule, my *confrères* carry the official packages in a despatch-box, which is just as obvious as a lady's jewel-bag in the hands of her maid. Everyone knows they are carrying something of value. They put a premium on dishonesty. Well, after I saw the 'Scrap of Paper' play, I determined to put the Government valuables in the most unlikely place that anyone would look for them. So I used to hide the documents they gave me inside my riding-boots, and small articles, like money or jewels, I carried in an old cigar-case. After I took to using my case for that purpose, I bought a new one, exactly like it, for my cigars. But to avoid mistakes, I had my initials placed on both sides of the new one, and the moment I touched the case, even in the dark, I could tell which it was by the raised initials.

"No one knew about this except the Queen's Messenger of whom I spoke. We once left Paris together on the Orient Express. I was going to Constantinople, and he was to stop off at Vienna. On the journey I told him of my peculiar way of hiding things, and showed him my cigar-case. If I recollect rightly, on that trip it held the Grand Cross of St. Michael and St. George, which the Queen was sending to our Ambassador. The Messenger was very much entertained at my scheme, and some months later when he met the Princess he told her about it as an amusing story. Of course, he had no idea she was a Russian spy. He didn't know anything at all about her, except that she was a very attractive woman. It was indiscreet, but he could not possibly have guessed that she could ever make any use of what he told her.

"Later, after the robbery, I remembered that I had informed this young chap of my secret hiding-place, and when I saw him again I asked him about it. He was greatly distressed and said he had never seen the importance of the secret. He remembered he had told several people of it, and among others the Princess Zichy. In that way I found out that it was she who had robbed me, and I know that from the moment I left London she was following me, and that she knew then that the diamonds were concealed in my cigar-case.

"My train for Nice left Paris at ten in the morning. When I travel at night I generally tell the *chef de gare* that I am a Queen's Messenger, and he gives me a compartment to myself. But in the daytime I take whatever offers. On this morning I had found an empty compartment, and I had tipped the guard to keep everyone else out, not from any fear of losing the diamonds, but because I wanted to smoke. He had locked the door, and as the last bell had rung, I supposed I was to travel alone, so I began to arrange my traps and make myself comfortable. The diamonds in the cigar-case were in the inside pocket of my waistcoat, and as they made a bulky package I took them out, intending to put them in my handbag. It is a small satchel like a bookmaker's, or those handbags that couriers carry. I wear it slung from a strap across my shoulder, and, no matter whether I am sitting or walking, it never leaves me.

"I took the cigar-case which held the necklace from my inside pocket, and the case which held the cigars out of the satchel, and while I was searching through it for a box of matches I laid the two cases beside me on the seat.

"At that moment the train started, but at the same instant there was a rattle at the lock of the compartment, and a couple of porters lifted and shoved a woman through the door and hurled her rugs and umbrellas in after her.

"Instinctively I reached for the diamonds. I shoved them quickly into the satchel, and, pushing them far down to the bottom of the bag, snapped the spring lock. Then I put the cigars in the pocket of my coat, but with the thought that now that I had a woman as a travelling companion, I should probably not be allowed to enjoy them.

"One of her pieces of luggage had fallen at my feet, and a roll of rugs had landed at my side. I thought if I hid the fact that the lady was not welcome, and at once started to be civil, she might permit me to smoke. So I picked her handbag off the floor and asked her where I might place it.

"As I spoke I looked at her for the first time and saw that she was a most remarkably handsome woman.

"She smiled charmingly and begged me not to disturb myself. Then she arranged her own things about her and, opening her dressing-bag, took out a gold cigarette-case.

"'Do you object to smoke?' she asked.

"I laughed and assured her I had been in great terror lest she might not allow me to smoke.

"'If you like cigarettes,' she said, 'will you try some of these? They are rolled especially for my husband in Russia, and they are supposed to be very good.'

"I thanked her and took one from her case, and I found it so much better than my own that I continued to smoke her cigarettes throughout the rest of the journey. I must say that we got on very well. I judged from the coronet on her cigarette-case, and from her manner, which was quite as well bred as that of any woman I ever met, that she was someone of importance, and though she seemed almost too good-looking to be respectable, I determined that she was some *grande dame* who was so assured of her position that she could afford to be unconventional. At first she read her novel, and then she made some comment on the scenery, and finally we began to discuss the current politics of the Continent. She talked of all the cities in Europe and seemed to know everyone worth knowing. But she volunteered nothing about herself except that she frequently made use of the expression, 'When my husband was stationed at Vienna,' or, 'When my husband was promoted to Rome.' Once she said to me, 'I have often seen you at Monte Carlo. I saw you when you won

"'Finally we began to discuss the current politics of the Continent.'"

the pigeon championship.' I told her that I was not a pigeon shot, and she gave a little start of surprise. 'Oh! I beg your pardon,' she said, 'I thought you were Morton Hamilton, the English champion.' As a matter of fact, I do look something like Hamilton, but I know now that her object was to make me think that she had no idea as to who I really was. She needn't have acted at all, for I certainly had no suspicions, and was only too pleased to have so charming a companion.

"The one thing that should have made me suspicious was the fact that at every station she made some trivial excuse to get me out of the compartment. She pretended that her maid was travelling behind us in one of the second-class carriages, and kept saying she could not imagine why the woman did not come to look after her; and if the maid did not turn up at the next stop, would I be so very kind as to get out and bring her whatever it was she pretended she wanted?

"I had taken my dressing-case from the rack to get out a novel, and had left it on the seat opposite to mine, and at the end of the compartment furthest from her. And once when I came back from buying her a cup of chocolate, or from some other fool errand, I found her standing at my end of the compartment with both hands on the dressing-bag. She looked at me without so much as winking an eye, and shoved the case carefully into a corner. 'Your bag slipped off on the floor,' she said. 'If you've got any bottles in it, you had better look and see that they're not broken.'

"And I give you my word, I was such an ass that I did open the case and look all through it. She must have thought I *was* a Juggins. I get hot all over whenever I remember it. But in spite of my dulness, and her cleverness, she couldn't gain anything by sending me away, because what she wanted was in the handbag, and every time she sent me away the handbag went with me.

"After the incident of the dressing-case her manner began to change. Either she had had time to look through it in my absence, or, when I was examining it for broken bottles, she had seen everything it held.

"From that moment she must have been certain that the cigar-case in which she knew I carried the diamonds was in the bag that was fastened to my body, and from that time on she probably was plotting how to get it from me.

"Her anxiety became most apparent. She dropped the great lady manner, and her charming condescension went with it. She ceased talking, and, when I spoke, answered me irritably or at random. No doubt her mind was entirely occupied with her plan. The end of our journey was drawing rapidly nearer, and her time for action was being cut down with the speed of the express train. Even I, unsuspicious as I was, noticed that something was very wrong with her. I really believe that before we reached Marseilles, if I had not, through my own stupidity, given her the chance she wanted, she might have stuck a knife in me and rolled me out on the rails. But as it was, I only thought that the long journey had tired her. I suggested that it was a very tedious trip, and asked her if she would allow me to offer her some of my cognac.

"She thanked me and said 'No,' and then suddenly her eyes lighted, and she exclaimed, 'Yes, thank you, if you will be so kind.'

"My flask was in the handbag, and I placed it on my lap, and with my thumb I slipped back the catch. As I keep my tickets and railroad guide in the bag, I am so constantly opening it that I never bother to lock it, and the fact that it is strapped to me has always been sufficient protection. But I can appreciate now what a satisfaction, and what a torment, too, it must have been to that woman when she saw that the bag opened without a key.

"While we were crossing the mountains I had felt rather chilly, and had been wearing a light racing coat. But after the lamps were lighted the compartment became very hot and stuffy, and I found the coat uncomfortable. So I stood up, and, after first slipping the strap of the bag over my head, I placed the bag in the seat next me and pulled off the racing coat. I don't blame myself for being careless; the bag was still within reach of my hand, and nothing would have happened if at that exact moment the train had not stopped at Arles. It was the combination of my removing the bag and our entering the station at the same instant which gave the Princess Zichy the chance she wanted to rob me.

"I needn't say that she was clever enough to take it. The train ran in the station at full speed and came to a sudden stop. I had just thrown my coat into the rack, and had reached out my hand for the bag. In another instant I should have had the strap around my shoulder. But at that moment the Princess threw open the door of the compartment and beckoned wildly at the people on the platform. 'Natalie!' she called, 'Natalie! here I am. Come here! This way!' She turned upon me in the greatest excitement. 'My maid!' she cried. 'She is looking for me. She passed the window without seeing me. Go, please, and bring her back.' She continued pointing out of the door and beckoning me with her other hand. There certainly was something about that woman's tone which made one jump. When she was giving orders, you had no chance to think of anything else. So I rushed out on my errand of mercy, and then rushed back again to ask what the maid looked like.

"'I must have rushed up to over twenty women and asked, "Are you Natalie?"'"

"'In black,' she answered, rising and blocking the door of the compartment. 'All in black, with a bonnet!'

"The train waited three minutes at Arles, and in that time I suppose I must have rushed up to over twenty women and asked, 'Are you Natalie?' The only reason I wasn't punched with an umbrella or handed over to the *gendarme* must have been that they probably thought I was crazy.

"When I jumped back into the compartment the Princess was seated where I had left her, but her eyes were burning with happiness. She placed her hand on my arm almost affectionately and said in a most hysterical way, 'You are very kind to me. I am so sorry to have troubled you.'

"I protested that every woman on the platform was dressed in black.

"'Indeed, I am so sorry,' she said, laughing; and she continued to laugh until she began to breathe so quickly that I thought she was going to faint.

"I can see now that the last part of that journey must have been a terrible half-hour for her. She had the cigar-case safe enough, but she knew that she herself was not safe. She knew if I were to open my bag, even at the last minute, and miss the case, I should know positively that she had taken it. I had placed the diamonds in the bag at the very moment she entered the compartment, and no one but our two selves had occupied it since. She knew that when we reached Marseilles she would either be twenty thousand pounds richer than when she left Paris, or that she would go to jail. That was the situation as she must have read it, and I don't envy her her state of mind during that last half-hour. It must have been hell.

"I saw that something was wrong, and in my innocence I even wondered if possibly my cognac had not been a little too strong. For she suddenly developed into a most brilliant conversationalist, and applauded and laughed at everything even I said, firing off questions at me like a machine-gun, so that I had no time to think of anything else but of what she was saying. Whenever I stirred, she stopped her chattering and leaned toward me, and watched me like a cat over a mouse-hole. I wondered how I could have considered her an agreeable travelling companion. I thought I should have preferred to be locked in with a lunatic. I don't like to think how she would have acted if I had made a move to examine the bag, but as I had it safely strapped around me again, I did not open it, and I reached Marseilles alive. As we drew into the station she shook hands with me and grinned at me like a Cheshire cat.

"'I cannot tell you,' she said, 'how much I have to thank you for.' What do you think of that for impudence?

"I offered to put her in a carriage, but she said she must find Natalie, and that she hoped we should meet again at the hotel. So I drove off by myself, wondering who she was, and whether Natalie was not her keeper.

"I had to wait several hours for the train to Nice, and as I wanted to stroll around the city, I thought I had better put the diamonds in the safe of the hotel. As soon as I reached my room I locked the door, placed the handbag on the table and opened it. I felt among the things at the top of it, but failed to touch the cigar-case. I shoved my hand in deeper and stirred the things about, but still I did not reach it. A cold wave swept down my spine, and a sort of emptiness came to the pit of my stomach. Then I turned red-hot and the sweat sprang out all over me. I wetted my lips with my tongue and said to myself, 'Don't be an ass! Pull yourself together, pull yourself together. Take the things out, one at a time. It's there, of course it's there. Don't be an ass!'

"So I put a brake on my nerves and began very carefully to pick out the things one by one, but after five seconds I could not stand it another instant, and I rushed across the room and threw out everything on the bed; but the diamonds were not among them. I pulled the things about and tore them open and shuffled and rearranged and sorted them, but it was no use. The cigar-case was gone. I threw everything in the dressing-case out on the floor, although I knew it was useless to look for it there. I knew that I had put it in the bag. I sat down and tried to think. I remembered I had put it in the satchel at Paris just as that woman had entered the compartment, and I had been alone with her ever since, so it was she who had robbed me. But how? It had never left my shoulder. And then I remembered that it had—that I had taken it off when I had changed my coat and for the few moments that I was searching for Natalie. I remembered that the woman had sent me on that goose-chase, and at every other station she had tried to get rid of me on some fool errand.

"I gave a roar like a mad bull and I jumped down the stairs six steps at a time.

"I demanded at the office if a distinguished

"'While I was standing there he must have given at least a hundred orders.'"

lady traveller, possibly a Russian, had just entered the hotel.

"As I expected, she had not. I sprang into a cab and inquired at two other hotels, and then I saw the folly of trying to catch her without outside help, and I ordered the fellow to gallop to the office of the Chief of Police. I told my story, and the ass in charge asked me to calm myself and wanted to take notes. I told him this was no time for taking notes, but for doing something. He got wrathy at that, and I demanded to be taken at once to his Chief. The Chief, he said, was very busy and could not see me. So I showed him my silver greyhound. In eleven years I had never used it but once before. I stated in pretty vigorous language that I was a Queen's Messenger, and that if the Chief of Police did not see me instantly he would lose his official head. The fellow jumped off his high horse at that and ran with me to his Chief—a smart young chap, a colonel in the army, and a very intelligent man.

"I explained that I had been robbed in a French railway carriage of a diamond necklace belonging to the Queen of England, which Her Majesty was sending as a present to the Czarina of Russia. I pointed out to him that if he succeeded in capturing the thief, he would be made for life and would receive the gratitude of three great Powers.

"He wasn't the sort that thinks second thoughts are best. He saw Russian and French decorations sprouting all over his chest, and he hit a bell and pressed buttons and yelled out orders like the captain of a penny steamer in a fog. He sent her description to all the city gates, and ordered all cabmen and railway porters to search all trains leaving Marseilles. He ordered all passengers on outgoing vessels to be examined, and telegraphed the proprietors of every hotel and pension to send him a complete list of their guests within the hour. While I was standing there he must have given at least a hundred orders, and sent out enough *commissaires*, *sergents de ville*, *gendarmes*, bicycle police, and plain-clothes Johnnies to have captured the entire German army. When they had gone he assured me that the woman was as good as arrested already. Indeed, officially, she was arrested; for she had no more chance of escape from Marseilles than from the Château D'If.

"He told me to return to my hotel and possess my soul in peace. Within an hour he assured me he would acquaint me with her arrest.

"I thanked him, and complimented him on his energy, and left him. But I didn't share in his confidence. I felt that she was a very clever woman and a match for any and all of us. It was all very well for him to be jubilant. He had not lost the diamonds, and had everything to gain if he found them; while I, even if he did recover the necklace, should only be where I was before I lost it, and if he did not recover it I was a ruined man. It was an awful facer for me. I had always prided myself on my record. In eleven years I had never mislaid an envelope nor missed taking the first train. And now I had failed in the most important commission that had ever been entrusted to me. And it wasn't a thing that could be hushed up, either. It was too conspicuous, too spectacular. It was sure to invite the widest notoriety. I saw myself ridiculed all over the Continent, and perhaps dismissed, even suspected of having taken the thing myself.

"I was walking in front of a lighted *café*, and I felt so sick and miserable that I stopped for a pick-me-up. Then I considered that if I took one drink I should probably, in my present state of mind. not want to stop under twenty, and I decided I had better leave it alone. But my nerves were jumping like those of a frightened rabbit, and I felt I must have something to quiet them or I should go crazy. I reached for my cigarette-case, but a cigarette seemed hardly adequate, so I put it back again and took out this cigar-case, in which I keep only the strongest and blackest cigars. I opened it and stuck in my fingers, but instead of a cigar they touched on a thin leather envelope. My heart stood perfectly still. I did not dare to look, but I dug my finger-nails into the letter and I felt layers of thin paper, then a layer of cotton, and then they scratched on the facets of the Czarina's diamonds!

"I stumbled as though I had been hit in the face and fell back into one of the chairs on the pavement. I tore off the wrappings and spread out the diamonds on the *café* table; I could not believe they were real. I twisted the necklace between my fingers, and crushed it between my palms, and tossed it up in the air. I believe I almost kissed it. The women in the *café* stood up on the chairs to see better, and laughed and screamed, and the people crowded so close around me that the waiters had to form a bodyguard. The proprietor thought there was a fight and called for the police. I was so happy I didn't care. I laughed, too, and gave the proprietor a handful of coin and told him to stand everyone a drink. Then I tumbled into a *fiacre* and galloped off to my friend the Chief of Police. I felt very sorry for him. He had been so happy at the chance I had given him, and he would be so disappointed when he learned I had sent him off on a false alarm.

"But now that I had the necklace I did not want him to find the woman. Indeed, I was most anxious that she should get clear away. For if she were caught, the truth would come out, and I was likely to get a sharp reprimand, and sure to be laughed at.

"I could see now how it had happened. In my haste to hide the diamonds when the woman was hustled into the carriage I had shoved the cigars into the satchel and the diamonds into the pocket of my coat. Now that I had the diamonds safe again it seemed a very natural mistake. But I doubted if the Foreign Office would think so. I was afraid it might not appreciate the beautiful

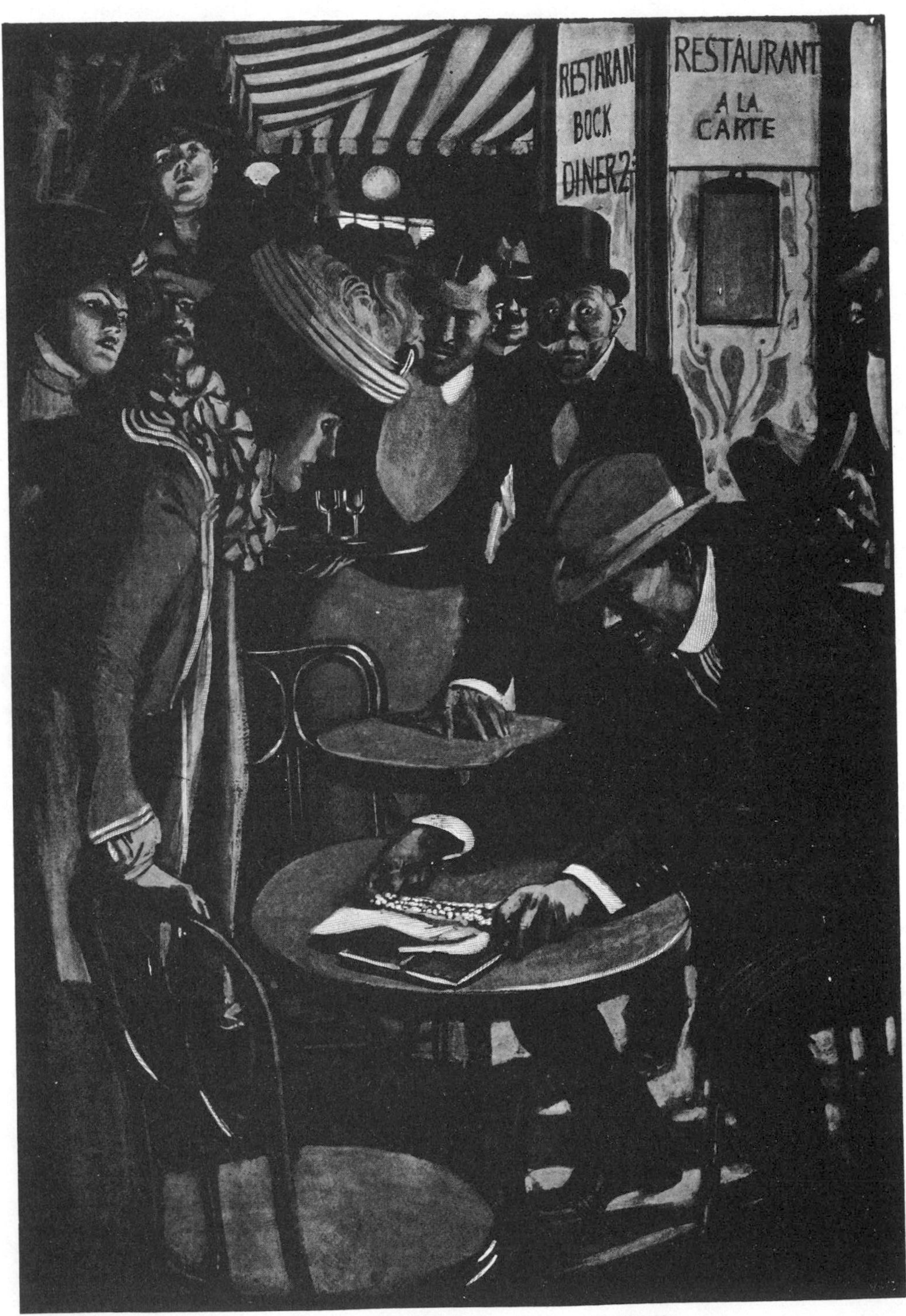

"'I spread out the diamonds on the *café* table.'"

simplicity of my secret hiding-place. So, when I reached the police station and found the Princess still at large, I was more than relieved.

"As I expected, the Chief was extremely chagrined when he learned of my mistake and that there was nothing for him to do. But I was feeling so happy myself that I hated to have anyone else miserable, so I suggested that this attempt to steal the Czarina's necklace might be only the first of a series of such attempts, and that I might still be in danger from an unscrupulous gang.

"I winked at the Chief and the Chief smiled at me, and we went to Nice together in a saloon car with a guard of twelve carabineers and twelve plain-clothes men, and the Chief and I drank champagne all the way. We marched together up to the hotel where the Russian Ambassador was stopping, closely surrounded by our escort of carabineers, and delivered the necklace with the most profound ceremony. The old Ambassador was immensely impressed, and when we hinted that already I had been made the object of an attack by robbers, he assured us that His Imperial Majesty would not prove ungrateful.

"I wrote a swinging personal letter about the invaluable services of the Chief to the French Minister of Foreign Affairs, and they gave him enough Russian and French medals to satisfy even a French soldier. So, though he never caught the woman, he received his just reward."

The Queen's Messenger paused and surveyed the faces of those about him in some embarrassment.

"But the worst of it is," he added, "that the story must have got about; for, while the Princess obtained nothing from me but a cigar-case and five excellent cigars, a few weeks after the coronation the Czar sent me a gold cigar-case with his monogram in diamonds. And I don't know yet whether that was a coincidence, or whether the Czar wanted me to know that he knew that I had been carrying the Czarina's diamonds in my pigskin cigar-case. What do you fellows think?"

IN THE FOG.

By RICHARD HARDING DAVIS

No. III.—THE SOLICITOR'S STORY.

SIR ANDREW rose, with disapproval written in every lineament.

"I thought your story would bear upon the murder," he said. "Had I imagined it would have nothing whatsoever to do with it, I would not have remained." He pushed back his chair and bowed stiffly. "I wish you 'Good-night,'" he said.

There was a chorus of remonstrance, and under cover of this and the Baronet's answering protests a servant for the second time slipped a piece of paper into the hand of the gentleman with the pearl stud. He read the lines written upon it and tore it into tiny fragments.

The youngest member, who had remained an interested but silent listener to the tale of the Queen's Messenger, raised his hand commandingly.

"Sir Andrew," he cried, "in justice to Lord Arthur Chetney I must ask you to be seated. He has been accused in our hearing of a most serious crime, and I insist that you remain until you have heard me clear his character."

"You?" cried the Baronet.

"Yes," answered the young man briskly. "I would have spoken sooner," he explained, "but that I thought this gentleman"—he inclined his head toward the Queen's Messenger—"was about to contribute some facts of which I was ignorant. He, however, has told us nothing, and so I will take up the tale at the point where Lieutenant Sears laid it down, and give you those details of which Lieutenant Sears is ignorant. It seems strange to you that I should be able to add the sequel to this story. But the coincidence, when explained, is obvious enough. I am the junior member of the law firm of Chudleigh and Chudleigh. We have been solicitors for the Chetneys for the last two hundred years. Nothing, no matter how unimportant, which concerns Lord Edam and his two sons is unknown to us, and naturally we are acquainted with every detail of the terrible catastrophe of last night."

The Baronet, bewildered but eager, sank back into his chair.

"Will you be long, sir?" he demanded.

"I shall endeavour to be brief," said the young solicitor; "and," he added, in a tone which gave his words almost the weight of a threat, "I promise to be interesting."

"There is no need to promise that," said Sir Andrew, "I find it much too interesting as it is." He glanced ruefully at the clock and turned his eyes quickly from it.

"Tell the driver of that hansom," he called to the servant, "that I take him by the hour."

"For the last three days," began young Mr. Chudleigh, "as you have probably read in the daily papers, the Marquis of Edam has been at the point of death, and his physicians have never left his house. Every hour he seemed to grow weaker; but although his bodily strength is apparently leaving him for ever, his mind has remained clear and active. Late yesterday evening word was received at our office that he wished my father to come at once to Chetney House and to bring with him certain papers. What these papers were is not essential; I mention them only to explain how it was that last night I happened to be at Lord Edam's bedside. I accompanied my father to Chetney House, but at the time we reached there Lord Edam was sleeping, and his physicians refused to have him awakened. My father urged that he should be allowed to receive Lord Edam's instructions concerning the documents, but the physicians would not disturb him, and we all gathered in the library to wait until he should awake of his own accord. It was about one o'clock in the morning, while we were still there, that

Inspector Lyle and the officers from Scotland Yard came to arrest Lord Arthur on the charge of murdering his brother. You can imagine our dismay and distress. Like everyone else, I had learned from the afternoon papers that Lord Chetney was not dead, but that he had returned to England. And on arriving at Chetney House I had been told that Lord Arthur had gone to the Bath Hotel to look for his brother and to inform him that if he wished to see their father alive he must come to him at once. Although it was now past one o'clock, Arthur had not returned. None of us knew where Madame Zichy had lived, so we could not go to recover Lord Chetney's body. We spent a most miserable night, hastening to the window whenever a cab came into the square, in the hope that it was Arthur returning, and endeavouring to explain away the facts that pointed to him as the murderer. I am a friend of Arthur's, I was with him at Harrow and at Oxford, and I refused to believe for an instant that he was capable of such a crime; but as a lawyer I could not but see that the circumstantial evidence was strongly against him.

"Toward early morning Lord Edam awoke, and in so much better a state of health that he refused to make the changes in the papers which he had intended, declaring that he was no nearer death than ourselves. Under other circumstances this happy change in him would have relieved us greatly, but none of us could think of anything save the death of his elder son and of the charge which hung over Arthur.

"As long as Inspector Lyle remained in the house my father decided that I, as one of the legal advisers of the family, should also remain there. But there was little for either of us to do. Arthur did not return, and nothing occurred until late this morning, when Lyle received word that the Russian servant had been arrested. He at once drove to Scotland Yard to question him. He came back to us in an hour and informed me that the servant had refused to tell anything of what had happened the night before, or of himself, or of the Princess Zichy. He would not even give them the address of her house.

"'He is in abject terror,' Lyle said. 'I assured him that he was not suspected of the crime, but he would tell me nothing.'

"There were no other developments until two o'clock this afternoon, when word was brought to us that Arthur had been found, and that he was lying in the Accident Ward of St. George's Hospital. Lyle and I drove there together, and found him propped up in bed with his head bound in a bandage. He had been brought to the hospital the night before by the driver of a hansom that had run over him in the fog. The cab-horse had kicked him on the head and he had been carried in unconscious. There was nothing on him to tell who he was, and it was not until he came to his senses this afternoon that the hospital authorities had been able to send word to his people. Lyle at once informed him that he was under arrest, and with what he was charged, and though the Inspector warned him to say nothing which might be used against him, I, as his solicitor, instructed him to speak freely and to tell us all he knew of the occurrences of last night. It was evident to anyone that the fact of his brother's death was of much greater concern to him than that he was accused of his murder.

"'That——' Arthur said contemptuously, 'that is nonsense! It is monstrous and cruel. We parted better friends than we have been for years. I will tell you all that happened—not to clear myself, but to help you to find out the truth.' His story is as follows: Yesterday afternoon, owing to his constant attendance on his father, he did not look at the evening papers, and it was not until after dinner, when the butler brought him one and told him of its contents, that he learned that his brother was alive and at the Bath Hotel. He drove there at once, but was told that about eight o'clock his brother had gone out, but without giving any clue to his destination. As Chetney had not at once come to see his father, Arthur decided that he was still angry with him, and his mind, turning naturally to the cause of their quarrel, determined him to look for Chetney at the home of the Princess Zichy.

"Her house had been pointed out to him, and, though he had never visited it, he had passed it many times and knew its exact location. He accordingly drove in that direction, as far as the fog would permit the hansom to go, and walked the rest of the way, reaching the house about nine o'clock. He rang, and was admitted by the Russian servant. The man took his card into the drawing-room, and at once his brother ran out and welcomed him. He was followed by the Princess Zichy, who also received Arthur most cordially.

"'You brothers will have much to talk about,' she said. 'I am going to the dining-room. When you have finished, let me know.'

"Sir Andrew rose, with disapproval written in every lineament. . . . He pushed back his chair and bowed stiffly. 'I wish you "Good-night."'"

"As soon as she had left them, Arthur told his brother that their father was not expected to outlive the night, and that he must come to him at once.

"'This is not the time to remember your quarrel,' Arthur said to him; 'you have come back from the dead only in time to make your peace with him before he dies.'

"Arthur says that Chetney was greatly moved at what he told him.

"'You entirely misunderstand me, Arthur,' he returned. 'I did not know the governor was ill, or I would have gone to him the instant I arrived. My only reason for not doing so was because I thought he was still angry with me. I shall return with you immediately, as soon as I have said good-bye to the Princess. It is a final good-bye. After to-night I shall never see her again.'

"'Do you mean that?' Arthur cried.

"'Yes,' Chetney answered. 'When I returned to London, I had no intention of seeking her again, and I am here only through a mistake.' He then told Arthur that he had separated from the Princess even before he went to Central Africa, and that, moreover, while at Cairo on his way south he had learned certain facts concerning her life there during the previous season which made it impossible for him ever to wish to see her again. Their separation was final and complete.

"'She deceived me cruelly,' he said; 'I cannot tell you how cruelly. During the two years when I was trying to obtain the governor's consent to our marriage she was in love with a Russian diplomat. During all that time he was secretly visiting her here in London, and her trip to Cairo was only an excuse to meet him there.'

"'Yet you are here with her to-night,' Arthur protested, 'only a few hours after your return!'

"'That is easily explained,' Chetney answered. 'I had just finished dinner to-night at the hotel when I received a note from her from this address. In it she said she had just learned of my arrival and begged me to come to her at once. She wrote that she was in great and present trouble, dying of an incurable illness, and without friends or money. She begged me, for the sake of old times, to come to her assistance. During the last two years in the jungle all my former feeling for Zichy has utterly passed away from me, but no one could have dismissed the appeal she made in that letter. So I drove here and found her, as you have seen her, quite as beautiful as ever she was, in very good health, and, from the look of the house, in no need of money.

"'I asked her what she meant by writing me that she was dying in a garret, and she laughed and said she had done so because she was afraid unless I thought she needed help I would not try to see her. That was where we were when you arrived. And now,' Chetney added, 'I will say good-bye to her, and you had better return home. No, you can trust me. I shall follow you at once. She has no influence over me now, but I believe, in spite of the way she has used me, that she is still fond of me after her queer fashion, and when she learns that this good-bye is final there may be a scene. And it is not fair to her that you should be here. So go home at once and tell the governor that I am following you in ten minutes.'

"'That,' said Arthur, 'is the way we parted. I never left him on more friendly terms. I was happy to see him alive again, I was happy to think he had returned in time to make up his quarrel with my father, and I was happy that at last he was clear of that woman. I was never better pleased with him in my life.' He turned to Inspector Lyle, who was sitting at the foot of the bed taking notes of all he told us.

"'Why, in the name of common-sense,' he cried, 'should I have chosen that moment of all others to send my brother back to the grave again?' For a moment the Inspector did not answer him. I do not know if any of you gentlemen are acquainted with Inspector Lyle, but if you are not, I should tell you that he is a very remarkable man. Our firm often applies to him for aid, and he has never failed us yet; my father has the greatest possible respect for him. Where he has the advantage over the ordinary police official is in the fact that he possesses imagination. He imagines himself to be the criminal, imagines how he would act under the same circumstances, and he imagines to such purpose that he generally finds the man he wants. I have often told Lyle that if he had not been a detective, he would have made a great success as a poet or a playwright.

"When Arthur turned on him, Lyle hesitated for a moment and then told him exactly what was the case against him.

"'Ever since your brother was reported as having died in Africa,' he said, 'your Lordship has been collecting money on *post obits*. Lord Chetney's arrival last night turned them into waste paper. You were suddenly in debt for thousands of pounds—for much more than you could ever possibly pay. No one knew that you and your brother had met at Madame Zichy's. But you knew that your father was not expected to outlive the night, and that if your brother were dead also, you would be saved from complete ruin, and that you would become the Marquis of Edam.'

"'Oh! that is how you have worked it out, is it?' Arthur cried. 'And for me to become Lord Edam, was it necessary that the woman should die, too?'

"'They will say,' Lyle answered, 'that she was a witness to the murder—that she would have told.'

"'Then why did I not kill the servant as well?' Arthur said.

"'He was asleep, and saw nothing.'

"'And you believe *that?*' Arthur demanded.

"'It is not a question of what I believe,' Lyle said gravely. 'It is a question for your peers.'

"'The man is insolent!' Arthur cried. 'The thing is monstrous! Horrible!'

"Before we could stop him, he sprang out of his cot and began pulling on his clothes. When the nurses tried to hold him down, he fought with them.

"'Do you think you can keep me here,' he shouted, 'when they are plotting to hang me? I am going with you to that house!' he cried to Lyle. 'When you find those bodies, I shall be beside you. It is my right. He is my brother. He has been murdered, and I can tell you who murdered him. That woman murdered him. She

"The Princess Zichy, who also received Arthur most cordially."

first ruined his life, and now she has killed him. For the last five years she has been plotting to make herself his wife, and last night, when he told her he had discovered the truth about the Russian, and that she would never see him again, she flew into a passion and stabbed him, and then, in terror of the gallows, killed herself. She murdered him, I tell you, and I promise you that we shall find the knife she used near her—perhaps still in her hand. What will you say to that ?'

"Lyle turned his head away and stared down at the floor. 'I might say,' he answered, 'that you placed it there.'

"Arthur gave a cry of anger and sprang at him, and then pitched forward into his arms. The blood was running from the cut under the bandage and he had fainted. Lyle carried him back to the bed again, and we left him with the police and the doctors and drove at once to the address he had given us. We found the house not three minutes' walk from St. George's Hospital. It stands in Trevor Terrace, that little row of houses set back from Knightsbridge with one end in Hill Street.

"As we left the hospital, Lyle had said to me, 'You must not blame me for treating him as I did. All is fair in this work, and if by angering that boy I could have made him commit himself, I was right in trying to do so ; though, I assure you, no one would be better pleased than myself if I could prove his theory to be correct. But we cannot tell. Everything depends upon what we see for ourselves within the next few minutes.'

"When we reached the house, Lyle broke open the fastenings of one of the windows on the ground floor, and, hidden by the trees in the garden, we scrambled in. We found ourselves in the reception-room, which was the first room on the right of the hall. The gas was still burning behind the coloured glass and red silk shades, and when the daylight streamed in after us, it gave the hall a hideously dissipated look, like the foyer of a theatre at a *matinée*, or the entrance to an all-day gambling hell. The house was oppressively silent, and because we knew why it was so silent we spoke in whispers. When Lyle turned the handle of the drawing-room door, I felt as though someone had put his hand upon my throat. But I followed close at his shoulder and saw, in the subdued light of many-tinted lamps, the body of Chetney at the foot of the divan, just as Lieutenant Sears has described it. In the drawing-room we found upon the floor the body of the Princess Zichy, her arms thrown out, and the blood from her heart frozen in a tiny line across her bare shoulder. But neither of us, although we searched the floor on our hands and knees, could find the weapon which had killed her.

"'For Arthur's sake,' I said, 'I would give a thousand pounds if we had found the knife in her hand, as he said we would.'

"'That we have not found it there,' Lyle answered, 'is to my mind the strongest proof that he is telling the truth—that he left the house before the murder took place. He is not a fool, and had he stabbed his brother and this woman he would have seen that by placing the knife near her he could help to make it appear as if she had killed Chetney and then committed suicide. Besides, Lord Arthur insisted that the evidence in his behalf would be our finding the knife here. He would not have urged that if he knew we would *not* find it, if he knew he himself had carried it away. This is no suicide. A suicide does not rise and hide the weapon with which he kills himself, and then lie down again. No, this has been a double murder, and we must look outside the house for the murderer.'

"While he was speaking, Lyle and I had been searching every corner, studying the details of each room. I was so afraid that, without telling me, he would make some deductions prejudicial to Arthur, that I never left his side. I was determined to see everything that he saw, and, if possible, to prevent his interpreting it in the wrong way. He finally finished his examination, and we sat down together in the drawing-room, and he took out his notebook and read aloud all Mr. Sears had told him of the murder, and what we had just learned from Arthur. We compared the two accounts, word for word, and weighed statement with statement. But I could not determine from anything Lyle said which of the two versions he had decided to believe.

"'We are trying to build a house of blocks,' he exclaimed, 'with half of the blocks missing. We have been considering two theories,' he went on : 'one that Lord Arthur is responsible for both murders, and the other that the dead woman in there is responsible for one of them, and has committed suicide ; but until the Russian servant is ready to talk, I shall refuse to believe in the guilt of either.'

"'What can you prove by him ?' I asked. 'He was drunk and asleep. He saw nothing.'

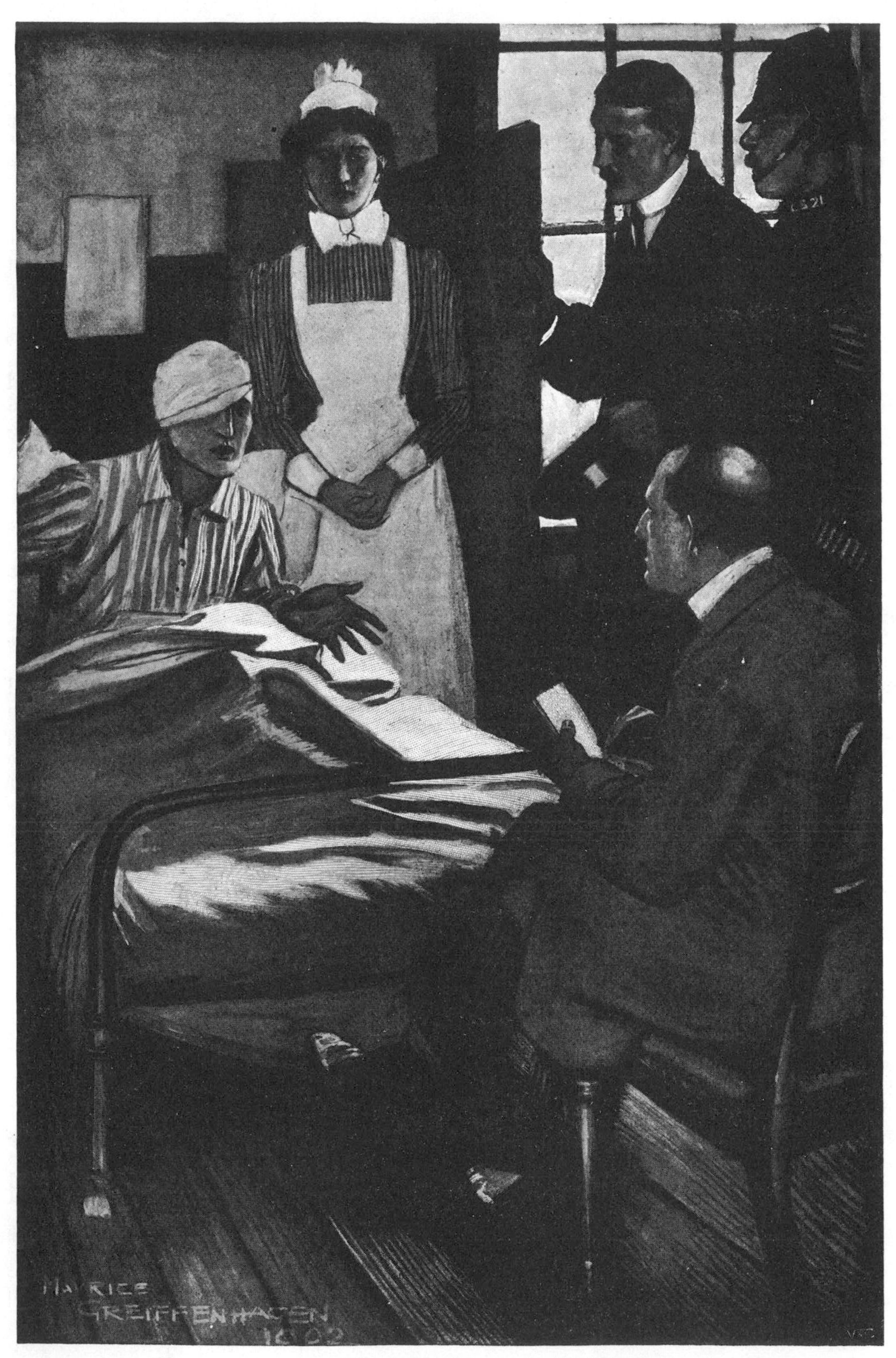

"'The thing is monstrous! Horrible!'"

"Lyle hesitated and then, as though he had made up his mind to be quite frank with me, spoke freely.

"'I do not know that he was either drunk or asleep," he answered. 'Lieutenant Sears describes him as a stupid boor. I am not satisfied that he is not a clever actor. What was his position in this house? What was his real duty here? Suppose it was not to guard this woman, but to watch her. Let us imagine that it was not the woman he served, but a master, and see where that leads us. For this house has a master, a mysterious, absentee landlord, who lives in St. Petersburg, the unknown Russian who came between Chetney and Zichy, and because of whom Chetney left her. He is the man who bought this house for Madame Zichy, who sent these rugs and curtains from Petersburg to furnish it for her after his own tastes, and, I believe, it was he also who placed the Russian servant here, ostensibly to serve the Princess, but in reality to spy upon her. At Scotland Yard we do not know who this gentleman is; the Russian police confess to equal ignorance concerning him. When Lord Chetney went to Africa, Madame Zichy lived in St. Petersburg; but there her receptions and dinners were so crowded with members of the nobility and of the army and diplomats, that among so many visitors the police could not learn which was the one for whom she most greatly cared.'

"Lyle pointed at the modern French paintings and the heavy silk rugs which hung upon the walls.

"'The unknown is a man of taste and of some fortune,' he said, 'not the sort of man to send a stupid peasant to guard the woman he loves. So I am not content to believe with Mr. Sears, that the man is a boor. I believe him instead to be a very clever ruffian. I believe him to be the protector of his master's honour, or, let us say, of his master's property, whether that property be silver plate or the woman his master loves. Last night, after Lord Arthur had gone away, the servant was left alone in this house with Lord Chetney and Madame Zichy. From where he sat in the hall he could hear Lord Chetney bidding her farewell; for, if my idea of him is correct, he understands English quite as well as you or I. Let us imagine that he heard her entreating Chetney not to leave her, reminding him of his former wish to marry her, and let us suppose that he hears Chetney denounce her, and tell her that at Cairo he has learned of this Russian admirer—the servant's master. He hears the woman declare that she has had no admirer but himself, that this unknown Russian was, and is, nothing to her, that there is no man she loves but him, and that she cannot live, knowing that he is alive, without his love. Suppose Chetney believed her, suppose his former infatuation for her returned, and that in a moment of weakness he forgave her and took her in his arms. That is the moment the Russian master has feared. It is to guard against it that he has placed his watch-dog over the Princess; and how do we know but that, when the moment came, the watch-dog served his master, as he saw his duty, and killed them both? What do you think?' Lyle demanded. 'Would not that explain both murders?'

"I was only too willing to hear any theory which pointed to anyone else as the criminal than Arthur, but Lyle's explanation was too utterly fantastic. I told him that he certainly showed imagination, but that he could not hang a man only for what he imagined he had done.

"'No,' Lyle answered, 'but I can frighten him by telling him what I think he has done, and now when I again question the Russian servant I will make it quite clear to him that I believe he is the murderer. I think that will open his mouth. A man will at least talk to defend himself. Come,' he said, 'we must return at once to Scotland Yard and see him. There is nothing more to do here.'

"He arose, and I followed him into the hall, and in another minute we should have been on our way to Scotland Yard. But just as he opened the street-door a postman halted at the gate of the garden and began fumbling with the latch.

"Lyle stopped, with an exclamation of chagrin.

"'How stupid of me!' he exclaimed. He turned quickly and pointed to a narrow slit cut in the brass plate of the front door. 'The house has a private letter-box,' he said, 'and I had not thought to look in it! If we had gone out as we came in, by the window, I should never have seen it. The moment I entered the house I should have thought of securing the letters which came this morning. I have been grossly careless.' He stepped back into the hall and pulled at the lid of the letter-box, which hung on the inside of the door, but it was tightly locked. At the same moment the postman came up the steps holding a letter. Without a word Lyle took it from his hand and began to examine it. It was addressed to the Princess Zichy, and on the back of the envelope was the name of a West End dressmaker.

"'That is of no use to me,' Lyle said. He took out his card and showed it to the postman. 'I am Inspector Lyle, from Scotland Yard,' he said. 'The people in this house are under arrest. Everything it contains is now in my keeping. Did you deliver any other letters here this morning?'

"The man looked frightened, but answered promptly that he was now upon his third round. He had made one postal delivery at seven that morning and another at eleven.

"'How many letters did you leave here?' Lyle asked.

"'About six altogether,' the man answered.

"'Did you put them through the door into the letter-box?'

"The postman said, 'Yes, I always slip them into the box, and ring and go away. The servants collect them from the inside.'

"'Have you noticed if any of the letters you leave here bear a Russian postage-stamp?' Lyle asked.

"The man answered, 'Oh, yes, sir, a great many.'

"'From the same person, would you say?'

"'The writing seems to be the same,' the man answered. 'They come regularly about once a week—one of those I delivered this morning had a Russian postmark.'

"'That will do,' said Lyle eagerly. 'Thank you, thank you very much.'

"He ran back into the hall and, pulling out his penknife, began to pick at the lock of the letter-box.

"'I have been supremely careless,' he said in great excitement. 'Twice before when people I wanted had flown from a house I have been able to follow them by putting a guard over their mail-box. These letters, which arrive regularly every week from Russia in the same handwriting—they can come but from one person. At least we shall now know the name of the master of this house. Undoubtedly it is one of his letters that the man placed here this morning. We may make a most important discovery.'

"As he was talking he was picking at the lock with his knife, but he was so impatient to reach the letters that he pressed too heavily on the blade and it broke in his hand. I took a step backward and drove my heel into the lock and burst it open. The lid flew back, and we pressed forward, and each ran his hand down into the letter-box. For a moment we were both too startled to move. The box was empty!

"I do not know how long we stood staring stupidly at each other, but it was Lyle who was the first to recover. He seized me by the arm and pointed excitedly into the empty box.

"'Do you appreciate what that means?' he cried. 'It means that someone has been here ahead of us. Someone has entered this house not three hours before we came, since eleven o'clock this morning.'

"'It was the Russian servant!' I exclaimed.

"'The Russian servant has been under arrest at Scotland Yard,' Lyle cried. 'He could not have taken the letters. Lord Arthur has been in his cot at the hospital. That is his *alibi*. There is someone else—someone we do not suspect—and that someone is the murderer. He came back here either to obtain those letters because he knew they would convict him, or to remove something he had left here at the time of the murder, something incriminating—the weapon, perhaps, or some personal article: a cigarette-case, a handkerchief with his name upon it, or a pair of gloves. Whatever it was, it must have been damning evidence against him to have made him take so desperate a chance.'

"'How do we know,' I whispered, 'that he is not hidden here now?'

"'No, I'll swear he is not!' Lyle answered. 'I may have bungled in some things, but I have searched this house thoroughly. Nevertheless,' he added, 'we must go over it again, from the cellar to the roof. We have the real clue now, and we must forget the others and work only it.' As he spoke he began again to search the drawing-room, turning over even the books on the tables and the music on the piano.

"'Whoever the man is,' he said over his shoulder, 'we know that he has a key to the front door and a key to the letter-box. That shows us he is either an inmate of the house or that he comes here when he wishes. The Russian says that he was the only servant in the house. Certainly we have found no evidence to show that any other servant slept here. There could be but one other person who would possess a key to the house and the letter-box—and he lives in St. Petersburg. At the time of the murder he was two thousand miles away.' Lyle interrupted himself suddenly with a sharp cry and turned upon me with his eyes flashing. 'But was he?' he cried. 'Was he? How do we know that last night he was not in London, in this very house when Zichy and Chetney met here?'

"He stood staring at me without seeing me, muttering and arguing with himself.

"'Don't speak to me!' he cried, as I ventured to interrupt him. 'I can see it now. It is all plain to me. It was not the servant, but his master, the Russian himself, and it was he who came back for the letters. He came back for them because he knew they would convict him. We must find them. We must have those letters. If we find the one with the Russian postmark, we shall have found the murderer.' He spoke like a madman, and as he spoke he ran around the room with one hand held out in front of him as you have seen a mind-reader at a theatre seeking for something hidden in the stalls. He pulled the old letters from the writing-desk and ran them over as swiftly as a gambler deals out cards; he dropped on his knees before the fireplace and dragged out the dead coals with his bare fingers, and then with a low, worried cry, like a hound on a scent, he ran back to the waste-paper basket and, lifting the papers from it, shook them out upon the floor. Instantly he gave a shout of triumph and, separating a number of torn pieces from the others, held them up before me.

"'Look!' he cried. 'Do you see? Here are five letters, torn across in two places. The Russian did not stop to read them, for, as you see, he has left them still sealed. I have been wrong. He did not return for the letters. He could not have known their value. He must have returned for some other reason, and, as he was leaving, saw the letter-box, and taking out the letters, held them together—so—and tore them twice across, and then, as the fire had gone out, tossed them into this basket. Look!' he cried, 'here in the upper corner of this piece is a Russian stamp. This is his own letter—unopened!'

"We examined the Russian stamp and found it had been cancelled in St. Petersburg four days ago. The back of the envelope bore the postmark of the branch station in Upper Sloane Street and was dated this morning. The envelope was of official blue paper, and we had no difficulty in finding the two other parts to it. We drew the torn pieces of the letter from them and joined them together side by side. There were but two lines of writing, and this was the message: 'I leave Petersburg on the night train, and I shall see you at Trevor Terrace after dinner Monday evening.'

"'That was last night!' Lyle cried. 'He arrived twelve hours ahead of his letter—but it came in time—it came in time to hang him!'"

The Baronet struck the table with his hand.

"The name!" he demanded. "How was it signed? What was the man's name?"

The young solicitor rose to his feet and, leaning forward, stretched out his arm. "There was no name," he cried. "The letter was signed with only two initials. But engraved at the top of the sheet was the man's address. That address was 'THE AMERICAN EMBASSY, ST. PETERSBURG, BUREAU OF THE NAVAL ATTACHÉ,' and the initials," he shouted, his voice rising into an exultant and bitter cry, "were those of the gentleman who sits opposite, who told us that he was the first to find the murdered bodies, the Naval Attaché to Russia, Lieutenant Ripley Sears!"

A strained and awful hush followed the solicitor's words, which seemed to vibrate in the air like a twanging bowstring which had just hurled its bolt. Sir Andrew, pale and staring, drew away with an exclamation of repulsion. His eyes were fastened upon the Naval Attaché with fascinated horror. But the American emitted a sigh of great content and sank comfortably into the arms of his chair. He clapped his hands softly together.

"Capital!" he murmured. "I give you my word I never guessed what you were driving at. You fooled me, I'll be hanged if you didn't—you certainly fooled me!"

The man with the pearl stud leaned forward with a nervous gesture. "Hush! be careful!" he whispered. But at that instant, for the third time, a servant hastening through the room handed him a piece of paper, which he scanned eagerly. The message on the paper read, "The light over the Commons is out. The House has risen."

The man with the black pearl gave a mighty shout and tossed the paper from him on the table.

"Hurrah!" he cried. "The House is up! We've won!" He caught up his glass and slapped the Naval Attache violently upon the shoulder. He nodded joyously at him, at the Solicitor, and at the Queen's Messenger. "Gentlemen, to you!" he cried; "my thanks and my congratulations!" He drank deep from the glass and breathed forth a long sigh of satisfaction and relief.

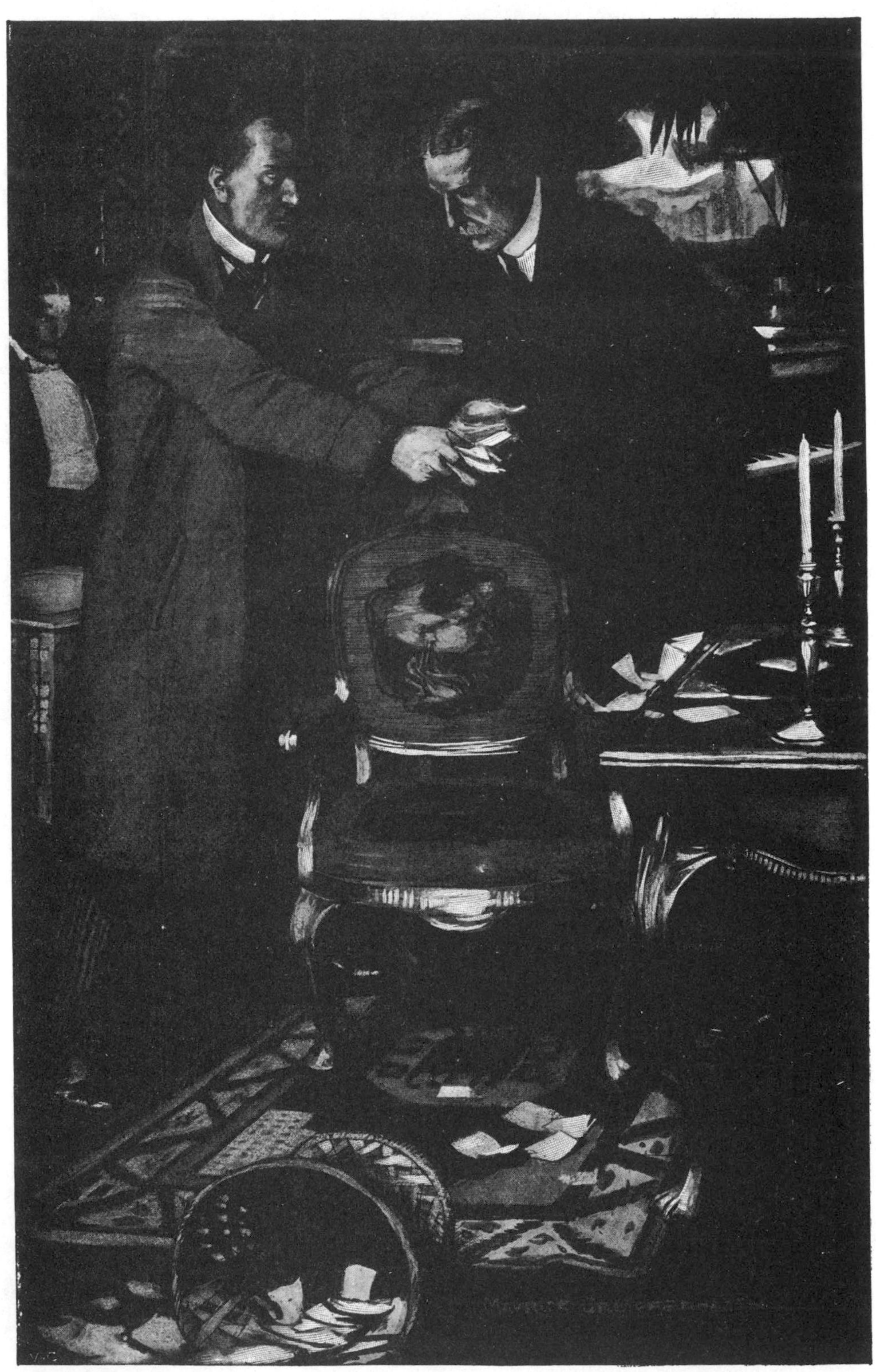

"'Look!' he cried. 'Do you see?'"

"But I say!" protested the Queen's Messenger, shaking his finger violently at the Solicitor, "that story won't do. You didn't play fair—and—and you talked so fast I couldn't make out what it was all about. I'll bet you that evidence wouldn't hold in a court of law—you couldn't hang a cat on such evidence. Your story is condemned tommy-rot. Now, my story might have happened, my story bore the mark——"

In the joy of creation the story-tellers had forgotten their audience, until a sudden exclamation from Sir Andrew caused them to turn guiltily toward him. His face was knit with lines of anger, doubt, and amazement.

"What does this mean?" he cried. "Is this a jest, or are you mad? If you know this man is a murderer, why is he at large? Is this a game you have been playing? Explain yourselves at once. What does it mean?"

The American, with first a glance at the others, rose and bowed courteously.

"I am not a murderer, Sir Andrew, believe me," he said; "you need not be alarmed. As a matter of fact, at this moment I am much more afraid of you than you could possibly be of me. I beg you please to be indulgent. I assure you we meant no disrespect. We have been matching stories, that is all, pretending that we are people we are not, endeavouring to entertain you with better detective tales than, for instance, the last one you read, 'The Great Rand Robbery.'"

The Baronet brushed his hand nervously across his forehead.

"Do you mean to tell me," he exclaimed, that none of this has happened? That Lord Chetney is not dead, that his solicitor did not find a letter of yours written from your post in Petersburg, and that just now, when he charged you with murder, he was in jest?"

"I am really very sorry," said the American, "but you see, sir, he could not have found a letter written by me in St. Petersburg, because I have never been in Petersburg. Until this week I have never been outside of my own country. I am not a naval officer. I am a writer of short stories. And to-night, when this gentleman told me that you were fond of detective stories, I thought it would be amusing to tell you one of mine—one I had just mapped out this afternoon."

"But Lord Chetney is a real person," interrupted the Baronet, "and he did go to Africa two years ago, and he was supposed to have died there, and his brother, Lord Arthur, has been the heir. And yesterday Chetney did return. I read it in the papers."

"So did I," assented the American soothingly. "And it struck me as being a very good plot for a story. I mean his unexpected return from the dead, and the probable disappointment of the younger brother. So I decided that the younger brother had better murder the elder one. The Princess Zichy I invented out of a clear sky. The fog I did not have to invent. Since last night I know all that there is to know about a London fog. I was lost in one for three hours."

The Baronet turned grimly upon the Queen's Messenger.

"But this gentleman," he protested, "he is not a writer of short stories; he is a member of the Foreign Office. I have seen him in Whitehall often, and, according to him, the Princess Zichy is not an invention. He says she is very well known—that she tried to rob him."

The servant of the Foreign Office looked unhappily at the Cabinet Minister and puffed nervously at his cigar.

"It's true, Sir Andrew, that I am a Queen's Messenger," he said appealingly, "and a Russian woman once did try to rob a Queen's Messenger in a railway carriage—only it did not happen to me, but to a pal of mine. The only Russian princess I ever knew called herself Zabrisky. You may have seen her. She used to do a dive from the roof of the Aquarium."

Sir Andrew, with a snort of indignation, fronted the young Solicitor.

"And I suppose yours was a cock-and-bull story, too?" he said. "Of course, it must have been, since Lord Chetney is not dead. But don't tell me," he protested, "that you are not Chudleigh's son, either."

"I'm sorry," said the youngest member, smiling in some embarrassment, "but my name is not Chudleigh. I assure you, though, that I know the family very well and that I am on very good terms with them."

"You should be!" exclaimed the Baronet; "and, judging from the liberties you take with the Chetneys, you had better be on very good terms with them, too."

The young man leaned back and glanced toward the servants at the far end of the room.

"It has been so long since I have been in the Club," he said, "that I doubt if even the waiters remember me. Perhaps Joseph may," he added. "Joseph!" he called, and at the word a servant stepped briskly forward.

The young man pointed to the stuffed head of a great lion which was suspended above the fireplace.

"Joseph," he said, "I want you to tell these gentlemen who shot that lion. Who presented it to the Grill?"

Joseph, unused to acting as master of ceremonies to members of the Club, shifted nervously from one foot to the other.

"Why, you—you did," he stammered.

"Of course I did!" exclaimed the young man. "I mean, what is the name of the man who shot it. Tell the gentlemen who I am. They wouldn't believe me."

"Who you are, my lord?" said Joseph. "You are Lord Edam's son, the Earl of Chetney."

"You must admit," said Lord Chetney, when the noise had died away, "that I couldn't remain dead while my little brother was accused of murder. I had to do something. Family pride demanded it. Now, Arthur, as the younger brother, can't afford to be squeamish, but personally I should hate to have a brother of mine hanged for murder."

"You certainly showed no scruples against hanging me," said the American, "but in the face of your evidence I admit my guilt, and I sentence myself to pay the full penalty of the law as we are made to pay it in my own country. The order of this Court is," he announced, "that Joseph shall bring me a wine-card, and that I sign it for five bottles of the Club's best champagne."

"Oh, no!" protested the man with the pearl stud, "it is not for *you* to sign it. In my opinion, it is Sir Andrew who should pay the costs. It is time you knew," he said, turning to that gentleman, "that unconsciously you have been the victim of what I may call a patriotic conspiracy. These stories have had a more serious purpose than merely to amuse. They have been told with the worthy object of detaining you from the House of Commons. I must explain to you that all through this evening I have had a servant waiting in Trafalgar Square with instructions to bring me word as soon as the light over the House of Commons had ceased to burn. The light is now out, and the object for which we plotted is attained."

The Baronet glanced keenly at the man with the black pearl and then quickly at his watch. The smile disappeared from his lips, and his face was set in stern and forbidding lines.

"And may I know," he asked icily, "what was the object of your plot?"

"A most worthy one," the other retorted. "Our object was to keep you from advocating the expenditure of many millions of the people's money upon more battleships. In a word, we have been working together to prevent you from passing the Navy Increase Bill."

Sir Andrew's face bloomed with brilliant colour. His body shook with suppressed emotion.

"My dear sir!" he cried, "you should spend more time at the House and less at your Club. The Navy Bill was brought up on its third reading at eight o'clock this evening. I spoke for three hours in its favour. My only reason for wishing to return again to the House to-night was to sup on the terrace with my old friend, Admiral Simons; for my work at the House was completed five hours ago, when the Navy Increase Bill was passed by an overwhelming majority."

The Baronet rose and bowed. "I have to thank you, sir," he said, "for a most interesting evening."

The American shoved the wine-card which Joseph had given him toward the gentleman with the black pearl.

"You sign it," he said.

THE END.

XIII

The Mystery of the Five Hundred Diamonds

ROBERT BARR

THE MYSTERY OF THE FIVE HUNDRED DIAMONDS.

By ROBERT BARR.

HEN I say I am called Valmont, the name will convey no impression to the reader, one way or another. My profession is that of private detective in London, and my professional name differs from that which I have just given you ; but if you ask any policeman in Paris who Valmont was, he will likely be able to tell you, unless he is a recent recruit. If you ask him where Valmont is now, he may not know, yet I have a good deal to do with the Parisian police.

For a period of seven years I was chief detective to the Government of France ; and if I am unable to prove myself a great crime-hunter, it is because the record of my career is in the secret archives of Paris.

I may say at the outset that I have no grievances to air. The French Government considered itself justified in dismissing me, and it did so. In this action it was quite within its right, and I should be the last to dispute that right ; but, on the other hand, I consider myself justified in publishing the following account of what actually occurred, especially as so many false rumours have been put abroad concerning the case. However, as I said at the beginning, I have no grievance, because my worldly affairs are now much more prosperous than they were in Paris, my intimate knowledge of that city and the country of which it is the capital having brought to me many cases with which I have dealt more or less successfully since I established myself in London.

Without further preliminary I shall at once plunge into an account of the case which a few years ago riveted the attention of the whole world.

The year 1893 was a prosperous twelve months for France. The weather was good, the harvest excellent, and the wine of that vintage is celebrated to this day. Everyone was well-off and reasonably happy, a marked contrast to the state of things a few years later, when dissension rent the country in twain.

Newspaper readers may remember that in '93 the Government of France fell heir to an unexpected treasure which set the whole civilized world agog, especially those inhabitants of it who are interested in historical relics. This was the finding of the diamond necklace in the Château de Chaumont, where it had lain for a century in a rubbish heap of an attic. I believe it has not been questioned that this was the veritable necklace which the Court jeweller, Boehmer, hoped to sell to Marie Antoinette, although how it came to be in the Château de Chaumont, no one has been able to form even a conjecture. For a century it was supposed that the necklace had been broken up in London, and its five hundred stones, great and small, sold separately. It has always seemed strange to me that the Countess de Lamotte-Valois, who was thought to have profited by the sale of these jewels, should not have abandoned France if she possessed money to leave that country, for exposure was inevitable if she remained. Indeed, the unfortunate woman was branded and imprisoned, and afterwards was dashed to death from the third storey of a London house, when, in the direst poverty, she sought escape from the consequences of debt.

I am not superstitious in the least, yet this celebrated piece of treasure-trove seems actually to have exerted a malign influence over everyone who had the misfortune to be connected with it. Indeed, in a small way, I who write these words suffered dismissal and disgrace, though I caught but one glimpse of this dazzling scintillation of jewels. The jeweller who made it met financial ruin ; the Queen for whom it was constructed was beheaded ; that high-born Prince Louis René Édouard, Cardinal de Rohan, who purchased it, was flung into prison ; the unfortunate Countess, who said she acted as go-between, clung for five awful minutes to a London window-sill before dropping to her death to the flags below ; and now, a hundred and eight years later, up comes this devil's display of fireworks to the light again.

Droulliard, the working man who found

the ancient box, seems to have prised it open and, ignorant though he was — he had probably never seen a diamond in his life before—realised that a fortune was in his grasp. The baleful light from the combination must have sent madness into his brain, working havoc therein as though they were those mysterious rays which scientists have recently discovered. He might quite easily have walked out of the main gate of the Château unsuspected and unquestioned with the diamonds concealed about his person, but instead of this he crept from the attic window on to the steep roof, slipped to the eaves, dropped and lay dead with a broken neck, while the necklace, intact, shimmered in the sunlight beside his body.

No matter where these jewels had been found, the Government had doubtless the first claim upon them ; but as the Château de Chaumont was an historical monument, and the property of France, there could be no question to whom the necklace belonged. The Government at once claimed it and ordered it to be sent by a trustworthy military man to Paris. It was carried safely and delivered promptly to the authorities by a young captain of artillery, to whom its custody had been entrusted.

In spite of its fall from the tall tower, neither case nor jewels was perceptibly damaged. The lock of the box had apparently been forced by Droulliard's hatchet, or perhaps by the clasp-knife found on his body. On reaching the ground, the lid had flown open and the necklace was thrown out.

I believe there was some discussion in the Cabinet regarding the fate of this ill-omened trophy, one section wishing it to be placed in a museum, on account of its historical interest, another advocating the breaking-up of the necklace and the selling of the diamonds for what they would fetch. But a third party maintained that the method to get the most money into the coffers of the country was to sell the necklace as it stood ; for as the world now contains so many rich amateurs who collected undoubted rarities regardless of expense, the historic associations of the jewelled collar would enhance the intrinsic value of the stones ; and this view prevailing, it was announced that the necklace would be sold by auction a month later in the rooms of Meyer, Renault and Co., in the Boulevard des Italiens, near the Bank of the Crédit-Lyonnais.

This announcement elicited much comment from the newspapers of all countries, and it seemed that from a financial point of view, at least, the decision of the Government had been wise, for it speedily became evident that a notable coterie of wealthy buyers would be congregated in Paris on the thirteenth, when the sale was to take place. But we of the inner circle were made aware of another result somewhat more disquieting, which was that the most expert criminals in the world were also gathering like vultures upon the fair city. The honour of France was at stake. Whoever bought that necklace must be assured of a safe conduct out of the country. Whatever happened afterwards we might view with equanimity, but while he was a resident of France his life and property must not be endangered. Thus it came about that I was given full authority to insure that neither murder nor theft, nor both combined, should be committed while the purchaser of the necklace remained within our boundaries, and for this purpose the police resources of France were placed unreservedly at my disposal. If I failed, there should be no one to blame but myself ; consequently, as I have remarked before, I do not complain of my dismissal by the Government.

The broken lock of the jewel-case had been very deftly repaired by an expert locksmith, who in executing his task was so unfortunate as to scratch a finger on the broken metal, whereupon blood poisoning set in, and although his life was saved, he was dismissed from the hospital with one arm gone, and his usefulness destroyed.

When the jeweller Boehmer made the necklace, he asked a hundred and sixty thousand pounds for it, but after years of disappointment he was content to sell it to Cardinal de Rohan for sixty-four thousand pounds, to be liquidated in three instalments, not one of which was ever paid. This latter amount was probably somewhere near the value of the five hundred and sixteen separate stones, one of which was of tremendous size, a very monarch of diamonds, holding its court among seventeen brilliants each as large as a filbert. This iridescent concentration of wealth was in my care, and I had to see to it that no harm came to the necklace or to its prospective owner until they had safely crossed the boundaries of France.

The four weeks previous to the thirteenth proved a busy and anxious time for me. Thousands, most of whom were actuated by mere curiosity, wished to view the diamonds. We were compelled to discriminate, and sometimes discriminated against the wrong person, which caused unpleasantness. Three distinct attempts were made to rob the safe, but luckily these were frustrated, and so we came unscathed to the eventful thirteenth of the month.

The sale was to take place at two o'clock, and on the morning of that day I took the somewhat tyrannical precaution to have the more dangerous of our own criminals, and as many of the foreigners as I could trump up charges against, laid by the heels, yet I knew very well it was not these rascals I had to fear, but the suave, well-groomed gentlemen, amply supplied with unimpeachable credentials, stopping at our fine hotels and living like princes. Many of these were foreigners against whom we could prove nothing, and whose arrest might land us into temporary international difficulties. Nevertheless, I had each of them shadowed, and on the morning of the thirteenth, if one of them had even disputed a cab fare, I should have had him in prison half an hour later, and taken the consequences; but these gentlemen are very shrewd and do not commit mistakes.

I made up a list of all the men in the world who were able or likely to purchase the necklace. Many of them would not be in person at the auction-rooms; their bidding would be done by agents. This simplified matters a good deal, for the agents kept me duly informed of their purposes, and, besides, an agent who handles treasure every week is an adept at the business, and does not need the protection which must surround an amateur who, in nine cases out of ten, has but scant idea of the dangers that threaten him, beyond knowing that if he goes down a dark street in a dangerous quarter, he is likely to be maltreated and robbed.

There were no less than sixteen clients, all told, who we learned were to attend personally on the day of the sale, any one of whom might well have made the purchase. The Marquis of Warlingham and Lord Oxtead, from England, were well-known jewel-fanciers, while at least half-a-dozen millionaires were expected from the United States, with a smattering from Germany, Austria, and Russia, and one each from Italy, Belgium, and Holland.

Admission to the auction-rooms was allowed by ticket only, to be applied for at least a week in advance, applications to be accompanied by satisfactory testimonials. It would possibly have surprised many of the rich men collected there to know that they sat cheek by jowl with some of the most noted thieves of England and America; but I allowed this for two reasons: first, I wished to keep these sharpers under my own eye until I knew who had bought the necklace; and secondly, I was desirous that they should not know they were suspected.

I had trusty men stationed outside on the Boulevard des Italiens, each of whom knew by sight most of the probable purchasers of the necklace. It was arranged that when the sale was over, I should walk out to the Boulevard alongside the man who was the new owner of the diamonds, and from that moment until he quitted France my men were not to lose sight of him if he took personal custody of the stones, instead of doing the sensible and proper thing of having them insured and forwarded to his residence by some responsible transit company, or depositing them in the bank. In fact, I took every precaution that occurred to me. All police Paris was on the *qui vive* and felt itself pitted against the scoundrelism of the world.

For one reason or another, it was nearly half-past two before the sale began. There had been considerable delay because of forged tickets, and, indeed, each order of admittance was so closely scrutinised that this in itself took a good deal more time than we anticipated. Every chair was occupied, and still a number of the visitors had to stand. I stationed myself by the swinging-doors at the entrance end of the hall, where I could command a view of the entire assemblage. Some of my men were standing with backs against the wall, whilst others were distributed amongst the chairs, all in plain clothes. During the sale, the diamonds themselves were not displayed, but the box containing them rested in front of the auctioneer, and three policemen in uniform stood guard on either side.

Very quietly the auctioneer said that there was no need for him to expatiate on the notable character of the treasure he had to offer for sale, and with this preliminary he requested them to bid. Someone said twenty thousand francs, which was received with much laughter; then the bidding went steadily on until it reached nine hundred thousand francs, which I knew to be less than half the reserve the Government had put upon the necklace. The contest advanced more slowly until the million and a half was touched, and there it hung fire for a time, while the auctioner remarked that this sum did not equal that which the maker of the necklace had finally been forced to accept for it. After another pause, he said that as the reserve was not exceeded, the necklace would be withdrawn, and probably never

"'One million dollars.'"

again offered for sale. He therefore urged those who were holding back to make their bid. At this the contest livened until the sum of two million three hundred thousand francs had been offered, and now I knew the necklace would be sold. Nearing the three million mark the competition thinned down to a few dealers from Hamburg and the Marquis of Warlingham, from England, when a voice that had not yet been heard in the auction-room said, in a tone of some impatience—

"One million dollars."

There was an instant hush, then the scribbling of pencils, as each person there reduced the sum to its equivalent in his own currency: pounds for the English, francs for the French, marks for the German, and so on. The aggressive tone and the clear-cut face of the bidder proclaimed him an American, not less than the financial denomination he had used. In a moment it was realised that his bid was a clear leap of more than two million francs, and a sigh went up from the audience as if this settled it, and the great sale was done. Nevertheless, the auctioneer's hammer hovered over the lid of his desk, and he looked up and down the long line of faces turned towards him. He seemed reluctant to tap the board, but there was no further price bid against this tremendous sum, and with a sharp click the mallet fell.

"What name?" he asked, bending over towards the customer.

"Cash," replied the American. "Here's the cheque for the amount. I'll take the diamonds with me."

"Your request is somewhat unusual," protested the auctioneer mildly.

"I know what you mean," interrupted the American—"you think the cheque may not be cashed. You will notice it is drawn on the Crédit-Lyonnais, which is practically next door. I must have the jewels with me. Send round your messenger with the cheque: it will take only a few minutes to find out whether or not the money is there to meet it. The necklace is mine, and I insist on having it."

The auctioneer with some demur handed the cheque to the representative of the French Government who was present, and this official himself went to the bank. There were some other things to be sold, and the auctioneer endeavoured to go on through the list, but no one paid the slightest attention to him.

Meanwhile I was studying the countenance of the man who had made the astounding bid, when I should instead have adjusted my preparations to meet the new conditions confronting me. Here was a man about whom we knew nothing whatever. I had come to the instant conclusion that he was a prince of criminals, and that some design, not at that moment fathomed by me, was on foot to get possession of the jewels. The handing up of the cheque was clearly a trick of some sort, and I fully expected the official to return and say the draft was good. I determined to prevent this man from getting the case until I knew more of his game. Quietly I removed from my place near the door to the auctioneer's desk, having two objects in view: first, to warn the auctioneer not to part with the treasure too easily; and secondly, to study the suspected man at closer range. Of all evil-doers, the American is most to be feared; he uses more ingenuity in the planning of his projects, and will take greater risks in carrying them out, than any other malefactor on earth. From my new station I saw I had two to deal with. The bidder had a keen, intellectual face, and refined, ladylike hands, clean and white, showing they had long been divorced from manual labour, if, indeed, they had ever done any useful work. Coolness and imperturbability were his beyond a doubt. The companion who sat at his right was of an entirely different stamp. His hands were hairy and sun-tanned; his face bore the stamp of grim determination and unflinching bravery. I knew that these two types usually hunted in couples—the one to scheme, the other to execute, and they always formed a combination dangerous to encounter and difficult to circumvent.

There was a buzz of conversation up and down the hall, and these two men talked together in low tones. I knew now that I was face to face with the most hazardous problem of my life.

"'You must not give up the necklace,' I said."

I whispered to the auctioneer, who bent his head to listen. He knew very well who I was, of course.

"You must not give up the necklace," I said.

He shrugged his shoulders.

"I am under the orders of the officials of the Ministry of the Interior. You must speak to him."

"I shall not fail to do so," I replied. "Nevertheless, do not give up the box too readily."

"I am helpless," he said with another shrug. "I obey the orders of the Government."

Seeing it was useless to parley further with the auctioneer, I set my wits to work to meet the new emergency. I felt convinced that the cheque would prove to be genuine, and that the fraud, wherever it lay, would be disclosed too late to be of service to the authorities. My duty, therefore, was to make sure we lost sight neither of the buyer nor the thing bought. Of course, I could not arrest him merely on suspicion; besides, it would make the Government the laughing-stock of the world if they were to sell a case of jewels and immediately arrest the buyer when they themselves had handed his purchase over to him; and ridicule kills in France. A breath of laughter will blow a Government out of existence in Paris much more effectually than a whiff of cannon-smoke. My duty, then, was to give the Government full warning, and never lose sight of my man until he was clear of France; then my responsibility was ended.

I took aside one of my own men in plain clothes and said to him—

"You have seen the American who has bought the necklace?"

"Yes, sir."

"Very well. Go outside quietly and station yourself there. He is likely to emerge presently with the casket in his possession. You are not to lose sight of either the man or the jewels. I shall follow him and be close behind him as he emerges, and you are to shadow us. If he parts with the case, you must be ready at a sign from me to follow either the man or the jewels. Do you understand?"

"Yes, sir," he answered, and left the room.

It is ever the unforeseen that baffles us: it is easy to be wise after the event. I should have sent two men, and I have often thought since how wise is the regulation of the Italian Government, which sends out its policemen in pairs. Or I should have given my man power to call for help; but even as it was, he did only half as well as I had a right to expect of him, and the blunder he committed by a moment's dull-witted hesitation. Ah, well! there is no use in scolding. After all, the result might have been the same.

Just as my man disappeared through the two folding-doors, the official from the Ministry of the Interior entered. I intercepted him about half-way between the door and the auctioneer.

"Possibly the cheque appears to be genuine," I whispered to him.

"Certainly," he replied pompously. He was a man greatly impressed with his own importance—a kind of character with whom it is always difficult to deal. Afterwards the Government claimed that this official had warned me, and the utterances of an empty-headed ass, "dressed in a little brief authority," as the English poet says, were looked upon as the epitome of wisdom.

"I advise you strongly not to hand over the necklace as has been requested," I went on.

"Why?" he asked.

"Because I am convinced the bidder is a criminal."

"If you have proof of that, arrest him."

"I have no proofs at the present moment, but I request you to delay the delivery of the goods."

"That is absurd!" he cried impatiently. "The necklace is his, not ours. The money has already been transferred to the account of the Government. We cannot retain the five million francs and refuse to hand over to him what he has bought with them"; and so the official left me standing there, nonplussed and anxious. The eyes of everyone in the room had been turned on us during our brief conversation, and now the official proceeded ostentatiously up the room with a grand air of importance; then, with a bow and a flourish of the hand, he said dramatically—

"The jewels belong to Monsieur."

The two Americans rose simultaneously, the taller holding out his hand while the auctioneer passed to him the case he had apparently paid so highly for. The American nonchalantly opened the box, and for the first time the electric radiance of the jewels burst upon that audience, each member of which craned his neck to behold it. It seemed to me a most reckless thing to do. He examined the jewels minutely for a few moments, then snapped the lid shut again and calmly put the box in his outside pocket; and I could not help noticing now that the light overcoat he wore had pockets made extraordinarily large, as if on purpose for this very case. And now this amazing man walked serenely down the room past miscreants who would have joyfully cut his throat for even the smallest diamond in that conglomeration; yet he did not take the trouble to put his hand on the pocket which contained the case, or in any way attempt to protect it. The assemblage seemed stricken dumb at his audacity. His friend followed closely at his heels, and the tall man disappeared through the folding-doors. Not so the other, however. He turned quickly and whipped two revolvers out of his pocket, which he presented at the astonished crowd. There had been a movement on the part of everyone to leave the room, but the sight of these deadly weapons confronting them made each one shrink into his place again.

The man with his back to the door spoke in a loud and domineering voice, asking the auctioneer to translate what he had to say into French and German. He spoke in English.

"These here shiners are valuable; they belong to my friend who has just gone out. Casting no reflections on the generality of people in this room, there are, nevertheless, half-a-dozen 'crooks' among us whom my friend wishes to avoid. Now, no honest man here will object to giving the buyer of that there trinket five clear minutes in which to get away. It's only the 'crooks' that can kick. I ask these five minutes as a favour, but if they are not granted, I am going to take them as a right. Any man who moves will get shot."

"I am an honest man," I cried, "and I object. I am chief detective of the Government. Stand aside; the police will protect your friend."

"Hold on, my son," warned the American, turning one weapon directly upon me, while the other held a sort of roving commission, pointing all over the room. "My friend is from New York, and he distrusts the police as much as he does the grafters. You may be twenty detectives, but if you move before that clock strikes three, I'll bring you down—and don't you forget it."

It is one thing to face death in a fierce struggle, but quite another to advance coldly upon it towards the muzzle of a pistol held so steadily that there could be no chance of escape. The gleam of determination in the man's eye convinced me he meant what he said. I did not consider then, nor have I considered since, that the next five minutes, precious as they were, would be worth paying my life for. Apparently everyone else was of my opinion, for none moved hand or foot until the clock slowly struck three.

"Thank you, gentlemen," said the American, as he vanished between the spring-doors. When I say vanished, I mean that word and no other, because my men outside saw nothing of this individual then or later. He vanished as if he had never existed, and it was some hours before we found how this had been accomplished.

I rushed out almost on his heels, as one might say, and hurriedly questioned my waiting men. They had all seen the tall American come out with the greatest leisureness and stroll towards the west. As he was not the man any of them were looking for, they paid no further attention to him, as, indeed, is the custom with our Parisian force. They have eyes for nothing but what they are sent to look for, and this trait has its drawbacks for their superiors.

I ran up the Boulevard, my whole thought intent on the diamonds and their bidder. I knew my subordinate in command of the men inside the hall would look after the scoundrel with the pistols. A short distance up I found the stupid fellow I had sent out, standing in a dazed manner at the corner of the Rue Michodière, gazing alternately towards the Place de l'Opéra and down the short street at whose corner he stood. The very fact that he was there was proof that he had failed.

"Where is that American?" I cried.

"He went down this street, sir."

"And why are you standing there like a fool?"

"I followed him this far, then a man came up the Rue Michodière, and without a word the American handed him the jewel-box, turning instantly down the street up which the other had come. The other jumped into a cab and drove towards the Place de l'Opéra."

"And what did you do? Stood here like a post, I suppose?"

"I didn't know what to do, sir. It all happened in a moment."

"Why didn't you follow the cab?"

"I didn't know which to follow, sir, and the cab was gone instantly while I watched the American."

"What was its number?"

"I don't know, sir."

"You clod! Why didn't you call one of our men, whoever was nearest, and leave him to follow the American while you followed the cab?"

"I did shout to the nearest man, sir, but he said you told him to stay there and watch the English lord; and even before he had said that, both American and cabman had disappeared."

"Was the man to whom he gave the box an American, too?"

"No, sir, he was French."

"How do you know?"

"By his appearance and the words he spoke."

"I thought you said he didn't speak?"

"He did not speak to the American, sir,

but he said to the cabman: 'Drive to the Madeline as quickly as you can.'"

"Describe the man."

"He was a head shorter than the American, wore a black beard and moustache rather neatly trimmed, and seemed to be a superior sort of artisan."

"You did not take the number of the cab. Should you know the cabman if you saw him again?"

"Yes, sir, I should."

Taking this fellow with me, I returned to the now empty auction-room and there gathered all my men about me. Each in his notebook took down descriptions of the cabman and his passenger from the lips of my incompetent spy; then I dictated a full description of the two Americans, and scattered my men to the various railway stations of the lines leading out of Paris, with orders to make inquiries of the police on duty there, and to arrest one or more of the four persons described, should they be so fortunate as to find any of them, which I much doubted.

I now learned how the man with the pistols vanished so completely as he did. My subordinate in the auction-room had speedily solved the mystery. To the left of the main entrance of the auction-room was a door that gave access to the premises in the rear. As the attendant in charge confessed when questioned, he had been bribed by the American earlier in the day to leave this side-door open and to allow the man to escape by the goods-entrance. Thus the ruffian had not appeared on the Boulevard at all, and so had not been observed by any of my men.

Taking my spy with me, I returned to my own office and sent an order throughout the city that every cabman who had been in the Boulevard des Italiens between half-past two and half-past three that afternoon was to report to me. The examination of these men proved a very tedious business indeed; but whatever other countries may say of us, we French are patient, and if the haystack is searched long enough, the needle will be found. I did not discover the needle I was looking for, but I came upon one quite as important, if not more so.

"'Any man who moves will get shot.'"

It was nearly ten o'clock at night when a cabman answered my oft-repeated question in the affirmative.

"Did you take up a passenger a few minutes past three o'clock on the Boulevard des Italiens, near the Crédit-Lyonnais? Had he a short, black beard? Did he carry a small box in his hand and order you to drive to the Madeline?"

The cabman seemed puzzled.

"He had a short, black beard when he got out of the cab," he replied.

"What do you mean by that?"

"I drive a closed cab, sir. When he got in, he was a smooth-faced gentleman; when he got out, he wore a short, black beard."

"Was he a Frenchman?"

"No, sir, he was a foreiguer—either English or American."

"Did he carry a box?"

"No, sir; he had in his hand a small handbag."

"Where did he tell you to drive?"

"He told me to follow the cab in front, which had just driven off very rapidly towards the Madeline. In fact, I heard the man such as you describe order the other cabman to drive to the Madeline. I had come up to the kerb when this man held up his hand for a cab, but the open cab cut in ahead of me. Just then my passenger stepped up and said in French, but with a foreign accent: 'Follow that cab wherever it goes.'"

I turned with some indignation to my spy.

"You told me," I said, "that the American had gone down a side street. Yet he evidently met a second man, obtained from him the handbag, turned back, and got into the closed cab directly behind you."

"Well, sir," stammered the man, "I could not look in two directions at the same time. The American certainly went down the side street, but of course I watched the cab which contained the jewels."

"And you saw nothing of the closed cab right at your elbow?"

"The Boulevard was full of cabs, sir, and the pavement crowded with passers-by, as it always is at that hour of the day; and I have only two eyes in my head."

"I am glad to know you had that many, for I was beginning to think you were blind."

Although I said this, I knew in my heart it was useless to censure the poor wretch, for the fault was entirely my own in not sending two men, and in failing to guess the possibility of the jewels and their owner being separated. Besides, here was a clue to my hand at last, and no time must be lost in following it up. So I continued my interrogation of the cabman.

"The other cab was an open vehicle, you say?"

"Yes, sir."

"You succeeded in following it?"

"Oh, yes, sir. At the Madeline the man in front re-directed the coachman, who turned to the left and drove to the Place de la Concorde, then up the Champs Élysées to the Arch, and so down the Avenue de la Grand Armée and the Avenue de Neuilly, where it came to a standstill. My fare got out, and I saw he wore a short, black beard, which he had evidently put on inside the cab. He gave me a ten-franc piece, which was very satisfactory."

"And the fare you were following? What did he do?"

"He got out, paid the cabman, went down the bank of the river, and on board a steam launch that seemed to be waiting for him."

"Did he look behind or appear to know that he was being followed?"

"No, sir."

"And your fare?"

"He ran after the first man and also went aboard the steam launch, which instantly started down the river."

"And that was the last you saw of them?"

"Yes, sir."

"At what time did you reach the Pont de Neuilly?"

"I do not know, sir; I had to drive rather fast, but the distance is seven or eight kilometres."

"You would do it under the hour?"

"Yes, certainly under the hour."

"Then you must have reached there about four o'clock?"

"It is very likely, sir."

The plan of the tall American was now perfectly clear to me, and it comprised nothing that was contrary to law. He had evidently placed his luggage on board the steam launch in the morning. The handbag had contained various materials which would enable him to disguise himself, and this bag he had probably left in some shop down the side street, or else someone was waiting with it for him. The giving of the treasure to another man was not so risky as it had at first appeared, because he instantly followed that man, who was probably his confidential servant. Despite the windings of the river, there was ample time for the launch to reach Havre before the American steamer sailed on Saturday morning. I surmised it was his intention to come alongside of the steamer before she left her berth in Havre harbour, and thus transfer himself and his belongings unperceived by anyone on watch at the land side of the liner. All this, of course, was perfectly justifiable, and was, in truth, a well-laid scheme for escaping observation. His only danger of being tracked was when he got into the cab. Once away from the neighbourhood of the Boulevard des Italiens, he was reasonably sure to evade pursuit, and the five minutes which his friend with the pistols had won for him gave him just about the time he needed to get as far as the Place Madeline, and after that everything was easy. Yet if it had not been for this five minutes secured by coercion, I should not have had the slightest excuse for arresting him. But he was accessory after the act in that piece of illegality—in fact, it was absolutely certain that he had been accessory before the act, and guilty of conspiracy with the man who had presented firearms to the auctioneer's audience, and who had interfered with an officer in the discharge of his duty by threatening me and my men. So I was now legally in the right if I arrested every person on board that steam launch.

With a map of the river before me, I proceeded to make some calculations. It was now nearly ten o'clock at night. The launch had had six hours to go at its utmost speed. It was doubtful if so small a vessel could make ten miles an hour, even with the current in its favour, which is rather sluggish because of the locks and the level country.

Sixty miles would place her beyond Meulan, which is fifty-eight miles from the Pont Royal, and, of course, a lesser distance from the Pont de Neuilly. But the navigation of the river is difficult at all times, and almost impossible after dark. There were chances of the boat running aground, and then there was the inevitable delay at the locks. So I estimated that the launch could not yet have reached Meulan, which was less than twenty-five miles from Paris by rail. Looking up the time-table, I saw there were still two trains to Meulan—the next at 10.25, which reached Meulan at 11.40. I had time to reach St. Lazarus station and there do some telegraphing before the train left.

"'When he got out, he wore a short, black beard.'"

With three of my assistants, I got into a cab and drove to the station, sending one of my men to hold the train while I went into the telegraph-office, cleared the wires, and got into communication with the lock-master at Meulan. He replied that no steam-launch had passed down since an hour before sunset. I then instructed him to allow the yacht to enter the lock, close the upper gate, let half of the water out, and hold the vessel there until I came. I also ordered the local Meulan police to send enough men to the lock to enforce this command. Lastly, I sent messages all along the river asking the police to report to me on the train the passage of the steam-launch.

The 10.25 is a slow train, stopping at every station. However, every drawback has its compensations, and these stoppages enabled me to receive and to send telegraphic messages. I was quite well aware that I might be on a fool's errand in going to Meulan. The yacht might turn before it had steamed a mile, and come back into Paris. There had been no time to learn whether this were so or not, if I was to catch the 10.25. Also it might have landed its passengers anywhere along the river. I may say at once that neither of these two things happened, and my calculations as to her movements were accurate to the letter. But a trap most carefully set may be prematurely sprung by inadvertence, or more often by the over-zeal of some stupid ass who fails to understand his instructions, or oversteps them if they are understood. I received a most annoying telegram from Denouval, a lock about thirteen miles above that of Meulan. The local policeman, arriving at the lock, found that the yacht had just cleared. The fool shouted to the captain to return, threatening him with all the pains and penalties of the law if he refused. The captain did refuse, rang on "Full speed ahead!" and disappeared in the darkness. Through this well-meant blunder of an understrapper, those on board the launch had received warning that we were on their track. I telegraphed to the lock-keeper at Denouval to allow no craft to pass towards Paris until further orders. We had the launch trapped in a thirteen-mile stretch of water, but the night was pitch dark, and passengers might be landed on either bank, with all France before them.

It was midnight when I reached the lock at Meulan, and, as I expected, nothing had been seen or heard of the launch. It gave me some satisfaction to telegraph to that dunderhead at Denouval to walk along the river-bank to Meulan and report if he learnt the launch's whereabouts. We took up our quarters in the lock-keeper's house and waited. There was little sense in sending men to scour the country at this time of night, for the pursued were on the alert and were not likely to allow themselves to be caught if they did go ashore. On the other hand, there was every chance that the captain would refuse to let them land, because he must know his vessel was in a trap from which he could not escape; and although the demand of the policeman at Denouval was quite unauthorised, nevertheless the captain must be well aware of his danger in refusing to obey that command. Even if he got away for the moment, he must know that arrest was certain and that his punishment would be severe. His only plea could be that he had not heard and understood the order to return. But this plea would be invalidated if he aided in the escape of two men who, he must now know, were wanted by the police. I was, therefore, very confident that if the men demanded to be set ashore, the captain would refuse when he had had time to think about his own danger. My estimate proved accurate, for towards one o'clock the lock-keeper came in and said the green and red lights of an approaching craft were visible, and as he spoke, the yacht whistled for the opening of the lock. I stood by the lock-keeper while he opened the gates; my men and the local police were concealed on each side of the lock. The launch came slowly in, and as soon as it had done so, I asked the captain to step ashore, which he did.

"I wish a word with you," I said. "Follow me."

I took him into the lock-keeper's house and closed the door.

"Where are you going?"

"To Havre."

"Where did you come from?"

"Paris."

"From what quay?"

"From the Pont de Neuilly."

"When did you leave there?"

"At five minutes to four o'clock this afternoon."

"Yesterday afternoon, you mean?"

"Yesterday afternoon."

"Who engaged you to make this voyage!"

"An American—I do not know his name."

"He paid you well, I suppose?"

"He paid me what I asked."

"Have you received the money?"

"Yes, sir."

"I may inform you, captain, that I am chief detective of the French Government, and that all the police of France at this moment are under my control. I ask you, therefore, to be careful of your answers. You were ordered by a policeman at Denouval to return. Why did you not do so?"

"The captain hesitated, turning his cap about in his hands."

"The lock-keeper ordered me to return, but as he had no right to order me, I went on."

"You know very well it was the police who ordered you, and you ignored the command. Again I ask you why you did so."

"I did not know it was the police."

"I thought you would say that. You knew very well, but were paid to take the risk, and it is likely to cost you dear. You had two passengers aboard?"

"Yes, sir."

"Did you put them ashore between here and Denouval?"

"No, sir, but one of them went overboard, and we couldn't find him again."

"Which one?"

"The short man."

"Then the American is still aboard?"

"What American, sir?"

"Captain, you must not trifle with me. The man who engaged you is still aboard."

"Oh, no, sir—he has never been aboard."

"Do you mean to tell me that the second man who came on your launch at the Pont de Neuilly is not the American who engaged you?"

"Oh, no; the American was a smooth-faced man, this man has a black beard."

"Yes, a false beard."

"I did not know that, sir. I understood from the American that I was to take but one passenger. One came aboard with a small box in his hand, the other with a small bag. Each claimed to be the passenger in question. I did not know what to do, so I left with both of them on board."

"Then the tall man with the beard is still with you?"

"Yes, sir."

"Well, captain, is there anything else you have to tell me? I think you will find it better in the end to make a clean breast of it."

The captain hesitated, turning his cap about in his hands for a few moments, then he said—

"I am not sure that the first passenger went overboard of his own accord. When the police hailed us at Denouval——"

"Ah! you knew it was the police, then?"

"I was afraid after I left it might have been. You see, when the bargain was made with me, the American said that if I reached Havre at a certain time, a thousand francs extra would be paid to me, so I was anxious to get along as quickly as I could. I told him it was dangerous to navigate the Seine at night, but he paid me well for attempting it. After the policeman called to us at Denouval, the man with the small box became very much excited and asked me to put him ashore, which I refused to do. The tall man appeared to be watching him, never letting him get far away. When I heard the splash in the water, I ran aft, and I saw the tall man putting the box which the other had held into his handbag, although I said nothing of it at the time. We cruised back and forward about the spot where the other man had gone overboard, but saw nothing more of him. Then I came on to Meulan, intending to give information about what I had seen. That is all I know of the matter, sir."

"Was the man who had the jewels a Frenchman?"

"What jewels, sir?"

"The man with the small box."

"Oh, yes, sir, he was French."

"You hinted that the foreigner threw him overboard. What grounds have you for such a belief if you did not see the struggle?"

"The night is very dark, sir, and I did not see what happened. I was at the wheel in the forward part of the launch, with my back turned to these two. I heard a scream, then a splash. If the man had jumped overboard as the other said, he would not have screamed. Besides, as I told you, when I ran aft, I saw the foreigner put the little box in his handbag, which he shut up quickly, as if he did not wish me to notice."

"Very good, captain. If you have told the truth, it will go easier with you in the investigation that is to follow."

I now turned the captain over to one of my men and ordered in the foreigner with his bag and bogus black whiskers. Before questioning him, I ordered him to open the handbag, which he did with evident reluctance. It was filled with false whiskers, false moustaches, and various bottles, but on top of them all lay the jewel-case. I raised the lid and displayed that accursed necklace. I looked up at the man, who stood there calmly enough, saying nothing in spite of the overwhelming evidence against him.

"Will you oblige me by removing those false whiskers?"

He did so at once, throwing them into the open bag. I knew the moment I saw him that he was not the American, and thus my theory had broken down—in one very important part, at least. Informing him who I was, and cautioning him to speak the truth, I asked how he came into possession of the jewels.

"Am I under arrest?" he asked.

"Certainly," I replied.

"Of what am I accused?"

"You are accused in the first place of having in your possession property which does not belong to you."

"I plead guilty to that. What in the second place?"

"In the second place, you may find yourself accused of murder."

"I am innocent of the second charge. The man jumped overboard."

"If that is true, why did he scream as he went over?"

"Because, too late to recover his balance, I seized this box and held it."

"He was in the rightful possession of the box; the owner gave it to him."

"I admit that; I saw the owner give it to him."

"Then why should he jump overboard?"

"I do not know. He seemed to become panic-stricken when the police at the last lock ordered us to return. He implored the captain to put him ashore, and from that moment I watched him keenly, expecting that if we drew near to the land, he would attempt to escape, as the captain had refused to beach the launch. He remained quiet for about half an hour, seated on a camp-chair by the rail, with his eyes turned towards the shore, trying, as I imagined, to penetrate the darkness and estimate the distance. Then suddenly he sprang up and made his dash. I was prepared, and instantly caught the box in his hand. He gave a half-turn, trying either to save himself or to retain the box, then with a scream went down shoulders first into the water. It all happened within a second after he leaped from his chair."

"You admit yourself, then, indirectly responsible for his drowning, at least?"

"I see no reason to suppose that the man was drowned. If able to swim, he could easily have reached the river-bank. If unable to swim, why should he attempt it encumbered by the box?"

"You believed he escaped, then?"

"I think so."

"It will be lucky for you should that prove to be the case."

"Certainly."

"How did you come to be in the yacht at all?"

"I shall give you a full account of the affair, concealing nothing. I am a private detective, with an office in London. I was certain that some attempt would be made by probably the most expert criminals at large to rob the possessor of this necklace. I came over to Paris, anticipating trouble, determined to keep an eye upon the jewel-case, if this proved possible. If the jewels were stolen, the crime was bound to be one of the most celebrated in legal annals. I was present during the sale and saw the buyer of the necklace. I followed the official who went to the Bank, and thus learned that the money was behind the cheque. I then stopped outside and waited for the buyer to appear. He had the case in his hand."

"In his pocket, you mean?"

"He had it in his hand when I saw him. Then the man who afterwards jumped overboard approached him, took the case without a word, held up his hand for a cab, and when an open vehicle approached the kerb, he stepped in, saying 'The Madeline.' I hailed a closed cab, instructed the cabman to follow the first, disguising myself with whiskers as near like those of the man in front as I had in my collection."

"Why did you do that?"

"As a detective, you should know why I did it. I wished as nearly as possible to resemble the man in front, so that if necessity arose I could pretend that I was the person commissioned to carry the jewel-case. As a matter of fact, the crisis arose when we came to the end of our cab journey. The captain did not know which was his true passenger, and so let us both aboard the launch. And now you have the whole story."

"An extremely improbable one, sir. Even by your own account, you had no right to interfere in this business at all."

"I quite agree with you there," he replied with great nonchalance, taking a card from his pocket-book, which he handed to me.

"That is my London address; you may make inquiries, and you will find I am exactly what I represent myself to be."

The first train for Paris left Meulan at eleven minutes past four in the morning. It was now a quarter after two. I left the captain, crew, and launch in charge of two of my men, with orders to proceed to Paris as soon as it was daylight. I, supported by the third man, waited at the station with our English prisoner, and reached Paris at half past five in the morning.

The English prisoner, though severely interrogated by the judge, stood by his story. Inquiry by the police in London proved that what he said of himself was true. His case, however, began to look very serious when two of the men from the launch asserted that they had seen him push the Frenchman overboard, and their statement could not be shaken. All our energies were bent for the next two weeks on trying to find something of the identity of the missing man, or to get any trace of the two Americans. If the tall American were alive, it seemed incredible that he should not have made application for his missing property.

All attempts to trace him by means of the Crédit-Lyonnais proved futile.

We made inquiries about every missing man in Paris, but also without result.

The case had excited much attention throughout the world, and doubtless was published in full in the American papers. The Englishman had been in custody three weeks when the Chief of Police of Paris received the following letter:—

"I raised the lid and displayed that accursed necklace."

"DEAR SIR,—On my arrival in New York by the English steamer *Lucania*, I was much amused to read in the papers accounts of the exploits of detectives, French and English. I am sorry that only one of them seems to be in prison; I think his French *confrère* ought to be there also. I regret exceedingly, however, that there is the rumour of the death, by drowning, of my friend, Eugène Dubois, of 375, Rue aux Juifs, Rouen. If this is indeed the case, he has met his death through the blunders of the police. Nevertheless, I wish you would communicate with his family at the address I have given, and assure them that I will make arrangements for their future support.

"I may say that I am a manufacturer of imitation diamonds, and, through extensive advertising, have accumulated a fortune of many millions. I was in Europe when the necklace was found, and had in my possession over a thousand imitation diamonds of my own manufacture. It occurred to me that here was the opportunity of the most magnificent advertisement in the world. I saw the necklace, received its measurements, and also obtained photographs of it taken by the French Government. Then I set my expert friend, Eugène Dubois, at work, and he made an imitation necklace so closely resembling the original that you apparently do not know it is the unreal you have in your possession. I was not nearly so much afraid of the villainy of the crooks as of the blundering of the police, who would have protected me with brass-band vehemence if I could not elude them. I knew that the detectives would overlook the obvious, but would at once follow a clue if I provided one for them. Consequently I laid my plans, just as you have discovered, and got Eugène Dubois up from Rouen to carry the case I gave him down to Havre. I had had another box prepared in brown paper with my address in New York written thereon. The moment I emerged from the auction-room, while my friend the cowboy was holding up the audience, I turned my face to the door, took out the genuine diamonds from the case and slipped it into the box I had prepared for mailing. Into the genuine case I put the bogus diamonds. After handing the box to Dubois, I turned down a side street, and then into another whose name I do not know, and there in a shop, with sealing-wax and string, did up my packet for posting. I labelled the package 'Books,' went to the nearest post-office, paid letter postage, and handed it over unregistered, as if it were of no particular value. After this I went to my rooms in the Grand Hotel, where I had been staying under my own name for more than a month. Next morning I took train for London, and the day after sailed from Liverpool on the *Lucania*. I arrived before the *Gascoigne*, which sailed from Havre on Saturday, met my box at the Customs-house, paid duty, and it now reposes in my safe. I intend to construct an imitation necklace which will be so like the genuine one that nobody can tell the two apart; then I shall come to Europe and exhibit the pair, for the publication of the truth of this matter will give me the greatest advertisement that ever was.

"Yours truly,

"JOHN P. HAZARD."

I at once communicated with Rouen and found Eugène Dubois all right. His first words were—

"I swear I did not steal the jewels."

He had swum ashore, tramped to Rouen, and kept quiet in great fear as to what would happen.

It took Mr. Hazard longer to make his imitation necklace that he supposed, and several years later he took passage with the two necklaces on the ill-fated steamer *Burgoyne*, and now rests beside them at the bottom of the Atlantic. As the English poet says—

Full many a gem of purest ray serene,
The daik, unfathom'd caves of ocear bear.

XIV

The Loot of Cities

ARNOLD BENNETT

THE LOOT OF CITIES:

THE ADVENTURES OF A MILLIONAIRE IN SEARCH OF JOY.

By ARNOLD BENNETT

No. I.—THE FIRE OF LONDON.

"YOU'RE wanted on the telephone, sir."

Mr. Bruce Bowring, managing director of the Consolidated Mining and Investment Corporation, Limited (capital two millions, in one-pound shares, which stood at twenty-seven-and-six), turned and gazed querulously across the electric-lit spaces of his superb private office at the confidential clerk who addressed him. Mr. Bowring, in shirt-sleeves before a Florentine mirror, was brushing his hair with the solicitude of a mother who has failed to rear most of a large family.

"Who is it?" he asked, as if that demand for him were the last straw but one. "Nearly seven on Friday evening!" he added, martyrised.

"I think a friend, sir."

The middle-aged financier dropped his gold-mounted brush and, wading through the deep pile of the Oriental carpet, passed into the telephone-cabinet and shut the door.

"Hallo!" he accosted the transmitter, resolved not to be angry with it. "Hal*lo!* Are you there? Yes, I'm Bowring. Who are you?"

"*Nrrrr*," the faint, unhuman voice of the receiver whispered in his ear. "*Nrrrr. Cluck.* I'm a friend."

"What name?"

"No name. I thought you might like to know that a determined robbery is going to be attempted to-night at your house in Lowndes Square—a robbery of cash—and before nine o'clock. *Nrrrr.* I thought you might like to know."

"Ah!" said Mr. Bowring to the transmitter.

The feeble exclamation was all he could achieve at first. In the confined, hot silence of the telephone-cabinet, this message, coming to him mysteriously out of the vast unknown of London, struck him with a sudden sick fear that perhaps his wondrously organised scheme might yet miscarry, even at the final moment. Why that night of all nights? And why before nine o'clock? Could it be that the secret was out, then?

"Any further interesting details?" he inquired, bracing himself to an assumption of imperturbable and gay coolness.

But there was no answer. And when after some difficulty he got the exchange-girl to disclose the number which had rung him up, he found that his interlocutor had been using a public call-office in Oxford Street. He returned to his room, donned his frock-coat, took a large envelope from a locked drawer and put it in his pocket, and sat down to think a little.

At that time Mr. Bruce Bowring was one of the most famous conjurers in the City. He had begun, ten years earlier, with nothing but a silk hat; and out of that empty hat had been produced, first the Hoop-La Limited, a South African gold-mine of numerous stamps and frequent dividends, then the Hoop-La No. 2 Limited, a mine with as many reincarnations as Buddha, and then a dazzling succession of mines and combinations of mines. The more the hat emptied itself, the more it was full; and the emerging objects (which now included the house in Lowndes Square and a perfect dream of a place in Hampshire) grew constantly larger, and the conjurer more impressive and persuasive, and the audience more enthusiastic in its applause. At last, with a unique flourish, and a new turning-up of sleeves to prove that there was no deception, had come out of the hat the C.M.I.C., a sort of incredibly enormous Union Jack, which enwrapped all the other objects in its splendid folds. The shares of the C.M.I.C. were affectionately known in the Kaffir circus as "Solids"; they yielded handsome though irregular dividends, earned chiefly by flotation and speculation; the circus believed in them. And in view of the annual meeting of shareholders to be held on the following Tuesday afternoon (the conjurer in the chair, and his hat on the table), the market price, after a period of depression, had stiffened.

Mr. Bowring's meditations were soon interrupted by a telegram. He opened it and read : "*Cook drunk again. Will dine with you Devonshire, seven-thirty. Impossible here. Have arranged about luggage.—Marie.*" Marie was Mr. Bowring's wife. He told himself that he felt greatly relieved by that telegram ; he clutched at it ; and his spirits seemed to rise. At any rate, since he would not now go near Lowndes Square, he could certainly laugh at the threatened robbery. He thought what a wonderful thing Providence was, after all.

"Just look at that," he said to his clerk, showing the telegram with a humorous affectation of dismay.

"Tut, tut," said the clerk, discreetly sympathetic towards his employer thus victimised by debauched cooks. "I suppose you're going down to Hampshire to-night as usual, sir ?"

Mr. Bowring replied that he was, and that everything appeared to be in order for the meeting, and that he should be back on Monday afternoon or, at the latest, very early on Tuesday.

Then, with a few parting instructions, and with that eagle glance round his own room and into circumjacent rooms which a truly efficient head of affairs never omits on leaving business for the week-end, Mr. Bowring sedately, yet magnificently, departed from the noble registered offices of the C.M.I.C.

"Why didn't Marie telephone instead of wiring ?" he mused, as his pair of greys whirled him and his coachman and his footman off to the Devonshire.

II.

THE Devonshire Mansion, a bright edifice of eleven storeys in the Foster and Dicksee style, constructional ironwork by Homan, lifts by Waygood, decorations by Waring, and terra-cotta by the rood, is situate on the edge of Hyde Park. It is a composite building. Its foundations are firmly fixed in the Tube railway ; above that comes the wine cellarage, then the vast laundry, and then (a row of windows scarcely level with the street) a sporting club, a billiard-room, a grill-room, and a cigarette-merchant whose name ends in "opoulos." On the first floor is the renowned Devonshire Mansion Restaurant. Always, in London, there is just one restaurant where, if you are an entirely correct person, "you can get a decent meal." The place changes from season to season, but there is never more than one of it at a time. That season it happened to be the Devonshire. (The *chef* of the Devonshire had invented tripe suppers, *tripes à la mode de Caen*, and these suppers—seven-and-six—had been the rage.) Consequently all entirely correct people fed as a matter of course at the Devonshire, since there was no other place fit to go to. The vogue of the restaurant favourably affected the vogue of the nine floors of furnished suites above the restaurant ; they were always full ; and the heavenward attics, where the servants took off their smart liveries and became human, held much wealth. The vogue of the restaurant also exercised a beneficial influence over the status of the Kitcat Club, which was a cock-and-hen club of the latest pattern and had its "house" on the third floor.

It was a little after half-past seven when Mr. Bruce Bowring haughtily ascended the grand staircase of this resort of opulence and paused for an instant near the immense fireplace at the summit (September was inclement, and a fire burned nicely) to inquire from the head-waiter whether Mrs. Bowring had secured a table. But Marie had not arrived—Marie, who was never late ! Uneasy and chagrined, he proceeded, under the escort of the head-waiter, to the glittering Salle Louis Quatorze and selected, because of his morning attire, a table half-hidden behind an onyx pillar. The great room was moderately full of fair women and possessive men, despite the month. Immediately afterwards a youngish couple (the man handsomer and better dressed than the woman) took the table on the other side of the pillar. Mr. Bowring waited five minutes, then he ordered Sole Mornay and a bottle of Romanée-Conti, and then he waited another five minutes. He went somewhat in fear of his wife and did not care to begin without her.

"Can't you read ?" It was the youngish man at the next table speaking in a raised voice to a squinting lackey with a telegraph-form in his hand. "'Solids ! Solids,' my friend. 'Sell—Solids—to—any—amount—to-morrow—and—Monday.' Got it ? Well, send it off at once."

"Quite clear, my lord," said the lackey, and fled. The youngish man gazed fixedly but absently at Mr. Bowring and seemed to see through him to the tapestry behind. Mr. Bowring, to his own keen annoyance, reddened. Partly to conceal the blush, and partly because it was a quarter to eight and there was the train to catch, he lowered his face and began upon the sole. A few min-

"'Can't you read? Sell—Solids—to—any—amount.'"

utes later the lackey returned, gave some change to the youngish man, and surprised Mr. Bowring by advancing towards him and handing him an envelope—an envelope which bore on its flap the legend "Kitcat Club." The note within was scribbled in pencil in his wife's handwriting, and ran: "*Just arrived. Delayed by luggage. I'm too nervous to face the restaurant, and am eating a chop here alone. The place is fortunately empty. Come and fetch me as soon as you're ready.*"

Mr. Bowring sighed angrily. He hated his wife's club, and this succession of messages telephonic, telegraphic, and caligraphic was exasperating him.

"No answer!" he ejaculated, and then he beckoned the lackey closer. "Who's that gentleman at the next table with the lady?" he murmured.

"I'm not rightly sure, sir," was the whispered reply. "Some authorities say he's the strong man at the Aquarium, while others affirm he's a sort of American millionaire."

"But you addressed him as 'my lord.'"

"Just then I thought he was the strong man, sir," said the lackey, retiring.

"My bill!" Mr. Bowring demanded fiercely of the waiter, and at the same time the youngish gentleman and his companion rose and departed.

At the lift Mr. Bowring found the squinting lackey in charge.

"You're the liftman, too?"

"To-night, sir, I am many things. The fact is, the regular liftman has got a couple of hours off—being the recent father of twins."

"Well—Kitcat Club."

The lift seemed to shoot far upwards, and Mr. Bowring thought the lackey had mistaken the floor, but on gaining the corridor he saw across the portals in front of him the remembered gold sign, "Kitcat Club. Members only." He pushed the door open and went in.

III.

INSTEAD of the familiar vestibule of his wife's club, Mr. Bowring discovered a small antechamber, and beyond, through a doorway half-screened by a *portière*, he had glimpses of a rich, rose-lit drawing-room. In the doorway, with one hand raised to the *portière*, stood the youngish man who had forced him to blush in the restaurant.

"I beg your pardon," said Mr. Bowring stiffly—"is this the Kitcat Club?"

The other man advanced to the outer door, his brilliant eyes fixed on Mr. Bowring's; his arm crept round the cheek of the door and came back bearing the gold sign; then he shut the door and locked it. "No, this isn't the Kitcat Club at all," he replied. "It is my flat. Come and sit down. I was expecting you."

"I shall do nothing of the kind," said Mr. Bowring disdainfully.

"But when I tell you that I know you are going to decamp to-night, Mr. Bowring——"

The youngish man smiled affably.

"Decamp?" The spine of the financier suddenly grew flaccid.

"I used the word."

"Who the devil are you?" snapped the financier, forcing his spine to rigidity.

"I am the 'friend' on the telephone. I specially wanted you at the Devonshire to-night, and I thought that the fear of a robbery at Lowndes Square might make your arrival here more certain. I am he who devised the story of the inebriated cook and favoured you with a telegram signed 'Marie.' I am the humorist who pretended in a loud voice to send off telegraphic instructions to sell 'Solids,' in order to watch your demeanour under the test. I am the expert who forged your wife's handwriting in a note from the Kitcat. I am the patron of the cross-eyed menial who gave you the note and who afterwards raised you too high in the lift. I am the artificer of this gold sign, an exact duplicate of the genuine one two floors below, which induced you to visit me. The sign alone cost me nine-and-six; the servant's livery came to two pounds fifteen. But I never consider expense when, by dint of a generous outlay, I can avoid violence. I hate violence." He gently waved the sign to and fro.

"Then my wife——" Mr. Bowring stammered in a panic rage.

"Is probably at Lowndes Square, wondering what on earth has happened to you."

Mr. Bowring took breath, remembered that he was a great man, and steadied himself.

"You must be mad," he remarked quietly. "Open this door at once."

"Perhaps," the stranger judicially admitted. "Perhaps a sort of madness. But do come and sit down. We have no time to lose."

Mr. Bowring gazed at that handsome face. with the fine nostrils, large mouth, and square, clean chin, and the dark eyes, the black hair, and long, black moustache; and he noticed the long, thin hands. "Decadent!" he decided. Nevertheless, and though it was with the air of indulging the caprice of a lunatic, he did in fact obey the stranger's request.

It was a beautiful Chippendale drawing-room that he entered. Near the hearth, to which a morsel of fire gave cheerfulness, were two easy-chairs, and between them a small table. Behind was extended a four-fold draught-screen.

"The revolver was raised."

"I can give you just five minutes," said Mr. Bowring, magisterially sitting down.

"They will suffice," the stranger responded, sitting down also. "You have in your pocket, Mr. Bowring—probably your breast-pocket—fifty Bank of England notes for a thousand pounds each, and a number of smaller notes amounting to another ten thousand."

"Well?"

"I must demand from you the first-named fifty."

Mr. Bowring, in the silence of the rose-lit drawing-room, thought of all the Devonshire Mansion, with its endless corridors and innumerable rooms, its acres of carpets, its forests of furniture, its gold and silver, and its jewels and its wines, its pretty women and possessive men—the whole humming microcosm founded on a unanimous pretence that the sacredness of property was a natural law. And he thought how disconcerting it was that he should be trapped there, helpless, in the very middle of the vast pretence, and forced to admit that the sacredness of property was a purely artificial convention.

"By what right do you make this demand?" he inquired, bravely sarcastic.

"By the right of my unique knowledge," said the stranger, with a bright smile. "Listen to what you and I alone know. You are at the end of the tether. The Consolidated is at the same spot. You have a past consisting chiefly of nineteen fraudulent flotations. You have paid dividends out of capital till there is no capital left. You have speculated and lost. You have cooked balance-sheets to a turn and ruined the eyesight of auditors with dust. You have lived like ten lords. Your houses are mortgaged. You own an unrivalled collection of unreceipted bills. You are worse than a common thief. (Excuse these personalities.)"

"My dear, good sir——" Mr. Bowring interrupted grandly.

"Permit me. What is more serious, your self-confidence has been gradually deserting you. At last, perceiving that some blundering person was bound soon to put his foot through the brittle shell of your ostentation and tread on nothing, and foreseeing for yourself an immediate future consisting chiefly of Holloway, you have, by a supreme effort of your genius, borrowed £60,000 from a bank on C.M.I.C. scrip, for a week (eh?), and you have arranged, you and your wife, to—melt into thin air. You will affect to set out as usual for your country place in Hampshire, but it is Southampton that will see you to-night, and Havre will see you to-morrow. You may run over to Paris to change some notes, but by Monday you will be on your way to——frankly, I don't know where; perhaps Monte Video. Of course, you take the risk of extradition, but the risk is preferable to the certainty that awaits you in England. I think you will elude extradition. If I thought otherwise, I should not have had you here to-night, because, once extradited, you might begin to amuse yourself by talking about me."

"So it's blackmail," said Mr. Bowring, grim.

The dark eyes opposite to him sparkled gaily.

"It desolates me," the youngish man observed, "to have to commit you to the deep with only ten thousand. But, really, not less than fifty thousand will requite me for the brain-tissue which I have expended in the study of your interesting situation."

Mr. Bowring consulted his watch.

"Come, now," he said huskily, "I'll give you ten thousand. I flatter myself I can look facts in the face, and so I'll give you ten thousand."

"My friend," answered the spider, "You are a judge of character. Do you honestly think I don't mean precisely what I say —to sixpence. It is eight-thirty. You are, if I may be allowed the remark, running it rather fine."

"And suppose I refuse to part?" said Mr. Bowring, after reflection. "What then?"

"I have confessed to you that I hate violence. You would therefore leave this room unmolested, but you wouldn't step off the island."

Mr. Bowring scanned the agreeable features of the stranger. Then, while the lifts were ascending and descending, and the wine was sparkling, and the jewels flashing, and gold chinking, and the pretty women being pretty, in all the four quarters of the Devonshire, Mr. Bruce Bowring in the silent parlour counted out fifty notes on to the table. After all, it was a fortune, that little pile of white on the crimson polished wood.

"*Bon voyage!*" said the stranger. "Don't imagine that I am not full of sympathy for you. I am. You have only been unfortunate. *Bon voyage!*"

"'I told him I wished to enter.'"

"No! By Heaven!" Mr. Bowring almost shouted, rushing back from the door, and drawing a revolver from his hip-pocket. "It's too much! I didn't mean to—but confound it! what's a revolver for?"

The youngish man jumped up quickly and put his hand on the notes.

"Violence is always foolish, Mr. Bowring," he murmured.

"Will you give them up, or won't you?"

"I won't."

The stranger's fine eyes seemed to glint with joy in the drama.

"Then——"

The revolver was raised, but in the same instant a tiny hand snatched it from the hand of Mr. Bowring, who turned and beheld by his side a woman. The huge screen sank slowly and noiselessly to the floor in the surprising manner peculiar to screens that have been overset.

Mr. Bowring cursed. "An accomplice! I might have guessed!" he grumbled in final disgust.

He ran to the door, unlocked it, and was no more seen.

IV.

THE lady was aged twenty-seven or so; of medium height, and slim, with a plain, very intelligent and expressive face, lighted by courageous, grey eyes and crowned with loose, abundant, fluffy hair. Perhaps it was the fluffy hair, perhaps it was the mouth that twitched as she dropped the revolver—who can say?—but the whole atmosphere of the rose-lit chamber was suddenly changed. The incalculable had invaded it.

"You seem surprised, Miss Fincastle," said the possessor of the bank-notes, laughing gaily.

"Surprised!" echoed the lady, controlling that mouth. "My dear Mr. Thorold, when, strictly as a journalist, I accepted your invitation, I did not anticipate this sequel; frankly I did not."

She tried to speak coldly and evenly, on the assumption that a journalist has no sex during business hours. But just then she happened to be neither less nor more a woman than a woman always is.

"If I have had the misfortune to annoy you——!" Thorold threw up his arms in gallant despair.

"Annoy is not the word," said Miss Fincastle, nervously smiling. "May I sit down? Thanks. Let us recount. You arrive in England, from somewhere, as the son and heir of the late Ahasueras Thorold, the New York operator, who died worth six million dollars. It becomes known that while in Algiers in the spring you stayed at the Hôtel St. James, famous as the scene of what is called the 'Algiers Mystery,' familiar to English newspaper-readers since last April. The editor of my journal therefore instructs me to obtain an interview with you. I do so. The first thing I discover is that, though an American, you have no American accent. You explain this by saying that since infancy you have always lived in Europe with your mother."

"But surely you do not doubt that I am Cecil Thorold," said the man. Their faces were approximate over the table.

"Of course not. I merely recount. To continue. I interview you as to the Algerian mystery and get some new items concerning it. Then you regale me with tea and your opinions, and my questions grow more personal. So it comes about that, strictly on behalf of my paper, I inquire what your recreations are. And suddenly you answer: 'Ah! My recreations! Come to dinner to-night, quite informally, and I will show you how I amuse myself!' I come. I dine. I am stuck behind that screen and told to listen. And—and—the millionaire proves to be nothing but a blackmailer."

"You must understand, my dear lady——"

"I understand everything, Mr. Thorold, except your object in admitting me to the scene."

"A whim!" cried Thorold vivaciously, "a freak of mine! Possibly due to the eternal and universal desire of man to show off before woman!"

The journalist tried to smile, but something in her face caused Thorold to run to a chiffonier.

"Drink this," he said, returning with a glass.

"I need nothing." The voice was a whisper.

"Oblige me."

Miss Fincastle drank and coughed.

"Why did you do it?" she asked sadly, looking at the notes.

"You don't mean to say," Thorold burst out, "that you are feeling sorry for Mr. Bruce Bowring? He has merely parted with what he stole. And the people from whom he stole, stole. All the activities which centre about the Stock Exchange are simply various manifestations of one primeval instinct. Suppose I had not—had not interfered. No one would have been a penny the better off except Mr. Bruce Bowring. Whereas——"

"You intend to restore this money to the Consolidated?" said Miss Fincastle eagerly.

"Not quite! The Consolidated doesn't deserve it. You must not regard its shareholders as a set of innocent shorn lambs. They knew the game. They went in for what they could get. Besides, how could I restore the money without giving myself away? I want the money myself."

"But you are a millionaire."

"It is precisely because I am a millionaire that I want more. All millionaires are like that."

"I am sorry to find you a thief, Mr. Thorold."

"A thief! No. I am only direct; I only avoid the middleman. At dinner, Miss Fincastle, you displayed somewhat advanced views about property, marriage, and the aristocracy of brains. You said that labels were for the stupid majority, and that the wise minority examined the ideas behind the labels. You label me a thief; but examine the idea, and you will perceive that you might as well call yourself a thief. Your newspaper every day suppresses the truth about the City, and it does so in order to live. In other words, it touches the pitch, it participates in the game. To-day it has a fifty-line advertisement of a false balance-sheet of the Consolidated, at two shillings a line. That five pounds, part of the loot of a great city, will help to pay you for your account of our interview this afternoon."

"Our interview to-night," Miss Fincastle corrected him stiffly, "and all that I have seen and heard."

At these words she stood up; and as Cecil Thorold gazed at her, his face changed.

"I shall begin to wish," he said slowly, "that I had deprived myself of the pleasure of your company this evening."

"You might have been a dead man had you done so," Miss Fincastle retorted; and observing his blank countenance, she touched the revolver. "Have you forgotten already?" she asked tartly.

"Of course it wasn't loaded," he remarked. "Of course I had seen to that earlier in the day. I am not such a bungler—— "

"Then I didn't save your life?"

"You force me to say that you did not, and to remind you that you gave me your word not to emerge from behind the screen. However, seeing the motive, I can only thank you for that lapse. The pity is that it hopelessly compromises you."

"Me?" exclaimed Miss Fincastle.

"You. Can't you see that you are in it, in this robbery, to give the thing a label. You were alone with the robber. You succoured the robber at a critical moment. . . . . 'Accomplice,' Mr. Bowring himself said. My dear journalist, the episode of the revolver, empty though the revolver was, seals your lips."

Miss Fincastle laughed rather hysterically, leaning over the table with her hands on it.

"My dear millionaire," she said rapidly, "you don't know the new journalism, to which I have the honour to belong. You would know it better had you lived more in New York. All I have to announce is that, compromised or not, a full account of this affair will appear in my paper to-morrow morning. No, I shall not inform the police. I am a journalist simply, but a journalist I *am*."

"And your promise, which you gave me before going behind the screen—your solemn promise that you would reveal nothing? I was loth to mention it."

"Some promises, Mr. Thorold, it is a duty to break; and it is my duty to break this one. I should never have given it had I had the slightest idea of the nature of your recreations."

Thorold still smiled, though faintly.

"Really, you know," he murmured, "this is getting just a little serious."

"It is very serious," she stammered.

And then Thorold noticed that the new journalist was softly weeping.

V.

THE door opened.

"Miss Kitty Sartorius," said the erstwhile liftman, who was now in plain clothes and had mysteriously ceased to squint.

A beautiful girl, a girl who had remarkable loveliness and was aware of it (one of the prettiest women of the Devonshire), ran impulsively into the room and caught Miss Fincastle by the hand.

"My dearest Eve, you're crying! What's the matter?"

"Lecky," said Thorold aside to the servant, "I told you to admit no one."

The beautiful blonde turned sharply to Thorold.

"I told him I wished to enter," she said imperiously, half closing her eyes.

"Yes, sir," said Lecky. "That was it. The lady wished to enter."

Thorold bowed.

"It was sufficient," he said. "That will do, Lecky."

"Yes, sir."

"But I say, Lecky, when next you address me publicly, try to remember that I am not in the peerage."

The servant squinted.

"Certainly, sir." And he retired.

"Now we are alone," said Miss Sartorius, "introduce us, Eve, and explain."

Miss Fincastle, having regained self-control, introduced her dear friend the radiant star of the Regency Theatre, and her acquaintance the millionaire.

"Eve didn't feel *quite* sure of you," the actress stated; "and so we arranged that if

"Put the fifty trifles in the grate."

she wasn't up at my flat by nine o'clock, I was to come down and reconnoitre. What have you been doing to make Eve cry?"

"Unintentional, I assure you——" Thorold began.

"There's something between you two," said Kitty Sartorius sagaciously, in significant accents. "What is it?"

She sat down, touched her picture hat, smoothed her white gown, and tapped her foot. "What is it, now? Mr. Thorold, I think *you* had better tell me."

Thorold raised his eyebrows and obediently commenced the narration, standing with his back to the fire.

"How perfectly splendid!" Kitty exclaimed. "I'm so glad you cornered Mr. Bowring. I met him one night and I thought he was horrid. And these are the notes? Well, of all the——!"

Thorold proceeded with his story.

"Oh, but you can't do *that*, Eve!" said Kitty, suddenly serious. "You can't go and split! It would mean all sorts of bother; your wretched newspaper would be sure to keep you hanging about in London, and we shouldn't be able to start on our holiday to-morrow. Eve and I are starting on quite a long tour to-morrow, Mr. Thorold; we begin with Ostend."

"Indeed!" said Thorold. "I, too, am going in that direction soon. Perhaps we may meet."

"I hope so," Kitty smiled, and then she looked at Eve Fincastle. "You really mustn't do *that*, Eve," she said.

"I must, I must!" Miss Fincastle insisted, clenching her hands.

"And she will," said Kitty tragically, after considering her friend's face. "She will, and our holiday's ruined. I see it—I see it plainly. She's in one of her stupid conscientious moods. She's fearfully advanced and careless and unconventional in theory, Eve is; but when it come to practice——! Mr. Thorold, you have just got everything into a dreadful knot. Why did you want those notes so very particularly?"

"I don't want them so very particularly."

"Well, anyhow, it's a most peculiar predicament. Mr. Bowring doesn't count, and this Consolidated thingummy isn't any the worse off. Nobody suffers who oughtn't to suffer. It's your unlawful gain that's wrong.

Why not pitch the wretched notes in the fire?" Kitty laughed at her own playful humour.

"Certainly," said Thorold. And with a quick movement he put the fifty trifles in the grate, where they made a bluish yellow flame.

Both the women screamed and sprang up.

"*Mr*. Thorold!"

"Mr. *Thorold!*" ("He's adorable!" Kitty breathed).

"The incident, I venture to hope, is now closed," said Thorold calmly, but with his dark eyes sparkling. "I must thank you both for a very enjoyable evening. Some day, perhaps, I may have an opportunity of further explaining my philosophy to you."

THE LOOT OF CITIES:

THE ADVENTURES OF A MILLIONAIRE IN SEARCH OF JOY.

By ARNOLD BENNETT

No. II.—A COMEDY ON THE GOLD COAST.

IT was five o'clock on an afternoon in mid-September, and a couple of American millionaires (they abounded that year, did millionaires) sat chatting together on the wide terrace which separates the entrance to the Kursaal from the promenade. Some yards away, against the balustrade of the terrace, in the natural, unconsidered attitude of one to whom short frocks are a matter of history, certainly, but very recent history, stood a charming and imperious girl; you could see that she was eating chocolate while meditating upon the riddle of life. The elder millionaire glanced at every pretty woman within view, excepting only the girl; but his companion seemed to be intent on counting the girl's chocolates.

The immense crystal dome of the Kursaal dominated the gold coast, and on either side of the great building were stretched out in a straight line the hotels, the restaurants, the *cafés*, the shops, the theatres, the concert-halls, and the pawnbrokers of the City of Pleasure—Ostend. At one extremity of that long array of ornate white architecture (which resembled the icing on a bride-cake more than the roofs of men) was the palace of a king; at the other were the lighthouse and the railway-signals, which guided into the city the continuously arriving cargoes of wealth, beauty, and desire. In front, the ocean, grey and lethargic, idly beat up a little genteel foam under the promenade for the wetting of pink feet and stylish bathing-costumes. And after a hard day's work, the sun, by arrangement with the authorities during August and September, was setting over the sea exactly opposite the superb portals of the Kursaal.

The younger of the millionaires was Cecil Thorold. The other, a man fifty-five or so, was Simeon Rainshore, father of the girl at the balustrade, and president of the famous Dry Goods Trust, of exciting memory. The contrast between the two men, alike only in extreme riches, was remarkable: Cecil still youthful, slim, dark, languid of movement, with delicate features, eyes almost Spanish, and an accent of purest English; and Rainshore with his nasal twang, his stout frame, his rounded, bluish-red chin, his little eyes, and that demeanour of false briskness by means of which ageing men seek to prove to themselves that they are as young as ever they were. Simeon had been a friend and opponent of Cecil's father's; in former days those twain had victimised each other for colossal sums. Consequently Simeon had been glad to meet the son of his dead antagonist, and, in less than a week of Ostend repose, despite a fundamental disparity of temperament, the formidable president and the Europeanised wanderer had achieved a sort of intimacy, an intimacy which was about to be intensified.

"The difference between you and me is this," Cecil was saying. "You exhaust yourself by making money among men who are all bent on making money, in a place specially set apart for the purpose. I amuse myself by making money among men who, having made or inherited money, are bent on spending it, in places specially set apart for the purpose. I take people off their guard. They don't precisely see me coming. I don't rent an office and put up a sign which is equivalent to announcing that the rest of the world had better look out for itself. Our codes are the same, but is not my way more original and more diverting? Look at this place. Half the wealth of Europe is collected here; the other half is at Trouville. The entire coast reeks of money; the sands are golden with it. You've only to put out your hand—so!"

"So?" ejaculated Rainshore, quizzical. "How? Show me?"

"Ah! That would be telling."

"I guess you wouldn't get much out of Simeon—not as much as your father did."

"Do you imagine I should try?" said Cecil gravely. "My amusements are always discreet."

"But you confess you are often bored. Now, on Wall Street we are never bored."

"Yes," Cecil admitted. "I embarked on these—these enterprises mainly to escape boredom."

"You ought to marry," said Rainshore pointedly. "You ought to marry, my friend."

"I have my yacht."

"No doubt. And she's a beauty, and feminine too; but not feminine enough. You ought to marry. Now, I'll——."

Mr. Rainshore paused. His daughter had suddenly ceased to eat chocolates and was leaning over the balustrade in order to converse with a tall, young man whose fair, tanned face and white hat overtopped the carved masonry and were thus visible to the millionaires. The latter glanced at one another and then glanced away, each slightly self-conscious.

"I thought Mr. Vaux-Lowry had left?" said Cecil.

"He came back last night," Rainshore replied curtly. "And he leaves again to-night."

"Then—then it's a match, after all!" Cecil ventured.

"Who says that?" was Simeon's sharp inquiry.

"The birds of the air whisper it. One heard it at every corner three days ago."

Rainshore turned his chair a little towards Cecil's. "You'll allow I ought to know something about it," he said. "Well, I tell you it's a lie."

"I'm sorry I mentioned it," Cecil apologised.

"Not at all," said Simeon, stroking his chin. "I'm glad you did. Because now you can just tell all the birds of the air direct from me that in this particular case there isn't going to be the usual alliance between the beauty and dollars of America and the aristocratic blood of Great Britain. Listen right here," he continued confidentially, like a man whose secret feelings have been inconveniencing him for several hours. "This young spark—mind, I've nothing against him!—asks me to consent to his engagement with Geraldine. I tell him that I intend to settle half a million dollars on my daughter, and that the man she marries must cover that half-million with another. He says he has a thousand a year of his own, pounds—just nice for Geraldine's gloves and candy!—and that he is the heir of his uncle, Lord Lowry; and that there is an entail; and that Lord Lowry is very rich, very old, and very unmarried; but that, being also very peculiar, he won't come down with any money. It occurs to me to remark: 'Suppose Lord Lowry marries and develops into the father of a man-child, where do *you* come in, Mr. Vaux-Lowry?' 'Oho! Lord Lowry marry! Impossible! Laughable!' Then Geraldine begins to worry at me, and her mother too. And so I kind of issue an ultimatum—namely, I will consent to an engagement without a settlement if, on the marriage, Lord Lowry will give a note of hand for half a million dollars to Geraldine, payable on *his* marriage. See? My lord's nephew goes off to persuade my lord, and returns with my lord's answer in an envelope sealed with the great seal. I open it and I read—this is what I read: 'To Mr. S. Rainshore, American draper. Sir—As a humorist you rank high. Accept the admiration of Your obedient servant, LOWRY.'"

The millionaire laughed.

"Oh! It's clever enough!" said Rainshore. "It's very English and grand. Dashed if I don't admire it! All the same, I've requested Mr. Vaux-Lowry, under the circumstances, to quit this town. I didn't show him the letter—no. I spared his delicate feelings. I merely told him Lord Lowry had refused, and that I would be ready to consider his application favourably any time when he happened to have half a million dollars in his pocket."

"And Miss Geraldine?"

"She's flying the red flag, but she knows when my back's against the wall. She knows her father. She'll recover. Great Scott! She's eighteen, he's twenty-one; the whole affair is a high farce. And, moreover, I guess I want Geraldine to marry an American, after all."

"And if she elopes?" Cecil murmured as if to himself, gazing at the set features of the girl, who was now alone once more.

"*Elopes?*"

Rainshore's face reddened as his mood shifted suddenly from indulgent cynicism to profound anger. Cecil was amazed at the transformation, until he remembered to have heard long ago that Simeon himself had eloped.

"It was just a fancy that flashed into my mind," Cecil smiled diplomatically.

"I should let it flash out again if I were you," said Rainshore with a certain grimness. And Cecil perceived the truth of the maxim that a parent can never forgive his own fault in his child.

II.

"YOU'VE come to sympathise with me," said Geraldine Rainshore calmly, as Cecil, leaving the father for a few moments, strolled across the terrace towards the daughter.

"It's my honest, kindly face that gives me away," he responded lightly. "But what am I to sympathise with you about?"

"'I tell you it's a lie.'"

"You know what," the girl said briefly.

They stood together near the balustrade, looking out over the sea into the crimson eye of the sun; and all the afternoon activities of Ostend were surging round them—the muffled sound of musical instruments from within the Kursaal, the shrill cries of late bathers from the shore, the toot of a tramway-horn to the left, the roar of a siren to the right, and everywhere the ceaseless hum of an existence at once gay, feverish, and futile; but Cecil was conscious of nothing but the individuality by his side. Some women, he reflected, are older at eighteen than they are at thirty-eight, and Geraldine was one of those. She happened to be very young and very old at the same time. She might be immature, crude, even gawky in her girlishness; but she was just then in the first flush of mentally realising the absolute independence of the human spirit. She had force, and she had also the enterprise to act on it.

As Cecil glanced at her intelligent, expressive face, he thought of her playing with life as a child plays with a razor.

"You mean——?" he inquired.

"I mean that father has been talking about me to you. I could tell by his eyes. Well?"

"Your directness unnerves me," he smiled.

"Pull yourself together, then, Mr. Thorold. Be a man."

"Will you let me treat you as a friend?"

"Why, yes," she said, "if you'll promise not to tell me I'm only eighteen."

"I am incapable of such rudeness," Cecil replied. "A woman is as old as she feels. You feel at least thirty; therefore you are at least thirty. This being understood, I am going to suggest, as a friend, that if you and Mr. Vaux-Lowry are—perhaps pardonably—contemplating any extreme step——"

"Extreme step, Mr. Thorold?"

"Anything rash."

"And suppose we are?" Geraldine demanded, raising her chin scornfully and defiantly and dangling her parasol.

"I should respectfully and confidentially advise you to refrain. Be content to wait, my dear, middle-aged woman. Your father may relent. And also, I have a notion that I may be able to—to——"

"Help us?"

"Possibly."

"You are real good," said Geraldine coldly. "But what gave you the idea that Harry and I were meaning to——?"

"Something in your eyes—your fine, daring eyes. I read you as you read your father, you see."

"Well, then, Mr. Thorold, there's something wrong with my fine, daring eyes. I'm just the last girl in all America to do anything—rash. Why! if I did anything rash, I'm sure I should feel ever afterwards as if I wanted to be excused off the very face of the earth. I'm that sort of girl. Do you think I don't know that father will give way? I guess he's just got to. With time and hammering, you can knock sense into the head of any parent."

"I apologise," said Cecil, both startled and convinced. "And I congratulate Mr. Vaux-Lowry."

"Say. You like Harry, don't you?"

"Very much. He's the ideal type of Englishman."

Geraldine nodded sweetly. "And so obedient! He does everything I tell him. He is leaving for England to-night, not because father asked him to, but because I did. I'm going to take mother to Brussels for a few days' shopping—lace, you know. That will give father an opportunity to meditate in solitude on his own greatness. Tell me, Mr. Thorold, do you consider that Harry and I would be justified in corresponding secretly?"

Cecil assumed a pose of judicial gravity.

"I think you would," he decided. "But don't tell anyone I said so."

"Not even Harry?"

She ran off into the Kursaal, saying she must seek her mother. But instead of seeking her mother, Geraldine passed straight through the concert-hall, where a thousand and one wondrously attired women were doing fancy needlework to the accompaniment of a band of music, into the maze of corridors beyond, and so to the rear entrance of the Kursaal on the Boulevard van Isoghem. Here she met Mr. Harry Vaux-Lowry, who was most obviously waiting for her. They crossed the road to the empty tramway waiting-room and entered it and sat down; and by the mere act of looking into each other's eyes, these two—the stiff, simple, honest-faced young Englishmen with "Oxford" written all over him, and the charming child of a civilisation equally proud, but with fewer conventions—suddenly transformed the little bureau into a Cupid's bower.

"It's just as I thought, you darling boy," Geraldine began to talk rapidly. "Father's the least bit in the world scared; and when he's scared, he's bound to confide in someone; and he's confided in that sweet Mr. Thorold. And Mr. Thorold has been requested to reason with me and advise me to be a good girl and wait. I know what *that* means. It means that father thinks we shall soon forget each other, my poor Harry. And I do believe it means that father wants me to marry Mr. Thorold."

"What did you say to him, dear?" the lover demanded, pale.

"Trust me to fool him, Harry. I simply walked round him. He thinks we're going to be very good and wait patiently. As if father ever *would* give way until he was forced!"

She laughed disdainfully. "So we're perfectly safe so long as we act with discretion. Now let's clearly understand. To-day's Monday. You return to England to-night."

"Yes. And I'll arrange about the licence and things."

"Your cousin Mary is just as important as the licence, Harry," said Geraldine primly.

"She will come. You may rely on her being at Ostend with me on Thursday."

"Very well. In the meantime, I behave as if life is a blank. Brussels will put them off the scent. Mother and I will return from there on Thursday afternoon. That night there is a *soirée dansante* at the Kursaal.

Mother will say she is too tired to go to it, but she will have to go all the same. I will dance before all men till a quarter to ten—I will even dance with Mr. Thorold. What a pity I can't dance before father, but he's certain to be in the gambling-rooms then, winning money; he always is at that hour! At a quarter to ten I will slip out, and you'll be here at this back door with a carriage. We drive to the quay and just catch the 11.5 steamer, and I meet your cousin Mary. On Friday morning we are married; and then, then we shall be in a position to talk to father. He'll pretend to be furious, but he can't say much, because he eloped himself. . . . Didn't you know?"

"Passed straight through the concert-hall."

"I didn't," said Harry, with a certain dryness.

"Oh, yes! It's in the family! But you needn't look so starched, my English lord." He took her hand. "You're sure your uncle won't disinherit you, or anything horrid of that kind?"

"He can't," said Harry.

"What a perfectly lovely country England is!" Geraldine exclaimed. "Fancy the poor old thing not being *able* to disinherit you! Why, it's just too delicious for words!"

And for some reason or other he kissed her violently.

Then an official entered the bureau and asked them if they wanted to go to Blankenburghe; because, if so, the tram was awaiting their distinguished pleasure. They looked at each other foolishly and sidled out, and the bureau ceased to be Cupid's bower.

III.

By Simeon's request, Cecil dined with the Rainshores that night at the Continental. After dinner they all sat out on the balcony and sustained themselves with coffee while watching the gay traffic of the Digue, the brilliant illumination of the Kursaal, and the distant lights on the invisible but murmuring sea. Geraldine was in one of her moods of philosophic pessimism, and would persist in dwelling on the uncertainty of riches and the vicissitudes of millionaires. She found a text in the famous Bowring case, of which the newspaper contained many interesting details.

"I wonder if he'll be caught?" she remarked.

"I wonder," said Cecil.

"What do you think, father?"

"I think you had better go to bed," Simeon replied.

The chit rose and kissed him duteously.

"Good night," she said. "Aren't you glad the sea keeps so calm?"

"Why?"

"Can you ask? Mr. Vaux-Lowry crosses to-night, and he's a dreadfully bad sailor. Come along, mother. Mr. Thorold, when mother and I return from Brussels, we shall expect to be taken for a cruise in the *Claribel*."

Simeon sighed with relief upon the departure of his family and began a fresh cigar. On the whole, his day had been rather too domestic. He was quite pleased when Cecil, having apparently by accident broached the subject of the Dry Goods Trust, proceeded to exhibit a minute curiosity concerning the past, the present, and the future of the greatest of all the Rainshore enterprises.

"Are you thinking of coming in?" Simeon demanded at length, pricking up his ears.

"No," said Cecil, "I'm thinking of going out. The fact is, I haven't mentioned it before, but I'm ready to sell a very large block of shares."

"The deuce you are!" Simeon exclaimed. "And what do you call a very large block?"

"Well," said Cecil, "it would cost me nearly half a million to take them up now."

"Dollars?"

"Pounds sterling. Twenty-five thousand shares, at 95⅜."

Rainshore whistled two bars of "Follow me!" from "The Belle of New York."

"Is this how you amuse yourself at Ostend?" he inquired.

Cecil smiled: "This is quite an exceptional transaction. And not too profitable, either."

"But you can't dump that lot on the market," Simeon protested.

"Yes, I can," said Cecil. "I must, and I will. There are reasons. You yourself wouldn't care to handle it, I suppose?"

The president of the Trust pondered.

"I'd handle it at 93⅜," he answered quietly.

"Oh, come! That's dropping two points!" said Cecil, shocked. "A minute ago you were prophesying a further rise."

Rainshore's face gleamed out momentarily in the darkness as he puffed at his cigar.

"If you must unload," he remarked, as if addressing the red end of the cigar, "I'm your man at 93⅜."

Cecil argued; but Simeon Rainshore never argued—it was not his method. In a quarter of an hour the younger man had contracted to sell twenty-five thousand shares of a hundred dollars each in the United States Dry Goods Trust at two points below the current market quotation, and six and five-eighths points below par.

The hoot of an outgoing steamer sounded across the city.

"'We shall expect to be taken for a cruise in the *Claribel*.'"

"I must go," said Cecil.

"You're in a mighty hurry," Simeon complained.

IV.

Five minutes later, Cecil was in his own rooms at the Hôtel de la Plage. Soon there was a discreet knock at the door.

"Come in, Lecky," he said.

It was his servant who entered, the small, thin man with very mobile eyes and of no particular age, who, in various capacities and incarnations—now as liftman, now as financial agent, now as no matter what—assisted Cecil in his diversions.

"Mr. Vaux-Lowry really did go by the boat, sir."

"Good. And you have given directions about the yacht?"

"The affair is in order."

"And you've procured one of Mr. Rainshore's Homburg hats?"

"It is in your dressing-room. There was no mark of identification on it. So, in order to smooth the difficulties of the police when they find it on the beach, I have taken the liberty of writing Mr. Rainshore's name on the lining."

"A kindly thought," said Cecil. "You'll catch the special G.S.N. steamer direct for London at 1 a.m. That will get you into town before two o'clock to-morrow afternoon. Things have turned out as I expected, and I've nothing else to say to you; but, before leaving me, perhaps you had better repeat your instructions."

"With pleasure, sir," said Lecky. "Tuesday afternoon.—I call at Cloak Lane and intimate that we want to sell Dry Goods shares. I ineffectually try to conceal a secret cause for alarm, and I gradually disclose the fact that we are very anxious indeed to sell really a lot of Dry Goods shares, in a hurry. I permit myself to be pumped, and the information is wormed out of me that Mr. Simeon Rainshore has disappeared, has possibly committed suicide; but that, at present, no one is aware of this except ourselves. I express doubts as to the soundness of the Trust, and I remark on the unfortunateness of this disappearance so soon after the lamentable panic connected with the lately vanished Bruce Bowring and his companies. I send our friends on 'Change with orders to see what they can do and to report. I then go to Birchin Lane and repeat the performance there without variation. Then I call at the City office of the *Evening Messenger* and talk privily in a despondent vein with the financial editor concerning the Trust, but I breathe not a word as to Mr. Rainshore's disappearance. Wednesday morning.—The rot in Dry Goods has set in sharply, but I am now, very foolishly, disposed to haggle about the selling price. Our friends urge me to accept what I can get, and I leave them, saying that I must telegraph to you. Wednesday afternoon.—I see a reporter of the *Morning Journal* and let out that Simeon Rainshore has disappeared. The *Journal* will wire to Ostend for confirmation, which confirmation it will receive. Thursday morning.—The bottom is knocked out of the price of Dry Goods shares. Then I am to call on our other friends in Throgmorton Street and tell them to buy, buy, buy, in London, New York, Paris, everywhere."

"Go in peace," said Cecil. If we are lucky, the price will drop to seventy."

V.

"I SEE, Mr. Thorold," said Geraldine Rainshore, "that you are about to ask me for the next dance. It is yours."

"You are the queen of diviners," Cecil replied, bowing.

It was precisely half-past nine on Thursday evening, and they had met in a corner of the pillared and balconied *salle de danse*, in the Kursaal behind the concert-hall. The slippery, glittering floor was crowded with dancers—the men in ordinary evening dress, the women very variously attired, save that nearly all wore picture-hats. Geraldine was in a white frock, high at the neck, with a large hat of black velvet; and amidst that brilliant, multicoloured, lighthearted throng, lit by the blaze of the electric chandeliers and swayed by the irresistible melody of the "Doctrinen" waltz, the young girl, simply dressed as she was, easily held her own.

"So you've come back from Brussels?" Cecil said, taking her arm and waist.

"Yes. We arrived just on time for dinner. But what have you been doing with father? We've seen nothing of him."

"Ah!" said Cecil mysteriously. "We've been on a little voyage, and, like you, we've only just returned."

"In the *Claribel?*"

He nodded.

"You might have waited," she pouted.

"Perhaps you wouldn't have liked it. Things happened, you know."

"Why, what? Do tell me."

"Well, you left your poor father alone, and he was moping all day on Tuesday. So on Tuesday night I had the happy idea of going out in the yacht to witness a sham night attack by the French Channel Squadron on Calais. I caught your honoured parent just as he was retiring to bed, and we went. He was only too glad. But we hadn't left the harbour much more than an hour and a half when our engines broke down."

"What fun! And at night, too!"

"Yes. Wasn't it? The shaft was broken. So we didn't see much of any night attack on Calais. Fortunately the weather was all that the weather ought to be when a ship's engines break down. Still, it took us over forty hours to repair—over forty hours! I'm proud we were able to do the thing without being ignominiously towed into port. But I fear your father may have grown a little impatient, though we had excellent views of Ostend and Dunkirk, and the passing vessels were a constant diversion."

"Was there plenty to eat?" Geraldine asked simply.

"Ample."

"Then father wouldn't really mind. When did you land?"

"About an hour ago. Your father did not expect you to-night, I fancy. He dressed and went straight to the tables. He has to make up for a night lost, you see."

They danced in silence for a few moments. and then suddenly Geraldine said—

"Will you excuse me? I feel tired. Good night."

The clock under the orchestra showed seventeen minutes to ten.

"Instantly?" Cecil queried.

"Instantly." And the girl added, with a hint of mischief in her voice, as she shook hands: "I look on you as quite a friend since our last little talk; so you will excuse this abruptness, won't you?"

He was about to answer when a sort of commotion arose near behind them. Still holding her hand, he turned to look.

"Why!" he said. "It's your mother! She must be unwell!"

Mrs. Rainshore, stout, and robed, as always, in tight, sumptuous black, sat among a little bevy of chaperons. She held a newspaper in trembling hands, and she was uttering a succession of staccato "Oh-oh's," while everyone in the vicinity gazed at her with alarm. Then she dropped the paper, and, murmuring "Simeon's dead!" sank gently to the polished floor just as Cecil and Geraldine approached.

Geraldine's first instinctive move was to seize the newspaper, which was that day's Paris edition of the *New York Herald*. She read the headlines in a flash: "Strange disappearance of Simeon Rainshore. Suicide feared. Takes advantage of his family's absence. Heavy drop in Dry Goods. Shares at 72 and still falling."

VI.

"MY good Rebecca, I assure you that I am alive."

This was Mr. Rainshore's attempt to calm the hysteric sobbing of his wife, who had recovered from her short swoon in the little retreat of the person who sold Tauchnitzes, picture-postcards, and French novels, between the main corridor and the reading-rooms. Geraldine and Cecil were also in the tiny chamber.

"As for this," Simeon continued, kicking the newspaper, "it's a singular thing that a man can't take a couple of days off without upsetting the entire universe. What should you do in my place, Thorold? This is the fault of your shaft."

"I should buy Dry Goods shares," said Cecil.

"And I will."

There was an imperative knock at the door. An official of police entered.

"Monsieur Ryneshor?"

"The same."

"We have received telegraphs from New York and Londres to demand if you are dead."

"I am not. I still live."

"But Monsieur's hat has been found on the beach."

"My hat?"

"It carries Monsieur's name."

"Then it isn't mine, sir."

"*Mais comment donc——?*"

"I tell you it isn't mine, sir."

"Don't be angry, Simeon," his wife pleaded between her sobs.

The exit of the official was immediately followed by another summons for admission, even more imperative. A lady entered and handed to Simeon a card: "Miss Eve Fincastle. *The Morning Journal.*"

"My paper——" she began.

"You wish to know if I exist, madam!" said Simeon.

"I——" Miss Fincastle caught sight of Cecil Thorold, paused, and bowed stiffly. Cecil bowed; he also blushed.

"I continue to exist, madam," Simeon proceeded. "I have not killed myself. But homicide of some sort is not improbable if—— In short, madam, good night!"

Miss Fincastle, with a long, searching, silent look at Cecil, departed.

"Bolt that door," said Simeon to his daughter.

Then there was a third knock, followed by a hammering.

"'Simeon's dead!'"

"Go away!" Simeon commanded.

"Open the door!" pleaded a muffled voice.

"It's Harry!" Geraldine whispered solemnly in Cecil's ear. "Please go and calm him. Tell him I say it's too late to-night."

Cecil went, astounded.

"What's happened to Geraldine?" cried the boy, extremely excited, in the corridor. "There are all sorts of rumours. Is she ill?"

Cecil gave an explanation, and in his turn asked for another one. "You look unnerved," he said. "What are you doing here? What is it? Come and have a drink, and tell me all, my young friend." And when, over cognac, he had learnt the details of a scheme which had no connection with his own, he exclaimed, with the utmost sincerity: "The minx! The minx!"

"What do you mean?" inquired Harry Vaux-Lowry.

"I mean that you and the minx have had the nearest possible shave of ruining your united careers. Listen to me. Give it up, my boy. I'll try to arrange things. You delivered a letter to the father-in-law of your desire a few days ago. I'll give you another one to deliver, and I fancy the result will be different."

The letter which Cecil wrote ran thus:—

"DEAR RAINSHORE,—I enclose cheque for £100,000. It represents part of the gold that can be picked up on the gold coast by putting out one's hand—so! You will observe that it is dated the day after the next settling-day of the London Stock Exchange. I contracted on Monday last to sell you 25,000 shares of a certain Trust at 93⅜. I did not possess the shares then, but my agents have to-day bought them for me at an average price of 72. I stand to realise, therefore, rather more than half a million dollars. The round half-million Mr. Vaux-Lowry happens to bring you in his pocket; you will not forget your promise to him that when he did so you would consider his application favourably. I wish to make no profit out of the little transaction, but I will venture to keep the balance for out-of-pocket expenses, such as mending the *Claribel's* shaft. (How convenient it is to have a yacht that will break down when required!) The shares will doubtless recover in due course; and I hope the reputation of the Trust may not suffer, and that for the sake of old times with my father you will regard the episode in its proper light and bear me no ill-will.

"Yours sincerely, C. THOROLD."

The next day the engagement of Mr. Harry Nigel Selincourt Vaux-Lowry and Miss Geraldine Rainshore was announced to two continents.

THE LOOT OF CITIES:

THE ADVENTURES OF A MILLIONAIRE IN SEARCH OF JOY

By ARNOLD BENNETT

III. A BRACELET AT BRUGES.

THE bracelet had fallen into the canal.

And the fact that the canal was the most picturesque canal in the old Flemish city of Bruges, and that the ripples caused by the splash of the bracelet had disturbed reflections of wondrous belfries, towers, steeples, and other unique examples of Gothic architecture, did nothing whatever to assuage the sudden agony of that disappearance. For the bracelet had been given to Kitty Sartorius by her grateful and lordly manager, Lionel Belmont (U.S.A.), upon the completion of the unexampled run of "The Delmonico Doll" at the Regency Theatre, London. And its diamonds were worth five hundred pounds, to say nothing of the gold.

The beautiful Kitty, and her friend Eve Fincastle the journalist, having exhausted Ostend, had duly arrived at Bruges in the course of their holiday tour. The question of Kitty's jewellery had arisen at the start. Kitty had insisted that she must travel with all her jewels, according to the custom of theatrical stars of great magnitude. Eve had equally insisted that Kitty must travel without jewels, and had exhorted her to remember the days of her simplicity. They compromised. Kitty was allowed to bring the bracelet, but nothing else save the usual half-dozen rings. The ravishing creature could not have persuaded herself to leave the bracelet behind, because it was so recent a gift and still new and strange and heavenly to her. But, since prudence forbade even Kitty to let the trifle lie about in hotel bedrooms, she was obliged always to wear it. And she had been wearing it this bright afternoon in early October when the girls, during a stroll, had met one of their new friends, Madame Lawrence, on the world-famous Quai du Rosaire, just at the back of the Hôtel de Ville and the Halles.

Madame Lawrence resided permanently in Bruges. She was between twenty-five and forty-five, dark, with the air of continually subduing a natural instinct to dash, and well dressed in black. Equally interested in the peerage and in the poor, she had made the acquaintance of Eve and Kitty at the Hôtel de la Grande Place, where she called from time to time to induce English travellers to buy genuine Bruges lace wrought under her own supervision by her own paupers. She was Belgian by birth, and when complimented on her fluent and correct English, she gave all the praise to her deceased husband, an English barrister. She had settled in Bruges like many people settle there, because Bruges is inexpensive, picturesque, and inordinately respectable; besides an English church and chaplain, it has two cathedrals and an episcopal palace with a real bishop in it.

"What an exquisite bracelet! May I look at it?"

It was these simple but ecstatic words, spoken with Madame Lawrence's charming foreign accent, which had begun the tragedy. The three women had stopped to admire the always admirable view from the little quay, and they were leaning over the rails when Kitty unclasped the bracelet for the inspection of the widow. The next instant there was a *plop!* an affrighted exclamation from Madame Lawrence in her native tongue, and the bracelet was engulfed before the very eyes of all three.

The three looked at each other, nonplussed. Then they looked around, but not a single person was in sight. Then, for some reason which doubtless psychology can explain, they stared hard at the water, though the water there was just as black and foul as it is everywhere else in the canal system of Bruges.

"Surely you've not dropped it!" Eve Fincastle exclaimed in a voice of horror. Yet she knew positively that Madame Lawrence had.

The delinquent took a handkerchief from her muff and sobbed into it. And between her sobs she murmured: "We must inform the police."

"Yes, of course," said Kitty, with the lightness of one to whom a five-hundred-pound bracelet is a bagatelle. "They'll fish it up in no time."

"Well," Eve decided, "you go to the police at once, Kitty; and Madame Lawrence will go with you, because she speaks French; and I'll stay here to mark the exact spot."

The other two started, but Madame Lawrence, after a few steps, put her hand to her side. "I can't," she sighed, pale. "I am too upset. I cannot walk. You go with Miss Sartorius," she said to Eve, "and I will stay." And she leaned heavily against the railings.

Eve and Kitty ran off, just as if it were an affair of seconds, and the bracelet had to be saved from drowning. But they had scarcely turned the corner, thirty yards away, when they reappeared in company with a high official of police, whom, by the most lucky chance in the world, they had encountered in the covered passage leading to the Place du Bourg. This official, instantly enslaved by Kitty's beauty, proved to be the very mirror of politeness and optimism. He took their names and addresses, and a full description of the bracelet, and informed them that at that place the canal was nine feet deep. He said that the bracelet should undoubtedly be recovered on the morrow, but that, as dusk was imminent, it would be futile to commence angling that night. In the meantime, the loss should be kept secret; and to make all sure, a succession of gendarmes should guard the spot during the night.

Kitty grew radiant and rewarded the gallant officer with smiles; Eve was satisfied; and the face of Madame Lawrence wore a less mournful hue.

"And now," said Kitty to Madame, when everything had been arranged, and the first of the gendarmes was duly installed at the exact spot against the railings, "you must come and take tea with us in our winter-garden; and be gay! Smile: I insist. And I insist that you don't worry."

Madame Lawrence tried feebly to smile.

"You are very good-natured," she stammered.

Which was decidedly true.

II.

THE winter-garden of the Hôtel de la Grande Place, referred to in all the hotel's advertisements, was merely the inner court of the hotel roofed in by glass at the height of the first storey. Cane flourished there, in the shape of lounge-chairs, but no other plant. One of the lounge-chairs was occupied when, just as the carillon in the belfry at the other end of the Place began to play Gounod's "Nazareth," indicating the hour of five o'clock, the three ladies entered the winter-garden. Apparently the toilettes of two of them had been adjusted and embellished as for a somewhat ceremonious occasion.

"Lo!" cried Kitty Sartorius, when she perceived the occupant of the chair, "the millionaire! Mr. Thorold, how charming of you to reappear like this! I invite you to tea."

Cecil Thorold rose with appropriate eagerness.

"Delighted!" he said, smiling, and then explained that he had arrived from Ostend about two hours before and had taken rooms in the hotel.

"You knew we were staying here?" Eve asked as he shook hands with her.

"No," he replied; "but I am very glad to find you again."

"Are you?" She spoke languidly, but her colour heightened and those eyes of hers sparkled.

"Madame Lawrence," Kitty chirruped, "let me present Mr. Cecil Thorold. He is appallingly rich, but we mustn't let that frighten us."

From a mouth less adorable than the mouth of Miss Sartorius such an introduction might have been judged lacking in the elements of good form, but for more than two years now Kitty had known that whatever she did or said was perfectly correct because she did or said it. The new acquaintances laughed amiably and a certain intimacy was at once established.

"Shall I order tea, dear?" Eve suggested.

"No, dear," said Kitty quietly. "We will wait for the Count."

"The Count?" demanded Cecil Thorold.

"The Comte d'Avrec," Kitty explained. "He is staying here."

"A French nobleman, doubtless?"

"Yes," said Kitty; and she added, "you will like him. He is an archæologist, and a musician—oh, and lots of things!"

"If I am one minute late, I entreat

"The next instant there was a *plop!*"

pardon," said a fine tenor voice at the door.

It was the Count. After he had been introduced to Madame Lawrence, and Cecil Thorold had been introduced to him, tea was served.

Now, the Comte d'Avrec was everything that a French count ought to be. As dark as Cecil Thorold, and even handsomer, he was a little older and a little taller than the millionaire, and a short, pointed, black beard, exquisitely trimmed, gave him an appearance of staid reliability which Cecil lacked. His bow was a vertebrate poem, his smile a consolation for all misfortunes, and he managed his hat, stick, gloves, and cup with the dazzling assurance of a conjurer. To observe him at afternoon tea was to be convinced that he had been specially created to shine gloriously in drawing-rooms, winter-gardens, and *tables d'hôte.* He was one of those men who always do the right thing at the right moment, who are capable of speaking an indefinite number of languages with absolute purity of accent (he spoke English much better than Madame Lawrence), and who can and do discourse with *verve* and accuracy on all sciences, arts, sports, and religions. In short, he was a phœnix of a count; and this was certainly the opinion of Miss Kitty Sartorius and of Miss Eve Fincastle, both of whom reckoned that what they did not know about men might be ignored. Kitty and the Count, it soon became evident, were mutually attracted; their souls were approaching each other with a velocity which increased inversely as the square of the lessening distance between them. And Eve was watching this approximation with undisguised interest and relish.

Nothing of the least importance occurred, save the Count's marvellous exhibition of how to behave at afternoon tea, until the refection was nearly over; and then, during a brief pause in the talk, Cecil, who was sitting to the left of Madame Lawrence, looked sharply round at the right shoulder of his tweed coat; he repeated the gesture a second and yet a third time.

"What is the matter with the man?" asked Eve Fincastle. Both she and Kitty were extremely bright, animated, and even excited.

"Nothing. I thought I saw something on my shoulder, that's all," said Cecil. "Ah! It's only a bit of thread." And he picked off the thread with his left hand and held it before Madame Lawrence. "See! It's a piece of thin black silk, knotted. At first I took it for an insect—you know how queer things look out of the corner of your eye. Pardon!" He had dropped the fragment on to Madame Lawrence's black silk dress. "Now it's lost."

"If you will excuse me, kind friends," said Madame Lawrence, "I will go." She spoke hurriedly and as though in mental distress.

"Poor thing!" Kitty Sartorius exclaimed when the widow had gone. "She's still dreadfully upset"; and Kitty and Eve proceeded jointly to relate the story of the diamond bracelet, upon which hitherto they had kept silence (though with difficulty), out of regard for Madame Lawrence's feelings.

Cecil made almost no comment.

The Count, with the sympathetic excitability of his race, walked up and down the winter-garden, asseverating earnestly that such clumsiness amounted to a crime; then he grew calm and confessed that he shared the optimism of the police as to the recovery of the bracelet; lastly he complimented Kitty on her equable demeanour under this affliction.

"Do you know, Count," said Cecil Thorold, later, after they had all four ascended to the drawing-room overlooking the Grande Place, "I was quite surprised when I saw at tea that you had to be introduced to Madame Lawrence."

"Why so, my dear Mr. Thorold?" the Count inquired suavely.

"I thought I had seen you together in Ostend a few days ago."

The Count shook his wonderful head.

"Perhaps you have a brother——?" Cecil paused.

"No," said the Count. "But it is a favourite theory of mine that everyone has his double somewhere in the world." Previously the Count had been discussing Planchette—he was a great authority on the supernatural, the sub-conscious, and the subliminal. He now deviated gracefully to the discussion of the theory of doubles.

"I suppose you aren't going out for a walk, dear, before dinner?" said Eve to Kitty.

"No, dear," said Kitty positively.

"I think I shall," said Eve.

And her glance at Cecil Thorold intimated in the plainest possible manner that she wished not only to have a companion for her stroll, but to leave Kitty and the Count in dual solitude.

"I shouldn't, if I were you, Miss Fincastle," Cecil remarked with calm and studied blindness. "It's risky here in the evenings—with these canals exhaling miasma and mosquitoes and bracelets and all sorts of things."

"I will take the risk, thank you," said Eve in an icy tone, and she haughtily departed; she would not cower before Cecil's millions. As for Cecil, he joined in the discussion of the theory of doubles.

III.

On the next afternoon but one, policemen were still fishing, without success, for the bracelet, and raising from the ancient duct long-buried odours which threatened to destroy the inhabitants of the quay. (When Kitty Sartorius had hinted that perhaps the authorities might see their way to drawing off the water from the canal, the authorities had intimated that the death-rate of Bruges was already as high as convenient.) Nevertheless, though nothing had happened, the situation had somehow developed, and in such a manner that the bracelet itself was in danger of being partially forgotten; and of all places in Bruges, the situation had developed on the top of the renowned Belfry which dominates the Grande Place in particular and the city in general.

The summit of the Belfry is three hundred and fifty feet high, and it is reached by four hundred and two winding stone steps, each a separate menace to life and limb. Eve Fincastle had climbed those steps alone, perhaps in quest of the view at the top, perhaps in quest of spiritual calm. She had not been leaning over the parapet more than a minute before Cecil Thorold had appeared, his field-glasses slung over his shoulder. They had begun to talk a little, but nervously and only in snatches. The wind blew free up there among the forty-eight bells, but the social atmosphere was oppressive.

"The Count is a most charming man," Eve was saying, as if in defence of the Count.

"He is," said Cecil; "I agree with you."

"Oh, no, you don't, Mr. Thorold! Oh, no, you don't!"

Then there was a pause, and the twain

"'Pardon! Now it's lost!'"

looked down upon Bruges, with its venerable streets, its grass-grown squares, its waterways, and its innumerable monuments, spread out maplike beneath them in the mellow October sunshine. Citizens passed along the thoroughfare in the semblance of tiny dwarfs.

"If you didn't hate him," said Eve, "you wouldn't behave as you do."

"How do I behave, then?"

Eve schooled her voice to an imitation of jocularity—

"All Tuesday evening, and all day yesterday, you couldn't leave them alone. You know you couldn't."

Five minutes later the conversation had shifted.

"You actually saw the bracelet fall into the canal?" said Cecil.

"I actually saw the bracelet fall into the canal. And no one could have got it out while Kitty and I were away, because we weren't away half a minute."

But they could not dismiss the subject of the Count, and presently he was again the topic.

"Naturally it would be a good match for the Count—for *any* man," said Eve; "but then it would also be a good match for Kitty. Of course, he is not so rich as some people, but he is rich."

Cecil examined the horizon with his glasses, and then the streets near the Grande Place.

"Rich, is he? I'm glad of it. By the by, he's gone to Ghent for the day, hasn't he?"

"Yes. He went by the 9.27, and returns by the 4.38."

Another pause.

"Well," said Cecil at length, handing the glasses to Eve Fincastle, "kindly glance down there. Follow the line of the Rue St. Nicolas. You see the cream-coloured house with the enclosed courtyard? Now,

"Making graceful and expressive signs to Kitty."

do you see two figures standing together near a door—a man and a woman, the woman on the steps? Who are they?"

"I can't see very well," said Eve.

"Oh, yes, my dear lady, you can," said Cecil. "These glasses are the very best. Try again."

"They look like the Comte d'Avrec and Madame Lawrence," Eve murmured.

"But the Count is on his way from Ghent! I see the steam of the 4.38 over there. The curious thing is that the Count entered the house of Madame Lawrence, to whom he was introduced for the first time the day before yesterday, at ten o'clock this morning. Yes. It would be a very good match for the Count. When one comes to think of it, it usually is that sort of man that contrives to marry a brilliant and successful actress. There! He's just leaving, isn't he? Now let us descend and listen to the recital of his day's doings in Ghent—shall we?"

"You mean to insinuate," Eve burst out in sudden wrath, "that the Count is an—an *adventurer*, and that Madame Lawrence—— Oh! Mr. Thorold!" She laughed condescendingly. "This jealousy is too absurd. Do you suppose I haven't noticed how impressed you were with Kitty at the Devonshire Mansion that night, and again at Ostend, and again here? You're simply carried away by jealousy; and you think because you are a millionaire you must have all you want. I haven't the slightest doubt that the Count——"

"Anyhow," said Cecil, "let us go down and hear about Ghent."

His eyes made a number of remarks (indulgent, angry, amused, protective, admiring, perspicacious, puzzled) too subtle for the medium of words.

They groped their way down to earth in silence, and it was in silence they crossed the Grande Place. The Count was seated on the *terrasse* in front of the hotel, with a liqueur glass before him, and he was making graceful and expressive signs to Kitty Sartorius, who leaned her marvellous beauty out of a first-storey window. He greeted Cecil Thorold and Eve with an equal grace.

"And how is Ghent?" Cecil inquired.

"Did you go to Ghent, after all, Count?" Eve put in. The Comte d'Avrec looked from one to another, and then, instead of replying, he sipped at his glass. "No," he said, "I didn't go. The rather curious fact is that I happened to meet Madame Lawrence, who offered to show me her collection of lace. I have been an amateur of lace for some years, and really Madame Lawrence's collection is amazing. You have seen it? No? You should do so. I'm afraid I have spent most of the day there."

When the Count had gone to join Kitty in the drawing-room, Eve Fincastle looked victoriously at Cecil, as if to demand of him: "Will you apologise?"

"My dear journalist," Cecil remarked simply, "you gave the show away."

* * * * *

That evening the continued obstinacy of the bracelet, which still refused to be caught, began at last to disturb the birdlike mind of Kitty Sartorius. Moreover, the secret was out, and the whole town of Bruges was discussing the episode and the chances of success.

"Let us consult Planchette," said the Count. The proposal was received with enthusiasm by Kitty. Eve had disappeared.

Planchette was produced; and when asked if the bracelet would be recovered, it wrote, under the hands of Kitty and the Count, a trembling "Yes." When asked: "By whom?" it wrote a word which faintly resembled "Avrec."

The Count stated that he should personally commence dragging operations at sunrise. "You will see," he said, "I shall succeed."

"Let me try this toy, may I?" Cecil asked blandly, and upon Kitty agreeing, he addressed Planchette in a clear voice: "Now, Planchette, who will restore the bracelet to its owner?"

And Planchette wrote "Thorold," but in characters as firm and regular as those of a copy-book.

"Mr. Thorold is laughing at us," observed the Count, imperturbably bland.

"How horrid you are, Mr. Thorold!" Kitty exclaimed.

IV.

Of the four persons more or less interested in the affair, three were secretly active that night, in and out of the hotel. Only Kitty Sartorius, chief mourner for the bracelet, slept placidly in her bed. It was towards three o'clock in the morning that a sort of preliminary crisis was reached.

From the multiplicity of doors which ventilate its rooms, one would imagine that the average foreign hotel must have been designed immediately after its architect had been to see a Palais Royal farce, in which every room opens into every other room in every act. The Hôtel de la Grande Place was not peculiar in this respect; it abounded in doors. All the chambers on the second storey, over the public rooms, fronting the Place, communicated one with the next, but naturally most of the communicating doors were locked. Cecil Thorold and the Comte d'Avrec had each a bedroom and a sitting-room on that floor. The Count's sitting-room adjoined Cecil's; and the door between was locked, and the key in the possession of the landlord.

Nevertheless, at three a.m. this particular door opened noiselessly from Cecil's side, and Cecil entered the domain of the Count. The moon shone, and Cecil could plainly see not only the silhouette of the Belfry across the Place, but also the principal objects within the room. He noticed the table in the middle, the large easy-chair turned towards the hearth, the old-fashioned sofa; but not a single article did he perceive which might have been the personal property of the Count. He cautiously passed across the room through the moonlight to the door of the Count's bedroom, which apparently, to his immense surprise, was not only shut, but locked, and the key in the lock on the sitting-room side. Silently unlocking it, he entered the bedroom and disappeared . . . .

In less than five minutes he crept back into the Count's sitting-room, closed the door and locked it.

"Odd!" he murmured reflectively; but he seemed quite happy.

There was a sudden movement in the region of the hearth, and a form rose from the arm-chair. Cecil rushed to the switch and turned on the electric light. Eve Fincastle stood before him. They faced each other.

"What are you doing here at this time, Miss Fincastle?" he asked sternly. "You can talk freely; the Count will not waken."

"I may ask you the same question," Eve replied with cold bitterness.

"Excuse me. You may not. You are a woman. This is the Count's room——"

"You are in error," she interrupted him. "It is not the Count's room. It is mine. Last night I told the Count I had some important writing to do, and I asked him as a favour to relinquish this room to me for twenty-four hours. He very kindly consented. He removed his belongings, handed me the key of that door, and the transfer was made in the hotel books. And now," she added, "may I inquire, Mr. Thorold, what you are doing in my room?"

"I—I thought it was the Count's," Cecil faltered, decidedly at a loss for a moment. "In offering my humblest apologies, permit me to say that I admire you, Miss Fincastle."

"I wish I could return the compliment," Eve exclaimed, and she repeated with almost plaintive sincerity: "I do wish I could."

Cecil raised his arms and let them fall to his side.

"You meant to catch me," he said. "You suspected something, then? The 'important writing' was an invention." And he added, with a faint smile: "You really ought not to have fallen asleep. Suppose I had not wakened you?"

"Please don't laugh, Mr. Thorold. Yes, I did suspect. There was something in the demeanour of your servant Lecky that gave me the idea. . . . I did mean to catch you. Why you, a millionaire, should be a burglar, I cannot understand. I never understood that incident at the Devonshire Mansion; it was beyond me. I am by no means sure that you didn't have a great deal to do with the Rainshore affair at Ostend. But that you should have stooped to slander is the worst. I confess you are a mystery. I confess that I can make no guess at the nature of your present scheme. And what I shall do, now that I have caught you, I don't know. I can't decide; I must think. If, however, anything is missing to-morrow morning, I shall be bound in any case to denounce you. You grasp that?"

"I grasp it perfectly, my dear journalist," Cecil replied. "And something will not improbably be missing. But take the advice of a burglar and a mystery, and go to bed. it is half past three."

And Eve went. And Cecil bowed her out and then retired to his own rooms. And the Count's apartment was left to the moonlight.

V.

"PLANCHETTE is a very safe prophet," said Cecil to Kitty Sartorius the next morning, "provided it has firm guidance."

They were at breakfast.

"What do you mean?"

"I mean that Planchette prophesied last night that I should restore to you your bracelet. I do."

He took the lovely gewgaw from his pocket and handed it to Kitty.

"Ho-ow did you find it, you dear thing?" Kitty stammered, trembling under the shock of joy.

"I fished it up out—out of the mire by a contrivance of my own."

"But when?"

"Oh! Very early. At three o'clock a.m. You see, I was determined to be first."

"In the dark, then?"

"I had a light. Don't you think I'm rather clever?"

Kitty's scene of ecstatic gratitude does not

"'You see everything plainly?"

come into the story. Suffice it to say that not until the moment of its restoration did she realise how precious the bracelet was to her.

It was ten o'clock before Eve descended. She had breakfasted in her room, and Kitty had already exhibited to her the prodigal bracelet.

"I particularly want you to go up the Belfry with me, Miss Fincastle," Cecil greeted her; and his tone was so serious and so urgent that she consented. They left Kitty playing waltzes on the piano in the drawing-room.

"And now, O man of mystery?" Eve questioned, when they had toiled to the summit, and saw the city and its dwarfs beneath them.

"We are in no danger of being disturbed here," Cecil began; "but I will make my explanation—the explanation which I certainly owe you—as brief as possible. Your Comte d'Avrec is an adventurer (please don't be angry), and your Madame Lawrence is an adventuress. I knew that I had seen them together. They work in concert, and for the most part make a living on the gaming-tables of Europe. Madame Lawrence was expelled from Monte Carlo last year for being too intimate with a croupier. You may be aware that at a roulette-table one can do a great deal with the aid of the croupier. Madame Lawrence appropriated the bracelet 'on her own,' as it were. The Count (he may be a real Count, for anything I know) heard first of that enterprise from the lips of Miss Sartorius. He was annoyed, angry—because he was really a little in love with your friend, and he saw golden prospects. It is just this fact—the Count's genuine passion for Miss Sartorius—that renders the case psychologically interesting. To proceed, Madame Lawrence became jealous. The Count spent six hours yesterday in trying to get the bracelet from her, and failed. He tried again last night, and succeeded, but not too easily, for he did not re-enter the hotel till after one o'clock. At first I thought he had succeeded in the daytime, and I had arranged accordingly, for I did not see why he should have the honour and glory of restoring the bracelet to its owner. Lecky and I fixed up a sleeping-draught for him. The minor details were simple. When you caught me this morning, the bracelet was in my pocket, and in its stead I had left a brief note for the perusal of the Count, which has had the singular effect of inducing him to decamp; probably he has not gone alone. But isn't it amusing that, since you so elaborately took his sitting-room, he will be convinced that you are a party to his undoing—you, his staunchest defender?"

Eve's face gradually broke into an embarrassed smile.

"You haven't explained," she said, "how Madame Lawrence got the bracelet."

"Come over here," Cecil answered. "Take these glasses and look down at the Quai du Rosaire. You see everything plainly?" Eve could, in fact, see on the quay the little mounds of mud which had been extracted from the canal in the quest of the bracelet. Cecil continued: "On my arrival in Bruges on Monday, I had a fancy to climb the Belfry at once. I witnessed the whole scene between you and Miss Sartorius and Madame Lawrence, through my glasses. Immediately your backs were turned, Madame Lawrence, her hands behind her, and her back against the railing, began to make a sort of rapid, drawing-up motion with her forearms. Then I saw a momentary glitter. . . . Considerably mystified, I visited the spot after you had left it, chatted with the gendarme on duty and got round him, and then it dawned on me that a robbery had been planned, prepared, and executed with extraordinary originality and ingenuity. A long, thin thread of black silk must have been ready tied to the railing, with perhaps a hook at the other end. As soon as Madame Lawrence held the bracelet, she attached the hook to it and dropped it. The silk, especially as it was the last thing in the world you would look for, would be as good as invisible. When you went for the police, Madame retrieved the bracelet, hid it in her muff, and broke off the silk. Only, in her haste, she left a bit of silk tied to the railing. That fragment I carried to the hotel. All along she must have been a little uneasy about me. . . . And that's all. Except that I wonder you thought I was jealous of the Count's attentions to your friend." He gazed at her admiringly.

"I'm glad you are not a thief, Mr. Thorold," said Eve.

"Well," Cecil smiled, "as for that, I left him a couple of louis for fares, and I shall pay his hotel bill."

"Why?"

"There were notes for nearly ten thousand francs with the bracelet. Ill-gotten gains, I am sure. A trifle, but the only reward I shall have for my trouble. I shall put them to good use." He laughed, serenely gay.

THE LOOT OF CITIES:

THE ADVENTURES OF A MILLIONAIRE IN SEARCH OF JOY.

By ARNOLD BENNETT

IV.—A SOLUTION OF THE ALGIERS MYSTERY.

"AND the launch?"

"I am unaware of the precise technical term, sir, but the launch awaits you. Perhaps I should have said it is alongside."

The reliable Lecky hated the sea; and when his master's excursions became marine, he always squinted more formidably and suddenly than usual, and added to his reliability a certain quality of ironic bitterness.

"My overcoat, please," said Cecil Thorold, who was in evening dress.

The apartment, large and low, was panelled with bird's-eye maple; divans ran along the walls, and above the divans orange curtains were drawn; the floor was hidden by the skins of wild African animals; in one corner was a Steinway piano, with the score of "The Orchid" open on the music-stand; in another lay a large, flat bowl filled with blossoms that do not bloom in England; the illumination, soft and yellow, came from behind the cornice of the room, being reflected therefrom downwards by the cream-coloured ceiling. Only by a faintly heard tremor of some gigantic but repressed force, and by a very slight unsteadiness on the part of the floor, could you have guessed that you were aboard a steam-yacht and not in a large, luxurious house.

Lecky, having arrayed the millionaire in overcoat, muffler, crush-hat, and white gloves, drew aside a *portière* and followed him up a flight of stairs. They stood on deck, surrounded by the mild but treacherous Algerian night. From the white double funnels a thin smoke oozed. On the white bridge, the second mate, a spectral figure, was testing the engine-room signals, and the sharp noise of the bell seemed to desecrate the mysterious silence of the bay; but there was no other sign of life; the waiting launch was completely hidden under the high bows of the *Claribel*. In distant regions of the deck, glimmering beams came oddly up from below, throwing into relief some part of a boat on its davits or a section of a mast.

Cecil looked about him, at the serried lights of the Boulevard Carnot, and the riding lanterns of the vessels in the harbour. Away to the left on the hill, a few gleams showed Mustapha Supérieure, where the great English hotels are; and ten miles further east, the lighthouse on Cape Matifou flashed its eternal message to the Mediterranean. He was on the verge of feeling poetic.

"Suppose anything happens while you are at this dance, sir?"

Lecky jerked his thumb in the direction of a small steamer which lay moored scarcely a cable's-length away, under the eastern jetty. "Suppose——?" He jerked his thumb again in exactly the same direction. His tone was still pessimistic and cynical.

"You had better fire our beautiful brass cannon," Cecil replied. "Have it fired three times. I shall hear it well enough up at Mustapha."

He descended carefully into the launch, and was whisked puffingly over the dark surface of the bay to the landing-stage, where he summoned a fiacre.

"Hôtel de ——" he instructed the driver.

And the driver smiled joyously; everyone who went to the Hôtel de —— was rich and lordly, and paid well, because the hill was long and steep and so hard on the poor Algerian horses.

II.

Every hotel up at Mustapha Supérieure has the finest view, the finest hygienic installation, and the finest cooking in Algeria; in other words, each is better than all the others.

Hence the Hôtel de —— could not be called " first among equals," since there are no equals, and one must be content to describe it as first among the unequalled. First it undoubtedly was—and perhaps will be again. Although it was new, it had what one visitor termed " that indefinable thing—*cachet*." It was frequented by the best people—namely, the richest people, the idlest people, the most arrogant people, the most bored people, the most titled people—that came to the southern shores of the Mediterranean in search of what they would never find—an escape from themselves. It was a vast building, planned on a scale of spaciousness only possible in a district where commercial crises have depressed the value of land, and it stood in the midst of a vast garden of oranges, lemons, and medlars. Every room—and there were three storeys and two hundred rooms—faced south: this was charged for in the bill. The public

" So he sat down beside her, and they talked."

rooms, Oriental in character, were immense and complete; they included a dining-room, a drawing-room, a reading-room, a smoking-room, a billiard-room, a bridge-room, a ping-pong-room, a concert-room (with resident orchestra), and a room where Aissouias, negroes, and other curiosities from the native town might perform before select parties. Thus it was entirely self-sufficient, and lacked nothing which is necessary to the proper existence of the best people. On Thursday nights, throughout the Season, there was a five-franc dance in the concert hall. You paid five francs, and ate and drank as much as you could while standing up at the supper-tables arrayed in the dining-room.

On a certain Thursday night in early January, this Anglo-Saxon microcosm, set so haughtily in a French colony between the Mediterranean and the Djujura Mountains (with the Sahara behind), was at its most brilliant. The hotel was crammed, the prices were high, and everybody was supremely conscious of doing the correct thing. The dance had begun somewhat earlier than usual, because the eagerness of the younger guests could not be restrained. And the orchestra seemed gayer, and the electric lights brighter, and the toilettes more resplendent that night. Of course, guests came in from the other hotels. Indeed, they came in to such an extent that to dance in the ballroom was an affair of compromise and ingenuity. And the other rooms were occupied, too. The bridge-players recked not of Terpsichore, the cheerful sound of ping-pong came regularly from the ping-pong-room; the retired Indian judge was giving points as usual in the billiard-room; and in the reading-room, the steadfast intellectuals were studying the *World* and the Paris *New York Herald*.

And all was English and American, pure Anglo-Saxon in thought and speech and gesture—save the manager of the hotel, who was Italian, the waiters, who were anything, and the wonderful concierge, who was everything.

As Cecil passed through the imposing suite of public rooms, he saw in the reading-room—posted so that no arrival could escape her eye—the elegant form of Mrs. Macalister, and, by way of a wild, impulsive freak, he stopped and talked to her, and ultimately sat down by her side.

Mrs. Macalister was one of those Englishwomen that are to be found only in large and fashionable hotels. Everything about her was mysterious, except the fact that she was in search of a second husband. She was tall, pretty, dashing, daring, well-dressed, well-informed, and, perhaps thirty-four. But no one had known her husband or her family, and no one knew her county, or the origin of her income, or how she got herself into the best cliques in the hotel. She had the air of being the merriest person in Algiers; really, she was one of the saddest, for the reason that every day left her older, and harder, and less likely to hook—well, to hook a millionaire. She had met Cecil Thorold at the dance of the previous week, and had clung to him so artfully that the coteries talked of it for three days, as Cecil well knew. And to-night he thought he might, as well as not, give Mrs. Macalister an hour's excitement of the chase, and the coteries another three days' employment.

So he sat down beside her, and they talked.

First she asked him whether he slept on his yacht or in the hotel; and he replied, sometimes in the hotel and sometimes on the yacht. Then she asked him where his bedroom was, and he said it was on the second floor, and she settled that it must be three doors from her own. Then they discussed bridge, the Fiscal Inquiry, the weather, dancing, food, the responsibilities of great wealth, Algerian railway-travelling, Cannes, gambling, Mr. Morley's "Life of Gladstone," and the extraordinary success of the hotel. Thus, quite inevitably, they reached the subject of the Algiers Mystery. During the Season, at any rate, no two guests in the hotel ever talked small-talk for more than ten minutes without reaching the subject of the Algiers Mystery.

For the hotel had itself been the scene of the Algiers Mystery, and the Algiers Mystery was at once the simplest, the most charming, and the most perplexing mystery in the world. One morning, the first of April in the previous year, an honest John Bull of a guest had come down to the hotel-office, and laying a five-pound note before the head clerk, had exclaimed: "I found that lying on my dressing-table. It isn't mine. It looks good enough, but I expect it's someone's joke." Seven other people that day confessed that they had found five-pound notes in their rooms, or pieces of paper that resembled five-pound notes. They compared these notes, and then the eight went off in a body down to an agency in the Boulevard de la République, and without the least demur the notes were changed for gold. On the second of April, twelve more people found five-pound notes in their rooms, now prominent on the bed, now secreted—as, for instance, under a candlestick. Cecil himself had been a recipient. Watches were set, but with no result whatever. In a week nearly seven hundred pounds had been distributed amongst the guests by the generous, invisible ghosts. It was magnificent, and it was very soon in every newspaper in England and America. Some of the guests did not "care" for it;

thought it "queer," and "uncanny," and not "nice," and these left. But the majority cared for it very much indeed, and remained till the utmost limit of the Season.

The rainfall of notes had not recommenced, so far, in the present Season. Nevertheless, the hotel had been thoroughly well patronised from November onwards, and there was scarcely a guest but who went to sleep at night hoping to descry a fiver in the morning.

"Advertisement!" said some perspicacious individuals. Of course, the explanation was an obvious one. But the manager had indignantly and honestly denied all knowledge of the business, and, moreover, not a single guest had caught a single note in the act of settling down. Further, the hotel changed hands and the manager left. The mystery, therefore, remained, a delightful topic always at hand for discussion.

After having chatted, Cecil Thorold and Mrs. Macalister danced—two dances. And the hotel began audibly to wonder that Cecil could be such a fool. When, at midnight, he retired to bed, many mothers of daughters and daughters of mothers were justifiably angry, and consoled themselves by saying that he had disappeared in order to hide the shame which must have suddenly overtaken him. As for Mrs. Macalister, she was radiant.

Safely in his room, Cecil locked and wedged the door, and opened the window and looked out from the balcony at the starry night. He could hear cats playing on the roof. He smiled when he thought of the things that Mrs. Macalister had said, and of the ardour of her glances. Then he felt sorry for her. Perhaps it was the whisky-and-soda which he had just drunk that momentarily warmed his heart towards the lonely creature. Only one item of her artless gossip had interested him—a statement that the new Italian manager had been ill in bed all day.

He emptied his pockets, and standing on a chair, he put his pocket-book on the top of the wardrobe, where no Algerian marauder would think of looking for it; his revolver he tucked under his pillow. In three minutes he was asleep.

III.

He was awakened by a vigorous pulling and shaking of his arm; and he, who usually woke wide at the least noise, came to his senses with difficulty. He looked up. The electric light had been turned on.

"There's a ghost in my room, Mr. Thorold! You'll forgive me—but I'm so—"

It was Mrs. Macalister, dishevelled and in white, who stood over him.

"This is really a bit too stiff," he thought vaguely and sleepily, regretting his impulsive flirtation of the previous evening. Then he collected himself and said sternly, severely, that if Mrs. Macalister would retire to the corridor, he would follow in a moment; he added that she might leave the door open if she felt afraid. Mrs. Macalister retired, sobbing, and Cecil arose. He went first to consult his watch; it was gone—a chronometer worth a couple of hundred pounds. He whistled, climbed on to a chair, and discovered that his pocket-book was no longer in a place of safety on the top of the wardrobe; it had contained something over five hundred pounds in a highly negotiable form. Picking up his overcoat, which lay on the floor, he found that the fur lining—a millionaire's fancy, which had cost him nearly a hundred and fifty pounds—had been cut away, and was no more to be seen. Even the revolver had departed from under his pillow!

"Well!" he murmured, "this is decidedly the grand manner."

Quite suddenly it occurred to him, as he noticed a peculiar taste in his mouth, that the whisky-and-soda had contained more than whisky-and-soda—he had been drugged! He tried to recall the face of the waiter who had served him. Eyeing the window and the door, he argued that the thief had entered by the former and departed by the latter. "But the pocket-book!" he mused. "I must have been watched!"

Mrs. Macalister, stripped now of all dash and all daring, could be heard in the corridor.

"Can she——?" He speculated for a moment, and then decided positively in the negative. Mrs. Macalister could have no design on anything but a bachelor's freedom.

He assumed his dressing-gown and slippers and went to her. The corridor was in darkness, but she stood in the light of his doorway.

"Now," he said, "this ghost of yours, dear lady!"

"You must go first," she whimpered. "I daren't. It was white . . . . but with a black face. It was at the window."

Cecil, getting a candle, obeyed. And having penetrated alone into the lady's chamber, he perceived, to begin with, that a pane had been pushed out of the window by the old, noiseless device of a sheet of

"Cecil and Mrs. Macalister danced."

someone with more appetite than a ghost that you saw. Perhaps an Arab."

She came in, femininely trusting to him; and between them they ascertained that she had lost a watch, sixteen rings, an opal necklace, and some money. Mrs. Macalister would not say how much money. "My resources are slight," she remarked. "I was expecting remittances."

Cecil thought: "This is not merely in the grand manner. If it fulfils its promise, it will prove to be one of the greatest things of the age."

He asked her to keep cool, not to be afraid, and to dress herself. Then he returned to his room

treacled paper, and then, examining the window more closely, he saw that, outside, a silk ladder depended from the roof and trailed in the balcony.

"Come in without fear," he said to the trembling widow. "It must have been

and dressed as quickly as he could. The hotel was absolutely quiet, but out of the depths below came the sound of a clock striking four. When, adequately but not æsthetically attired, he opened his door again, another door near by also opened, and Cecil saw a man's head.

"I say," drawled the man's head, "excuse me, but have *you* noticed anything?"

"Why? What?"

"Well, I've been robbed!"

The Englishman laughed awkwardly, apologetically, as though ashamed to have to confess that he had been victimised.

"Much?" Cecil inquired.

"Two hundred or so. No joke, you know."

"So have I been robbed," said Cecil. "Let us go downstairs. Got a candle? These corridors are usually lighted all night."

"Perhaps our thief has been at the switches," said the Englishman.

"Say our thieves," Cecil corrected.

"You think there was more than one?"

"I think there were more than half a dozen," Cecil replied.

The Englishman was dressed, and the two descended together, candles in hand, forgetting the lone lady. But the lone lady had no intention of being forgotten, and she came after them, almost screaming. They had not reached the ground floor before three other doors had opened and three other victims proclaimed themselves.

Cecil led the way through the splendid saloons, now so ghostly in their elegance, which only three hours before had been the illuminated scene of such polite revelry. Ere he reached the entrance-hall, where a solitary jet was burning, the assistant-concierge (one of those officials who seem never to sleep) advanced towards him, demanding in his broken English what was the matter.

"There have been thieves in the hotel," said Cecil. "Waken the concierge."

From that point, events succeeded each other in a sort of complex rapidity. Mrs. Macalister fainted at the door of the billiard-room and was laid out on a billiard-table, with a white ball between her shoulders. The head concierge was not in his narrow bed in the alcove by the main entrance, and he could not be found. Nor could the Italian manager be found (though he was supposed to be ill in bed), nor the Italian manager's wife. Two stablemen were searched out from somewhere; also a cook. And then the Englishman who had lost two hundred or so went forth into the Algerian night to bring a gendarme from the post in the Rue d'Isly.

Cecil Thorold contented himself with talking to people as, in ones and twos, and in various stages of incorrectness, they came into the public rooms, now brilliantly lighted. All who came had been robbed. What surprised him was the slowness of the hotel to wake up. There were two hundred and twenty guests in the place. Of these, in a quarter of an hour, perhaps fifteen had risen. The remainder were apparently oblivious of the fact that something very extraordinary, and something probably very interesting to them personally, had occurred and was occurring.

"Why! It's a conspiracy, sir. It's a conspiracy, that's what it is!" decided the Indian judge.

"Gang is a shorter word," Cecil observed, and a young girl in a macintosh giggled.

Sleepy *employés* now began to appear, and the rumour ran that six waiters and a chambermaid were missing. Mrs. Macalister rallied from the billiard-table and came into the drawing-room, where most of the company had gathered. Cecil yawned (the influence of the drug was still upon him) as she approached him and weakly spoke. He answered absently; he was engaged in watching the demeanour of these idlers on the face of the earth—how incapable they seemed of any initiative, and yet with what magnificent Britannic phlegm they endured the strange situation! The talking was neither loud nor impassioned.

Then the low, distant sound of a cannon was heard. Once, twice, thrice.

Silence ensued.

"Heavens!" sighed Mrs. Macalister, swaying towards Cecil. "What can that be?"

He avoided her, hurried out of the room, and snatched somebody else's hat from the hat-racks in the hall. But just as he was turning the handle of the main door of the hotel, the Englishman who had lost two hundred or so returned out of the Algerian night with an inspector of police. The latter courteously requested Cecil not to leave the building, as he must open the inquiry (*ouvrir l'enquête*) at once. Cecil was obliged, regretfully, to comply.

The inspector of police then commenced his labours. He telephoned (no one had thought of the telephone) for assistance and asked the Central Bureau to watch the railway station, the port, and the stage-coaches. He acquired the names and addresses of *tout le monde*. He made catalogues of articles. He locked all the servants in the ping-pong-room. He took down narratives, beginning with Cecil's. And while the functionary was engaged with Mrs. Macalister, Cecil quietly but firmly disappeared.

"In various stages of incorrectness, they came into the public rooms."

"The *Claribel* picked up the boat of the *Perroquet Vert.*"

After his departure, the affair loomed larger and larger in mere magnitude, but nothing that came to light altered its leading characteristics. A wholesale robbery had been planned with the most minute care and knowledge, and executed with the most daring skill. Some ten persons—the manager and his wife, a chambermaid, six waiters, and the concierge—seemed to have been concerned in the enterprise, excluding Mrs. Macalister's Arab and no doubt other assistants. (The guests suddenly remembered how superior the concierge and the waiters had been to the ordinary concierge and waiter!) At a quarter past five o'clock, the police had ascertained that a hundred rooms had been entered, and horrified guests were still descending! The occupants of many rooms, however, made no response to a summons to awake. These, it was discovered afterwards, had either, like Cecil, received a sedative unawares, or they had been neatly gagged and bound. In the result, the list of missing valuables comprised nearly two hundred watches, eight hundred rings, a hundred and fifty other articles of jewellery, several thousand pounds' worth of furs, three thousand pounds in coin, and twenty-one thousand pounds in banknotes and other forms of currency. One lady, a doctor's wife, said she had been robbed of eight hundred pounds in Bank of England notes, but her story obtained little credit; other tales of enormous loss, chiefly by women, were also taken with salt. When the dawn began, at about six o'clock, an official examination of the façade of the hotel indicated that nearly every room had been invaded by the balconied window, either from the roof or from the ground. But the stone flags of the terrace, and the beautifully asphalted pathways of the garden disclosed no trace of the plunderers.

"I guess your British habit of sleeping with the window open don't cut much ice to-day, anyhow!" said an American from Indianapolis to the company.

That morning no omnibus from the hotel arrived at the station to catch the six-thirty train which takes two days to ramble to Tunis and to Biskra. And all the liveried porters talked together in excited Swiss-German.

IV.

"My compliments to Captain Black," said Cecil Thorold, "and repeat to him that all I want him to do is to kept her in sight. He needn't overhaul her too much."

"Precisely, sir." Lecky bowed; he was pale.

"And you had better lie down."

"I thank you, sir, but I find a recumbent position inconvenient. Perpetual motion seems more agreeable."

Cecil was back in the large, low room panelled with bird's-eye maple. Below him the power of two thousand horses drove through the nocturnal Mediterranean swell his *Claribel* of a thousand tons. Thirty men were awake and active on board her, and twenty slept in the vast, clean forecastle, with electric lights blazing six inches above their noses. He lit a cigarette, and going to the piano, struck a few chords from "The Orchid"; but since the music would not remain on the stand, he abandoned that attempt and lay down on a divan to think.

He had reached the harbour, from the hotel, in twenty minutes, partly on foot at racing speed, and partly in an Arab cart, also at racing speed. The *Claribel's* launch awaited him, and in another five minutes the launch was slung to her davits, and the *Claribel* under way. He learnt that the small and sinister vessel, the *Perroquet Vert* (of Oran), which he and his men had been watching for several days, had slipped unostentatiously between the southern and eastern jetties, had stopped for a few minutes to hold converse with a boat that had put off from the neighbourhood of Lower Mustapha, and had then pointed her head north-west, as though for some port in the province of Oran or in Morocco.

And in the rings of cigarette-smoke which he made, Cecil seemed now to see clearly the whole business. He had never relaxed his interest in the affair of the five-pound notes. He had vaguely suspected it to be part of some large scheme; he had presumed, on slight grounds, a connection between the *Perroquet Vert* and the Italian manager of the hotel. Nay, more, he had felt sure that some great stroke was about to be accomplished. But of precise knowledge, of satisfactory theory, of definite expectation, he had had none—until Mrs. Macalister, that unconscious and man-hunting agent of Destiny, had fortunately wakened him in the nick of time. Had it not been for his flirtation of the previous evening, he might still be asleep in his bed at the hotel . . . . He perceived the entire plan. The five-pound notes had been mysteriously scattered, certainly to advertise the hotel, but only to advertise it for a particular and colossal end, to fill it full and overflowing with fat victims. The situation had been thoroughly studied in all its details, and the task had been divided and allotted to various brains. Every room must have been examined, watched, and separately plotted against; the habits and idiosyncrasy of every victim must have been individually weighed and considered. Nothing, no trifle, could have been forgotten. And then some supreme intelligence had drawn the threads together and woven them swiftly into the pattern of a single night, almost a single hour! . . . . And the loot (Cecil could estimate it pretty accurately) had been transported down the hill to Mustapha Inférieure, tossed into a boat, and so to the *Perroquet Vert*. And the *Perroquet Vert*, with loot and looters on board, was bound, probably, for one of those obscure and infamous ports of Oran or Morocco—Tenez, Mostaganem, Beni Sar, Melilla, or the city of Oran, or Tangier itself! He knew something of the Spanish and Maltese dens of Oran and Tangier, the clearing-houses for stolen goods of two continents, and the impregnable refuge of scores of ingenious villains.

And when he reflected upon the grandeur and immensity of the scheme, so simple in its essence, and so leisurely in its achievement, like most grand schemes; when he reflected upon the imagination which had been necessary even to conceive it, and the generalship which had been necessary to its successful conclusion, he murmured admiringly—

"The man who thought of that and did it may be a scoundrel; but he is also an artist, and a great one!"

And just because he, Cecil Thorold, was a millionaire, and possessed a hundred-thousand-pound toy, which could do nineteen knots an hour, and cost fifteen hundred pounds a month to run, he was about to defeat that great artist and nullify that great scheme, and incidentally to retrieve his watch, his revolver, his fur, and his five hundred pounds. He had only to follow, and to warn one of the French torpedo-boats which are always patrolling the coast between Algiers and Oran, and the bubble would burst!

He sighed for the doomed artist; and he wondered what that victimised crowd of European loungers, who lounged sadly round the Mediterranean in winter, and sadly round northern Europe in summer, had done in their languid and luxurious lives that they should be saved, after all, from the pillage to which the great artist in theft had subjected them!

Then Lecky re-entered the state-room.

"We shall have a difficulty in keeping the *Perroquet Vert* in sight, sir."

"What!" exclaimed Cecil. "That tub! That coffin! You don't mean she can do twenty knots?"

"Exactly, sir. Coffin! It—I mean she—is sinking."

Cecil ran on deck. Dawn was breaking over Matifou, and a faint, cold, grey light touched here and there the heaving sea. His captain spoke and pointed. Ahead, right ahead, less than a mile away, the *Perroquet Vert* was sinking by the stern, and even as they gazed at her, a little boat detached itself from her side in the haze of the morning mist; and she sank, disappeared, vanished amid a cloud of escaping steam. They were four miles north-east of Cape Caxine. Two miles further westward, a big Dominion liner, bound direct for Algiers from the New World, was approaching and had observed the catastrophe — for she altered her course. In a few minutes, the *Claribel* picked up the boat of the *Perroquet Vert*. It contained three Arabs.

V.

THE tale told by the Arabs (two of them were brothers, and all three came from Oran) fully sustained Cecil Thorold's theory of the spoliation of the hotel. Naturally they pretended at first to an entire innocence concerning the schemes of those who had charge of the *Perroquet Vert*. The two brothers, who were black with coal-dust when rescued, swore that they had been physically forced to work in the stokehold; but ultimately all three had to admit a knowledge of things which was decidedly incriminating, and all three got three years' imprisonment. The only part of the Algiers mystery which remained a mystery was the cause of the sinking of the *Perroquet Vert*. Whether she was thoroughly unseaworthy (she had been picked up cheap at Melilla), or whether someone (not on board) had deliberately arranged her destruction, perhaps to satisfy a Moorish vengeance, was not ascertained. The three Arabs could only be persuaded to say that there had been eleven Europeans and seven natives on the ship, and that they alone, by the mercy of Allah, had escaped from the swift catastrophe.

The hotel underwent an acute crisis, from which, however, it is emerging. For over a week a number of the pillaged guests discussed a diving enterprise of salvage. But the estimates were too high, and it came to nothing. So they all, Cecil included, began to get used to the idea of possessing irrecoverable property to the value of forty thousand pounds in the Mediterranean. A superb business in telegraphed remittances was done for several days. The fifteen beings who had accompanied the *Perroquet Vert* to the bottom were scarcely thought of, for it was almost universally agreed that the way of transgressors is and ought to be hard.

As for Cecil Thorold, the adventure, at first so full of the promise of joy, left him melancholy, until an unexpected sequel diverted the channel of his thoughts.

THE LOOT OF CITIES:

THE ADVENTURES OF A MILLIONAIRE IN SEARCH OF JOY.

By ARNOLD BENNETT

No. V.—IN THE CAPITAL OF THE SAHARA.

MRS. MACALISTER turned with sudden eagerness and alarm towards Cecil Thorold—the crowd on the lawn in front of the railings was so dense that only heads could be moved—and she said excitedly—

"I'm sure I can see my ghost across there!"

She indicated with her agreeable snub nose the opposite side of the course.

"Your ghost?" Cecil questioned, puzzled for a moment by this extraordinary remark.

Then the Arab horsemen swept by in a cloud of dust and of thunder, and monopolised the attention of the lawn and the grand-stand, and the *élite* of Biskra crammed thereon and therein. They had one more lap to accomplish for the Prix de la Ville.

Biskra is an oasis in the desert, and the capital of the Algerian Sahara. Two days' journey by train from Algiers, over the Djujura Ranges, it is the last outpost of the Algerian State Railways. It has a hundred and sixty thousand palm-trees; but the first symptom of Biskra to be observed from the approaching first-class carriage is the chimney of the electric-light plant. Besides the hundred and sixty thousand palm-trees, it possesses half-a-dozen large hotels, five native villages, a fort, huge barracks, a very ornamental town-hall, shops for photographic materials, a whole street of dancing-girls, the finest winter climate in all Africa, and a gambling Casino. It is a unique thing in oases. It completely upsets the conventional idea of an oasis as a pool of water bordered with a few date-palms, and the limitless desert all round! Nevertheless, though Biskra as much resembles Paris as it resembles the conventional idea of an oasis, it is genuine enough, and the limitless desert is, in fact, all around. You may walk out into the desert and meet a motor-car manœuvring in the sand; but the sand remains the sand, and the desert remains the desert, and the Sahara, more majestic than the sea itself, refuses to be cheapened by the pneumatic tyres of a Mercedes, or the blue rays of the electric light, or the feet of English, French, and Germans wandering in search of novelty—it persists in being august.

Once a year, in February, Biskra becomes really and excessively excited, and the occasion is its annual two-day race-meeting. Then the tribes and their chieftains and their horses and their camels arrive magically out of the four corners of the desert and fill the oasis. And the English, French, and Germans arrive from the Mediterranean coast, with their trunks and their civilisation, and crowd the hotels till beds in Biskra are precious beyond rubies. And under the tropical sun, East and West meet magnificently in the afternoon on the racecourse to the north of the European reserve. And the tribesmen, their scraggy steeds trailing superb horsecloths, are arranged in hundreds behind the motor-cars and landaus, with the *pari-mutuel* in full-swing twenty yards away. And the dancing-girls, the renowned Ouled-Nails, covered with gold coins and with muslin in high, crude, violent purples, greens, vermilions, shriek and whinny on their benches just opposite the grand-stand, where the Western women, arrayed in the toilettes of Worth, Doucet, and Redfern, quiz them through their glasses. And fringing all is a crowd of the adventurers and rascals of two continents, the dark and the light. And in the background the palms wave eternally in the breeze. And to the east the Aurès mountains, snow-capped, rise in hues of saffron and pale rose, like stage-mountains, against the sapphire sky. And to the south a line of telegraph-poles lessens and disappears over the verge into the inmost heart of the mysterious and unchangeable Sahara.

It was amid this singular scene that Mrs. Macalister made to Cecil Thorold her bizarre remark about a ghost.

"What ghost?" the millionaire repeated, when the horsemen had passed.

Then he remembered that on the famous night, now nearly a month ago, when the hotel at Algiers was literally sacked by an organised band of depredators, and valuables to the tune of forty thousand pounds disappeared, Mrs. Macalister had given the first alarm by crying out that there was a ghost in her room.

"Ah!" He smiled easily, condescendingly, to this pertinacious widow, who had been pursuing him, so fruitlessly, for four mortal weeks, from Algiers to Tunis, from Tunis back to Constantine, and from Constantine here to Biskra. "All Arabs look more or less alike, you know."

"But——"

"Yes," he said again. "They all look alike, to us, like Chinamen."

Considering that he himself, from his own yacht, had witnessed the total loss in the Mediterranean of the vessel which contained the plunder and the fleeing band of thieves; considering that his own yacht had rescued the only three survivors of that shipwreck, and that these survivors had made a full confession, and had, only two days since, been duly sentenced by the criminal court at Algiers—he did not feel inclined to minister to Mrs. Macalister's feminine fancies.

"Did you ever see an Arab with a mole on his chin?" asked Mrs. Macalister.

"No, I never did."

"Well, my Arab had a mole on his chin, and that is why I am sure it was he that I saw a minute ago—over there. No, he's gone now!"

The competing horsemen appeared round the bend for the last time, the dancing-girls whinnied in their high treble, the crowd roared, and the Prix de la Ville was won and lost. It was the final race on the card, and in the *mêlée* which followed, Cecil became separated from his adorer. She was to depart on the morrow by the six a.m. train. "Urgent business," she said. She had given up the chase of the millionaire. "Perhaps she's out of funds, poor thing!" he reflected. "Anyhow, I hope I may never see her again." As a matter of fact, he never did see her again. She passed out of his life as casually as she had come into it.

He strolled slowly towards the hotel through the perturbed crowd of Arabs, Europeans, carriages, camels, horses, and motor-cars. The mounted tribesmen were in a state of intense excitement, and were continually burning powder in that mad fashion which seems to afford a peculiar joy to the Arab soul. From time to time a tribesman would break out of the ranks of his clan, and, spurring his horse and dropping the reins on the animal's neck, would fire revolvers from both hands as he flew over the rough ground. It was unrivalled horsemanship, and Cecil admired immensely the manner in which, at the end of the frenzied performance, these men, drunk with powder, would wheel their horses sharply while at full gallop, and stop dead.

And then, as one man, who had passed him like a hurricane, turned, paused, and jogged back to his tribe, Cecil saw that he had a mole on his chin. He stood still to watch the splendid fellow, and he noticed something far more important than the mole—he perceived that the revolver in the man's right hand had a chased butt.

"I can't swear to it," Cecil mused. "But if that isn't my revolver, stolen from under my pillow at the hotel at Algiers, on the tenth of January last, my name is Norval, and not Thorold."

And the whole edifice of his ideas concerning the robbery at the hotel began to shake.

"That revolver ought to be at the bottom of the Mediterranean," he said to himself; "and so ought Mrs. Macalister's man with the mole, according to the accepted theory of the crime and the story of the survivors of the shipwreck of the *Perroquet Vert*."

He walked on, keeping the man in sight.

"Suppose," he murmured—"suppose all that stuff isn't at the bottom of the Mediterranean, after all?"

A hundred yards further on, he happened to meet one of the white-clad native guides attached to the Royal Hotel, where he had lunched. The guide saluted and offered service, as all the Biskra guides do on all occasions. Cecil's reply was to point out the man with the mole.

"You see him, Mahomet," said Cecil. "Make no mistake. Find out what tribe he belongs to, where he comes from, and where he sleeps in Biskra, and I will give you a sovereign. Meet me at the Casino to-night at ten."

Mahomet grinned an honest grin and promised to earn the sovereign.

Cecil stopped an empty landau and drove hurriedly to the station to meet the afternoon train from civilisation. He had arrived

"He perceived that the revolver in the man's right hand had a chased butt."

in Biskra that morning by road from El Kantara, and Lecky was coming by the afternoon train with the luggage. On seeing him, he gave that invaluable factotum some surprising orders.

In addition to Lecky, the millionaire observed among the passengers descending from the train two other people who were known to him; but he carefully hid himself from these ladies. In three minutes he had disappeared into the nocturnal whirl and uproar of Biskra, solely bent on proving or disproving the truth of a brand-new theory concerning the historic sack of the Algiers hotel.

But that night he waited in vain for Mahomet at the packed Casino, where the Arab chieftains and the English gentlemen, alike in their tremendous calm, were losing money at *petits chevaux* with all the imperturbability of stone statutes.

II.

NOR did Cecil see anything of Mahomet during the next day, and he had reasons for not making inquiries about him at the Royal Hotel. But at night, as he was crossing the deserted market, Mahomet came up to him suddenly out of nowhere, and, grinning the eternal, honest, foolish grin, said in his odd English—

"I have found—him."

"Where?"

"Come," said Mahomet mysteriously. The Eastern guide loves to be mysterious.

Cecil followed him far down the carnivalesque street of the Ouled-Nails, where tom-toms and nameless instruments of music sounded from every other house, and the *premières danseuses* of the Sahara showed themselves gorgeously behind grilles, like beautiful animals in cages. Then Mahomet entered a crowded *café*, passed through it, and pushing aside a suspended mat at the other end, bade Cecil proceed further. Cecil touched his revolver (his new revolver), to make sure of its company, and proceeded further. He found himself in a low Oriental room, lighted by an odorous English lamp with a circular wick, and furnished with a fine carpet and two bedroom chairs certainly made in Curtain Road, Shoreditch—a room characteristic of Biskra. On one chair sat a man. But this person was not Mrs. Macalister's man with a mole. He was obviously a Frenchman, by his dress, gestures, and speech. He greeted the millionaire in French and then dropped into English—excellently grammatical and often idiomatic English, spoken with a strong French accent. He was rather a little man, thin, grey, and vivacious.

"Give yourself the pain of sitting down," said the Frenchman. "I am glad to see you. You may be able to help us."

"You have the advantage of me," Cecil replied, smiling.

"Perhaps," said the Frenchman. "You came to Biskra yesterday, Mr. Thorold, with the intention of staying at the Royal Hotel, where rooms were engaged for you. But yesterday afternoon you went to the station to meet your servant, and you ordered him to return to Constantine with your luggage and to await your instructions there. You then took a handbag and went to the Casino Hotel, and you managed, by means of diplomacy and of money, to get a bed in the *salle à manger*. It was all they could do for you. You gave the name of Collins. Biskra, therefore, is not officially aware of the presence of Mr. Cecil Thorold, the millionaire; while Mr. Collins is free to carry on his researches, to appear and to disappear as it pleases him."

"Yes," Cecil remarked. "You have got that fairly right. But may I ask——"

"Let us come to business at once," said the Frenchman, politely interrupting him. "Is this your watch?"

He dramatically pulled a watch and chain from his pocket.

"It is," said Cecil quietly. He refrained from embroidering the affirmative with exclamations. "It was stolen from my bedroom at Algiers, with my revolver, some fur, and a quantity of money, on the tenth of January."

"You are surprised to find that it is not sunk in the Mediterranean?"

"Thirty hours ago I should have been surprised," said Cecil. "Now I am not."

"And why not now?"

"Because I have formed a new theory. But have the goodness to give me the watch."

"I cannot," said the Frenchman graciously—"not at present."

There was a pause. The sound of music was heard from the *café*.

"But, my dear sir, I insist." Cecil spoke positively.

The Frenchman laughed. "I will be perfectly frank with you, Mr. Thorold. Your cleverness in forming a new theory of the great robbery merits all my candour. My name is Sylvain, and I am head of the detective-force of Algiers—*Chef de la Sureté*. You will perceive that I cannot part with

"'Is this your watch?'"

the watch without proper formalities. Mr. Thorold, the robbery at the hotel was a work of the highest criminal art. Possibly I had better tell you the nature of our recent discoveries."

"I always thought well of the robbery," Cecil observed, "and my opinion of it is rising. Pray continue."

"According to your new theory, Mr. Thorold, how many persons were on board the *Perroquet Vert* when she began to sink?"

"Three," said Cecil promptly, as though answering a conundrum.

The Frenchman beamed. "You are admirable," he exclaimed. "Yes, instead of eighteen, there were three. The wreck of the *Perroquet Vert* was carefully prearranged; the visit of the boat to the *Perroquet Vert* off Mustapha Inférieure was what you call, I believe, a 'plant.' The stolen goods never left dry land. There were three Arabs only on the *Perroquet Vert*—one to steer her, and the other two in the engine-room. And these three were very careful to get themselves saved. They scuttled their ship in sight of your yacht and of another vessel. There is no doubt, Mr. Thorold," the Frenchman smiled with a hint of irony, "that the thieves were fully *au courant* with your doings on the *Claribel*. The shipwreck was done deliberately, with you and your yacht for an audience. It was a masterly stroke," he proceeded almost enthusiastically, "for it had the effect, not merely of drawing away suspicion from the true direction, but of putting an end to all further inquiries. Were not the goods at the bottom of the sea, and the thieves drowned? What motive could the police have for further activity? In six months—nay, three months—all the notes and securities could be safely negotiated, because no measures would have to be taken to stop them. Why take measures to stop notes that are at the bottom of the sea?"

"But the three survivors who are now in prison," Cecil said. "Their behaviour, their lying, needs some accounting for."

"Quite simple," the Frenchman went on. "They are in prison for three years. What is that to an Arab? He will suffer it with stoicism. Say that ten thousand francs are deposited with each of their families. When they come out, they are rich for life. At a cost of thirty thousand francs and the price of the ship—say another thirty thousand—the thieves reasonably expected to obtain absolute security."

"It was a heroic idea!" said Cecil.

"It was," said the Frenchman. "But it has failed."

"Evidently. But why?"

"Can you ask? You know as well as I do! It has failed, partly because there were too many persons in the secret, partly because of the Arab love of display on great occasions, and partly because of a mole on a man's chin."

"By the way, that was the man I came here to see," Cecil remarked.

"He is arrested," said the Frenchman curtly, and then he sighed. "The booty was not guarded with sufficient restrictions. It was not kept in bulk. One thief probably said: 'I cannot do without this lovely watch.' And another said: 'What a revolver! I must have it.' Ah! The Arab, the Arab! The Europeans ought to have provided for that. That is where they were foolish—the idiots! The idiots!" he repeated angrily.

"You seem annoyed."

"Mr. Thorold, I am a poet in these things. It annoys me to see a fine composition ruined by bad construction in the fifth act. . . . . However, as Chief of the Surety, I rejoice."

"You have located the thieves and the plunder?"

"I think I have. Certainly I have captured two of the thieves and several articles. The bulk lies at——" He stopped and looked round. "Mr. Thorold, may I rely on you? I know, perhaps, more than you think of your powers. May I rely on you?"

"You may," said Cecil.

"You will hold yourself at my disposition during to-morrow, to assist me?"

"With pleasure."

"Then let us take coffee. In the morning, I shall have acquired certain precise information which at the moment I lack. Let us take coffee."

III.

On the following morning, somewhat early, while walking near Mecid, one of the tiny outlying villages of the oasis, Cecil met Eve Fincastle and Kitty Sartorius, whom he had not spoken with since the affair of the bracelet at Bruges, though he had heard from them and had, indeed, seen them at the station two days before. Eve Fincastle had fallen rather seriously ill at Mentone, and the holiday of the two girls, which should have finished before the end of the year, was prolonged. Financially, the enforced leisure was a matter of trifling importance to Kitty Sartorius, who had insisted on remaining with her friend, much to the disgust of her London manager. But the journalist's resources were less royal, and Eve considered herself fortunate that she had obtained from her newspaper some special descriptive correspondence in Algeria. It was this commission which had brought her, and Kitty with her, in the natural course of an Algerian tour, to Biskra.

Cecil was charmed to see his acquaintances; for Eve interested him, and Kitty's beauty (it goes without saying) dazzled him. Nevertheless, he had been, as it were, hiding himself, and, in his character as an amateur of the loot of cities, he would have preferred to have met them on some morning other than that particular morning.

"You will go with us to Sidi Okba, won't you, to-day?" said Kitty, after they had talked a while. "We've secured a carriage, and I'm dying for a drive in the real, true desert."

"Sorry I can't," said Cecil.

"Oh, but——" Eve Fincastle began, and stopped.

"Of course you can," said Kitty imperiously. "You must. We leave to-morrow—we're only here for two days—for Algiers and France. Another two days in Paris, and then London, my darling London, and work! So it's understood?"

"It desolates me," said Cecil. "But I can't go with you to Sidi Okba to-day."

They both saw that he meant to refuse them.

"That settles it, then," Eve agreed quietly.

"You're horrid, Mr. Thorold," said the bewitching actress. "And if you imagine for a single moment we haven't seen that you've been keeping out of our way, you're mistaken. You must have noticed us at the station. Eve thinks you've got another of your——"

"No, I don't, Kitty," said Eve quickly.

"If Miss Fincastle suspects that I've got another of my——" he paused humorously, "Miss Fincastle is right. I *have* got another of my—— I throw myself on your magnanimity. I am staying in Biskra under the name of Collins, and my time, like my name, is not my own."

"In that case," Eve remarked, "we will pass on."

And they shook hands, with a certain frigidity on the part of the two girls.

During the morning, M. Sylvain made no sign, and Cecil lunched in solitude at the Dar Eef, adjoining the Casino. The races being over, streams of natives, with their tents and their quadrupeds, were leaving Biskra for the desert; they made an interminable procession which could be seen from the window of the Dar Eef coffee-room. Cecil was idly watching this procession, when a hand touched his shoulder. He turned and saw a gendarme.

"Monsieur Collang?" questioned the gendarme.

Cecil assented.

"*Voulez-vous avoir l'obligeance de me suivre, monsieur?*"

Cecil obediently followed, and found in

"Drew another revolver from his own pocket and winked."

the street M. Sylvain, well wrapped up, and seated in an open carriage.

"I have need of you," said M. Sylvain. "Can you come at once?"

"Certainly."

In two minutes they were driving away together into the desert.

"Our destination is Sidi Okba," said M. Sylvain. "A curious place."

The road (so called) led across the Biskra River (so called), and then in a straight line eastwards. The river had about the depth of a dinner-plate. As for the road, in some parts it not merely failed to be a road—it was nothing but virgin desert, intact: at its best it was a heaving and treacherous mixture of sand and pebbles, through which, and not over which, the two unhappy horses had to drag M. Sylvain's unfortunate open carriage.

M. Sylvain himself drove.

"I am well acquainted with this part of the desert," he said. "We have strange cases sometimes. And when I am on important business, I never trust an Arab. By the way, you have a revolver? I do not anticipate danger, but——"

"I have one," said Cecil.

"And it is loaded?"

Cecil took the weapon from his hip pocket and examined it.

"It is loaded," he said.

"Good!" exclaimed the Frenchman, and then he turned to the gendarme, who was sitting as impassively as the leaps and bounds of the carriage would allow, on a small seat immediately behind the other two, and demanded of him in French whether his revolver also was loaded. The man gave a respectful affirmative. "Good!" exclaimed M. Sylvain again, and launched into a description of the wondrous gardens of the Comte Landon, whose walls, on the confines of the oasis, they were just passing.

Straight in front could be seen a short line of palm-trees, waving in the desert breeze under the desert sun, and Cecil asked what they were.

"Sidi Okba," replied M. Sylvain. "The hundred and eighty thousand palms of the desert city of Sidi Okba. They seem near to you, no doubt, but we shall travel twenty kilometres before we reach them. The effect of nearness is due to the singular quality of the atmosphere. It is a two hours' journey."

"Then do we return in the dark?" Cecil inquired.

"If we are lucky, we may return at once, and arrive in Biskra at dusk. If not—well, we shall spend the night in Sidi Okba. You object?"

"Not at all."

"A curious place," observed M. Sylvain.

Soon they had left behind all trace of the oasis, and were in the "real, true desert." They met and passed native equipages and strings of camels, and from time to time on either hand at short distances from the road could be seen the encampments of wandering tribes. And after interminable joltings, in which M. Sylvain, his guest, and his gendarme were frequently hurled at each other's heads with excessive violence, the short line of palm-trees began to seem a little nearer and to occupy a little more of the horizon. And then they could descry the wall of the city. And at last they reached its gate and the beggars squatting within its gate.

"Cecil snatched at the revolver."

"Descend!" M. Sylvain ordered his subordinate.

The man disappeared, and M. Sylvain and Cecil drove into the city; they met several carriages of Biskra visitors just setting forth on the return journey.

In insisting that Sidi Okba was a curious place, M. Sylvain did not exaggerate. It is an Eastern town of the most antique sort, built solely of mud, with the simplicity, the foulness, the smells, and the avowed and the secret horrors which might be expected in a community which has not altered its habits in any particular for a thousand years. During several months of each year it is visited daily by Europeans (its mosque is the oldest Mohammedan building in Africa, therefore no respectable tourist dares to miss it), and yet it remains absolutely uninfluenced by European notions. The European person must take his food with him; he is allowed to eat it in the garden of a *café* which is European as far as its sign and its counter, but no further; he could not eat it in the *café* itself. This *café* is the mark which civilisation has succeeded in making on Sidi Okba in ten centuries.

As Cecil drove with M. Sylvain through the narrow, winding street, he acutely felt the East closing in upon him; and, since the sun was getting low over the palm-trees, he was glad to have the detective by his side.

They arrived at the wretched *café*. A pair-horse vehicle, with the horses' heads towards Biskra, was waiting at the door. Unspeakable lanes, fetid, winding, sinister, and strangely peopled, led away in several directions.

M. Sylvain glanced about him.

"We shall succeed," he murmured cheerfully. "Follow me."

And they went into the mark of civilisation, and saw the counter, and a female creature behind the bar, and, through another door, a glimpse of the garden beyond.

"Follow me," murmured M. Sylvain again, opening another door to the left into a dark passage. "Straight on. There is a room at the other end."

They vanished.

In a few seconds M. Sylvain returned into the *café*.

IV.

Now, in the garden were Eve Fincastle and Kitty Sartorius, tying up some wraps preparatory to their departure for Biskra. They caught sight of Cecil Thorold and his companion entering the *café*, and they were surprised to find the millionaire in Sidi Okba after his refusal to accompany them.

Through the back door of the *café* they saw Cecil's companion reappear out of the passage. They saw the creature behind the counter stoop and produce a revolver and then offer it to the Frenchman with a furtive movement. They saw that the Frenchman declined it, and drew another revolver from his own pocket and winked. And the character of the wink given by the Frenchman to the woman made them turn pale under the sudden, knifelike thrust of an awful suspicion.

The Frenchman looked up and perceived the girls in the garden, and one glance at Kitty's beauty was not enough for him.

"Can you keep him here a minute while I warn Mr. Thorold?" said Eve quickly.

Kitty Sartorius nodded and began to smile on the Frenchman; she then lifted her finger beckoningly. If millions had depended on his refusal, it is doubtful whether he would have resisted that charming gesture. (Not for nothing did Kitty Sartorius receive a hundred a week at the Regency Theatre.) In a moment the Frenchman was talking to her, and she had enveloped him in a golden mist of enchantment.

Guided by a profound instinct, Eve ran up the passage and into the room where Cecil was awaiting the return of his M. Sylvain.

"Come out!" she whispered passionately, as if between violent anger and dreadful alarm. "You are trapped—you, with your schemes!"

"Trapped!" he exclaimed, smiling. "Not at all. I have my revolver!" His hand touched his pocket. "By Jove! I haven't! It's gone!"

The miraculous change in his face was of the highest interest.

"Come out!" she cried. "Our carriage is waiting!"

In the *café*, Kitty Sartorius was talking to the Frenchman. She stroked his sleeve with her gloved hand, and he, the Frenchman, still held the revolver which he had displayed to the woman of the counter.

Inspired by the consummate and swiftly aroused emotion of that moment, Cecil snatched at the revolver. The three friends walked hastily to the street, jumped into the carriage, and drove away. Already, as they approached the city gate, they could see the white tower of the Royal Hotel at Biskra shining across the desert like a promise of security. . . .

The whole episode had lasted perhaps two minutes, but they were minutes of such intense and blinding revelation as Cecil had never before experienced. He sighed with relief as he lay back in the carriage.

"And that's the man," he meditated, astounded, "who must have planned the robbery at the hotel! And I never suspected it! I never suspected that his gendarme was a sham! I wonder whether his murder of me would have been as leisurely and artistic as his method of trapping me! I wonder! . . . Well, this time I have certainly enjoyed myself."

Then he gazed at Eve Fincastle.

The women said nothing for a long time, and even then the talk was of trifles.

V.

Eve Fincastle had gone up on to the vast, flat roof of the Royal Hotel, and Cecil, knowing that she was there, followed. The sun had just set, and Biskra lay spread out below them in the rich autumn light which already, eastwards, had turned to sapphire. They could still see the line of the palm-trees of Sidi Okba, and in another direction, the long, lonely road to Figuig, stretching across the desert like a rope which had been flung from heaven on the waste of sand. The Aurès mountains were black and jagged. Nearer, immediately under them, was the various life of the great oasis, and the sounds of that life—human speech, the rattle of carriages, the grunts of camels in the camel-enclosure, the whistling of an engine at the station, the melancholy wails of hawkers—ascended softly in the twilight of the Sahara.

Cecil approached her, but she did not turn towards him.

"I want to thank you," he started.

She made no movement, and then suddenly she burst out. "Why do you continue with these shameful plots and schemes?" she demanded, looking always steadily away from him. "Why do you disgrace yourself? Was this another theft, another blackmailing, another affair like that at Ostend? Why——" She stopped, deeply disturbed, unable to control herself.

"My dear journalist," he said quietly, "you don't understand. Let me tell you."

He gave her his history, from the night-summons by Mrs. Macalister to that same afternoon.

She faced him.

"I'm so glad," she murmured. "You can't imagine——"

"I want to thank you for saving my life," he said again.

She began to cry; her body shook; she hid her face.

"But——" he stammered awkwardly.

"It wasn't I who saved your life," she said, sobbing passionately. "I wasn't beautiful enough. Only Kitty could have done it. Only a beautiful woman could have kept that man——"

"I know all about it, my dear girl," Cecil silenced her disavowal. Something moved him to take her hand. She smiled sadly, not resisting. "You must excuse me," she murmured. "I'm not myself to-night . . . It's because of the excitement . . . . Anyhow, I'm glad you haven't taken any 'loot' this time."

"But I have," he protested. (He was surprised to find his voice trembling.)

"What?"

"This." He pressed her hand tenderly.

"That?" She looked at her hand, lying in his, as though she had never seen it before.

"Eve," he whispered.

* * * * *

About two-thirds of the loot of the hotel robbery was ultimately recovered; not at Sidi Okba, but in the cellars of the hotel itself. From first to last that robbery was a masterpiece of audacity. Its originator, the *soi-disant* M. Sylvain, head of the Algiers detective-force, is still at large.

THE LOOT OF CITIES:

THE ADVENTURES OF A MILLIONAIRE IN SEARCH OF JOY.

By ARNOLD BENNETT

VI.—"LO! 'TWAS A GALA NIGHT!"

PARIS. And not merely Paris, but Paris *en fête*, Paris decorated, Paris idle, Paris determined to enjoy itself, and succeeding brilliantly. Venetian masts of red and gold lined the gay pavements of the *grands boulevards* and the Avenue de l'Opéra; and suspended from these in every direction, transverse and lateral, hung garlands of flowers whose petals were of coloured paper, and whose hearts were electric globes that in the evening would burst into flame. The effect of the city's toilette reached the extreme of opulence, for no expense had been spared. Paris was welcoming monarchs, and had spent two million francs in obedience to the maxim that what is worth doing at all is worth doing well.

The Grand Hotel, with its eight hundred rooms full of English and Americans, at the upper end of the Avenue de l'Opéra, looked down at the Grand Hotel du Louvre, with its four hundred rooms full of English and Americans, at the lower end of the Avenue de l'Opéra. These two establishments had the best views in the whole city; and perhaps the finest view of all was that obtainable from a certain second floor window of the Grand Hotel, precisely at the corner of the Boulevard des Capucines and the Rue Auber. From this window one could see the boulevards in both directions, the Opéra, the Place de l'Opéra, the Avenue de l'Opéra, the Rue du Quatre Septembre, and the multitudinous life of these vivid thoroughfares — the glittering *cafés*, the dazzling shops, the painted *kiosks*, the lumbering omnibuses, the gliding trams, the hooting automobiles, the swift and careless cabs, the private carriages, the suicidal bicycles, the newsmen, the toysellers, the touts, the beggars, and all the holiday crowd, sombre men and radiant women, chattering, laughing, bustling, staring, drinking, under the innumerable tricolours and garlands of paper flowers.

That particular view was a millionaire's view, and it happened to be the temporary property of Cecil Thorold, who was enjoying it and the afternoon sun, at the open window, with three companions. Eve Fincastle looked at it with the analytic eye of the journalist, while Kitty Sartorius, as was quite proper for an actress, deemed it a sort of frame for herself, as she leaned over the balcony like a *Juliet* on the stage. The third guest in Cecil's sitting-room was Lionel Belmont, the Napoleonic Anglo-American theatrical manager, in whose crown Kitty herself was the chief star. Mr. Belmont, a big, burly, good-humoured, shrewd man of something over forty, said he had come to Paris on business. But for two days the business had been solely to look after Kitty Sartorius and minister to her caprices. At the present moment his share of the view consisted mainly of Kitty; in the same way Cecil's share of the view consisted mainly of Eve Fincastle; but this at least was right and decorous, for the betrothal of the millionaire and the journalist had been definitely announced. Otherwise Eve would have been back at work in Fleet Street a week ago.

"The gala performance is to-night, isn't it?" said Eve, gazing at the vast and superbly ornamented Opera House.

"Yes," said Cecil.

"What a pity we can't be there! I should so have liked to see the young Queen in evening dress. And they say the interior decorations——"

"Nothing simpler," said Cecil. "If you want to go, dear, let us go."

Kitty Sartorius looked round quickly. "Mr. Belmont has tried to get seats, and can't. Haven't you, Bel? You know the whole audience is invited. The invitations are issued by the Minister of Fine Arts."

"Still, in Paris, anything can be got by paying for it," Cecil insisted.

"My dear young friend," said Lionel Belmont, "I guess if seats were to be had, I should have struck one or two yesterday.

I put no limit on the price, and I reckon I ought to know what theatre prices run to. Over at the Metropolitan in New York I've seen a box change hands at two thousand dollars, for one night."

"Nevertheless——" Cecil began again.

"And the performance starting in six hours from now!" Lionel Belmont exclaimed. "Not much!"

But Cecil persisted.

"Seen the *Herald* to-day?" Belmont questioned. "No? Well, listen. This will interest you." He drew a paper from his pocket and read: "Seats for the Opéra Gala. The traffic in seats for the gala performance at the Opéra during the last Royal Visit to Paris aroused considerable comment and not a little dissatisfaction. Nothing, however, was done, and the traffic in seats for to-night's spectacle, at which the President and their Imperial Majesties will be present, has, it is said, amounted to a scandal. Of course, the offer so suddenly made, five days ago, by Madame Félise and Mademoiselle Malva, the two greatest living dramatic sopranos, to take part in the performance, immediately and enormously intensified interest in the affair, for never yet have these two supreme artists appeared in the same theatre on the same night. No theatre could afford the luxury. Our readers may remember that in our columns and in the columns of the *Figaro* there appeared four days ago an advertisement to the following effect: '*A box, also two orchestra stalls, for the Opéra Gala, to be disposed of, owing to illness. Apply*, 155, *Rue de la Paix*.' We sent four several reporters to answer that advertisement. The first was offered a stage-box for seven thousand five hundred francs, and two orchestra stalls in the second row for twelve hundred and fifty francs. The second was offered a box opposite the stage on the second tier, and two stalls in the seventh row. The third had the chance of four stalls in the back row and a small box just behind them; the fourth was offered something else. The thing was obviously, therefore, a regular agency. Everybody is asking: 'How were these seats obtained? From the Ministry of Fine Arts, or from the *invités?*' Echo answers 'How?' The authorities, however, are stated to have interfered at last and to have put an end to this buying and selling of what should be an honourable distinction."

"Bravo!" said Cecil.

"And that's so!" Belmont remarked, dropping the paper. "I went to 155, Rue de la Paix myself yesterday, and was told that nothing whatever was to be had, not at any price."

"Perhaps you didn't offer enough," said Cecil.

"Moreover, I notice the advertisement does not appear to-day. I guess the authorities have crumpled it up."

"Still——" Cecil went on monotonously.

"Look here," said Belmont, grim and a little nettled. "Just to cut it short, I'll bet you a two-hundred-dollar dinner at Paillard's that you can't get seats for to-night —not even two, let alone four."

"You really want to bet?"

"Well," drawled Belmont with a certain irony, slightly imitating Cecil's manner, "it means something to eat for these ladies."

"I accept," said Cecil. And he rang the bell.

II.

"LECKY," Cecil said to his valet, who had entered the room, "I want you to go to No. 155, Rue de la Paix, and find out on which floor they are disposing of seats for the Opéra to-night. When you have found out, I want you to get me four seats—preferably a box. Understand?"

The servant stared at his master, squinting violently for a few seconds. Then he replied suddenly, as though light had just dawned on him. "Exactly, sir. You intend to be present at the gala performance?"

"You have successfully grasped my intention," said Cecil. "Present my card." He scribbled a word or two on a card and gave it to the man.

"And the price, sir?"

"You still have that blank cheque on the Crédit Lyonnais that I gave you yesterday morning. Use that."

"Yes, sir. Then there is the question of my French, sir, my feeble French—a delicate plant."

"My friend," Belmont put in, "I will accompany you as interpreter. I should like to see this thing through."

Lecky bowed and gave up squinting.

In three minutes (for they had only to go round the corner), Lionel Belmont and Lecky were in a room on the fourth floor of 155, Rue de la Paix. It had the appearance of an ordinary drawing-room, save that it contained an office-table; at this table sat a young man, French.

"You wish, messieurs?" said the young man.

"Have the goodness to interpret for me," said Lecky to the Napoleon of Anglo-Saxon

" Belmont had the ecstasy of paying the bill."

theatres. "Mr. Cecil Thorold, of the Devonshire Mansion, London, the Grand Hotel, Paris, the Hôtel Continental, Rome, and the Ghezireh Palace Hotel, Cairo, presents his compliments, and wishes a box for the gala performance at the Opéra to-night."

Belmont translated, while Lecky handed the card.

"Owing to the unfortunate indisposition of a Minister and his wife," replied the young man gravely, having perused the card, "it happens that I have a stage-box on the second tier.

"You told me yesterday——" Belmont began.

"I will take it," said Lecky in a sort of French, interrupting his interpreter. "The price? And a pen!"

"The price is twenty-five thousand francs."

"Gemini!" Belmont exclaimed in American. "This is Paris, and no mistake!"

"Yes," said Lecky, as he filled up the blank cheque, "Paris still succeeds in being Paris. I have noticed it before, Mr. Belmont, if you will pardon the liberty."

The young man opened a drawer and handed to Lecky a magnificent gilt card, signed by the Minister of Fine Arts, which Lecky hid within his breast.

"That signature of the Minister is genuine, eh?" Belmont asked the young man.

"I answer for it," said the young man, smiling imperturbably.

"The deuce you do!" Belmont murmured.

So the four friends dined at Paillard's at the rate of about a dollar and a half a mouthful, and the mystified Belmont, who was not in the habit of being mystified, and so felt it, had the ecstasy of paying the bill.

III.

It was nine o'clock when they entered the magnificent precincts of the Opera House. Like everybody else, they went very early—the performance was not to commence until nine-thirty—in order to see and be seen to the fullest possible extent. A week had elapsed since the two girls had arrived from Algiers in Paris, under the escort of Cecil Thorold, and in that time they had not been idle. Kitty Sartorius had spent tolerable sums at the best *modistes* in the Rue de la Paix and the establishments in the Rue de la Chaussée d'Antin, while Eve had bought one frock (a dream, needless to say) and had also been nearly covered with jewellery by her betrothed. That afternoon, between the bet and the dinner, Cecil had made more than one mysterious disappearance. He finally came back with a diamond tiara for his dear journalist. "You ridiculous thing!" exclaimed the dear journalist, kissing him. It thus occurred that Eve, usually so severe of aspect, had more jewels than she could wear, while Kitty, accustomed to display, had practically nothing but her famous bracelet. Eve insisted on pooling the lot, and dividing equally, for the gala.

Consequently the party presented a very pretty appearance as it ascended the celebrated grand staircase of the Opéra, wreathed to-night in flowers. Lionel Belmont, with Kitty on his arm, was in high spirits, uplifted, joyous; but Cecil himself seemed to be a little nervous, and this nervousness communicated itself to Eve Fincastle—or perhaps Eve was rather overpowered by her tiara. At the head of the staircase was a notice requesting everyone to be seated at nine-twenty-five, previous to the arrival of the President and the Imperial guests of the Republic.

The row of officials at the *controle* took the expensive gilt card from Cecil, examined it, returned it, and bowed low with an intimation that he should turn to the right and climb two floors; and the party proceeded further into the interior of the great building. The immense corridors and *foyers* and stairs were crowded with a collection of the best-known people and the best-dressed people and the most wealthy people in Paris. It was a gathering of all the renowns. The garish, gorgeous Opéra seemed to be changed that night into something new and strange. Even those shabby old harridans, the box-openers, the *ouvreuses*, wore bows of red-white-and-blue and smiled effusively in expectation of tips inconceivably large.

"*Tiens!*" exclaimed the box-opener who had taken charge of Cecil's party, as she unlocked the door of the box.

And well might she exclaim, for the box (No. 74—no possible error) was already occupied by a lady and two gentlemen, who were talking rather loudly in French! Cecil undoubtedly turned pale, while Lionel Belmont laughed within his moustache.

"These people have made a mistake," Cecil was saying to the *ouvreuse*, when a male official in evening dress approached him with an air of importance.

"Pardon, monsieur. You are Monsieur Cecil Thorold?"

"I am," said Cecil.

"Will you kindly follow me? Monsieur the Directeur wishes to see you."

"You are expected, evidently," said Lionel Belmont. The girls kept apart, as girls should in these crises between men.

"I have a ticket for this box," Cecil remarked to the official. "And I wish first to take possession of it."

"It is precisely that point which Monsieur the Directeur wishes to discuss with Monsieur," rejoined the official, ineffably suave. He turned with a wonderful bow to the girls, and added with that politeness of which the French alone have the secret: "Perhaps, in the meantime, these ladies would like to see the view of the Avenue de l'Opéra from the balcony? The illuminations have begun, and the effect is certainly charming."

Cecil bit his lip.

"Yes," he said. "Belmont, take them."

So, while Lionel Belmont escorted the girls to the balcony, there to discuss the startling situation and to watch the Imperial party drive up the resplendent, fairylike, and unique avenue, Cecil followed the official.

He was guided along various passages and round unnumbered corners to the rear part of the colossal building. There, in a sumptuous bureau, the official introduced him to a still higher official, the Directeur, who had a decoration and a long, white moustache.

"Monsieur," said this latter, "I am desolated to have to inform you that the Minister of Fine Arts has withdrawn his original invitation for Box No. 74 to-night."

"I have received no intimation of the withdrawal," Cecil replied.

"No. Because the original invitation was not issued to you," said the Directeur, excited and nervous. "The Minister of Fine Arts instructs me to inform you that his invitation to meet the President and their Imperial Majesties cannot be bought and sold."

"But is it not notorious that many such invitations have been bought and sold?"

"It is, unfortunately, too notorious."

"The box was already occupied."

Here the Directeur looked at his watch and rang a bell impatiently.

"Then why am I singled out?"

The Directeur gazed blandly at Cecil. "The reason, perhaps, is best known to yourself," said he, and he rang the bell again.

"I appear to incommode you," Cecil remarked. "Permit me to retire."

"Not at all, I assure you," said the Directeur. "On the contrary. I am a little agitated on account of the non-arrival of Mademoiselle Malva."

A minor functionary entered.

"She has come?"

"No, Monsieur the Directeur."

"And it is nine-fifteen! *Sapristi!*"

The functionary departed.

"The invitation to Box No. 74," proceeded the Directeur, commanding himself, "was sold for two thousand francs. Allow me to hand you notes for the amount, dear monsieur."

"But I paid twenty-five thousand," said Cecil, smiling.

"It is conceivable. But the Minister can only concern himself with the original figure. You refuse the notes?"

"By no means," said Cecil, accepting them. "But I have brought here to-night three guests, including two ladies. Imagine my position"

"I imagine it," the Directeur responded. "But you will not deny that the Minister has always the right to cancel an invitation. Seats ought to be sold subject to the contingency of that right being exercised."

At that moment still another official plunged into the room.

"She is not here yet!" He sighed, as if in extremity.

"It is unfortunate," Cecil sympathetically put in.

"It is more than unfortunate, dear monsieur," said the Directeur, gesticulating. "It is unthinkable. The performance *must* begin at nine-thirty, and it *must* begin with the garden scene from 'Faust,' in which Mademoiselle Malva takes *Marguerite*."

"Why not change the order?" Cecil suggested.

"Impossible. There are only two other items. The first act of 'Lohengrin,' with Madame Félise, and the ballet 'Sylvia.' We cannot commence with the ballet. No one ever heard of such a thing. And do you suppose that Félise will sing before Malva? Not for millions. Not for a throne. The etiquette of sopranos is stricter than that of Courts. Besides, to-night we cannot have a German opera preceding a French one."

"Then the President and their Majesties will have to wait a little, till Malva arrives," Cecil said.

"Their Majesties wait! Impossible!"

"Impossible!" echoed the other official, aghast.

Two more officials entered. And the atmosphere of alarm, of being scotched, of being up a tree of incredible height, the atmosphere which at that moment permeated the whole of the vast region behind the scenes of the Paris Opéra, seemed to rush with them into the bureau of the Directeur and to concentrate itself there.

"Nine-twenty! And she couldn't dress in less than fifteen minutes."

"You have sent to the Hotel du Louvre?" the Directeur questioned despairingly.

"Yes, Monsieur the Directeur. She left there two hours ago."

Cecil coughed.

"I could have told you as much," he remarked very distinctly.

"What!" cried the Directeur. "You know Mademoiselle Malva?"

"She is among my intimate friends," said Cecil smoothly.

"Perhaps you know where she is?"

"I have a most accurate idea," said Cecil.

"Where?"

"I will tell you when I am seated in my box with my friends," Cecil answered.

"Dear monsieur," panted the Directeur, "tell us at once! I give you my word of honour that you shall have your box."

Cecil bowed.

"Certainly," he said. "I may remark that I had gathered information which led me to anticipate this difficulty with the Minister of Fine Arts——"

"But Malva, Malva—where is she?"

"Be at ease. It is only nine-twenty-three, and Mademoiselle Malva is less than three minutes away, and ready dressed. I was observing that I had gathered information which led me to anticipate this difficulty with the Minister of Fine Arts, and accordingly I took measures to protect myself. There is no such thing as absolute arbitrary power, dear Directeur, even in a republic, and I have proved it. Mademoiselle Malva is in room No. 429 at the Grand Hotel, across the road. . . . Stay, she will not come without this note."

He handed out a small, folded letter from his waistcoat pocket.

Then he added: "Adieu, Monsieur the Directeur. You have just time to reach the State entrance in order to welcome the Presidential and Imperial party."

At nine-thirty, Cecil and his friends were ushered by a trinity of subservient officials into their box, which had been mysteriously emptied of its previous occupants. And at the same moment the monarchs, with monarchal punctuality, accompanied by the President, entered the Presidential box in the middle of the grand tier of the superb auditorium. The distinguished and dazzling audience rose to its feet, and the band played the National Anthem.

"You fixed it up, then?" Belmont whispered under cover of the National Anthem. He was beaten, after all.

"Oh, yes!" said Cecil lightly. "A trivial misconception, nothing more. And I have made a little out of it, too."

"Indeed! Much?"

"No, not much! Two thousand francs. But you must remember that I have been less than half an hour in making them."

The curtain rose on the garden scene from "Faust."

IV.

"My dear," said Eve.

When a woman has been definitely linked with a man, either by betrothal or by marriage, there are moments, especially at the commencement, when she assumes an air and a tone of absolute exclusive possession of him. It is a wonderful trick, which no male can successfully imitate, try how he will. One of these moments had arrived in the history of Eve Fincastle and her millionaire lover. They sat in a large, deserted public room, all gold, of the Grand Hotel. It was midnight less a quarter, and they had just returned, somewhat excited and flushed, from the glories of the gala performances. During the latter part of the evening, Eve had been absent from Cecil's box for nearly half an hour.

Kitty Sartorius and Lionel Belmont were conversing in an adjoining *salon*.

"Yes," said Cecil.

"Are you quite, quite sure that you love me?"

Only one answer is possible to such a question. Cecil gave it.

"That is all very well," Eve pursued with equal gravity and charm. "But it was really tremendously sudden, wasn't it? I can't think what you see in me, dearest."

"My dear Eve," Cecil observed, holding her hand, "the best things, the most enduring things, very often occur suddenly."

"Say you love me," she persisted.

So he said it, this time. Then her gravity deepened, though she smiled.

"You've given up all those—those schemes and things of yours, haven't you?" she questioned.

"Absolutely," he replied.

"My dear, I'm so glad. I never could understand why—— "

"Listen," he said. "What was I to do? I was rich. I was bored. I had no great attainments. I was interested in life and in the arts, but not desperately, not vitally. You may, perhaps, say I should have taken up philanthropy. Well, I'm not built that way. I can't help it, but I'm not a born philanthropist, and the philanthropist without a gift for philanthropy usually does vastly more harm than good. I might have gone into business. Well, I should only have doubled my millions, while boring myself all the time. Yet the instinct which I inherited from my father, the great American instinct to be a little cleverer and smarter than someone else, drove me to action. It was part of my character, and one can't get away from one's character. So finally I took to these rather original 'schemes,' as you call them. They had the advantage of being exciting and sometimes dangerous, and though they were often profitable, they were not too profitable. In short, they amused me and gave me joy. They also gave me *you*."

"Another official plunged into the room."

Eve smiled again, but without committing herself.

"But you have abandoned them now completely?" she said.

"Oh, yes," he answered.

"Then what about this Opéra affair to-night?" She sprang the question on him sharply. She did her best to look severe, but the endeavour ended with a laugh.

"I meant to tell you," he said. "But how—how did you know? How did you guess?"

"You forget that I am still a journalist," she replied, "and still on the staff of my paper. I wished to interview Malva to-night for the *Journal*, and I did so. It was she who let out things. She thought I knew all about it; and when she saw that I didn't, she stopped and advised me mysteriously to consult you for details."

"It was the scandal at the gala performance last autumn that gave me an action for making a corner in seats at the very next gala performance that should ever occur at the Paris Opéra," Cecil began his confession. "I knew that seats could be got direct from more or less minor officials at the Ministry of Fine Arts, and also that a large proportion of the people invited to these performances were prepared to sell their seats. You can't imagine how venal certain circles are in Paris. It just happened that the details and date of to-night's performance were announced on the day we arrived here. I could not resist the chance. Now you comprehend sundry strange absences of mine during the week. I went to a reporter on the *Echo de Paris* whom I knew and who knows everybody. And we got out a list of the people likely to be invited and likely to be willing to sell their seats. We also opened negotiations at the Ministry."

"'Managers don't go scattering five-hundred-pound bracelets for nothing.'"

"How on earth do these ideas occur to you?" asked Eve.

"How can I tell?" Cecil answered. "It is because they occur to me that I am I—you see. Well, in twenty-four hours my reporter and two of his friends had interviewed half the interviewable people in Paris, and the Minister of Fine Arts had sent out his invitations, and I had obtained the refusal of over three hundred seats, at a total cost of about seventy-five thousand francs. Then I saw that my friend the incomparable Malva was staying at the Ritz, and the keystone idea of the entire affair presented itself to me. I got her to offer to sing. Of course, her rival Félise could not be behind her in a patriotic desire to cement the friendliness of two great nations. The gala performance blossomed into a terrific boom We took a kind of office in the Rue de la Paix. We advertised very discreetly. Every evening, after bidding you 'Good-night,' I saw my reporter and Lecky, and arranged the development of the campaign. In three days we had sold all our seats, except one box, which I kept, for something like two hundred thousand francs."

"Then this afternoon you merely bought the box from yourself?"

"Exactly, my love. I had meant the surprise of getting a box to come a little later than it did—say at dinner; but you and Belmont, between you, forced it on."

"And that is all?"

"Not quite. The minions of the Minister of Fine Arts were extremely cross. And they meant to revenge themselves on me by depriving me of my box at the last moment. However, I got wind of that, and by the simplest possible arrangement with Malva I protected myself. The scheme—my last bachelor fling, Eve—has been a great success, and the official world of Paris has been taught a lesson which may lead to excellent results."

"And you have cleared a hundred and twenty-five thousand francs?"

"By no means. The profits of these undertakings are the least part of them. The expenses are heavy. I reckon the expenses will be nearly forty thousand francs. Then I must give Malva a necklace, and that necklace must cost twenty-five thousand francs."

"That leaves sixty thousand clear?" said Eve.

"Say sixty-two thousand."

"Why?"

"I was forgetting an extra two thousand made this evening."

"And your other 'schemes'?" Eve continued her cross-examination. "How much have they yielded?"

"The Devonshire House scheme was a dead loss. My dear, why did you lead me to destroy that fifty thousand pounds? Waste not, want not. There may come a day when we shall need that fifty thousand pounds, and then——"

"Don't be funny," said Eve. "I am serious—very serious."

"Well, Ostend and Mr. Rainshore yielded twenty-one thousand pounds net. Bruges and the bracelet yielded nine thousand five hundred francs. Algiers and Biskra resulted in a loss of——"

"Never mind the losses," Eve interrupted. "Are there any more gains?"

"Yes, a few. At Rome last year I somehow managed to clear fifty thousand francs. Then there was an episode at the Chancellory at Berlin. And——"

"Tell me the total gains, my love," said Eve—"the gross gains."

Cecil consulted a pocket-book.

"A trifle," he answered. "Between thirty-eight and forty thousand pounds."

"My dear Cecil," the girl said, "call it forty thousand—a million francs—and give me a cheque. Do you mind?"

"I shall be charmed, my darling."

"And when we get to London," Eve finished, "I will hand it over to the hospitals anonymously."

He paused, gazed at her, and kissed her.

Then Kitty Sartorius entered, a marvellous vision, with Belmont in her wake. Kitty glanced hesitatingly at the massive and good-humoured Lionel.

"The fact is——" said Kitty, and paused.

"We are engaged," said Lionel. "You aren't surprised?"

"Our warmest congratulations!" Cecil observed. "No. We can't truthfully say that we are staggered. It is in the secret nature of things that a leading lady must marry her manager—a universal law that may not be transgressed."

"Moreover," said Eve later, in Cecil's private ear, as they were separating for the night, "we might have guessed much earlier. Theatrical managers don't go scattering five-hundred-pound bracelets all over the place merely for business reasons."

"But he only scattered one, my dear," Cecil murmured.

"Yes, well. That's what I mean."

XV

The Hammerpond Mystery

H.G. WELLS

The Hammerpond Park Burglary

The Tale of an Artistic Crime.

By H. G. Wells.

IT is a moot point whether burglary is to be considered as a sport, a trade, or an art. For a trade, the technique is scarcely rigid enough, and its claims to be considered an art are vitiated by the mercenary element that qualifies its triumphs. On the whole it seems to be most justly ranked as sport, a sport for which no rules are at present formulated, and of which the prizes are distributed in an extremely informal manner. It was this informality of burglary that led to the regrettable extinction of two promising beginners at Hammerpond Park.

The stakes offered in this affair consisted chiefly of diamonds and other personal *bric-à-brac* belonging to the newly married Lady Aveling. Lady Aveling, as the reader will remember, was the only daughter of Mrs. Montague Pangs, the well-known hostess. Her marriage to Lord Aveling was extensively advertised in the papers, as well as the quantity and quality of her wedding presents, and the fact that the honeymoon was to be spent at Hammerpond.

The announcement of these valuable prizes created a considerable sensation in the small circle in which Mr. Teddy Watkins was the undisputed leader, and it was decided that, accompanied by a duly qualified assistant, he should visit the village of Hammerpond in his professional capacity.

Being a man of naturally retiring and modest disposition, Mr. Watkins determined to make his visit *incog.*, and after due consideration of the conditions of his enterprise, he selected the *rôle* of a landscape artist and the unassuming surname of Smith. He preceded his assistant, who, it was decided, should join him only on the last afternoon of his stay at Hammerpond.

Now the village of Hammerpond is, perhaps, one of the prettiest little corners in Sussex; many thatched houses still survive, the flint-built church, with its tall spire nestling under the down, is one of the finest and least restored in the county, and the beech-woods and bracken jungles through which the road runs to the great house are singularly rich in what the vulgar artist and photographer call "bits." So that Mr. Watkins, on his arrival with two virgin canvases, a brand-new easel, a paint-box, portmanteau, an ingenious little ladder made in sections (after the pattern of the late lamented master, Charles Peace), crowbar, and wire coils, found himself welcomed with effusion and some curiosity by half-a-dozen other brethren of the brush. It rendered the disguise he had chosen unexpectedly plausible, but it inflicted upon him a considerable amount of æsthetic conversation for which he was very imperfectly prepared.

"Have you exhibited very much?" said young Porson in the bar-parlour of the "Coach and Horses," where Mr. Watkins was skilfully accumulating local information on the night of his arrival.

"Very little," said Mr. Watkins, "just a snack here and there."

"Academy?"

"In course. *And* at the Crystal Palace."

"Did they hang you well?" said Porson.

"Don't rot," said Mr. Watkins; "I don't like it."

"I mean did they put you in a good place?"

"Whadyer mean?" said Mr. Watkins suspiciously. "One 'ud think you were trying to make out I'd been put away."

Porson had been brought up by aunts, and was a gentlemanly young man even for an artist; he did not know what being "put away" meant, but he thought it best to explain that he intended nothing of the sort. As the question of hanging seemed a sore point with Mr. Watkins, he tried to divert the conversation a little.

"Do you do figure-work at all?"

"No, never had a head for figures," said Mr. Watkins, "my miss — Mrs. Smith, I mean, does all that."

"She paints too!" said Porson. "That's rather jolly."

"Very," said Mr. Watkins, though he really did not think so, and, feeling the conversation was drifting a little beyond his grasp, added: "I came down here to paint Hammerpond House by moonlight."

"Really!" said Porson. "That's rather a novel idea."

"Yes," said Mr. Watkins, "I thought it rather a good notion when it occurred to me. I expect to begin to-morrow night."

"What! You don't mean to paint in the open, by night?"

"I do, though."

"But how will you see your canvas?"

"Have a bloomin' cop's—" began Mr. Watkins, rising too quickly to the question, and then, realising this, bawled to Miss Durgan for another glass of beer. "I'm going to have a thing called a dark lantern," he said to Porson.

"But it's about new moon now," objected Porson. "There won't be any moon."

"There'll be the house," said Watkins, "at any rate. I'm goin', you see, to paint the house first and the moon afterwards."

"Oh!" said Porson, too staggered to continue the conversation.

"They doo say," said old Durgan, the landlord, who had maintained a respectful

"Have you exhibited very much?" said young Porson in the bar-parlour of the "Coach and Horses."

silence during the technical conversation, "as there's no less than three p'licemen from 'Azleworth on dewty every night in the house—'count of this Lady Aveling 'n her jewellery. One'm won fower-and-six last night, off second footman—tossin'."

Towards sunset next day Mr. Watkins, virgin canvas, easel, and a very considerable case of other appliances in hand, strolled up the pleasant pathway through the beech-woods to Hammerpond Park, and pitched his apparatus in a strategic position commanding the house. Here he was observed by Mr. Raphael Sant, who was returning across the park from a study of the chalk-pits. His curiosity having been fired by Porson's account of the new arrival, he turned aside with the idea of discussing nocturnal art.

Mr. Watkins was apparently unaware of his approach. A friendly conversation with Lady Hammerpond's butler had just terminated, and that individual, surrounded by the three pet dogs, which it was his duty to take for an airing after dinner had been served, was receding in the distance. Mr. Watkins was mixing colour with an air of great industry. Sant, approaching more nearly, was surprised to see the colour in question was as harsh and brilliant an emerald green as it is possible to imagine. Having cultivated an extreme sensibility to colour from his earliest years, he drew the air in sharply between his teeth at the very first glimpse of this brew. Mr. Watkins turned round. He looked annoyed.

"What on earth are you going to do with that *beastly* green?" said Sant.

Mr. Watkins realised that his zeal to appear busy in the eyes of the butler had evidently betrayed him into some technical error. He looked at Sant and hesitated.

"Pardon my rudeness," said Sant; "but really that green is altogether too amazing. It came as a shock. What *do* you mean to do with it?"

Mr. Watkins was collecting his resources. Nothing could save the situation but decision. "If you come here interrupting my work," he said, "I'm a-goin' to paint your face with it."

Sant retired, for he was a humorist and a peaceful man. Going down the hill, he met Porson and Wainwright. "Either that man is a genius or he is a dangerous lunatic," said he. "Just go up and look at his green." And he continued his way, his countenance brightened by a pleasant anticipation of a cheerful affray round an easel in the gloaming, and the shedding of much green paint.

But to Porson and Wainwright Mr. Watkins was less aggressive, and explained that the green was intended to be the first coating of his picture. It was, he admitted in response to a remark, an absolutely new method, invented by himself. But subsequently he became more reticent; he explained he was not going to tell every passer-by the secret of his own particular style, and added some scathing remarks upon the meanness of people "hanging about" to pick up such tricks of the masters as they could, which immediately relieved him of their company.

Twilight deepened, first one then another star appeared. The rooks amid the tall trees to the left of the house had long since lapsed into slumbrous silence, the house itself lost all the details of its architecture and became a dark grey outline, and then the windows of the salon shone out brilliantly, the conservatory was lighted up, and here and there a bedroom window burnt yellow. Had anyone approached the easel in the park it would have been found deserted. One brief uncivil word in brilliant green sullied the purity of its canvas. Mr. Watkins was busy in the shrubbery with his assistant, who had discreetly joined him from the carriage-drive.

Mr. Watkins was inclined to be self-congratulatory upon the ingenious device by which he had carried all his apparatus boldly, and in the sight of all men, right up to the scene of operations. "That's the dressing-room," he said to his assistant, "and, as soon as the maid takes the candle away and goes down to supper, we'll call in. My! how nice the house do look to be sure, against the starlight, and with all its windows and lights! Swop me, Jim, I almost wish I *was* a painter-chap. Have you fixed that there wire across the path from the laundry?"

He cautiously approached the house until he stood below the dressing-room window, and began to put together his folding ladder. He was much too experienced a practitioner to feel any unusual excitement. Jim was reconnoitring the smoking-room. Suddenly, close beside Mr. Watkins in the bushes, there was a violent crash and a stifled curse. Someone had tumbled over the wire which his assistant had just arranged. He heard feet running on the gravel pathway beyond.

Mr. Watkins, like all true artists, was a singularly shy man, and he incontinently dropped his folding ladder and began running circumspectly through the shrubbery. He was indistinctly aware of two people hot upon his heels, and he fancied that he distinguished the outline of his assistant in front of him. In another moment he had vaulted the low stone wall bounding the shrubbery, and was in the open park. Two thuds on the turf followed his own leap.

Mr. Watkins' memory of the incidents of the next two minutes is extremely vague.

It was a close chase in the darkness through the trees. Mr. Watkins was a loosely-built man and in good training, and he gained hand-over-hand upon the hoarsely panting figure in front. Neither spoke, but, as Mr. Watkins pulled up alongside, a qualm of awful doubt came over him. The other man turned his head at the same moment and gave an exclamation of surprise. "It's not Jim," thought Mr. Watkins, and simultaneously the stranger flung himself, as it were, at Watkins' knees, and they were forthwith grappling on the ground together. "Lend a hand, Bill," cried the stranger as the third man came up. And Bill did—two hands in fact, and some accentuated feet. The fourth man, presumably Jim, had apparently turned aside, and made off in a different direction. At any rate, he did not join the trio.

Mr. Watkins' memory of the incidents of the next two minutes is extremely vague. He has a dim recollection of having his thumb in the corner of the mouth of the first man, and feeling anxious about its safety, and for some seconds at least he held the head of the gentleman answering to the name of Bill to the ground by the hair. He was also kicked in a great number of different places, apparently by a vast multitude of people. Then the gentleman who was not Bill got his knee below Mr. Watkins' diaphragm, and tried to curl him up upon it.

When his sensations became less entangled he was sitting upon the turf, and eight or ten men—the night was dark, and he was rather too confused to count—standing round him, apparently waiting for him to recover. He mournfully assumed that he was captured, and would probably have made some philosophical reflections on the fickleness of fortune, had not his internal sensations

Mr Watkins was made much of in the salon.

disinclined him for speech. He noticed very quickly that his wrists were not handcuffed, and then a flask of brandy was put in his hands. This touched him a little—it was such unexpected kindness.

"He's a-comin' round," said a voice which he fancied he recognised as belonging to the Hammerpond second footman.

"We've got them, sir, both of 'em," said the Hammerpond butler, the man who had handed him the flask. "Thanks to *you*."

No one answered this remark. Yet he failed to see how it applied to him.

"He's fair dazed," said a strange voice; "the villains half-murdered him."

Mr. Teddy Watkins decided to remain fair dazed until he had a better grasp of the situation. He perceived that two of the black figures round him stood side by side with a dejected air, and there was something in the carriage of their shoulders that suggested to his experienced eye hands that were bound together. Two! In a flash he rose to his position. He emptied the little flask and staggered—obsequious hands assisted him—to his feet. There was a sympathetic murmur.

"Shake hands, sir, shake hands," said one of the figures near him. "Permit me to introduce myself. I am very greatly indebted to you. It was the jewels of my wife, Lady Aveling, which attracted these scoundrels to the house."

"Very glad to make your lordship's acquaintance," said Teddy Watkins.

"I presume you saw the rascals making for the shrubbery, and dropped down on them?"

"That's exactly how it happened," said Mr. Watkins.

"You should have waited till they got in at the window," said Lord Aveling; "they would get it hotter if they had actually committed the burglary. And it was lucky for you two of the policemen were out by the gates, and followed up the three of you. I doubt if you could have secured the two of them—though it was confoundedly plucky of you, all the same."

"Yes, I ought to have thought of all that," said Mr. Watkins; "but one can't think of everythink."

"Certainly not," said Lord Aveling. "I am afraid they have mauled you a little," he added. The party was now moving towards the house. "You walk rather lame. May I offer you my arm?"

And instead of entering Hammerpond House by the dressing-room window, Mr. Watkins entered it—slightly intoxicated, and inclined to cheerfulness again—on the arm of a real live peer, and by the front door. "This," thought Mr. Watkins, "is burgling in style!"

The "scoundrels," seen by the gaslight, proved to be mere local amateurs unknown to Mr. Watkins, and they were taken down into the pantry, and there watched over by the three policemen, two gamekeepers with loaded guns, the butler, an ostler, and a carman, until the dawn allowed of their removal to Hazelhurst police-station.

Mr. Watkins was made much of in the salon. They devoted a sofa to him, and would not hear of a return to the village that night. Lady Aveling was sure he was brilliantly original, and said her idea of Turner was just such another rough, half-inebriated, deep-eyed, brave, and clever man.

Someone brought up a remarkable little folding-ladder that had been picked up in the shrubbery, and showed him how it was put together. They also described how wires had been found in the shrubbery, evidently placed there to trip-up unwary pursuers. It was lucky he had escaped these snares. And they showed him the jewels.

Mr. Watkins had the sense not to talk too much, and in any conversational difficulty fell back on his internal pains. At last he was seized with stiffness in the back, and yawning. Everyone suddenly awoke to the fact that it was a shame to keep him talking after his affray, so he retired early to his room, the little red room next to Lord Aveling's suite.

* * * * *

The dawn found a deserted easel bearing a canvas with a green inscription, in the Hammerpond Park, and it found Hammerpond House in commotion. But if the dawn found Mr. Teddy Watkins and the Aveling diamonds, it did not communicate the information to the police.